"You are free to take your rights."

He looked at her reflection in the mirror; standing so passively, arms at her sides; a sort of self-abnegating surrender. To him! There rose before him a vision of two countesses who once almost gouged each other's eyes out for the favors of his couch.

In a flash of revelation he saw her as she had been the day she had accepted his proposal of marriage. That hectic gesture; the glove withdrawn, the hand proferred in surrender. By heaven, *she had sold herself to him* . . .

He turned from the mirror and seized her dress at the neck. With one savage wrench he tore the stately robe apart from neck to hem. For a moment he stared at her splendid, youthful body. He felt a sense of renewed potency and vigor as he pulled her towards the bed. . . .

The Flower of the Storm

A breathtaking novel
of hot-blooded desire and epic adventure

The Flower
of the
Storm

(Formerly: *The Big Wind*)

Beatrice Coogan

BALLANTINE BOOKS • NEW YORK

Library of Congress Catalog Card Number: 68-14173

ISBN 0-345-27368-0

This edition published by arrangement with Arlington Books Ltd.

Manufactured in the United States of America

First Ballantine Books Edition: March 1978

PART ONE
6th January, 1839

CHAPTER 1

Another crash shook the long row of windows in the drawing-room. This time there was a rending and splitting that was unmistakable. The young man in the great winged chair by the fire laid down his book. It was useless trying to concentrate with that wind howling outside.

'I'll hold a crown that is one of the oaks near the house.' He drew the heavy folds of Italian velvet from the window nearest the fireplace and unlatched the iron bars that held the shutters across the glass.

He peered out. In the three-quarters of an hour since the shutters had been barred the configuration of the near landscape had changed. Something blotted out the lawn. He had the impression that the lawn was no longer there. He rubbed the glass impatiently with his fingers and strained to pick out the two long rows of black shapes where the avenue ran between the trees. Here and there he discerned the tall outline of a tree, but the familiar form of the colonnade was not there. There were unfamiliar spaces and he knew that every space was a fallen tree.

His eyes travelled back to the centre front. Then he realised that the weird hulk that distorted the scene was the base of the giant oak tree standing up-ended, its torn-out roots in mid-air, its leafy branches down in a black cavity that had been a smooth velvet pleasance eight minutes ago.

As he looked, a great squalling gust of wind came screaming across the park and hurled itself against the glass. He was flung backwards against a table. The heavy silver candelabrum that stood there was overturned. At the same time there was a crashing sound of breaking glass and into the room came showers of leaves, sticks, stones and big lumps of clay. The green velvet hangings ballooned inward and tossed priceless bric-à-brac from tables and mantelpiece. Lighted candles were knocked from their sconces. The great five-foot chandelier of Waterford cut

7

glass swung wildly from the ceiling. Hundreds of its dangling pieces swirled together, making a musical swan-song before they crashed to destruction against walls and mirrors and the uncarpeted spaces of the floor.

When the frightened servants burst open the door the draught created a whirlwind that sent fresh destruction all through the elegant room. The green curtains lashed out in fury against the walls and their tasselled ends reaching to the mantel piece sent shepherdesses and goddesses flying to the mosaic hearth tiles in smithereens. ' 'Tis the end of the world, Sir Roderick,' cried the old butler. His master, cursing himself for his folly in opening the shutters, was now trying to close them.

'Come and help me and stop talking nonsense,' he cried. Another gust of wind sent the shutters flying into their faces and went roaring and whistling round the house and down the chimneys. 'You there!' Sir Roderick roared at the footman who was aimlessly picking up broken china and glass. 'Drag in these big chairs from the hall and put them against these shutters. And you, young Thomas,' he called to the knife boy who was crouching in terror beside a curio cabinet, 'go and help him. When they had succeeded in securing the bars across the shutters they had to hold their arms against the wood. Despite the strength of the iron bars, the wind hurling itself through the glassless window was straining the shutters inwards until they creaked aloud.

The footman and the boy came slowly across the room gasping with the effort of dragging one of the heavy Flemish choir stalls that were used as hall chairs. They placed it against the barred shutters and went back to the hall for the rest. Backwards and forwards they went, helped by the master and the butler, until there was a chair at every window and two at the one that was broken.

As the men were about to leave the room the door opened and the six-foot figure of Mrs. Stacey, the cook, came in followed by a group of servant girls. They all held rosary beads. The butler, leading the outgoing procession stood transfixed. Their audacity recalled him to his dignity as Commander-in-Chief of the staff. The kitchen had actually come unbidden to the drawing-room! It was as unheard-of and as horrifying as the storm that raged outside.

He looked up at the towering cook. 'Is it mad you are?' he

issed. But Mrs. Stacey for once ignored him. With hands still lasped as though in prayer and the rosary beads entwined bout her fingers she went beseechingly towards her master, ddressing her prayers to him instead of to her Maker.

'Sir Roderick, acquanie, I ask your pardon for makin' so bold. ut don't ask us to stay down there. The water is a foot deep on he kitchen floor....'

'Water? Where is it coming from?'

'I don't know where it came from, Sir Roderick. It just ppeared in the kitchen without sound or warning....'

An elderly housemaid pressed forward. 'There was a roar like under and then, God between us and all harm, the door pened by itself and the water flowed in.'

Sir Roderick thrust through the press of jabbering servants. Why was I not told of this before?' The butler tried to explain him that it was to tell him about the flooding in the kitchen at he came up in the first instance, but Mrs. Stacey's voice rowned his. When she realised that she was expected to follow er master downstairs she became hysterical and screamed at the p of her voice about tombstones.

'The yard is full of tombstones, your Honour,' said a maid. They are floatin' about on the water.'

Mrs. Stacey reached out a restraining hand. 'Sir Roderick, are it wasn't the water I was afraid of, an' I'm not afeared of ything on two feet, or four neither, but the prophecies of aint Columcille have come to pass this night. The graves have pened and the holy tombstones have travelled across near a undred acres of land. The like was never known. The corpses at own them tombstones will be here next.'

Sir Roderick had turned from her impatiently and started own the passage towards the back stairs. From over his head a oice called to him quietly. Mrs. Mansfield, the housekeeper, as leaning over the banisters of the main staircase.

'Sir Roderick, will you send for Dr. Mitchell for her Lady-ip?'

'Dr. Mitchell?' In the sudden turmoil of the storm he had rgotten that Margaret had not been feeling too well after din-er. Her back had ached from bending over the big embroidery ame and she had gone up to rest for a while on the chaise-ngue. 'Is there anything amiss with her Ladyship?' he cried as e rushed past the housekeeper two steps at a time.

'It is her, her——' the prim spinster, for all her housekeeper title of Mrs., stood groping to express herself delicately.

'Speak up, woman!' he yelled. She shrank back against th banisters. 'It is her condition, Sir Roderick. The storm ha started her confinement.'

In the bedroom, a tall, beautiful girl was clutching the corne of the mantelpiece. She came towards him, her eyes dilated wi fear. 'Oh, Roderick, what is happening outside? Is the worl mad, or is it coming to an end?'

He put his arms around her and soothed her. 'It is only storm.' There was a deafening roar outside and the room seeme to shake. The girl gave a low moan of pain. He held her fro him and looked into her face. She was deathly pale. 'Margare is this true what Mrs. Mansfield says? Surely it could not be f another month?' The storm crashed again around the hou and she fell against him.

'Roderick, send for Dr. Mitchell and have him bring a nurse

'But—the trained nurse from Dublin will be here on Mo day.'

'Monday will be too late. Hurry, Roderick, hurry.'

He kissed her. 'Don't worry, my darling. Dr. Mitchell and nurse will be with you in no time.' And while he reassured h he thought of the fallen trees and the floods and doubted in h heart that the elderly doctor would get through this storm hell.

Downstairs in the servants' regions he found men, wome and children thronging the passages and back stairs and eve pantry room that had a step above ground level. John Carmod the gardener, came forward holding a wailing child in his arm He looked like a man who had come face to face with th supernatural. His teeth chattered as he endeavoured to expla the presence of himself and his entire family in his maste house.

'The roof was lifted off, your Honour, like the lid of a box. blew up in the sky like a loose hand-cock of hay and at the sam time the back wall of the house crashed down an' meself an' t wife an' two of the children were thrun' out of the bed to t ground. This gossoon has his little leg crushed.'

Others were crowding round with their incredible accounts havoc. Some had their roofs blown off. Others had awaken from exhausted sleep to find that their beds had turned in

10

afts that bore them hither and thither on a strange sea of water
hat had appeared like a ghostly visitation from another world.

All of them sought to draw close to the young man who was
he mainstay of their lives, to draw comfort from his presence as
vell as shelter from his house. But their master could spare
hem no comfort.

'Is John Dermody here?' he called above the clamour. But
ohn Dermody, the coachman, was the only employee who was
1ot present. He slept over the coach-house beside the stables in a
heltered corner of the yard. The waters had not reached him.
Roderick sent a footman to fetch him.

No other mission but that of bringing aid to the lady of the
1ouse who was facing her trouble more than a month before her
ime would have induced the young footman out of doors to
ace the tombstones, and maybe their owners! As he waded knee-
leep in water across the yard, with head down against the
nurderous blast, a white object with the outline of a human
1ody floated towards him and he was knocked face downward
n the water. Shivering with fear and cold he struggled to his
cnees and recognised the object that had up-ended him. It was a
vhite marble tombstone surmounted by a man's head.

Before he could stand upright another white object, soft and
lammy, floated towards him and knocked him sideways. He
elt the hideous sensation of its dank hair on his cheeks and
nuffling his mouth. Holy Mother of God, Mrs. Stacey was
ight. The prophecies had come true! The corpses had come for
heir tombstones.

Screaming like a madman, he floundered to the coach-house
nd hammered in a frenzy at its door. Big John Dermody was
s calm as when he sat aloft on the driver's seat of the fine
arriage in gorgeous livery and cockaded hat, holding the reins
vith the dignified mien of a Roman charioteer.

Since the storm began he had moved continuously from box
o box, soothing the frightened horses. Now he soothed the half-
razed footman who clung to him jabbering about a tombstone
hat had knocked him flat on his face. 'And the corp' that
wned it came along next and hit me across the face.'

''Tis no corp', avic, leastways not a human one. It's only a
·oor drowned sheep. Look at it and let the fear go out of you.'
Ie forced the lad to look over his shoulder where even in the
.arkness he could discern the outlines of more sheep tossed

hither and thither in the swirling waters.

'Think of what their loss means to the master! All these fine ewes that would be lambin' in two months more!'

Mention of his master recalled the footman to his errand. 'Oh, Mr. Dermody, the tombstones and the corpses put it out o' my head what I came for. The Sir bid me tell you yoke the best carriage and go at once for Dr. Mitchell. Ye're to drive like mad. He's in a terrible state.'

Big John held the footman at arms'-length. 'Pull yoursel' together and give your message. Is the Sir hurt? And if so why should the carriage go for Dr. Mitchell. Isn't it on horseback he'd come, or drive his own Back-to-back?'

''Tis for the convaynence of bringing the midwife and the doctor gettin' a bit ould in himself for the night that's in it.'

'Midwife? What are ye ravin' about? Amn't I meetin' the Dublin coach for her on Monday?'

'Monday will be too late for her Ladyship. The poor Lady-craythur has come to her confinement with the dint of the storm.' The coachman waited for no more. He bade him fetch Mike O'Driscoll, the head groom. The footman started to ex postulate, but for once the coachman abandoned his calm and gave a roar that sent the footman floundering on his way.

A moment later Mike O'Driscoll was holding the frightened leaders as they reared and plunged, his own fear forgotten in his concern for the horses he loved. Big John, in the act of leading out two more horses, spied two people coming round the side o' the house towards the back door. At the same moment the lanterns suspended from the overhanging roof of the stable swung wildly in a great roaring blast of wind and crashed to the floor, leaving them all in complete darkness. The horse screamed and plunged wildly. Other horses trembling in their stalls heard the screams and their hooves could be heard above the storm as they lashed them in terror against walls and doors.

Big John called towards the two figures to come and help with the horses. They were the gate lodge-keeper and his wife. The man held a whimpering puppy under one arm and a pic ture under the other. The woman held a basket containing a hen and chicks in one hand and in the other she clutched a big china teapot. They had come to join the homeless at the Big House. Their snug lodge was levelled to the ground and their tale of havoc chilled Big John's stout heart the hope of bringing

12

help to his young mistress. The huge trees that stood on either side of the entrance gates were uprooted and lay, one above the other, across the entrance. It was the same, they said, all along the avenue. It was blocked every few yards with fallen trees. No vehicle could get past.

He considered the possibility of getting out by the back avenue to the by-road but abandoned the idea. The artificial pond for driving the carriage through to wash the mud from the wheels was in that part of the stableyard. It was now a lake. The back drive followed the course of the land where the river seemed to have burst its banks near the graveyard. Big John led the horses back to their stalls, then waded towards the house to hold counsel with his master.

Sir Roderick, returning from reassuring his wife that help would soon be on its way, was feeling more competent to cope with the plight of his helpless employees. Mrs. Stacey, after hearing the lodge-keepers' report, had gone into wilder flights of hysteria. The child with the crushed leg was wailing unceasingly. Other children, hungry, sleepy and rain-sodden, joined in a chorus of wails. Hannah Riorden, the elderly housemaid who had spoken to Sir Roderick about the flooding in the kitchen, was on her knees giving out the Rosary at the top of her voice. The sight of Big John Dermody towering above the throng, when he should be well out on the high road, pulled Sir Roderick up in dismay.

'Did you not receive my orders to take the carriage for the doctor and midwife?' Disappointment lashed his anger to fury. Never before had he spoken in anger to his coachman. And even as he spoke, he sensed that his orders were beyond obedience. Big John Dermody was not readily deterred.

'If it would be agreeable to you, Sir Roderick,' he said when he explained their tree-beleaguered plight, 'I thought to saddle the Rajah and ride to Templetown. I'd reach the road by taking the fields.'

'The Rajah is too heavy. If you must ride, take the new sorrel. It has speed.'

'Beggin' your pardon, Sir Roderick. It's not speed that counts tonight. It is strength.'

'Oh, for God's sake,' Roderick shouted, 'don't stand there arguing with me, get on a horse and fetch the doctor. It is life or death, man!' Big John strode down the passage to the back

13

door. As he opened it a gust of wind sent him staggering backwards, and his weight brought down the lithe body of his master who had followed him on an impulse. 'John,' he said as he rose, and there was no anger now, only appeal, 'do you think you can make it?'

For a brief moment the two men looked out into the wild darkness. Sleet drove through the open door and saturated their garments. But the horror of the night was in its sound. Down the long slopes from the graveyard came a screaming wind that ended in a kind of mad laughter as it whirled in and out through the treetops. There were whining creaks as heavy branches were torn from the trunks and sent whirling through the air, while from below came the agonised protests of the great deep roots that were being dragged from the earth that had held them for over a hundred years.

As the two men stood there helpless and awed, the master for the first time in his life felt his own unimportance. It seemed so absurd for one to assert authority over the other. The servant sensed his master's abasement. He turned towards him. 'Have no fear, Sir Roderick, I'll make it all right.'

The moment of revelation passed, master and man fitted back into perspective.

'God carry you safely,' said Sir Roderick. He turned to his demoralised workfolk.

Fear had dredged the soul of young Thomas, the knife boy and courier-drudge of Mrs. Stacey and the butler. He accepted unquestioningly their pronouncement that the world would end tonight. How else could it be? Had he not seen the black clouds, blacker than the eyes of man had ever seen before, as he ran back across the short cut through the bog this evening; after he had delivered the mistress's message to old Lady Cullen at Crannagh Hall? Now here was the great castle that had withstood the might of Cromwell, shaking like the hairy skeough grass that grows on top of the bog. And, God be praised, the graves had opened and the Dead were out there in the yard, waiting to be judged!

Suddenly he was exalted by a strange, new courage. There was no need to have to die now and have to go through all the grimness of funeral and the dreaded grave. He would be judged in life, right here in Kilsheelin Castle, and then go on straight up to Heaven. Not even a delay for a while in Purgatory, because Purgatory would be done away with after the Last Judgment. Of course there would still be Hell. But sure he hadn't a in on his soul. Or hadn't he? His mind quailed at the recollection of the audacious act he had committed about a fortnight ago, only a day after his foster-mother had brought him here before she left for America. He had come upon the Sir's 'necessary' built out of sight down the garden. He had often heard about the hole in a board that gentlemen used and the temptation had proved too much. He had actually tiptoed inside and—behaved like a gentleman!

The Sir was returning from the back door. The lad braced himself. Any moment now he would stand in the Presence of the Lord of Creation! For the first time he raised his voice unbidden to the Lord of the castle.

'Sir—yer Honour!' The haughty face looking down at him brought back servitude to his fear-purged soul. He backed and gulped. Pity stirred his master. 'What is it, lad?'

Thomas gulped again. 'Will the judgment be here, yer Honour? Sure we'd never get to the Valley of Jostlers tonight?'

'Jostlers? What is the boy talking about?'

Mrs. Stacey rose from her knees. 'He means the Valley of Jehosaphus where we'll all be judged this night, your Honour, sthore.' His Honour gave a roar that sent Mrs. Stacey down on her knees again, and reduced the voices and the wailings to silence; all but the injured child. 'If I hear another word of that kind of talk from you, I'll have you locked outside with the tombstones. Their owners will direct you to the Valley of Jehosaphus!' Mrs. Stacey made the sign of the cross in speechless dread.

'Patrick claimed from the Almighty three favours....' The voice came to them on a rush of icy wind. Struggling through the open door was the wild figure of an old man, dragging a harp. His white hair was wet on his shoulders, his bardic cloak lashed out behind. 'The bard!' gasped young Thomas, rushing across to close the door and help with the harp. 'Aye,' said the old man grimly, 'the bard of the O'Carrolls left to drown alone, forgotten.' They had all forgotten the family bard outside in his own special quarters at the extreme end of the east wing. '—that in the seventh year before the Day of Judgment,' continued the old man, regardless of Mrs. Stacey's fresh outcry, 'the land of Ireland would be engulfed in a mighty tidal wave so that no man of Ireland might know the terrors of the Last Day——'

The assurance brought no comfort to the assembly. It was showing signs of hysteria. Sir Roderick broke in impatiently on the prophetic utterances, 'For Heaven's sake, Bard, stop talking nonsense and——' He was at a loss what to suggest the old man should do. He mustn't leave him here; the bard was too sensitive about his position in the household. 'Come upstairs,' he finished. The bard shook his wet locks. 'It was ever the duty of the bard to inspire and give courage. I will stay with the helpless.' Sir Roderick felt something like a smile. The dignified minstrel was in dread of going from the company of the serving staff to sit alone in bardic state. 'Have no fear, woman!' he said to the cook. 'This is not the final floodwater—the storm that comes in its fury between the day of the Sun's death—the twenty-second day of December—and Twelfth Night; is but the Wild Huntsman, rushing by on his eight-footed steed.'

His master turned to leave, then stopped and raised his voice above the intoning of the bard's mysticisms. 'Look at that fire!' he roared.

Of the eight fires that burned in separate heaps of turf along the great hearth, a pot or kettle swinging from a crane over each pile, only two were smoking. Not a red spark in the great furnace of fires that had burned night and day, unquenched through the generations. Rain and sleet and stones were pouring down the chimney.

He bade them light the fires and hold themselves in readiness for their mistress's requirements. To the butler he gave instructions for food and drink for the homeless. As he passed the man who held the suffering child, he placed a hand upon his shoulder. 'The doctor will be here soon,' he said gently. 'He will see to the little one.' The man looked at him with grateful eyes. 'God bless your Honour.'

CHAPTER 2

Mrs. Mansfield removed Margaret's gown of blue brocade. Even in this moment of stress she let her hand linger lovingly over the raised embroidery of coral and gold bullion fringing. One by one she removed the silken petticoats flounced with Brussels lace that the young bride had brought from her Belgian home. From in front of the fire, where it was airing, she took a nightgown of finest silk and the wrapper of white cashmere, all ruffles and ribbons.

As the girl reached out her arms to place them in the sleeves, the housekeeper thought how helpless she looked, standing there ill and lonely, far from her native land. For a moment she was tempted to take her in her arms and give her comfort. But tradition prevailed.

Service in Kilsheelin Castle was not casual or slapdash. The young Sir, for all his books and paintings and music-playing, was formal and exacted a correct disposition from his servants. And her Ladyship was very foreign even though her father, an officer in the French army, had been Irish, and her mother was half Irish. She had a funny accent and she did not seem to understand Ireland or the Irish.

As lovingly as a caress Mrs. Mansfield tied the wrapper loosely round the girl and made a pretty bow under her chin with the ribbons of the dainty nightcap. Then she drew the mounting steps to the bedside. 'Let you go up these now and lie down,' she coaxed, 'and your trouble will be over before it has time to start.'

Just as Margaret put her foot on the first step to make the ascent of the bed, a thunderous crash shook the castle. The room vibrated. Margaret pitched forward, clutching one of the bedposts. It moved and something came away in her hand. A shriek escaped her. She thought the great bed was crushing down upon her.

Candle sconces were thrown on the floor. Down the chimney

came a deafening noise like a bombardment from Heaven Something fell on the stone hearth with a resounding crash. A black cloud of smoke blew across the room. Candles were blown out and from somewhere near she heard a low moan. 'Mrs Mansfield,' she called. There was no answer.

She struggled to rise and in the light of one broken candle hanging loosely in the brass arm of a big walnut sconce lying on the carpet, its candles quenched, she saw the prostrate body of Mrs. Mansfield. The housekeeper's head was in the shadow of the open door of the wardrobe where she had turned to put away the blue gown. The girl could not see the blood.

She rose to her feet, terrified to hold on to anything lest it give way and bring her down again. The whole castle was an inferno of roaring winds. Every blast was followed by crashes from roof to cellar as if the wind were carrying out a systematic dismantling of the castle and all its proud possessions.

She stood there alone in the smoke-darkened room and suddenly her calm broke. 'Rodereeck,' she screamed, 'Rod-er-ee-eek.' She dragged out the last syllable in a thin, long-drawn pleading. But the sound was not thin enough to pierce the massive door that was voicing its own groans against the merciless battering.

At last he came. For a moment he stood aghast. Like the lawn outside, the contours of the room had changed since he last saw it. It had lost its familiar outline. The furniture that, for him, had represented form and symmetry since his earliest recollections, had somehow vanished.

Heavy objects loomed in disorder from the floor. The only object that was upright was the tall fourposter bed, its white canopies and curtains gleaming ghostly in the darkness.

He moved towards it to his wife. Then he saw her standing motionless at the far side. She had ceased to cry out. She could feel her throat torn and a sensation like blood in her mouth. Some fundamental instinct caused her to marshal her energy and emotion for the ordeal that was yet to come.

She raised her arms to him. As he drew her to him the thing she held fell from her hand. It was the fluted top of the bedpost with its gay carvings of acanthus leaves and bunches of grapes.

'Rodereeck, do not ever leave me again,' she whispered.

'My poor little love. I won't leave you, and soon the doctor will be here.' Dear God, he seemed to be repeating that assur-

nce all night. He pressed his cheek to hers and then he became
ware that Mrs. Mansfield was not in the room.

'Where is Mrs. Mansfield? I cautioned her not to leave you.'
Margaret turned her head towards the housekeeper's pros-
rate form. 'She's there,' she whispered.

He looked over her shoulder. The broken candle gave a spurt
f flame and this time Margaret saw the blood. It had almost
overed Mrs. Mansfield's gentle face. Margaret fell against
Roderick in a dead faint.

He placed her on the bed and ran to the head of the stairs.
Across the banisters he saw the servants in the hall below. A
group of them surged up the stairs. He was almost relieved to
ee Mrs. Stacey in the vanguard. Was she not his own foster-
mother? She had borne children. She would sustain Margaret.
As they approached within two steps of him, a long thin whistle
of wind came in an icy blast down the two open storeys of the
hallway. A huge painting by Reubens—a Madonna and Child—
swung from the wall and crashed at their feet.

The sound of Mrs. Stacey's lamentations challenged the
wind. 'It's a sign!' she yelled. 'When a picture falls there'll be a
death in the house. Oh! The poor young mistress!'

Roderick suppressed his urge to strangle her. There was no
hope of help for Margaret from this quarter! Sternly he
ordered the butler to have the cook battened downstairs and on
no account to let her within sound of her Ladyship for the rest
of the night.

In a few moments it seemed as if the omen was fulfilled. The
servants shivered as Mrs. Mansfield's lifeless body was borne
past.

Hannah, the most responsible of the womenfolk, took over
the vigil in her mistress's room.

Sir Roderick strained his ears towards the windows that he
did not dare to open. If only he could stand at a window and
watch out for the doctor! The very motions of watching would
be an outlet for this tension.

He kept on chafing Margaret's wrists while Hannah dabbed
vinegar on her forehead and held smelling-salts to her nose.
'There must be something I can do,' he told himself, but his
confused brain offered no suggestion. He felt trapped. The roaring of the wind did not unnerve him, nor the crashes. But when
it came in long thin screeches down the length of the denuded

19

park and crashed against the windows with a wild laughin
sound like the mocking of demons, he wanted to run and bur
his ears.

Hannah had lit fresh candles and now he recognised th
bulky mass that lay on the hearthstone and blocked up th
entire fireplace. It was a section of the tessellated tower that ha
blown down the chimney, crushing the fireplace to rubble. Fo
the first time he realised that the castle·was in danger! It ha
stood up through the centuries against raids and wars an
sieges. It had escaped the ravages of Cromwell. Now the ele
ments had hurled themselves against its powerful battlements.

Roderick pulled desperately at the heavy masonry to free th
chimney opening and clear the room of swirling smoke. From
the bedside a sharp yelp of pain told him that Margaret ha
regained consciousness. He moved back to her.

'Are you in pain?' he asked her, and thought immediately
what a stupid question to put to a woman in her condition!

'It is not the pain that disturbs me. It is the shaking of th
bed. I fear that I shall be thrown down and the child be kille
before it is born.'

He reached out as if to steady the shaking of the huge
mahogany bed that held his wife's frail body. Oh, for the soun
of hooves! But there was nothing to be heard above the fierce
sound of thundering winds, the crashing of falling timber and a
great wailing as though all the Banshees of the race of the
Tuatha de Danaan were outside, keening, not for one soul but
for the souls of all the people in the world. Was it the end of an
era? Or was the cook right? Was it the end of the world?

The bed rocked and Margaret moaned again. She thought
longingly of the snug sleeping berths built into the wall, one
above the other in the room she had shared with her sister in the
Belgian villa overlooking the Lake of Nightingales.

In lulls between storm and pain, she thought that Yvette was
popping little hard objects like beads on to her face from the
berth above. Yvette was always tossing things down at her!
Margaret put up her hand and pushed away the pieces of
flowers and fruit that so embellished the reeds and fluted
columns of the bed. Mr. Chippendale had never envisaged a
wind that could blow his carvings about like *papier-mâché*.

A freakish wind blew round the room in all directions. With a
weird whistling sound it scattered candles and ornaments again

20

and with a long-drawn scream it loosened the carved crane from the great headboard—intended by its designer to be the emblem of care and watchfulness. It fell straight on Margaret.

It was more than she could bear. She threw herself into her husband's arms and implored him to take her to some safe place. He held her to him and tried to think of some refuge. Some place where she could lie in safety to endure the pain and fear.

He thought of the flooded basement, the wrecked drawing-room, the bedrooms all around her, all shaking and shuddering and clanging. At last he thought of something. Because of the flooding, most of the household and refugees were now in the front hall, and the passages behind it. He called some of the men and had them remove the big Flanders tick and place it with all its bolsters and pillows on the floor in a corner of the room furthest from the window and fire. While he directed the men he held Margaret in his arms and his heart contracted as he felt her agony.

Where was Big John?

In the tempest Big John thanked the good God that the master had allowed him to take the Rajah. No other horse in the castle stalls could have stood up to this storm: no other horse in Ireland!

Three times they made the road, only to be driven back to the fields by the barriers of uprooted trees. The fields were completely under water. Sometimes the seventeen-and-a-half hands horse sank ot his shoulders. Big John spurred him, but feared to dismount lest he be sucked under. It went to his heart to add his weight to the struggle of the horse as he floundered to lift himself and his rider from the down-suck of bog. Once, when the powerful horse could struggle no longer and it looked as if itself and rider must perish in the morass, a wind came thundering across the earth like thousands of horsemen. A rick of turf stood near the submerged horse and rider. In an instant it was tossed in the air and a shower of black sods were scattered around them for hundreds of yards. A sod struck Big John on the side of the head and he felt stunned for a moment and dropped the reins. Instantly he felt the horse lifted bodily out of the swamp. It gave a whinnying cry that chilled his veins.

Somehow they found firm footing and rode forward. And now a faint glow rose in the darkness and lit the way before them. As he drew near he saw that it was Carney's shebeen on fire. A group of men and women stood helplessly watching the flames. As they saw the horseman approach they ran to him. Carney recognised Big John and asked him to help with the flames.

'The lads were playing Twenty-Five for a leg of mutton and all of a sudden a great wind blew down the chimney. There was a fire on the hearth that would roast an ox an' Felix Downey had just banged the Five of Hearts on the table when the flames flew around the room and before we knew where we wor me house was on fire.' Then he said simply, 'I've no house now, Mr. Dermody.'

Big John felt the pathos of the simple statement. 'God knows,' he answered, 'I'd like to give a hand but I must go for the doctor. Her Ladyship is in a bad way. The child is coming before its time and it has taken me an hour to get this far.'

John Carney forgot his own trouble in his sympathy for the sweet young Ladyship. 'Go on your way and God be with you,' he said. 'There is nothing you can do here.' His wife and two other women crowded round the horse's head, full of concern for her Ladyship.

'God carry you safely,' they cried as he urged Rajah forward.

To right and left of him cabins were levelled to the ground or on fire. Once he passed a group of naked children shivering and crying in front of the ruins of a group of cabins. And once, as the horse took a fallen tree in a jump, he fell from the saddle and his shoulder gave him fierce pain. The side of his head was aching, too, where the sod of turf had struck him. He did not notice that blood poured over his ear on to his shoulder.

Templetown was close now but all he could see was a great red glow in the sky and clouds of smoke. The wind had shifted from southwest to sheer west and was blowing louder and wilder. Showers of stones and branches blew about him incessantly—once a brick hit Rajah on the head and it reared and plunged panic-stricken. Big John held on madly, the force of his hold torturing his injured shoulder.

Dr. Mitchell lived on the Mall. Big John never remembered how he got there. It hadn't occurred to him that midst this havoc and disaster others would have need of the doctor. When a servant told him that the doctor was not at home, the utter dismay unmanned him. He suddenly felt the pain in the side of

22

his head and for a moment his knees sagged with weakness and exhaustion.

The doctor had gone to the barracks near the Mall where a sentry box had been lifted from the ground and blown down the street with the sentry still inside.

When Big John came upon Dr. Mitchell, he was bending over a policeman who had been helping with the sentry and had got his leg and thigh broken. The wind-borne sentry, miraculously unhurt, was helping him. A group of frightened, wailing children were waiting by the road.

'Is it mad you are,' the doctor said, 'to talk of going to a confinement on a night like this.'

'Her Ladyship is bad,' urged Big John. 'It's a month before her time an' the midwife not due from Dublin till Monday. Night or no night, the child must be loosed.'

The doctor straightened his back. 'I'm not talking about the night, I'm talking about its victims. Listen to these children. Do you know what's wrong with them? They're blind.' The force of the wind had dashed fiery ash into the eyes of the terrified, homeless children.

Dr. Mitchell never knew how near he was to being lifted bodily into Big John's arms and brought off by force. 'For the love of God, Dr. Mitchell, come with me! I wouldn't face Sir Roderick. He's counting on my word, an' I never broke it yet.'

'Yourself and your word,' shouted the doctor. 'God damn it into hell and out of hell! Can't you see I'm wanted worse here? Anyone can have a baby.'

The sentry chuckled. He was feeling very happy about being alive. 'I couldn't,' he said.

A military surgeon came on the scene to attend the sentry. He had striven through the storm from a card party outside the town. The sight of him cheered Dr. Mitchell. For the first time he noticed the blood on Big John's face, and that he swayed as he stood.

'Come up to the house till I look at you,' he said more kindly. 'We'll tackle the baby afterwards.'

CHAPTER 3

Margaret, lying in the comparative security of the floor, at last became aware of the storm that was rending her body. Until now the tumult and the swaying had imbued her with an all pervading fear that dulled her sense of physical pain. Now pain was in possession. Although outside the storm was approaching the highest pitch of its fury, it was in abeyance for her. As tree by tree was uprooted and the earth seemed to groan with anguish, the child within her clamoured, pain by pain, for the gift of life.

She tugged at the pretty bow beneath her chin. Her husband leaned over, glad to be of some help. But the neat bow of Mrs. Mansfield's contriving eluded his fingers and he bungled. In a frenzy of pain Margaret tore the ribbons from the cap.

His ineptitude upset Roderick beyond all proportion. He rose from his crouching position. The noise began to beat against his brain. Panic assailed him. It must be the end of all creation. How could a man-made world survive when all Nature was crashing? Why then should this futile anguish be forced upon the being he loved so dearly? The child was being born to die! Still, in birth was hope. Let the world crash! Margaret would bring new life and a new world. She was like Eve outside her lost Eden expecting, not just her first babe, but the first babe of the human race.

For a moment the storm seemed to quiet, lull, then all the winds converged about the castle and hurled themselves with a murderous roaring upon walls and roofs and windows. Roderick staggered backwards to the door and leaned there, his hands about his ears, until there was an easing. Then quietly he slipped from the room to see what fresh disaster had befallen.

In the front hall servitors and tenants were clinging together for support and comfort. Children still wailed but the injured child lay in a half-fainting stupor. He splashed his way to the back door. He must see what was happening outside! He *must* get a respite from this prisonhouse of storm! But the opened

24

door yielded nothing but darkness and rain and icy, screaming winds. Above the wind he detected a scream more eerie still. It was the screaming of horses in terror. In despair he turned inward only to hear the worst scream of all, the first long-drawn scream of abandon echoing down through the spaces from his wife's room.

As he reached her door Hannah came to him. 'For God's sake, your Honour, Sir, will you send someone for Mag Miney. 'Tis gettin' terrible an' I'm no use. 'Tis no easy birth.'

'Surely you don't mean that old witch near the front lodge?'

'The same one, your Honour. She's a great hand at childbedding. Her Ladyship's past carin', Sir Roderick. Let you go in God's name!'

What Hannah said was true. Margaret was past caring. And she had ceased to be his Margaret. Her face was purple and swollen. Her fine nostrils were distended and coarsened. Her sensitively curved mouth was a maw from which animal sounds emerged.

Young Thomas begged to be allowed to accompany his master on the ride to the midwife. It was a proud moment for the boy when the groom hoisted him up in front of Roderick and placed a burning turf sod on a stave in his hand to guide them.

Sir Roderick knew every inch of his estate but Thomas knew it better. At least until tonight.

Showers of sparks from the smouldering sod made a trail of light for them. It gave a thin, flickering light for a few yards. 'The path is gone,' Thomas said, peering forward. 'It was there this evening and I coming back from Lady Cullen's.'

'Were you at Lady Cullen's today?' Close as they were together he had to bend his ear to the boy's mouth to hear his reply.

' 'Twas something your own Ladyship was sending her for "little Christmas". A grand little box from Belgium and a bit of chaney in it.' Thomas had thought the handsome box grander than the china ornament it contained.

Little Christmas! Of course! This was the feast of the Epiphany. Or had been. They must be well into the small hours of another day. Roderick fumbled inside his cloak for his watch and held it towards the light. Half-past two and the night stretched long in front of them though they had lived through

Eternity.

There was no need to skirt the estate wall. It was no longer there. The horse was stumbling over the big stones that had held the privacy of the estate in their long-knit framework. Once it baulked and shivered. The dancing sparks showed them a dead cow.

'There's her house,' said Thomas, and as the lanthorn picked out a house he crossed himself. Sir Roderick saw the gesture.

'If you are afraid to go in for her I shall go myself.'

'No, indeed, your Honour, it is just a habit I have when I pass her house. I'm afraid of no human being tonight. What can anyone do to you fornint that big wind?'

His master's face relaxed into its first smile for many an hour at the unconscious irony of the lad's logic.

'It is better that I stay with the horse,' he said. Young Thomas jumped down and disappeared in the wake of the sparks from the burning sod.

A moment later an old crone stood beside the horse and peered up at its rider. 'Is it a thing that the great lady of Kilsheelin Castle has need of Mag Miney this night?' He could not see her face but there was mockery in the cackling voice.

'Is it true that you have skill in childbirth?' he demanded coldly.

'Aye, 'tis true an' many a one has blessed that skill without any big wind blowing. Oh, I . . .' he cut her short.

'Come with me at once.'

Thomas helped her up behind the Sir. Her body reeked vilely. There was a stench from the basket that she carried that made him want to retch. She was chuckling away to herself at the idea of riding behind the Lord of Kilsheelin when suddenly her chuckling ceased. The wind was veering from southeast to southwest. Suddenly a fierce blast came from the west and the two winds met in a whirlwind that drove the breath from horse and riders. The horse was flung back on its haunches and brought the old woman to the ground. The boy was on the ground helping the maddened horse. The master dismounted and pulled on the reins with all his strength.

Then it happened. A wild whistling filled the air and before their eyes the field in front of them rose from the earth and soared into the sky. It paused motionless for an instant, suspended in the grasp of the whirlwind, then soared away into the

26

western darkness; acres of unbroken sod and grass floating through the sky like a magic carpet.

The three stood speechless, the little knife boy and the witch and the Lord of the soil, their eyes straining upwards through the darkness. Suddenly a cry burst from the man, 'My land, my land! It is not possible!'

The boy clutched him, forgetful of rank. 'We're left behind,' he wailed. 'The whole world is going up into heaven and we are left behind.'

Behind them the old woman was keening and mumbling. 'You have angered them, Sir Roderick O'Carroll. There was Hungry Grass in that field. Grass where fairies hold their revels. They make hungry those who walk upon it. You walked on it with your proud feet and you cut down the ring of hawthorn trees. Never before have sperrits taken a man's land. I wish you no harm, but no man can prosper after the sperrits have taken his land.'

'Shut up, you old harpy!' Roderick struggled with the horse that was pawing for a footing, its hind legs on solid ground, its front lunging over the brink where the field had disappeared.

At last they reached the stable yard. When the old woman entered the kitchen the people there edged away from her contact. They edged further still when she placed her basket on the table and drew from it a mess of unsalted butter, rancid and green. She had herbs as well and took them to the pot that hung over one of the fires that smoked without blazing.

Mrs. Stacey turned the fanwheel to make a flame and watched every movement the old creature made. When she threw a handful of raspberry leaves into the water the cook was reassured. She grew fearful again when strange leaves with strange smells were added.

Sir Roderick came in from the stable and stopped short at the sight of the old woman bending over the fire. 'Why has she not been taken at once to her Ladyship?' he demanded.

'She'll have need for what I'm making. I'm ready now if you'll show me the way.' She poured the brew into a jug and taking up the foul butter mess she followed the Sir.

'She'll put a spell on the child if ever she brings it to the world,' hissed the big cook.

The lodge-keeper's wife nodded agreement. 'She'll leave a changeling in its place. It's not the first time she has done it.'

Mrs. Stacey drew her chair near her and looked fearfully towards the door.

'The Sir can scoff at the prophecies but did he ever think he'd live to see the day when Mag Miney would bring home the heir of Kilsheelin?'

''Tis the truth you're sayin', Mrs. Stacey. But did any of us think we'd live to see a wind like the one that's blowing to-night?'

'Mrs. Murray, acquanie,' the cook bent towards her and lowered her voice, 'the prophecies are comin' back to me. There was some I couldn't remember.' She enumerated on her fingers. 'The graves will open...' Mrs. Murray nodded, '... that has happened without a doubt.' The cook pressed down her index finger. 'The Russians will water their horses on the shores of Lough Neagh, and ...' she pressed on her big second finger until it cracked, 'women will walk the earth in trousers!'

Mrs. Murray gasped. 'God forgive you, Mary Anne Stacey, Saint Columcille had something better to do with his time than making that kind of prophecy. I can see reason in the graves opening. It has happened before an' I've seen the tombstones meself tonight. The Russians might come too. Didn't the Danes come? And Cromwell? And Strongbow? Maybe the Russians will have a try too. Much good may it do them! But if the world won't end until womankind walks the face of the earth in—throusers! Then you can take it from me now, Mary Anne Stacey, the world will *never* end!' She shook the water from her feet, gathered up her basket of chirping chickens and their squawking mother and went from the kitchen.

In the bedroom Sir Roderick found his wife kneeling on the Flemish tick, unrecognisable. The frilly nightcap was gone. The glossy hair was bedraggled and dank. The puffed face shone with the dew of labour. The old woman held the jug to her lips. 'Take this, asthore!' The girl turned wild eyes towards her. 'Maman!' she gasped. But she saw only a dirty old woman with a lump of rancid butter and a jug.

Sir Roderick moved down to the drawing-room but turned back at the sight of its havoc. He went on to the dining-room. It did not seem so bad here. At least in the darkness there was form and line. He called for lights and as the footman lit candles he felt relief to see the long table and the familiar chairs reflecting the light in their dark surfaces of Domingo mahogany. He never liked Domingo mahogany. It was a post-Cromwellian innovation. He had intended to replace it with something lighter. Then he remembered his treeless land and the field that had blown away before his eyes. My God! What a fantasy! Did it really happen? He would know tomorrow, if tomorrow ever came. He was too tired to think of tomorrow. He stretched his arms out on the table and laid his head on them. In a moment he was asleep.

It was half-past five when the footman called to say that Big John had arrived with the doctor. The doctor had gone straight upstairs. Roderick hurried up and as he knocked at the bedroom door he realised that it was the first time that night that he had done so. There was no wind roaring outside.

Dr. Mitchell opened the door. 'I'm sorry that I could not be here to deliver the child but everything seems to be all right. My God! What are you doing?' There was a roaring now and it was not the wind. He strode across the room and knocked from old Mag's hand the butter she was about to use to heal the lacerated tissue. He turned back to Sir Roderick. 'If I was not in time to deliver the child, thank God I've been in time to save your wife from childbed fever. Stinking butter! No wonder wimmen die! Get out!' he bawled.

And then from the bed came a sound that gladdened the ears of the man who had lived through a night of fearsome sounds. It was the sound of a new-born baby's cry. He made a quick move in its direction but the doctor waved him back.

'Leave us a while. There is nothing to worry about.'

Roderick's step was light as he moved down the stairs. As he passed old Mag muttering and groaning with the effort of the unaccustomed steps his heart smote him. It was sorry treatment to give the poor creature who had brought his child through storm into the world. He paused to give her a gold piece, then hurried from her blessings; and her smell.

As she came chuckling into the kitchen, Mrs. Stacey stopped turning the fanwheel on the fires that now blazed, all eight of them.

'Is there anything in it yet?' she asked Mag. Big John put down the mug of tea he was sipping.

Mag placed the butter with tender care into her basket while the kitchen reeked. 'To be sure there is. I done what I came to do.'

'Praises be to God,' said the coachman, rising to his feet. 'Is it an heir or a child?'

' 'Tis a child that's in it.'

Mrs. Stacey dropped the wheel handle and straightening up in her chair. 'Welcome be the holy will of God,' she said with pious disappointment. 'Sure, isn't it better than nothing?'

A bell swung wildly in the row that hung near the door. Before its tongue could clatter the Sir himself gave tongue from the library door. 'Hegarty! The flag!'

The butler came shivering and blinking from his pantry. He had slept through the last episode of the drama. The flag! Cead mile curses! The heir was born and he not standing by to hoist the flag!

But there was no getting to hoist it. The turret stairs was blocked with part of the turret itself. None of the men could squeeze past; not even the gossoons, Mickey-the-turf and Johnny-the-buckets. 'Where's that new gossoon, the knife boy?' the butler demanded. 'Surely he is small enough to make his way to the turret.'

Young Thomas was found stretched across two wooden chairs under a big cloak. The Sir, it seems, had noticed him there when he passed with the doctor and had bidden someone to put a covering over him. The old-fashioned man's 'trusty' that had trailed about him the day a few weeks back when a respectable-looking woman had brought him to Mrs. Mansfield, trailed from him again as he edged his small body past the massive piece of turret that jammed the stairway. Young Thomas raised the standard of the O'Carrolls and watched it float high above the broken turret. He could see the family arms and the picture of the hawk and although he couldn't read he knew that the words beneath were 'An seabac abu' the rallying cry of the O'Carrolls—The hawk to victory!

The storm, like the lady of the castle, was spent. The air was still, a sigh of a breeze scarcely unfurled the folds of Saint Patrick's blue. Down in the great yard, workers and homeless tenants gazed up in awe. The wonder of it surged through the shivering Thomas. They were looking up at the flag that none but he could raise! The newcomer to the castle! Its smallest and youngest member except for that other newcomer, the girl-child whose birth he was proclaiming. He turned suddenly and edged down again. From the turret entrance he could see the hall door standing open. There was no one around. Instead of going down the servants' stairway he came forward and put a timid bare foot on the top step of the grand staircase. Fearfully he craned over each shoulder, then with a swoop he bunched the old 'trusty' up under his armpit and skeeted down the stairs.

He walked backwards over the gravel to the lawn, his face straining upwards intent on viewing his handiwork, oblivious of Roderick who stood gazing at the flag. Roderick looked down at the small boy who appeared suddenly beside him, draped in a garment belonging to the past century and to God knows whom else. About three feet of brown frieze fell in a train behind and left two little skinny legs unhampered and unsheltered. 'So it's you again!' said Roderick.

Young Thomas gave a frightened glance sideways and was reassured. He resumed his rapt contemplation of his achievement. This wasn't any of the staff hierarchy. It was only the Sir, God-like and remote and unlikely to threaten a body with a skelp on the lug. 'Yes, your Honour's Sir, it's me,' he said; 'and,' he continued, pointing an arm upward and letting another few yards of the frieze flop to the grass, 'it was me that raised that flag. Not a one in the whole castle but me was able to do it. Only for me the world'd never know that we have a little colleen-uasail—a girl of the nobility inside in the castle.'

Sir Roderick looked down at the grotesquerie of brown frieze and muddy flesh that had travelled with him in some perimeter of space and time while the world had fought against the heavens for its existence. A figment of the night's fantasy! He handed Thomas a crown piece.

The child looked down at the big coin and, like his master, wondered if this too were a figment of the night. Only he didn't think in terms of figments. He wondered if his Honour's Nobility had been having a swig of the bottle on account of the great event. 'You haven't a sup taken, your Honour's Sir?'

His Honour told him not to be so demmed impertinent or he would take back the money.

'It's not-imperance—your Honour's Sir. Gentlemen throws money in drink; but not this much. Look at the size of it!' It covered the small hand he held up. He also held up two fan-fringed eyes so blue that they held Sir Roderick's gaze. 'I wouldn't like to take—to take, an—advantage.' The big word was hauled up with a jerk from mud squelched toes.

'Thank you,' his master replied. 'But I shouldn't be too conscientious about—advantages. Just grab them.'

Young Thomas grabbed so tightly that he let his 'trusty' fall where it would. 'I will, your Honour's Sir,' he breathed, and shot off, but stumbled over the 'trusty'. Out of its folds a muffled voice insisted, 'Oh then, indeed and indeed I will.'

Roderick watched amused as the small object scuttled away cautiously ahead of its own fanned-out tail, like some little brown thing of the earth; not a fox, not with those blue and candid eyes; a squirrel perhaps, or maybe, a leprechaun.

CHAPTER 4

Men worked furiously to make a passage for the Sir as he rode out to seek a foster-mother for his daughter. This mission, he thought, was all of a piece with the mess of unreadiness into which Nature had plunged all of them. He chucked his horse to order. There was no need for it to take fright at the little doe whose gentle eyes pleaded timidly from a lifeless body.

Everything had been so neatly planned. Months ago he had arranged the novel luxury of a Professed Nurse-Tender trained at Doctor Mosse's famous lying-in hospital beside Dublin's Rotunda Gardens. No handy woman for his lovely Margaret! Instead, she had been delivered by the black arts—and hands of an old witch who was even now standing at the gates of the castle watching the men remove the topmost tree that blocked the entrance, and boasting of her role in the night's drama.

Roderick cleared the underneath tree and cantered down the carriage road. He halted in sudden amazement. How could I possibly have gone astray, he wondered! He had turned into a tiny boreen known as the Wolf Track. Long after the last wolf had been exterminated from the Tipperary hills at the turn of the previous century the Kilsheelin O'Carrolls had kept alive the rumour of the wolves that had originally beaten this track. The scare intimidated all unwarranted approach to the black density of forests that screened the existence of the Catholic O'Carrolls hostile powers. But now Roderick felt disorientated. Trees and familiar landmarks had vanished overnight. He found himself looking at strange vistas. He could see the windings of the four crossroads that met at Kilsheelin Cross. He could glimpse, for the first time, the distant turrets of Strague Castle.

Strague Castle was one of the survivors of the thirteen castles of the O'Carrolls. Its branch had held through the centuries a recurring record of treachery. Or was it, Roderick reflected, just practical expediency? When Cromwell rode up to its door the owner had played the game. A smiling welcome and, My castle

33

is at your disposal, Lord Cromwell. It worked. When Cromwell rode out the gate again with his sword and his Bible and his wart and with his soldiery all refreshed, Calvagh O'Carroll was still in possession of Strague Castle.

A century later, while another owner was serving in Austria, his youngest son turned Protestant and claimed thereby the castle. From a nearby cabin where the absent owner had spent his early childhood in the old foster-age custom of the nobility, his peasant foster-brother set out for Austria to warn him. O'Carroll hastened home but was denied admission to his castle by his own son. He was forced to shelter in the cabin of his fosterage. A few months later, broken-hearted, he died there in the arms of his foster-brother.

Again, just thirty-eight years ago this very month, when the Irish Parliament was voted out of Ireland by the infamous Act of Union with the British Parliament, the father of the present owner voted against his country. As a bribe for betraying it into its present beggary and decay he had been given the peerage of Strague, suitably financed.

Yet, Roderick reflected, not all Strague O'Carrolls had been traitorous. Generations of its occupiers had averted the eyes of authority from the castle of the Catholic O'Carrolls living their hidden lives behind a wooden curtain of almost inpenetrable forests. Planter statesmen and lawyers, vague about the land they were seizing and reparcelling, looked no further than Strague Castle with its loyal Protestant inmates. They remained unaware of the life that teemed beyond that wooden curtain which each succeeding generation trained to grow taller and denser and blacker about the hidden castle of Kilsheelin. From beneath the leafy folds its sons had slipped out by night to Europe, fighting on its battlefields, Spain, Austria, France, Holland; basking in the glitter of its court life; from time to time they would return, along this very track, bringing with them the gossip of the countries of their affiliation, their languages and their culture.

He turned in his saddle. Like a woman surprised half-dressed, Kilsheelin Castle was standing partly exposed. Never before from this point had one been able to glimpse even a stone of its structure. Now the remaining trees hung about it, brown and dishevelled like inadequate garments. Like the brown trusty around the urchin who had raised that blue flag fluttering there

bove a broken turret. My God, what an indignity! That mini-
ure ragamuffin! This storm had certainly acted like a dredger;
sting strange elements up through the cool, proud surface of
oderick's life.

The flag recalled him to the existence of his premature
aughter and her needs. These treeless vistas had beguiled him
own vistas of time! The man he had come to see hailed him
om the roof he was repairing and started to climb down. Black
at Ryan was Sir Roderick's foster-brother. The custom of
osterage had died out before Roderick's birth but when business
ad taken the elder Sir to the Continent after Roderick's birth,
e took his fragile wife with him and left the baby at the house
f Black Pat's father to be nursed by his widowed sister, Mrs.
tacey. Mrs. Stacey had lost her baby as well as her husband, so
hat Roderick received the clamouring tide of her love. He had
rown up with her dark-skinned, black-haired nephew, Pat;
ogether they raided the castle orchard, poached its streams, and
hen they encountered Sir Dominic, the heir would touch his
orelock to him as Black Pat did, not realising that the grand
entleman in the carriage or on horseback was his own father.
Vhen the time came for Roderick to return to the castle, Mrs.
tacey, rather than be parted from her foster-son, took service
here.

'God save you, Sir Roderick,' greeted Black Pat. ''Tis an ill
vind blows no one good. I could be almost thankful to last
ight's big wind for blowing you my way.'

Black Pat wanted to know if there was any truth in the story
bout the flying field. There was an element of fear in his
mazement when Roderick assured him that there was nearly
ve acres of truth in the story. 'They say you cut down the ring
f hawthorn trees beside the Hungry Grass.'

Roderick smiled amusedly. 'So you still give in to pisho-
uerie?'

'Not a whole lot, but,' Black Pat shook his head slowly, 'I'd
ut down a forest of oaks before I'd cut a hawthorn tree.'

Roderick returned to his mission. Mrs. Stacey had told him
hat Black Pat's wife had a young baby. She might make a
uitable foster-mother. 'She will need to come at once,' he said.
The child is very tiny. She has come six weeks ahead of
chedule. It was the storm.'

Black Pat's face closed. For a fleeting moment it showed

something that eluded Roderick. His wife, he said promptly
had weaned their baby. The impression persisted with Roderic
that there was an element of—reluctance? An independen
devil, Black Pat! But this was no time for independence. Ha
he some kind of idea that his wife was above being wet nurse t
his landlord's child? Black Pat was speaking quickly. Hi
neighbour's wife—widowed in the storm—was nursing an in
fant. She would be an admirable wet nurse. All at once Blac
Pat could not do enough for his foster-brother. He would ten
to the woman's livestock while she would be at the castle; woul
repair her roof; tend her farm. This was the Black Pat who ha
risked his life for Roderick. There seemed to be but one poin
where his loyalty halted. As Roderick turned out on to th
carriage road he realised that he had not met his foster-brother'
wife.

Roderick could scarcely get passage through his own land
There were crowds milling about. News of the uprooted fiel
seemed to have gone far and wide. They gazed with awe at th
pit-like wilderness strewn with rubble and boulders and tree
and lifeless carcasses. O'Driscoll, the groom, came to him wit
the information that the field itself had fallen unbroken on
small farm at Poolgower, four miles off. O'Driscoll had wagon
yoked in readiness for the Sir's instructions to recover his soil.

At Poolgower the crowds were greater. The receiving end o
the marvel held more spectacle. A field of grassland fallen from
the clouds of heaven!

'My men will remove it now,' Sir Roderick said to Jame
Keating, the owner of the farm. The man eyed him levelly for
moment. 'By whose authority?' he demanded.

Roderick gave an impatient frown. 'By mine, of course,' h
gestured O'Driscoll towards the field. He had expected to find i
lying loose and broken upon the surface, but the might of th
blast had impacted it into the earth as though it had been ther
always. O'Driscoll looked at it in bewilderment. 'It is not goin
to be so easy as we thought, your Honour's Sir,' he said.

Keating barred his way. 'I'm glad that you realise it is no
going to be so easy,' he said grimly. 'I dare any man of you t
put a foot into that field.' Behind him a tall, lantern-jawe
young man, obviously a son, sauntered forward. He held a fowl
ing-piece nonchalantly through the crook of his arm as thoug
he were off for a bang at a rabbit. By a strange coincidence a few

36

more young men happened along with casually-cocked fowling-pieces as though they also were off for a few pot-shots. Roderick sized up the situation. The possibility of anyone dreaming of trying to retain the field had never occurred to him. He curbed his fury and spoke coldly. 'Do you not realise that this is my property blown here by a freak of nature?'

'I realise,' Keating replied, 'that this is my property.' He indicated a few poor fields bordering the bog. 'And that,' he said, pointing to the greenest one, 'is something that fell from the heavens; an act of God. It is best not to dispute the actions of God.'

Rage swept through Roderick. A short while back he had mused on how his ancestors had clung to their land through the centuries in the face of every menace. Not a foot had they yielded! Did this hind presume to hold a parcel of its acreage that had strayed by freakish chance? 'By God,' he cried. 'I'll dispute your action.' He signalled his men to return home. There was no hope of achieving anything at this moment. 'I shall return,' he said to Keating, 'when the crowd has dispersed.'

On his return he encountered Black Pat again. He had brought the foster-mother to the castle. 'Are you off to see the peep show?' he asked him.

Black Pat turned blacker still. 'You have no call to say such a thing to me, Rody O'Carroll.' In the quick hurt of his sensitivity he addressed his landlord as he had done in those young days of fosterage. 'I wouldn't be wanting to see—or hear—that a dog belonging to you was sick.'

Roderick went to his study. There was much to be done. The land would have to be recovered. Mrs. Mansfield's death would have to be reported. There would be an inquest. He was interrupted by the bard who appeared full of reproach that no formal announcement had been made to him of the birth of the child. 'I who recorded the genealogy of your father aye, and your grandfather, for my own father had gone blind at the time.' There was no harp in his apartment fit to play a note in honour of the great event. The small harps were flung 'trinacaila', their frames battered, their strings awry. The great family harp stood in two feet of water. The bard held the piano in scorn and of course the bagpipes were only for lesser folk. 'And I assume,' said the old gentleman slyly, 'that the wine cellar has fared as badly. We may not even drink to the great occasion.'

Roderick took the hint. He led them inward and rang for the butler. Black Pat hung back, but the bard harangued him upon the ties of fosterage. 'The little cailinuasail above is your foster second cousin. The link,' he said, 'extended in fosterage to one hundred degrees whereas in blood it stopped short at twenty degrees.' They drank the health of the infant girl and it looked as though the old man would drink the health of all her preceding generations. He was aghast to hear about the field. Not at the manner of its going, but that Sir Roderick should be so puerile as to consider falling back upon the quill of any attorney for its recovery. 'Has the Wild Huntsman dismantled your gunroom?' he asked. 'The O'Carroll Ribeach went out and bade the English quit his land when Queen Elizabeth divided Tipperary among four men of Cheshire. And they quit!'

Roderick rose to end the genealogical survey. 'Unfortunately, Bard,' he smiled, 'it is not Queen Elizabeth this time. It is the Wild Huntsman who has chosen to divide my land. And this Keating man of Poolgower is proving more formidable than the four men of Cheshire.'

Sir Roderick, gazing bleakly through the window at his wastelands, watched scores of men cutting up the great trunks that lay across the carriageway and piling them along the sides. Away to the left beyond the park, groups of people were standing round talking and pointing, and behaving rather like spectators at a hurling match. Two horsemen rode past the massive iron gates that lay on the ground. Roderick saw that one was a policeman, guessed the other was the Coroner come about Mrs. Mansfield.

Mr. O'Neill-Balfe sipped a glass of Roderick's claret appreciatively, toasted the birth of the child, and listened to the details of the housekeeper's death. 'I'll see her,' he said. 'And after that I have just one more storm inquest in this district. A man called Lucas has reported that his wife and newly-born infant were washed from their bed and drowned. Meantime,' he raised his glass, 'I drink to the birth that defied the storm.' Then he remembered the field. 'I take it that it is some exaggeration of superstitious peasants?'

Sir Roderick shrugged. 'I wish it *were* an exaggeration. Before my very eyes I saw a section of my land—about five acres— scooped out of the ground and carried through the air. It travelled across the park and over the western turret out of sight.'

'Astounding!'

'What is more astounding still is that it travelled four miles before it alighted on the farm of James Keating of Poolgower. I rode over there yesterday and saw it; a field of green, fattening grass among a few little fields no better than bog. I see little hope of retrieving it. It has been planted there with the same force that lifted it from my territory; and the sightseers are aiding and abetting him; tramping it deeper into his possession.'

The Coroner had the impression that his host was speaking to himself. Aiding and abetting? What strange language! But then the poor young gentleman had been through a dreadful ordeal; he must have incurred immense financial loss. Roderick suddenly recollected himself. 'You see the people are going there in their hundreds. I don't suppose anything like it has ever happened before.'

When the Coroner had departed, Roderick seated himself at his desk and made an entry in a big black book.

'On the night of January the Sixth in the Year of Our Lord, One Thousand Eight Hundred and Thirty-Nine a great wind blew across Ireland. It has caused havoc and disaster and the loss of many lives; how many it is not yet known. In the course of this storm five acres of the land that my forefathers have held through the centuries against all unwarranted approach, were raised skywards in my presence and borne out of my sight. On the Seventh of January, this same year, I rode forth to the farm of James Keating of Poolgower and there did see my own land lying unbroken as it had left me. I pray that this act of Nature will not affect the lives of those whose heritage has been so strangely visited.'

He closed the book and then almost as an afterthought, re-opened it and wrote, 'The stress of the storm brought my wife to labour before her time. Our housekeeper, Julia Mansfield, was killed in my wife's presence while tending her. Towards morning my wife gave birth to a daughter.'

As he re-read what he had just written its significance smote him. He was the youngest and only survivor of his parent's five children. The doctor doubted the likelihood of Margaret's bearing another child and so the record of the birth of his daughter, Sterrin, read like another incident of the storm. The record of the birth of a son and heir would have been a different matter. No storm would have taken precedence over *that* event.

CHAPTER 5

The Dublin Mail Coach came clattering down the Market Square, scattering mud from wheels and hooves in all directions. A bigger cheer than usual went up from the crowd of ostlers and hangers-on outside Mullaly's Coaching Inn. The coach was three days late and the whole town was out to greet its arrival.

The most imposing of all the waiting vehicles was that driven by Big John Dermody, of Kilsheelin Castle. Not, indeed that it was the grandest, because he merely drove a one horse back-to-back. But he sat so regally, holding the long whip upright like a spear, that he gave prestige to any equippage.

The 'Scout', otherwise John Doyle, the shoemaker from Love Lane, a temperamental shoemaker and a master pedant, never missed the arrival or departure of a mail coach. He checked the identity of each passenger who descended from the coach, his occupation and mission, as though it were his paid calling. The various drivers, guards and ostlers passed on to him all the recent news from Dublin, and all possible information about the passengers. The drivers of waiting vehicles yielded, often unwittingly, all available information about those for whom they waited. But never would Big John divulge an iota of gossip.

It was obvious to the Scout that it was no member of the family, nor of the Quality, that Big John awaited, because he was only driving a back-to-back. Although, argued the Scout, the Sir was not above using the back-to-back; but in that event Big John would be wearing his tall hat, not the Hardy Bastard, which was the colloquial description of the pot-shaped half caroline the coachman was wearing.

However, news of the storm in Dublin and en route was of primary importance just now. The identity of passengers must wait. The last blast of the bugle had scarcely died away when the Scout had his foot on the step sacred to the driver.

'God save ye! We thought you must have blown away altogether, or did yet get e'er a blast of the wind there at all?'

'Don't be talkin',' said the driver; 'tis a sight for sore eyes to
see you. It does me heart good to see the faces of friends when
there's so many on my route that I'll never see again after that
same wind.' He threw the reins to an ostler and stood up stiffly.
'Mr. Doyle, you have often heard me spake of Murty Kava-
nagh?'

'Of Naas?'

'The same. He's gone.'

'Is it kilt you mean?'

'That's what I *do* mean, and so is his wife kilt, and his two
children, and the house they lived in is gone and the town it
stood in is gone.'

'The town of Naas is it you mean?'

'There is no town of Naas in it now. Every house in it is
levelled to the ground.'

'Praises be to the Hand of God. . . .'

Before he could pass comment there was a cheer from the
crowd bustling about the coach. He stepped back and looked
towards the alighting passengers. A tall man towering above the
rest was being received with homage by the owner of the inn. In
the brief exchange of news the crowd had swelled and the Scout
had found himself pushed to the outside. A rich stentorian
voice rolled over the craning heads. The Scout, flailing right
and left with his elbows, cried out: 'There is only one voice like
that in all Ireland.'

Behind him the driver, his prestige disregarded, and fighting
his own passage through the crowd, gasped into the Scout's
prim: 'There is only one Liberator in Ireland.' The Scout tried
to answer, but his mouth was full of the elbow of a buxom lady
in a bright red cloak who requested him not to eat the elbow off
her.

'Madam,' said he, 'you have, no doubt, a tasty elbow, but
Saint Thomas says that a thing which is not in its own place is
an abomination. I'd be thankful if you'd keep your elbow to
yourself.'

The lady's face went redder than her cloak. 'How dare you
call me an abomination!'

The Scout made a breast-stroke away from her. His feet were
off the ground and he was literally swimming forward in the

throng. 'That,' he answered, 'was merely a Thomasian figure of speech.' He grabbed at the cape of the driver's coat as he jostled past him. 'You are the cause of all this. Why didn't you inform me that the great Daniel O'Connell, the Liberator of Ireland, was on your mail coach instead of talking of trivialities like the big wind?'

'Faith, 'twas the same "triviality" brought him here in my mail coach. The wheel of his own coach went over a hole in the road. The linch-pin came out of the wheel, and the whole side of the carriage went over into the ditch.'

They reached the forefront of the crowd and stood looking up in awe of the world's greatest personality, the uncrowned King of Ireland, Daniel O'Connell. There he stood in their own home town, unheralded except by the trumpeting blasts of the wind that had brought him to their midst.

As he spoke the aristocrats paused with feet on their carriage steps in the act of departure. The voice that no orator ever equalled rolled across the square and every voice and sound was hushed. To most of them he was but a legend: the man who had liberated them from the savagery of the Penal Code.

He grieved with them over the anguish that had come to them in the wake of the storm. A voice in the crowd yelled 'Sure you would have prevented it yourself if you could, Dan.'

'I would, God knows.'

His tones fell softer but still all-pervading. 'There is nothing I would not do to prevent further suffering to my sorely tried countrymen.'

Loud cheering stopped him for nearly five minutes. He held up his hand and there was silence. 'When the hand of man is raised against you, I defend you with every breath of my being.'

The Scout could contain himself no longer. He ran forward and grasped the Liberator's flowing cloak. 'You've done that, sir,' he panted. 'No man ever did more for his fellow-men.'

The pat that the great orator gave to the Scout's shoulder 'went', as he said to the mail-coach driver, 'to me very soul, and it will vibrate down through the generations that, plaze God, will follow me.'

The Liberator resumed. 'When the Hand of God is raised above us we can but bow our heads and say, Thy will be done. In Dublin alone I have addressed six hundred people made homeless by the storm. Not a stone left of the habitations in which they were born and reared. I have seen the drowned bodies of men and women washed forth from the homes along the Liffey quays. Some of my fellow members coming from their constituencies in the West and South have told, in Dublin, tales that are too harrowing for your ears. In some towns the fires blazed unremittingly from eleven o'clock at night until six o'clock next morning. In Loughrea the fire burned all night, and the aid of every possible member of the male population was of no avail. When one half of the town was destroyed and the fire had been almost extinguished, the wind changed and fanned the flames in the opposite direction until the other half of the town was consumed.'

Then he went on to tell them a tale of an anticlimax to the Penal System. The people of one small town had completed, just before Christmas, the first church that had been built there since the persecutions of previous centuries had razed its monasteries and abbeys. It had been built by the efforts and labour and contributions of the poorest of people. 'This Christmas Day gone past,' he cried, and now the beautiful voice throbbed with feeling; there were no more oratorical tricks, no phrase-making, and as always when he was deeply moved, its melting pathos plucked at the heart strings of his listeners, 'for the first time in more than a century and a half the congregation knelt before an altar that was not erected in a cave, or a garret. There was no curtain hung between the priest and his flock to enable them to swear with truth, if put to it, that they knew not the identity of the Mass celebrant.'

He caught up a handful of the folds of his great cloak and threw them across his shoulder. Not a soul in the outermost edges of the multitude missed one breath that now came in tremulous tones. 'On the night of Epiphany, that Feast that celebrates the Coming of the Wise Kings with their offerings that were the symbols of Faith and Homage and Self-denial, on that night as you all know too well the big wind blew.' He dropped his voice almost to a whisper, but not a syllable was missed. 'That little church was blown to pieces. The stones that were hand carved with love and devotion were scattered for miles across the countryside. There is nothing left of that great act of faith and human endeavour.'

He raised his voice in sudden thundering. 'Who will rebuild that church? Where are the lords of that soil and the rightful protectors of its people?'

Now the Scout and the enlightened ones knew where he was leading their thoughts. He was on his pet theme: the Repeal of the Act of Union that had deprived Ireland of its native government, and transferred its legislature to England.

'They have abandoned the country that they have betrayed. These landlords are the perpetrators of the Union that has caused misery they shirk to share. They do not like to stand in the sphere of their own infamy. They have taken shelter in England where there are no hungry Irish faces to look shame upon them. They are gone where they can enjoy in peace the plunder of the betrayal, where they can squander in luxuries the rack-rents that their agents wring from their impoverished tenants in Ireland.'

From the centre of the crowd came a cat-call. It was Sealy Ring, a middleman, notorious for his exploitation of the tenants of his absentee employer.

The crowd would have lynched him, but the voice that had held them spellbound was now wheedling. O'Connell had pushed the enormous chimney-pot hat to a rakish angle that displayed the rich dark curls, powdered with silver. He dropped into the vernacular brogue. 'Lave him be, boys,' he shouted. 'Sure I can't find a wisp of hay for every ass that brays!'

As the crowd laughed and cheered he tried to move away, but there wasn't space in front of him to move a foot. In vain did the innkeeper and ostlers and police cry, 'Make way for the Liberator!' Finally he was lifted up on the shoulders of some men and borne into the hall of the inn.

The excitement over, Big John sought out Mrs. Hogan, the nurse from Dublin who was astonished to learn that the infant O'Carroll had already arrived at Kilsheelin Castle.

'It will be a gathering of the giants! How I wish I could come downstairs for the dinner.' Margaret addressed the remark to her husband's back. Mr. O'Connell and the member for Tipperary, Mr. Richard Lalor Sheil, were coming to dine at Kilsheelin Castle. She wished Roderick would not keep looking out of the window at that field. Every time he came into the room he moved as though drawn from her bedside to that window. It was sad to think that the giant oak was uprooted on which he had carved their entwined hearts and initials. The lovely tea-parties they used to have under its branches! She sighed. Immediately he came to her.

'Are you tired, darling?' He placed his hand on the hair that hung smooth and glossy again across her shoulders. She reached up and took his hand.

'I was just thinking of the day that you carved our names under that funny twisted branch on the lovely tree that has gone.'

Now he sighed. 'There are a great many lovely trees gone.' He had given her no idea of the extent of the damage. She did not know there had been lives lost. She knew that the turret had been hit because a piece of it had actually come down the chimney into her room. She knew that a number of trees had been blown down; but she did not know that the number ran into thousands. She knew, too, that some beasts had been killed, but she had not been told that a great herd of cattle had been either drowned or killed by falling trees and flying missiles.

She would have been distressed to know that the herdsman who did the killing had been hard set to find a sheep to kill for tomorrow's dinner for such distinguished guests. The thought of the dinner made her sigh again, and the sigh made him laugh. He slipped his arm around her shoulder.

'What a dismal duet! We seem to do nothing but sigh at each other. Wait until you see Mr. O'Connell. He will blow away your sighs. He comes into a room like a current of fresh air, and everything and everyone brightens and quickens.'

She snuggled into him. 'You admire him so much that I feel a little jealous!'

'Good! It is good for my morale to know that I can make beautiful women jealous. But I remember when I was about fifteen father introduced me to Daniel O'Connell. I thought he was a most superb specimen, powerful shoulders, eyes and lips that a woman would admire.'

'Do you think that I shall?'

'You shall not. But it was his voice that I remember most. It possessed a cadence that was unforgettable. I noticed it again the other evening.'

'He seems to have been your hero. Who was your heroine?'

'My heroine was a brown-haired demoiselle whom I saw one day skating on a lake in Belgium. I watched until she came out of the Park of Nightingales with her mama and her sister and her fierce old *bonne* who was carrying their skates. They all got into a *voiture* and drove off. I followed it on foot at a gallop until it stopped outside a certain villa in the Place de l'Église. She is still my heroine.'

She put up her hand and entwined her fingers in his. 'I was no heroine on Sunday night.'

He held her to him. 'You were magnificent. I can't bear to think of what you went through on that night of horror.'

They were silent for a moment until with a little shiver she said, 'Let us forget it. Let us talk of the preparations for tomorrow's dinner party. *O mon Dieu!* If only Mrs. Mansfield were better! Mrs. Stacey is so *gauche*. How is *la pauvre* Mansfield?'

Sir Roderick went to the window again. Let us forget it, he thought, bitterly. Let us forget it and how is *la pauvre* Mansfield? Where shall I seek forgetfulness? Out there in the peaceful landscape of my demesne? Out among my fallen trees, my cattle! Out in the arid bed of my wind-stolen land! Margaret assessed his graceful outline, tall, lithe, a fraction under six feet, the dark pallor of his complexion framed in side-whiskers, the thick, upswept hair, not black, not brown. She could not see the long blue-grey eyes but she knew that they did not hold that lazy look of his that women found so fascinating.

'Rodereeck,' she called in sudden panic, 'why do you not answer me?'

He turned to her. 'What was it you asked me? Oh yes, Mrs. Mansfield. She is getting on all right.'

'But Rodereeck, you said, and so did the doctor, that she was slightly stunned, and that she had sprained her shoulder under the big brass candle-holder, Rodereeck.' She pronounced his name the way she now did in stress or pleading. 'Are you keeping something from me?'

For a moment he thought of telling her the truth. Someone of the staff was sure to let it out. No one ever spoke of the housekeeper without saying, 'Poor Mrs. Mansfield, God rest her.' Then he looked at her dilated pupils, and remembered the strange way she had looked yesterday when she said she thought the bed was swaying, and had made a gesture towards the bed pillar as though to support herself. He came over to her with a quick stride. 'Of course I'm not keeping anything back, you silly girl. But it is more than a sprain. Her shoulder appears to be broken. She—she was too stunned to allow of a closer examination that first morning. I had such a job procuring a foster nurse for my daughter that I did not discover the extent of Mrs. Mansfield's injuries until Dr. Mitchell's visit yesterday.'

'Roderick, you look so—so *triste* when you look through that window out at your great inheritance. I feel that you grieve that it was not a son—oh!' Tension had quickened the dull pain that had never left her head since some moment after one of the crashes during that awful night. Roderick turned at the sound. He had indeed been grieving that the child was not a son. Inheritance, did she say! Who was to inherit what? He that troubleth his house, said the proverb, shall inherit the wind. Heaven knows I have never troubled my house!

He took a silk handkerchief from his pocket and wiped away her tears. 'If I seem strange and preoccupied it is because there should be the slightest dwindling of that heritage for our child. Surely you do not think that I could be disappointed with that solitary little blossom that dared the elements.'

There came a knock at the door and Nurse Hogan came in with the child. Margaret took it in her arms. 'It is the tiniest baby I have ever seen.'

'Your Ladyship, for a baby that has come nearly six weeks before its time it is coming on wonderfully.'

Sir Roderick touched the tiny cheek. 'Do you know, Margaret,' he said, 'I have a dreadful suspicion that we have a red-haired woman in the family.'

'Don't you like red hair? Let me see. Maman and Papa are both brown, very brown. Yvette is golden. *Grand'mère* du Clos was dark, and I do not know what colour *Grand'mère* O'Regan was. She had died in Ireland before Papa left there. But he always said that I resembled her the most.'

'She must have been pretty.'

The nurse stood by and marvelled at the way the Quality paid compliments to each other, an' they married, the same as if they were only courting.

'What colour was your father's hair, Roderick? I know about your mother's black ringlets. I love to look at her portrait. Why is there no portrait of your father? He seems to have been such a beau. All those brocaded coats and satin breeches in his powder closet. A man like that should have several portraits.'

'There must be a portrait in Dublin somewhere,' he replied, 'if only I could find it. There is an entry in his book, sixteen

pounds to the Painter for my Portrait. I believe he must have
sat for it in Dublin, and it was never claimed. They both caugh
the cholera almost immediately after his return from his las
trip to Dublin.'

'It is all so sad.' Margaret pressed the baby's soft cheek
against her own. 'To die so young and not be able to wear al
those lovely clothes. There is a white satin dress in you
maman's chest, and never have I seen in Belgium upon any
grande dame a gown so *magnifique*. Such exquisite Spanish
lace! And a stomacher of real brilliants, and the train is embroidered in coral and gold.'

'You shall wear it when you go to the Castle Drawing-Room.

'Oh la, Roderick, but it is *demodée*. It must be unpicked and
made all over again, Rodereeck!' Her voice went high and thin
'This bed, it is not safe! It sways.' Her face went pale and
strained.

'Darling, I should not have let you talk so much.' He
beckoned to the nurse. 'Give her the medicine the doctor pre-
scribed. It will make her sleep.'

He watched while the nurse administered the soothing
draught. Gradually Margaret became calm and drowsy.

The kitchen was alive with bustle. The news of the visit o
Daniel O'Connell had lifted its atmosphere from the gloom and
the desolation wrought by the storm and by the death of Mrs
Mansfield, whose calm personality had been the support and
guidance of the staff. Michael, the turf boy, kept coming in and
out with baskets of turf which he built up in neat stacks inside
the chimney walls. They were sopping wet, and the ovens buil
into the thickness of the kitchen walls had to be heated fo
baking. The bastibles that hung over the fires on the hearth had
previously been sufficient to bake enough bread for the household. But now six of them, and a big griddle as well were going
all day to keep the homeless workers and tenants supplied.

The Liberator's visit was like the coming of royalty. 'O'Connell is King of Ireland,' George the Fourth had wailed when he
had signed the Emancipation Bill. And King he had been eve
since to the prostrate millions he had raised to human status
The chatelaine of the castle was ill; its housekeeper dead; its
butler numbed with shock and cold. The cessations of the
hearth fires had jolted the poor man in mind and body. Apar
from freezing his bones and tubes it had cast him breathless int

a void, as a fish is cast from its breathing element of water into the stifling void of air. The hearth fire of cabin or castle never dies. In the Kilsheelin kitchen there had been the sustained warmth of centuries of fires that had burned winter and summer, day and night. The butler would never forget the night of the big wind; not for its havoc but for the icy halt in the historicity of his world.

Mrs. Stacey was whipping a syllabub and telling the assembly that she wouldn't take twenty golden guineas to walk in the field that 'they' had taken. The dish nearly fell from her hand when she saw the Sir standing in front of her. He asked her in Gaelic about tomorrow's menu. She enumerated the dishes. Hare soup, four geese (and the caraway seeds for stuffing, all washed away out of the cupboard), a boiled ham and a ham baked in cider, a side and hind quarters of mutton—and not a beast fit to kill for beef. 'Is naire orm! There is shame on me. 'Tis a mean boards your Honour's Sir. Not a taste of fish either.'

'Ni fear cuirin na cuideas,' he soothed her. Enough is as good as a feast.

'Enough!' she exclaimed. 'The Liberator's own cook would not insult a guest by sending meat to the table without the elegance of a fish course. And it isn't one kind of fish that she'd send up but often twenty.'

The Liberator, her master pointed out, had the Atlantic at his back door; not to mention the streams and rivers that raced against each other to bring fish down the slopes of his wild mountain territory. 'And the Liberator's cook could not hold a rush dip to the dinner that you can cook, Mo Banaltra.'

The cook's eyes felt a rush of tears. It was many a year now since her haughty young master had addressed her as his balantra. When he had been a little boy in fosterage under her brother's roof he had called her nothing else. That day when Sir Dominic had brought him back here to the castle, the lonely little boy had called out so poignantly for his banaltra that she had surrendered the independence of her own home life to be with him here. She reached up and touched his hand that rested so affectionately upon her shoulder.

'Have no fear for tomorrow night, Dalta ma croidte. Fosterson of my heart.'

CHAPTER 6

The first guest into the drawing-room was old Lady Cullen followed at an interval of six paces by Lord Cullen. The old gentleman still dressed like a Georgian buck. He gleamed from wig to shoe buckle. The only dull thing about him was the socket on each side of his nose where a roguish eye was sunk too deep to display its twinkle.

'Incredible,' he cackled as he minced across the carpet. 'I thought that we had sustained considerable damage at Crannagh Hall but, egad, it was only the sigh of a zephyr compared to what I have seen as we drove up your avenue. Felicitations.'

Roderick didn't feel that the storm's havoc was anything to be felicitated upon. But the old dandy proceeded. 'Fancy being presented with a daughter in the midst of such a tempest! What a wonderful lady is your charming wife! An amazing feat, egad!'

'Shut up, Cullen,' said his own wife. 'The girl had no alternative once it started. Take me to her, Rody.'

On the way up he requested the old lady not to allude to the housekeeper's death. 'She does not know that Mrs. Mansfield is dead.'

'What do you take me for?' Lady Cullen demanded. 'An omadhawn?' In the bedroom she noted the distended pupils and the constant tremor of Margaret's lips. But she hugged her briskly and closed the baby's fingers over a gold four-pound piece for luck.

'Have you decided what you are going to call her?'

Margaret admitted that they had not. 'She came before we had decided.'

'Everything is topsy-turvy,' Lady Cullen observed. 'In the ordinary course of etiquette, a lady should not receive until she is at least a month confined; of course, if I were a proper lady I would not attempt to pay a call at this stage, but when we heard of the arrival and I knew that the weather was rather bad that night, I insisted on accompanying Cullen when Roderick invited him to dine with Mr. O'Connell. What a man that is!'

'Yes. I feel that I ought to make an effort to rise and give him fitting welcome.'

'Don't think of such a crazy notion.'

'Ah, but he is almost like royalty. In Belgium he was one of the names they chose when they were seeking a candidate to elect as King.'

'He is greater than royalty. He is the saviour of Ireland. When I think of the tribulations we have endured! I have known relatives of mine to be disposed and imprisoned because it became known that they had made wills leaving their own property to their families. Yes, I have known a relative of mine to be beaten to death because he carried a walking stick. The Penal System regarded a walking stick in the hand of a Catholic as the bearing of arms.'

Margaret began to show signs of restlessness and the nurse glided over to her. Lady Cullen took the hint. 'I'd better go down in case Cullen is putting his foot in it. Do you know, my dear, I always knew he was an idiot but latterly he is becoming an eejit.' She stopped and kissed her young kinswoman. 'Hurry and get well, my dear, before the next Drawing-Room. Remember, I'm going to present you.'

When she had gone Nurse Hogan took a liberty for the first time. She had noticed that strained look come on her patient's face when the old lady spoke of beatings and cruelties.

'Herself and her Penal talk!' she exploded. 'Couldn't she talk of something pleasant and natural like—like the weather?'

Margaret smiled. 'She *did* talk about the weather. She said it was rather bad last Friday night, and it was. No matter what *divertissement* you create!' She caught the nurse's hand. 'Mrs. Hogan, you won't leave me? I get so frightened and you seem to understand. Were you frightened that night?'

'I was, my Lady, very frightened.'

'Did you have an unpleasant experience?'

The nurse did not answer for a second, then she said quietly, 'Yes, my Lady, I had an unpleasant experience.'

'What is it? Tell me please.' The nurse turned towards the window. With the trees gone it was possible to see right down to the entrance and she saw, to her surprise that it was crammed with people and beyond the broken boundary wall the road was

51

dense with people. She turned back ... startled.

'Your Ladyship, it is not going to be a very private visit. The demesne is thronged with people. Perhaps Sir Roderick does not know. The window under this is shuttered because of broken glass. It will be terrible for you if they start cheering and shouting.'

'Oh, I hope they do cheer. That kind of noise does not disturb me. I hate wailing winds and I fear being trapped in something that sways back or throws me into some dark, smoky place.'

A knock admitted Hannah preceding the footman who nearly staggered under the weight of a massive silver tray laden with food.

The nurse was glad of the interruption. It was a relief to tuck a big napkin under her Ladyship's pretty chin and coax her to try a tiny taste of all the lovely food that Mrs. Stacey sent in such quantities.

Lady Cullen arrived back in the drawing-room just in time to check her husband's footwork. He had been hopping around the room exclaiming and simpering over every battered shred of priceless bric-à-brac. Sir Roderick, wincing as each fresh *objet de vertu* was held before the quizzing glass, felt that all that was needed was a hammer to complete the picture of a little, wizened dealer crying, 'Fifteenth-century Portuguese—er—somewhat damaged,' and dropping a priceless heirloom for some contemptible bid.

Sir Roderick was relieved by the old lady's return. Behind her the butler was announcing, 'The Messieurs de Guider'. Two middle-aged gentlemen, dressed exactly alike in bright-blue frock coats with brass buttons and wearing dark brown wigs, came forward with solemn faces. They greeted Sir Roderick as though they were offering condolences to the bereaved.

'A terrible sight!' The elder twin waved his hand towards the window to indicate the havoc he had seen outside. When the younger one said to Sir Roderick, 'I'm sorry for your trouble,' his host half expected him to add, 'I'm a friend of the corpse's,' like one of the tenants at a wakehouse.

A cheer from the waiting crowd at the gateway announced Mr. O'Connell's approach. The old bard moved out of the shadow of the hallway to play a welcoming air. The avenue had been sufficiently cleared to make it possible for a carriage to get through. But it was not timber but a solid phalanx of human beings that impeded the carriage bearing the Liberator.

Sir Roderick, standing at the porch with his guests, was perturbed at the spectacle. 'A gentleman should have some privacy in his own grounds,' said Lord Cullen.

His host, with a sweep towards the half-upright gates and the big gaps in the high wall that exposed the house to the highway, said ruefully, 'There is not much privacy there and anyway, Mr. O'Connell is a public institution. He belongs to *them*.' He nodded his head towards the crowd.

The yard at the back emptied itself of workers. From across the fields tenants, men, women and children came streaming. They finally took the horses from the shafts and drew the carriage themselves. Every few yards men jostled to share the honour of drawing the Liberator. Through the park rang the incessant cries of 'Long live O'Connell! Long live the Liberator of Ireland!'

Sir Roderick came forward and bowed with a dignity that was almost reverence. Lady Cullen curtsied as though to royalty and her husband made a leg. The two gentlemen in blue bowed with courtly grace.

'This is a proud day for my house, sir,' said Roderick, 'I only wish that it were in more fitting shape for your reception, but you have come in the wake of the storm.' As he stepped back at the drawing-room door to admit Mr. O'Connell and his host, Mr. Richard Lalor Sheil, he waved his hand with a sweep of display, 'We are compelled to receive you in its track.'

The great pile of glass in the corner caught the visitor's eyes. 'Ah,' cried Mr. O'Connell, 'that superb chandelier! There is nothing grander in Dublin Castle. I remember it in your father's time. He was very proud of it.'

'Both his grandfather and father were great collectors,' said Mr. Lalor Sheil. 'This is a treasure house of lovely things. Roderick has the collecting urge too. Have you made any additions lately, Roderick?'

Lord Cullen pointed his cane handle towards the ceiling and cackled heartily, 'A most valuable specimen.' He kept on cackling at his own joke about the baby until his wife jogged his elbow and sent snuff down his ruffles.

'May I be privileged to view the specimen and its fair producer?' said Mr. O'Connell. 'It is not customary I know to intrude so soon but I must leave for London in a few days. It may be a long time again before I have the pleasure of meeting your wife and her baby.'

'If you will come this way, sir, my wife will be honoured.'

As they ascended the stairs Mr. O'Connell continued, 'Her father and my brother, Maurice, and myself only narrowly escaped being guillotined when we were trying to get from Douai College to Calais. It was the day Louis the Sixteenth was executed in Paris.'

Margaret's pale face flushed to receive such a personage in such a place and in *such* an illness. Mr. O'Connell kissed the hand she shyly extended. He spoke to her in French. 'I crave a thousand pardons for such an indelicate intrusion. But I had to see the charming chatelaine and now that I have seen her I know that my impeachment of etiquette was worthy of the risk.' He turned to Sir Roderick. 'You have made a worthy contribution to your forefathers' collection of the beautiful. Allow me to congratulate you.'

He turned back to Margaret. 'You have the same glossy, brown hair as your grandmother Madame The O'Regan. Her son, your gallant father, God rest him, and my brother and myself hid in the same haystack from the revolutionaries when we were making our escape from the college.'

'I have often heard him speak of that day, Monsieur O'Connell,' said Margaret.

O'Connell was delighted. 'Now you don't say! It makes me glad and proud to know that he held me in his memory.'

'He held you in his memory with great affection,' she answered.

'Sir Roderick, it was worth my risking your sweet lady's displeasure to come to her bower and learn that I had not been forgotten by that brave soldier and Irishman, Colonel Michael O'Regan. And now, where is his grandchild?' He took the tiny baby in his arms.

'Little flower of the storm,' he murmured. 'What name have you chosen for the little treasure?' he asked.

'We have not decided, sir. She came impetuously and her coming had to take second place to the storm,' answered the father.

'Poor little mite, she had a trying passage. I know what I would call her if she were mine.'

Sir Roderick turned eagerly to his wife. 'Darling, shall we ask Mr. O'Connell to choose a name?'

Margaret's laugh rang out in all its former exuberance. 'Oh, Roderick!" she cried, 'veritably Mr. O'Connell has more weighty things to settle than the matter of a baby's name.'

'Forgive me for daring to contradict a lady, and one so lovely and charming, but a baby's name is a very important matter. I believe that a name influences the life of its owner for all time, be it long or short. I think if I owned this little one I should be tempted to call in Blaw-na-Sthurrim.'

'Sther-een!' Margaret wrinkled her brows. 'It sounds very long and difficult. I could never pronounce such a name.'

'Stherrin is the Western pronunciation,' said the Liberator. 'Have you not acquired the Gaelic? How do you conduct your household?'

Mr. O'Connell had taken it for granted that Margaret, despite her continental birth would have been familiar with Gaelic. 'The butler speaks French,' she explained, 'and Mrs. Mansfield speaks English. What does the name mean?'

'It means,' said her husband, 'Flower of the Storm.'

'And,' said Mr. O'Connell, 'you may take the flower part for granted and call her just Sthurrim.'

'Mr. O'Connell, do you know I like the meaning of the name. I should like to think of her growing up strong and vigorous like her name. She is so tiny now.'

'She will outgrow that fault, dear lady, and she will have the strength of the storm and the courage of her forebears and she already shows signs of the beauty of her mother.'

'Sther-een,' Margaret kept repeating the name, struggling with the pronunciation.

'I like the way you say it best, darling,' Roderick said. 'Sterrin it shall be.'

The Liberator took a gallant leave of Margaret and returned to the company below. The new name and its owner were toasted in the dining-room by Richard Lalor Sheil. 'Wait!' cried Sir Roderick, as Richard was about to raise his glass. 'We'll drink from the Mether Cup. It is one of the baubles that the storm has left intact.'

He took from the sideboard a big quadrangular-shaped cup made of yew wood. A silver-mounted handle was fitted on each of the four sides. Mr. O'Connell leaned across to examine it.

55

'Did Cromwell have a sup out of that?' he asked. 'There is some story, is there not, that your illustrious ancestor Taidgh Ruadh O'Carroll was inhospitable enough to refuse the poor man a drink when he paid a courtesy call to the castle?'

'He did not exactly *refuse*, but when old Boney-face demanded that he send his servants with refreshments to his men, my little red-headed ancestor planted his feet across the width of the porch and said: "There is a great mortality upon my house. I am the last of my household that the plague has left standing and I fear I shall not stand upright much longer." '

'Did he fall for the ruse?' asked Stephen de Guider.

'Like a shot. Cromwell jumped up on his horse and said that neither he nor his men would taste anything from a pesty house. But he promised to call again.'

He filled the Mether Cup with wine. 'He never returned.' He placed the big square cup in front of his cousin. 'I must confess, Richard,' he said, and there was a faintly bitter twist to his smile, 'that of all the uninvited guests who have come with covetousness in their hearts, the first to succeed in wresting a portion of my land from me was the one who came last night week—The Big Wind.'

Richard Lalor Sheil rose to his feet. He knew that his cousin regarded the loss of the few acres as something sinister and supernatural so he refrained from those picturesque phrases that enchanted his hearers in the House of Commons. 'May all your misfortune blow away with the field. When Nature robbed the cradle of your land, a sweet hostage was placed in the cradle that held your own body. We drink to Sterrin!'

He moved the cup towards Lady Cullen. She placed her hand on one of the handles and took a sip. 'To Sterrin,' she cried.

The cup went round the table. 'To Sterrin, God bless her,' cried the Liberator in ringing tones.

CHAPTER 7

It was the Feast of Epiphany again. Were it not for the obligation to hear mass, Sir Roderick would have wished the day to drop unnoticed into the passing week; no reminiscences; no associations.

For long after last Epiphany Margaret had drooped like a flower crushed by the storm, and when her body had recovered from the birth of Sterrin, her mind's vigour had lagged behind. There had been times when Roderick had feared that she might carry a permanent scar to shadow the brightness of her mind. She had become subject to violent pains and whirrings in her head. They gave her the sensation, amounting almost to hallucination, that she was a small boat, rudderless and oarless, tossing on a wild sea at the mercy of the winds.

But gradually that quality of winsome serenity that had so intrigued Roderick began to return. Margaret had entered gaily into all the Christmas festivities, but on Christmas night while the bard was playing to them in the drawing-room a gust of wind rattled the windows and the old man stopped his music. He wandered off into a lot of old 'rawmaish' about the Wild Huntsman on his Eight-footed Steed who rides forth between the date of the sun's death in the middle of December and the Twelfth Day. Margaret grew strained again and started to watch for a recurrence of the terrible storm that she assumed must be a fixture of the Irish calendar and clime.

Roderick had outraged the bard by ordering the hanger-on musician Paddy-the-rat from the kitchen to play his lively jigs and reels. He banned all further references to the Big Wind, even references to the baby's birth. He kept Margaret on the go so much during those twelve visiting days of Christmas when every house stood open and everyone visited everyone else that the twelfth and last day came upon her unawares. All she realised was that two of the most glittering and sought-after-hostesses of the garrison society were coming for this new-fashioned afternoon tea that she found so delightful.

Roderick had told her he would be late today. He did not say why, but Margaret was sure it had something to do with the Whiteboys. She was not precisely sure what the Whiteboys were, but Roderick had explained to her that they were an organisation whose stated purpose was to protest against unfair landlords, but who now seemed interested in little else but violence. They roamed the countryside, their faces blackened, wearing white shirts over their outer garments. They seemed more interested in crime than causes, and left terror and sometimes death in their wake. Margaret didn't like to think about them. She wondered if she would ever get used to this strange country. Whether her love for her handsome, sensitive husband would overcome her fear of the land and the people he loved so much. She wished he were with her now to help her entertain her guests.

In the drawing-room Thomas the knife boy was helping the footman to light the one hundred and forty-seven candles that was all the chandelier could now hold.

'It is a poor light compared to what used to be in it before this night twelvemonths,' said the footman, looking up regretfully at the depleted chandelier. 'Three hundred and fifty candles I used to light on it.' He sighed gustily.

Young Thomas dutifully echoed his superior's sigh with more force than sadness. It blew out his taper whose holder was taller than himself. 'It must have been a great blaze,' he said. 'Mrs. Stacey says that it is unlucky to keep a thing after it is broken. She says it should be broken into three more pieces and then thrown out.'

The footman said that Mrs. Stacey said more than her prayers. 'People couldn't be expected to throw out a thing like that as if it were a broken mug.'

Young Thomas looked up dreamingly at the shapely tree of gleaming glass and colour that had so many of its branches and blossoms blighted. 'I suppose,' he said, 'that people who are born into owning grandeur like that have to bide with it when it meets misfortune. They probably have to accept whatever bad luck it brings.'

The footman leaned on the long lighter and looked sternly at the lad. 'I'm thinkin' it is too much time that you have on your hands since you went out with the Sir on the front of his horse.

It's not right for the likes of you to be lyin' lazin' in bed until half-past six in the mornin's and wastin' time when you *are* up, learnin' to write off them tombstones. What would Nurse Hogan say if she knew?'

But Nurse Hogan did know. She had come upon him one day when no one was about, labouring over a sheet of brown paper in the coachhouse. On rows of uneven lines scrawled with white chalk were written in great sprawling words 'Richardus O'Carroll nobilis de Kilsheelin 1672 and William O'Carroll, Kilsheelin, Gentleman, who was happily emigrated to the Kingdom of Heaven Anno Domini 1701.' Along the wall in front of the copypaper were ranged the tombstones uprooted by the Big Wind.

The sight of the nameless waif teaching himself to write had stirred the aching roots of her heart. It recalled the studious young son who had been hurled from her life the night the tombstones had been uprooted. Had she protested there would have been an end to young Thomas's writing accomplishment; because the nurse had become almost indispensable to Lady O'Carroll. So deftly had she fitted into the household that she had taken over Mrs. Mansfield's post with almost companion status.

A tinkle of bells and a frou-frou of silk warned the footman and his helper that Lady O'Carroll had entered the room. Thomas wondered how her Ladyship's feet operated. She seemed to float along in a limbless sort of way. Only the bells and keys in her chatelaine belt suggested movement.

The boy had never before been so close to her Ladyship. He had only peeped through banisters or around corners at a remote and rustling graciousness, a wafting of fragrance, a tinkling of sound like the music heard at fairy raths. He gazed raptly at her foreign-seeming complexion and her great brown eyes, and the tall lighter in his hand became a lance uplifted.

She gazed about her to make sure that there was no nook or corner left unlighted to shadow fearsomeness. Lighted candelabra stood on every table and cabinet. She pointed to a branch of lights and bade the footman place them in a distant corner. That was better! Now there wasn't a dark shadow in all the room.

A carriage jingled to a halt outside the window. A charming young officer whom she had met during the week at a military hunt breakfast was handing out someone dressed in a ravishing black velvet hat with a sable cloak. Margaret gave a discreet peep from behind the hangings. She made little smoothing movements with her fingers down the fifteen bows that reached from her collar to the first frill of her skirt, then the butler announced, 'Mrs. Appleyard, Mrs. Kennedy-Sherwin and Lieutenant Fitzharding-Smith.'

Mrs. Appleyard drew Margaret under the brim of her hat and dabbed her cheek with the edge of her own. 'Sweet Lady O'Carroll! How charming you look! So *ingénue*! And that exquisite gown! I don't have to ask if it is French. Only a Parisian dressmaker could have dreamed of those fascinating bows marching all the way up the façade——'

'Like a flight of silken steps.' Margaret pretended not to hear the interruption. There was so much open admiration in the young lieutenant's eyes that he might mean something subtle.

She turned to Mrs. Kennedy-Sherwin and was relieved at the sight of her small, frilly bonnet that could not sweep her inside its brim. But the vivacious little brunette was not at all the embracing type. She was contented to compliment Margaret on her shy waistline.

Margaret decided that this phrase had better be ignored also. She wasn't sure what a 'shy' waistline was. One never could be quite sure with the garrison colony. They were so gay and modern. She just smiled and welcomed her but gave an involuntary look towards her waistline.

Lieutenant Fitzharding-Smith followed her glance and as he bowed over her hand he said, 'You must know, Lady O'Carroll, that a lady's waist has the shy quality of the violet that shrinks but is never shrunken.'

Margaret was glad when the arrival of tea gave her a chance to barricade herself behind the big tea urn. Her sense of fun had survived her rigid upbringing but had yielded no tricks of repartee.

She sipped her unsweetened tea and nibbled at the lump of sugar on her saucer and listened to the gay gossip that held wisps of scandal. Captain Bellamy had called out Captain Hatton of the Thirty-first and when he flicked his sword through his opponent's scalp and displayed on its tip a lock of rich, but false, brown hair called out, 'I am quite satisfied.'

'He had never been really satisfied about its genuineness

before,' Lieutenant Fitzharding-Smith explained in case the joke missed his hostess.

'He must think me very stupid,' she thought. Aloud she remarked, 'Wasn't it a leetle unkind? And also, why did he not wear a wig instead of a toupee?'

'Because, my dear,' said Mrs. Kennedy-Sherwin, 'he had not yet accustomed himself to the premature loss of a very handsome head of hair.'

Margaret was glad now that Roderick was detained, even though the nasty threats from the Whiteboy organisation did worry her. Roderick had never expressed any disapproval of Mrs. Appleyard and her set but he showed no urge towards friendship there. He would certainly disapprove of such idle chatter.

It was a relief when Hegarty came in to say that Nurse Hogan wished to know if she would have Miss Sterrin brought down.

Miss Sterrin, in her nursemaid's arms and marshalled by Nurse Hogan, gazed with complete composure out of deep blue eyes that subdued her audience into silence. They grouped around the stage of her beauty and paid tribute.

Lieutenant Fitzharding-Smith put a finger under her chin and Sterrin effortlessly and noiselessly vomited a few bubbles of milk pudding over his finger on to the frills of Malines lace. 'When she is the toast of the country I shall boast of this condescension,' he said as he brought the silk handkerchief into action again.

Nurse Hogan was contrite. 'Has she over-eaten again?' Margaret asked.

She turned apologetically to her guests. 'She eats enormously for a baby but she was so tiny when she was born that it is good to see her thriving so.'

'What a quaint name,' said Mrs. Kennedy-Sherwin, 'is it some name of your family in Belgium?'

Margaret explained the storm significance of the name. 'My dear,' said Mrs. Appleyard, 'you were the heroine of the hour. We were having a card party when a courier came for the surgeon. The roof of the guardhouse had blown in and the men were being blown around like leaves. Lord knows how many limbs were broken.'

'It was such fun,' said Mrs. Kennedy-Sherwin. 'All the guests had to stay overnight. There were four of us in Cynthia's bedroom and the men were sleeping on couches in the drawing-room.'

'Yes, "the flying sentry" came home to find his bedroom gone and his wife standing on the part of the floor that had not crashed to the floor beneath. By Jove, it was deuced funny to see her standing there in her nightgown. One wall, all flowery wallpaper, stood behind her. The other three, and the roof, all gone.' Nurse Hogan's hand trembled.

Margaret took the baby. She looked down tensely at the red gold curls. Through them she saw a bedroom floor and a woman lying in shadow, blood smearing the hot candle wax.

Nurse Hogan moved to her. 'Shall I take her now, your Ladyship?'

Lieutenant Fitzharding-Smith noticed Margaret's pallor. As Nurse Hogan took the baby from her mother, the lieutenant stepped towards her and made a sweeping bow. 'Allow me to pay a small tribute to one whom I shall not dare to approach when this dawning beauty has reached its full noontide.' He suddenly produced a silver flower, tulip shaped, with a mother-of-pearl handle set round with tiny bells that tinkled sweetly.

Margaret looked up at him and her eyes were wide with gratitude; for his sensitive timing. She had thought she was going to faint. How could he have known that it was the baby's birthday? And how could she admit to any of them that she, its mother, had forgotten what day it was! What had that terrible storm done to her?

She looked deep into Lieutenant Fitzharding-Smith's eyes with affection. The officer did not dare to interpret her look for what it seemed to express. But he was conscious of some deep emotion behind those lovely eyes. He felt colour heating his cheeks and his pulse quickened.

The baby broke the tension with a musical cascade from the costly 'rattle' he had given her. The nurse adjusted a white fur hood over the red gold curls against the chill air of the passages and stairs. As the little procession left the drawing-room a silvery sound of bells wafted back. Margaret gave a happy little laugh. 'I love tinkling sounds! Every time that I shall hear these bells I shall feel compelled to think of you.'

'Compelled!' His eyebrows registered mock dismay. 'Only under compulsion shall I be remembered?'

'*Mais non!*' she cried. 'You mock my English. It is when I desire to say something—*très gentil*—that I sometimes put into it my foot and I say instead something *gauche.*'

'You could not say anything *gauche* however hard you tried.' There was homage in his voice and eyes. Abruptly he turned the topic to door-knockers. He had been hauled before the colonel for his part in a door-knocker raid the night before. 'We really expected to be confined to barracks this week. We bagged fifteen knockers. Every house in the Mall except Dr. Mitchell's and only ten-shillings fine! It was deucedly cheap! I was afraid I should have had to miss the Moonlight Ball. Are you going, Lady O'Carroll?'

Before she could reply Sir Roderick entered the room. Despite the courtesy of his greeting the tempo of the little gathering abated. Margaret noted with an inward sigh the stern look that had become so habitual since that horrid storm.

The small talk faltered like a song gone out of tune. Lieutenant Fitzharding-Smith decided to come to the rescue with something solid and man-to-man. 'I believe, sir,' he said, 'that you are having difficulty with that fellow who grabbed your land?' To judge from his host's expression the young man felt that it might have been wiser to stick to the Moonlight Ball theme.

Mrs. Kennedy-Sherwin saved Roderick the necessity of replying by announcing that she had eaten all the French bonbons. He turned at once to ring and have the bonbonnière replenished, but she had started to draw on her pelisse. He turned back to assist her. Margaret looked bleak as Lieutenant Fitzharding-Smith collected the big sable muff that was en suite with Mrs. Appleyard's collar. Her little festivity was ending!

To prolong the moment of departure rather than of necessity, she led the ladies to the little ante-room where her father-in-law's friends used to put the last touches to their toilets before entering the drawing-room.

They chattered with restored vivacity as they titivated before the mirror on the wig-powder stand. Margaret watched closely as Mrs. Appleyard took the little ewer of rosewater from the lower tier and poured some into the basin on the top tier. What would happen if she wet her complexion? Rumour had it that the blonde beauty used not only 'visage powder' but rouge!

But the lady just wet her fingertips, peered into the mirror and said she looked a hag. Her hostess courteously repudiated such a suggestion, and her friend neither agreeing nor disagreeing told her to cheer up, the violets would soon be in season.

'Violets!' said Margaret, intrigued at the hint of a new beauty tip. 'Do they help?'

'Of course,' shrilled Mrs. Kennedy-Sherwin. 'Fancy your not knowing! It is the most marvellous lotion. Violets boiled in milk with—— Oh, my gracious! What is that?'

A dull explosive sound followed by a crash sounded from across the hall in the direction of the drawing-room. Margaret leaned back against the wig block, her face ashen . 'Quick! She's going to faint.' Mrs. Appleyard pulled smelling-salts from her muff and Mrs. Sherwin opened the door to peep out.

Footsteps pounded across the hall. 'La!' she cried. 'Where are the gentlemen off to? They are simply racing out.'

The two men were barely in time to see the white-clad figures of men running into the shrubbery. They could hear them calling to others to go back that there were military after them.

Sir Roderick laid a restraining hand upon the younger man's shoulder. 'Put away your pistol. I don't want bloodshed if I can avoid it. They will only shed more blood in retaliation! Perhaps my wife's or my child's.'

'Surely not, sir! Pardon my saying it, but I thought that they did not attack their own—er—I mean you are a Catholic like themselves, I thought that they respected their own co-religionists.'

'They don't care whom they attack. They have lost sight of the original grievance that started the Whiteboy movement. It is no longer a matter of tithes or evictions or any other agrarian discontent. It is sheer brutality for its own sake.' He climbed a little knoll in the shrubbery, and peered. 'I'll hold a crown that tall fellow is a son of Keating's. The white shirt doesn't cover that new suit.' He had noticed it at Mass today. He found himself noticing the most ordinary details about this family whose existence he had scarcely noticed previously. His face was bitter as he stepped off the knoll.

Sir Roderick suddenly became aware of his guest's scrutiny. 'Forgive my preoccupation with my own affairs. It is a churlish way to treat a guest. I have reason to be glad of your presence here today. The minute they saw the colour of your uniform coming round the terrace they took to their heels. They probably thought I had a company of military installed for protection.'

'I'm deuced glad I was here, sir. Would it not be a wise precaution to arrange to have a company of military posted here?'

'No, I'll deal with them myself. We have lived in harmony with our tenants throughout the generations. It is inconceivable now that I should protect myself from them with military display. No O'Carroll of Kilsheelin has even been known to evict a tenant or raise a rent and Heaven knows we have held our lands with stress and strait.'

'But, sir, I hope you won't think it devilishly impertinent of me to point out the risk that you mentioned yourself a moment ago. You spoke of the danger to your wife and child. Surely any suspicion of danger to them would outweigh any feudal conception of protectiveness towards your tenantry?'

Sir Roderick realised that the young man spoke truly. His own obstinacy and possessiveness was exposing his sweet Margaret and her little storm flower to danger. In a friendlier tone he said, 'I do not anticipate a recurrence of such raids. Tonight has a special significance. It is an anniversary and—a warning—— We had better return to the ladies. Let us hope they heard nothing.'

He did not catch what his companion was saying about a cockfight the next morning. He was thinking if it had only been any of the fields stretching away behind the castle! But it had to be from those too few fertile acres to the front.

They found the drawing-room all aflutter. Mrs. Appleyard, with gold-topped smelling-salts still in play, stood over Margaret. Mrs. Kennedy-Sherwin sat beside her on the couch holding her hand and giving it little pats, and Mrs. Hogan hovered anxiously in the background.

In the centre of the room the butler supervised the sweeping up of broken glass. Overhead, a mutilated branch had lost twelve blossoms that had held twelve lights.

'Are you all right, my darling?' Sir Roderick bent over Margaret and Mrs. Appleyard looked in solemn wonder at that tone and gaze of deepest love that she, the golden toast, had never evoked in any man.

Margaret looked up wild-eyed. 'Oh, Roderick. It is the same all over again. It is not Sterrin's birthday. It is the anniversary of the storm. The crash, that smell, the scorching, and all that candlegrease on the carpet. It is just like when Mrs. Mansfield——'

He wished the visitors in Timbuctoo that he might take her in his arms. But little Mrs. Kennedy-Sherwin gave things a practical turn by announcing that she felt faint. Above the sixteen-inch waistline her heart was feeling the protesting pressure of the potato bread. In that moment of drama she was able to swoon into a most ladylike faint.

Margaret was immediately on her feet, all attendance and concern. Mrs. Appleyard transferred the smelling salts to the petite nostrils that had a tendency to quiver despite their owner's efforts to maintain a wan stillness. Lieutenant Fitzharding-Smith chafed the tiny wrists that lay so pathetically in his palm. Nurse Hogan hurried in with burnt feathers. Margaret unfastened as many buttons as modesty would allow. Roderick, relieved that the poor little lady had averted a complete breakdown, brought more cushions in an excess of gratitude while Mrs. Kennedy-Sherwin felt that this was the most successful faint she had ever had in her life.

The visitors made their farewells with practised grace. Lieutenant Fitzharding-Smith bent low over his hostess's flaccid hand. Little Mrs. Kennedy-Sherwin murmured something about the morrow's cockfight breakfast and an opera performance at Sir Jocelyn Devine's in Kilkenny. Roderick tried to frame a refusal that would not sound too unfriendly. Nurse Hogan helped Margaret upstairs.

Roderick hurried his guests to their carriage, and waved them on their way. Returning, he noticed a man standing by the gate. George Lucas was his name and he was seeking employment.

He told Roderick that he was one of the twenty farmers who had been evicted by Major Darby because a sheep had been stolen. The evictions had disgusted Roderick; the farmers involved were decent, honest men. Darby was the type of landlord who regarded his tenants as being a lower species than his livestock.

Roderick was not impressed by Lucas, a small man with small eyes that had the blue-black sheen of the beetle. His wife, he said, had given birth to a child the night of the Big Wind; when he returned after seeking help for her he found that she and the child that had been born in his absence had both been drowned by the sudden flood that had washed them from the bed.

It was obvious that the man was pressing an affinity with Sir Roderick's own experiences. The poor devil had been tragically dealt with by that freak storm; but, between workers and hangers-on Roderick already had more workers than work. The man persisted. He had been, he said, a skilled bricklayer before he had acquired the farm. He looked pointedly at the section of boundary wall that still gaped on the 'Sir's road' since the Big Wind. He wouldn't dream of a tradesman's wages, just a farm worker's, or less.

The man seemed to speak by insinuations. Roderick knew that he was referring to the fact that the skilled men who had been engaged to rebuild the wall had left it one third finished and rushed off to where bricklayers had been rumoured to get as much as seven and six a day for repairing storm damage. Lucas was effusive when Roderick agreed to employ him. 'Your Honour's Sir will never regret this turn,' he said.

Roderick looked into the small eyes. 'I trust,' he replied coldly, 'that you will never give me cause for regret.'

That night when he wrote in his black book, it was to enter: 'George Lucas is to work for me until after the harvest at five shillings per week and his victuals. I am to keep back sixpence a week to be sure of his not going. If he goes he forfeits sixpence per week.' Roderick looked long at the last entry. It was the first time that he had ever made use of this condition in the terms of a man's employment.

CHAPTER 8

Sterrin came scrambling up the back stairs in answer to her name.

'So you've been in the kitchen again! What were you doing there?'

'Helping young Thomas to clean the knives.'

'What!' Nurse Hogan was aghast. 'The idea of you demeaning yourself at such a task! And don't you know that you are not supposed to go to the kitchen?'

Sterrin sighed, 'All the fun is in the kitchen.' She strained up to the mirror on the nurse's dressing-table and sighed again. 'I wish I hadn't red hair. The fairies are always trying to steal red-haired babies. They have their eye on me.' The nurse knew where this bit of pishoguerie was coming from. She resolved to speak to Mrs. Stacey.

'Sit down, Miss Sterrin. I have something to say to you. No, don't lean forward with your elbows on your knees like an old man smoking a pipe. Sit upright and fold your hands the way you were taught to.'

The nurse marvelled anew at the startling contrast between the child's vivid red hair and jet-black brows. Sometimes it was hard to realise that Miss Sterrin was only a child. She was so much a—a person. And that clear voice of hers never fumbled a word and never prattled baby talk.

'Miss Sterrin, you know that your papa and mamma may be going to Dublin after Christmas?'

Sterrin nodded. 'Mamma is going to the castle to curtsey to the lady who rules over Ireland while the Queen is busy keeping her eye on England.'.

'Who on earth told you such a thing?'

'Young Thomas.' Before the nurse could remonstrate about her associates, Sterrin's eyes spilled over. The nurse's heart smote her. The child rarely cried or made demands. It often seemed to the nurse as though the child lacked the security of direct and all-enveloping love. Her parents' love came to her through the muffling sense of their disappointment that she had not been a boy: and then they were so wrapped up in each other!

'I shall be very lonely when everybody goes away. You and Papa and Mamma.'

The nurse hugged the warm, heaving body; she thought of how her frozen heart had responded to its warmth the first night she arrived at the castle. The child's mother too, for all her grandeur and her possessions had a lost, helpless look in her lovely brown eyes that had made an appeal to one who had thought never again to respond to human emotion.

Did you have an unpleasant experience that night? her Ladyship had asked. Nurse Hogan gripped the child closer as though to protect herself from the memory of that experience. Unpleasant! It was unpleasant to have the roof ripped from above your head; unpleasant to be hurled in your bed with your husband and your child down through ceiling after ceiling to the basement. She thought now of the day when she returned from the funeral of her husband and son and passed the bustle of a waiting mail coach. Someone had shouted something about Templetown. The name had penetrated her numbed brain. That was the place where she had been engaged to go as Nurse-Tender for the confinement of a lady of title! She had lost that too; everything and everyone. Then she heard someone expostulating with the guard who was insisting that those who had paid to travel on Monday must get the first preference. As she stood on the sidewalk looking at the gaping rooms of her roofless home, a thought crawled like some unexpected living thing across the ruin of her world. *She* had paid to travel last Monday. The mail coach had not been able to travel until now. Husband, child, home, purse, all swept away. All she possessed in the world was a claim to a seat in that mail coach!

Sterrin wriggled. 'You are squeezing me.' The nurse came back to the present. Her grip relaxed. She held Sterrin from her and looked into her face. 'Listen to me, Miss Sterrin, if you promise to be very good and to keep away from the kitchen and never do anything so unladylike as to clean knives, I think I could get your mamma to agree to take you to Dublin.' It was Sterrin's turn to squeeze hard. Then with an 'Up the White-boys!' that went ringing round the room and down the passages, she went head over heels in a cartwheel of pantalettes and petticoats.

The nurse grabbed her. 'Miss Sterrin, you limb of the devil who taught you to say that? Was it young Thomas?'

Sterrin shook her head. 'Young Thomas does not say bad words. Sometimes he speaks like Papa.' The nurse agreed, mentally.

'Was it Mickey the turf boy?'

'No. He merely taught me how to say the divil damn me ould brogues and——'

'That will do. Don't you know that these "Whiteboys" are wicked men?'

'Some of them are gentlemen.'

'Gentlemen can be wicked too, Miss Sterrin.'

'That's a sin.'

The nurse gave her a shake. 'Don't you know that the White-boys nearly killed your mamma?' Sterrin's face masked over with an impenetrable stillness that always baffled the nurse. 'What would your mamma say if she were to hear you shouting that terrible catchcry?'

'She would say, "Oh, la, la, the bed it is shaking".'

'You unnatural child. You little know what your poor mam-ma went through so that you could come into this world she——'

'I know what young Thomas went through. He suffered a terrible lot to bring me down into the world; just as much a Mamma did. She was in bed but he was out in the storm and he never blames me for headaches or for the big wind blowing—— The nurse was about to shake her quiet when the white stillness of the small face broke up into tears. 'Sit down, Alannah,' the nurse said gently. 'Give me your solemn promise that you will never again say "Up the Whiteboys".'

'May I stick to the chair if I ever say "Up-the-Whiteboys" again.' Sterrin raised herself slightly and gave an apprehensive glance towards the part of her that covered the cushion.

'Now promise that you will never go into the kitchen again.'

Sterrin's eyes widened with dismay; then her mouth bunched 'Promise!'

Sterrin raised herself slightly above the chair. 'May I stick to the chair that I am sitting upon if I ever go into the kitchen again.' The nurse was not too enthusiastic about the wording but she knew that it was solemnly binding with those from whom Miss Sterrin had acquired it. 'Very well, now come with me to your mamma's boudoir and we'll see whether she'll take you to Dublin.'

'Hist!' Thomas, sweeping hot ashes from the recessed wall ovens, turned towards the sound. Miss Sterrin's head was inside the kitchen door. The part of her that 'might stick to the chair' was well outside in the passage. He shook his head to her beckoning. 'Come on in here yourself,' he said.

'Do,' urged the cook. She was wrapping a big currant soda cake in a cloth to steam. 'Come in and I'll cut you a piece of currant cake, Miss Sterrin, gra' gal.' She had a hundred forms of address for the child, but Sterrin liked best 'gra' gal' that was a diminutive of 'bright love'.

'I dare not,' Sterrin whispered. 'I promised Nurse. I swore a mighty oath.'

'Was it "that I may stick to the chair"?'

Sterrin nodded. 'But,' she temporised, looking towards the steaming cake, 'I wasn't actually *sitting* on the chair when I swore.'

Thomas suspended his besom. 'That's cheating,' he said.

The cook buttered a slice of the hot cake and sent Thomas out with it. 'Maybe you had better stick to your word for a few days until the strength has left it, Miss Sterrin, aquanie. Wait!' She handed another slice to young Thomas, 'I can't have your own mouth watering.'

Sterrin squatted in virtue at the foot of the back stairs while the knife boy leaned against the banister. 'Why,' she demanded, 'are you demeaning yourself doing Mickey-the-turf's work?'

'He has the smallpox.'

'Isn't a knife boy high-classer than a turf boy?'

'Of course.'

'Well, if Mickey-the-turf dies, what will happen?'

'In that event Johnny-the-buckets will be promoted in his place and young Johnny-the-rat will be promoted to the buckets.'

They sat in silence pondering on the possible changes in the lower echelons of the kitchen staff. 'Wah——' She paused to swallow the last piece of cake, then stooped and wiped her mouth with the plainest of her petticoats. 'Miss Sterrin, that is

71

a most unladylike thing to do,' he remonstrated.

'Huh!' she snorted. 'I saw you blowing your nose like this.' She put a finger to the side of her nose and gave a convincing demonstration. He ate in silence while the shamed flush covered all his face; then he pointed out that those who *could* afford handkerchiefs of fine cambric didn't seem to know what to do with them. 'Wiping your mouth on your petticoat! Nasty little——' He stopped.

'Knife boys have no right to call ladies "nasty little——" ' She put her elbows on her knees and leaned her chin in her hands. 'Nasty little what?' she wheedled. He moved off. Over his shoulder he said, 'At least you don't have to worry about wiping the soles of your shoes.' She turned up the soles of her little slippers, 'Why not?'

'Because you can always wipe them on the knife boy.'

'Young Thomas,' she called after him, 'don't look so cross with me. I'm going to Dublin too.'

He stopped with his last piece of cake suspended at his lips. 'You're not?'

'I *am* so; and you needn't pretend that you are not sorry. You *look* sad.'

'I—of course I'm not sorry. Now I shall be able to get my work done instead of always getting into trouble.' Upstairs Nurse Hogan's voice could be heard calling. 'Are you down there again, Miss Sterrin?' Her charge had to content herself with sticking her tongue out at Thomas and then scampering out the back entrance.

A moment later she walked demurely in the front door sniffing a flower. The nurse gave her a speculative look and ordered her upstairs to have her hands washed for her embroidery lesson.

The long-planned journey to Dublin was halted almost at the outset by crowds. Every kind of vehicle from carriages to donkey carts filled the highway; and all the time people kept streaming from fields and side roads.

At the crossroads the carriages of Lord Cullen and Lord Strague waited by arrangement. Lord Strague was in a towering rage. 'You must change your route,' was his greeting. 'The police tell me there are forty thousand assembled in Roscrea already. There's no knowing how many are ahead of us. I've

72

seen eighty thousand turn out to meet the fellow in Glasgow.'

The 'fellow' proved to be Father Matthew, the apostle of temperance. The priest, urged by the Quakers of Cork some years before, had started a movement to cope with the problem of drunkenness. The movement had spread like a flame, not only over Ireland, but over England and Scotland. A police officer came up and advised Sir Roderick to postpone his journey. The roads were impassable. Margaret could have wept aloud.

But the journey was not postponed. Lord Strague, a distillery owner whose receipts had been reduced to a fraction by the temperance campaign, finally stopped inveighing against the priest and the stupid people who were flocking to take his pledge against alcohol. His cousin, Sir Jocelyn Devine, he told Sir Roderick, has extended an invitation to them to journey across country and spend the night at his mansion in Kilkenny where he was entertaining a house-party for the Carlow Races. 'He has engaged that Hungarian musician chap to play——' A squeal from inside his carriage interrupted him and Mrs. Kennedy-Sherwin's head came through. 'La, Lady O'Carroll,' she shrilled, 'don't you just long to see Mr. Lizst? He played in Dublin last week and I'm told his long golden hair is too——' Lord Strague motioned the coachman and the elegant bonnet receded to permit his Lordship to resume his place.

Margaret was thrilled. Hien! The visit was proving to be one of the blessings of temperance. Her small daughter, however, shadowed the prospect by recounting the legend of Sir Jocelyn's mansion. According to the bard, it was haunted by the cries of little children who had been compelled by Sir Jocelyn's ancestor to dance on red hot gridirons for the entertainment of his guests. Her papa rapped out sharply that little girls should be seen and not heard and remarked to Margaret that the child's head was overstuffed with bardic mythology. But Lady Cullen, that evening in the drawing-room, fluttered rays of truth on the tale from behind her fan. She leaned across Margaret to tell her grandniece whom she was presenting at the vice-regal drawing-room, how her own aunt, a cousin of the then viceroy, had got him to investigate the story and proved it to be only too grimly true. Fortunately for Margaret, at that moment the host announced the Hungarian musician ... and a small, pasty-faced boy of about twelve dressed in a black velvet suit, bowed and

73

seated himself at the piano.

He wasn't Mr. Lizst, but he was Hungarian, and he had played last week before Queen Victoria and the Prince Consort. Margaret, watching the dull, white face had the impression that the boy was maintaining the ghostly tradition of child performers. Roderick saw her lips tremble; then at a gust of wind against the shutters, he saw that she barely repressed a shriek.

It was the same as last year, and every year on this date, the sixth of January, she could not forget—even in this splendid social setting—that this was the date of the Big Storm that had almost unhinged her mind; and again as on previous years, he recalled as an afterthought that this was also the date of their daughter's birth. Tonight she was four years old.

Sir Jocelyn, believed to be Ireland's wealthiest landlord, could not allow for any plan of his to be disrupted. It was somewhat later before his guests discovered for themselves that Mr. Lizst, on his way to an engagement in the North of Ireland had been hauled from his carriage by a crowd of Orangemen and was within inches of being ducked in a pond when his identity was discovered. Because he was a splendid personage in a splendid equippage, some of the Orange brethren had come to the wishful conclusion that he was Daniel O'Connell. Meantime Sir Jocelyn produced another Hungarian musician.

Next morning his carriage led the cavalcade along the road to the race-course....

CHAPTER 9

Dublin was a pleasing surprise to Margaret. She had expected to see a decaying capital with grass-grown streets. But there was nothing of this about the stately houses that lined the street. Roderick explained that all these houses had been overhauled and refurbished for the visit, some years back, of George the Fourth. The stonework, the graceful fanlights were all in perfect condition; and already the wrought iron lamps outside the Adamesque and Venetian doorways were cheerfully alight. Sackville Street, the centre of its great expanse—the widest street in Europe, her papa used to tell her—held a tree-lined mall where fashionable ladies promenaded on the arms of their escorts.

Roderick's old lady cousins, with whom they were to spend the season, had implemented the warmth of their welcome by ordering a second fire in the grate at the far end of their spacious drawing-room. Its chimney protested against this strange invasion of heat and sent it back into the room in clouds of smoke. Margaret, entering the room, had the impression of two quaint figures in bygone finery extending arms to her from mists of time. The mists dispersed in puffs down into her eyes, nostrils and throat; everywhere but the chimney. But they cast no cloud upon her delight at this charming room whose walls had the friendliness to permit a muted penetration of the cheery street cries and music.

Just to sit at her bedroom window in this pleasant house brought joy to Margaret. The park outside held no grey tinge from a lost field; no shadowy figures conjured out of eerie tales of hauntings. Only the sounds of children trundling hoops beside streamered nursemaids wheeling elegant basinettes; of vendors crying, 'Malahide oysters, threepence a dozen, Dublin Bay Herrings a penny a dozen!'; the pieman calling his hot jam puffs a penny each, the dairyman crying 'Milk-o', and always that distant diapason of the street musicians.

Sterrin asked her something but Margaret didn't reply. She was intrigued watching the manoeuvres of a beautifully-dressed girl and her beau trying to elude their fat chaperone. They slipped down a shady avenue near the park railings and the chaperone continued walking on the main avenue for yards before she discovered their evasion. Margaret went off into peals of mirth at the spectacle of the chaperone doubling back in her tracks looking, in swaying hoops, like a large, agitated duck.

'What is it, *chérie*?' Sterrin had asked again if she might go out and put her ear to the roadway to listen for Papa's returning carriage. Margaret went off into fresh peals at the thought of her small daughter, like the *garçonnerie* at Kilsheelin, listening for the sound of her papa's carriage from among all the wheel-rattling and hoofbeats of a city's traffic.

Roderick was late. He had gone to the Grecian Club with Lord Cullen. He was also a little bit drunk.

He drew Margaret to him.

'Here is the lovely girl all aglow from skating on the lake of Nightingales, I am happy to meet you again.' He kissed her long and tenderly.

'Oh, you silly Roderick, I am not a nightingale and I do not sing.'

'There were swans on that lake. You are like a swan but not so white.'

'Hein? Not as white. That is not a *bon mot*.'

'Yes it is. The whiteness of a swan is too stark for a lovely lady. It would give her a white-washed look. Now, let me see.' He took her face in his hands and scrutinised it. 'Yours is a creamy whiteness. Still, that's not right either. There's a yellow in cream. That's because little flecks of butter come through.'

She laughed delightedly. 'Oh, la, la, now it is you who are the charming Irlandais who followed me home to the Place de l'Eglise, M'sieu. I am enchanted to meet you again!' She kissed him.

'Egad,' he cried gaily, 'this is yet another reunion. What a pity Lord Cullen is not here. It would give me an excuse to roar "Bumpers Gentlemen!" Ugh!' He put his hand to his head. The very mention of bumpers sent wine blasts through it.

She shivered. 'Roderick, ma chree—I *am* getting good at the Gaelic, am I not?—Roderick, ma chree, do not let us talk of things that are sad and sinister.'

'Ah, now I know your shade of white,' he said next morning as he picked up a tall glass filled with a yellowish fluid. 'It is the whiteness of a pearl from a very rare oyster that has blood in its veins that tints the translucence of its pearl. And now, my pearly swan, will you be good enough to throw this out of the window.' He handed her the glass.

'What on earth is this, Roderick? Ugh! It has an ugly smell.'

'It is a concoction that the old ladies used to make up for the gentlemen when they had advanced far in their cups the night before. Give it to the fig tree.' He stretched and yawned.

Margaret waited at the window for a chance to douche the fig tree that grew out of the cobbled backyard. She did not mind Big John, busy moving to and fro from the stables to the coach-house, but the coachman belonging to the cousins was also moving in and out of the yard all the time, making a fuss about their solitary horse that had to be housed in the coach-house to make room for the Kilsheelin horses. Neighbouring windows found occasion to open more frequently than usual now that the Misses O'Carroll's yard had come alive. And Maryjoe, the maid who was not exactly a housekeeper, but ranked higher than the professed cook, seemed suddenly to have a great deal of business to take her from the kitchen door to the little drying green near the stables and Big John.

Roderick emerged from the small dressing-room in trousers and ruffled shirt. He started to tell her about the interesting people he had met at the 'Grecian' the previous night. '... and I saw the poet James Clarence Mangan. He looked like the walking sublimation of tragedy.'

Maryjoe disappeared at last and Margaret douched the fig tree. 'In future,' she remarked, 'you must drink your medicine. Is that the gentleman who wrote "My Dark Rosaleen"?' She opened a little gold casket and popped a chocolate into her mouth. 'I prefer the poetry of the other gentleman who writes for the "Nation". I doted on his poem about Owen Roe O'Neill.'

Roderick looked at her in amazement. 'The Lament For Owen Roe O'Neill', the first ballad Mr. Davis had written, was designed solely for the purpose of rousing patriotic fire ... 'May God wither up their hearts!', it clamoured. 'May their blood cease to flow, May they walk in living death who murdered Owen Roe'. Hardly the kind of thing to appeal to a lady like Margaret who vapoured at the mention of blood.

'Will you tell me, mo craiveen cno, why do you, of all people, say that you dote on such blood-curdling fare?'

'What does "mo craiveen cno" mean?'

'It means literally, my cluster of nuts. Figuratively, it means my nut-brown maid. That's you. Answer my question.'

He was disappointed when she explained that her interest was merely because of an association. Some Belgian school friends who were descendants of Owen Roe had been full of legends about Earl O'Neill.

'Oh,' he said, 'is that all! I had hoped it stirred some flame deep below that calm and pearly surface.'

She watched him silently as he eased his shapely figure into his body coat and smoothed down its velvet lapels. She flicked his silk ruffles into place. 'Roderick, you are disappointed. I lack that—*flamme* you speak of.'

He held her at arm's-length gazing into those enormous brown eyes. 'My share of the world, my nut-brown maid, in your tranquil depths I am completely at peace. As for *flamme*, you have more than enough to consume me.'

She couldn't leave it at that. She couldn't resist that age-old question to which Adam was the only man who could give a truthful negative. 'Was I really the first woman in your life? Surely there must have been someone before—before I skated into your view? Some of these dashing horsewomen you so admire out hunting. I'm so terrified of horses!'

Funny she should mention that! As though thinking aloud, he had reminisced about a girl he had once seen in the hunting field. He had assisted her when her horse stumbled and she became unseated. For an exciting moment they had ridden stirrup to stirrup and then—the scene came back. He forgot Margaret; forgot his surroundings and saw a laughing sprite tossing a gay glance over her shoulder at him from tiptilted eyes before she disappeared into a spinney.

'Was she pretty?'

'M'm. Her eyes were—' he almost said 'unforgettable'. After all, their unforgettableness had been drowned in the limpid depths of the wonderful brown eyes that were gazing up at him now.

A brief encounter: but it had been his initiation to romance. Over-serious for his age from a lonely childhood bereft of brothers and sisters; burdened too soon with responsibility, he had known a moment of shattering joy when he had picked the little huntswoman from the ground. Instead of setting her upon her feet he had gone on holding her in his arms while someone steadied her mount. She had spoken to him from the saddle, but he had been too intent upon watching her eyes. Yes, they *were* unforgettable; they held three colours merged into a woodland hazel that was not of autumn but of spring when the bluebells—green-sheathed—tinted the brown tree boles. 'Her eyes were—what?' He came back to the brown eyes that probed, apprehensive of that moment of past romance. 'I'm not certain, but I am positive that yours are—glorious.'

But she must probe deeper. 'And did you meet her afterwards?'

'Never.'

Margaret did not fail to note the wistfulness in the word that betrayed a bygone regret. 'What was her name?'

'Mansfield, I believe. What does it matter? Now I have you.' He kissed her. 'Mo cuid de'n saoghail! My share of the world. My completely satisfying share of the world.' He gave her a little push. 'Be off now and put your hair in curling rags until tomorrow night.'

'Curling rags! *Tiens!* There is a very grand hairdresser coming tomorrow afternoon to curl me before I dress.' But inside her Margaret felt something like a shiver. It had been a near thing; that encounter with the hunting miss.

'I think that she went back to school.'

So he was still thinking of her! Of his hunting miss! Thank heavens she had had to return to school! Margaret could too readily envisage Roderick watching the girl, entranced: as he had watched her when he saw her that first time skating over the frozen lake in the park at Anvers.

He didn't think it necessary to tell her that the lovely little face under the feathered riding hat had tossed its beckoning eyes into his dreams. That he had ridden his horse exhausted to trace where she lived—to the banks of the Ara River where her house stood in its enclasping trees. But the woodland sprite had vanished forever.

Its apparition still made a haunting in Margaret as she dressed for her shopping expedition.

'What colour was her hair?' He put an arm about her waist and drew her down the stairs.

'Whose hair? Oh! fair, I think.'

'And, was it straight or curly?' Roderick hadn't dreamed that his passing recollection would have aroused such a passion of curiosity.

'I—forget.' A sudden vision of wind-tossed curls glinted across his memory. 'Curly, I think.' He put a finger on the smooth brown coils beneath her bonnet. 'Forget her, my cluster of brown nuts. She will never trouble you; a wraith of forgotten memory! You are my reality.'

The cousins, cloaked and bonneted, watched them descend the stairs, his arm about her waist. 'They are *so* in love!' they breathed, unanimous in thought and word and wistful longings undefined.

Hester stuck her head out of the carriage to ask Roderick if he had taken the potion. Roderick assured her that he had. Then Sarah's head came out and she said that her dear papa always said that it went to his very roots whenever he felt indisposed the morning after he had—after he had entertained gentlemen to supper!

Roderick assured her that it had gone to the roots of this morning's recipient. 'My anxious spouse saw to that. Didn't you, Margaret?' He gestured the coachman on and as he turned back to the door his eye fell on the knocker. 'By jove, solid gold!' He examined the heavy ring held in the mouth of a lion. It was tempting Providence, he thought, to allow that to hang there in these modern times when no footman slept inside the door on his trestle bed. A good thing the knocker-snatching young subalterns from Templetown were not knocking about!

He had scarcely closed the door before a knocker-snatching young subaltern from Templetown grasped the ring, then halted in surprise. 'By jove, solid gold!'

On the inside, Roderick heard his words thrown back and wondered if the door held an echo like that place in Killarney. He reopened it just as Lieutenant Fitzharding-Smith was about to let the ring crash against the lion's brazen neck. 'I wouldn't advise you to try any funning with that,' was his greeting.

Lieutenant Fitzharding-Smith felt that the greeting was not in the tradition of Fine Old Irish Hospitality. 'Oh, sir, I wouldn't *dream* of anything like that.'

'No, by all accounts you don't waste time dreaming in the presence of door-knockers. You act, forcibly.'

Roderick continued to stand in the doorway.

'It was such a fine morning,' the lieutenant said, puzzled by Roderick's discourtesy, 'that I thought I'd take a walk in this charming square. I had no idea it was so close to Mr. Gresham's.'

Sir Roderick looked significantly at the dove-grey moistness of the unbeckoning morn. 'Too bad that you've missed the ladies. They've gone shopping. I was about to fill in these cards for the Levée and Drawing-room,' he said.

'Oh, please don't let me detain you,' said the guest. He went on detaining him, then looked with amazement at the parcel he was holding in his hand as though he wondered how it had come to be there. 'These are chocolates. I thought that Sterrin might like them.'

Roderick was finding his own discourtesy a strain.

'Won't you come in a while?'

'I mustn't detain you,' said the lieutenant, promptly following him into the dining-room. Roderick moved to the sideboard.

'Brandy, say you? It is such a fine—such a raw morning. Or would you prefer claret?'

The officer preferred brandy. The Dublin claret, he thought, compared unfavourably with the claret in the South of Ireland and particularly with that served at Kilsheelin Castle. The young gentleman considered that deucedly splendid claret!

Roderick thawed. He considered the Dublin claret was hogwash. But he did not think it necessary to explain that the Kilsheelin brand came by night off a French boat to a Waterford cove called Straud-na-Coaleen, whose full name and meaning was The Strand of the Little Peoples' Music. An underground cave and passage from the fairies' strand conveyed it to cellars of his uncle's home there. Instead, he called out to Sterrin who was passing the door.

She came in dressed in her fur-trimmed cloak of green velvet, and curtsied. Each of them felt as he gazed at the perfect features set in gleaming red curls so admirably framed in her green hood, that he was looking not at just a lovely child but at the beginnings of a poised and lovely lady. She carried two sticks pointed at each end. Big John, she explained, had whittled them for her so that she could play tipcat with the children in the park. Lieutenant Fitzharding-Smith handed her the parcel. 'These are for a good little girl,' he said, feeling that he

81

was talking like an impertinent buffoon.

'I'm afraid I *have* been rather good since I came to Dublin,' said Sterrin in a tone that suggested there was no possibility here of being otherwise. She undid the parcel and gasped at the sight of the satin-covered box, then she looked up at him seriously.

'But this is a grown-up lady's box. Is it really for me?'

Her papa hastened to assure her that it was. Who else would Lieutenant Fitzharding-Smith want to bring such a nice box of chocolates to? I'll hold a crown, he thought, that they were never intended for Sterrin.

In an excess of gratitude Sterrin invited the young officer to join her for a game of tipcat in the park. He accepted with unexpected alacrity. It would give him an excuse to escort Sterrin back to the house later.

Into his damned barrow, thought Roderick, as he made his way to the study at the top of the house. A queer place to have a study! No. 9 was not really a terrace house. It had stood here before the square had been erected. It held nooks and crannies not required by modern life.

Roderick sauntered round the room examining the floral designs on the bog oak panelling. Suddenly, there was a clicking sound under his fingers and the panel gave way, revealing a room exactly like the study, the same sloping ceiling and panelled walls, except that in the ceiling there was a large sky-light window.

This must be the room where his grandfather's marriage had taken place. It was bare of furniture except for a low tapestry-covered seat, a chair and a plain chest of drawers made of bog oak, but without any carving or adornment. Roderick ran his fingers over the top surface until he found what he suspected, a spring that lifted the plain top, revealing below a beautifully-carved altar piece. It was a relic from the Penal days when the Protestant O'Carrolls made it possible for their Catholic kinsmen to have Mass there, and a look-out warned them of danger so that the lid went down hurriedly upon an innocuous looking chest and the priest made his escape through the skylight.

He opened all the drawers and rummaged through them until he found another spring that released a panel. From behind it he drew two dust covered miniatures and a small, thick diary.

When the dust, almost hard from damp, had been scraped

away from the miniatures he looked at his grandfather's face. Except for the elaborately curled wig, and, yes, the contours of the face were a little softer, the lips a trifle fuller, Roderick felt that he might be looking at his own portrait. The second miniature held his grandmother's lovely face framed by her famous black ringlets.

Roderick leafed through the diary. It was his grandfather's. Much of it was in French, but there were a few references to 'Straud-na-Coaleen' that Roderick had been thinking about scarcely an hour ago. There were references to hours and tides and a few times the name of a boat and its skipper and its cargoes of silk and brandy and wine. One item had such a nonchalant and unrevealing tone that Roderick wondered that his grandfather had troubled to record the event—'June sixteenth, year of Our Lord Seventeen seventy-nine I did give satisfaction to Asculph O'Flaherty this morning in the Barley Fields below the Rotunda Gardens where Doctor Mosse has his Lying-in hospital. His pistols were more than one foot long. Like all Galway gentlemen his skill lies in the sword. Pray God he recovers.' Your pious prayers, it seems were not answered, Roderick recalled.

The next day's item followed in unemotional routine, 'June seventeenth, I was married to Miss Beamon Blake at my brother's new house in Dublin——' A light filtered through into Roderick's mind. Miss Blake penniless, but beautiful, had been a Galway lady; from an estate close to that of the hapless Asculph whose skill, to his misfortune, had lain in the sword. The duel and the marriage were not unrelated!

'—The ceremony was performed by Mr. O'Loughlin at nine o'clock at night, he then leaving by the roof to ride by night to my Uncle John's estate at Annestown in the County Waterford to await the "Francoise" for Bordeaux, he not being a registered priest. I gave my wife a diamond necklace from the sale of the oaks by the field of the Hungry Grass. The design was in keeping. She looked pretty in a white demask redingote and a petticoat. I was bravely dressed in a buff cloth suit with waistcoat of satin, much trimmed with gold——' And as though conscience had pricked at the despoiling of the land, there was a note in brackets. '(With the slackening of the Penal savageries there is scarcely the old need for the concealment of our existence in a dark cloak of forestry. "He that troubleth his house," saith the proverb of the bravely dressed and likewise gold-vested Solomon, "shall inherit the wind.")' Only, thought Roderick, rising to his feet, it was I who inherited the wind. Not even the demned necklace. Wonder what became of it! It had not been among the meagre jewels he had taken over from his own mother. There had never been a reference to the necklace. Probably sold to meet some other eventuality! He pushed the diary far back into the concealed nook and his finger gripped something cold. It was a necklace of diamond oak leaves strung together by links of gold and with a cluster of diamond acorns forming a pendant. The design is in keeping! In keeping with the oaks; not with the lady's dress as Roderick had assumed. 'Grandpapa,' he breathed, 'I—I almost apologise for questioning your prodigality. You loved her very beautifully—your Beamon!' The necklace appeared to have been pushed hurriedly, and unexpectedly out of sight. His grandfather must have been compelled to make one of his hurried flights from the country. Possibly on account of that duel . . .

Roderick hurried excitedly to the stairhead as the butler was admitting the ladies. Then he frowned. Lieutenant Fitzharding-Smith, holding Sterrin's hand, had arrived at the same moment. Blast the young squirt! He needn't think he was going to introduce the Templetown garrison customs into his household. It might be *bon ton* for officers' wives to have a sort of *cupidon déchaîné*, in the form of a young subaltern, in tow. But this would not do for *his* wife!

He pocketed the diamond plantation. The news of his dramatic discovery must wait.

Later he realised that the young officer's presence had saved him from releasing the diamonds like a charge of bullets. The cousins themselves might have hidden them there for safety. For some reason or other, the diamonds must have been willed to *them*. But the ladies, when they heard of them, were as surprised as he had been. Who but Roderick had a right to them, they said? The diamond leaves and acorns of the Kilsheelin oaks! Miss Sarah suggested that he keep them a secret from Margaret until she was dressed and ready for her Presentation the next night. Roderick agreed, but he whistled as he bounded up the stairs, and sang as he dressed for this evening's dinner party at the Liberator's great house in Merrion Square.

There had been times when deep in the pre-Celtic roots of his being Roderick had wished that he had not cut the hawthorn trees that used to grow in the field of the Hungry Grass. He knew well that the servants and tenants and even some of the neighbouring gentry attributed the field's misadventure to his own high-handedness with that mystic circle and all that it might enclose.

Now, he felt something ridiculously like relief to know that it was his romantic grandfather who had exposed the field to the merry orgies of the big wind. But as he rode with Margaret to dinner at Mr. O'Connell's town house in Merrion Square he felt as though a sparkle from the romanticism of that superb recklessness had suddenly shone out through the years to en-glamour his love for his own wife.

Margaret was conscious of his suppressed excitement but she put it down to the general excitement that was abroad since Mr. O'Connell's dramatic announcement. He had stated publicly that this very year of 1843 would see the repeal of the Act of Union. The announcement had sent a wild, concerted throb of hope through all the populace. At every street corner that they passed, glee-men were singing the songs they had composed overnight to commemorate the announcement. Their ragged children were doing a roaring trade selling the printed version at a penny a sheet.

The usual crowd of sightseers, native and foreign, that waited nightly for a glimpse of the great man had swelled tonight to a multitude. The gig lights twinkled on the livery facings of the Liberator's servants as they went from carriage to carriage, haranguing the onlookers and forging a path for the guests.

Roderick's spirits responded to the surging hope. 'The Repeal for 1843!' cried the crowd. Why not? he thought! Must Ireland's agony drag on till the world itself dissolves? At some time, in some year, it must end. Why *not* 1843? As he crossed the hall in the wake of the servants he felt as though he were moving bodily towards the starting point of some new and glorious era.

The feeling persisted as he mounted the stairs. The drawing-room was suddenly more than a place of flooding candle-glow, of colour and silk and firelight and laughter. It was a gay rally-ing ground for the commencement of the new Ireland. The greeting that burst from him to his host echoed the catch-cry from outside. '1843, then, Liberator!' he cried.

The Liberator gave a hand to each of them and drew them towards the company. 'Leave numerals to describe other years, Sir Roderick,' he smiled, 'this is Repeal Year. Mark my words.'

The party seemed to have divided itself into two groups. The older guests were more noticeable at the top fireplace. But the hilarity in the region of the fire that blazed at the lower end of the room was exclusively youthful.

'That's Davis down there reciting one of his own lampoons.' The host indicated a young man surrounded by a group that hung, with obvious delight, on his every word.

Roderick had not expected to see Davis here. The young leader begrudged time spent away from his gigantic task of nation building. His counselling, advising, writing; training the minds of the people for the new, freer life that was to come; training his colleagues for the higher duties that lay ahead. 'By Jove, sir,' said Roderick, 'I had not expected the pleasure of meeting this new planet. Lady O'Carroll will be thrilled. She is an ardent admirer of his poems; particularly his more blood-thirsty ones. Aren't you, my dear?'

The Liberator sighed gustily. 'That is the trouble. His poems are too bloodthirsty; too revolutionary for my purpose.' Davis made no secret of his impatience with O'Connell's peaceful methods of attaining Repeal.

Their host moved off having disposed of Roderick between a Protestant parson and a Catholic priest and bestowed the gift of Lady O'Carroll's company upon a French count. Roderick finally met Davis and fell under his spell. Here, he thought, was a force; no fiery revolutionary here! So much for rumour! He had heard that Davis was a religious bigot, opposed to O'Connell's Catholicism. The high-minded young genius who clasped his hand with the warmth of friendship would be as incapable of being anti-Catholic as he would be of being anti-Irish. Nothing that was ignoble, thought Roderick, could exist behind that broad brow. He felt again the exhilaration he had felt outside. A movement with two such leaders could not fail. But should two such leaders clash? 'Well then,' thought Roderick, as he gazed into the friendly countenance, the blue eyes set in a framework of solid strength, 'well then, I should hate to have the choice of fealty thrust upon me.'

Their meeting was interrupted by a weird-looking figure who passed between them and went up to his host with an apology for his dress. Instead of the conventional black evening suit, the long, lugubrious-looking gentleman was wearing a blue body coat with great, gilt buttons, white duck trousers and Wellington boots. Just then a footman hurried up and Roderick caught the words he whispered in agitated Gaelic to his master, 'Will your Honour's Liberator come out and save Mr. Steele's hat.'

So this was the famous Tom Steele! The Cambridge graduate who might have been a great inventor if he had not chosen to go a-windmill tilting. He had mortgaged his ancestral estates in County Clare to the tune of ten thousand pounds in order to aid the Spanish insurgents against Frederick the Seventh. What he had salvaged from the wreck of his fortune he had, Protestant, though he was, poured into O'Connell's movement for Catholic emancipation. 'There was a great inventor lost in him,' Davis commented to Roderick. 'But the only thing he has invented in recent years is his title for the self-made role of Head Pacificator of Ireland and the Repeal Funeral; and of course, the only time he ever varies the uniform for which he has excused himself to our host is when he drapes it in funereal black, as well as his carriage, horses, and coachmen and drives off to the scene of some agrarian outrage to reproach the transgressors and show them that they have put the Repeal into mourning.'

The self-styled Head Pacificator of Ireland returned with a very high white-peaked hat held tenderly in both hands. Behind his back O'Connell wagged an admonitory finger at some of the students near the end fireplace.

'Well, Pacificator,' said Davis, 'I hear you have been conducting one of your funeral services today. I trust the evil-doers were duly grief-stricken.'

'Aye,' said the Head Pacificator, 'I brought home to them the harm they were doing to the cause of Repeal and to the noble efforts of the Liberator. There won't be another outrage there again.'

'Come, Tom,' Davis laughed, 'do you really believe that your parade of funeral grief will suppress the impulses of resentment under which these men labour?'

'I *do* believe, Doubting Thomas, that the bloodless method by which our leader liberated his people from centuries of bondage and blood-letting will prevail once more, in his efforts for Repeal.' He raised his voice so that its lugubrious utterances boomed through the room. 'They will benefit more from the words of my funeral service than from your warmongering squibs.'

As the servant was helping Margaret to salmon, the Liberator turned to her and told her to wish. 'It is the first of this year's catch.'

From the end of the table Steele boomed up, 'I can guess what your wish is, Liberator.'

'You can indeed,' said O'Connell. He held a piece of salmon suspended on a fork, 'My wish is the Repeal for 1843.'

'Oh, Mr. O'Connell,' she cried, 'you should never reveal your wish. It is unlucky.' But all the glasses were raised though it was early for toasts. 'To the Repeal!' thundered the young men.

CHAPTER 10

The afternoon of the great presentation, Margaret locked herself away from human gaze to cover her face in a plaster of flowers and lotion. Roderick argued that it was ridiculous to apply plaster to skin that was flawless and Margaret argued back that because of that very fact a plaster was necessary. One did not bring one's everyday face, flawless or otherwise, to the vice-regal throne of Dublin Castle. Roderick took himself off on mysterious business of his own. The Mesdames O'Carroll retired for their nap and Sterrin was left to mope.

Dublin had begun to pall on Sterrin. The fashionable Mountjoy Square could not offer the sustained interests of the square that formed the stable yard behind Kilsheelin Castle. There was life and clatter there all day; shops too, the estate carpenter's shop, the forge where, for a small sum, tenants could order anything from a scythe to a thimble, the slaughter-house where they bought venison for a penny a pound. Slaughter-house! As if by miracle the word brought into view the spectacle of a messenger boy kicking a cow's bladder along the pavement towards the house. She strained on tiptoe to peep through the window. Miraculously the boy stopped at this very railing, then disappeared down the area. She tiptoed down the stairs and struggled with the hall door. The effort was a lesson in life for Sterrin. It was the first time she had ever opened a door. Always they opened to her approach. The boy was nowhere in sight but the bladder lay unguarded on the step all bloodstained and ballooned. She drew back her foot and kicked. Something banged against the drawing-room window as the footman was in the act of setting a tray before his mistresses. The next minute the house was in an uproar. The footman disappeared from the room with the announcement that 'Miss Sterrin is kilt!' The ladies joined by Margaret could just glimpse Sterrin lying on her back while a fierce and ragged boy stood over her saying something about a red-haired rip!

Miss Sarah paused in her swoon to watch Sterrin rise, push a ringlet from her bloodstained nose and inform her adversary that she was about to 'break his canister'. The term was unfamiliar to the Dublin gurrier. It was only after Sterrin's fist had shot out and landed on his nose that enlightenment dawned. Just then a grandiose personage alighted from a carriage and ordered the footman to haul him inside. With sinking terror the urchin saw himself leaving his beloved Dublin slums on a convict ship. 'Don't send me "over", your Honour's Nobility,' he sobbed.

Nurse Hogan discovered that the blood on Sterrin's nose was from the rebound of the bladder. She hastened to exonerate the poor ragamuffin. He was finding it hard to convince the gentleman that he had not laid a finger upon his daughter. ' 'Twas the bladder that bumped age'n her, your Nobility,' he pleaded. 'I only gave her one little shove an' she up an' hot me an' if she hot me nothin' at all furder I'd have no snotther left.'

He went on his way with his pocket enriched by Sir Roderick's shilling and his vocabulary enriched by what he assumed to be the Quality's word for describing ones snotther. He could be heard challenging a gurrier who had designs on the bladder to hit it a kick at the risk of having his canister broken!

Miss Sarah was the only one of the three swooning ladies who showed no signs of recovering. Burnt feathers to the nose and smelling salts were all right for ordinary vapours; but for a first-class faint like this, something stronger was demanded and she wasn't going to be baulked of her cure. Her wan lips parted, Roderick stooped to catch the tremulous whisper. 'The French cabinet,' she murmured. In a corner of a painted cabinet he found a brandy bottle three-quarters full. Halfway through the second glass she allowed herself to return to full consciousness.

She looked up as Margaret bent to apologise for Sterrin and gave a squawk. 'Your face!' she gasped and swooned off again. Roderick looked across at his wife. The candles had not yet been lighted. In the twilight her face was purplish and splotchy. He stared horrified. Once before he had seen her look this way! That night, before he set out for the witch for Sterrin's birth. Sterrin! What had the brat brought on her mother? Tonight of all nights. He rounded on the child where she stood apart, her face a white gleam in the dimness. 'Go to your room, Miss,' he roared. 'I'll deal with you later.' Just then the butler appeared with lighted sconces and announced the hairdresser. Margaret clapped her hands to her face. '*Dieu!*' she cried. 'I had thought to have this stuff off my face before he arrived.' She started to pick off the violet petals that had been brewed in the lotion for her complexion. The butler lapsed into speech. 'And me to be thinking that it was the cholera that her Ladyship was gettin'.'

Margaret hesitated at the door. 'Cousin Hester, do you think it is really necessary for me to have a hairdresser? I'm sure he will frizz me. I vow I should hate to be frizzed.'

Miss Hester was shocked. 'My dear, think of your lappets and your feathers! You *must* have curls and pouffes to hold them——'

'Besides,' murmured the invalid, 'curls are so ladylike and so dainty I'm sure Roderick would prefer you with curls. Wouldn't you, Roderick?'

Margaret wondered if the question would remind him of that hefty hey-nonny-nonny huntswoman with the curls who had managed to fall off her horse into his arms. For a second she thought to dismiss the hairdresser. She didn't want curls!

But Roderick looked lovingly at her, clotted cream, withered petals and all. 'I prefer her hair when it is in two glossy plaits hanging down over her shoulders,' he said. The suggested intimacy of his words sent Sarah burrowing in her reticule for a fan to cool her blushes. But suddenly the brandy altered her viewpoint. She stopped groping and began to giggle.

At last the long tulle lappets and the regulation three feathers were pinned in place on the shining curls. The inmost petticoat of horsehair weighted at the hem with a thick straw plait was covered with a succession of petticoats, from muslin ones to those of lace-edged silk that increased in elegance towards the final one of satin, quilted to the knees and fortified above and below the waist with whalebones placed a hand's length apart. While Margaret relaxed in a wrapper before donning the tour de force of the white satin presentation gown, Roderick came into the room. 'Shut your eyes,' he ordered. He clipped on her wrist a gold bracelet set with diamonds. She turned to him with a cry of sheer delight. His kiss stifled her outcry about its beauty, its costliness. 'The bangle is my own presentation gift. Close your eyes again.'

This time when she opened them she made no outcry. The glory of the necklace that he had hung about her throat evoked

91

the supreme tribute of unvoiced rapture. The row of candles on the dressing-table were duplicated by the mirror's reflection. Roderick, standing behind her chair, had the impression of an altar alight with candles before the rapt face that was enshrined by the mirror. She touched one of the diamond leaves that shimmered on her throat. 'Roderick!' she breathed but could not go on. Instead she rose and put her arms about him. He held her from him at arm's-length, fearful of disturbing her court coiffure, and told her the story of the diamonds.

'The oaks of Kilsheelin,' she murmured when he had finished. 'The diamond oaks! I feel so unworthy of them.' He risked her *grande toilette* to crush her to him and tell her that it was the diamonds that were unworthy. And while they stood thus together they did not notice the little figure that came in and stood watching them wistfully, then tiptoed away.

She was lurking in the shadows of the corridor when they emerged in the full ceremonial of court dress. Her papa was superb in velvet court dress under a cloak, swung casually back from the gold clasps that held it at his throat. Her mother with her regal plumes and lappets and an ermine cloak over her white satin gown was like a snow queen. Sterrin couldn't restrain herself. 'Oh, Mamma,' she cried. 'You look like a beautiful queen and Papa looks like a prince, and I'm sorry for kicking a common boy's bladder and giving everyone vapours.'

Margaret had forgotten all about Sterrin's disgrace. 'Where on earth have you been?'

'I have been waiting to be dealt with—by Papa. Nurse said that it meant a spanking.'

Roderick's heart smote him. 'Perhaps Nurse mistook me. I may have said that little ladies who kicked cows' bladders on city pavements *deserved* to be slapped.' He wondered if he had ever kicked a cow's bladder with Black Pat. Margaret laid aside her bouquet and held out her arms. The pathos of the child! Waiting in misery to receive her punishment while she herself was receiving gifts and love! She kissed her. 'Promise that you will never do such a thing again.'

'I promise,' said Sterrin, then temporised. 'I promise never to kick a cow's bladder on a city street pavement.' That didn't include the Kilsheelin slaughter-house where the bladders were bigger and bloodier.

'Hm,' said her papa, noting the reservations. He kissed her

92

and told her he would take her to the Rotunda gardens next afternoon to see the dancing bear.

Sterrin was thrilled until she remembered something. 'Lieutenant Fitzharding-Smith has promised to go with Nurse Hogan and me tomorrow to help me choose a book for young Thomas. Perhaps you would come instead and afterwards we could see the bear?'

'No,' said papa. 'I'm afraid that I am not sufficiently conversant with the literary taste of young Thomas.'

He swept her a mock bow and gave his arm to her mamma. There were exclamations of admiration from passers by as the two were lighted to the carriage by the butler and footman holding aloft great brass lanterns. Even Big John relaxed his wonted dignity to stare from one to the other with prideful admiration. He had never before seen the young Sir dressed this way. A cold rain was falling and her Ladyship reminded him to put on his oilskin cape. His gratitude was respectful but his refusal was firm. Big John was driving to the court of Dublin Castle. The Kilsheelin livery would not be covered tonight. Not if it was the Big Wind itself that blew!

He drove them through avenues of spectators; Dubliners of all classes, but mostly the patient Lazaruses snatching the dazzling glimpses vouchsafed them from the Dives' carriages. There was no begrudging in their looks. Only the eagerness for life's pageantry hinted by the sparkle of a diamond on a white neck, the gleam of a gold epaulette on a scarlet tunic. The lights of hundreds of carriages, the street lights, the opened candle-lit windows filled with craning heads had transported them out of the sleety greyness of the January night into a brightness that was climeless and timeless.

At last the wide staircase of the State Apartments unrolled its blaze of scarlet carpet before Margaret. Footmen in maroon coats and salmon breeches stood on every landing; more scarlet glared out from big, fur-hatted guardsmen. All these shades would clash horribly in the daytime, she thought, but now, in the benign sheen from thousands of candles in blue and gilt candelabra all tints were blended.

In a cloakroom she found Lady Cullen shedding layers of cloaks on to the attending servants, and they went together to take their places in the procession. It was a long and painful ritual.

Margaret began to feel wilted. It was a full half-hour since the procession had made a further move. It was all right, she reflected, for girls seeking husbands to endure this elegant hardship but, she had—Roderick! And, without any of this; just a quick encounter in the brisk exhilarating air of the ice rink. She looked up at the candles bending in the stifling heat. The shoulders of the gentlemen's court suits were frosted with the drippings. Roderick's shoulders had been frosted that day at the ice rink. Something pricked at the back of her ankles. Like a pin! Could anything have come undone? In panic she went over the list of her petticoats. Her long drawers were secured twice around her waist with running string. She never tolerated pins. Nothing but buttons stoutly sewn. When the procession moved again she could feel the pricking all around her ankles. *Dieu!* The whalebones in her petticoat couldn't possibly have come undone! Suddenly she realised that it was the straw plait in the hem of her horsehair petticoat. The press of bodies was crushing it into her flesh. And, horrors! Despite all the perfume sachets that had been sewn into the plait it was giving out a whiff! She looked about her. But in that atmosphere of sublimated humanity the straw in one lady's petticoat made neither reck nor reek. She flinched, someone in front was looking around and whispering over her shoulder. Margaret thought in agony that she had noticed, but she merely said, 'Fancy all this fuss for the sake of being kissed by the Viceroy!' Margaret could have sworn that the girl had rouge on. A few minutes later, she was certain.

The throne had come into view. The Viceroy in blue coat and white knee breeches was not looking too appreciative as he stooped to exercise his privilege of kissing each debutante on either cheek. The Vicereine, a-gleam with teeth and diamonds looked indulgently at the ceremonial caress.

'He has my sympathy,' whispered one of the Honourable Mesdames in the estrade behind Her Excellency. A debutante was raising a face ravaged by smallpox beyond the shelter of lappet or ringlet and the Viceroy bent in service to his Queen.

When the Viceroy straightened after bestowing the ceremonial kiss on Margaret's neighbour's cheeks there was a distinct smudge of red on his upper lip!

The stentorian voice of the chamberlain called out: 'Lady O'Carroll presented by Lady Cullen.' The aides-de-camp were spreading out the glory of her train. Pray Heaven, thought Margaret as she went down into the billows of her satin, that he won't kiss rouge on to my cheeks! But the Vicereine had seen the smudge and murmured something through lips that continued to smile. His Excellency rubbed a handkerchief over his lips and the beautiful Lady O'Carroll received a kiss that was unsullied and—unhurried!

CHAPTER 11

Next day, Mr. O'Connell called to collect Sir Roderick, who had promised to join the Repeal Association at the bi-weekly meeting at the Corn Exchange. The cousins were thrilled to see him and called his attention to their father's sword hanging over the fireplace.

'We hung Papa's sword there, Mr. O'Connell, the day the Union was signed forty-three years ago,' said Hester. 'You would have been too young then to be concerned with the significance of the Union.'

'Too young!' cried O'Connell. 'In troth, madam, I was not. When I saw the new royal standard go up over Dublin Castle on that first day, and heard the artillery thundering from Phoenix Park and the bells of Saint Patrick's Cathedral sounding their *carillon de joie* for Ireland's degradation, I swore that I would devote my life to restoring our stolen freedom.'

'You certainly succeeded,' said Sir Roderick, 'when you won the victory of centuries with Catholic emancipation. But surely a second victory so soon is too much to envisage!'

The Liberator put his hand on the younger man's shoulder. 'The road to freedom has been opened. By the same method that we won the right to practise our religion, we will win the right to govern in our own parliament; not by bloodshed or violence or turbulence, but by legal, peaceable and constitutional means alone.'

He took his leave of the ladies and swung Sterrin on his shoulders for a pick-a-back down the stairs. On an impulse as he kissed her goodbye he turned to her parents and said, 'Why not take her along with us to witness your initiation? It will be something for her to remember later when prosperity has returned with the parliament that she saw her papa vow his services to its achievement.' As he watched her skedaddle up the stairs for her bonnet, he murmured, 'There is something about that child that I find arresting. Perhaps it is that, like myself,

96

she was hurled into life by storm.'

In the Ladies' Gallery at the Corn Exchange, sitting between her mother and Lady Cullen, Sterrin listened wide-eyed to the sound of her father's name sent in clarion tones down the thronged hall as the Liberator introduced that 'distinguished and honourable gentleman, Sir Roderick O'Carroll of Kilsheelin Castle, Templetown'. Her embarrassed Papa had not anticipated rising to confront such a throng of people. He was glad when he could sit down and listen to the Liberator.

O'Connell was declaiming that in the last war with France, Ireland had supplied the general and two-thirds of the officers and men in the English Army and Navy. A clock struck. O'Connell fumbled automatically for his watch. 'And yet, she has no parliament——' then stopped dead and whispered.

Before he could resume Tom Steele was on his feet. His lugubrious voice, cracked with emotion, was announcing, 'Sacred Heavens! Have I lived to see this day of woe! A transaction unparalleled in the annals of infamy has occurred in this hall to the country's Liberator, my august leader!'

A gasp went through the audience. Roderick rose and looked anxiously towards the gallery that held his wife and child. He had exposed them to danger by bringing them! Surely Steele was speaking of attempted assassination. Steele drew his hands across his face but his voice still held tears as he said brokenly, 'The watch of the illustrious Liberator has been stolen from his pocket!'

The Liberator calmed the pandemonium. In the gallery, Mrs. Kennedy-Sherwin whispered to Margaret that there was nothing to fear. The audience was soon lost in O'Connell's vituperative eloquence against Wellington and Peel. Roderick, chuckling away, found himself crushed sideways by a powerful gentleman. He was holding aloft a gold watch which he placed in front of the Liberator. Up jumped Tom Steele, his hand on his sword. 'Name the base miscreant! He is not fit to live!'

'It was found, sir,' said the gentleman calmly, 'under your pillow in your bedroom.'

Later in the Ladies' Gallery a toast to Father Matthew, the Temperance leader, was drunk with tea while the band played 'Ned Gower's Farewell to Whiskey'. 'It appears to be a lingering "Farewell",' said Lady Cullen looking down at Lord Cullen who rose more unsteadily to raise his bumper each time the toast was repeated. When the band changed to 'We'll Never Get Drunk Again', she saw him go down for the third time and disappear beneath the table. There was nothing she could do about it because O'Connell was on his feet reading a report on Ireland written by some gentleman sent over by *The Times*.

'He says here,' cried O'Connell, 'that Irish women are ugly.' There was an angry roar. Then every gentleman rose to his feet and raised his glass towards the ladies: Margaret lifted her fan in front of her face and there was a fluttering as all the ladies did likewise against the onslaught of all these staring gentlemen. Sterrin looked up over her head to see what it was that some of the gentlemen were actually pointing at. It was a great bunch of mistletoe.

'I'll die! I vow I shall die,' wailed Mrs. Kennedy Sherwin.

'Not likely,' said Lady Cullen.

The Liberator, eager to get home to his correspondence, could not see the cause of the commotion that barred his way; but as the wardens with Tom Steele booming, 'Make way for the Liberator!' cleared a path, the cause came in sight. He strode forward and placed his hand on the shoulder of the gallant who was bending over Mrs. Kennedy-Sherwin under the mistletoe. 'Young man,' he cried, 'make way for the Liberator!' Mrs. Kennedy-Sherwin found herself engulfed in the tidal wave of the Liberator's amorous kisses.

'Come,' said Margaret to Sterrin. 'We have had enough excitement for today. Let us find your father.'

It had been a puzzling day, Sterrin thought, as she and Margaret pushed their way through the crowd. She would be glad to find her father, of course, but gladder still if Margaret had said: 'We have had enough of Dublin. Let us go back to Kilsheelin.'

CHAPTER 12

Young Thomas crouched with his ear to the ground. 'Ah, here they are,' he murmured. He had caught a faint subterranean rumble. They would soon be here. Young Thomas was to serve the marriage mass of Ulick Prendergast's daughter. He knew the Latin and the priest had asked him to assist.

He straightened and resumed his arm swinging and stamping up and down past the back lodge. It must be half-past five by now, thought he. The night still held the dawn in its dark grip.

A few minutes later there was a gruff, 'Whoa there,' and Ulick Prendergast's side-car reined in.

Thomas stepped forward with a God-save-you. The gruff voice said, 'God save you kindly. Let you get up on this side. Why weren't you at the cross?'

The devil whip you! thought Thomas; and I obliging you! 'The priest told me,' he answered civilly, 'that you'd pick me up at the back lodge at half-past five.'

'It would have shortened the journey had you waited at the cross.' The prosperous old farmer was as economical of words and time on the wedding morning of his only child as on all other occasions.

An overhanging branch spent a spray of drops over their heads. The still figure on the far side moved to avoid them. She seemed to have a queer, bulky shape, and like her father, nothing much to say for herself. Maybe she was wondering what kind of a man she was to marry. Maybe she had not seen him yet!

Thomas sighed as he thought of the romances that he read about in books. It seemed that only the Quality could have Love Matches! Sometimes in the kitchen Mrs. Stacey talked of the love match between the Sir and her Ladyship. How he had seen her floating over a frozen lake in a wonderful place called the Park of Nightingales; how he had stood transfixed at the sight of her loveliness; waited while her servant removed her skates, then followed her carriage all the way to her home. Her Ladyship, they said, had peeped the Sir out of the corner of her bonnet and it was love at first sight with her too.

It would be the same with Miss Sterrin. One day she would come galloping down the high road on her horse and some rich nobleman with a sword at his side and silver spurs jingling against a fine black horse would fall madly in love with her. Miss Sterrin for some reason or other would be dressed like her ancestress in a green cloak embroidered with the seven colours that only those of royal blood used to wear; and it flying from her shoulders and her red curls flying in the wind; the way Athele O'Carroll must have looked when she dashed on her horse through the woods to warn her father, the little red-haired Sir Timothy, that Cromwell was riding for Kilsheelin.

A little sound from the far side of the car interrupted Thomas's daydreams. The girl had started to say something, then stopped. The church spire was in view; the end of her life! The familiar life of home, girlhood, convent, home again, her cosy bedroom above the ceiling of which lay a paradise of bees. Thomas heard the little sobbing sigh.

From another direction three men and a boy were driving towards the church. The driver, James Keating of Poolgower, looked across the well at his second son, John. 'You won't change your mind about Dublin?'

'No.' The small monosyllable was gorged with emotion: anger; resentment; despair.

The eldest son, James's James, turned round to his brother. 'People will think that we are doing things mean.'

'I don't give a tinker's curse what people think.'

They were trying to get the bridegroom to go to Dublin for the Bed of Honour. A cold bed, he thought. He had no heart to go away with a woman he had never set eyes on. He had never dreamed of a match for years to come. He, a younger son with no prospects; but neither had he dreamed of this unexpected legacy of a farm from his uncle. Overnight he had become a man of property. Overnight too, almost, the matchmakers had come to 'draw down' talk of a match with the daughter of the rich and miserly Ulick Prendergast. He was lucky, they told him. A nice-looking girl with everything that a man could wish for! What did they know about a moment of dance? What a man might wish for? The face that had haunted him for months floated back. With it came the golden scene around the Platform Dance; the girl he had faced in the Change Partners; a laughing, breathless moment as he swung her off her feet, then gripped her tight until she had steadied herself, then a shocked voice summoning her back to her parents' phaeton.

The car halted. They were at the church. John stepped down.

A sudden squall of wind and rain blew across the chapel yard. 'We may as well move inside,' said James Keating. Inside! Not even the preface of a meeting in the chapel yard! By God! Was he mad to have consented to this marriage barter? Hadn't he finished with his father's tyranny when he acquired a farm of his own? Scenes from a life that was over flashed across John's mind; that first sight of the field that had fallen to them from the skies; a resplendent officer springing eagerly up the steps of the Protestant church, smiling, because he was going to marry the woman of his choice; and again, recurring, unforgettable—a laughing colleen swinging in his arms to the sound of fiddles; losing her footing so that his hold on her tightened to a caress, a mingling of laughter, a brushing of soft hair against his cheek —'There is no sense.' John started to shout but no one noticed anything because his voice scraped through on a low pitch. 'There is no sense in getting wet out here.'

During the Kyrie he peeped sideways from under his hands. That must be she in the blue bonnet! Her head was bowed and the bonnet brim covered her face completely.

But her right eye had found a peephole through the involutions of the velvet ruching beneath her brim. It strained for a sight of the bald head, the toothlessness that had caused a bride to fly from this very church two weeks ago. In the last panic-stricken stretch of the journey she had resigned herself to some such destiny. The peephole showed her a young man with glossy hair, lots of it, one wide shoulder—and the other one must be just as wide—covered in the finest chocolate-coloured broadcloth with a velvet collar.

Life flowed back into her veins. It gave her strength to lift her head and look full at his face. It couldn't be! It couldn't! The stranger whom she could not forget! ' 'Tis a sin for me to let thought of that face into my mind this morning.' But the rosary beads no longer hung limply from her hands. They danced. All that it needed was music. And the heart inside of

101

her was filled with music!

Through the third and fourth finger of his left hand he had glimpsed a pair of small white hands. Hm! Very white indeed for a farmer's daughter who did the amount of work that was claimed for her at the matchmaking. His eyes slewed up higher.

The blue bonnet turned full face at the eye between his fingers. His heart gave a mighty thud across the width of his chest. I'm dreaming, he cried out in the silence of his mind. This morning of all mornings, I ought not to have let that face into my mind!

But the face wasn't in his mind at all. It was there across the aisle. It was beside him at the altar. The little hand that lay in his for the ring was the one he had clasped on the platform dance at the Crossroads last August.

'You wouldn't read better in a love-story,' said the bridesmaid to the best man at the breakfast table. Old Ulick unscrewed something between a snort and a chuckle. 'Truth,' he said, 'is always stranger and better than fiction.' For it was old Ulick himself who had made the love-story come true. He had recognised the boy who had danced at the Crossroads with his daughter; knew his family's history and had watched its industriousness. The moment the inheritance of the farm had made the lad eligible, Ulick had despatched his emissaries for the 'drawing down'.

James Keating took out his timepiece. 'There will be a Bianconi at the cross in three-quarters of an hour. It catches the mail coach at Thurles—but I keep forgetting; you are not going on the mail coach.'

The bride turned towards him with shining eyes. Joy and relief had distilled a radiance that glowed around her like a halo.

'Of course, we are going on the mail coach,' she said.

'Of course, we are going on the mail coach,' chorused her husband.

Thomas tried to make his farewell to Mrs. Prendergast. He had been in a state of dread since he discovered the identity of the bridegroom. What would become of him if the Sir were to learn that he had served at a Wedding Mass for a son of James Keating; the land-grabber of Poolgower, brother of the man who had led the Whiteboy raid on the castle and barely missed shooting her Ladyship!

Mrs. Prendergast was pressing food on Thomas, recognising the boy, and James Keating sensed the cause of his reluctance to accept. 'Perhaps,' he remarked coldly, 'the lad would feel more at home in the kitchen.'

Thomas felt his cheeks stinging. This was the first time his servitude had been cast at him as a stigma.

'Thank you, sir,' he said quietly. 'I'll just break my fast with the three sips of water and then I'll be on my way.'

The girls were sorry to see him leave the parlour. They had thought him some nice-spoken college boy. A youth called Tim Lonergan, the son of a well-to-do farmer, had seen the hurt flush on Thomas's face. He slipped out after him. 'There is more 'divarshun here in the kitchen,' he remarked. Young Donal Keating, a boy of about ten or eleven had seen the slight but when he tried to follow Thomas, his father drew him back. 'Stay where you belong!' he ordered. 'Let us hope that you will serve the next Wedding Mass in the family.'

There was always more fun in the kitchen; away from the priest and the parents and the uncles and aunts, and these uppish merchants, like the ones inside, who bought the Prendergast farm produce; and the schoolmaster who was using long words that people only pretended to understand and quoting, 'Let me not to the marriage of true minds admit impediment', whatever that meant.

There were no poetic subtleties in the kitchen where two long tables, end to end, had two people squashed together on every chair. Half a dozen girls were pelting backwards and forwards from the fire to the table and 'Let go of me arm or I'll let this spill on you, gravy and all,' was the prelude to every helping of roast meat that they tried to place in front of the boys. It wasn't bad enough having their faces roasted off them bending over the blazing turf and from the steam from kettles and bastables hanging from every hook on the crane, but every time one of them passed the tables with a plate of roast meat, a hand reached out to catch her or an arm shot around her waist or some other piece of dluderin' by play. Never had gaiety entered the scene of a wedding so early in the day. It had burst out from the morn's unexpected romance like the sudden flowering of a Nordic summer.

Nora Campion, one of John Keating's cousins, put another leg of chicken on the plate of a man who had danced in the very

Cashel Sets where the bridal pair had met. 'Lay that across your lips,' she said, 'and tell us all about it.'

He drew her swiftly to his knee and was just telling her that he would prefer to put his lips to better use when her mother came down from the parlour with an empty teapot for replenishing. 'Nora!' roared Mrs. Campion.

'Well, I must say that's a nice way to behave and the priest in the parlour!' But she wasn't as cross as she pretended. She lifted up her padded silk skirt and pinned it round her waist showing a black silk petticoat that was as grand again. 'Move up there, lads,' she said to the boys who were having snacks at the fire until there would be space at the tables. 'Make a space for me here and tell me the story of the bride and groom.'

They were all so full of gallantry and tea and currant cake and port wine that they jumped to her request and left the form without balance so that her huge weight landed on the floor. Young Thomas joined the dozen young men who dashed to haul her up. 'I'm tellin' you,' she gasped as she restored herself and her seven petticoats, 'that if it had been myself John Keating had to swing in the Cashel Sets he wouldn't forget me either. Go on, anyway, and tell us all about it, for it has all the love and none of the poverty and heartache of a young couple that runs away and gets cut off, like the little lady that ran off with Sir Roderick O'Carroll's foster-brother, Black Pat Ryan. *She's* cut off with a vengeance; cut off from her family and cut off from them she's married into because she's too genteel to mix with them. Go on with your story!'

The story was still in the telling when Thomas slipped unnoticed from the kitchen. 'Twould be powerful to linger for the dancing! The squeak of bagpipes and the preparatory scrape of fiddles were all that troubled to follow him out to the road to entice him back. But it was powerful, too, to be alone to ponder on what he had heard the bridegroom whisper to the bride as he lifted her on to the car after the ceremony.

'We must have been meant for each other from the beginning,' John Keating had murmured, 'from before we met at the Crossroads dance; before ever we were born.'

Could such a thing be? Could two people be destined that way for each other? True, the Keatings since the windfall of the field had become steadily prosperous; but John had been reared poor and hard. He could never have raised his eyes to a well-to-do, well-educated girl like Miss Prendergast. Yet it had happened; before Thomas's eyes. Just as it had happened before Thomas's eyes, the miracle of the field flying from the castle through the skies to the Keatings. And here was Thomas assisting at the Wedding Mass of one of those on whom the field had descended! A link in the strange trend of events that had started on the night of the Big Wind!

He vaulted a high ditch. Why should the Keating wedding cause his heart to surge with a gladness that held a sense of hope?

In the castle kitchen he was plied with questions about the wedding. When he mentioned the bridegroom's name, Mr. Hegarty lowered the tongs and dropped the red ember it held, without lighting his pipe. Slowly he turned in the chair, revolving himself by his grip on the arms. He gazed long at Thomas and his words, when they came, were grim with outrage.

'Do you mean to stand there and coolly admit that you went forth from *this* house; *this* house, I say, and in the time that belongs to the service of Sir Roderick O'Carroll, you accommodated James Keating of Poolgower by assisting at the marriage of his son?'

Thomas's heart quailed but immediately steadied. It was unjust to accuse him of disloyalty to the Sir. He, who alone of all of them, had been witness to the terrible thing that had happened on that night. None but he had heard the cry of anguish that had burst from their restrained and haughty master when he saw his land torn from his ground and borne from him across the sky to James Keating of Poolgower?

Very quietly came his answer and Mrs. Stacey thought to herself that the Sir would not speak more proudly.

'You all know,' he said, 'that the priest's servant boy left word here on Sunday that I was to meet Ulick Prendergast at the back lodge at half-past five this morning to go serve a Mass at his daughter's marriage. I was fully vested in soutane and surplice in the sacristy when I heard the name of the man she was to marry. Would you have me profane the Mass by refusing to serve? The Sir himself would not carry enmity that far.'

The Sir himself would not look more haughty, thought the butler. There's blood in that lad! But he merely said that there would be law and order in this kitchen from this day forth.

CHAPTER 13

It was the gayest Season that Dublin had seen for forty years. The Tolka was frozen for weeks. There were skating parties every day and Lady O'Carroll was the acknowledged belle of the rink. Spectators stood to watch her as she cut intricate figures or waltzed to the music of mandolins.

Roderick could scarcely take his eyes from her as she skimmed over the ice; lovelier, livelier even, than on that day in Antwerp when she had captured his heart. Incredible to associate this glowing girl with the melancholy being, all fears and clutchings; crying out, wild-eyed at the repairing of the castle wall lest it close her in.

Braziers burned along the banks and hot chestnut vendors did a roaring trade. Vendors of all kinds were doing a roaring trade everywhere. Never had such money poured into the tills of Dublin shops. Never since the parliament house in College Green had closed its Ionis porticos on the last member, and the life force of a splendid nation had drained its way across the seas to another land. But now by the dedicated life force of one man those porticos would open soon again, those rusted mill wheels on the Tolka would turn again. Already the feeble pulse of a nation was strengthening. The word Repeal was breathed on the frosted breaths of the skaters. The messenger boys and waggoners sang the word through the streets in their glee songs. Margaret and Roderick heard the Repeal cry echoing down the Dublin hills to the accompaniment of sleigh bells. They heard it at *soirée*s in Merrion Square; at military balls; at hunt breakfasts.

This Repeal business, Sterrin thought, seemed to be benefiting everyone but herself. It was merely keeping *her* cooped up in a house that had neither park nor stable and where the only person remotely near her own age was her own mamma! How did they manage to have their knives cleaned? No knife boy and as for a turf boy! Black coal was emptied through a grating on the

106

front steps into a cellar beside the kitchen. Not that it would have mattered about there being no turf boy, if they had a knife boy, and if the knife boy was young Thomas. 'Papa,' she asked suddenly. 'If Big John were to wash the smell of the horses off himself would he become a gentleman?'

'Egad!' said her startled papa. 'I don't think that Big John needs any deodorising to make him a gentleman.'

'What does that mean?'

'It means that Big John, in his own way, is a gentleman already.'

'By the powers of war!'

Her papa told her sternly that little ladies did not say 'By the powers of war' and Sterrin argued that in that case Big John could not be a gentleman, since he always expressed surprise with that exclamation. Sir Roderick sighed. 'Sterrin,' he asked gently this time, 'has anyone ever told you that little girls should be seen and not heard?'

'Yes, Papa,' she informed him. 'Someone tells me that every day.'

It was Sterrin's turn to sigh. She had heard Maryjoe tell the Professed Cook that the fishmonger had made so much money supplying stinking fish to the military barracks and to all the extra festivities in connection with Repeal, that he had bought a big house in Ballsbridge, and as soon as he had the smell of the fish washed off him he would become a gentleman. It wasn't so much about Big John that Sterrin had wanted to know, it was about young Thomas. But, one couldn't mention *him* that way to Papa. If young Thomas, she pondered, were to wash the smell of the knives from him would he become a gentleman? But then young Thomas did not smell of knives. And he needed no washing. His hands were never dirty and his hair was always brushed back into shiny curls and he spoke nicely. He had learned how to read and read an awful lot of books like Trinity gentlemen. Yet *he* wasn't a gentleman! She sighed again and decided to leave the problem until she would be grown up.

Her father noted the sigh and took sudden stock of his daughter's small figure, so remotely still. Was it stillness or was it intimidation from constant repression? For her age she possessed unusual powers of observation. Had she been a boy one might have enjoyed developing such powers. But a girl, and a pretty one, had no need for any developing of the intellect. It

107

might, heaven forbid, make her a blue-stocking!

He turned towards the door and the sight of his wife's charming figure dressed for an afternoon's promenade. 'What say you, my dear,' he called out, 'that we bring this little person with us. Her cheeks seem too peaked and her brain too active.'

When her mamma consented, Sterrin, in an excess of gratitude promised to be seen and not heard. And, as her papa escorted his ladies down the steps, one on either arm, she added for good measure. 'And I promise also, not to be young more than once.'

'A most praiseworthy undertaking,' her father assured her. 'Attempts at repeating youth are rarely successful and always unattractive.'

'Then do you think,' Mamma asked him, 'that I ought to change this bonnet? I am perhaps a *leetle* too old for its frivolity?'

Sterrin suddenly experienced that shut-out feeling that came so often when she was with her parents. Papa was looking completely away from her towards his wife's slim figure and at her girlish face beneath the new bonnet of golden chip. But it was a relief to hear him assure Mamma that *she* would never grow old.

The shut-out feeling soon passed for there was a lilt in the air of Dublin these days. Other ladies promenading along the Sackville Street Mall had, like Margaret, laid aside their hoods and velvet bonnets for chip ones decked with flowers. There were flowers already in the window boxes of those mansions that were still maintained as dower houses by the great ladies of the past.

More spectators than usual, Roderick thought, were watching the arrival of the mail coaches. The attraction was the Shrovetide brides in their unmistakable blue bonnets arriving from their country weddings for the Bed of Honour.

'It is almost like watching a play,' said Margaret. Roderick agreed. All the laughter and quips as one blue-bonneted figure after another was swung to the ground by her brand-new husband, lent a kind of ballet effect.

He squired his ladies around about and they sauntered back in the wake of those honeymooners who were making for Mr. Gresham's inn where the Bed of Honour would contain the irreducible minimum of fleas. At the door of the inn one bridegroom was pleading with the innkeeper. But Mr. Gresham kept shaking his head. Between the Castle season and the Repeal movement it was becoming necessary to make reservations in advance. 'These days,' they heard him say, 'honeymoons should not be left to chance, unless,' he smiled, 'yours happens to be a runaway one.' The bride was blushing furiously while the groom protested. Then as Mr. Gresham turned to indicate another inn, the groom's face showed full and Roderick stopped dead. 'I'll wager five crowns that fellow is a Keating of Poolgower!' he exclaimed. 'And, ye gods! The bride is old Prendergast's daughter. The Keating land grabber must be prospering; a honeymoon at Gresham's no less!'

Margaret looked from the pretty, radiant face of the bride to Roderick's; black with anger. 'Roderick,' she pleaded, 'the girl is lovely, and quite genteel. I believe that she was at school with the De Lacey girls. Don't grudge them their happiness. Neither of these had anything to do with your land.'

He strode on and for a second both Sterrin and her mamma lost their hold of his arm. 'Forgive me,' he said as he slowed for them. 'But a man's land is sacred; every acre of it. As sacred almost as——' He was nearly going to say as sacred as a man's wife but he was halted again in mid-sentence. The weirdest-looking equipage came galloping towards them.

It had all the appurtenances of a funeral coach; plumed horses, crepe-swathed driver. But when the mad rocking of the coach parted the drawn curtains, Margaret and Roderick recognised to their great delight the gloomy figure of Tom Steele, the Head Pacificator of Ireland.

He sat with arms folded on chest; uniform covered in a long black cloak, peaked cap bending with crepe. The Repeal movement was in deep and angry mourning.

When they reached home they found Lady Cullen's grand-nephew, Patrick, and a group of fellow students of Trinity in the drawing-room. Then the explanation for Thomas Steele's funeral dash came out. The Whiteboys were active again. They had fired into the de Guider's house a few nights before wounding Stephen de Guider and mutilating scores of his cattle. 'Tom Steele's animated corpse went down in the Repeal Hearse this afternoon.'

The news revived in Margaret all the sinister associations that made her dread to return to Kilsheelin. That night there was a beating in her brain that mounted into deafening crashes. The cousins brewed the leaves of the small ivy. It was soothing, they assured Roderick, when the mind was disturbed. They didn't say that it was listed in their herb book as 'a cure for the madness'. But the sleep vouchsafed to Margaret by the ivy brew was vivid with the images of white-clad men with blackened faces, and with the red-dripping horror of mutilated animals. And the sounds of screaming winds and screaming cattle that awakened her were still tearing from her own throat when sleep had gone.

Sterrin, awakened by the cries, crouched outside her parents' bedroom. Once its door opened and she saw her mother's face; wild-looking and unfamiliar. Papa was trying to hold her in his arms and where Mamma's hands gripped his shoulders, the cloth of his robe was torn.

CHAPTER 14

He had the whole white world to himself. The farmsteads with their roofs of golden thatch were glamorised into fairy palaces of white and gold. As he swung down the road his mood burst into song. The one that Mr. Davis had written under the inspiration of the three hundred Greeks who had died at Thermopelae and the three Romans who had held the Sublician Bridge. . . .

> *'When boyhood's fire was in my blood,*
> *I read of ancient freemen,*
> *For Greece and Rome who bravely stood*
> *Three hundred men, and three men.'*

A carriage came round the bend towards him. Heads craned from the windows at the sound of the magnificent voice echoing through the white stillness. Fiona De Lacey, going to her first Moonlight Ball, called excitedly over her shoulder to her sister Eithne. 'Quick! Who is that divine young gentleman?'

Eithne squeezed into the window space. 'I declare I've never seen him before. Perhaps he is some visitor to Kilsheelin. My goodness, isn't he handsome! And what a voice!'

'Let's have a look.' Their brother gave them a privileged push. 'Humph, he's a mere youngster! Probably he's that chap from Eton who is staying with Lord Strague's son. Thinks he owns the bally ground he walks on!'

The three offspring of a squireen sent their varying looks of envy, longing and admiration after the knife boy from the kitchen of Kilsheelin Castle until he was out of sight.

'I'd vow,' declared Fiona, 'that he is going to keep a love tryst.' She groped in her muff for the flannel-wrapped hot brick and gave herself up to romantic longings.

Young Thomas, following his own voice and awakening the echoes would have welcomed any other tryst than this one to

111

scout and scavenge for news about the unromantic preludes to Kitty Dowling's proposed marriage. Particularly this perfect night! They weren't that badly off for news in the kitchen, he thought. If Kitty Dowling was going to marry a rich old man, that was her affair. He didn't want any part of it. Yet he could not deny Mrs. Stacey her gossip and, therefore, found himself on his way to the Dowlings to deliver some dripping. 'Be sure to tell them it's our extra,' Mrs. Stacey had warned him.

Dowling's dog ran out barking as young Thomas opened the gate.

'God save all here,' said Thomas as he stepped in the house. The girl stooping over a pot on the hearth looked up, startled. She pushed back the jet-black curl that had fallen over her nose and answered.

'God save you kindly.'

Her mother, mixing a soda cake at the table took her thumb out of the heap of soda she was about to crush in her left palm. She let her 'God save you' slip abstractedly through her open curiosity.

He stated his errand with such deprecatory civility that the two women were delighted to relieve Mrs. Stacey of the problem of her superfluous dripping. 'Musha,' said Mrs. Dowling with great relief. 'Sit down there at the fire and take the weight off your legs. Didn't I think for a minnit that you were a gentleman.'

'You had me fooled, too,' said Kitty. 'Was it you we heard singing "A Nation Once Again"?'

'I'm afraid I did not realise that I was making so much noise.'

'Noise is it?' said Mrs. Dowling. ' 'Twas the grandest singing. Sure we thought it might be some of the quality going to the Moonlight Ball in the town. Though I was fearful too that it might be one of the Whiteboys. 'Tis the sort of night they would be up to their andramartins only there isn't one of them could sing like that.'

Two men, father and son obviously, came from an adjoining room. They didn't see young Thomas sitting in the gloom of the chimney nook. 'Kitty,' cried her father, 'haven't you got your good gown on yet. And look at your hair. It is to shame us you would?'

'Whisht John,' cautioned his wife, 'we've company.' Her husband craned and recognised young Thomas. He had seen him

112

often in the farmyard in the castle.

'God save you, you're welcome here,' he said, but he was abstracted. There was too much at stake tonight. Men were coming to draw down a match between his daughter and the richest man in the barony and here she was dressed as if she were going out to feed pigs.

'Go wash your face and put on your Sunday gown,' he said to her in a low, tense voice. Kitty kicked off her low shoes and put her feet into a big, dirty pair of boots belonging to her father that were drying by the hearth.

'What are you doin'?' he asked. 'They'll be here in a minute.'

'I've to go out to the byre to set these eggs under the cluckin' hen.'

'That'll hold till tomorrow.'

'No,' said Kitty, moving to the door. 'She'll have gone off the cluck.'

She tied a canvas apron round her waist and ignored their protests. As she took up a lantern and left the room, she said, 'I'm dressed well enough for another woman's leavings.'

The brown hen pushed every egg under her puffy chest with as much cackling and scolding as though she had laid them herself. She had barely poked the thirteenth under the fertile heat of her feathers and given an ungrateful peck at Kitty's hand when a low whistle sounded from the orchard.

She blew out the lantern as she came into the moonlight from the dark byre, and hurried under the apple trees. The moon was making a kind of fireworks display out of the little waterfall and sending up shafts and sparks of silver flame. But it etched too clearly the tall figure of Mark Hennessey, who had been courting her for two years.

'Mark,' she whispered, 'you could be seen a mile off.'

He stepped backwards over the little stream and drew her after him into the field below, and under the shade of a great beech tree. 'Have they bid for you yet?' he asked her as he drew her into his arms.

Her head was down on his shoulder and she left it there as she answered down between the frieze and the fresh skin of that grand body that would never hold her close again.

'I don't know. I've not been within. I made an excuse to set eggs under a clucker. Something told me you'd come. Oh, Mark!' The words came tenser and forced her breath in quivers

113

against the back of his neck.

'To think this is the last time we'll be together. 'Twould have been as well if I'd stayed inside but I had to torture myself with the look of you and the feel of you. I had to kiss you goodbye.'

He turned his head sideways and pressed kisses into her black ringlets. 'You said last Sunday week that you'd run away with me.'

She drew away and as she stood before him he thought her ringlets looked like shining ebony in the moonlight and the severe beauty of her features was etched like a marble statue.

'That was before the cow died, and before the proctor thought the place looked so tasty that we ought to be payin' more tithes to the parson and the agent thought we ought to be payin' more rent to the landlord. It broke my heart to uproot the grand shrubs I got from Miss Cullen. Every time she passed on her horse, she'd turn down the boreen to see how they were doin' and she vowed that they throve better in the shelter of our yard than in the glass house at Crannagh Abbey. 'Twas the same with the slippings I got from Miss De Lacey. I had to pull them up and we had to muck up the whitewash and paint, and leave the gate hanging on one hinge and be the dirty Irish we are expected to be.'

'Sh, you'll be heard.' Her voice had risen and her breast was heaving. 'I know,' he soothed. 'Whisht, wasn't I forgetting what I came for.' He took a purse from his pocket and took out three bank-notes. 'Look!'

She took the notes in her hand and read clearly in the white light the three inscriptions of twenty pounds. Her eyes were wide with question.

'Mark is it, is it the Big Wind again?' He nodded. 'Where did you find them?'

'In the field at the bottom of Graffin's Hill. I was slashing briars on the headlands and I saw something white, two pieces of white. They were stuck within the heart of the hedge. I thought immediately of the two ten-pound notes Jack Ryan found last year and he toppin' thistles.'

'But, Mark, are you right to keep it? Could anyone claim it? Don't you remember the trouble there was about the gold that was found?'

'That was different. That was Mr. de Guider's gold beyond a doubt and it was found on his own grounds. Now this money

114

was in a spot in the hedge that's in direct line with my Uncle Larry's house and, look here!' He pulled out the purse again and held up something between his finger and thumb. 'They are biteens of feathers that were stuck inside two of the notes that were rolled up together——'

'Your Uncle Larry's mattress that was blown down the hill?'

He nodded again. 'There's no knowin' what money he had sewn up in the feathers. He always made it an excuse that he meant to leave me plenty only for what blew away that night. Still, it didn't keep him from leavin' what was left to his wife's nephew.'

'An' all the work you used to do! Well, 'tis an ill wind that blows no one good. I'm glad from my heart for you, Mark asthore, but,' her voice broke, 'I suppose it is America for you now.'

He drew her back into his arms and held her face upturned so that the moon glorified the beauty of every feature that he inventoried. The blue eyes, the straight Grecian nose, the perfect teeth that gleamed through half parted lips. He thought with sickness of this flower being thrown away on Owen Heffernan's dunghill! Suddenly he crushed her to him and kissed her as he had never kissed her since the first time their lips had gently met in the orchard.

She pushed him from her, panting and frightened of the strange unfamiliar stirrings within herself. 'Mark.' He had never been like this before in all the tender courting of the last two years.

He was panting hard but he held her from him now and gripped her hands till they hurt. 'Kitty, I can make a bid for you tonight. Sixty pounds and the few I've saved isn't much against fifty-four acres of land that's as good as the Golden Vale, and I believe he has a stocking of gold forbye. But, Kitty, my life's love,' he drew her again into his arms. 'I've love enough to cover every one of his acres. It's piled as rich in my heart as all his hoard of gold.'

She pulled herself from him and looked back at the pretty house with braided thatch and latticed windows that stood in its generous yard under the shade of the silvery orchard. There was taste and industry there.

'The talk of this marriage has lifted the dread from their hearts. Two years ago 'twas the sow. Last year our fine horse

115

and then a cow. And when the cow died last week and they dropped its carcass into the quarry, the schoolchildren said, "There's another beast in Dowling's graveyard." I could see that eviction was staring my mother and father in the eyes. One bad season now, and what would pay the rent and tithes? My father was born here and my mother came here to live when her own father was evicted. I'd rather see them shot the way her father was shot that day than see them walk down the boreen for the last time and turn their heads for the work house.' She put her face into her hands.

He drew down her hands. ' 'Twill be the same to me as if you were shot, the day you drive down the boreen on Owen Heffernan's phaeton on your weddin' drive.'

'Stop!' She clung to him. 'Oh, Mark, what can we do?'

'Kitty, 'tis the way I was thinkin', the other one of the ould Clarke couple is dead and the cottage is vacant. It's not much more than a cabin——'

'But we'd be together. We'd know our youth together.'

'And we have strength enough to rise up out of poverty——'

Someone called. They turned to see Niall coming down the orchard path. 'Kitty,' he called, 'there's money bid for you.' She turned to step over the stream but Mark held her. 'Give me an answer one way or the other. If you go this way we'll never meet again.'

Niall reached out his hand and pulled her over the stream. 'Come on, girl,' he said, 'there is a gentleman widin, with a face that would stop a funeral and he's gettin' impatient.' He turned to Mark. 'God save you, Mark. 'Twould be a nice night for the coortin' if there was no matchmakin'. Romance isn't for the likes of us.'

She turned back to Mark. 'There's a boy inside coordheecing. A respectable boy in service at the castle. Thomas his name is.'

'Young Thomas, I know him.'

'I'll give him a message for you and he'll tell you what happens tonight. Wait for him at the low part of the castle wall on the Sir's road.'

> *'When I was poor,'* sang young Thomas,
> *'Your father's door*
> *Was closed against your constant lover;*

> *With care and pain*
> *I tried in vain*
> *My fortune to recover.'*

'Musha, there was flour in the potatoes tonight,' said Mark Hennessey, stepping out from the shadow of the tree that grew high over the castle wall. ' 'Tis well for you that has the heart to sing so gay.'

'There was indeed flour in the potatoes tonight,' said Thomas. 'I never tasted finer. And the butter was made by the finest butter-maker in all the country——'

Mark interrupted angrily. 'You are playin' tricks with me. Did she give you e'er a message for me?'

'She did. But first she gave a message to Mr. Heffernan. She gave it to him personally.' Young Thomas chuckled.

'Go on. It's easy for you to laugh. What did she say to him?'

'When he had complimented her on her butter, he very generously urged us all to put plenty of it on our potatoes as the butter-maker would soon be removing to his less hospitable roof.'

'An' did he admit that much against himself?'

'Not in so much words. But he left us in no doubt that when that butter was being made by *his* wife, it would not be put down so lavishly with the potatoes for "coordheecers".'

'His wife?' The words jerked out hoarsely as Mark turned away. 'Ye need say no more. Good night to ye.'

Young Thomas kept up with him. 'If it's all the same to you, Mark, I'd as lief give the message I was given. 'Twould only be civil.'

Mark halted. 'Say it quick and be finished with it.'

'She bade me tell you hurry and get Clarke's cottage before anyone else grabs it and she made me promise to serve the Mass at your wedding.'

Mark swung round and grasped young Thomas's arm in a vice. 'Is she goin' to run off with me you mean?'

'She'll tell you that tomorrow night. You are to be down the orchard at the same time and you are to be sure and have word about the cottage.'

'I'll be there, and I'll have the few lines of writing for the cottage. May God increase you, young Thomas, whoever you are——' Thomas stiffened.

117

'Don't take offence, avic,' cried Mark, ''tis long sorry I'd be to belittle you. But look there.' He swung his hand in the direction of the Devil's Bit. 'My great-grand-uncle was said to be the handsomest officer in the French army. His people owned all that land as far as your eye can see but the gentility is gone thin in us with hardship and poverty and no learnin'. What I mean is that you have it in you as strong as 'twas bred. You're not like the others up there. I'll always be your friend if you want one and 'tis proud I am that you'll serve me Weddin' Mass. God be with you.'

Young Thomas still jangled a little under the reference to his unknown origin, until he had vaulted the wall. The familiar park scene had its unfailing effect upon him of soothing graciousness. He brushed the brambles from his knees and resumed his song:

> 'Far, far away,
> By night and day
> I toiled to win a golden treasure,
> And golden gains,
> Repaid my pains
> In fair and shining measure.'

When the song reached the back courtyard, Mr. Hegarty stopped translating the newspaper into Gaelic for his underlings and laid down the *Freeman's Journal*. 'I'll repay that lad's pains, and in a spot where he'll repair his breeches.' He looked sternly over his steel glasses. 'A nice hour, a nice hour,' he repeated, 'for a boy of your age to be nightwalking.'

And who sent me nightwalking? thought the culprit. 'I couldn't help it, sir,' he said. 'They made me wait for the potatoes.'

'Musha, what else would they do,' cried Mrs. Stacey. 'An' was it praties they had? But sure of course, what else would they have an' it only a "drawin' down". Sit in and tell us all.'

He told them all and an hour later when the first sleepy crow sounded from the hen shed, Ellen, the parlour maid, as she rose nearly brought her hands together in applause. 'Do you know,' she said, 'you had me forgettin' where I was. I was between two minds whether it was to genuflect, I should, like comin' out of the Church, or to clap like the end of a play.'

'But what I can't understand,' said Mrs. Stacey, 'is, how did

Kitty come to have her Sunday gown on her and the red shoes from France and her hair brushed down around her, seeing that she left the kitchen in her sack "praskeen" and her father's brogues; and she to say before she went to set the hen that she was dressed well enough for another woman's leavings?'

Young Thomas sighed. This was the third time he had described that scene. Though indeed it has stirred himself so much that he had been lost in the telling. There had been something so unusual in the way Kitty had let the long ringlets fall, brushed, but ungathered down her back, that although his own curls swept back down only to the top of his collar, the eyes of his audience seemed to see through him the long, black ringlets flowing over the blue gown as Kitty emerged from her room and confronted Owen Heffernan with her scorn of his 'evicted land.' She had heard all from Niall. 'The first time I call to your husband's house, Kitty,' Niall had said, 'I'll be wearing a white shirt on the outside of me clothes and black on my face, and I won't go alone.'

It was unfortunate for Owen that Kitty Dowling herself of all people, had been witness to the eviction of Widow Fogarty, one of his tenants. She stood before him and spoiled the good of the fine potatoes and butter and sweet milk, as she told him how the bailiff's man had kneaded the woman's knuckles with his own until she released her frantic grip of the latch she would never raise again. How she had watched the widow kissing the grass that grew inside the yard gate, as they pushed her through with her children clinging to her skirts. It was an accepted caress. 'But do you think,' said Kitty, 'that I'd walk in on that grass that she was pushed from to fall flat on the road with weakness and heartbreak. How dare you come to this house for me...? I'd rather go to my grave!'

His kitchen audience could see the two matchmakers wilting in their chairs. And then young Thomas described how the old suitor turned back from the door as he was about to leave and shouted 'An' me to be near buyin' a new suit for this! 'Twas God done it that I hadn't the money from me, and the suit on me back tonight....'

'Suit, inagh!' Kitty had cried. ' 'Tisn't a suit but a shroud you'll be needin' when the cross[1] is painted on your door....'

[1] Crosses were painted on the doors of farmers who bought the land of their evicted neighbours.

He wondered privately would Kitty have been so accusingly dramatic if there were no handsome lover waiting in the orchard. He yawned. What was Mrs. Stacey saying? Surely she didn't want him to go over all that again.

'An' I suppose,' said Ellen, 'that Kitty showed off the hair and the gown and shoes to grig him, let him see what he was missin'.'

'No,' said young Thomas, rising sleepily, 'I think the idea was prompted by her strong sense of drama.' And off he went to bed where he dreamed all night long of joyous weddings in Dublin.

CHAPTER 15

Lady O'Carroll gripped the bedpost while Nurse Hogan pulled on her corset laces. The gown for the big event of the Dublin season drooped on its dummy. 'Try again, Nurse Hogan!' But it was no use. Every time the Nurse tugged, her Ladyship heaved. 'I'll die if I have to miss the Melon Show at Lord Cloncurry's,' Margaret moaned.

'My dear, you look awful,' said Mrs. Kennedy-Sherwin, calling on her way to the Show. 'I must rush, there will be such a squeeze that my gown will be hidden out of sight if I am not there early. It is the first in Dublin—my gown *à la Marie Antoinette* that permits the petticoat to be glimpsed. I brought it back from Paris. The first there too, except the Comtesse de Clery's—but no one saw hers. His Majesty—you know who, State visit, no names, no pack drill—slipped her out on the balcony but the Queen slipped after them and locked the window. They were out on the balcony all night, dare not tap. Now she won't be coming to Ireland for the Repeal rally; caught a chill, Comte de Clery is coming alone. I'll tell you all this evening. My dear, you do look awful. Better stay at home if what I suspect ails you.'

'Could she be right?' Margaret asked the Nurse later. 'All that nausea? And my wedding ring finger is paining exactly as it used to before Sterrin.'

'You know what Dr. Mitchell said, your Ladyship. It is out of the question. No, it is only all the flies on the meat this hot weather.'

It was a woebegone and bedraggled Mrs. Kennedy-Sherwin who called on the way back from the Melon Show.

'What on earth happened?' gasped Margaret. 'Surely the rain didn't do *that*?' She pointed to the crushed and sodden bonnet that the little lady held fastidiously away from herself by the top of a streamer.

'My *bonnet-babet-blonde* is ...' she started to wail, but was

121

silenced by the usually complacent Jeremy.

'Stop wailing about your wretched bonnet!' he snapped. 'You are lucky to be alive.'

His wife beckoned Margaret behind a screen and explained the mystery. As their carriage had driven along the sea road a maid had come to an upper window to empty a chamber-pot into the sea. It slipped from her grip and came hurtling down over the carriages.

'The horses reared up, then bolted! A most aristocratic-looking house, Lady O'Carroll; *and* all the contents!'

'Of the house?'

'Don't be absurd, Lady O'Carroll! Of the—the THING! And to think,' she wept, 'that the Lord Lieutenant never saw it.'

'The—the THING?' choked Margaret.

'Lady O'Carroll! How *could* you? As if His Excellency would look at—— No, I mean my *bonnet-babet-blonde*. I had hoped it would be the first to be seen in Ireland. They were only starting to be the rage in Paris when we were leaving there. And as for my Marie Antoinette——' She broke down completely. The fate of the gown *à la Marie Antoinette* was too much for her. It was intended to electrify the guests at the Melon Show, the great outdoor event that highlighted the Dublin season. According to its great Parisian designer, the gown was a daring innovation that 'permitted the ankles to be glimpsed'.

And here, hadn't the rain driven the guests indoors? And Mrs. Kennedy-Sherwin found herself jostled into a nook in an upper corridor where the gown itself was not glimpsed, much less the provocative ankles it had dared to reveal.

'Just think,' she sobbed, 'of my having to arrive *bareheaded* in the full afternoon! I shall never lift my head again!'

'You were brave,' soothed Margaret, 'to face it at all with your head uncovered.'

'*And* her ankles uncovered!' said Lady Cullen, appearing round the screen. 'There is, after all, a Providence that designs our ends; both ends!'

That evening in the drawing-room Captain Kennedy-Sherwin was telling Roderick about the stampede at the Melon Show when word came just as the refreshments were being handed round, that the Host, Lord Cloncurry and several other gentlemen including the Liberator and his son, had been deprived of their office as Magistrate.

'By gad, that is a portentous move. It is the first step that the government has taken against the Repeal Movement——'

'It has ruined my Marie Antoinette gown from Paris,' said Mrs. Kennedy-Sherwin emerging from the screen. Sir Roderick swept her a bow. 'And what,' he asked her, 'is the latest from Paris, apart from that exquisite gown?'

'In Paris,' the Captain interposed, 'the talk, as in Dublin, is all Repeal. The leader of the French radicals, Ledru Rollins has announced his intention of coming to Dublin to present in person the big sum of money that his party has collected for the cause.'

'Repeal indeed!' shrilled Mrs. Kennedy-Sherwin. 'Everyone of the "*haut ton*" is more concerned with the scandal of the Comtesse de Clery locked out on a balcony with His Majesty with nothing but her satin gown *à la Marie Antoinette*—the *dernier cri* in fashion, that permits the petticoat to be glimpsed underneath.'

'Hmph!' said Lady Cullen, who was in Dublin trousseau shopping for her niece Patricia. 'It is just as well that she is not coming here. Dublin balconies can be very chilly during a Repeal reception; and so can Dublin hostesses, should they catch their menfolk "glimpsing" the petticoats of their lady guests.'

'Repeal receptions,' cried La Petite. 'One might as well be gowned "a la red petticoat" for all those repealers note of a lady's gown. It is amazing the way politics divert gentlemen from their normal interests.'

Some of the French party had arrived already. Americans who had attended the week-long meeting in New York addressed by the President and had heard his threat to seize Canada with American arms if force was used against the repeal movement, were thronging into Dublin. So were English statesmen. Extra boats brought English holiday-makers. There was to be a great rally at Tara.

'Roderick, could I not travel to Tara with you,' pleaded Margaret, 'while the road is still clear?' Roderick was going in his official capacity as Warden in the Liberator's cortège. It would be a gruelling journey. and Margaret's pale and peaky looks made him fear another of her wild spasms.

'My darling, there is no such thing as a clear road within twenty-five miles of Tara. People have been bivouacking in the

123

fields for days past. Look at these.' They were driving through Sackville Street where formations of dust-grimed figures streamed endlessly by as though they had marched through many nights to the Assumption Day meeting. An event, he thought, to speak of to one's sons. 'Though I vow,' he said aloud, 'that I should like Sterrin to witness it. It will be an epic of history. Perhaps we could go the canal route. I'll try to find a way.'

He found the Grand Canal harbour and a long stretch of the canal packed with gaily decorated flyboats from the Barrow and Suir and even the Shannon. They had cruised up through Munster and Leinster and dropped their passengers at points of vantage, then continued on to Dublin to ply for more. But every seat and space was sold out.

As Big John watched the Sir moving from boat to boat through disappointed crowds he spied a limping figure that he recognised. He was the skipper of a canal boat and was the same Carney that had lost his shebeen the night of the Big Wind. He tossed the reins to Joseph and talked with his old acquaintance. He pointed to Sterrin and reminisced of his experience on the night of her birth.

'And you tell me she was born in that storm?'

The skipper saluted Roderick. 'Your coachman has told me of your Honour's difficulty.' He dropped his voice. 'There's talk of running a new barge on Assumption Eve. There are no bookings for there's nothing fixed—but your Honour's name will be the first down. A fine Milesian name for such a journey.' He saluted Sterrin. 'We'll weather the storm again, Little Lady.'

But there was no storm. It was a golden day when the sound of the harbour clock, striking two, drew a long, musical blast over the waters and streets from the postilion's bugle. He squared his shoulders in the new blue livery, drew his whip downwards across the towing horse and out into the waters slipped the *Colleen Bawn* at a good four miles an hour. Cheering crowds on either bank wished her Godspeed on her maiden voyage, and incoming boats sounded courtesy blasts. Rowing boats gave the only impression of movement and the sun glittering on the harp of the Repeal flag gave the suggestion of a flutter on the *Colleen Bawn*'s pennants.

'We are going to take a speed test between the twelfth and thirteenth lock,' announced Sterrin, returning from her proud position beside the skipper.

Margaret had dozed from the somnolent heat and the gentle movement and the incessant muffled thud of the Repeal marchers on the grassy banks. Sometimes the formation would break and banners were unshouldered while the thirsty and exhausted sat round three-legged pots over picnic fires. The smell of home-cured bacon cooking on bolsters of cabbage challenged the strong fragrance from hedgerow and hayfield.

When the *Colleen* emerged into the thirteenth lock even Repeal yielded place to the speed test. The skipper grasped the steering lever and fixed his eyes on the great turnip watch suspended from a nail before him. An elderly English Earl brought forth his gold repeater. Other gentlemen did likewise. And foreigners, thinking it was part of the Repeal agitation, solemnly produced their watches. The skipper of Lord Cloncurry's boat, where it stood in readiness at the private landing of his country estate, gave a courtesy blast to the *Colleen* that nearly up-ended her tow horse and diverted her course. But the thirteenth lock was achieved with a flourish and a triumphant blast and the captain announced an average speed of four and a half miles an hour. When the cheering ceased and flagons had been distributed with the Company's compliments, the Earl said they would have clocked five miles per hour only for that damned horn that upset the tow horse.

The skipper agreed and returned to his instructions from this amazing young lady who was born the night he lost his old home. It had never dawned on him that moths and butterflies had names and significance until she pointed to a butterfly that had lighted on his steering arm.

'That's called "Skipper" like you,' she remarked. 'It's a male butterfly, you know,' and then proceeded to enlighten him about Meadow Browns and Green Artillerys and Red Admirals until a little old woman in a big white apron loomed up and demanded her American letter. The boat slowed while the captain harangued Mrs. McNally.

Did she think that the *Colleen Bawn* on her maiden voyage, bearing the Quality for all ends of the earth to Tara of the Kings, should slow up to deliver Mrs. McNally's letter from her daughter in America?

Mrs. McNally did. 'And the two loaves of baker's bread I left word you were to pick up for me at the thirteenth lock.'

The skipper nearly hit the bank. 'Are you aware that between the twelfth and thirteenth locks there was history being made? The *Colleen Bawn* achieved a speed never before accomplished by any vessel on these waters. She made five miles an hour.'

Mrs. McNally looked pathetically at the letter in her hand. The skipper was pulling out without reading it. The postilion urged the horse from a walk to a trot and Mrs. McNally had to run alongside to keep up.

'Sure there's no one left in the townland that could read it for me,' she pleaded. 'They are all gone to Tara and there's none left but a handful of children to help me to milk all the neighbour's cows and feed their stock.'

'I'll read it on the way back.' But she urged that she'd die with the dint of waiting to know how her daughter fared.

'And the child expected and all! At my age,' she urged, 'the next day might never come at all.'

'She's quite right,' said the English Earl who, along with Sterrin, had taken up a position next to captain. 'The old may not indulge in the luxury of postponement. Read the woman's letter.'

Margaret, with all due sympathy to the old lady, considered this a bit high-handed. The skipper pondered a suitable comment about the Grand Canal Company's time to quell Lord-do-as-I-tell-you when Sterrin tapped him and said, 'Please read the poor old woman's letter.'

'Dear Mother,' he read. 'I hope this finds you as it leaves me, a bit weak after the birth but in good health. . . .'

'Thanks be to God,' cried Mrs. McNally. 'Is it a boy or a child?'

The skipper glanced over the top of the page and resumed.

'Michael John was on special duty at the big meeting here in New York in aid of Repeal. . . .' Cheers burst from the craning heads in the Steerage while the captain courteously explained to the First Class that Michael John was the writer's husband and a policeman.

'Go on,' urged the old woman.

'Go on,' said the Steerage.

'He was that near to Mr. Tyler who is the President of America that he could have put out his hand and touched him. "On the question of Irish Repeal," said the President, "I am no halfway man." '

126

The skipper paused for the cheers from the First and Steerage to subside. He was beginning to enjoy his position.

'Go on!' yelled the Steerage. 'What does she say next?'

'She says,' he resumed, ' "did you get the woollen combinations I sent?" ' Mrs. McNally nodded repeatedly.

'Indeed, 'twas them kept the life in me last winter. 'Twas only in the real hot weather of last week'—her eyes, unquesting, met those of the Earl's—'that I left them off.'

The Earl bowed. 'I should think it would be good weather for washing them too!'

She agreed. 'They'd dry in a night, but,' she turned back to the skipper, 'you didn't say yet if it is a child or a boy?'

The skipper frowned in perplexity. 'It's neither—or else it's spelled wrong. D-a-n-i-e-l-l-e, after the Liberator I suppose...'

Quite unexpectedly the elegant Lady O'Carroll intervened with the information that Danielle was a girl's name. 'The feminine of Daniel.'

'Did she say how she got over the confinement?' urged Mrs. McNally.

'There's details in that, not fit for public hearing. There's been enough of indelicate things aired.'

He pulled out midstream though the voices of the Steerage protested that 'they' had not been washed much less aired.

Down in the cushioned saloon the pint of wine that accompanied the regular four-and-tenpenny dinner of turkey and boiled ham and mutton was extended without limit and there were sweetmeats and all kinds of dainties. The party grew more friendly as it dwindled to disembark passengers at private landing stages where gaily decorated boats awaited the morrow's journey. On drifted the boat in a haze of golden sunset. The marchers on the bank merged into the velvety darkness. Their grass-muffled footfalls sounded the heart beat of a nation. Music spurted from the hayfields and waned into distant roads. From a boreen a torchlight procession wended its way over a bridge. Lights gleaming through the boughs on every shoulder gave the impression of an illuminated forest moving through the darkness. Out from its curtain veil stepped that incurable romantic, the moon, and it bade the martial airs give place to love songs.

'It reminds me of Venice,' said the voice of the Earl. From the floorboards with her head on her mother's knee the sleepy voice of Sterrin murmured, 'I wish young Thomas were here.'

As Roderick drove through dawn-hazed Dublin to the Mass in the privileged oratory of the Liberator's town house, he had the impression that the familiar streets had been transformed into forest glades. The fantasy persisted in the bouquet of flowers handed by a pretty girl to each guest of the breakfast party given in honour of the Liberator by Mr. McGarry of Baggot Street. When the corner of his eye caught a colourful figure in the balcony of the dining-room window, Roderick thought for a frivolous moment he was seeing the Marie Antoinette gown that 'graciously permitted the petticoats to be glimpsed'. But when the host appeared with the Liberator a burst of bardic music brought into view a full-dress harpist who played throughout the breakfast.

The Liberator's own bard occupied a carriage to himself at the head of the long procession that awaited the moment of departure from Merrion Square. Roderick and Patrick Cullen and other members of the bodyguard disputed minutes from conflicting timepieces. But the Head Pacificator, with great gold hunter extended, arbitrated the ultimate moment. At exactly eight forty-five, to the drop of Tom Steele's peace bough, the Liberator ascended his four-horse charit. The picked musicians entered the carriage behind and the two-hundred-carriage cortège moved out.

The sudden thunder of cheers that seemed to come from the skies made Roderick look up. The roof of every tall house was thronged. Every window was blocked with people waving handkerchiefs and flags. The sidewalks had disappeared beneath a solid mass of cheering, waving humanity. He turned to Patrick and expressed a doubt that there might not be so vast a crowd at Tara.

But it looked as if no one had stayed at home. Horses were rearing up and up-ending vehicles at the tumult of cheering that rose and swelled through every green-clad street and everywere was the all-pervading odour of flowers and foliage and fresh dung.

When Tara hill came in sight, Roderick stood up and his figure came in view of the men who marched behind the Templetown band. They gave the O'Carroll rallying cry: it was taken up and sent back to him by the curly-headed giant, John Holohan from Upper Kilsheelin who bore the satin banner on

128

which Master Hennessey's niece had embroidered in gold, 'O'Connell Monarch of the Irish Heart'.

Acres away Sterrin pulled her mamma's gown. 'Papa must be coming near,' she said excitedly. 'I hear the O'Carroll cry.'

'An seabac Abu!' came the rallying cry of the ancient O'Carrolls—'The hawk to victory!'

'And what's more,' said Sterrin, 'that's Felix Downey. He can split a glass with his voice.'

And for the second time Big John encountered Felix marching along the high road with a leg of mutton on his shoulder. 'It's becoming a habit with you, Felix,' he greeted. Beside Felix marched the Scout with one of the most unique of the humorous banners that interspersed those of silken seriousness. 'Made to my own design by James Wright,' he explained as he lowered the great five-foot-square loaf impaled upon the staff that supported his weary form.

Roderick, still standing, raised a white flag and one of the Repeal Cavalry on the hill took the signal and gave the word of command as the ten thousand waiting horsemen moved forward to escort the leader. Over the central plains of Ireland surged the acclaim of one million voices like the sound, not of many waters, but of many oceans. Again and again the old harper touched the chords but the sound died on the strings.

The ruddy face of the Liberator paled as he stood in moved silence. No High King ever witnessed such a spectacle from his subjects converging upon his palace from the four highways of Ireland that once led to Tara.

Sterrin was amazed to see so many English ladies and gentlemen as well as Irish blow their noses and dab their eyes the way grown-ups did when they didn't want to let on they were crying. Lady Cullen did not care who saw her tears. Neither did her husband. When he watched through his glass the Trades of Drogheda carry their flags to the summit and plant them round the Stone of Destiny so that the colours drooped forward in a mourning circle, it was not of the kings of Ireland that were crowned on the Stone that he thought but of the Honourable Edward Cullen, slim and fair and dandified who lay with the United Irishmen who fell there in ninety-eight. Through the glass he watched the group of Protestant men escort old James O'Byrne of Wicklow and place their Orange flag beside his green one on the stone. It was their womenfolk who had flung themselves in supplication before the redcoat soldiers for the life of James's seventeen-year-old son. But the boy was hanged before his kitchen door and the Protestant women had died in vain beneath the horses' feet.

Major de Courcey lowered the telescope to Sterrin's eyes and pointed out the different Guilds that marched behind their banners. 'These are the shoemakers and I think that the ones behind are the glassblowers.'

'And who are the giants with the funny hats?'

'They are not giants,' he laughed. 'They are the coppersmiths. They wear the tallest hats in Europe—in fact in the whole world.'

'I wish they'd take them off. I cannot see what is happening in front of them.' And as if they had heard her, the barrier of towering hats vanished as every man uncovered to the tinkling of the Mass bell. The priest ascended the central altar and a million people knelt in prayer.

CHAPTER 16

Sterrin was amazed to see how tall young Thomas had grown while she was away in Dublin. And it wasn't so much his height; something about his face! He no longer looked as though he belonged with the *garçonnerie*, the little turf and water carriers and all the other juvenile odd-jobbers of the kitchen. He had a grown-up expression, sort of proud looking; almost like Papa's. It gave her a feeling she was too young to recognise as dismay lest he might withdraw that protective companionability for which she had been so homesick in Dublin.

But when she sought him out a few minutes after her homecoming, his face lit up. He had been dreading the change that the high living in Dublin might have made in her. As the carriage drove up he had glimpsed her in a big flowered hat and new fashionable clothes, looking proud and unsmiling like the Honourable Miss Athele O'Carroll of Strague Castle who wouldn't dream of speaking to a knife boy except to give an order. But Sterrin was merely cramped from the journey and aching from the pressure of the hat ribbons tied under her chin.

'Did you like the book I sent you?' she demanded.

'I read it three times,' he told her. 'I'll read it again for you.'

But she knew all about the story. Ignatius, the Misses O'Carrolls' footman had told it to her three times. 'Ignatius saw the ghost and met the gentleman who wrote the story.'

'Met Sir Walter Scott?'

'Yes, he visited Tyrone House long ago when Ignatius worked there and he asked him all about the ghost that haunts it.'

'Sapristi! Fancy meeting the gentleman who wrote all those marvellous books!'

'What does Sapristi mean?'

'Oh, it is said in books. It is more dashing than Egad and By Jove.'

Sterrin looked at him with knit brows. 'You are a funny knife

131

boy,' she said at last. 'There were no knife boys in Dublin but when we went to lunch in Celbridge Abbey we saw the ghost of a lady called Vanessa—we didn't exactly see her ghost, we saw her bower in the garden where she does her haunting, but I met a knife boy there. *He* didn't say Sapristi. He said Begob, and he had a dirty nose—— Come back, it is very bad manners to walk off when a lady is speaking to you. Where are you going?'

'To clean my nose.'

'But it is not—— Oh, I didn't think you would start being cross with me so soon. I learned my alphabet so that I would be able to write to you. I learned to write "cat" and "dog" but when I started to write a letter to you these words were no use.'

He turned back. This was not the welcome he had planned. Life had quickened again for him when he had glimpsed her a while back; just as it had quickened the morning after the Big Wind when he had brought two copper jugs of hot water to an upstairs room and he had glimpsed the lovely baby that had come on the storm's last gasp. The tiredness of the night had fallen from him, and the castle itself, because that little being would dwell there henceforth, had acquired an interest that had waned only when the carriage disappeared through the gates last January. Now she was back and here he was displaying boorish resentment! As though *he* had any right to resent anything that she might choose to say!

'Look,' he said. 'Come out here till I show you something.' He led her across the yard to the smith's shed where two massive iron supports had been forged to support the trunk of the great oak that used to stand in the centre of the lawn. 'Why,' she gasped. 'It has come to life again. It looks like a great big seat growing out of the ground with branches on it.'

'That is exactly what it is meant to look like,' he said, 'and see here.' He showed her the initials entwined in a heart that her papa had carved when he first brought her mamma to Kilsheelin.

When the fallen oaks had been taken away to some cabinet maker the Sir had ordered that this one was not to be removed. He had given no further instructions about it and it had lain in a corner of the yard forgotten until young Thomas, looking at the initials one day, thought it a pity to see this record of romance lying neglected. He had shown the initials to Rafferty the castle carpenter and asked him how the tree might be preserved. When Rafferty suggested a seat young Thomas had brought a book from the library showing a sketch of a pulpit in a church in Belgium. It seemed to be scooped out of a tree that had all its branches still growing. It was just the kind of fanciful work that appealed to Rafferty. He was only happy when he was given some lovely period piece to repair or preserve.

Roderick looked with wonder at young Thomas when Rafferty said that *his* was the inspiration for the magnificent structure. The surface of the great trunk had been hollowed and planed, and some of its branches had been cunningly contrived with the aid of skilled carving to appear to be growing from it in a graceful intertwining pattern. The trunk had not, as Thomas had assumed, gone unnoticed by Sir Roderick. Oftimes as he passed it lying there he would recall its grandeur in life; recall, too, that it had been the sound of its crash that had caused him to open the window and admit the storm's first onslaught. The initials he had carved, his own and those of his lovely bride, faced him now from the centre of the seat's back. And this gracious thought had come from the little ragamuffin who had scuttled away that morning in a trail of brown trusty like—like? Roderick couldn't remember what he had reminded him of then and he could not recall what, or whom, he reminded him of now; that wide brow, the poise of lip, the sensitive nostril; someone? 'Thank you, Thomas,' he said quietly. 'I appreciate your thought—and your perception.'

He couldn't know either that Thomas felt a thrill of pleasure that the 'young' had, for the first time been omitted. He couldn't know that the sensitivity that he had noticed for the first time had been sculpted forth by himself. It had started when, as he led the doctor to tend Big John's shoulder after that night ride he had seen the child lying across two wooden chairs in a sleep of prostration and had given a curt order that the boy be covered. When the nameless waif heard later who it was who had been responsible for the luxury of a tarpaulin rug, his awe had merged into an agony of gratitude that had awakened the questing clamour of his intellect.

The seat was placed where it had stood in life. Cushions were placed in its couched length and here Margaret lay in the sunny days that stretched into mid-September, cherished and tended, her mind relaxed in the detachment of waiting motherhood.

Returning to Kilsheelin had been, after all her fears, a joyous experience. The people had stopped working in the fields and run towards the roadside as their carriage passed. Some of them gave great shouts of 'Repeal' as they ran, 'as though,' Roderick had said, 'we had Repeal packed safely in one of our valises'.

It was good to come home when the fruits of the earth were coming home. From where she lay she could see the carts laden with sheaves coming across the fields to the yard. Later she heard the sound of laughter and merriment as extra hands joined the workers in the yard for the threshing. No tortured lowings sounded from the fields these nights. The country under the discipline of Repeal was crimeless.

The season's toil came to a glorious climax with the dance at the end of the ten days' threshing. Sky and earth were bathed in the refulgent brightness of the harvest moon as Margaret lay under the flowered drapes of her bed and listened to the music of fiddles and melodeons and bagpipes that came through the open window.

Suddenly there was a hush in the laughter and the twanging. A ripple of musical sound throbbed out on the air, and Margaret knew that the bard had condescended to grace the dance with his presence. A little cloud came over her mood. The bard played such sad music! But no sadness came from the harp strings. Its music was part of the lyric of the night. Three notes formed the prelude; the first low and deep, the second tender and the third so full of life and passion that the leaves ceased their whispering and the birds in their nests were beguiled into sending back sleepy trills.

When the clapping had subsided the strings throbbed out again in a melody that surprised Margaret, for she knew the bard dismissed Moore's melodies as modern and trivial. But she was still more surprised when a young voice took up the refrain.

'Believe me if all those endearing young charms'

'Roderick,' she called towards the dressing-room. He came in his robe and stood listening at the window until the song ended.

'Who on earth,' she asked him, 'owns that delightful voice?'

He turned from the window and discarded his robe. 'I have an idea that it is the property of our highly individual knife boy.'

134

'Then, you knew that he could sing like that?'

He snuffed candles and got into bed. No darkening followed their quenching; just a lovely slow whitening as the moon's rays took over. 'Darling,' he said flinging his arm across the pillow, 'you should always wear moonlight.' He kissed her and sighed pleasantly. 'It has been a long day.' He had been abroad since dawn. She repeated her question about young Thomas. 'Yes,' he murmured sleepily. 'Lady Cullen mentioned to me that she had heard him sing at the Crossroads dancing last *Corpus Christi*. She said she slowed the brougham to listen to him. I meant to speak to Hegarty about it. I won't have my staff clowning for the public. The business of the seat put his bad behaviour out of my head.'

'The seat was a graceful thought, Roderick, for a young kitchen boy! It reminds me of Bruckstruyn's famous pulpit at Malines.'

Much later, when she thought he was asleep, Margaret heard a muffled voice, from the pillows, say, 'There must be quite a lot about that boy that I don't know.'

Next day he learned something about his knife boy that Thomas had prayed might never reach the Sir's ears. It was gale day. Tenants came in a steady trickle and lingered over their payments longer than usual. They all wanted to talk about Repeal. All of them wore Repeal buttons in their lapels. Those of them who had not been to the Monster Meeting at Tara had been to the nearby town of Cashel on *Corpus Christi* when O'Connell had addressed four hundred thousand people. Roderick was glad to see Black Pat. The bellrope was tugged straight away for refreshments and over their glasses they reminisced pleasantly. He asked about his wife whom he had not yet met, and about the farm occupied by Sterrin's wet nurse, Mrs. Conry. It was worrying him. It was not being worked satisfactorily except for whatever assistance Black Pat could give, and for over a year no rent had been paid.

'We'll make a match for her,' said Black Pat, getting to his feet. 'There's nothing like a husband for taking the bare look off a woman.' Roderick assured him that he was more concerned about having the bare look removed from the farm.

No farmer had ever been evicted from the Kilsheelin estate, but no landlord could be expected to allow one of his holdings to go to rack and ruin. Mrs. Conry had gradually come to

135

identify herself with Black Pat's fosterage connection because he had continued to sow and save her crops since the day she became Sterrin's wet nurse. Roderick decided to go and see her right away. When he rang for his horse the servant who answered said that George Lucas was outside, pleading for an interview.

The name conveyed nothing to Sir Roderick. He had forgotten about the small dark man to whom he had given temporary employment after being evicted with nineteen others by Major Darby because a sheep had been stolen. Lucas came in twisting his hairskin cap in his hand; but he came right to the point. He wanted permission to marry into the Widow Conry's farm.

It should be the solution to the problem. The man was a good worker, honest, conscientious. Demmit, he didn't have to be likeable as well! Roderick studied the little face, neither young nor old, smooth yet finely shrivelled like an apple pulled too soon. The thin hair was blue-black and the small eyes had a blue-black sheen. Like a beetle, Roderick thought. Aloud he said, 'There are tenants of my own with sons who have a stronger claim on any vacant farm.'

The man gave the cap another twist. 'With respects to your Honour's Sir, you wouldn't say that they would have a stronger claim than Miss Sterrin's foster-mother?' Blast the fellow's presumption! Roderick curbed an inclination to have him thrown out. Why did it have to be Sterrin's foster-mother-of-sorts who had captured his farming fancy? And what could a fine-looking woman see in this little yellow bittern? Curtly he told him to return next day. Meanwhile he would talk to Black Pat. Roderick didn't believe in interfering in the lives—and loves—of his tenants. Once, in his schooldays he had encountered an entire family cast from their home because the father permitted the eldest daughter to marry without first seeking his landlord's consent. The feudal brutality of the incident had sickened him. But Mrs. Conry had a claim on his interest—he looked up impatiently. Hadn't the fellow gone yet....!

'Your Honour—Herself—my Intended, bid me ask your permission to have the young scholar that cleans your knives serve the Wedding Mass.'

Roderick frowned, 'I don't supply Mass servers. You may go.' So his knife boy was a scholar as well as a singer! The man

136

turned back at the door and there was a blue-black glitter in the small eyes. Roderick had a sudden mnemonic flash of very young days and Black Pat showing him a particularly ugly beetle called the 'darraghadheal'. If one killed it in a special way and repeated a stipulated number of Our Fathers and Hail Marys one would be forgiven the Seven Deadly Sins because, Black Pat explained, the 'darraghadheal' had led the soldiers up to the spot in Gethsemane where Our Lord was praying.

'It was only, your Honour,' the man was saying, 'that my Intended was in the church last Shrovetide when the lad served the Wedding Mass for James Keating's son and Miss Prendergast.' He bobbed a half curtsey and went out. Roderick strode to the bellrope. 'Mass Server!' he fumed. 'He'll be a notice server when I'm finished with him.'

Sterrin rushed after young Thomas when the unprecedented summons came for him to appear at once before the Sir. Her papa closed the heavy door in her face. No inkling escaped through its panels or keyhole. She tore round to the open window where she caught some of his angry words. '... damnation ... cheapening my service ... singing to Crossroad gatherings ... not paid to acquire a classical education ... Latin! ... to be availed of for the weddings of every Tom, Dick and Harry!'

Sterrin thought that young Thomas looked quite different. The white tenseness of his face made him look like someone else altogether. Her papa had the same impression. Another countenance seemed to be straining out through the blanched face of the knife boy; one strangely familiar. The impression persisted in the boy's answer.

'The Latin was availed of your Honour's Sir, by the priest, and for the purpose of serving his Mass.'

'You are insolent,' said Sir Roderick confounded by the simple dignity of the reply. His accusation sounded as unjust in his own ears as in those of his daughter—and, in his knife boy's. 'How old are you?' he demanded.

Thomas was confused. 'I—I'm not sure, your Honour's Sir.'

'You are old enough,' his master told him coldly, 'to know where your loyalty should lie. I will have no disloyalty in my service. You may go.'

There was an awful finality about the words. Thomas took it that he was to go from his master's service as well as from his presence.

Another door closed against Sterrin—but not deliberately—as she chased after Thomas. She pushed this one open and found him sitting on his bed forlornly; his eyes fixed on the granite floor where pieces of mica sparkled from the care he lavished on every cherished inch of his precious little cubicle of a room.

'Is he sending you away?' she asked solemnly. He gave no answer. His throat was too full; all the way back to the desolation that ranged about his heart. 'Young Thomas!' she pleaded. He squeezed his eyes tight until they felt cleared of the prickling moisture. All his book-learning and visioning had turned into comical presumption; comical to others. He was just a lonely, friendless boy, panic-stricken at the thought of leaving his beloved home.

'Damnation, Thomas, answer me!'

He opened his eyes. 'So you heard!'

'There were some other words like that but I couldn't catch them while I was climbing to the window-sill. Young Thomas, why did you keep it secret from me? About those weddings I mean. I wouldn't have told, even about the Keatings although they are our enemies.'

'It must have been that sneaky little Lucas who told. He has been a-courting your foster-mother while you were in Dublin. I suppose he's been here looking for permission to marry into her place. I hope he doesn't get it. He is not the type of our tenants.'

Our tenants! The phrase brought him to his feet. 'I'd better pack my belongings.' He looked around at them; the bar of perfumed soap beside the cracked Doulton basin, discarded from upstairs. The cigar box beside it held the two linen handkerchiefs purchased since Miss Sterrin's reference to the knife boy with the snotty nose. Beneath the stand the pair of boots made by the Scout of finest leather reserved for the Quality. He looked hesitantly at the surtout hanging behind the door. It was scarcely his—to take away. It had descended upon him, taken in and up, when her Ladyship had ordered new livery with special padding for the coachman's injured shoulder.

He turned away to the galleried table, minus a leg. On it lay the treasure that no one could prevent him from taking away; unless perhaps the donor decided to do so.

But the sight of her gift *Saint John's Eve* fondled in his hands sent her hurtling up the back stairs to seek the intervention of Nurse Hogan. There was no use approaching that fierce, unfamiliar-looking papa who mouthed blasts and damnations.

Nurse Hogan was aghast. Young Thomas dismissed! Young Thomas was dear to her. When she first came he was the only one of the Gaelic-speaking gossoons who could speak English to her. He was the only one also who had no background, no relatives, not even a name. No one knew anything about him. He had arrived here shortly before herself. Anything that might have been known about him had died with the housekeeper on the night of the Big Wind. His plight had gone to her heart. She it was who had first indulged his studiousness. It was she who had got him promoted from the toleration of hanger-on status to the payroll of staff. She made a quick swish towards her Ladyship's boudoir. But the Sir was there, deep in conversation and looking in no mood to brook interruption.

'Roderick,' Margaret was pleading, 'don't let that storm twist you as it has twisted me.' He looked at her startled. She had never before referred to her attacks so positively. Nothing seemed more unlikely than that there should be any disturbance in the placid serenity of this sweet being. The boudoir expressed that same serenity. She had been sitting at her spinet when he entered. She preferred its music to that of the grand piano in the drawing-room. The harp she regarded as too solemn and dramatic. She liked tinkling things, the music boxes that she collected, the little silver bells she wore on her chatelaine belt. They heralded her approach in chime with the soft sussurus of her silken skirts. Nothing ominous about such sounds; nothing twisted!

'After all,' she went on, 'other people didn't go round demanding their trees when they flew away from them that night.'

There was a knock at the door and Sterrin entered.

She could not stand the strain any longer. Young Thomas had decided to go at once without begging, he said. Mrs. Stacey had broken into tears and lamentation when he bade her good-bye and when he turned to Sterrin she made another dash for the stairs determined to brave her father's ire. She dropped a specially deep curtsey first to her mamma, then to her papa.

'Papa,' she began, 'I've come to crave a boon of you.' She wasn't too sure what a boon was but in the story-books that were read to her the princesses generally said the word when they wanted to get something out of their royal papas. She

139

poured out a graphic and not too coherent description of young Thomas's merits, his unremitting toil, the grief of Papa's foster-mother, Mrs. Stacey, and finally the pathos of his plight driven forth to wander homeless in the snow.

Her papa maintained a serious front and indicated the golden September sunshine that streamed through the open windows. The weather conditions, he pointed out, were ideal for a homeless wanderer. There seemed little likelihood of snow. She had to yield the point. Her papa was always right. But it said snow in the story where the scullion, who was really an enchanted prince, was being cast forth for raising his eyes towards the king's daughter. That was the worst of the written word. It seemed to have no bearing on real life; like c-a-t and d-o-g and m-a-t that she had laboured over only to find that they were silly when it had come to writing a letter to young Thomas.

Roderick sent Sterrin from the room, but he was smiling. He went to the gun-room and dismantled a fowling-piece, then sent an order to have it cleaned by young Thomas; as though nothing had happened.

Roderick did not smile after his talk with Black Pat about Lucas.

'She'll have no one, Master Rody, but Lucas.' Black Pat was gloomy, too. 'She believes that he was meant for her by Heaven. The Big Wind that took her husband and child from her took wife and child from Lucas. 'Tis fate she says.'

Roderick sighed resignedly. 'By gad, Pat, fate or the Big Wind has caused me enough of trouble without blowing that beetle on my property.' He felt something absurdly like a premonition as he watched Black Pat walk down the road. Roderick gave George Lucas permission to marry Mrs. Conry, and allowed the 'darraghadheal' to burrow quietly into the Kilsheelin estate.

CHAPTER 17

Thomas was to go to Dublin for the great rally that was to terminate the open-air agitation of Repeal Year. Roderick had decided that he could use the lad's resourcefulness—and horsemanship—in what some newspaper reporter had humorously described as the 'Repeal Cavalry'.

Thomas was stunned with joy. He was to be supplied with an armlet that would identify him as a 'Courier'. He would convey messages through that mighty throng! He was to play his minute part in this final display that would preface the liberation of his country!

Thomas dared to feel pity for the great Mr. Hegarty; for all of his friends in the kitchen. Carrying out their routine tasks; nothing seemed to have changed for them. They were unconscious of the glory that had burst upon his soul. He rushed to tell his marvellous news to Sterrin.

She looked at him in wonder. He was the same young Thomas—but—he was all shiny; not polish shiny but like the glow around people in holy pictures.

'Think of it, Miss Sterrin,' he said when he had poured out the news. 'Not just going to Dublin, but taking part in such a gathering; the biggest ever in the world. Me! The million that was at Tara will only be a handful to this last rally. It is like a play staged by history; the last act of a long drama and *I'll* be there—on the stage.' He turned away to the window, embarrassed. For the first time in his life he had opened his heart to another. But even to her there were still things he could not say aloud. He gripped the iron hasp of the window. Even if she were old enough to understand, he could never tell her what it was that was bringing tears to his eyes.

This wasn't just the flamboyant ardour of youthful patriotism. He had felt like this once before; the time he had awakened after the storm night, cramped from lying across two hard chairs but snug from the unaccustomed covering that had been

141

tucked around him. By order of no less a person than his Honour, the Sir! Then, like now, he had felt that he—belonged.

No, Miss Sterrin would never understand what it was to feel like this. She'd need to be a waif, homeless, nameless, forever blowing her heart breaths upon the window pane to peep in from outside.

'The castle will seem queer with you away.' The wistful voice dropped into the surge of his thoughts. He turned. She *did* look poorly. And he revelling in his own good fortune.

'I shall be terribly lonely for you,' she continued.

'That's just because you're feeling low. You'll be all right by the time I'm leaving and you won't mind.' His sympathy was automatic. She had said something that had lifted his new-found sense of belonging—to the point of elation. This great castle would seem different to someone because it was without *him*! Miss Sterrin to be lonely for *him*! For young Thomas the knife boy!

Sterrin out-sighed him, 'When Papa is away Mamma doesn't seem to notice that I am here at all. I have to ask her everything twice and then she—she almost snaps because she has to come out of her thoughts to answer me.'

'Fancy you noticing that!'

She leaned up on her elbow. 'Why? Had you noticed it too?'

He moved to the fireplace. 'I'm noticing that it is time I did something about making a fire. A big blazing fire will put these queer thoughts out of your head.'

'And will you read a book to me?'

'If Nurse Hogan allows, *and* if I can manage the time.'

As he was leaving the room she called out, 'Young Thomas, if a dragon were to run away with me would you rescue me?'

He paused to consider the question. 'If the dragon wore trousers I probably would. But they usually wear scales.'

On the journey to Dublin he thought on what she had said about her mamma almost snapping at her in her papa's absence because she had to 'come out of her thoughts' to answer Sterrin. The idea seemed to suggest a chink in the structure of Miss Sterrin's love-guarded life; a chink to admit the grey chill of—outsideness, that he knew so well. Of course, the Sir and her Ladyship *were* very wrapped up in each other. Different from

142

anything he had ever observed among the Quality who came to stay at the castle; even honeymooners. They were like the sweethearts in books whose love-story ended in marriage and the information that 'they lived happily ever after'. Thomas was always exasperated at that unsatisfactory phrase. Why couldn't the author go on and let one glimpse that happy-ever-after? But now, in Kilsheelin Castle he was glimpsing it all the time.

Once in the turbulent city, Thomas forgot his carriage decorum. His head kept moving from one side to the other as though it were on a swivel. 'It is not always like this,' Mike O'Driscoll explained. 'Dublin has never seen such crowds before. Look at that!' He flicked the whip in the direction of the Customs House where the great bulk of a man-of-war loomed over vessels flying the flags of all nations. 'It has never seen the like of that either. I wonder what it is there for.'

Roderick's travelling companion, his neighbour Mr. Delaney, wondered also. He was like an emancipated schoolboy. He leaned from one window to the other and talked uninhibitedly to strangers in the carriages that crawled on either side. They dropped him at the crumbling mansion that had been his grandfather's town residence, and was now occupied by a recluse kinsman. Before entering it he made Roderick promise to collect him later and go to the Crow Street Theatre where the famous actor Thomas Young was billed to play. 'He has changed his name,' he said. 'Married the wealthy Mrs. Winterbottom last month and has assumed her name.'

Sir Roderick was amazed. 'How could a man who has made his own name so famous, throw it aside at the whim of a rich widow?'

Thomas withdrew his head from the rumble and drew forth Mr. Delaney's carpet bag. Ye Gods! thought the nameless knife boy. Fancy throwing away any name, famous or humble; one's own rightful name! The new caroline hat that made him look so tall and grown up had fallen over his eyes. A woman who walked alone winked at the graceful youth who was straightening his hat over crisp curls.

'That lady must have mistaken me for someone else,' said Thomas when he remounted. O'Driscoll spat. 'The whipster! Keep your eyes straight ahead the way you were trained avic. That's no lady.'

'No, I suppose not,' agreed Thomas. 'Ladies don't wink.'

Later as O'Driscoll turned the horses away from the theatre after dropping the two gentlemen, Thomas looked longingly back.

'Surely,' cried O'Driscoll, ' 'tisn't wantin' to shut yourself up in a playhouse you are with all that divarshun goin' on in the streets.'

Thomas sighed. 'I'd give anything to see the acting of a great man like Mr. Young.'

'Whoa!' called O'Driscoll to the horses. 'You needn't give anything except whatever it costs to go in by that door.' He pointed his whip to the gallery entrance. 'But you can give me your word that you'll slip out before the last word is spoke on the stage and be on that kerb to open the carriage door when the gentlemen come out.'

A grateful Thomas arrived panting at the back row of the gallery just as the manager had come before the curtain to announce the change in the famous actor's name. He apologised that there had not been sufficient time to alter the billing. Then the curtain slowly rose. Thomas gazed and his whole world receded. He stood at the rails like some bewitched mortal gazing across the threshold of the fairy land of Hy Brazil.

The witty interruptions of the surrounding 'gods' scarce reached his consciousness. But in the middle of the last act, he was shattered to reality; the central character—played by Mr. Young—was lamenting his lost youth. 'Then, alas,' he wailed, 'I was young——' and across his sentence the raucous voice of Thomas's neighbour yelled, 'And now you're Winterbottom!' The house exploded into laughter. Thomas slipped out during the uproar.

'You kept your word,' said O'Driscoll as Thomas climbed up beside him. 'Are you satisfied now?'

'Yes, Mr. O'Driscoll,' said Thomas leaning back blissfully, 'very, very satisfied——' There was a sound of laughter from the theatre and he turned to the sight of Sir Roderick and Mr. Delaney emerging arm-in-arm; still hilarious over the interruption which they decided was a better finish than waiting for the finale.

When Thomas had shut them in he resumed his seat and went on talking as if he had not been interrupted. 'After all, what's in a name?' he demanded from the uplifted tail of the livery stable horse. 'A rose under any other name would smell as sweet and Mr. Young under any other name would sound as sweet. The actor's the thing, not the name——'

From the corner of his mouth, O'Driscoll hissed. 'It's a bad sign when a lad of your age talks to himself. It wasn't natural for a gossoon to shut himself up in a playhouse and the whole world walkin' outside. What playhouse could give that divarshun?' He gestured towards the kerbs.

Along the kerbs every instrument from a harp to a tin whistle was striving for supremacy. And every one seemed to have its own followers. The girls and youths from the country danced jigs and reels around the fiddlers. The overseas stranger favoured the Celtic harp.

'Mm,' Thomas murmured, 'but then I shall have an opportunity of seeing them all, both the world and the musicians, at the meeting on Sunday. I might never again have the opportunity of seeing Thomas Young act.'

But neither the world, nor the musicians—nor Thomas—saw the meeting at Clontarf.

The next day, when he emerged from Conciliation Hall after receiving his armlet and instructions, no one would dream that he was other than one of the vast troop of well-to-do young horsemen who voluntarily attended all the Monster meetings under the adhesive nickname of the Repeal Cavalry.

'Where do you think you are going?' an angry voice interrupted his rapt admiration of his armlet. He stepped apologetically from the path of a big, important-looking personage. 'What does *that* indicate?' The man pointed to the armlet. Thomas explained. 'And you are a member of this "Cavalry"?' Very emphatically Thomas assured him that he was. 'You seem very proud of your assignment. Your name, Mr. Cavalryman?' The question was demanded in that tone of authority to which Thomas was accustomed to give prompt answer.

'Young, er——' The proud cavalryman had no name to offer but the classification that distinguished him from the boys who carried the turf and water. 'Young——' he stammered, and the gentleman's eyes narrowed at the evasion. Thomas's embarrassed eyes fell on the poster announcing the order of tomorrow's rally. They were interspersed with hand bills that blazed the two words to which he responded in lieu of a name. Only they were in reverse. Thomas Young instead of 'young Thomas'! And the posters announced the actor as dispensing

145

with the name. Thomas turned and smiled at the big man. 'My name,' he smiled, 'is Thomas Young.'

The gentleman looked silently at Thomas, then gestured one of the policemen and murmured something. The policeman stepped nearer to Thomas.

There had been a titter from some of the young Repeal horsemen when Thomas read out the actor's name. 'I say,' called one of them, thinking Thomas was a bit of a blade. 'You had some nerve to twit a big gun like him!' Thomas learned with shock that he had been misleading one of the police chiefs from Dublin Castle.

'It would have been wiser to have given your own name,' said an older man. 'Also it was indiscreet to make any reference to the term "Cavalry". The Liberator has protested to the newspaper that coined the phrase. He says it could readily give the government the opening they are looking for. It could be construed into something martial; something challenging. And there *is* something afoot. Why all these extra police and military twenty-four hours before the meeting?'

The answer followed in the wake of a galloping horseman who drew rein outside the Corn Exchange and rushed inside. By obvious arrangement the police chief and convoy of police moved after him. Thomas found himself back in the hall propelled inwards by the rush of Repealers sensing trouble. Up in the gallery reserved on festive occasions for ladies, he could see Sir Roderick with Mr. Delaney and a party of provincial gentlemen talking and sending out bursts of laughter through cigar smoke. But everyone went still as the messenger strode purposefully to the Liberator and placed a document before him.

All eyes were focused on O'Connell as he scanned its contents. It took but a second; then he spoke quietly; just a few words, but they were heard through the hall, from the back where Thomas stood to the gallery where Sir Roderick and the others were now on their feet. 'This must be obeyed,' they heard him say. 'They have declared the meeting at Clontarf illegal.'

The scratching of the quill could be heard as the secretary furiously wrote to the Liberator's dictation; a clattering broke the stunned silence as Sir Roderick and the others came tearing down the stairs. Men were crowding to read the document, then turning to look at each other.

'Surely, the Liberator will not obey this!' cried Sir Roderick.

'They cannot forbid the public the right of assembly.'

But the messenger had already left for the printers with O'Connell's appeal to the people not to assemble. The gathering was banned.

With sinking dread Thomas heard voices say that it was a whimsical phrase 'Repeal Cavalry' that had given the government the pretext it needed. 'You see now,' said the young horseman who had thought Thomas had been merely twitting the police chief about his name. 'He was trying to trap you into a definite statement that you belonged to the cavalry.'

Thomas reeled. He had betrayed his great trust! Heaven, could it possibly have been his abysmal folly that had crashed this sublime finale! He turned and forced his way blindly towards the crowded entrance.

'Young Thomas!' Sir Roderick's peremptory summons halted his knife boy's despairing flight.

He was despatched with those who were posted to the Naas road to meet the contingents from the South and bid them return to their homes. At every approach to the city, North, South, East and West, the Wardens repelled the processions marching behind their banners and bands.

Once during a lull while they waited for fresh contingents, the two law students who were with Thomas beguiled their deflated spirits with anecdotes of their background. Thomas listened amazed. The brilliance of their banter was like a shower of intellectual fireworks that made a responsive sparkling in his own intellect. In the darkness he became disorientated. His background receded. He scarcely realised that he was joining in their sallies with a delicacy of wit that delighted them. Then the marching feet sounded again. 'No meeting?' The weary men who had walked from the extremest points of the country could not believe their ears.

By dawn Thomas was exhausted. But his work was accomplished. He had helped to stem the vanguard. The posters would do the rest. They were up now in every village within twenty miles of Dublin.

As he turned for Dublin he heard his name called and his tired eyes strained through a mask of dust to recognise a lad from Upper Kilsheelin. It was Tim Lonergan, the well-to-do farmer's son whom he had met at the Prendergast–Keating wedding.

'Why should we go back?' demanded Tim furiously. 'Why shouldn't we fight them? There is an army of us on the march.'

'Hush,' said Thomas who knew now that this gruelling vigilance of Wardens had been to forestall any clash between the marchers and the military. 'Is it with your peace twigs you'd fight the army that's mustered back there with cannon and rifle and ships of war? Don't speak of fighting. That is all they want. One shot will bring down the avalanche.'

'Avalanche!' Tim spat the word. He threw his withered peace bough from him and faced for home without a word of farewell.

CHAPTER 18

Thomas had almost forgotten the incident with the police chief on the day before the rally that never took place when he was summoned by the Sir to the drawing-room. Mr. Lalor-Shiel, the member for Dungarvin, was with Sir Roderick. As Thomas entered the room the two gentlemen looked very fixedly at him. Thomas had the sudden feeling that the Member's call had something to do with himself.

The news was shattering. The Liberator had been arrested. The Government had charged him with conspiracy to excite rebellion.

Mr. Lalor-Shiel, who had been briefed to defend Mr. John O'Connell, the Liberator's son—also under arrest—had heard that enquiries were being made about his cousin, Sir Roderick O'Carroll. A young gentleman who was seen to have been in close company of Sir Roderick at the Corn Exchange and to have taken whispered instructions from him had deliberately given the police a false name. Enquiries at the home of Sir Roderick's kinswomen, the Misses O'Carroll of Mountjoy Square, had disclosed that no person of the name had either stayed there or called. The police suspected that the name given was a taunt to themselves; it was the name emblazoned on the walls of the Corn Exchange announcing the visit of the famous actor Thomas Young. The police didn't like being taunted. They had compiled a formidable dossier about the Repeal activities of Sir Roderick O'Carroll.

The Sir's face was white with anger as he questioned his presumptuous servant. Thomas's face was whiter still. He had believed that all that 'cavalry' business had gone unnoticed. The whole world knew now that the government had pounced upon the excuse offered by the term when some Repeal secretary had used it in drawing up the programmes and positions for the meeting.

'I have had to speak to you before about your presumptuous

activities,' fumed the Sir. 'Do you realise what you have done?'

Before Thomas could reply, the piping voice of Mr. Lalor-Shiel addressed him. 'Do you realise that you have brought your master under suspicion. That he may be arrested?'

Thomas realised but one thing; that he wanted to die! There and now on the Aubusson carpet that he had swept so often; he ought to have concerned himself solely with sweeping and with every other servile chore, instead of book-learning and politics—the Sir arrested! The great, kind Sir beloved of all his employees and tenants. Miss Sterrin's papa! Into his numb brain crawled the Scout's oft-repeated misquotation of Saint Thomas —'A thing which is not in its own place is an abomination.' That's what I am—an abomination!

Mr. Lalor-Shiel was repeating the question. 'Why didn't you give your own name?' He had been expecting to see some cocky servant, brash and glib and ready to break down into whining denials. But here was natural dignity. Not just the kind acquired in genteel service. He noted the fine head; the sensitive mouth and nostrils. He noted how the shamed colour overflowed into the blenched face as the boy said, 'I have no name of my own, sir.'

'If,' he said on a less reproachful note, 'you felt it necessary to assume a name, why pick on one so illustrious? You might as well have said you were the Duke of Wellington.' When Thomas explained, Lalor-Shiel, laughed outright. 'Mr. Young,' said Thomas, naïvely, 'didn't want his name any more.'

Thomas explained the impulse that had caused him to give the name that had stared out at him from the wall behind the police officer. 'The words of the name were so familiar to me, Sir. They were those by which I am called. I merely reversed them.'

When Thomas had left the room, Lalor-Shiel turned with quirked brow to Roderick. 'Where on earth did you get him, Rody? Who is he?'

Roderick was striding up and down, his mind in a whirl. One of the gentlemen arrested with the Liberator had joined the movement only five days before; had attended the Corn Exchange but once. What chance had Roderick? Deep in the affairs of the movement since his enrolment? It was no satisfaction to him to hear Lalor-Shiel just now quote the Liberator in saying that Sir Roderick O'Carroll's road arrangements for the proclaimed meeting, and the subsequent dispersals had been a 'masterpiece of organisation'. A masterpiece that might land him in jail!

'Where did I get who? Good heavens, I don't know where half of them came from! The kitchen is always full of God-save-all-here's and hangers-on and little run-around gossoons.' He resumed his pacing, then stopped. 'Yes, I believe the lad was a protégé of Mrs. Mansfield's—our housekeeper you remember who was killed the night of the Big Wind? Some woman brought him to her; his mother probably. She was leaving for America; probably intended sending for him; never heard of again.'

'He reminds me of someone——'

'Forget him, Richard. It was most kind of you to come and warn me. Forgive my testiness. Were it not for the state of Margaret's health I might find the incident piquant especially about the name that—"Mr. Young didn't want any more".' He told him about the witticism from the 'gods' at the expense of Mr. Young's name. 'Now that you recall it to me, young Thomas or "Thomas Young" is even younger than I thought. He is tall for his age. I forced the predicament upon him. He is resourceful; too damned resourceful.' He pulled the bellrope. 'Let's have what Lord Cullen calls a Bumper.'

Next morning after a fear-racked night, Thomas spied Constable Humphreys walking up the avenue in the wake of a mounted Sub-Inspector of Police. They were coming for him!

He removed his apron. In a silver cover dish he saw the reflection of curls falling over his forehead. He smoothed them back. As he rubbed his moist palms on the roller towel he wondered would there be time to say goodbye to Miss Sterrin. But, hadn't the Sir sent for him last night and warned him not to utter a breath of this! He must go without seeing her! And when he returned, when his sentence was served—but then the Sir might not take him back into his service! Anyway she'd be gone by then; married to—— 'The Sir wants you in the library, immediately.'

By the time he reached the library, the Sir had given the Sub-Inspector the full details about the alleged false name business.

'Nevertheless, if you don't mind, Sir Roderick,' said the grandiose official, 'I shall call upon my constable to corroborate.'

Constable Humphreys confirmed that he recognised the youth as one whom he had known for some years and whom he had 'invariably heard apostrophised by estimable and noted persons in Templetown, as "young Thomas".'

'Do you know of any surname or patronymic?' asked his superior.

The constable wished that he had thought up 'patronymic' himself; but he fished out a beauty from his erudite jaws. 'I have never heard of the existence of any other nomenclature,' he said. Where the hell, thought Roderick, does he get them?

The officer was perplexed. 'This, of course, alters the charge of false representation—somewhat. But, there is still the *intent to mislead,* by the juxtaposition of words.'

'Mislead whom?' asked Roderick irritably and changing the juxtaposition of his feet. They were itching to put a toe through all this bumptious pedantry. He brusquely pointed out that his servant, Thomas, brought to Dublin for the first time had been warned to show caution if any stranger addressed him. 'How could the boy possibly know that your superior was other than a civilian?'

The Sub-Inspector bowed and wished Sir Roderick good day. At the door he turned. He had thought of another reason for attaching Thomas to the ironmongery that peeped through the silk folds of the handkerchief up the constable's cuff.

'He may be required to give evidence at the trials. I take it that he will not seek to absent himself?'

Sir Roderick pulled the bellrope significantly. 'I vouch for my servant,' he said.

Thomas looked down at the carpet. Again, he wished he could lie down on it and die. This time in gratitude to the wonderful, omnipotent Sir! He raised his eyes for the onslaught, but the face before him was smiling. The Sir was thinking that the knife boy's face was as fine-drawn as one of his own blades. It would stand no more sharpening. 'We must see about having you brought to the christening font,' he said. 'Can't have people coming here talking about nomenclature before breakfast. Puts me off my food!'

Thomas dared not stir from the castle lest he be summoned to Dublin as a witness. But the trial was postponed. It was discovered that hundreds of Catholic names that should have been on the panel of jurors had never been listed. The only Catholic names listed belonged to people who had been dead for years. So the Crown was reluctantly compelled to concede a postponement until January.

Not since the inquests on Mrs. Mansfield and the others after the Big Wind had a policeman been seen near the castle. Now they had become a daily spectacle. Sometimes from a window Thomas would glimpse the top of a shako as the police peeped over the opening that had been partially built up after that night. On Christmas Eve he almost bumped into his friend Sergeant Flynn patrolling with the pedantic constable. He jumped back as if he were stung. This meant that he would be under house guard for the lovely twelve days of Christmas when everyone went to and fro visiting all the time and only the most essential work was performed. Golden Meadows would be keeping open house; on a big scale. Tim Lonergan had mentioned something about taking him along with the Wren Boys and Mummers. To parade around the countryside behind the omadhawn; playing every instrument that would give music! Every house open to them to come in and play and dance and feast! Oh well, he sighed to himself as he cleaned a knife with a raw potato. I cannot have it every way! I cannot take part in the history of my country and then go cod-acting around the countryside with the Wren boys!

The Sir frowned as he encountered the police patrol on the little bridle road. Was a gentleman to have no privacy even on Christmas Eve? The Sir's road was private property. A concession to the public. Not a right. He barely returned the salute. The sergeant looked after the proud figure. The Sir had always reined in for a passing word with him. He watched him stop no less than three times to chat with farmers and to their wives and children ensconsed on feather mattresses that were covered with Christmas shopping.

'This,' said the sergeant to his subordinate, 'is one of the times when I hate my job. When I realise that a policeman is, after all, merely a spy on his fellow-men.'

Roderick's ill humour melted in the all-pervading atmosphere of good cheer. All the way to Templetown he was hailed; by farmers, their waggons or phaetons laden with good things. At every boreen entrance groups of children watched out for their homing parents and the big three-quart cans of sweets and the bottles of lemonade with the glass marbles in the necks of them.

Two little boys on top of a fence tugged their forelocks to him and their little 'big' sister gave him a radiant smile. As he slowed they jumped down and ran over to him. 'We got the sheep,' said one of the boys. They were Black Pat's children! Every tenant had been given a joint of meat but Black Pat had been sent a whole sheep. 'Oh boys, o' boys,' said the older lad, 'but we'll have "maw galore"!'[1]

Unlike the children of other tenants they were completely uninhibited in his presence. They chattered to him about the good things that their mammy and daddy would bring them from town. But when he produced silver coins and the little boys thrust out chubby palms their sister stopped them, 'Mammy does not allow us to accept money,' she said. This was something out of the ordinary! Roderick decided that he must meet this mammy of theirs. 'It is a great pity,' said the little girl, her bright eyes fixed on the money.

Her brother solved the problem. 'Father Hickey gives us money when we answer our catechism. Mammy doesn't mind that.'

'All right,' said Sir Roderick. 'Who made the world?'

They told him with one concerted gasp.

'How many Gods are there?' He asked the older.

'One, of course.'

'Why are you so positive?'

Adam's eyes devoured the half-crown, but the big word had him baffled. His little brother put up his hand. 'Please, your Honour, I'm not posibet. I'm a good boy. An' there couldn't be two Gods because they'd fight. Thanks very much, your Honour.' He turned and raced homeward in case his Honour might change his mind. The little girl looked at her landlord reproachfully. 'You shouldn't have given him a prize for that answer,' she said. 'It is not in the book.'

'I know,' said Roderick apologetically. 'But his prize was not for catechism. It was for logic.' He dropped a half-crown into her pocket and gave another to Adam.

He rode home in good humour, the police forgotten, until he reached the entrance to the bridle road. The peaks of two shakos made a gleam in the twilight. He swerved back and rode in through the main gates.

[1] Plenty of good things.

154

In January, Roderick and young Thomas rode to Dublin for the Liberator's trial. Young Thomas had thought his hero might be driven to the trial in some kind of tumbril. But, in fact, O'Connell approached the court in triumph, seated in the Lord Mayor's coach, surrounded by the city fathers. As he entered the courtroom, the members of the Bar rose to their feet. Young Thomas and the Sir joined the witnesses and spectators in shouting: 'Long live O'Connell and Repeal.'

But they had to quit the trial almost before it began. While listening to arguments over prospective jurors, Roderick noticed his neighbour's son, Hubert De Lacey, making his way towards him through the crowded room. Hubert had a message. It was from Nurse Hogan.

The note read—'Your Honour's Sir. I am not happy about Her Ladyship.' He turned swiftly. His neighbour's son Hubert De Lacey was behind him. Roderick left the court-room with Hubert to question him. His mother, Hubert said, had called on Lady O'Carroll yesterday. The nurse, when she heard that Hubert was coming up to the trials had slipped him this note.

Thought Roderick, as the horses were lashed homeward, I had no right to linger there with Margaret in stark terror! Fighting back incipient madness. Women were known to go mad in childbirth. Or, would there be any hereditary——? There was so little about her that he knew really, before that day when he had been halted by the sight of her, floating over the ice. The scene had enraptured him, the red glow of charcoal braziers burning along the lake side, chestnut roasting, musicians playing violins and mandolins. And Margaret! So lovely, so serene! All he knew was that he had loved her from that moment with a sort of predestined love that had permeated his whole existence ever since. No, there was no hereditary taint. It was Nature itself that had gone mad that night when Margaret's malady had started. The spectacle of the housekeeper's pitiful death in the presence of Margaret's agony would have unhinged a stronger mind. Dr. Mitchell often wondered if Lady O'Carroll could have been struck by a heavy splinter of the massive turret. Anything could have happened to her in that inferno through which poor Sterrin had struggled for the gift of life! And then that Whiteboy raid by the Keating brute!

As he and Thomas approached the gates a scurry of gossoons rose up from the roadway and raced up the avenue. There must

155

be something terrible amiss. He forgot that whenever he returned from Dublin, gossoons were in the habit of wagering their treasures against the first one to catch the carriage sound and reach the castle with the news.

Margaret was haggard and wild-looking. She clung to him speechlessly. Nurse Hogan told him later that there had been a storm the night before Mrs. De Lacey had called. Her Ladyship's palms had bled from the effort to keep calm. 'At last, Sir Roderick,' said the nurse, 'she insisted upon getting up, late and dark as it was. I couldn't stop her. She walked in the park in the open space where there are no trees. She said if the child must come in the storm it would be born where nothing could fall upon its birth or upon its mother. It was terrible, your Honour; to think of a child born in a field like an animal; with respects to you, Sir Roderick, that was why I took the liberty of sending the note by Mr. De Lacey.

'You did quite right,' he told her.

The nurse asked him for the recipe for the brewed leaves of the ground ivy. She couldn't find it, she said, in her Ladyship's herb book.

Roderick had told Margaret nothing about the recipe that his cousins had given him for her malady. He had entered it into his own black record book. When he had scribbled it out for the nurse, she went almost stealthily through the woods and gathered the plant herself; then brewed it in the privacy of her own room. Though she was a scientifically trained Ladies' Nurse-Tender, she appreciated that the illness that attacks the mind must be treated secretly.

In the following days, Roderick went no further from the castle than the estate bounds. Margaret grew more distraught. Every gust of wind that blew across the treeless lawns made her dread a storm that would hurl her travail into some windswept gehenna of desolation. Once, by mistake, Roderick, with a gun under his arm, a brace of dogs at his heels, and Mike O'Driscoll alongside with the shot and powder, crossed into the neighbouring estate. He realised his trespass as he was about to aim at a mallard.

'Go on, your Honour's Sir,' urged Mike, disgusted at seeing his master lower the gun. 'You might as well have a bang as any of the other scoundrels that do be poaching.'

Before his master could assess the significance of the remark, a figure appeared at the foot of the hill and waved.

'It's young Thomas!' cried O'Driscoll. 'Her Ladyship must——'

Roderick made to jump back into his own territory, missed his footing and landed up to his waist in bog. 'Get me out!' he yelled. O'Driscoll tugged futilely while his frenzied master sank deeper.

'You see,' explained O'Driscoll, 'it is always easier to pull a gentleman out of a bog when he falls in head first.'

Roderick, when he eventually surfaced, regretted that he had not the time to push O'Driscoll in head first. 'I'll be more accommodating the next time,' he spluttered as he rushed down the hill. He left pools of water on the bedroom carpet. Margaret looked up startled at the spectacle of the black-faced, grimy apparition that stood over her.

'You don't think that you are going to kiss a freshly accouched lady in *that* condition?' The doctor nodded towards the little powder room. 'Your son is having a bath in there. You ought to join him. You could do with a bath yourself.'

When Thomas returned with the barrels of porter and jars of port wine for the tenants' celebration, he saw Miss Sterrin standing gazing upwards at the flag flying from the turret. He crossed to her side. 'It was I,' he said, 'who raised the flag when you were born.'

She nodded. 'I know. But it was Papa's own self who raised it today. You see this is a more important event.'

'Nonsense. You were the first-born. Your birth was a far more important event.'

'But there were no celebrations.'

Thomas pointed out that there had been a death in the household. 'Poor Mrs. Mansfield!' he sighed. 'It was unfortunate for me that she died then. She knew who I was.' Sterrin looked at him speculatively.

'Do you think you might be a prince in disguise?'

He shook his head. 'I've given up that idea. You see Miss Sterrin, if I were, she would not have put me to clean the knives.'

CHAPTER 19

One early morning the following week, on the way home from Templetown, driving his flour-laden wagon, Thomas saw a crowd gathered on the main street near the Dublin Road. The Scout was there holding a sheaf of papers. Thomas drew rein and watched as the Scout read furiously then looked at his audience.

'Listen to these sacred words!' he cried. 'The Liberator has been sentenced to jail.'

The words that the Scout had picked out were the ones that O'Connell had used to comfort his weeping daughters as he stepped across the threshold of Richmond jail. 'Thank God I am in jail for Ireland.' A woman fell to her knees with a wailing 'Vo, Vo!'

A shop assistant, taking down the shutters of a shop window, tucked up his blue apron and ran with the news to his employers. Next minute he was being helped by other assistants to put back the shutters. Soon every shop in Templetown was closed and shuttered again. The Scout's grief was palatably seasoned with pride as he watched the Repeal flag mount slowly over the Assembly Rooms to ride at half-mast for the 'newses' that the Scout Doyle had brought to Templetown!

Clattering of hooves sounded and the Scout hurried to where the future Lord Cullen, his horses a-foam, was reining to a halt. 'God save Your Honour,' he greeted him.

'God blast you, Doyle,' replied the Honourable Patrick. The moment he sighted the kneeling people he knew that he had been forestalled. He was not the first with news.

It had been like this in Dublin yesterday; people dropping on their knees as the news hit them: regardless of their surroundings. The one who had secured them their liberty to pray in public had lost his own liberty! Their idol, their high priest, now he had become their martyr. Their hereditary sense of tragedy was consummated in this imprisonment.

158

Patrick Cullen and scores of his fellow Young Irelanders had ridden through the night for the honour of being the first with the news to their native towns. The Scout looked at the special copy of *Nation* that Davis had rushed into print—in green ink—the moment sentence had been passed. He repressed a shudder at the thought of how near he had been to the loss of the golden sovereign with which he had bribed a night wagoner to bring him the first news of the verdict—and his fame. Another five minutes and to the Honourable Mister Cullen would have gone the glory of broadcasting the news in a blaze of emerald. 'Green ink!' he gasped. 'Why wasn't I told?'

'An oversight on the part of Mr. Davis, no doubt,' said Patrick sarcastically.

The damned newsmongering shopmaker had crashed his elaborate plans. Along his route he had barely slowed at the gate lodges of a few friends like the Delaneys to send up urgent invitations to dine at Crannagh Abbey that afternoon. Now the Scout was clambering up the fat sides of a big white horse to ride to Kilsheelin Castle.

'Always a white steed for the man who rides forth on high errand,' he was saying to the ostler.

Roderick, a rod on his shoulders, was emerging from the hall door when the Scout came clattering up the front avenue, no less! The Scout was disgusted at the cart-hose which came to a solid stop when its rider hoped to rein it to its fat haunches and send a dramatic spray of gravel over the surge of his news. ' 'Tis well your Honour's Sir is not a Greek noble,' he started off, 'or I should be beheaded for the tidings that I bear.'

His head was still intact when he led his charger to the kitchen door. The staff stood round him, spellbound at his 'newses'. Gradually stable and bar, saddlery and forge emptied into the yard, their occupants crowding the kitchen door and passage. It was the Scout's finest hour. 'They have caged the eagle of Derrynane,' he orated. 'They have silenced the voice that thundered more fiercely than the waves that beat upon his own wild mountain of Coomakishka——' He paused to wipe his eyes. 'Me eyes are wet,' he keened, 'and me throat is dry——' The butler took the hint.

Johnny-the-buckets laid down the laden pails he had held suspended throughout the dramatic oration. For the first time in his brief career he raised his voice in the kitchen councils.

159

'Misther Doyle,' he quavered, 'does that mean that the Penal days will come back? Will we have to hear Mass in caves again?'

Young Thomas drew a large cut potato down from the blade of a knife, then cast it into the pile of cut potatoes at his feet. 'No, o man of the buckets!' he cried, with a brandishing flourish of the knife. 'The Liberator, like the dead Cid, will be stronger than ever in captivity.'

The Scout didn't like to be placed at a disadvantage by having to admit that he didn't know who the dead 'Syd' was. He drained his glass and instead, asked the youth how often would them cut potatoes be used on the knives.

'They'll never again be used,' Thomas informed him. Instead of being downcast like the others he was feeling an inner exaltation. He, alone of them, had touched the outer slopes of this great climax. 'They have served their purpose. This blade,' he said raising it aloft, 'would reject a sullied spud just as a well-bred horse will reject the oats from which it has previously fed.'

Begob, thought the Scout, there's blood in that lad! Aloud he remarked that his ould pig wouldn't reject a 'sullied spud'. He rode home with a sackful of them in front of his white charger.

The castle was in the throes of a great campaign of prayer and devotions. Roderick had invoked its privilege of having Mass celebrated in the oratory. Every morning it was offered for the Liberator's deliverance. Tenants and neighbours came fasting. The congregation overflowed on to the gallery and down the stairs and hallway. Breakfasts went on until early afternoon. When the petition went to the House of Lords the church ordered a special nine-day novena of prayer throughout the land to implore that justice might be done. Sir Roderick gave out the novena prayers at night. Work finished early; workers streamed in and knelt on the lawn below the oratory window. The wagonette load of De Lacey's, instead of going home after the midday breakfast, stayed on for the evening novena so that breakfast ran into dinner. It was like a medieval feast of the church.

The summer days were passed, but the earth still paused on its axis to begin the long descent towards the cold and darkness of winter. Sterrin's young mind was awed by the solemnity of it all. She was strangely moved by the sound of prayer that came

160

in on a murmuring wave through the oratory window. Her ear caught the faint difference in the usual responses. When her papa gave the invocation of the old Gaelic litany, 'Oh greatest of women!'—instead of the usual Guide orainn. 'Pray for us,' the people answered Guide air. 'Pray for him.' When he came to 'Loose the enslaved! Appease for us the Judge with Thy prayers and with Thy intercession!' the familiar words took on a special significance. The voices soared with greater intensity to blend with the same pleas rising from homes and churches throughout the land in a great pyramid of prayer.

In other lands, throughout Europe, in America, the churches offered prayers and masses, but Ireland was a nation on its knees.

For thirty years this man had been the nation's right arm, wresting with it, one after another, Ireland's plundered rights from the flames of an English Parliament lighted to consume them. Statesmen might oppose this petition, lawyers disprove it. *The Times* might scoff, but this kneeling populace, a people cast in an ancient mould, almost without a counterpart in the world, prayed with sublime and simple faith, for a miracle.

On the eve of the close of the novena, the eighth night, the Scout decided to perform his devotions at Kilsheelin. He might pick up a crumb of 'newses' as to how the petition was being received in London.

Towards the end of the litany the man beside him seemed suddenly to be directing his prayers sideways instead of upwards. His elbow seemed to drive them with a holy beat into the Scout's lean ribs. 'Would you mind prayin' upwards,' hissed the exasperated Scout. Another poke and a compelling upward look brought the Scout's eye aloft. 'The flag of privilege!' he gasped. Ireland's ancient flag in the delicate tint called Saint Patrick's blue was being slowly hoisted above the turret.

In the oratory Sterrin thought that her papa was gabbling the prayers. Margaret glanced sideways at him. Never since she had skated with him in Belgium during their romance had she seen him like this; so flushed and boyish. Thomas, emerging from the turret staircase, had to squeeze a space for himself at the entrance to the accompaniment of 'Hush's' and 'Whists'. The prayers were almost over, but he had accomplished his trust. To him, again, had fallen the glory of hoisting the flag that proclaimed a great occasion. His responses were mechanical as

161

he waited for the announcement that would explain the quick, secret command issued to him as the Sir hurried past him from the library to the oratory.

Sir Roderick was almost breathless as he rose from his knees and strode to the open window. 'Tomorrow,' he called to the kneeling throng, 'will be the last day of this special devotion offered for the success of this petition that has gone to the House of Lords. Tomorrow,' he cried on a louder note, 'our prayers will be offered in thanksgiving, because'—he paused—'the Liberator has been set free!'

He put out a hand to quell the uproar and told them not to leave without refreshments. Behind him, Phineas De Lacey, still on his knees, held his face in his hands to conceal the tears. A few minutes later he was dancing a slip jig on the gallery. Sterrin, instead of being lighted to bed, was lighted by torchlights to the great pyramid of branches that awaited the ceremonial kindling from the taper that young Thomas handed to her papa.

CHAPTER 20

Roderick was glad when all the fanfaronade had subsided. Now maybe he could get down to the business of the estate, and find some time to spend with Dominic, his newborn son.

Black Pat had been on to him to let him buy a blood horse he had spoken of selling. Roderick had doubts. It was a horse for a gentleman—and at a gentleman's price. Still, for old times' sake, he supposed he would have to let Black Pat have it at his own price!

Roderick's thoughts went back to childhood when he had fostered under Black Pat's roof. Even then Black Pat had been fearless with horses. And it would seem that his foster-brother's little runaway bride was fearless that way too.

Roderick had been astounded to find a reference to Black Pat's bride in his father's black book, of all places! The girl had been the daughter of well-to-do people in the South Riding. When they could not persuade her to marry the rich suitor of their choice they called in the parish priest to add the weight of his influence. While the parents were receiving the priest she slipped through a window and made off on the priest's horse to Black Pat.

A runaway marriage was something to talk of for nine days of wonder. But to run away on the priest's horse! That had been something to whisper about in dread. Supposing, went the whisper, that the priest had needed his horse for some sudden and sacred purpose! Rumour strengthened the 'supposing' into a fact. Someone *had* died without a priest, it stated, because of the girl's profane act. Her family had written her off. There would be no record of having the manuscript that chronicled her family's history from one generation to another.

But Sir Dominic had recorded her in his book when she married his tenant. Her high spirits had intrigued him. And because of his strong sense of the tie of fosterage, he had given an attractive farm to Black Pat. Under the details of tenancy he

163

had written, 'I trust that its heritage will recompense his little wife Nonie—for the fine heritage she has abandoned in the cause of love.'

Roderick, too, had been intrigued—and annoyed! Fancy Black Pat being the hero of such rich romance! Extraordinary that he had never mentioned anything of it to him! Roderick could scarcely realise the extent to which he had grown up and away from the little boy who used to trot like an affectionate puppy at the heels of Black Pat. Nor, that his remote and arrogant mien was intimidating to the tenants who had been accustomed to the affability of his father.

He decided to ask Black Pat for her maiden name and fill it in the blank.

He turned the pages back. So much of his father came through the flowing handwriting. There were several references to Malachy. His father had set great store by the fosterage tie. Malachy had been the son of the house where he had fostered until he was eight years old. He seemed to have kept up the link with him until Malachy left to join the Austrian army. 'I had no shame,' he wrote, 'for the tears I shed at parting with my dear foster-brother.' Further on Roderick read the record of Malachy's death in Austria. Underneath, his father had inscribed the old Gaelic saying—'Dear to a man is his brother; but his foster-brother is the marrow of his heart.'

There was a knock and Hegarty admitted George Lucas to pay his rent.

'I brought it before,' he explained, 'but your Honour was—absent.'

Roderick noticed the deliberate hesitation. No other tenant would have used the word. It savoured of 'absenteeism'.

'Your Honour!'

'What is it?' Roderick was making out the receipt. He felt ashamed of his own brusquerie.

'Herself was wondering that Miss Sterrin hadn't called to see her new little foster-sister.'

'Her what?'

'Aye, foster-sister. Near two months she is now.'

Blast the fellow's impudence! To claim the kinship of fosterage because his wife had been Sterrin's wet nurse!

'... But his foster-brother is the marrow of his heart!' Roderick couldn't imagine the 'Darraghadheal' being the marrow of any man's heart. Coldly he yielded to tradition. 'I'm sure that her Ladyship will arrange for Miss Sterrin to visit the infant.'

Margaret was contrite when she heard about the new baby. She was anxious not to offend any customs. Her Papa used to tell them such droll things in Antwerp about the farmhouse in County Clare when *his* father had been fostered! 'And I cannot go today. I am—what is it, head upon heels? All this excitement.'

Roderick looked at her. She was holding her own baby son, Dominic. Her gazelle eyes were sheening with vibrancy. Excitement suited her. Life could be stolid in Antwerp. It wasn't all ice skating!

'Don't worry,' he said. 'The fellow had a cheek to remind me. Let Sterrin drive that way with the new governess. It will soothe them to have her call so promptly.'

As the pony phaeton was approaching Ryan's, Black Pat rode towards them at a sauntering canter, his pipe in the corner of his mouth. He doffed his hat to them and Sterrin impishly doffed her bonnet. Black Pat always made her feel mischievous. He looked at her uncovered head with the most comical consternation, then wheeled round and went pelting back.

There was not time to query his strange behaviour because it had caused the pony to bolt. By the time it had quietened they had reached Lucas's. Lucas was not so soothed by the visit as her Papa had suggested. He felt it a slight that it was an employee, however genteel, who had accompanied Miss Sterrin. He liked to boast to people that he was the foster-father of Sir Roderick O'Carroll's child. When he married her wet nurse he had envisioned perquisites and gifts.

The baby, Sterrin informed her mamma later, was like a halfpenny orange. 'Not even a penny one?' asked her papa. 'By the way,' he went on, 'did you happen to see Black Pat?' When she told him about his strange behaviour he rode down prepared to tell him that he had changed his mind about the horse. The sound of a violin playing 'Love's Young Dream' came to him as he rode into his foster-brother's yard.

Black Pat was all apologies. 'But sure, Sir Rody, everyone knows that if a body meets up with a redhaired woman on the way to make a deal there is nothing for it but to turn straight back.'

'What the devil ...!' From behind him a clear voice interrupted. 'It is most unbecoming of Pat to speak in such a way of your daughter, Sir Roderick.'

A tiny figure had appeared at the doorway. It was Mrs. Black Pat. A green cloak, hastily donned, was being tied at the neck with a green velvet bow. The voice, in clear and faultless diction, was emerging from the depths of the velvet-lined hood that almost covered the wearer's face. As she crossed the yard towards him the flash of her shoe buckle made a ripple in the symphony of the greens she wore; green leather shoes, green cloak; deeper green in the velvet that banded hem and hood. Something of woodland occurred to him as he saluted her; no brim-touching, but a full uncovering with a sweep that he had scarcely thought to make towards Black Pat Ryan's wife. 'Such silly superstition!' she said and proceeded to run her hand over his mount in the most expert manner. He might as well not have been there!

'I hope,' Roderick said coolly, 'that you don't think this is the horse that I am selling to your husband.' The hood didn't turn but the voice inside said just as coolly, 'Of course not! This beauty is something too special for *our* barnyard.'

'Hmph!' He thought. 'You seem a bit too special yourself for this barnyard!' He wondered if she, too, were a beauty; but short of bending down and peering inside the green twilight of her hood there was no way of knowing. Anyway it did not matter. He was feeling strangely rasped.

It did not help his mood, when, as he entered the house for the drink that must ratify the sale, a potato came flying out and barely missed his eye. The culprit came forward and chucked down a black curly forelock in salute. He was the chubby little boy whose logic had once earned him a half-crown from Roderick. 'It wasn't you I aimed to hit, your Honour,' he assured his father's overlord. 'It was Norisheen.' His sister rose from the music box she was playing in the parlour and curtsied. 'Adam,' she informed Roderick, 'could not hit a haystack.' She made a quick escape and left him alone with the tinkling strains of 'Love's Young Dream'.

Shiny objects highlighted the gloom of the long, narrow room: a trinket box in chased silver on the cabinet; heavy silver candlesticks on the mantelpiece. Trifling but unexpected. And most unexpected were the water colours. The shimmer of their

166

gilt frames drew his eyes. Egad! How did such artistry come to be on Black Pat's walls? From the end of the room a duet of children's voices informed him that the pictures had been painted by their mammy. Roderick turned in time to see two small nightclad figures who had been peeping at him from an end room. Immediately they jumped back on to a huge feather mattress and proceeded to turn somersaults.

Their father came in with the whiskey and explained that they had the chincough. 'Aye,' he went on as Roderick continued to study the paintings, 'herself drew them. A great notion she has for drawin' and colourin' and the like.' He said it as though they were something to be indulged and dismissed like the chincough.

Again Roderick was conscious of that rasped sensation. But just then he heard an alarmed stamping from the direction of the hitching post. He dashed to it in time to see Norisheen slide down the offside of his precious filly and vanish through the hedge. He had sprung into the saddle before he realised that it was Mrs. Ryan who was holding the bridle; in spite of his anger he was amazed to see how strangely quiet and timid the animal had gone under her soothing pats. Normally it would still be performing a dance of terror on its hind legs.

'Do please forgive us; all of us, Sir Roderick!' A white cheek came out from the hood and rubbed itself on the animal's velvet muzzle. 'I can't think,' said the voice from under the horse's neck, 'how that child came to take such an outrageous liberty.'

He had a suspicion that she was laughing at him. 'Can't you?' he exclaimed crisply. He jerked the horse's head round and the white cheek beneath it disappeared into its hood the way a snail's head vanishes into its shell at the approach of a human. 'Trot, Mammy; trot, foal!' he flung back at her over his shoulder. At the gate he turned back. She was still standing there. Like a miniature in a green plush frame, he thought! He had intended complimenting her upon her artistic skill. To atone for his brusqueness he doffed his hat in a high sweep and rode out, musing upon this highly individual household. Too demned individual—its juvenile members—and—— Suddenly his smile tightened. The darraghadheal, he thought, and nodded casually.

George Lucas uncovered to his landlord but the black eyes held no friendship; only the blue-green shimmer of the beetle.

The darraghadheal had been observing the friendly visit his neighbour had received from the Sir. Black Pat's roars of laughter; the child's easy familiarity. Mounting the Sir's horse, no less! There were landlords who would evict for the like. This was the kind of association he had visualised when he married the foster-nurse of the Sir's child. The Sir sweeping off his hat to Black Pat's wife as though she were a very grand lady!

Black Pat Ryan, the little man argued bitterly to himself as he gazed after the arrogant figure on the superb horse, was after all only the nephew of the Sir's foster-mother. Not her own child, as his was the child of Miss Sterrin O'Carroll's foster-mother; and the recognition she gets—on this same day that the Sir himself visits his foster-brother—is a prim call from a patronising bitch of a governess!

Roderick rode on, oblivious of the thoughts that were twisting the mind of this newcomer to his estate who saw himself as a 'millteoir orda'.[1] He basked in the gentle warmth of Saint Martin's summer; golden weather, soft and silent. A film of mist lay on the Devil's Bit. All day in the woods flakes of gold fell gently, making a golden carpet beneath a golden canopy.

Tenants looked up as Sir Roderick passed and halted the stroke of the flail to give him a 'Dia agat'. This was the finest hour of the year. Their hearts rejoiced at the spectacle of land pleasantly burdened with the produce of their toil; gardens of stubble covered with 'shocks' of wheat, oats and barley; fields of potatoes where the pits full packed were already raised. There was a silence about Golden Meadows that proclaimed an early harvest saved and stored and the family off with their neighbours, the Ulick Prendergasts and the Campions, to their lodges at Tramore for the sea water. Never had Roderick seen the thatched roofs look so attractive. There was Black Pat again working his field. But what on earth was he up to?

Black Pat was standing in front of his spade that stood upright in the ground. For a moment he stood that way, motionless. Then he doffed his hat skywards, spat on either hand, rubbed them together, then plunged the spade deep into the earth. Roderick waited tensed, sharing with his foster-brother this moment of homely drama. Black Pat was performing the opening ceremony of his potato harvest. And it was a

[1] Brother to the Great.

good one. He raised the first stalk high and shook from it a shower of potatoes. Roderick spurred onwards with a sense of gladness.

As he cantered home, he realised that he had forgotten to ask Black Pat for his wife's maiden name for the record book. Whoever she was, he thought as he hummed the tune, his foster-brother had captured a prize. Roderick had the impression that Black Pat was being deliberately reticent about his wife. He never presumed on the old association and now it looked as though he was reluctant to foist his wife's superiority upon the notice of his landlord. An independent devil!

'Love's Young Dream' beat the rhythm of his homeward canter. It must have been Black Pat's wife who had been playing the violin! When young Thomas came to take his horse the Sir was humming ... 'when my dream of life from morn till night, was love, still love.'

Sterrin came through a wicket gate with her governess. He asked her what she had learned that morning and regretted the query. 'Love's Young Dream' retreated before the flow of her learning. There were, she told him, nine hundred and fifty-two publications in Great Britain. A new kind of beehive had been invented—and, oh yes, Sterrin had also learned the exact day upon which the snake emerges from its winter sleep.

Miss Ferguson-Coyne found her employer's obvious amazement flattering. 'I feel,' she said, 'that the study of nature is most broadening to the mind of a child.' An overhead whirring made him look up. Sterrin sent a long whistle skywards. The governess was shocked. 'Ladies don't whistle.' Sterrin looked at her curiously, 'What other way could one call to a jack snipe?'

Roderick followed the course of the snipe until they disappeared into the wood, 'Yes, Miss Ferguson-Coyne,' he said at last, 'the study of nature is indeed broadening to the mind.' He gestured towards the golden woods. '... earth crammed with heaven and every common bush afire with God; but only he who sees takes off his shoes.' He looked lazily through long lashes at the confused blue-stocking. 'The snake must be one of those who "sees". He *does* take off his skin. Doesn't he?'

The governess took Sterrin's hand. 'It is getting chilly out here.'

Her employer looked after her. 'I'll wager it is chilly!' He chuckled. It must be! 'For a woman who studies the undressing habits of snakes.' From under the horse's head came a suppressed snort. Roderick had forgotten the knife boy. He wheeled. 'If you have digested your nature study, my lad, take that filly around to the stables.'

The year's procession moved on until it caught up with Little Christmas. Margaret and Roderick were going to a whist party at De Lacey's. It would be Margaret's first outing since the birth of Dominic. There would be carpet dancing as well and games and forfeits—and feasting! Margaret shuddered pleasantly at the thought of the De Lacey menus. Their dining-room suggested a butcher's stall to her. Only that the carcasses were cooked and they sprawled from under silver cover dishes instead of hanging from hooks.

But the gaily repressed shudder at the sight of roasts was different from that which convulsed her when the winds blew about the castle on the feast of the Epiphany. Every gust and scurry presaged a recurrence of the night that Sterrin was born. People overlooked the fact that Little Christmas was Sterrin's birthday. It was the anniversary of the ordeal that her Ladyship endured over Miss Sterrin. For poor Sterrin it was a day of undefined guilt. Every time her mamma tapped the barometer or dropped something or stifled a scream Sterrin knew that it was because of something terrible that she—Sterrin—had in some way, caused to happen on this day to her own mamma!

But on this particular birthday she was summoned to the hall door and there was Big John leading a Connemara pony up and down.

The mountainy man who brought her said something about the pony having fairy blood; Big John couldn't follow the man's Connaught gaelic.

It was with reluctance that Sterrin accompanied her parents to the party. Normally she would have been delighted. Mrs. De Lacey had sent a last-minute request that she be brought as she had abandoned the idea of sending Bunzy and the younger ones to bed. Every bedroom would be occupied by overnight guests. Last year every step of the stairs and upper corridor had been a 'sit-outery' for couples. The youngsters hadn't slept a wink; nor tried to.

The mountainy man had made another sale. Immediately Sterrin arrived at Kilincarrig Lodge she was led out to the stables in an aura of mystery and lanthorn light. Bunzy's new pony was bigger than Sterrin's. 'But that,' Sterrin suggested, 'is probably because it is pure mortal. Mine has fairy blood.'

'If that be so,' Bunzy said, 'your pony can't be a thoroughbred.' Sterrin didn't like the sound of that at all. The infusion of fairy blood made her pony a more rarefied thoroughbred! 'No ordinary thoroughbred could catch up on a fairy pony. It would leave them all behind,' she argued.

'But supposing,' said the logical Bunzy, 'that it left them so far behind that it never came back? Supposing,' she whispered with awful solemnity and holding the lanthorn close to Sterrin's face, 'that it were to vanish with you on its back?'

Sterrin preferred not to consider the supposition. She shivered. 'It is cold out here.' But inside in the glow of the candle-lit hall her courage returned. Her mamma was crowing with laughter as Mr. De Lacey strained on tiptoes to kiss her under the mistletoe. A big blue punch bowl, the biggest Sterrin had ever seen, was steaming on a wainscoted seat inside the hall door. Every new arrival had to sample it before removing a stitch of wrapping. Whether the punch was lowered willingly or under good-humoured coercion the tone of the night was established. Hilarity began on the threshold.

One didn't have to pretend to be cold to cover one's fear in this bright warm din of music and chatter and protective grown-ups, all of them happy; some of them in fits laughing at being forced to swallow a 'toshkeen' or to yield a kiss under the mistletoe! 'Besides,' said Sterrin blandly resuming their discussion in the pony stall, 'I don't believe in fairies.' Not just now!

'Be careful!' Bunzy hissed into her ear. 'Red-headed children are not safe from the fairies until they are seven.' And suddenly Sterrin was conscious of freedom from the lifelong fear. 'They can't touch me ever again. I'm seven tonight!'

Winter lingered too long like a guest that has outworn its welcome. In early March the mountains were still clothed in dazzling white and the pale spring sunlight fell about them like a vesture of gold. 'Mountains,' Roderick told Sterrin, 'are never more sublime than when wrapped in snow.'

He held her leading rein as they skirted the ploughlands, and while he trained her to ride he imbued in her the love and the lore of the land. Everywhere the lesser farmers were rushing to get the last drill closed before Saint Patrick's day. He slowed and watched the seed fall gently into his beloved soil, to be held in tender consummation until the harvest. 'Only there, Gra' gal,' he said, 'lies true fulfilment.'

Saint Patrick's Eve was a raw day. In the afternoon as Roderick approached Black Pat's on the homeward ride, Sterrin far behind him, a group of girls ran with a scurry of laughter across the road and into the house. Suddenly he slowed and frowned. A cordon of green wool was stretched in a barrier across the tiny road. If he hadn't slowed in time the horse might have taken fright!

This Ryan Dhuv household would need to have its 'vivre' toned down! 'Will you kindly remove this demned thing!' he called out. Alarmed squeals sounded behind the topiaried hedge. There was a further scurry as the girls rushed to the door. Before it closed he heard an unmistakable voice urge them to go on back and 'claim their footing'!

Footing! His frown was chased by a smile. Not since he was a child had he seen the green thread across the road on Saint Patrick's Eve and the spinning girls claiming a shilling for 'footing'. If the stranger were handsome he was let pass on the forfeit of a kiss. His father had always paid with a kiss; and his progress on Saint Patrick's Eve had been slow. There were always a lot of green barriers in Sir Dominic's path.

A small figure came out of the house. 'They have no courage, Sir Roderick,' said Mrs. Ryan.

'Who are they?' he asked. She told him they were friends on a visit for the Holy Day. He didn't catch what she said. He was thinking that it was difficult to believe that this immature little figure had produced one child; much less six! Instead of the matron's high-cauled cap she wore a dainty babet; just like the ones Margaret wore. For the first time he saw her face. High cheek bones, long eyes demurely veiled, a pointed chin. They sketched a picture in his memory. Scarcely a picture, an impression, of prick-eared laughing fauns flitting through trees. He couldn't be mistaken, no one else could claim those woodland hazel eyes. The memory of that magic moment so many years ago came flooding back. 'So it's you!' he said softly.

She lifted the long lashes slowly. A wicked gleam slipped out. 'Fancy your remembering me!'

'I——' He was about to say that he had wondered what had become of her after that day in the hunting field! Better say nothing. Let the encounter go on lying in the tomb of memory.

He went on looking into her eyes. Yes, there were still three colours in their depth. Woodland colours. The green of leaves in a brown pool; blue from the faint reflection of bluebells on its brink.

She held up her hand. 'The shilling! I'll collect it for them, though they don't deserve it.'

He dropped back the shilling he had been drawing from his pocket. 'I haven't got a shilling. You must collect the forfeit instead.'

She looked up at him, dainty and cool as a goldfish. 'There is no necessity for you to pay forfeit on this road.' This was his own road. Narrow and rough, and rugged—and proud!

And the 'footing' was for handsome strangers. Like the one in the hunting field. So, she thought, he remembered! It had been like a caress when he had lifted her after she had fallen from her horse. And when he had dropped on his knee to let her remount it had seemed like an act of homage.

She looked at the green ball in her hand. What had prompted her to his folly? 'I'll remove it.' She started to roll up the ball.

He seized her wrist. 'Now, who has no courage?' She pressed her face into the horse's cheek. Did he think to snatch a kiss from a wayside wench! She'd let him see!

But all that she let him see above the velvet muzzle was one eye charged with provocative deviltry. He jerked up Thuckeen's head and brought down his own.

The kiss lasted through an eternity of seconds. There had not been enough time in Nonie's life to discover that a kiss could be so overpowering and yet so gentle. Pat's kisses had never caused this tumult.

When she thought it had subsided she looked up. But it had swept the colours in her eyes together and tossed them to the surface. It requires an artist to mix colours; something like that was his impression. It wasn't a conscious boast. But it was so obvious that Black Pat was no artist.

He has availed of his landlord's privilege, she thought, and murmured, '*Droit de seigneur*.' She dropped him a mock curtsey. 'I'm honoured—your Honour!'

He frowned. He felt rasped again; the same feeling he had known the day he had sold them the horse. But now as he looked at the porcelain figurine with the honey gold hair he

173

recognised the feeling for what it was; the irritation that an artist feels at the spectacle of a lovely picture crudely framed.

'Blame yourself! Briseann an ducas tre suleann an cat,' he said and soared over the cordon. He couldn't wait for her to wind up the demned worsted. He had to ride those dangerous currents out of his veins.

Behind her there was a clattering as Black Pat rode into the yard. He called her name but she took no notice. Why had Sir Roderick quoted that Gaelic saying. 'Nature breaks out through the eyes of a cat'?

'I didn't expect that from you, Nonie.' The gravel-voiced constriction in Pat's voice made her turn at last. She scrutinised the lean dark features. He was wearing his good broadcloth for the evening's festivities. He did justice, she thought, to well-cut clothes; lithe and well knit; sat his fine horse with the same easy grace as his aristocratic foster-brother. The grace but not the graces! She turned and looked after the receding horseman. There rode all the grace of life that had been envisaged in the romantic heart of the girl who had eloped with Black Pat.

'And I didn't expect it from Rody O'Carroll either.'

'Didn't you, Pat?' she answered him at last, in a funny, quiet little voice. 'But people are never quite what they are expected to be. Neither is life.' He felt that her eyes, so unusually bright, were looking through and beyond him. If she saw him at all, it was to take his measure with the man whose kiss had made her eyes look as they did.

Suddenly they became aware of him. 'Don't be so serious, Pat duv,' she cried and her voice had resumed its normal brightness. 'It was the girl inside who tied the wool across the road. I've never seen the custom before—of course, we lived quite a good stretch in from the road.'

'Aye,' he said and the gravel still dried his voice, 'there was an avenue between you and the road.'

Sterrin rode towards her papa and asked him what was the green thing across the road. He suppressed the inclination to tell her that little girls should be seen and not heard.

'I suppose,' she reflected when he had explained the old custom, 'that those kind of people would prefer the shilling to a kiss.'

Those kind of people! Little Oenone, elegant, poised, accomplished; overflowing with that elusive, indefinable quality of feminine allure. How many shillings in the dowry she had spurned for love's kiss?

'Which would you prefer? The kiss or the shilling?'

'The shilling, of course,' she said hopefully.

For the second time the same shilling was pondered in his fingers, then dropped. No bribery, he decided.

They turned into the Sir's road. Over the gap in the wall they could see the 'garconnerie' led by young Thomas picking baskets of shamrocks.

'You won't need that much,' she called.

'Won't we?' said Thomas who hadn't glimpsed the Sir. 'All the Delaney young ladies have arrived and a carriageful of De Laceys and——' Sterrin gave a cry of delight as she spied Bunzy riding towards her on her Connemara pony.

'Mamma allowed me to ride with Hubert behind the carriage and she says that I can stay the night if I am asked.'

Roderick popped his head over the wall. 'Well,' he gasped in mock amazement. 'If it isn't little Miss Bunzy. Let us hope that you are going to do us the honour of staying over for the feast-day.' Bunzy gasped out an excited assurance then galloped off to inform her mamma that she had been invited to stay.

Margaret was entertaining Saint Patrick's Day celebrants in the drawing-room. Roderick made his way to the library by the back and took down the book of records. The excited tingling in his finger made him riffle the pages. Here it was! The entry about Black Pat's lease. '...and I trust that its heritage will compensate his little wife, Nonie ... for the heritage that she has abandoned in the cause of love'.

What kind of pompous sentiment was that for his father to record? The heritage of a little wayside farmhouse and a half-dozen brats fathered by a rustic. And what kind of a lady had she been? Where was her fastidiousness? Galloping off after the fellow. He caught sight of himself in a mirror. And she galloped in the opposite direction from you! *You* had to do the galloping after *her*! What the devil am I talking about? He closed the book with a snap and got to his feet. Then sat down again and opened it and filled in her surname in the space left by his father; Mansfield. It looked strange there, the solitary word in its green ink that was a conceit of Davis's for Repeal Year; and the Nonie didn't suit it. Probably a crudity of Black Pat's. But it suited *Her*; pert, provocative! Very painstakingly he squeezed

175

in over the surname the name that he had taken care to ascertain after the hunting incident—Oenone. Miss Oenone Mansfield! And now she was Nonie Black Pat Ryan. The distinctive name looked as strange, pushed in there between the rather faded lines of his father's writing as its owner had looked down in the little farmhouse in her green gown, staring out at him from those marvellous eyes. He closed the book with a snap. What the devil had the love ramifications of his tenants got to do with *him*? He was making too much about a seasonable kiss; footing or mistletoe or whatever it was! Whatever it was it still made a tingling on his lips as he went to meet his guests.

At the drawing-room door he stopped amazed. This was something different from the usual Saint Patrick's Eve celebrations. A batch of Delaney girls came round him, all sporting the usual streams of green ribbon from shoulders to hem. But it was the gentlemen who had given him the sudden impression of splendour.

Patrick Cullen in the elegant uniform suggested by Davis to attract the young nobility to Repeal's '*corps d'elite*' was leading forward Lord Templetown's son and heir resplendent in the new uniform.

'They make me feel positively dowdy,' said Fiona De Lacey. Her father assured her that she would feel dowdier still by the time that he had paid the tailor for Hubert's uniform.

'Forty-five guineas for the jacket alone. Me! who has not had a new suit since I was married!'

Roderick linked his arm and drew him towards the mether cup for the ceremonial drowning of the shamrock.

'Don't worry, Phineas,' he said. 'You'll get it all back on the first wave of Repeal.'

CHAPTER 21

The grain harvest that Fall had been a plenteous one. Soon it would be potato-digging time, the 'poor man's harvest'. Roderick rode down to see Black Pat. He slowed to look across a hedge at Black Pat's mare. It was in foal by the thoroughbred he had sold them. A fine mare. They had a profit-making strain there.

When he rode out on to their roadway he heard violin music from the house. It had a happy sound. The life she had chosen must hold for her some meaning. Was there meaning he wondered in that tune she had chosen? 'Love's Young Dream' again. Because he was tempted to linger he touched his spurs to his mount and pressed on. 'No,' he hummed, 'that hallowed form is ne'er forgot. Which first love traced...' He broke off. If that hallowed form down there in the field was Black Pat's, it was behaving deucedly extraordinary!

Black Pat was running from one drill to the next digging a few stalks and tossing them aside. Then he jumped across more drills and started to dig like a maniac. Roderick set his mount to the hedge and cantered up the headland. Black Pat, completely oblivious of his landlord's presence, flung stalk after stalk from his spade, then with a sobbing gasp he flung the spade from him in a wide sweep.

It landed at the horse's feet. The animal reared up on its hind legs and almost unseated Roderick. Black Pat turned to the spectacle of the great horse plunging high and menacing above him. 'The Black Horseman!' he screamed. 'Vo, Vo! The Black Horseman that rides across the land scattering Pestilence and Death and Starvation!'

Down in the opening, as he knelt over the drills Roderick saw heaps of black, slimy mess. They were the fruits of the healthy, firm potatoes he had seen go down in this field on Saint Patrick's Eve ... He averted his head from the stench.

Black Pat was feeling ashamed of his outburst. He held the

177

bridle while Sir Roderick mounted and at last he found voice to say in Gaelic. 'The dogs have not eaten up the end of the year.' Roderick assured him that he would not see him short. A good thing that the castle crop was so good! O'Driscoll had turned up a few stalks this morning for a preview of the crop. They had been laden with the finest potatoes. It looked as if there might be need of them all; if there were other cases like Black Pat's.

He reached the Cobs where his own potato fields lay. 'Good God!' He flung himself from the horse. 'Those leaves have the same spots as Ryan's.'

The leaves that had bloomed green and healthy in the morning looked now as if acid had been poured on them. He pulled up a stalk. It shrivelled in his hand. Even while he held it the potatoes blackened and melted!

He sprang on to a bank and called some workmen to bring spades. They dug as madly as had Black Pat. The results were the same. What had been firm tubers this morning were now a putrid mess. Was this another trick of nature? Like the one that had deprived him of his field. 'By God! She won't trick me again!' he said aloud.

The men looked at each other. But that was their last idle moment. All night the torches blazed in the potato fields. Indoor and outdoor staff worked like fiends. In the lurid glare their faces reminded young Thomas glancing up from his spade, of the fiends in the illustrations of the 'Inferno' in the library, driving their tripods into hell's flames. But these were desperate men fighting with unrelenting spades the evil force that threatened from the earth. The scene reminded Margaret of the time in her childhood when she had been visiting in Holland and had seen men fighting back the sea from the gorged dykes.

By morning one quarter of the crop was saved. The rest was corruption. It was disaster for the tenants.

At Christmas, after Roderick had added potatoes to the tenants' usual gift of meat, there was none left for his own family. Perhaps, after Saint Stephen's Day, he would ride over to Queen's County and purchase a few tons of Mr. Delaney's famous 'Queen's County Champions'.

Hounds met on Kilsheelin's lawn on Saint Stephen's morning. The mist-enshrouded symphony of creaking and jinglings and yaps livened to the gay exchange of greetings. Carriages kept streaming up the avenue. The dereliction of the potato field gave way to the gaiety of the hunting field. Roderick, in the act of pouring a stirrup cup for Lord Templetown, stopped suddenly. 'Egad!' exclaimed his Lordship. 'What a pair! What a matched pair! Whose turnout is it, Sir Roderick?' An imposing-looking equipage was whirring up the avenue followed by a pair of grooms with a blanketed horse apiece.

Roderick peered with flagon suspended. A small figure in mulberry stepped down and opened the door with a flourish. The outline of the lady who emerged was sculpted in the perfection of her riding habit.

'God save you, Roddy!' she called. 'I see that I am in time for the stirrup juice.'

Roderick offered the flagon and doffed his hunting cap. 'By the piper that played before Moses, if it isn't Mrs. Delaney.'

'I don't blame your surprise, Roddy,' she said. 'It is not often that we take the moths from the carriage. I thought we would pay you proper respect for a change. And—I have a small favour to ask.'

Roderick sketched an elaborate bow. 'You have but to name it.'

She waved away the mounting block and sprang into the saddle. 'Oh,' she said offhandedly. 'I only want you to sell me a few tons of spuds.'

'Is that all?'

'Be careful there, Roddy. You're spilling the wine. Yes, that's all.'

After the hunt Mrs. Delaney canvassed every gentleman of her acquaintance for potatoes. But they all had the same story. Their potatoes had failed. Lord Cullen had fared worst. He had saved his entire crop sound. But when the pits had been opened at Christmas to distribute potatoes among the tenants, there wasn't a sound one there. They had rotted in the pits. 'And they were perfect going in. My steward graded them meticulously.'

They trotted round to the front of the castle. Mrs. Appleyard was being helped from her mount by a military groom. 'Oh la!' she cried. 'What solemn faces! Whatever can you gentlemen be discussing?'

'Just potatoes, dear lady,' said Lord Templetown getting stiffly from his saddle.

'Potatoes!' shrilled Mrs. Kennedy-Sherwin. 'What a dull

179

topic.'

'Conversation, dear lady, is always dull when gentlemen are left together. It will brighten now under the radiance of your presence.' His tone was like a chuck under the chin.

She purred. It only needed well-trimmed compliments to bring her into full sparkle after the excitement of the hunt. 'Flatterer!' she cooed. 'And anyway there are lots more interesting vegetables. Myself, I prefer artichokes.'

'Ah, but what an adorably selective palate,' piped in Lord Cullen.

The delighted little flirt noticed that even the unassailable Sir Roderick was smiling at her. Quite a conquest.

His smile was for his thoughts. What would Black Pat say if he were to suggest artichokes to him? Or, better still. Asparagus! And then he recalled that Black Pat had a wife who had not always been beyond the possibility of—asparagus, who still retained an allure more subtle than this little siren's. Better not draw *that* covert! 'Papa!' Sterrin galloped up all excitement. 'The Wren Boys are coming!'

Up the avenue, to the music of fiddles and bagpipes came the traditional Saint Stephen's Day procession of youths and girls. The grotesque 'Omadhawn', a sack over his body with holes for his arms, his face masked like the jester of medieval processions, kept order by capering about and belabouring everyone with a cow's bladder tied to a stick. 'The wren, the wren, the king of all birds,' they chanted. 'On Saint Stephen's Day was caught in the furse. Although he is little; his family is great. Rise up Lords and Ladies and give us a treat!'

Roderick lightened as he led them inward for the usual reception. The blight of the potatoes had not blighted their spirits. He could still remember how proud he had felt as a small boy trotting up the avenue in the wake of the Wren boys with Black Pat; he felt just as awed as the others at the castle's grandeur. Consciousness of the knowledge that he was its heir had not dawned; only consciousness of the fact that he alone of the small boys who ran in the wake of the procession was privileged by the leader to be let carry the holly branch that held the wren.

It was held now by John Holohan who had carried the Templetown banner so high at Tara's meeting. The ladies' eyes ranged interestedly over his six feet five inches. A scarlet sash was draped bandillero fashion across his shoulders. When he removed his ribbon-decked hat, his hair sprang out in thick rings about his forehead.

'All he needs,' murmured Mrs. Kennedy-Sherwin, 'is a toga.'

'Must you be so classically blue-stocking?' drawled her friend.

Dominic Landy, the Omadhawn, signalled the musicians and marshalled his followers into dance formation. John Holohan laid aside his holly bush and bowed before Lady O'Carroll for the honour of leading her out.

'How delightfully arcadian!' said Mrs. Appleyard to Lieutenant Fitzharding-Smith.

'And,' said Mrs. Kennedy-Sherwin, 'she needs neither hounds nor huntsmen to draw her coverts.'

The Lieutenant looked longingly towards the lady of his hopeless devotion. 'Lady O'Carroll is more shepherdess than huntress,' he sighed.

'And you,' said Mrs. Kennedy-Sherwin, 'are more sheep than huntsman.'

He sprang to his feet. 'Lady fair, were a gentleman to make that statement I should call him out. I demand that you give me satisfaction by allowing me to *lead* you out.'

Roderick gave his hand to a golden-haired girl in a scarlet cloak. When she laid aside her cloak and moved into the centre of the hall there was something like a gasp. Her hair cascaded in golden waves down to the first frill of her gown. Lieutenant Fitzharding-Smith hummed the aria from Handel. 'And the glory of golden hair.' Margaret was minded of the kneeling Magdalen.

When the food was served, Roderick noticed that things were different with the gay dancers and mummers. The flush of the dance receding from John Holohan's face left it white and thin. The same with all the others. Their faces all too pallidly etched. They were showing the shortage of potatoes. Some of these six-footers would eat two dozen twice a day.

To Sterrin's surprise the ponyman from the mountain appeared again a month later. He had no ponies; just two wild-looking boys and three little girls who shivered together under the shawl for which their mother had no further need.

They told Mrs. Stacey about the shawl as they sat huddled in the chimney nook gazing with awe at the row of fires. Eight fires! Blazing separately and sending separate spirals of smoke up the vast chimney; as vast as six of their native cabins put together.

The praties had gone black in the ground. Attracta the oldest, had told her; just as they had on everyone else in the parish. Then the landlord, Lord Campbell who had been absent in England so long that none of the children had ever seen him, decided to come back. Lady Campbell was bringing thirty guests and the mountain was wanted for a shoot. So the tenants houses had to be knocked down. Mameen had been sick and when the police and bailiff came on Christmas Eve to put them out, Attracta had pleaded with them to let mameen stay the night and the rest would go. There was a wild storm blowing in from the Atlantic; terrible sleet and rain. One could hear the souls in purgatory crying in the wind.[1] But mameen had to get out.

Daddy carried her down the track to the foot of the hill and she was still in sight of the house when she died. The smallest child interrupted to say that her mameen didn't want to die. She had cried! Mary Josephine, the middle girl, turned on her and said that it was a terrible thing to say about mameen. She didn't mind dying only for leaving them behind without food. At this stage of the recital, Mrs. Stacey and all the female staff were crying.

The rush light had been lighting in every window on the mountain, Rosheen said, so that the Blessed Virgin and Iosagain[2] and Saint Joseph would be able to find their way if they were looking for shelter. Mameen had watched every light go out one by one as the houses fell beneath the crowbar. Then when the last twinkle vanished into darkness she lay back in Daddy's arms and died.

But it was only when they reached the workhouse thirty-eight miles further, that they knew the real anguish of parting. The girls must go with the hard-faced woman and live separately from Daddy and the boys. Pakie had set up a wailing cry for Attracta who had mothered him when he fretted for mameen. The gates had started to shut out the wild mountains that dared not give them shelter. The hard-faced woman was drawing

[1] A Connemara belief that the wailing of the wind is the souls in Purgatory pleading for prayers.

[2] Iosagain—Eesagain means Little Jesus.

away the girls. They were to wear the pauper jerkin. They were to give up mameen's shawl.

The shawl decided all of them; with one swift thought as uniting as its own warm folds. Attracta drew it tight around the three pairs of shoulders and Daddy put a hand on the nearest one and said, 'We'll not be stoppin'.'

'And that is all very sad,' said Sir Roderick when Sterrin had poured out the whole story verbatim. She was helping him to tie flies in the gun room. 'But my own tenants have the first claim on my charity.'

'But, Papa——'

'Sweetheart, the roads of Connaught are thronged with starving people making for the districts where the potatoes have not failed and where bread and meal have not reached famine prices. We must christen our own children first. We cannot afford to adopt a family of bachachs.'

'Oh, Papa, the Scallys are not beggars. No beggar would breed such ponies and—their mother's shawl is not a beggar-woman's. It is wundruss.'

But her papa was adamant. They would have to go out of that fever hut. What would happen if any of the servants were to contract fever, now that the fever hospital was full and all these sick and semi-starving people moving along the road to the workhouse?

She went and perched on the arm of his chair. 'Don't dare to wheedle me,' he said, drawing her into his arm. Margaret came in and demanded her embroidery scissors.

'I would ask the blacksmith to make scissors for your flies but I am too superstitious. A sharp instrument might cut our love.'

He reached up and touched the brown coils under the prim babet. 'Vulcan himself could not contrive an instrument sharp enough to cut our love.'

'Good!' cried Sterrin clambering down. 'Then the Scallys may stay.'

'Come back, you baggage!' he called. 'I tell you I cannot pay my way. I shall soon be touching my hat to the bank manager.'

Sterrin sighed gustily. 'What a pity the bank manager is not a lady! You might try paying your way the way you paid your footing to Mrs. Black Pat.'

'Footing?' Margaret was mystified. Sterrin explained. Vividly. Roderick put up his hand again. This time to ease out the ominous crease forming between the brown eyes.

'It is just an old Irish custom,' he expostulated. 'Like you kissing Mr. De Lacey under the mistletoe.'

'I did not kees!' Margaret always went very foreign when she was angry. 'I was keesed—and Mr. De Lacey is fat, and he is bald where his wig slips!'

Sterrin sought to reassure her mamma. 'But Mrs. Black Pat is not fat, nor bald. She has golden hair, and it curls without rags or paper, her daughter says.' Her mamma didn't seem to find the information helpful, so Sterrin pressed on. 'She dresses very nicely, and speaks nicely too. She is much highclasser than Black Pat.'

Margaret walked slowly to the table and dropped the scissors with a little clank in front of Roderick. 'Keep it,' she said. 'I give it to you.'

He quirked his eyebrows. 'And what about cutting our love?'

'It ees cut! In hafs! By you! Foo-ting, *Hein!*' The little bugle and bells in her key belt mingled angrily as the door closed.

Roderick looked back to his amazed daughter. 'My dear,' he said untenderly, "will you never learn that little girls should be seen and not heard.' Particularly, he added to himself, when they *have* seen!

CHAPTER 22

The 'footing' incident caused the first discord in the lilt of their marriage. Margaret got so bogged down in her resentment that she couldn't extricate herself. She devoted herself to little Dominic, so much so that Sterrin felt jealous and out of sorts watching her mother wheel him about in a basinette and sing him to sleep every night. Roderick was desperately busy trying to cope with the prevailing distress; organising relief schemes, attending to the purchase and sowing of tested seeds, supervising the cleansing of the soil after its terrible disease.

He took the time off to greet the Liberator along with Phineas De Lacey and other landlords at the Thurles railway terminus where O'Connell would entrain on his journey to Westminster to plead for help for Ireland. Roderick held that a government's first duty was to save life. A national disaster like this, he urged, ought not to be left to the efforts of private individuals.

Roderick felt sad as he gripped O'Connell's hand. The Liberator was showing the effects of his imprisonment. The winter that ought to have been spent in convalescing from its effects had been spent in relieving the distress of his own people. His blue eyes looked unlikely to cause him further criticism on the score of roving over the curves of a pretty woman. He possessed as many faults as the soil from which he sprang, but lack of charity or generosity could not be listed against him. He had brought a doctor at his own expense to cope with an outbreak of fever in his district. He had ordered wholesale slaughtering of beeves and mutton; dispatched blankets to the remotest parts of his wild mountain territory. Out of the purblind depths of his own charity, he held that all charity should be voluntary and private. Organised charity, he insisted, offended human dignity.

He listened wearily to the difficulties and suggestions pressed by Roderick's deputation. At stages all the way from County Kerry he had met similar deputations.

But once in England, O'Connell threw off his weariness. At Westminster, he was once more the incarnation of Ireland; seeing with its eyes, enduring its sufferings. He reminded the House that the potato had failed in Europe. The countries afflicted had closed their ports to the export of grain until their populations were fed; had ceased distilling; had lowered the price of bread. Why could not this be done for Ireland?

He raised again the wondrous and witching voice of a mighty orator, riveting the attention of the world, drawing all eyes towards Ireland. But Parliament averted its gaze, and told O'Connell and the world that the possibility of a famine in Ireland was a 'baseless vision'!

Roderick watched with panic in his heart as the stock in his granary dwindled. He would have to buy grain; And with what? Only a third of his tenants had paid rent! He was feeding most of them. A line of tenants moved up for the meal that Lady O'Carroll doled out. She glanced up and caught his cold expression and her face hardened. But he saw only their substance that was draining away through her hands. A baseless vision indeed! God knows he didn't begrudge the poor devils their bit! But he had a wife and two children and a heritage to guard. A man should christen his own child first. He became aware of his wife's angry scrutiny and turned away.

She watched him ride across the fields and jump the ditch into the old road that had once been a wolf track. Somewhere in that direction lived that Ryan woman! Margaret had pieced her story together; a product of a boarding school for Young Ladies! Hein! Nothing very ladylike about flaunting herself on the roadway to be kissed by passing strangers. His foster-brother's wife! Perhaps his footing was not just an annual affair! Had Roderick gone footing now? Immediately she was ashamed of the thought, but it rankled.

Roderick rode to the townland called the Cobs where he was experimenting with potatoes in lea soil that had not been ploughed in twenty-five years. The Cobs lay behind Black Pat's farm. He could see the horse he had sold them. But no sign of the mare. It ought to have foaled before now. He thought for a moment to call and have a look at the foal but he spied O'Driscoll waiting for him. As he skirted the Ryan haggard he heard the tinkle of the music box.

Margaret heard it too as she came along the little road in the brougham. A cluster of 'half-acre' holdings lay beyond Ryan's house. Their occupants were depending entirely upon the food she dispensed at the castle every day. There were some who were unfit to come for it. Margaret, straining after the distant speck that she could still see bobbing up and down inside the hedge, experienced an urge of charity that was strangely sudden. She ordered the brougham and packed a basket with food.

The Ryan children, peeping through the hedge, saw the fine brougham lurching along their rutted boreen. They raced in the back way to tell their mother. 'And she has a big basket of goodies! She must have heard that we are in hardship,' said the eldest girl, Norisheen. Her mother rounded on her. Had she breathed it to a soul that things were not well with them? Had any of them? But they assured her that they had let no one know that food was short. 'We tell them, coming from school, that we have fresh meat every day and soda currant cake and roast chicken——' Nonie hushed them. The phantom menu was torturing. 'And,' she chided them, 'it is dreadfully bad manners to speak outside of what you eat.' She strained on tiptoe in the shadow of the window hangings. She had never seen his wife. Perhaps she might be bringing the children some dainties? It would be terrible to accept anyone's charity. Still, Pat was his foster-brother. Sir Roderick would be bound to feel concern if he had heard that the foal had been still-born and the mare had died, and that they had lost a cow; that pigs had rooted among the rotten slime in the potato drills and had died; that catastrophes had rained upon them!

She smoothed her hair. But I won't go out to my lady's carriage to receive her charity with a curtsey. I'll stay here and accept it graciously; a gift for the children from their father's foster-brother! She ordered the younger children down to the kitchen, 'And, turn off that music box! No, leave it on.' It lent an air of unconcern; a background for conversation. You like music, I see? Oh yes, I adore Mozart; especially his Fantasia in C Minor.

Lady O'Carroll looked straight ahead. The corner of her right eye had glimpsed the toparied hedge, the patches of grass cut in the semblance of a lawn; the window boxes; and even a Chinese rose blooming away regardless of season. Out of place, like its owner! All of a sudden Margaret would have given her back teeth to glimpse this little person whom Roderick had lifted in his arms from the road. She turned full face and looked at the house as the brougham passed it. Margaret felt a surge of rage. It gave her gentle face the look that the peeping Nonie took to be its habitual arrogance.

Fantasia! It played past Nonie's door in an orchestration of creaks and jingles and wheels and hoof beats. She had known many a secret moment of homesickness and heartsickness, but never anything like the desolation she felt as she stood now in the shadow of the curtains; steeled to accept the charity that— that had no intention of coming her way!

She, too, was angry. Hell roast you for a Belgian barbarian! But, she strained after the carriage, its outline was blurred with her own tears, she is lovely! Those eyes and hair against the skin! Chocolates and cream!

The metaphor recalled her to her constant niggling for something dainty to eat. She looked up at the beam from where, last year, a row of bacon flitches had hung. Would she dare to cut a piece from the solitary diminishing flitch? And with Pat away, too! But then, he was probably guzzling delicious food at her Auntie's in County Cork. He was staying there on his way to purchase seed potatoes from the Maharees in Kerry; the one place where the potatoes had not failed. Her idea, that! Another of her extravagances, like the horse. No, the horse had been Pat's extravagance. She whirled from the thought of the horse and their pipe dream of wealth from its stock. 'Stop that crying, Norisheen!' she said in a quaky voice. 'Did you actually think that I would accept food from anyone? Come on and help me beat eggs. I'll make pancakes for supper.'

Children are so pathetically easy to please, she thought, as she sloshed off a layer of bacon to try the pancakes. They were prancing with joy. Pancakes—and with rashers! They hadn't tasted the like since the pigs had died after eating the black potatoes.

A thought strove treacherously to rise and remind her that she herself had been easy to please a while back. What more than a child had she been when she let herself in for this— squalor!

The savoury smell from the pan restored her good humour. As she beat the eggs she carolled the song her mother's mother once sang long ago while her servants spun—

> *'Now hasten ye women*
> *Ye want not for bread*
> *The good wheels are steady*
> *Go spin the fine thread.'*

Margaret, driving back, heard the blithe words. So did Roderick on his way to speak to Pat. The lively clatter of eggs beating and laughter and the savoury smell came to him as he rode into Ryan's backyard from the fields. His father used to hum a song like that. He had told Roderick that his own mother used to sing it to her spinning women. It was heartening in this semi-starvation to hear that gay voice that dare sing. 'Ye want not for bread.' He started to dismount, then he saw the brougham.

He jumped on to the boreen and reined in beside the brougham. 'What on earth brings you down this way?' he demanded.

Margaret was deep in reverie. There was pitiful poverty in the cabins she had just visited. And then to hear that song 'Ye want not for bread'. Such bad form! Whatever her upbringing, the huz-zee was *déclassée*. A wayside Loreli trying to lure passing gentlemen—Margaret looked up startled. 'I don't have to ask what brings *you* this way.' She glanced back significantly towards the Ryan house.

He looked at her silently. 'No,' he said, at last. 'You don't have to ask. You prefer to find out for yourself.' She flinched at the hurtful suggestion—spying! It was incredible; also it was true. But Roderick was not troubling to make suggestions. 'If you must come spying this way,' he stated positively, 'don't take the brougham. This road will break the springs.' He spurred his mount and shot out in front.

Big John thought it was very unlike the Sir to shoot up a spray of puddle with his horse's hind feet. Her Ladyship was forced to dab her face with her handkerchief. She was still dabbing when he reined to at the hall door, and her eyes were red.

Life could not wait for moods and misunderstandings. As days passed, more and more people made claims on Roderick's time and stocks. Margaret's food distribution dragged on later each morning. The backache acquired at Dominic's birth grew chronic from the prolonged standing. And Dominic, too, felt the strain. His chubby face lengthened and he missed his mother.

Nurse Hogan came one day to tell Margaret that the celery was finished. Last week it had been the cauliflower. There was nothing now but the more drab vegetables—cabbage, turnips and onions. Bacon was scarce because the pigs that had been fattened for killing before Christmas, had got hold of those dreadful black potatoes and died. Margaret thought wistfully of the prodigal slaughtering of pigs during the prayers for the Liberator's release. Who would ever dream that feasting could turn so quickly to fasting? But who would ever dream that potatoes could make such a difference? To everyone, to an entire way of life! It had something to do with national economy, Roderick said. Meantime, Margaret hated cabbage; silently.

Sterrin too hated cabbage. But not silently. She expressed her aversion so volubly that both parents levelled their jagged tempers at her. Roderick was missing the potatoes. He frequently ate them three times a day, and always twice.

'You should be thankful,' he told her, 'that you have so much other food. There are millions who have nothing whatever to replace their potatoes.'

Her mamma told her sternly that she should be prepared to make sacrifices. Sterrin promptly sacrificed a heap of cabbage over the side of her plate. She tried to make Dominic eat it and offered him a little when he cried. She was tempted to warn her parents and governess that it contained a segment of caterpillar. There was bound to be some more in the dish. But it was bad manners to allude to the presence of such unscheduled species of cooked life in the vegetables until after people had eaten them. Anyway it would do Miss Ferguson-Coyne no harm to eat some of the Nature Stuff she was always preaching about.

She shoved a few spoonfuls of rice into her pocket. It wouldn't proclaim its presence so messily since it had no cream. There was so much milk being doled out that cream was reserved for butter-making only. For the past fortnight, Sterrin had been hoarding bread and butter and cheese and odd bits of meat to deposit in the hollow of a tree for the Ryan children. It was a deadly secret. The Ryans were awfully jolly. They said the quaintest things. The big girl could sketch and play the violin. In a couple of years when her parents made lots of money from selling blood stock horses, she would go to a boarding school. Meantime, her mother would skin them all alive if she knew that they were accepting food from anyone.

But Nonie knew all about the secret feasts. The younger ones had let it slip. She pretended not to hear and turned a blind eye. Let them have whatever they could. As long as she wasn't supposed to know and as long as that philandering father of Miss Sterrin O'Carroll and her stuck-up mother knew nothing.

Sterrin placed a layer of crocuses inside the lid of her basket of food. By right, she thought, they should be roses. The saintly Queen Elizabeth of Hungary, it seems, used to bring a basket of food to some poor people. One day, her cruel, wicked husband intercepted her and demanded to see what was in the basket. And, lo, when she raised the lid there was nothing there but roses.

It was young Thomas who intercepted Sterrin. He whisked her cloak from the suspicious-looking hummock in front of her saddle. 'Crocuses my eye! Who do you think you are? Queen Elizabeth of Hungary?'

'Who do you think *you* are?' She flashed and saw his hurt flush. *He* might risk the liberty of putting such a question to her. But never she to him. It cut too near the bone of the nameless scullion.

'Anyway,' he called after her, 'your charity is misplaced. The Ryans have rich relations.' The young Ryans had a way of making Thomas feel his position. Their mother looked through him as though he were not there. And Black Pat would nod casually as he rode by on his fine horse.

Now from a distance he watched Miss Sterrin deposit the food in the hollow trunk of a tree. From nowhere the Ryan children appeared and fell to like wolves.

Riding back, Sterrin heard footsteps following her from behind the hedge. A wild-looking, long-haired boy was watching her with a passion of intensity. The Scallys, the mountain children, were still ensconced in the fever hut under the lea of the hill out of sight of the castle and—the Sir!

'What are you following me for?' she called sharply. It must have been this Nosey Parker who had told young Thomas about her feeding the Ryans.

He looked blankly at her as she reproached his ingratitude. He understood only the Connaught Gaelic. But Attracta was picking up the Munster Gaelic. She came forward and explained that the sight of Sighle, Sterrin's pony, made the lad homesick for his mameen and his wild mountains. Especially as Sighle had been such a pet; she being a half capaill jisge.[1] Her sire had been one of the fairy horses that come up out of Loch Corrib on moonlight nights. He had come one night to the pony shed when Sighle's mother was horsing and Sighle was their offspring. Daddy had kept the shed locked after that but when the water horse came up out of the lake again Sighle's mother beat down the door with her own hoofs and went off with it. Mameen followed them but it was no use. With her own eyes she had seen the little mare go into the lake with the fairy horse and the water closed over their heads forever.

'Mameen took the little foal that she left behind, into the kitchen on moonlight nights and let it sleep in the chimney corner where the capail usige couldn't get at it. It became a great pet.' The boy reached timidly and stroked Sighle's nose.

Sterrin was disturbed, 'I didn't realise that there was so much fairy blood in Sighle.'

'As long as you keep away from water, your Honour's Miss,' Attracta assured her. 'But, of course, meanin' no disrespect to you, the colour of your hair might draw the fairies.'

Sterrin looked over her shoulder, 'Nonsense!' she said, 'I'm over age for their power. I'm past seven.' But she hurried the pony's homeward pace.

Young Thomas was sympathetic about the homesickness of the Scally boy. 'I could let him help me with Sighle.' The little pony had become his special care. He had advanced in all directions from the knife chore though its title persisted. 'I could do with an assistant,' he said grandiosely.

'Thomas,' she breathed, 'I knew you'd think of something. I don't know what I'd do without you.'

He whisked off the saddle and started to rub the pony. 'You have her sweating terribly,' he grumbled. It was not for him to reply that he didn't know what he'd do but for her own small self. When he was at his chores and she came down the stairs—a speck on its scaled expanse—when she entered a room, stole into the kitchen, the stable, it was like when the grand actors and actresses from England came on to the stage in the Assembly Rooms; peopling its emptiness, colouring its everyday drabness. 'And there are no water horses in Lough Bawn for you to worry about. The lake has disappeared again.'

[1] A water horse of fairy origin.

She went off, relieved. Every few years Lough Bawn had a habit of disappearing for a whole year. Scientists gave all sorts of explanations, but the locals knew that it merely was Peig the fairy woman retrieving what was her own. Long ago when water was scarce here she had carried the lake to them, all the way from Killarney, in her apron. And who could blame her if she took it back the same way now and then?

Thomas drove the governess chaise past the vanished lake that afternoon. The sight of its empty bed would assuage Miss Sterrin's fear of lurking steeds of the 'Sheeogue'. Miss Ferguson-Coyne held forth about secret streams and suctions and volcanic forces, Thomas glanced over his shoulder at Miss Sterrin, as they passed the pathetic stirabout line on Major Darby's estate—

'It's the Funny man!' she cried.

She was looking at Dominic Landy, the 'funny man' who had been dressed up as the clown in the Wren boys' procession on Saint Stephen's Day. Dominic cut no gay capers now. His hat was low over his eyes; his head deep in his collar for fear of being recognised taking charity. Fancy a good farmer like Dominic in a stirabout line! It was only the very poor with no land except potato patches who came for free stirabout to Major Darby.

People looked expectantly towards the sound of the wheels then turned back disheartened. A great cauldron was smoking away its substance over a barbecue fire. The smell tormented those who shivered in the afternoon wind waiting to break the day's fast. 'Oh God, why doesn't he come?' a woman cried. No one dared touch the cauldron till Darby himself arrived. Some- one cried: 'Here he is!' A big heavily-built man, with moustaches branching like plough handles, sauntered across the yard, tapping his leggings with his crop. Hunger emboldened one man to reproach, 'We're here this two hours, your Honour.' His landlord looked at him as though he were some new species of flea. Leisurely he went through his pockets until he found a toothpick. Then, more leisurely, he proceeded to free his teeth from the clingings of a substantial meal. Thomas's hands clenched on the reins. Dominic Landy's hands clenched too, but slithered open from the clammy moisture of febrile hunger.

Darby dropped the ladle into the cauldron and called out the cry that summons pigs to the swill. 'Suck! Suck! Suck!' he

193

yelled.

Dominic stepped from his place near the head of the line. 'That's no way to address human beings.' His voice meant to be defiant, but weakness caused it to be cracked and shrill.

Darby let the porridge pour slowly back into the cauldron. 'If you don't like the way I issue my invitations,' he sneered, 'you don't have to accept my hospitality.' From behind, a voice softly counselled Dominic to patience. It had taken him weeks of hunger, and those last three days of complete starvation before he could face in here for the brew of charity. Now, some-one had moved into his place. 'Get back there to the end of the line!' Darby suddenly snapped. 'Or get out.'

'All right, I'll get out. Keep your pig's swill. I want no man's charity.' The words echoed bravely round the spaces reserved for the dignity of his soul. He marched to their sound as tired soldiers march to the strains of their martial music. All the way down he marched; not Dominic Landy, of course, but the Wren boys' Omadhawn, the jester without his cap and bells; down to the very end of the queue.

Next day Sterrin tiptoeing upstairs with head down, bumped into Miss Ferguson-Coyne. 'What have you in that pocket?'

From the left pocket, bulging and discoloured, came creeping, crawling, buzzing, caterpillars, crickets, ladybirds, the live col-lection of Sterrin's own private brand of nature study.

'Not that pocket!' The governess' hand shot out and grabbed the pocket that Sterrin clutched. She squealed. Something moist and clammy had met her fingers. 'Another frog! If you dare to put it in my bed——' Sterrin struggled.

'I'm going to my own room. Word of honour. It is a matter of life or death.'

The governess was becoming used to her pupil's dramatic phraseology. Sterrin bolted her door. From her pocket she took two wobbling blobs, one large and white, one small and red, and placed them before the statue of the Child Jesus. The scene she had witnessed at Darby's on Saint Stephen's Day, the suffering, haggard look of poor nice Dominic Landy who had singled her out to dance with, called for a sacrifice of something she loved. Jelly! 'Oh please Iosagain, accept my sacrifice for the suffering people and avert famine and if you like jelly, I'll make the soupreem sacrifice on Friday, if we get any, and keep you a bigger piece, Amen.' A piece of fluff clung to the jelly. She

194

licked it off and turned away, then turned back to ensure with another lick that there was no more fluff. Sacrifice, mamma had said, was the highest form of prayer. Jelly certainly was the highest form of sacrifice. An hour later, when she peeped in, the blobs had vanished. Her sacrifice had been accepted.

She heard a noise outside the window which faced the Sir's Road. There was something happening out there. Down the road a posse of redcoats and constabulary marched. In their midst walked Dominic Landy. In handcuffs. Behind walked a tearful woman and two girls.

Across the fields Papa was galloping like mad, scattering the Ryan children in all directions. He jumped the hedge and pulled his horse across the width of the road. It barred the passage of a giant of a man who was following the soldiers. 'Go back, Holohan!' She heard Papa shout. 'Go back, I tell you. There is nothing you can do. Don't implicate yourself!'

John Holohan came on unheeding; white fury on his face. Sir Roderick swooped and caught his collar. 'Do you want to drag your own mother at the heels of a procession like that?'

The big man slumped. Helplessly he stood watching them take his friend to jail; to the convict ship; for fourteen years.

Dominic had suffered beyond endurance. Last night, his mind festering and his brain poisoned from the fumes of a swilled-out stomach, he had attacked the grain carts.

Lord Strague had tried the case this morning. It was over when Roderick, appealed to by Dominic's friends, had arrived at the Petty Sessions Court. Darby's evidence had been overpowering. Incitement, insolence, obstruction of his benevolence in feeding his tenants.

When Roderick told Lord Strague the true facts, his kinsman yawned. 'Always said Darby was an outsider. Damned bad form.' Roderick blazed with impotent rage. 'By God, Strague, had Darby been killed for calling a man as one calls a pig to the swill I'd have pronounced it justifiable homicide—*with* a strong recommendation for mercy.'

At dinner Roderick was morose. He pushed the half-eaten food aside and called for cheese. The butler looked appealingly towards her Ladyship and vanished. 'There is no cheese,' she said. Roderick's dismay was comical. Margaret herself made the cheese from an old Flemish recipe that she would not divulge to the Cook. No potatoes was an act of God. But no cheese was an

195

act of—of feminine vindictiveness! He glared at her. She glared back. Did he think she was some little housewife, to make cheese—like bread—at the top of her voice for passers-by to hear and halt?

He started to tell her what he *did* think. Then realised the goggle-eyed presence of his daughter. It was only since relationship with Roderick had become strained that Margaret had started to let Sterrin join them at meals when there were no guests. 'Are you aware,' he asked Margaret, 'that your daughter is handing out cheese, and bread and butter in basketfuls, to the Ryan children?'

Margaret looked slowly at her daughter as if she were Judas or his agent, the daraghadeel. The girl, she thought, was the picture of her father, only for the red hair. They were all alike, these O'Carrolls; secretive.

Sterrin quailed under the unusual scrutiny that was followed by a severe lecture. At last she made her curtsey, managed to palm her father's rejected jelly and made off with it to her sacrificial shrine. Mamma was unfair! She had told her weeks ago to share with the needy and to make sacrifices. Now she eats the head off a body for just being—obedient.

Carefully, Sterrin divided the jelly between the statue and herself. The Divine Child seemed to be finding her sacrifice very acceptable. She eyed the statue and the generous blob that was richly flavoured with port to make up for the shortage of cream. For how long more must she make these sacrifices? They were yielding no results. Look what had happened to poor Dominic Landy! And now she must go out and break it to the Ryans that she was forbidden to bring them any more food.

The two little Ryan boys and their youngest sister broke into tears when she told them. They climbed up and looked into the hollow where the food was usually concealed. They couldn't believe that there would be no more feasts. The older ones tried to put a face on their disappointment and say that it was really quite all right. They had just finished their dinner. But Sterrin was doubtful. There was a quaver like tears in their voices and despite what Mamma had said about them having plenty and having rich relations to help, they *looked* hungry. Or else sick!

She drew out three bull's-eyes she had been keeping for Sunday. 'Here,' she gasped, catching up on them, 'you could have one between every two of you and share licks. There is a lot of licking in a bull's-eye.'

And then something tragic happened. Young Pat claimed first suck of the one he shared with his brother. While Adam watched Pat's lips with slavering gums, there was a sudden gulp. The beautiful sweet had slithered unsucked, unsavoured, down into the empty void of Pat's stomach! Adam screamed. He rose on tiptoes and looked into his brother's mouth as he had looked down the tree trunk. Pat walked slowly home, cheated, betrayed. Every step of the way he could see it, a hard dark thing, squatting in the middle of his empty stomach; gloating over the slow delights it had withheld. Nonie heard Adam's cries. There was no turning a deaf ear now. The whole story came out in sobbing gasps. '... and the girl-with-the-red-hair's father saw the food and told her mother to forbid it.'

The shamed flush burned Nonie's cheeks. The children watched her nervously as she stormed about the house. Would she skin them alive? But Nonie was thinking of that 'footing' kiss. And she to think that it was a token of their meeting on the hunting field. She was just the tenant's wife who had caught the lewd attention of her landlord as he passed. The devil fly away with him, and his stuck-up foreign wife with her big brown eyes like a cow with colic. Himself and his forget-me-not blue eyes. Raking through a body, making her so churned up that she had gone off with the next horseman to gallop into her life. And look where *that* gallop had landed her!

The children's scared faces halted her thoughts. Lord, she hadn't realised that their faces were so pinched and their stomachs so swollen out. It was that new yellow meal from India. It swelled people up but left them hungry. She counted the few shillings left from the sovereign that her mother had secreted in the cast-off clothes sent by her sister. Nonie's father had died and his eldest daughter was in grim possession of the home—and of her mother. There was no danger that the mother's relenting charity would be allowed to reach the outcast.

Ten minutes later Nonie was emerging from the little all-purpose shop at Upper Kilsheelin just as Lady O'Carroll's brougham was drawing up.

Margaret had run out of wool. She was constantly knitting for the poor who had not been able to buy wool last winter. Now she would have to drive on to Templetown. It didn't

197

soothe her annoyance to be told by the shopkeeper that if she had been five minutes earlier she could have forestalled Mrs. Black Pat Ryan. Mrs. Black Pat had bought up her entire stock of yarn. 'I don't know why she needed so much. But sure, she always buys big.'

Nonie made a pleasing picture knitting on the porch as Lady O'Carroll approached. A wealth of yarn overflowed from a pretty work basket. A pale green shawl from India draped the shabbiness of her gown. The grease from the heel of the flitch of bacon hastily rubbed on the pan at the first sound of the wheels, sent the odour of frying bacon out through the opened door.

Margaret's misgivings over Sterrin and the food business subsided. There was no want here. She stole a glance at the gold head that hadn't bothered to look up for the overlord's carriage. The *mignon* type! *Petite!* About twenty-six, she would be. Looks eighteen!

Without warning the head came up. Too late Margaret looked straight ahead. She could have sworn there was mocking laughter in those tiptilted eyes. No slightest bow or acknowledgment of her landlord's wife. Just cool appraisement.

A horse pushed its head over the hedge and whinnied at the carriage horse. What a superb animal to grace a small farmer's haggert, Margaret thought. It lent a kind of cachet to the place. This must be the horse that Roderick had sold to Black Pat. He must think much of this foster-brother. Or is it that he thinks much—too much—of his foster-sister-in-law.

The smell from the empty pan was torturing the children. 'It is carrying pride too far, Nonie,' said Black Pat. Nonie was gazing after the carriage. I might have been sitting there instead of My Fine Lady! Too late had she heard that the week after the hunting encounter, young Mr. O'Carroll, the son of Sir Dominic O'Carroll, had twice been seen on the opposite bank of the river that flowed in front of the lawn at home. That lovely little river! Trickling its green depths between the willows.

Eyes staring through her brain made her turn from the window. She couldn't read the look in her husband's eyes. She busied herself mixing a handful of precious flour with yellow meal and sour milk to spread on the pan before the grease would evaporate. It would beguile the children's hunger.

'You are a nice one to talk of pride. You had only to ask him to let you have meal, aye, and stock, on credit till the harvest. What need was there to be first with the rent? He is not just a landlord to you. He was fostered in your home.'

'Aye,' said Pat, and his tone was bitter. 'Like the River Shannon was fostered in a pool like a pot at the butt of a hill.' He stood up and it was to himself that he talked as he went out. 'The stream goes out from the field that fostered it and becomes a river; full of power—and treachery.'

Day and night Nonie worked at the knitting. Stockings lengthened and multiplied from her needle until she had a basketful to carry to Templetown. By night she flitted in the shadow of a wall across the barrack square to the married quarters. But there were others before her. Respectable farmers' wives bartering their crochet and lace-edged clothes, exquisitely worked cuffs and collars and fichus and babets, for the price of a few loaves!

An opened door revealed an unmistakable profile. Nonie crouched back. She recognised Pat's beautiful cousin, Kitty, the wife of Mark Hennessey. Kitty was offering a sergeant's wife an embroidered cloth with a fall of lace nearly half a yard deep. The woman quoted a price and Kitty, too proud and too weary to huxter, accepted. A cloth that might grace a banquet changed hands for a florin.

Eightpence a dozen Nonie got for her stockings; if only she might have retained a few pairs for the children. The quartermaster's wife glimpsed the wistful little face as it turned back into the shadows. 'Here, little girl,' she called after her. 'Here's a halfpenny for yourself. Don't hand it up to your mammy.'

Nonie thanked her sweetly. The woman's husband who had made a fortune on handovers for contracts met a child gazing apparently rapt, at the halfpenny in the middle of her small palm. He dropped another one on top of it. 'Now you have a whole penny.'

In the street the little jets of repressed laughter were followed by repressed tears. The butcher, putting up the shutters saw her wipe them as she glimpsed the piece of beef that lay lonely on a slab. 'H-how much is it?' The pretty voice caught on a little hegging breath. 'Here, take it home to your mammy.' He pushed it into her basket. 'Take this too.' He shoved a big piece of suet after the beef.

A bianconi overtook her on the road home. The driver mistook her for a child and since Mr. Bianconi's instructions were never to pass by a woman carrying a baby nor a child that was heavily laden, she was still clutching her two halfpennies when she dismounted. 'Unless ye become as little children,' she grinned ruefully.

The girl has the divine gift of comedy, thought Sir Roderick O'Carroll. The lights of the bianconi and of his own carriage showed him the glitter of curls and of smiling teeth. She sees her life as a joke; not a calamity. Nonie started to decline the lift he offered but he had taken the basket from her. 'It is heavy,' he exclaimed, 'much too heavy for you!'

'The children will soon lighten it,' she said. Then in case he got the impression of want, she added casually, 'It is amazing how much children eat.'

'Tell me,' he leaned towards her, 'what were you laughing at just now?' The darkness held them in its intimacy. It showed up that distant gleam of romance that had been stillborn.

'Nothing much. The driver mistook me for a child and would not take my fare. I omitted to enlighten him.'

'I can understand why he made the error.'

But there was nothing childlike in the voice that replied. The former Oenone Mansfield had suddenly enough of patronage; halfpennies, hunks of beef, *and* his Sirship's carriage. Cool, educated, its accent as dignified as his own, her voice assailed him. 'Can I help the impression that people choose to take of me? I can assure you that I don't seek to make an impression, of any kind, on anyone.' She groped for the basket. The carriage was slowing in to the castle gates but already she was on the road pulling at the big, uncouth basket.

'Allow me.' Demmit, this was absurd! Behaving as though he were squiring a lady with a rose basket. She looked at the basket he held towards her. Bulging loaves had forced up the lid. Suddenly she put her hands inside her hood and inside her lovely golden hair. There was frenzy in the gesture as though she were gripping something in there that wanted to burst out and prevent her from resuming this uncouth burden that typified her life.

He sensed the anguish on her old–young face and his interest quickened as it would not to a happy woman. Then the proud imp of comedy returned to her. It prompted her to take her leave with a gesture of equality. Instead of grasping the handle, she arched her wrist high in the fashionable over-a-five-bar-gate handshake.

He matched her gesture with his own. Very deliberately, he shifted the basket to his left hand. As his lips touched her fingers, she felt a curious pulsation as of frozen ground that feels the first warm breath of Spring. Before he could speak, she had snatched the basket and vanished into the darkness; just as she had vanished from the hunting field into the darkness of the spinney.

Kitty Hennessey had returned from Templetown and invited young Thomas to sup with them. She smiled as Mark stopped in the act of pouring the watery porridge. 'Baker's bread!' He stared unbelieving. It was weeks since he had seen soda bread; much less baker's!

'Yes,' said Kitty nonchalantly. 'I got some in the town. Draw in your chair, young Thomas.'

Thomas thought her face looked transparent. He wondered what she had parted with to get the bread. But it was good to see her eat so heartily. He didn't know that the quickening of a second child was quickening her constant hunger. She did not thrill to these stirrings as she had for Theobald's when Thomas had sung the proud songs of Mr. Davis, and her heart had surged with hope. Vo, Vo, for the heritage she had envisaged in their strains. Vo, vo, for the great man who wrote them!

After supper, the Hennesseys walked to the gate with young Thomas. 'May God fasten the life strong in you,' Mark said to him in Gaelic.

Thomas looked back at them, standing there so splendid, both of them; so brave! To his own surprise he cried out, 'Sursum corda!'

Mark looked long after the boy. 'It is a pity,' he said musingly, 'to see him a servant boy. He has the makings of a priest. Aren't those Latin words in the Mass, Kitty?'

'Yes,' she said. 'Raise up your hearts, they mean. But a priest, inagh! That boy was made for woman's love.'

As Mark barred the door for the night, he turned on a sudden. 'Kitty,' he asked, 'what did you sell to buy that bread?'

She shrugged the heirloom from her vision. 'A bit of sewing,' she answered.

At Kilsheelin, Sterrin was wondering how long more would

she have to continue her sacrifice. Lent was over, but still she made sacrifice. Bits of chocolate pudding, anything that she really relished. And still no sign of Divine Clemency. She peeped into her room. It would be too soon to expect her offering to be taken. She had left it barely ten minutes ago. But, always she hugged the hope that some day she might catch Little Jesus unawares, in the act of eating the jelly!

It was not the Iosagain the Holy Child whom she caught unawares. It was Mickey-the-turf. She stood rooted with horror at the spectacle of his sacrilege.

She strode to him and jerked up his face. Desperately he strove with his turf-mouldy cuff to wipe a white smear of blancmange from mouth and chin. But the turf mould had blended with the blancmange and gave him a bearded, sinister look that was Judas-like. 'You caluminator!' she fumed. 'You blasphemer! You adulterer!'

Mickey-the-turf quailed. Only from the pulpit when it shook with the exhortations of the missioner had he ever heard such awful words.

'May it choke you!' she cried. She lashed him forth with her crop as the money-changers had been lashed forth by Him Whom she had hoped to appease by sustaining Him in His desert fast.

'No wonder people are still suffering!' she sobbed to Thomas, whom she had found in the pantry, polishing silver.

Never in the unconscious arrogance of her brief existence had she known what it was to be tricked and humiliated. She had been so utterly buoyed up by her sacrifice: 'And Iosagain never got one little bit!' The big tears spilled over. They wet her face. Her body shuddered in the way of those who seldom cry.

Thomas patted the hand that still rested on his arm. He had never seen her weep like this. Her Ladyship's full soft eyes could moisten easily. But Miss Sterrin's more deeply set, guarded their tears in their own depths. He scraped his throat. 'Don't cry, Miss Sterrin, asthore,' he murmured hoarsely, uncertain whether to offer her Mickey-the-turf's head on the salver he had been polishing or kill her a half-dozen dragons.

Roderick, on his way to the gun-room, paused at the sound of his daughter's sobs coming from the silver pantry across the passage. He heard young Thomas say gently, 'Miss Sterrin, maybe you have been too righteous about the sacrifice of your nice jelly.'

'Righteous?'

'The kind of goodness that the Proud Pharisee felt.'

'Young Thomas! How could you compare me with that craw-thumping hypocrite?' A deep sigh wafted across to the gunroom. 'Ah, young Thomas, I thought that you at least would understand. At night in bed I keep seeing Dominic Landy's face among the soldiers; it reminds me of Our Lord going to Calvary. The young Ryans' faces too. They were so disappointed when they heard that I must not bring them any more food. You see, I didn't *want* people to know that I was sacrificing my jelly. I didn't tell even you, young Thomas.'

'A pity you didn't. But don't fret, Miss Sterrin. You *made* the sacrifice. You will get your reward, and,' he added grimly, 'so will Mickey-the-turf.'

Roderick was dubious about that 'I didn't tell even *you*, young Thomas,' but he must warn her not to lie awake at nights over the young Ryans. There were too many children in real need. He recalled their mother's laden basket. That he ought not to have allowed her to carry? Demmit this was farcical. He couldn't go round the country carrying market baskets. Why in hell's gates hadn't she been away from home the day Black Pat had clattered into her father's yard on business? As she had been when Black Pat's foster-brother had ridden by.

Tomorrow was Gale Day. He must enquire from Black Pat if there was anything that he lacked. But in the morning Black Pat's rent was brought to the library by the butler.

'Mr. Ryan duv was, in a hurry, your Honour's Sir. He could not wait.'

CHAPTER 23

On May the twenty-fourth Margaret handed over the food ladling to Nurse Hogan.

She came to the library door to ask Roderick if he would soon be ready to start for town. The puzzled frown he gave her was for the bank manager's letter he was reading; not as he assumed, for herself. 'Blast the fellow,' he muttered aloud. 'Banks are for giving money; not for demanding it from their own clients.'

Margaret didn't give him time to compliment her on looking so exceptionally chic and pretty, with a great spray of tea roses on her carriage cloak and an old-gold chip bonnet tied with cherry coloured ribbons. She left the room and let the door close sharply behind her.

Roderick's frown was deeper still as he emerged from the bank in Templetown. He bumped into Phineas De Lacey on the porch of the bank's building. Phineas made no secret of his mission. He was seeking to get another mortgage on his estate. Only a few tenants had paid rent this Gale Day. He had been carrying the rest on his back all winter. 'Do you think anything will come of O'Connell's petition in the House today?' Phineas asked. The Liberator, baulked at every measure for alleviating the present distress, was to ask in the House that the Crown rents arising from the woods and forests in Ireland be retained there to pay the interest on the loan that the country had been forced to raise at its own expense.

Long bugle blasts drowned Roderick's reply. The mail coach was making a resplendent entry into the main street. The special greys reserved for the Queen's birthday made a great clattering. Both driver and guard wore new coats with scarlet facings. Bouquets drooped on their chests. Military parades and bands appeared but the usual crowds were missing. Only the Scout Doyle maintained the festive zeal. He stood at the coach landing depot wearing his Sunday 'hardy bastard', and plum-coloured body coat, and remembered to say, 'Well may you wear,' towards the coach-driver's new coat before asking for the passenger list.

Roderick had forgotten about the Queen's birthday. So that was why Margaret had asked him about going to town! Every year he had escorted her to see the parades, and meet her friends. He glanced up and saw Big John's cockade towering above the other coachmen outside the Mall coffee house.

He saw Margaret standing inside the door, the centre of fuss and greetings. There wasn't an available table. The place was packed with the garrison ladies—all sporting the red, white and blue colours—and their escorts and parties of loyal County folk.

Roderick was angered to see Margaret venturing there alone. But she wasn't alone for long. Lieutenant Fitzharding-Smith was instantly on his feet, summoning waiters and calling loudly for a table. Virginia Kennedy-Sherwin tried to make room but waiters came edging with a table over their heads, their feet tripping over swords.

Before Roderick could accept the Lieutenant's invitation to join them Margaret declined for him. 'Roderick is busy, Basil dear,' she cooed, giving the full battery of her wonderful eyes to the enraptured young officer. 'He has to give a lot of time to his tenants these days. Haven't you, Roderick?'

While the waiters manipulated the table, Roderick managed to murmur, 'Two can play at that game, my Lady.'

She flinched inwardly at the implied threat, but smiled sweetly and said, 'I know. The second one has started to play.'

He strode out fuming. The military parades had passed out of sight, but another parade came past Roderick, straggling in the opposite direction ... no bands, no banners. They were the poorest farmers who could not wait for the approaching crop that promised so abundantly. They were walking towards the poor-house. The Repeal buttons in their rags proclaimed that they had marched in the hope and glory of Repeal year. Now they moved to the music of the birthday salvoes—'like throngs of tattered beggars following, where late went by the pageant of a king'. Hope had left them and even as they made their way towards a living death, O'Connell, at Westminster, was told that the seventy-four thousand pounds rent from the yellow woods of Ireland must be applied towards improving Her Majesty's castle at Windsor and to the aggrandisement of Trafalgar

205

Square.

Sir Roderick's mood darkened when, at Kilsheelin, Hegarty told him that onions were the only vegetables left for dinner. Kilsheelin Castle without vegetables! It was fantastic.

'Sure we've been feeding an army, your Honour's Sir. A few showers after all this sun,' murmured the butler, 'and the peas will be bursting their pods.'

His master snorted. 'Live horse and you'll get grass.' He was dining alone. Her Ladyship, Hegarty was informed, was Mrs. Kennedy-Sherwin's guest at a garrison Birthday dinner. Miss Sterrin was staying the night at Kilcarrig Lodge with Miss Bunzy De Lacey. The onions, the butler assured him were most palatable when baked in their coats in the turf embers and served with butter.

'And savin' your Honour's presence,' murmured Hegarty confidentially, 'they are less objectionable that way—afterwards!'

Onions tended to reminisce; a fact to which Margaret delicately objected when kissed. Well, she was not likely to be kissed within the memory of these onions. With savage relish Roderick ate the whole dishful.

It was late when he stamped into his dressing-room and tugged the bell rope. When no one answered he stuck his head out the door and bellowed for someone to come and help him off with his jack boots! By right I should have a properly trained body servant, he grumbled, but at this rate of prosperity I'm damned lucky to have a body! 'Young Thomas!' he roared.

It was Margaret who came through the door. She stooped swiftly to draw off the obstinate boot but drew back at the anger of the face that almost touched hers. He misunderstood. 'I'm sorry,' he was coldly polite. 'I have not been fortunate enough to go-a-feasting. You see, Her Majesty and her Government have overlooked the fact that their first duty of governing is to save human life. I have therefore been so busy saving the lives of Her Majesty's subjects, that I have been compelled to eat onions on her birthday! I'm told they are objectionable—afterwards.'

She gripped his boot and lied bravely. 'Roderick, I—I have been eating onions too.'

'Indeed! How very inelegant—afterwards.'

'I mean,' she gripped harder, squatting at his feet, her big eyes pleading into his, 'I mean, when two people eat onions—

206

they don't notice——'

He extended his foot. 'Woman!' he ordered. 'Pull off that boot!' She tugged hard and fell backwards clutching the boot to her chest. He lifted her up, boot and all, and kissed her. Next minute the boot went sailing out through the window.

Young Thomas came racing around the corner of the castle. 'The Sir is roaring for you,' Johnny-the-buckets informed him. 'He is going to kill you.'

'He *has* killed me,' said young Thomas as a riding boot came through the air and hit him. He caught it without stopping and raced up the back stairs three at a time. 'Your Honour,' he called softly when his third knock went unanswered.

Through the closed door, his Honour told him to go to the devil.

The rain came and supplied the necessary swelling to the peas and beans. Then the sun returned and ripened vegetables earlier than ever before as though to make up for the earth's severity in the Autumn.

Margaret sighed as she watched the fine crop of peas dwindle down. She had distributed most of them to her tenants to help them over the last lap towards their own harvest. There would be no drying of beans and peas on the bleach greens for next winter! What matter! They had kept hunger at bay and— Roderick and she were back in their love again!

She accompanied him to Dublin when he journeyed to a special Repeal meeting. The Liberator was alarmed by the tone of the Young Ireland party in the *Nation*. It was becoming menacingly martial. He had written to his son John from England and ordered the meeting convened. In Conciliation Hall, Roderick listened to John O'Connell's warning that these militant young men could imperil his great movement for a bloodless regeneration of the country. He called upon every member of the Repeal Association to come and renew his pledge against physical force.

Outside Conciliation Hall, young Thomas sat on the carriage with the driver, sleepily recalling the day he had rushed panic-stricken from the hall thinking that it was he who had halted the march of Repeal. Suddenly he sat straight up. Through the open windows a voice came ringing.

'Abhor the sword, my Lord. Stigmatise the sword! ... No

my Lord, for at its blow and in the quivering of its crimson light a giant nation sprang from the waters of the Atlantic and by its redeeming magic the fettered Colony became a daring free Republic....' Thomas listened spellbound. Here was the authentic voice of youth, intrepid, defiant; calling on youth! Suddenly it broke off.

In the Ladies' Gallery Margaret was listening enthralled. She didn't understand half of it; she never did—of this kind of thing! But had this young gentleman, Thomas Francis Meagher, been but half so romantic looking as he was, she would still have been enthralled. For he had started to talk about her beloved Antwerp. '... I learned,' he cried, 'the first part of a nation's creed upon the ramparts of Antwerp ... stigmatise the sword! No, my Lord, for it scourged the Dutch marauders out of the old towns of Belgium; back into their own phlegmatic swamps! I honour the Belgians. I will not stigmatise the means by which they obtained a citizen King——'

The spell was broken. John O'Connell, acting in his father's absence, broke in to protest. 'These sentiments imperil the Association. Either Meagher or I quit the Hall.'

Roderick watched the young orator leave. With him went the leader Smith-O'Brien and Mitchell and Gavan Duffy; out from the Hall and the movement it housed. They took with them their brilliance and their bravery. Despite the July sunshine, the glow had gone from the Hall. He felt an urge to follow them. This pledge against force suddenly seemed to mock all the lessons of history. It seemed as pedantic and as pompous as—as John O'Connell himself; sitting there, envisaging himself in his father's cloak.

On the return drive Margaret was indignant that the oratory should have been stemmed in its Belgian sequence. 'I think it is very bad form of Mr. John O'Connell. He forgets that when we won our freedom in Belgium—*with* the sword—that we paid his father the tribute of nominating him for election as our King!'

Belgium and home had been much in her thoughts lately. Her mother had been ailing and Margaret had longed to visit her but the thought of the sea, the winds, the swaying boat! They were too terrifying to be faced alone. And, Roderick, could not have been spared during the recent emergency.

One lovely Sunday afternoon a few weeks later, she decided

to broach the matter. Roderick lay stretched in a garden chair feeling at peace with all the world. The worst was over. He had almost dragged his tenants through the last threat of famine. And now there was abundance in sight. Never had he seen such crops. Through half-closed lids he enjoyed the spectacle of his wife approaching him. In her white gown of striped muslin, tight-waisted and billowing, her country hat of white straw with its fall of white lace round the brim, she had a bridal air. He told her so.

'I am—a bride—again,' she twinkled. She bent over Dominic in his basinette beside the 'big wind seat'. 'I vow I shall have no favourites,' she cooed to him, 'but you make it difficult for me.'

Margaret lifted the baby and seated herself beside Roderick. From nowhere Pakie Scally appeared and stood behind them swishing off midges.

'And brides,' resumed Margaret, 'go on honeymoons.'

'Honeymoons?' Roderick was dangling his hunter over Dominic who clutched it and said 'Tick! tick!' It was a perfect moment for suggesting a trip to Belgium.

Roderick's first thought was the expense. Where would the money come from? He had spoken the words before he realised.

She apologised. 'I ought to have remembered what a time you've had. No rents coming in and everything going out——But'—she faltered—'it's been so long; nine years!'

He sat up and looked at her. She was as slenderly graceful as when he had first glimpsed her gliding over the ice at Antwerp; the heart-shaped face just as lovely! Was it nine years since then?

'We will go to Belgium,' he announced. 'No.' He placed a hand over her lips. 'You deserve a break away from this country. It has tossed you about too often; it treated you to a display of fireworks when you arrived that nearly sent you into Kingdom come; then climaxes and anti-climaxes. And you've worked like a galley slave all this year. Hasn't she, Mister?'

'Tick, tick,' replied Dominic, reaching to clutch the big watch that his father still dangled over him.

'Then that's settled. We go to Antwerp next month.'

'But, Roderick, the money!'

'My love, it is middle class to speak of money. And besides, in all the nine years you have been with me I have never seen better crops. We shall have a bumper harvest. When it is gathered and the rents flowing in we shall go sailing up the Scheldt; all four of us.'

Her eyes shone out at him. 'To see Maman again,' she breathed, 'to bring her our children!' She was near to tears. Hannah came for the baby.

'Come,' said Roderick. 'Let's go for a stroll.'

As Margaret adjusted the tapestry that draped the back of the big seat he stooped to study the scene she had embroidered. She had depicted the great tree exactly as it had stood in the centre of the lawn. Under its branches a girl watched while a man carved their intertwined initials. Beyond stretched the avenue with the trees meeting overhead as they used to, and in the distance the gateway under the arch formed by the sentinel tree at either pillar.

'It is exactly as it used to be. I have not fully appreciated your beautiful industriousness.'

They strolled through the pastures to where the first corn lay cut. Finches and chaffinches hopped songless and businesslike among the husks. He helped her on to a bank that throbbed with bees and flies. Grasshoppers did their best in the way of chirrups to make up for August's lack of bird-song. Margaret watched Roderick as his eyes roved over the fields. The love of the land lay deep and dark within him.

'Look, Margaret.' He waved towards the golden heads of wheat that bent towards each other. 'Don't they resemble a conclave of crowned kings?'

'La, la,' she cried gaily. 'I wish I could see things as you do. It must be the Belgian strain that curbs my Celtic vision.' Belgium, she thought. I shall be there soon. Soon! The words made a song in her heart that stripped the fields of mystique.

'Watch the way their leaves tremble,' he said. 'Even in this heat! They are trembling at their own power.'

'What a fanciful thought, Roderick!'

'It is not fanciful, Margaret. It is terribly real. No monarch on earth wields such power as these golden sceptres of wheat. If they were to lose, suddenly, their crown of golden grain, who would fill the hungry mouths of a starving world?'

A burst of music sounded. From the high bank where they stood they could see figures forming up on the dance platform at the crossroads.

'It has been many a long Sunday since they've held the platform dance. Thank goodness they have the heart to dance again. Shouldn't fancy myself dancing in this steaming heat!' He jumped down and held out his arms for her. 'Let's go and watch.'

Horses were tethered at the four roads that converged at the cross. Townspeople looked on from their phaetons and passing strangers reined in to watch the spectacle of a crossroad dance. Even the old people were there, lured by the lovely weather and the gladsome sight of the rich crops.

In the interlude, the piper, Owen Meagher, who was believed to have been taught his music by the fairies, played a solo.

Margaret murmured to Roderick that she could quite believe that the Good People had been his teachers. The sound made her think of the dancing of fairies and the singing of elves. Later, the long-haired girl who had danced at the castle did a Double Jig with John Holohan. Margaret and Roderick left the crossroads as Big John sang a selection which made the people roar at its wry humour.

'*The Wedding of Ballyporeen*'
'... *There was bacon and greens but the turkey was spoilt Potatoes dressed every way, roasted and boiled ...*'

Roderick led Margaret back along the bridle path to the Cobs where the potato field lay.

'We can take the short cut through Black Pat Ryan's,' he said.

Nonie had seen the elegant couple passing down through the fields. The sight of them, he with his arm around her waist, she floating like thistledown in her fashionable gown, struck at her heart.

For better or worse! One might as well have taken the nun's vow and coarse habit. Its renunciation of fashionable gowns would not have been more irrevocable than her marriage vows. She turned away. Gowns indeed! In a few more days her darlings would have food; solid food. A plate of floury potatoes just now would be more acceptable to herself than a silk gown.

She tried to busy herself. There was so little to do. The dishes were so easy to wash these days. No grease; no soiled cutlery; no pigs to boil for; no yarn to knit stockings. She looked idly through the window. He was coming this way! And the white gown floating behind; and he stopping every minute to help her over a twig or a pebble. She squeezed her eyes against the sight. Poor Pat for all his kindness would never dream of stepping back to allow her to pass first through that little gap! Damn them! Traipsing coolly through *her* land; making her mourn the refinements that she thought to forget.

She closed the door and drew down the fiddle. Roderick and Margaret turned towards the house as they heard the music, but they could only glimpse a bent gold head. Roderick's lips twitched. The tune was old and saucy—

> *'I met a fair Rosy by a mulberry tree,*
> *And though Mass was my notion*
> *My devotion was she——'*

He burst out laughing. 'She's a minx!'

'A huzz-ee,' said Margaret. She hadn't realised that the unfamiliar path would have led her past this door.

He drew her over another stile. Black Pat was sitting on the ground looking at his potato field. 'Be generous, Margaret! Remember, we are on the first stage of our honeymoon.' The sight of Black Pat watching his potatoes smote her. They had so little! While she—Belgium! Her mind made joyful plans about clothes.

'I see you are keeping a close eye on your potatoes, Pat.' Roderick called out.

Pat rose unhurriedly to his feet. 'No child ever got better mindin', Sir Roderick. A few more days of this heat and they'll be leppin' out of their skins.'

The pair strolled on arm in arm. Sterrin's voice called. She came up holding out Margaret's vinaigrette. 'You left it on the Big-Wind-seat.'

Roderick took her hand and sauntered along, his senses drowsed by the mingled scent of woodbine and hawthorn and the particularly strong-scented wild stock that grew on the hedge by the bog road.

'What a horrible smell!' said Margaret. 'Let's go back.' She was deep now in Sterrin's Belgium wardrobe.

Roderick broke off a blossom. 'It *is* rather pungent, love, but I must confess I find it pleasing.' Sterrin squealed with laughter.

'Silly Papa! Not *that* smell. . . . The one from the potato fields.'

'Potato fields?' he spoke quietly, but no longer sleepily.

'Yes,' she said. 'I rode there this afternoon. I had to turn back from the smell. That is why when I saw you heading for the Cobs I brought Mamma's vinaigrette.'

Black Pat's planning was simpler than Lady O'Carroll's field. Smoking his first pipe of tobacco for months, he planned about his fine potato crop. The priest had given him the tobacco today when he called for a birth certificate for Norisheen's Confirmation. He had filled his pockets with biscuits for the children. And the delight of them! Like Christmas they had said! But not like last Christmas. Well, next Christmas would be different; a goose in the bastable again; and dumplings with caraway seeds. Shamefacedly, he puffed out a cloud of smoke. Mean it was, for a respectable man to give his mind to thoughts of food. Like a bachach!

He smiled as he looked at the proud foliage of his potatoes. They had repaid his extravagance, the long journey to Kerry for seed potatoes from the Maharees! No rich farmer in the three parishes had dreamt of doing such a thing. Not even the Sir. Oh, little Nonie had big ways! He engulfed the landscape in smoke.

Black Pat looked over his shoulder. The castle Quality were behaving very strangely. Miss Sterrin was running towards the castle. The Sir was running in the opposite direction and her Ladyship was just standin' there; sniffin' elegantly at her smelling salts. He shrugged and resumed his seat and his pipe. There was no accountin' for the whimsies of the Quality. A few minutes later he was on his feet looking curiously over the hedge; just as Roderick had gazed at his own extraordinary behaviour last Autumn. Big John, on a horse that he hadn't taken time to saddle, had led Thuckeen up to the Sir. Pat could see the Sir riding the headlands of the Cobs hither and thither; mounting and dismounting. Now he was coming this way! Suddenly the great black horse rose over the hedge and skidded to its haunches beside Pat.

'Ryan!' called Sir Roderick. 'Go down there and see your potatoes are all right.'

'My potatoes, Sir Roderick! Sure——'

'Go on!'

Black Pat turned and ran. 'There's nothing wrong with my

213

potatoes!' he shouted. He pulled a piece of furze from a gap. It resisted and he forced through. He raced across the next field and through the hedge without making for the gap. He reached his field unaware that his face and hands were bleeding. 'There's nothing wrong with my potatoes!' he sobbed at the first drill. There was no tobacco smoke to kill the smell that rose and smote him to the earth!

Nonie found him there when she came to call him to the watery porridge. He refused to stir; just lay babbling and bleeding. Stiffly, like an old woman, she stooped and pulled a stalk from the earth. It was laden with fine potatoes. She gripped one. There was a squelch as her fingers closed over slime. She shook her hand to free it from the abomination, the stench. Before her eyes, the mess that had been a firm potato dropped in black splodges into a deep, gaping hole. She screamed. It was a haunting! The orchards of hell were forcing their evil fruit up through the earth! She fled.

Roderick turned in the saddle and looked back at his stricken fields. Beyond lay the sprawling colony of tiny holdings that had only potato patches. Their occupants, and as many more, to be fed by him! For ever! Was it some other phase of time or was it this very afternoon that he had talked whimsicalities about golden crowns filled with wheat to feed a starving world?

His glance fell on the face of the big coachman. There was a horror upon it this lovely evening that the terrible night of the Big Wind had not been able to produce. There was horror, too, on that lad's face. And on his hands! Young Thomas came over and spoke to his master without being addressed; just as he had spoken to him that night when the storm had swept all men to one level of helplessness. 'I saw them move, your Honour's Sir.' He shook his hands to free them of slime. 'Before my eyes they decomposed; like—like an apparition—of some——'

'Of some spectre,' said his master. 'The spectre of famine.'

Thomas stole out at dusk to see how things fared with Kitty and Mark at the little cottage at Knockgraffin. Mrs. Stacey slipped him a wedge of cake for Kitty. 'I saw her go down to the platform dance this afternoon. The creature looked like a brooch.' Thomas understood. He had glimpsed Kitty at Mass this morning and her profile had looked like a cameo brooch etched whitely against the black background of her hair.

He rushed through unaccustomed short cuts to warn Mark to get his potatoes out of the ground.

A motionless figure of a man stood silhouetted against the darkening light in the potato patch. It was Mark, his head bowed into the crook of the arm that leaned on the spade handle. With that awful smell coming from the opening around the spade the melancholy figure might well have exhumed the body of a loved one.

Thomas, scraping words of pity, might as well not have been there. He moved on into the house. Kitty was kneeling by the cradle, her cheeks pressed to the baby's. She turned at his step. 'God save you, Thomas! I knew you'd come.'

He drew her to her feet. 'You'll be cramped sitting there. Mark is taking it hard.'

'It is a wonder he hasn't gone mad. His poor body is only a husk; too weak to sustain a strong mind. Coax him inside, Thomas. I'll brighten the fire.'

He took the support of the spade from Mark and led him in. Kitty was turning the fanwheel. Fresh sods of turf stood upright, their heads together over the reddening embers.

Mark watched smoke dance up the chimney in patterned puffs. 'It was a trick,' he croaked, 'a mean, low trick of nature, codding our hungry hearts up to the eyes with the kind of sunshine that brings abundance. It made me dance—dance!' His voice thinned upwards. 'That's how tricksters fool men into putting their savings into a scheme that isn't there—— What in the name of God are you doing with that kettle, Thomas!?'

Thomas had swung a kettle of water on to the crane over the blaze. 'Are you dreamin', Thomas?' cried Kitty. There was hysteria in her laugh. She had retched as she turned in the boreen after the dance and the silent messenger of the Blight had sneaked down the pathway to greet them with its evil-smelling tidings. Her mind had retched too, in hysteria. She was drained, exhausted. There was no tea in the house. Why was Thomas boiling water?

Thomas scalded the teapot. 'We'll find use for the kettle,' he smiled. He took tea from a screw of paper in his pocket. The brew was weak but cheerful and there were still a few grains to lighten the despondency of the morrow.

Kitty's old warm smile shone through her tears as she took

the cup from him and the plate with the generous slice of cake. She cut it into three wafer-thin slices and when Theobald whimpered again, she took him up and fed him crumb by crumb.

Thomas watched with pity the way the child devoured the crumbs. The tiny features were perfect; like Kitty's, the same black curls. But the lovely roses had faded from the once chubby cheeks. They were as yellow as the Indian meal his little stomach rejected.

As they walked to the gate with him, Kitty said suddenly, 'Isn't it strange! This—calamity reminds me somehow of the Big Wind. That came suddenly, too; out of the sky in the evening. I was bolting the henhouse and suddenly I was flung along the yard and round the gable end of the house and the heavens were roaring as though God Himself were angry. Not that I associate the thing that has come out of the ground this evening with God.'

Thomas looked back and sketched a restricted wave. He didn't call *Sursum corda* this time. Lift up your heart, inagh.

He vaulted a fence. From the sheaves of corn a company of black-headed gulls rose silently to the night sky. Thomas suddenly stopped dead, his scalp prickling. A white wraith had appeared before him. Up and down it moved, wafting, swaying but never budging from the space before him; almost eye-level.

He forced himself to move forward, his heart racing with dread. He that had no fears of the night! And then he realised what it was. How often had he stopped to watch that marvel of nature, the dance of the ghost moths. He forged ahead. He mustn't let the evening's disaster unman him. But the dread was on him. From the fetid fields the smell rose up to waft through the night mist like a ghostly haunting of the landscape.

Sir Roderick was out at dawn. He checked on every drill. He had planted twice last year's potato crop. Not a drill had escaped! It was the same with the tenants. They wandered dispiritedly through their drills stopping here and there to pick up a blackened stalk. He looked across to Golden Meadows. Mr. Lonergan was walking slowly across a field, his head down. Roderick rode up the short avenue to Ulick Prendergast's farmhouse. The old man was sitting bolt upright on his horse, tight-lipped and grim. He uncovered silently and Roderick waited for him to speak. Ulick spoke only when he had something to say.

'It is like the Wrath to come,' he said, 'no one round here has escaped.'

A stream of callers surged up the avenue all day; landlords doing the rounds; ascertaining how other estates had fared; what measures to take.

'I'll evict,' cried Major Darby. There was panic in the threat. 'I couldn't carry through another season without rents.'

Roderick wasn't certain himself how far he could carry mercy. But he remembered Darby's tenant, Dominic Landy. 'Our first concern,' he said coldly, 'is to save human life.'

'That's all very well,' Darby thrust. 'But carrying uneconomic tenants on our backs is weakness. A weak landlord is a bad landlord.'

'Property,' Lord Templetown reminded him, 'imposes responsibilities. We can make no plans until we know the extent of the Blight. If it is nationwide, then the government will take over.'

'The government,' said Phineas De Lacey dully, 'will tell us again that the Blight is "a baseless vision".' There was a white despair on the cheerful ruddy countenance.

The Scout was not the only one who awaited the mail coach in the evening. A crowd of respectable townspeople waited anxiously for its news. The Scout almost scaled the sacred heights of the driver's seat. But ritual was upheld. The reins were handed to the ostler. The white gloves that remained immaculate no matter how black the potato, were slowly removed. Then the driver informed the Scout that the nine mail coaches that had checked in at the Dublin Depot this morning had all carried the same tale of disaster. The Blight had struck all over Ireland.

CHAPTER 24

'She gave them some broth without any bread. And she whipped them all soundly. And put them to bed.' Roderick couldn't believe his eyes. And yet it was true. He was standing at Arbour Hill in Dublin watching her Excellency the Vicereine dip the ladle into the first Government Soup for the famine victims. The ceremony was being held on the eve of Roderick's return to Kilsheelin after the Landlords' Protest meeting. His neighbours, the de Guiders, had come with him. The Government had not acceded to their petitions for help to combat the famine. But, it had made the gesture of sending Monsieur Soyer, the chef of the Reform Club, to show the starving Irish how to live on a soup containing three ounces of solid food to one ounce of water! 'A French chef, my dear!' murmured Miss Hester.

There he stood on a platform above the pit at Arbour Hill barracks where the bodies of the insurgents of '98 had been buried by their executioners. It seemed like a symbol of forgiveness that the spot should have been chosen by the Government for this act of benevolence. Palms and flowers adorned the sides. In the centre stood the Lord Lieutenant and his lady, flanked by the ladies-in-waiting and by aides-de-camp in the glory of full-dress uniform. Her Excellency, the Vicereine, was dressed for the occasion in a high-necked robe with but one velvet-edged flounce. It conveyed a dignified impression of subdued restraint. It reproached the fashionably-dressed ladies present in their many-flounced silken gowns. A military band brought from England for the event, played a selection of operatic and patriotic airs. The Union Jack blew in the wind over the bubbling cauldron. The great French chef came before the footlights and stirred the life-giving brew.

He flavoured and sipped; it was good! With a gesture of satisfaction he turned and bowed low to her Excellency. The band muted its airs. The bandmaster raised his baton. There was a rumbling and a crashing. All the gentlemen withdrew their supporting arms from their ladies and went rigid at the opening bars of God Save The Queen.

The semi-starving withdrew their support from the starving. The cripples straightened over their crutches. Hungry old veterans decorated by Wellington drew in their empty stomachs and stood erect to the anthem that had marched them to many a victory.

As the First Lady moved forward inside her swaying skirt, Sarah whispered, 'Hester, observe how the skirt swings. Her Excellency must be wearing one of those new "watch-spring" petticoats.'

The chef drew the ladle that was chained to the cauldron. Like a knight surrendering his sword he proffered it to the Vicereine. Slowly she dipped it into the Elixir of Irish life. Roderick turned to watch the first of the multitude led forward. It had woman's clothes and the face of a skeleton. Miss Sarah fumbled for her smelling salts.

As the gracious figure in the austere robe of blue barege dipped the ladle and slowly brought it towards those pallid lips, a young *beau* in front of Roderick murmured, 'Angel of mercy.' The charming girl on his arm gave an audible sob. The ladies were not the only ones moved to tears by the beautiful charity of this noble lady. Roderick noticed one young aide-de-camp furtively wiping a tear.

Whether it was that she was overcome with compassion; whether it was revulsion at the contortions of the terrible face as the mouth opened to receive the soup; or whether it was simply that she had filled the ladle too generously—the Vicereine's hand trembled and a few drops of soup fell on that exquisite gown!

The lady showed the iron training of vice-royalty. She went on holding the ladle while the creature took an unappreciatively long time about consuming the nourishment that she should have been gulping frantically.

'That lovely gown!' exclaimed Miss Hester. 'The dreadful soup is still dripping on it.'

'Don't worry, Cousin Hester,' soothed Roderick. 'It is not strong enough to stain.' And grimly he added: 'They ought to have strengthened it with bones from the pit.' Among the bones of '98 rebels executed were the Vicereine stood were those of his uncle the red-haired Calvagh O'Carroll who had blandly helped the hangman to tie the knot.

The young English gentleman in front glared challengingly back at Roderick. He was a recruit of the twelve-thousand-strong army of highly-paid officials who had crossed over to cope with the famine crisis.

'Shall we move, Sir Roderick?' Stephen de Guider was nervous lest the young blade call out Sir Roderick. People were edging away.

Roderick drew Miss Sarah forward. Her face had the look that always told Mike O'Driscoll that the Sir was ready to 'shoot a flea off the tail of a snipe'. 'Stand aside, sir,' he said to the young gentleman.

On the homeward journey Roderick and James de Guider passed crowds of starving men moving wearily along the roads to the Relief Works Schemes. Sleek and well-dressed officials put them through a catechism of insolent questions that began with the inevitable, 'Why should a big able-bodied man like you seek Relief Work?' And always it was answered with the patient statement that echoed through the millions. 'Ta ocras orm!' 'The hunger is on me!'

At Kilsheelin, Margaret sat at the window for a sight of Roderick's returning carriage. She was physically exhausted. The gloom of those daily scenes in the yard had darkened her spirits. She longed for Roderick.

Suddenly she saw a figure creep through the grey light of the fields. The silence was pierced by the agonising scream of an animal in torture. Dear God, it was starting again! The White-boys! The terrible mutilations! She pressed her hands over her ears so that they heard only her own screams.

When Roderick entered his wife's lovely white room with its gilded harp and its spinet and its glow of fire and candlelight, she was swaying in Nurse Hogan's arms. Horror was in Margaret's great soft eyes, in her voice whose screams had been muffled from him against Nurse Hogan's shoulder. 'Maman!' she screamed. Always before it had been 'Roder-eeck!' But now she cried out for Maman whom she would have been with, but for this terrible famine.

She quietened in his arms. The tenseness went from her body. He could feel its own warm seductiveness flow back. Too late.

She had merely unburdened her strain on to his overburdened shoulders. There was no escape for him, anywhere, from this seeping, all-pervading horror.

Roderick knew the sickening truth about the cry that Margaret had heard. It was not the Whiteboys this time, but desperate women who stole through the fields by night to draw blood from cattle to mix with meal for their hungry children!

Big John was first on the spot from which the cries had sounded. He found an emaciated old woman lying near the wounded animal. 'It wasn't for myself I did it,' she whispered. He recognised Mrs. Downey, the mother of Felix and Jim. 'The gossoons were fading before my eyes. I couldn't stand the look on their faces,' she whispered. He carried her to the cabin that had replaced the house blown down the night of the Big Wind. He had not been able to stop that night and help her because of his hurry to get help for her Ladyship. The next day she was dead.

Hers was the first famine death in Kilsheelin. The frenzied animal had lashed out and caught her temple. Though she died from her own criminal act, Mr. O'Neill-Balfe brought in a verdict of Death From Famine.

'The hunger is on me,' was the cry of the famine. Repeal was forgotten as men and women scrounged and battled to survive.

Nonie Ryan was desperate. There was nothing left to sell. She had written home at last for help, but there was no word back. 'We can wait no longer then,' she told Pat, '*He* is giving employment, draining that snipe bog of his.'

Pat looked at her squatting on the straw paliasse, her feet tucked under her like a little fairy woman. He reached and plucked the feather that clung to a tear at the end of her dainty nose. Feathers; they were every place since she sold the fine down stuffing of their marriage bed. 'Love!' he muttered aloud. 'Bad 'cess to it for the love that made me take you away from full and plenty. All right, I'll get work.'

Outside he gripped the gatepost to cough, and where he spat there was blood. Her head came through the window. 'Pat! I'd do it again—priest's horse and all—if—if I had the energy.'

His smile flashed back and his shoulders straightened.

But he went in the opposite direction from Kilsheelin; on to Major Darby's and his 'famine folly'. For sixpence a day—and a halfpenny docked by the pay clerk—men were building a thing called an obelisk. He cast a longing upward glance at the bog that Sir Rody O'Carroll was paying sevenpence a day for draining, no pay clerk to pocket his cut, and only a few fields away instead of this two-mile trudge! He halted uncertain and then it came back to him, as vivid as hunger; the scene on that Saint Patrick's Eve. Footing kiss how-are-you! Hadn't he seen their two faces? Like of people's that had found each other after being lost; the slow way their mouths had come towards each other and clung; and the eyes of her, longing after the fine horseman of her own kind till he was out of sight. Black Pat turned away. ' "Dear to a man's heart",' he quoted, ' "is his brother; but his foster-brother is the marrow of his heart". And you were the marrow of my heart, Rody O'Carroll. I little thought you'd ever play me false.'

For Margaret, her turn of duty at the soup cauldron at Templetown served as some relief from the horror around her. Despite misery and sorrow and often repulsive spectacles, when Mrs. Kennedy-Sherwin was ladling there was bound to be diversion. Nothing seemed to depress the little lady. She took her place behind the cauldron in the most startling confections as though she were presiding behind the silver tea urn in her own drawing-room. The Misses Cherry and Berry Comerford and Mrs. Enright in their big callimanco aprons had given up trying to impress her with their disapproving sniffs. She just didn't care. And there was never a shortage of gentlemen. When passing officers saw the vivacious chatterbox at the ladle they dismounted and leaned nonchalantly against their mounts, roaring with laughter at her sallies. Even the scarecrows laughed gaily when it was she who filled their soup cans. All the world loves laughter.

The scarecrows laughed now at Mrs. Enright pinned up for all the world to see the announcement that a sum of money had come unsought from a strange body of people in faraway New York. They called themselves the Independent Order of Odd Fellows.

What kind of fellows could they be at all, marvelled the hungry ones! The Scout enlightened them. They were a benevolent body of gentlemen who were handicapped by certain mental disability. '... what you ignoramuses might describe as being a—a bit touched here.' He tapped his chimney pot and the crowd roared. 'But,' he went on sternly, 'the great free land of America permits all men to go free and therefore these—these kindly gentlemen though they are—intellectually—like—like Billy Din there——' Billy smiled his silly smile and said that they were good gentlemen and '. . . they wouldn't hurt me foot,' the Scout continued, 'are allowed freedom to indulge the Christian impulses of their generous hearts.'

After his oration, the Scout would have liked a drop of the soup that smelled so temptingly. But it was the brew of charity; and the Scout styled himself a landlord. Didn't he own his own tiny house in Love Lane? And the lean-to-shanty beside it that was let at two shillings a month!

Young Thomas moved in a rasping trance—only one thing was clear. He was grateful for the memory of the leisurely—the cultured—life he had known before the famine. Now he milked cows in the sheds of his master's friends. He felt humble as he dispensed charity to industrious farmers. Those outstretched hands had cultivated their owners' soil whilst he had eaten the soft bread of servitude. Ah well! He didn't eat much soft bread now! No lazy reading; no pleasant chats with Miss Sterrin. No existence of his own. He saw few of his friends. As for Kitty and Mark, he put the thought of them from him with panic. God alone knew how things fared with them.

Kitty watched a shadow fall across her doorway. Her heart lifted. A coordheecer? Young Thomas maybe! She hadn't seen him for months.

'God save you,' said the man at the door. 'I'm looking for a colleen named Molly Slattery.' The implements of his trade protruded from the satchel on his shoulder. 'Has Molly the fever?' she asked. At least this was 'newses' of some kind. All 'newses' were bad these times! 'They don't wait for fever now to get their hair cut. There is a length of food value in hers, I'm told.' He watched the nervous play of Kitty's fingers through the black ringlets.

'How—how much will you give me for it?'

'Two shillings.'

She dropped her hand. Woman's vanity shot the listlessness from her voice. 'What do you think you are buying? A boneen?'

'By the frost, ma'am! 'Twould take a better head of hair than yours to buy a little pig these days.' He turned to the door. 'I must be on my way. Mrs. Campion has five daughters down— bad. She wants the hair off them before night. Not lookin' for money *she* is. Only waitin' for the relief I'll give.' He watched her features straining out at him from the thin skin of her face.

'The Campions!' she scoffed. 'Who would want to buy yellow hair?'

'Two and six, then,' he called. From the cradle the hungry wailing started again. The travelling barber gave a sympathetic, 'Tck, tck, I won't be keepin' you, ma'am. You'll be wantin' to get the child's supper.' His eyes slewed deliberately round a circuit that embraced the empty hearth, the door that swung from an empty cupboard. 'The mothers of hungry children haven't time to be bargaining about their hair.'

She turned frantically from the cradle and pulled the pins from her hair. 'How many mothers of hungry children have hair like that to bargain for? Four shillings,' she challenged.

He stepped back into the room and took out his purse. 'Sit down,' he said.

She kept her eyes squeezed tight until she heard the closing of the door. When she opened them the room was empty, but four silver shillings brightened the table.

The door opened again. 'Where did you say the Slattery girl lived?'

'I didn't say.' She wasn't going to have the plunder of Molly Slattery's cloak of hair on her conscience. What will Mark say, she thought, as she trekked home with her purchases? He was proud of her beautiful hair. But Mark merely asked her in amazement where had she got the beautiful food.

'I bought it.'

He looked round the bare room. 'With what, in the name of God?'

'With a bit of myself.'

People spoke strangely these times. He hoped there was nothing queer going on in Kitty's head. He peered out at her over the wooden porringer. There *was* something queer about her. 'Kitty!' he shouted suddenly. 'Kitty, cailin duv machree!' Dark girl of my heart! 'Your beautiful hair!'

By Christmas night when Young Thomas saw the Hennesseys, the cut ends of Kitty's hair had curled around her ears. The

224

graceful line of her neck and shoulder stood out uncluttered.

He was delighted by Kitty's short hair and reproached Mark for lacking an eye for beauty.

'Never let it grow again,' he told Kitty.

He had brought them some news and diversion along with a few stolen pieces from his own festive dinner-plate. He told them that John Holohan had left for America on Christmas Eve, that Molly Slattery had gone with him, leaving her mother keening inconsolably, as she watched the coach carrying the two away.

Thomas dared not delay. Christmas Day, except for the meat and apple dumpling, had been the same as every other day. Harder. Every house on the estate had its gift delivered. And the stirabout line had been served in the evening as well as in the morning. It had reached from the back door to the back lodge.

As he hurried through the darkness the rush lights—despite death and disaster—still shone from the cottages to light the Holy Family.

Roderick was forced to mortgage the castle. At night in the library the faces of his ancestors reproached him from their frames. Men had gone on dying, they said, all the centuries that this castle had gone on enduring.

'I know,' answered Roderick aloud. 'But one cannot lean against the walls of a castle and watch men die of hunger; *and* women; *and* children!'

His eyes roved round the walls to O'Carroll Ribbeach who, when Queen Elizabeth had divided Tipperary among three men of Cheshire had ridden forth astounded at the trespass and bade the English quit his land; the 'Handsome O'Carroll' whose descendant had signed the American Declaration of Independence; on to a dandy in a gorgeous waistcoat—'*You* cannot afford to reproach me, Grandfather. You began this ramp. It was you who contrived an entry for the demolition forces. You betrayed us to the gales of the Big Wind. A forest of oaks for a necklace.' He stopped dead. The diamond necklace! It could avert this disaster. The diamond oaks of Kilsheelin could give back shelter to the castle. There was still time.

He hurried upstairs to discuss the idea with Margaret. From the shadowy drapes of the fourposter her quiet breathing came to him. As he bent over her she gave a little moan of exhaustion.

He turned and descended to the library to deal with his mail.

The letter on top of the pile that awaited him bore no post-mark. Some local letter, he presumed, delivered by hand. As he tossed it aside to deal with the more distant ones he noticed the inscription on the back, 'American Postage to Ireland Suspended'. Inside was a draft drawn on an American bank for more than two thousand pounds. No name; just 'Anonymous sympathiser'.

For a brief moment Roderick felt a sense of privilege. Not because he had been the one entrusted with this magnificent contribution; but because apart from the impersonal transactions of the bank concerned, no one but God knew the donor's identity. No single word of thanks required; while the papers of the three kingdoms proclaimed the generosity of Her Majesty for her paltry contribution to her starving subjects!

He looked through the other letters. A shilling from a poor widow in England; a day's wages from a London counting clerk. On one piece of paper was scribbled, 'Poor Erin! I give you the first fruits of my first song.' It was signed 'English Songwriter'.

And then came a letter that he must answer. It came from the Protestant Archdeacon of an English cathedral and it was signed Roderick Carroll-Greyson. His offering, eight hundred pounds, was the Famine Collection from the morning and afternoon services last Sunday.

'My Carroll ancestors,' wrote the Archdeacon, 'came originally from Tipperary.... Perhaps in happier days we may meet....'

How pleasant it would be to invite the gentleman here! Would such a thing be possible ever again? Greetings and returning visits! Lavish hospitality on one's board. God! He put his head down on his arms. He felt hemmed in by horror; fought back an adolescent urge to run away from it all.

He shook the feeling from him and took the next letter. American, the same superscription on the back; 'Postage to Ireland Suspended'. There was a grandeur of spirit behind these words that appealed to Roderick. Here in Ireland every effort in the cause of charity was arrested by officialdom. Relief schemes mouldered on office files. Subscriptions were passed slowly from one department to another. Cargoes of benevolence lay unloaded while heads of departments pondered the problem of distribution and transport. And in America! an institute of State set aside! the word IRELAND on any crate, packet, or letter—a password for priority and free transport!

The letter was from Miss Maryanne O'Regan of Virginia. '... the talk is all of the great calamity in Ireland.... The Governor of Virginia held a big meeting ... all the big plantation owners.... It was agreed to send the *Raleigh* with several thousand tons of kiln-dried corn and rice and pickled pork.' Roderick smiled as he read. '... we held a quilting bee in the drawing-room and all the young ladies with copperplate writing were set to write instructions on how to cook the food, as I believe the Irish people have never seen any food but potatoes....' There was a subscription enclosed and then a postscript. Had the consignment of foodstuffs, addressed personally to himself, arrived? An official notification amid the correspondence informed him that a large consignment from Virginia, America, still awaited collection.

Immediately he gave orders for men to accompany him before dawn to Waterford dock. This valuable contribution had lain too long. He thought with panic of the grain ship of the Sultan of Turkey; the first in the sea-race of mercy to arrive; a feast for the rats because the English soldiery refused to unload it!

Roderick primed his pistols in readiness and left the rest of the letters to be dealt with by the De Lacey girls tomorrow. They would need more help at the rate subscriptions were coming in. There were so few well-educated young ladies available. Suddenly for the first time in months he thought of Mrs. Black Pat Ryan. *She* could be useful to cope with correspondence! He hadn't seen any of the family for months—a year, nearly. Although Black Pat sent his rent to the dot of Gale day. Never an hour behind.

Roderick could not know that the rent had come from the sale of the fine horse. Nonie looked out forlornly at the empty paddock. That speculation had failed; like the speculation of that journey for seed potatoes, at twice the cost of anyone else's. And Pat, at last, had to join the ranks of respectable farmers who were seeking Relief Work.

She moistened her lips and grimaced at the taste of her tongue. She drank a few sips of water but the clatter of her cup against the bucket brought in the children, their stomachs in

227

their eyes. She dare not rattle a utensil. 'Bread'n butter,' said the youngest. It was not a request; just a reaction to the clatter that her mind connected with the preparations for a meal. Outside there was a scuffling and Adam ran off somewhere screaming.

'Mammy,' said Norisheen firmly, 'I'll go to the castle and stand in the line. This is the day they give soup as well as meal. I'll bring home a canful.'

Nonie tried to keep her home. Her sister had written to say that she had posted foodstuff.

'The hunger is on me,' insisted Norisheen.

Her mother pressed her hands to her temples. 'Go on then,' she said dully. She turned from the sight of the girl's departure; with a can that had once held sweets for Christmas. The hunger is on me! The hunger is on me! The refrain mounted in a mocking crescendo. 'And how,' she cried aloud, 'am I to take the hunger from them?'

From the straw palliasse in the room beyond the parlour little Pat answered, 'You need take no hunger from me, Mammy. It has gone away.'

She had not noticed that he had gone to lie down. What was he saying? The hunger has gone away. Oh no, not that! She stooped and put her arms about him. 'You *are* hungry, my darling; and the food from your auntie will be here any minute. I'll cook lovely things.'

'I'm not hungry,' he whispered. The words chilled her heart with dread. This was the terrible stage of the famine. First the gnawing, constant hunger, then wild, devouring hunger. Then apathy and prostration. The juices ceased to make clamour. The tongue dried up; so did hope; so did life. It was the triumph of the famine. When it took back the hunger it had created.

She crushed him to her. 'You *are* hungry, gra' 'gal. You *are*. I'll get you——' What could she get him? And then at last she was glad that Norisheen had gone to beg for charity. 'I'll get you soup. Sleep now. When you waken, Norisheen will be here with the soup. I'll sing you to sleep love'—'Oh little head of gold! Oh candle of my house!' she sang, and her voice was like the releasing of a rusted lock. He *was* the candle of her house; the only bright head midst her dark brood. 'Oh! moths on the window fold your wings. . . .' He was looking at her strangely; unblinkingly. 'Oh! plover and oh! curlew over my house do not travel . . .' She stopped to catch what he was saying. Something

228

about three grains of oats. Dear God, the famine fever must be on him!

She looked wildly towards the window. Someone was on the roadway. It couldn't be Norisheen yet. She laid down the child and went to the door. Had God guided someone this way? A woman, tall and graceful, was gliding over the road like—an apparition. Like the Mother of Iosagain when She came to a cottage and soothed the wailing babe beside its sick mother; and when She had gone they both awakened to health!

The woman glanced at the open door and murmured something; but kept on. A vision indeed, thought Nonie as she closed the door! The vision of Lady O'Carroll was not for her or her child!

CHAPTER 25

Margaret had decided to seek out Mrs. Holohan. Though she was not a tenant, Margaret could not forget the woman's face as it looked after the car that was taking her son to exile. She shuddered as she thought of the way she would feel if she were separated from Dominic or Sterrin.

Margaret went by the short cut that she had taken with Roderick to the Crossroads dance the evening of the Blight. It led on to the road past Black Pat's door. The house seemed strangely quiet. As she past the door it opened with a rush and Mrs. Black Pat came out. Margaret gave her a good afternoon and went on without stopping. Behind her she could hear the door close with a crash.

He full lips tightened. This little Ryan person was *mauvais ton*. Why won't she realise her position? The absurdity of seizing every occasion to flounce and flaunt.

There was no sign of life at Mrs. Holohan's. Margaret relinquished the knocker. As she turned away, she thought she heard the sound of a moan inside ... she raised the latch and found Mrs. Holohan lying on the empty hearth. Even the water bucket was empty. Margaret wasted precious moments searching outside for a well. If only she could get her to the castle! If this were a main road! But there wasn't a soul nor a vehicle on this bye-road.

She suddenly remembered the soup kitchen outside Aughnacoll Church. A souperism centre where soup was given to the starving provided they abjured Catholicism; still, they would hardly try to induce a woman almost *in extremis* to apostasise! The place was only half a mile off, and Mrs. Holohan was barely the weight of her own clothes.

When Margaret arrived at the outskirts of the crowd people thought she was carrying a bundle of clothes. It was impossible to get through to the cauldron. The waiting was interminable. Famished Catholics thought to change their religion for the duration of the meal. 'I'm a Protestant,' they clamoured. But it wasn't that easy. They had to answer a long questionnaire. Only those who could produce written proof from a clergyman or authoritative person that they had attended church services were fed promptly.

Margaret's arms ached. She set Mrs. Holohan on her feet but she swayed and her pallor was getting terrible. The man in front was carrying a full-grown adult who pressed bonily against Margaret; and smelled abominably. Why on earth didn't I chance the journey home, she fumed! I could have got her as far as that—Mrs. Ryan. At least she would have given her nourishment.

She strained on tiptoe to attract the attention of a Souper. At the cauldron an emaciated wretch was pleading and expostulating. The soup, withheld while they catechised him, was tantalising.

Before Margaret could see what was happening, pandemonium had broken loose. The man had grasped the cauldron in a frenzy and upset its contents. People cupped the spilt fluid in their hands. They flung themselves down and lapped it like animals. They had reverted to untamed savagery.

Lady O'Carroll was knocked down. Mercifully someone lifted her burden. But a worse burden fell on her; pinned her down. The body that the man in front of her had carried. A dead body! Its face grinned into hers. Its incontinence fouled her clothes. She screeched and clawed from under the clamping grip. She found herself running down an empty road; running from the terrible Thing behind her; from the terrible screams that filled her ears. Gradually she realised that they were her own.

A blind, intuitive memory led her suddenly from the road on to the field path. The sight of a pretty, braided roof recalled her to a sense of control. There was no disapproval in her now. Here was a gladsome house! It had never sounded the hunger cry; only music and life; life!

She saw a carriage stop. The small figure that emerged carrying a child was Virginia Kennedy-Sherwin's. Dazedly, Margaret followed her inside and down a passage. She glimpsed two figures on something that was neither bed nor couch. She saw Mrs. Kennedy-Sherwin lay the child beside the two figures and turn to hold someone else in her arms. Margaret put her hands to her ears. The screams had started again. But it was just one long wail of uttermost despair. Long after it ceased a small figure confronted her.

'You have come too late, Lady O'Carroll,' said Mrs. Pat Ryan Duv. 'Go now!' Lady O'Carroll obeyed.

At the clanging of the bell Nurse Hogan rushed to the landing. Her Ladyship at last! She watched her pass Hegarty without speaking and skim up the stairs.

Lady O'Carroll offered no explanation for the clay-sodden shoes, the torn flounces; for the incredible filth of her pelisse and robe. 'Tell them to bring me a bath,' was all she said.

Roderick's spirits lifted as he came into the drawing-room. It was heavenly to come back to this calm and lovely woman. The little susurrus of her silken skirts as she moved forward and back over the embroidery frame made a shoheen-sho lullaby in his ears. Waterford had been hell. The whining and begging and keening around the docks! And passing Darby's place on the way back he had passed men building a Famine Folly, a spiral-shaped excrescence, neither decorative nor useful. One of the workmen had uncovered and given him a God-save-you. Roderick did not know who he was. There had been something vaguely familiar about him; but the characteristics that distinguished one human being from another had left all their faces. They all had the angular outline and stretched skin of death's anatomy.

It must be ages since he had seen Margaret at her embroidery frame; ages, too, since she had worn a silken gown. 'Hm!' he sniffed as he stooped to kiss her. 'We are very fragrant this evening—and, very decorative. Are we expecting company?'

She touched a wing of grey in the black of his hair. 'No one ...' The butler interrupted with a tray. 'I took the liberty, your Ladyship,' he said, noticing her surprised expression. The new-fangled afternoon tea had been stopped since the famine, but her appearance when she returned had shocked him. 'It's killin' ye'rselves ye both are.'

Margaret had none of the usual chatter about the Soup Kitchen. 'Anything strange?' Roderick asked her and immediately thought how meaningless the phrase had become. Everything was strange. People looked strange, those strange-looking men building a strange-looking obelisk. Only what was normal

232

held novelty. Like Margaret's silk gown and her embroidery frame!

'No——' The tea she was pouring slopped over into the saucer. 'Nothing strange, except a letter for you from Cousin Hester.'

His cousin, he read, had instructed her bank manager to send him one hundred pounds; she had already donated five hundred pounds to the Central Fund in Dublin. 'They can ill afford that,' he commented. Suddenly he burst out laughing. 'Listen to this; apparently despite famine and pestilence there had been no diminution in the Castle's splendours for the Second Drawing-room. '"There was only one unfortunate incident,"' he read out. '"A line of Debutantes' carriages got caught up in a line of sick carts but they managed to get to Saint Patrick's Hall in time to make their curtsies——"' Roderick looked up. 'The debutantes, I assume my love, not the sick carts.' Margaret was looking into space. More strangeness! She normally revelled in such social titbits. '"Her Excellency,"' he went on, '"was influenced, it is generally assumed, in her choice of dress by the melancholy state of the country. She *actually wore black*! An overskirt and corsage of black Gros D'Afrique lined with ..."' what is it Hegarty?'

The butler wished to enquire on behalf of some man downstairs if Mr. Pat Ryan—Black Pat—were employed in Sir Roderick's Bog Reclamation Scheme. He was wanted at home. There was trouble there.

Black Pat! Roderick remembered that he must call there tonight and enlist Mrs. Black Pat's service for the famine correspondence. What was the fellow talking about? Black Pat doing Relief Work! There must be some mistake. Surely, if Black Pat needed employment he would have come to me. 'One of Mr. Black Pat Ryan's children is dead,' said Hegarty sadly.

'Dead!' The word struck with all its former starkness. It had no connection with the Dead he had driven past today, with the undeliberate indifference of helplessness. 'It must be fever.' Roderick rose to his feet. Fever was now taking high toll from homes that were well above the margin of hunger. 'Don't worry, my dear. I'll avoid contact with infection as much as possible. But this is one sick house I must visit.'

In the hallway he glanced up towards a sound in the gallery. Through a cloud of perfumed steam he saw two servants carrying a laden bath towards the back staircase.

At Black Pat's he stood where Margaret had stood at the entrance to the long shadowy room. Through the open door in the room beyond he could see the little figures on the straw. The day that he had sold the horse they had been there too; with the chin-cough. But not on straw, on a mountainous feather bed; turning cartwheels and pelting a potato that had barely missed his own eye. They had told him proudly that it was their mammy who had painted the pictures he had been admiring. And suddenly the recollection made him conscious of the bareness about him; blank spaces where those skilful paintings had hung; the silver trinket box that had caught his attention was gone; the silver candlesticks, the lustres, the rosewood music box. 'Yes, they've all been eaten.'

He turned startled. He hadn't noticed her there, crouching down beside the straw. They've all been eaten! And the whole structure of his existence; his very home was the heritage of his own children consumed in his efforts against such hunger. He strode towards her. 'Why didn't you tell me? Why didn't you come like the others? Why didn't you bring *them*?'

'To the stirabout line?' It brought her to her feet.

'Yes, the stirabout line. It keeps people alive. Not pride.'

'Pride? There are other kinds of pride. The pride that made you forbid your daughter to share her food with my children. The pride that caused your wife to drive past doing the Grande Dame. If only she had stopped this afternoon, she might have saved one of them, but when she did condescend to come—it was too late.'

Margaret had been here? 'Was Lady O'Carroll here? This afternoon?'

She nodded. 'Not to see me or mine. She saw Mrs. Kennedy-Sherwin carrying Adam in—Adam——' She would have sunk but he caught her. It was like holding a bird whose nest had been plundered; no substance, just a trembling beat of life. 'I had no right to speak to you like that,' she murmured hoarsely, 'but when you accused me of letting my darlings die. If only Pat were here! Why doesn't he come?'

His arm tightened around her. She rested against him with a queer little peaceful flutter of breath. He put his hand on her hair. There was a dankness in the soft curls. Dear God, had that impish sprite become this broken fragment of womanhood?

234

Was this the fearless girl who had sprung from his knee and gone riding off into the spinney; tossing back over her shoulder a laughing, beckoning glance from will-o-the-wisp eyes?

Suddenly something happened to him that had not happened since his mother and father had died one after the other. Tears gushed from beneath his lashes and fell upon her face.

In a sudden passion of tenderness he pressed her to him and when he stooped to murmur, 'I'll find Black Pat for you, little Nonie,' his lips brushed her cheek.

On the way out he stopped dead. Two sleeping heads showed above the ledge of the settle bed. On either side of the ingle were two more sleeping figures. One was the oldest girl. The other, no bigger, but dressed in the height of bedraggled fashion, was the irresistible Mrs. Kennedy-Sherwin! Her little face was strained and its tearmarks were frankly smudged. She reminded him of a kitten that had been out all night in the bushes. A smile softened his lips. One could always count upon her to evoke a smile! He removed his hat again and doffed it in salute towards a very gallant little lady. Then he thought of Margaret —in festive gown, bathed in perfume!

He found Black Pat. It was easier to recognise him now. The strain had gone from his features. He lay with three others at the foot of the potbellied monstrosity that had become their tombstone!

It was a long time before Roderick remembered to uncover. He bashed his gloved hand across the obelisk and cursed. He cursed the system. He cursed the government that forced men to raise monuments to their own hunger until their dead bodies formed its pedestal. He cursed himself who had let the friend of his childhood die; for the simple want of food! The untrammelled presence of death released memories long-forgotten. Scenes and recollections beat upon him like blows. Foster-brother! The word mocked him; 'Dear to a man—is his brother; but his foster-brother is the marrow of his heart!'

The first sleepy cock-crow was sounding from the fowl sheds as Roderick's footsteps came up the stairs. They passed Margaret's door and moved into the adjoining dressing-room. She stood and waited. She could hear him moving about. Then there was silence. She turned, disheartened, to put out the lamp. It was starting all over again! Just like that other time. And over the same person. She switched the reflections from her

235

confused mind. They were sacrilegious in the face of this afternoon's tragedy; and, he argued, how many nights had not Roderick gone to his dressing-room after dealing with the Famine subscriptions rather than disturb her? He was probably exhausted. She relit the spirit lamp. She would take him a hot drink and she would tell him what had happened to her this afternoon; what she could remember, because her head was queer and more confused than ever before.

Behind her the door opened. She tossed the plaits from about her face and turned eagerly. He made no move to come in, just stood there and looked with a certain fixity at the equipment for the soothing draughts that she sometimes brewed in the night hours.

'You knew didn't you, that there were three children dead?'

'Roderick!'—Oh, how was she going to explain if he stood there looking at her like that.

She was wearing an intricately embroidered white wrapper tied with a girdle of plaited ribbons in every pastel tint. Her chestnut plants had the gleam of a well-groomed horse. Margaret was always well groomed; even in *deshabille*. No curling papers rattling and bulging under her nightcap; no acrid smell of lotions. The sensuous appeal of her beauty was almost overpowering. But Roderick had been emptied of emotions tonight. Above his foster-brother's body; and when he had caught Nonie as she sank after he had told her what he had to tell her, he had felt that his own soul had approached that region that holds the hosts of the dead. The beauty of this woman who had hastened from that hecatomb to perfume her body and deck it with silk had no power of appeal to him.

He made no effort to spare her the details of the Ryan tragedy and all that had led to it. 'And you assured me that they had plenty, that——'

'But I thought——'

'You thought! All you thought was that I was philandering. It has taken four dead bodies; four splendid lives to convince you that they were trying to cover their hunger with decent pride.'

He turned to the door then turned back. 'But,' he said, 'it wasn't really hunger that caused their deaths——'

'Oh!' The sound came from her in a little breath of relief. Anything but hunger! 'Was it fever?'

'Not fever,' he said looking at her levelly. 'Jealousy!'

She stared in stunned silence at the door that had closed on the terrible word. When she ran to it at last with a long-drawn 'Roder-eeck' she was answered by the slam of a bolt.

The Coroner's verdict was Wilful Murder By Her Majesty's Government of the four Ryan Duvs. His own censure was couched in such strong terms that it was feared that he would be charged with treason, staunch Protestant loyalist though he was. But Mr. O'Neill-Balfe had been unmanned by the findings of the autopsy on little Adam Ryan. Three grains of oats had been found in his empty stomach. He had snatched them from his brother and run away, then some stranger had given him a lift to Templetown Soup Kitchen where Mrs. Kennedy-Sherwin had found him collapsed and had taken him home to his mother.

A few nights later Sterrin awoke screaming from a nightmare. Roderick found her apologising abjectly to Nurse Hogan who was reproaching her for the fright she had given her poor mamma, and her mamma was saying that she must get another governess immediately. Miss Ferguson-Coyne had returned to Dublin that day in hysterics. She had been driving Dominic and Sterrin in the pony chaise when Wright's bread van came towards them. From nowhere a fierce mob had suddenly collected. They attacked the driver and tore the bread from the van and from each other like savages. When the pony bolted, Miss Ferguson-Coyne had lost all control. Sterrin had had to seize the reins and cope with her terrified brother. 'It is a terrible thing, Papa, when a grown-up is frightened.'

The child's world had been taken from beneath her. The white guilt on her face infuriated him. What were they doing to the stalwart little girl who would follow him on her pony over high jumps without a quiver? Another child victim of appeasement. He put an arm about her and told the nurse in a tone of dismissal that included Margaret, that he would see to Miss Sterrin.

'And that poor little Ryan boy,' Sterrin said. 'When his brother swallowed down the bull's eye he ran away from him that day also. Just as he must have done with those three grains of oats.'

For the first time, Roderick heard the story of the bull's eye.

237

'It was the day you told me not to bring them any more food—Is your hand hurting, Papa?' Unconsciously he had put the side of his hand to his mouth. Where he had struck it against the obelisk. 'Folly.' There was a wound.

She went on. 'Did you know, Papa, that their mamma used to ride to hounds like a lady?'

His lips sucked the cut: she could hear the hurt breath.

'Norisheen told me. Her papa bought a blood horse so that he could breed from it and soon she would ride again like a lady.'

His mind went back to the 'footing' kiss. It takes an artist, he had thought as he looked into the blending colours in her eyes, to mix colours. And, presuming bounder that he was, he had dared to assume that *he* himself was that artist! Not Black Pat who could make this grand fling in the cause of love's romance! Like Roderick's grandfather and the oaks!

'It is a terrible thing, Papa, when a sweet slips down one's throat before one has tasted it. *I* know.'

He looked down at the promise of beauty in the too-thin face. 'I hope, my stormling, that the sweets of life will not continue to evade you before you have savoured them!'

He tucked the clothes about her. 'Forget all this ullagoaning. Forget governesses too. Tomorrow your knife boy squire must take you bird-nesting. The tomtits have started house-hunting. Perhaps you may encounter that domesticated pair you saw last year.'

He knocked at Margaret's door and entered. Her heart lifted, but she curbed the smile that was starting. She wasn't going to fall on his neck straight away. She——

'I want no further talk of governesses,' he was saying. 'No child who has to witness the squeamishness of its elders will acquire self-control. An adult should stand up to things—at least in front of a child. Good night.'

Twelve little black eyes gazed unblinkingly at Sterrin from the tom-tit's nest at Golden Meadow. But they were not tom-tit's eyes? Mrs. Lonergan with a maid, was ladling porridge to a queue. She hurried up, all apologies. She could not invite them in, she crooned. Mr. Lonergan was down with 'The Sickness'. It was most catching. Tim came along and explained that the tom-tits had cleared off last year before their family was half reared. They had let the nest to a field mouse. 'They climb up by that,' he said indicating a currant bush.

Blackcurrant bushes as ladders for revolting little field mice had no interest for Sterrin. They only interested her as the source of blackcurrant tarts. All the way over she had been thinking of that delicious tart that Mrs. Lonergan had once given them. 'Oh dear,' she sighed aloud, 'you have no idea how disappointed I feel.' None whatever, she thought!

Tim led them by a right-of-way into the De Lacey estate. There was a joyful hail and Hubert De Lacey and two of his sisters came hurrying down the avenue. Sterrin's spirits rose. She hadn't been inside anyone's house for over a year. Paying calls or dropping-in was a thing of the past.

Hubert offered to recompense their disappointment about the tom-tits with a sight of something very rare. But Sterrin hastily interposed with a polite enquiry about his parents and a pointed glance towards the pretty white house in the trees. 'A sparrow-hawk's nest,' went on Hubert. Fiona, murmuring something about her mamma being indisposed, led the way very purposefully after her brother towards a rocky crag.

High above them, two fierce eyes watched and suddenly swooped. The sparrow-hawk had spotted a prey. Next minute a poor curlew was twisting backwards and forwards in the grip of those terrible claws. Sterrin lashed out with her whip but the curlew lay with its tender breast cut off as neatly as if it had been carved with a knife.

'If you don't mind,' said Sterrin politely. 'I'd rather not see the nest today.' A row of drops of blood picked out its lie 'that has taken away my appetite'.

'I wish,' sighed the uninhibited Bunzy, 'that it would take away mine—I'm always—ouch!' Her sister's elbow discouraged further disclosures.

When Thomas saw the faint flush on the faces of Fiona and Hubert he remembered suddenly the whisper that De Lacey's live-stock had been impounded for debt. There was not a beast in sight; not a clatter of maid or workman.

'You must excuse us, Master Hubert and Miss Fiona,' he said. 'The bard warned me to have Miss Sterrin back for a harp lesson. He is terribly crotchety.'

When they were out of earshot Sterrin demanded what the devil's father did he mean by telling such a fib. 'I had to say something,' he said, 'with you harping on about appetites and hunger. It is bad manners to drop in uninvited on people these times. The De Laceys were mortified at not being able to ask you in. And when Mrs. Lonergan couldn't invite you in you looked fit to join the stirabout line.'

'I had been hoping for a piece of tart, like that blackcurrant tart we got there before,' she admitted. 'The thought of nice food—a tart or cake it makes my mouth water. It always waters now when I think of food—nice food.'

Thomas was too embarrassed to reply. Miss Sterrin's confession of hunger made him feel the way he did whenever he surprised her in the garden on her way to the 'Necessary'. It had never occurred to him that she—that any of the family—might know what it was to feel hunger. The famine might have altered their existence. No more visitors, or visiting; no balls or whist. No dainties; bread measured by the slice. All the game poached despite the beeves and sheep that were slaughtered all the time to feed the hungry. But hunger! He studied the thin outline of her face. Not a pick on it. And its whiteness was thin, too. It used to look like the top of the milk.

He scraped his throat. 'What about tickling a trout? I'll make a fire.'

'A secret picnic? Just the two of us.' But, as suddenly as it had come, the light went from her face. 'Papa would be horrified. A gentleman would not disturb a trout just now.'

'I am not a gentleman; and—you are hungry.'

The trout he caught was well over two pounds but his fingers after the icy water could scarcely hold it for cleaning. She took his hand between her own and chafed it, and when she stooped and blew upon his fingers, the little warm breathings were as if, for him alone, the sun had suddenly shone down out of the January sky and warmed his being and filled it full with gladness. He gave his throat another scrape. 'I—er—it will be able to hold the trout now.' He gave the hand a businesslike shake then prepared the fish and gathered twigs and lit them with sparks from the iron tip of his heel and all the time he hummed and whistled as gay as the voice of the young stream that went sparkling and gurgling between miniature rocks.

When he proffered her the sizzling fish on a big dock leaf, she insisted upon him cutting half for himself.

'You surely don't think that I would sit and eat in front of you!' she exclaimed.

Thomas refrained from pointing out that it was his lot in life to serve her while she ate in front of him. But just now he felt disorientated. Away from servitude; away from the famine; alone in a world that held Miss Sterrin and himself in the warm circle of the dancing flames.

'I wish,' said Sterrin and 'twas as though she spoke his thoughts, 'that we could stay here forever.' It was so bright and cosy here with young Thomas; away from that awful stirabout line and the sad, sick faces. Just young Thomas and herself sharing the lovely big fire and the lovely trout. A shadow loomed over the flames and a voice said, 'God save you, Miss.'

'Cead mile curses!' murmured young Thomas. 'It is the "Darraghadheal".'

George Lucas was standing on the other side of the stream. 'A nice little picnic ye're havin'. It does a body good to see children havin' a bit of comfort an' so many starving! The poor little Ryan Duv children! Three grains of oats, God bless us! I'm sure the Sir would not have objected to them trespassing here for a bit of fish; his foster-brother's children!'

Young Thomas jumped to his feet to remonstrate but Sterrin silenced him with a gesture. 'You have no right to be here. My father permits no right of way on either side of this stream.'

Thomas was surprised at the man's quick look of alarm. He started muttering something about taking a short cut back. His wife had had a child this morning. 'Another covala—foster-sister—for you, Miss Sterrin,' he called over his shoulder.

Thomas watched the retreating figure through narrowed eyes. 'I'd swear that fellow was up to something. Covala, indeed! Makes me sick the way he keeps trying to claim fostership with you just because his wife was your wet-nurse. There's no such thing, these modern times.'

'There was such a thing between Papa and Black Pat. That's what Lucas was hinting at—blaming Papa for—' She swung into the saddle 'Hell roast the "Darraghadheal"! I was so happy!'

Thomas scattered the fire with a kick. Happy! He had never been so happy in all his born days. 'May the devil roast crabs in his——' He stopped aghast. But his lapse into coarseness had dispelled the cloud evoked by Lucas. Sterrin was flopped over the pony's head in peals of laughter.

241

There was no laughter the next afternoon as Sterrin followed humbly in the heels of young Thomas. She had never seen him cry before. The sight of his tears stirred her deeply. It was the funeral of little Theobald, Kitty's and Mark's firstborn. He had died while Sterrin and Thomas were picnicking by the stream. It was Thomas who had discovered it, for he had run to the Hennessey's the moment he and Sterrin had returned to the castle. He didn't know what had prompted him to steal that hour to see how things fared at the cottage. As he reached the door a weird-looking dog was dragging the sweet, small body of his god-child across the threshold and from the room beyond came sounds of moans.

Kitty was lying in the fresh agony that had come upon her when she realised that the child in her arms was dead. As the slow grinding pains became unbearable she had let the dead body slip to the floor. Pain by pain she was forced to yield to the demands of the one who was clamouring inexorably for the grim heritage abandoned by her firstborn.

They buried little Theobald in a tiny space behind the tombstone that said 'William O'Carroll, Gentleman of Kilsheelin who was emigrated to heaven in the Year of Our Lord 1678'. As Thomas dug the little grave he recalled how, when he was learning to write from the tombstones, he used to think that poor people emigrated to America and rich people to heaven.

When the box was covered, Sterrin stooped and with great reverence placed her spray of hothouse lilies on the tiny mound. It was then that Mark broke down completely. He threw himself upon his knees and sobbed; for the little one who had been born to die; for Kitty; for himself; for the inescapable anguish of life.

Sterrin blenched. It was terrible to hear a big man sob like that. Thomas looked at her whitened face. This was no place for her! And there would be murder over rifling the glass house for the precious lilies, but she had insisted. Someone, she said, must represent the family in Mamma and Papa's absence, and do the right thing by young Thomas's godchild. She had shown the gardener the same look of Christian ferocity that she had shown Mickey-the-turf when he had stolen her sacrificial jelly.

Thomas dropped down beside Mark. What prayers could he say? The soul of the little white blossom that had bloomed and faded needed no forgiving. He prayed that God might comfort

Kitty, lying up there spent, the new-born child in her arms.

Sterrin decided to kneel also; although she had been taught that one did not pray for the soul of an infant. Praying for the souls in Purgatory always reminded her of the salts mixed with senna that she drank once a week while Nurse Hogan held her nose and told her to 'offer it up for the souls in Purgatory'.

After the ceremony Mark hurried back to Darby's Scheme for Unproductive Labour. Major Darby had been shot at last night and there was a rumour that all pay was being stopped as a reprisal. Mark found Sir Roderick O'Carroll there demanding the wages that had been refused to Black Pat's widow.

'Who is responsible for that whiskey hut?' Sir Roderick demanded.

The paymaster flushed. From behind a voice called 'That's what I should like to know also.' It was Father Hickey. The priest had driven out with his friend Master Hennessey, to upbraid the men whom he suspected of being implicated in the shooting of Darby. The sight of the whiskey huts grieved him. Every Unproductive Labour Scheme had a whiskey hut, erected by unscrupulous pay clerks to seduce money from hungry, exhausted men who had not touched alcohol since the Temperance Campaign. 'I wouldn't mind,' said the priest to Sir Roderick, 'but it is rank poison.'

The pay clerk bridled. 'It is a harmless recipe,' he said, 'it gives the men warmth.'

'Harmless!' cried the priest. 'Warms them? Maddens them! Kills them!' He produced a slip of paper. 'Listen to this,' and he started to read a recipe. 'Here,' he said to the schoolmaster, 'You read it, I've left my spectacles at home.'

'One gallon of fresh, fiery whiskey,' intoned the schoolmaster as though he were giving out a problem in Euclid. 'A pint of rum, two ounces of corrosive sublimates. Three gallons of water——'

'It is whiskey like that,' interrupted Father Hickey, 'that makes you shoot your landlords.'

'Aye,' said the master flourishing the slip of paper, 'and it is whiskey like that that makes you *miss* them.'

Father Hickey and Master Hennessey drove on to the scene of the evictions that had caused the shooting. For a moment they thought they must have taken the wrong turn. A hamlet of houses that had crowned the low hill had disappeared.

243

A woman and a boy came away from a heap of rubble.

'Was that your home?' the priest asked.

'Yes, your Reverence,' she whispered. He asked was there any place to which he could drive her.'

'Only to the poorhouse, your Reverence; if they will take us.'

He bade the boy hop up behind. The boy seized the rail and swung but fell back. 'I'm sorry, your Reverence,' he apologised, 'the hunger is on me.' The master lifted the big, gangling boy in his arms. He was no heavier than a baby. 'Did I ever slap you at school?' he asked. The boy gave a grin that made wrinkles across his face. 'You did, faith, Master,' he croaked. 'You walloped us every morning. To make spartans of us, you said.'

The lad hastened to make amends! 'But you gave me ginger lumps, Master,' he assured him.

'Did I now? And what betrayed me into such weakness?'

'Because I was always the first of the lads from Gort-na-roe and I always brought two sods of turf.'

The master drew a check handkerchief from his tail pocket and blew loudly. 'That's right,' he said, 'terribly lazy lads they were from Gort-na-roe, and only one sod of turf under their oxters.'

A group of homeless looked up expectantly at the car but the priest shook his head, 'No room,' he said. He looked at the grasslands that had held colonies of homes. 'No room in their own green valleys; no room on the roadside; no room in the workhouse. May the God of all consolation find room for them in Heaven.'

The woman shuddered with cold. She had kept vigil all night by her demolished home. The priest put his surtout about her. A newspaper fell from its pocket. The master took it up and glanced through it. 'Well, Father,' he commented, 'at least they are finding room for them in America. Listen to the latest emigration figures. According to *The Times* in less than five months, three hundred thousand people have left Cove for America. And listen to this!' cried the master excitedly. '*The Times* had turned prophet! "In one more generation",' he read, ' "the Irish Celts will be as obsolete in Ireland as the Phoenicians in Cornwall and the Catholic religion will be as forgotten as the worship of Astarte." ' He crumpled the paper. 'What do you think of that, Father Hickey?'

The priest flicked the reins. 'Have you ever read the *Religio Medici*, Master?' he said, ' "Men are lived over again",' he quoted, ' "the world is now as it was in ages past." '

'Bedad, Father, I think I'll write a letter to *The Times* and quote that. That will wake the prophet up. He'll need a caput-geredormitor after it to make him sleep.'

'A what?' said the priest.

'Oh, that's a grand word I got from Constable Humphreys.'

'Sounds like him. That fellow thinks with his jaws.' Father Hickey reined in at his door and sighed. His housekeeper was standing at the door wearing a disapproving look. Two more hungry people to be fed! Out of what?

'Would you like me take them for a bit to my house?' whispered the master sympathetically. The priest straightened his shoulders for the fray. 'They are my guests,' he insisted. He walked them to the door.

The housekeeper eyed them and then the priest. 'How many times have I told your Reverence that you should christen your own child first?' she muttered.

'How many times have I told you,' he replied, 'that you should choose a more seemly metaphor.'

Roderick, on his way back from the Relief works had scarcely cleared the bay hedge when he was greeted by the gardener with a complaint about the lilies.

He stormed into the drawing-room. Sterrin was playing with Dominic. Margaret was bent over her embroidery. 'Will you kindly restrain your impulses to strew the graves of the dead with lilies from my glass houses,' Roderick shouted. 'I've given my trees to make coffins; my food; gone without rents; but I'm damned if I'll supply funeral lilies!'

Sterrin stood up respectfully to answer the charge. Papa must indeed be angry if he would curse a damn before Mamma. 'The lilies were for the grave of young Thomas's godchild.'

'Young Thomas!' her father exploded. 'Where the devil did *he* get a godchild?'

Sterrin proceeded again to give chapter and verse of Mark and Kitty's love-story that had ended in the Wedding Mass that young Thomas had served.

'The lovely girl in the scarlet cloak,' said her mamma, 'the one we saw at the fair?'

'Yes, Mamma.' Sterrin pressed home her advantage. 'And her baby Theobald, Thomas's godchild, was born the same day as Dominic.'

Margaret's eyes went towards Roderick but met no response.

'And Theobald,' continued Sterrin, 'died of hunger but they got a new baby this morning. I thought that you would not like the old one to be thrown into the Dead Pit——' Margaret's wince cut through but Sterrin forged on to her final point. 'After all, Papa, young Thomas is of our household.'

Roderick's brows shot up. Despite her recent display of fear his small daughter was indeed cast in the heroic mould. Of our household! 'All right, Sterrin,' he yielded. '*Noblesse oblige!* But in future will you confine your tributes to primroses.'

'In faith, Papa, I prefer primroses. Let us hope that the new baby will not need flowers.'

Margaret said that she would take Nurse Hogan and drive to see this Kitty. Roderick was once more struck by the shape of his wife's face. It looked as if it might have been outlined by one of those little heart-shaped patty tins for cakes. And the rich magnolia tint of her skin had turned lime white.

'You must not overtire yourself,' he said. It was the first remark that he had addressed to her since the Ryan tragedy. Fatigue and the continuous association with suffering had drained his voice of emotion; but she thought his dull tone meant sarcasm.

'I don't mind "overtiring" myself. But I have no intention of hunting out distress that is hidden under the silly pretence of genteelness.' Her breathing made the bugles and bells on her key belt tinkle. 'No hardship that I have known of has gone un-aided. No one who comes to me is ever refused, and *mon Dieu*, they come to me all the time.' Her eyes were two brown blobs of anger. 'Your—protégée, or whatever she is to you—allowed her husband and children to die for the sake of her *bourgeois* pride——'

'Stop!' he shouted. 'I won't allow——'

'*Hein!*' She ignored his interruption. 'I'd ask for food if *I* were hungry.' She whisked out in a whirl of hoops and jingles.

'I believe that you would,' he said to the door she slammed behind her.

Sterrin was still in the room; too paralysed to move. Papa shouting at Mamma; and Mamma shouting back! Roderick's conscience smote him at the sight of her fear. He put his arm about her and soothed her as he had done when she had awakened from the nightmare.

'Papa,' she breathed in an awed whisper. 'Did Mrs. Black Pat really do that? Did she let her husband and little children die?'

He found himself defending Nonie to his child. He told her what he had managed to glean; that Nonie *had* sought help from her parents but they had been ill at the time and had died, one after the other; that she did not know that Black Pat had the lung disease. It was deep in his branch of the Ryans; in his children, too. A few days' shortage would finish them. 'And,' said Sterrin placatingly, 'there is a curse on her, Mrs. Stacey says because she stole the Parish Priest's horse to run away with——' Sterrin flinched. Her papa had roared 'Stop!' at her the way he had at Mamma.

'Don't ever repeat that sinful nonsense again!' He softened at the sight of her face. 'Promise me, Sterrin,' he said more gently.

As he was leaving the room, she said: 'The De Laceys would not admit that they were hungry either but I met Bunzy this morning at our secret meeting place—oh, I never brought food to her, Papa.'

He stopped dead. What was the child saying? The *De Laceys* hungry! What was going on around him? His neighbours in need; his foster-kin dying of hunger while he was succouring strangers! Like the shoemaker's family that goes unshod.

'They are not hungry any more now that Mr. Lubey has bought their estate for a cucumber estate. Bunzy's Papa made her promise not to tell anyone and Bunzy made me promise——'

Out of the chaos Roderick recalled someone, somewhere, saying that there was a risk that Phineas De Lacey's place might be liable for sale under this new Encumbered Estates Act that was about to pass into law. An act that would give the court the right to sell land that had been in a family for centuries.

'Bunzy said that Mr. Lubey would prefer Kilsheelin Castle, but——'

Her papa let out a roar that sent the chandelier swinging and singing. 'By the living God! *Would* he! He'll never warm his a——' Sterrin saw her papa's mouth open to say the shocking word but instead he just said '*Ah*-hem.'

When the door had banged after him and the chandelier now danced to its own singing she put her hand over her mouth to

247

cover the snicker, 'Fancy Papa *knowing* a word like that!'

Roderick went down the park at a mad gallop, then wheeled. There was someone he was to see but he couldn't think who or where? He faced Thuckeen into the niche where the wall had been but partially restored. 'Why didn't I build that up long ago!' He always asked himself the same question when he faced the jump. And always when Thuckeen bunched her dainty hooves and soared over he was answered and restored by a sense of exaltation. He looked back as he landed and caught the quick glimpse of turret and roof that the niche afforded. So the gombeen man had dared to raise his eyes to them. By God! 'Yup Thuckeen!'

When he reached Black Pat's empty house, he realised his mission. Nonie was still at Mrs. Kennedy-Sherwin's of course, and the three surviving children. Her brother, a doctor and his wife, would be at Mrs. Kennedy-Sherwin's this afternoon. Roderick wanted to see what the brother was prepared to do for his sister and her orphans before taking action himself. He reined a moment and looked at the shut house. The Chinese roses bloomed on unconcernedly. Life and death were the same to them. They bloomed both summer and winter beneath the window.

One morning a few weeks later Roderick, in a cape-collared coat and holding a wide-brimmed hat, unbolted his dressing-room door. That coat gives him an air, thought Margaret. She was sitting up in bed sipping *café-au-lait*. Or does he give *it* an air? Anyway he had come back to her! She pursed her lips to check their smiling.

'I merely wished to tell you that I am off to Cork and shall not be back until tomorrow. I am despatching some tenants to America. Young Thomas will accompany me.'

'But you despatched them a week ago!' There had been a general exodus from the estates of Kilsheelin and Lord Temple-town and Lord Cullen. The three landlords had assisted with passage money and travelled with the emigrants to the port of embarkation.

'Mrs. Ryan and her children are going to America with Mark Hennessey and his wife.'

Her cup went down with a bang. 'Is this necessary?' He misunderstood her.

'Mrs. Ryan is unable to work the farm and too poor to employ labour.'

She shrugged aside his explanation. 'Is it necessary for you to see them off personally?'

'I might remind you that this particular family has a claim upon mine.'

'You don't *haf* to remind me' she panted, going foreign in her anger, 'that Mrs. Ryan has a claim on you.'

He was walking over to kiss her goodbye but instead turned and strode from the room.

CHAPTER 26

Nonie raised her foot to ascend the gangway. A bell sounded. It made a clanging in her heart. Was it too late to turn back? Now! Before this foot took the step? *He* had paid their passage money; had sent money ahead to a New York bank. She glanced over her shoulder to where he had halted to speak to a dandified gentleman, with shapely legs cased in black silk stockings. She knew that face, beautiful as a woman's: Father Matthew's! He had pleaded, she had heard, for her forgiveness with her father when he visited his relative's estate near her home; had tried to put down the terrible story that the priest had failed to reach a dying person because she had stolen his horse. Her father had placed the finest horse in his stables at the priest's disposal. He had made all the right gestures—except the divine gesture of forgiveness to his daughter.

A porter with head bent forward under a laden sack jostled her backwards. She touched the sack to steady herself. 'What is in it?' she asked suddenly.

'Oats,' he told her. Oats! All the seas of the world tumbled about her heart. Nausea awoke in her body. She stumbled forward. She couldn't get away quickly enough. 'Three grains of oats!' She didn't realise that she had spoken aloud. A firm hand took hold of her and led her on to the deck.

'Do you wish to change your mind? It is not too late.'

She looked so young and unprotected to go out into that void with her little ones and there was menace that chilled Roderick in the way the ocean had started to wave its white locks. He had asked her this before—if she wished to change her mind—and she had answered him repeatedly that no ocean was wide enough to put between her and the hungry land that had devoured her loved ones. But as she looked up into his eyes now she knew that now more than ever she must get away.

'Tell me one thing before I go,' she said. The stretched look had gone from her lips. They had resumed their shapely curving. While she spoke he watched the glancing movement of her perfect teeth. 'Do you still think that it was I—that the children——' It was torture still to speak of them, 'that my pride caused their death?'

He became aware of the terrible words these lips were forming. Did he think? Good God, had he said such a thing to this little blossom? If he had it must have been in the delirium of his own strain and horror that night. He started to reassure her.

'I did seek help—from my people. It came too late——'

He urged her to forget the past. He almost said that the past was a mistake. As if one could dismiss a past that was charged with the weight of those four lives! But whatever the past, there was, he felt, a positive future ahead of her. There must be; not just because of these strangely beautiful eyes; not even because of the spirit that had endured for so long. Long before the famine had added to her privations, she had had an indestructible reserve of the quality of feminine seductiveness that would always, everywhere, enlist men to her defence.

'You belong with the future. Remember that—Nonie.' The sound of her name faltering from his lips filled her with a wistfulness that was a separate thing from that other all-pervading sense of sorrow that never left her.

Roderick suddenly realised that she was parted from the Hennesseys. They were in the Steerage penned up with the crying children and keening ancients. Above the din Mark suddenly heard his name called. Sir Roderick O'Carroll arranged with one of the ship's officers for Mark and Kitty to join the First Class.

Then it was the final moment; when all the impersonal things are said: You have that address? You are sure you have enough of money? You will let me know the moment you arrive? But all the time inside, other thoughts are jostling in a panic to get out; to utter personal things. Like tiny stars, the brief seconds that had brought their lives together broke and illumined his memory. He longed to tell her that life had not quenched their light; he bent over her.

'Nonie!'

'Rody!'

A bugle sounded and a wild lament rose from the quayside.

The Hennesseys came aloft, dazzled by the sudden light. For an insane moment Kitty had the impression that Sir Roderick

O'Carroll was kissing Mrs. Black Pat Ryan goodbye. Then he vanished in the throng.

Young Thomas, standing on the dock, saw Mark and Kitty reappear. He craned eagerly over those in front. He longed to call out something; to go on talking in a link of words to hold them to him a while longer; but nothing would rise out of the arid desolation that was within him—desolation and joy, too. He touched his cheek. He had never known a human caress until the moment when he had reached out his hand to Kitty and instead of taking it she had flung her arm about him and pressed him to her and on the cheek that she had kissed she had left a tear.

A child groped past him and staggered. He steadied her and a woman murmured thanks and told him that the child had been partially blinded when the town of Loughrea in Galway had been set afire by the Big Wind. From every part of Ireland the emigrants continued to arrive, some well-dressed, some gentry already beggared by the famine. They gazed with haggard wonder at the foodstuffs piled along the quayside for shipment abroad; thousands of tons of grain were being loaded on to ships for England. Beside the emigrant ship a military transport ship was being provisioned for the West Indies. Emigrants watched the hams hauled aboard by the hundred, the firkins of butter. English soldiers guarded the wagons of corn grown by the starving emigrants; herds of cattle were driven aboard; even the skins of the asses that the emigrants had used for food were being shipped. They thought the sight was a progression of the food dreams that had haunted their existence night and day; a phantasmagoria of food stretching out before their eyes into the infinity of the ocean. A thin foreign voice called over their bedevilled sense for 'the cream for the officers' table!' Cream in scientifically sealed tins went aloft so that the officers would have fresh cream on the high seas! Was the like ever heard?

'Where did this food come from?' It was a man from the fertile county of Wexford who spoke. Wexford men providently equipped for American employment with the tools of their calling gazed unbelievingly at the English soldier's food. Where did it come from? What country could produce such food? And when they were told, their faces lost that look born of a submission to a calamity that they had deemed an act of God. There was a buzz of angry comment. These men had endured longer than the other emigrants. For, strangely, it had been in their own fertile Wexford with its people noted for husbandry, that the potato had first failed. They half turned and looked whence they had come, as though they thought to return and demand their rights.

Father Matthew, who attended all the emigrant departure ships, comforting those who had taken the pledge for him in all parts of the country during his campaigns, watched them take the last four steps. On their faces he could see the mutiny of their hearts. He murmured, 'Caelum non animum mutant qui trans mare current.'

Thomas, standing sideways from the priest, his eyes glued to the ship, caught the words and half understood them. Something, he thought, about those who must go over the seas, something to do with those chaps going batty at the sight of all that food and dragging the bitterness of what it had conveyed to them across the world to another land.

He took a frantic step forward. The boat had started to move and Kitty called out to him. Beside him the priest's Latin still sounded, but now it spoke a blessing and Thomas fought clear of the surge that blocked his throat. His own voice startled him as it went across the space of water: 'Sursum corda!'

The clear, brave cry startled Roderick too as he made his way towards his knife boy. Roderick was amazed at the vibrancy more than the words, that had escaped in a kind of cadence from the voice of subdued servitude. But he stared at crowds pressed against the railings of the deck, hoping for a glimpse of Noni, but he could not find her tiny figure. He felt a strange sense of finality, as if a large part of his life had been cut away. He stepped forward, raised his hat, holding it high above his head and remained immobile and unseeing as the ship moved away from the harbour. Not until Father Matthew touched his shoulder the second time and asked if he would share his luncheon did Roderick return to his surroundings.

CHAPTER 27

Margaret looked up with an expression of delight. Lieutenant Fitzharding-Smith had come spanking into the drawing-room. He dropped a kiss on Sterrin's nose, a box of chocolates on her lap then bowed low over her mamma's hand. It was ages since he had been here. And it would be ages before she would see him again. He was leaving for India!

Margaret, when he told her, forgot to withdraw her hand. All those years she had taken the friendship of this charming young officer so much for granted. And now when life was so grey and stark he was going away.

'To India!' she cried in dismay. 'Oh, Basil, I shall miss you terribly.'

No one heard Roderick come into the room. He had some idea of surprising her; of slipping up behind her at the embroidery frame and throwing his arms around her. On the way homewards he had decided that this childish situation must go no further. Two people concentrating on petty grievances in the midst of a people's agony. He had not waited to remove his cloak. He was still holding his beaver.

He went on holding it. One could scarcely throw reconciling arms around a wife who was clinging to another man's hand assuring him that she would miss him terribly.

'I trust,' he said coldly, 'that I am not intruding.'

'Don't worry,' she said, with matching coldness, and then she remembered that she, too, had planned a different greeting. She had planned to run and kiss him and afterwards try to make him understand the way things had befallen on that terrible afternoon of the Ryan tragedy. But here he was as unapproachable as ever!

'Basil is going to India,' she explained briefly.

'Oh! When are you off, Fitz?' Roderick would like to have sounded more regretful but he was conscious only of his everlasting fatigue. Anyway, departures had lost their former significance.

The Lieutenant explained that his draft had been ordered to Vizagapatam in a fortnight. 'We leave for Cork tomorrow.' As he looked round the room after Roderick had left to remove his travelling clothes, his thoughts went back to the first day that he entered it and saw Lady O'Carroll, in a 'robe de style' with little bows running like steps of stairs from the waist to the neck. His first impression had been—a beautiful girl in a beautiful room. But he had made some facetious remark and she had not liked it. The brittle badinage of the garrison had left him unready for such superlative graciousness blended with the naturalness of a pleasing child. When the lovely baby had been brought and placed in her arms he had thought of her as a madonna. Later when she had lain, pale and terrified, amid the broken glass from the chandelier after the Whiteboys' raid, his heart yearned for her. She had become his ideal of womanhood but, despite the smirks of the garrison set, it had never occurred to him to contemplate an illicit flirtation.

He sighed, 'I'm going to miss all this. You have no idea how much you have meant to me since that first afternoon that I came here.'

Margaret fought her tears as she bade him farewell. She watched him ride down the avenue until he passed out of sight. Roderick stood behind her. 'How could you?' she sobbed. 'Hinting and gibing! He shan't trouble you again. You might have been generous.'

Roderick had seen too many tears in the past months to be moved by those in his wife's beautiful eyes.

'I might remind you,' he said coldly, 'that there was little generosity shown to those who left here yesterday to face a grimmer voyage. But rest assured that Lieutenant Fitzharding-Smith will travel comfortably. Fresh cream for the officers' coffee on the high seas! By gad, what will they think of next? Forgive me, I must not intrude upon the sacredness of your grief.'

He strode to the dining-room and pulled the bellrope. He was hungry. Lunch at Father Matthew's had been sparse. He sat before the dark expanse of Domingo mahogany, weary and dispirited. Suddenly he put his head down on his arms and as he did so he experienced the sentient feeling of familiarity; and then he remembered. The night of the Big Wind he had sat like this; in this posture; feeling the same, racked and drained; life an arid desolation. Father Matthew had said at lunch that the famine was another big wind only that its blast was foetid like the simoon[1] of the desert. Roderick recalled the invigorating uplift and resurgence that the Liberator and Father Matthew had brought to the land. The famine had killed all that. It had tainted both earth and people. He thought of the separate hell of each father and mother. How could *we* hope to escape? We are tainted, Margaret and I. The Big Wind was the bard's 'wild huntsman' careering on his eight-footed steed. But the famine was—a serpent, leaving a wake of slime.

Sterrin, too, watched with sadness as Lieutenant Firzharding-Smith rode down the avenue. On a sudden she streaked across the park and jumped up on to the gap in the wall. He saw the red head pop up in the gap as he rode past the Scis Road and looked back for a last look where the castle came into view again. On a sudden he, too, turned in towards the gap, reached up and took her face between his hands. 'Goodbye, you sweet child,' he said. 'When next we meet I shall have to stand on a chair to see Miss Sterrin O'Carroll, the belle of the county, go past.' When the last hoof-beat had died away she turned forlornly and looked towards the castle. Everyone was leaving. Suddenly she remembered young Thomas. Her gloom lightened. There was always young Thomas.

He was in his room. When he had returned after taking leave of Kitty and Mark he felt that he must get away from the kitchen atmosphere. This was one of the times when he was conscious of not belonging there. But then, he belonged nowhere. He turned on the pillow to look through the window at the distant hillside speck that had been for so long his focal point of outlook; up there he had known complete and easeful equality with his fellow beings. A knock shattered his reflections. The devil whip them! The Sir himself said that I was to have a rest!

His pull at the door brought Sterrin inwards, clinging to the knob. Sterrin let out a gusty sigh. 'I'm feeling terribly dovroanach,' she said. Thomas's sigh mingled with hers. 'I'm feeling dovroanach myself,' he said.

'Did you know,' she asked him, 'that the De Laceys are going to America and Lieutenant Fitzharding-Smith to India?'

[1] Ahor, dust-laden wind of the Arabian desert.

He didn't know. Tiredness came back in waves. He sat on the side of the bed but remembered his manners and stood up again. 'Is Master Hubert going too?'

She nodded. 'All of them. All our friends are going; yours and mine. Soon, young Thomas, we shall have no one left but each other.'

He looked at her silently. She was getting long and leggy. It might be the famine, of course. But it might also be that she had begun to grow up. Another two or three inches would make the world of difference; the difference between her world and his. But what was it that she had said? No one left but each other? A warm glow spread through him. 'Miss Sterrin,' he cried, no longer dovroanach, no longer even tired. 'Your papa said that I was to have the rest of the evening off. Maybe Mr. O'Driscoll would allow me to exercise the old Rajah. We could ride to Lissnastreenagh. The blossoms are out.'

As they cantered across the fields their youthful sorrows went floating off into the May sunshine. They dismounted at the fairy rath and looked down. It was eerily beautiful. The trees grew in a perfect circle around the edge, their branches so closely woven that they formed a flowered canopy overhead. The floor of the hollow was covered with pink and white blossoms. All the time as they gazed petals kept dropping in a snow of fragrance. By June the bowl-shaped hollow would be filled to the brink. Thomas reached to break off a stem, but Sterrin gripped his wrist. 'It is unlucky to touch a blossom,' she warned.

'That is superstition,' he said. 'How can one avoid touching them? Look.' A blossom had fallen on his shoulder.

'That's different,' she said. 'The bard says that if a blossom falls on you it is a sign that you will marry your true love. But if you pick one yourself, it will bring you bad luck.'

Young Thomas sniffed disdainfully. 'The bard lives in a dream world of pishoguerie.' He was holding the Rajah's reins over his shoulder but as he removed them to remount he took care not to dislodge the blossom that had fallen there.

On their return, she pulled up suddenly by the side of the stream. 'Look!' she cried. 'The fly is risen!' He reined in beside her to watch the first flight of the mayfly soaring up dizzy with light and air after the long, strange life beneath the darkness of the waters. She flicked the reins. 'I must hurry and tell Papa.' There was a traditional glory in being the first with that ritual

257

cry, 'The fly is risen!'

'I'm afraid,' said Thomas dully, 'that there is only one cry now that your papa can heed.' Involuntarily she slowed. Even *she* understood that everything in life seemed to be subordinated to the unceasing famine cry, Ta ocras orm! The hunger is on me!

Near home they came upon another rare sight. The bard, wrapped in his saffron cloak, was pacing a plateau above a small tributary of the trout stream. 'And where were ye, children?' he asked. When they told him he peered at Thomas. 'Ye have no call going there, a comely youth like yourself, O'Carroll Og. You might be spirited away by the Speir-bhean.' He merged off into a spate of words that held more of dreaming sound than of sense. In spite of themselves, its witchery beat gently into the young minds of his listeners. Out of its cadence came the likeness of the Fairy Queen, the Speir-bhean. Beautiful in every way she was. Her hair golden, flowing in trembling waves to the ground; her eyebrows a curved stroke, deadly as an arrow; her skin white as the foam of a wild lake. The beauty of her eyes had laid a hundred men in weakness.

Thomas, feeling in danger of being drowsed into a weakness himself, stemmed the flow of vowel music. 'We won't go there again, Bard.'

'That's right, O'Carroll Og. Let ye take yer divarsion here on the Hill of The Embroidering Women where the Bride's price used to be paid. There is water here when ye race yer horses.' He was looking down into the stream that had been there when the great Aonachs of bygone centuries had been held here and the horses and great hounds had raced on its banks and the Levantine merchants had waited patiently to sell their jewels to the ladies from all the thirteen castles of the O'Carrolls, who were contesting for the embroidery prize that the High King himself would bestow.

'The poor bard,' commented Sterrin when they were out of earshot. 'Isn't it funny the way he mixes you up with the family? He is doting.' She cantered ahead and cleared the bay hedge. Thomas looked after her. She *might* have remembered that the Rajah could not take the jump.

'Why didn't you wait for me?' he said when he reached the yard.

She raised her black brows at him and dismounted without

258

answering. He flushed and stooped to unfasten the horse's girths. She came over and looked down at him. 'Isn't it funny the way the bard can never remember your name? He remembers everyone else's.'

He went on unloosening straps, then from underneath the horse he said, 'It is extremely funny.' He rose to his feet. 'You see,' he continued as he led off the horse. 'I happen to be the only one who has no name for him to remember.'

CHAPTER 28

For the first time in his memory, the Scout had missed the arrival of the mail coach on the birthday of the reigning monarch. He had felt so strangely weak that he had been compelled to send his son to deputise. And the spalpeen hadn't gleaned an iota of news.

'I have to see to everything myself,' the Scout told Constable Humphreys as he made his way to the inn.

The ostler at the inn could tell him nothing but news of the plague. 'Thirty died above yesterday.' The ostler nodded towards the fever hospital. The Scout turned from him. 'Do you call *that* "newses".' When he had moved on the ostler remembered something. He removed his straw from his mouth and called out. 'There is a cake at the coffee house might be worthy of your interest.'

'Cake!' The Scout halted and lashed the fellow's insolence. Cake! He that had been first with the nation's most momentous newses, that had bribed a wagoner with a golden sovereign to bring him the first word of the Liberator's sentence! That had been first out of Kilsheelin Castle to carry to Templetown the newses of his release! He drew his sleeve across his eyes.

The ostler uncovered. There would be no thunder in the House of Commons today. The Liberator had made his last speech. In a voice scarce more than a cracked whisper he had pleaded for food for his starving people. The desolation of his land that he was powerless to alleviate was slowly tearing O'Connell's heart asunder. He had stood in the House a drooping figure of pathos as he stretched out trembling arms in supplication '. . . I call upon you to recollect that I predict with the sincerest conviction that one-fourth of her population will perish unless you come to her relief. . . .' It was his final effort. A few days later he was dead.

The ostler knew those words like his prayers; like a holy prophecy that had come true. 'Vo, vo, to the great man that's gone. May the angels spread his bed in Heaven!'

'Amen!' said the Scout. 'And you offer me cake!' He turned very slowly.

'Faith, I didn't,' cried the astonished ostler.

'Figuratively speaking,' said the Scout. 'Not,' he continued, out of hearing, 'that I'd object strongly if a hunk were offered to me just now—in substance.'

The coffee house was deserted. Half the officers were down with plague, the waiter told him. None of the gentry had come. The Scout turned away. 'Twas amazing the weight of this old hat of his. He had gone a few paces when he turned nonchalantly. Was there any special sort of food on the menu today; a special cake or the like? He wasn't going to ask direct about the cake, the ostler might have been having him on.

The waiter told him that a duke had got his cook to make a birthday cake for the Queen and she couldn't reach on eatin' it. It had been put up for auction and knocked down to the Colonel of the Ninety-third and he over in London on holidays. He had sent it back ahead of him to have a raffle here today for the famine. He thought the usual crowd would be here. The waiter drew back a screen and revealed the tallest cake the Scout had ever seen.

'By the powers of wars!' Weariness fell away from the Scout. 'Sure the little lady—no disrespect to her Majesty—would need a ladder to climb up to that.' It was level with the top of his hardy bastard.

Five feet eight in height it was, the waiter told him proudly, and nine feet six in circumference. The statues round the first tier were the Nine Muses. The top tier represented Mount Parnassus.

'And the lad sittin' on it, holdin' that yoke like a harp, is called Apollo. Belike he's the Queen's Bard.'

'Belike,' said the Scout scathingly.

Next morning the Vicar found the Scout in a classical delirium.

'God save you, Mr. Debenham,' he raved. 'Will you have a piece of Terpsichore. No, I don't blame you. Sure your poor throat is burning and she is terribly sugary.'

The Vicar lifted him on to the front of his horse and rode with him to the hospital. 'Take him to the quarry,' the doctor ordered. The Vicar continued to stand at the ward door holding the Scout's bony weight, doubting his own hearing.

'Yes, the quarry,' repeated the doctor. 'Out there!' He waved impatiently in the direction of the window. 'There's no more room in the hospital.'

The Scout peered up at the grass and lichened wall of the quarry that rose up sheer to meet a dappled sky. 'Apollo with his lyre,' he croaked. It was young Thomas, poised on the brim of the quarry with prong suspended, after dropping down some of the straw that it was now his daily chore to bring to the hospital to help the shortage. He gazed in amazement at the extraordinary spectacle of the Scout being lowered into the quarry by the Vicar. To lie sick in the open quarry!

It was the first piece of 'newses' to interest the kitchen for a long time. Men in fever put out to lie in the open air! 'Twas as bad as an eviction.

'Even cattle,' said the butler, 'are brought in from the fields in sickness.'

That night after the kitchen rosary he added the Scout's name to the long list of Souls to be prayed for. But next day when Thomas returned with a special load of straw for the quarry, the Scout's soul was still there. So was his body. It was there until it was able to clamber out embodying its own incredible 'newses'; a living legend, the Scout Doyle who had been put to die with other plague victims in a quarry outside the hospital! Who throve and recovered—the others too—while men died hourly in the reeking wards across the yard!

Sir Roderick stopped dead at the spectacle of the big white structure that towered from the dining-table. 'What in Heaven's name is that?' he exploded. Lieutenant Fitzharding-Smith, Margaret informed him, had purchased hundreds of tickets for a cake raffled for the Relief Fund. He had directed before he left that if one of them were lucky the cake was to be delivered to Kilsheelin Castle.

'And who is going to eat that—that iced orgy?' he asked.

'I thought we might give a treat to the tenants' children.' She could have bitten her tongue. Instantly his bitter expression told her that he was thinking of those three dead children; seeing them as he had last seen them!

'Quite in the Marie Antoinette tradition,' he said at last. 'A child with an empty stomach *would* prefer a hunk of that monstrosity to—to—three grains of oats.'

She put her hands over her face, 'Roderick, stop! Stop reminding me! I *need* no reminding. That is why I thought to give those other ones a treat.' It had been a joy to come home from her grim tasks in that deserted town and find this gorgeous spectacle almost blotting out the light from the dining-room windows. But now she knew that it would not blot out the spectacle she wanted to forget. Nothing ever would.

Roderick had moved to a window that overlooked the Sir's Road. 'Look, Margaret!' A bread van, its driver flanked by policemen holding carbines, was passing. 'James Wright dare not let his plain bread out on the road without police protection. If hungry people saw this——' He was going to use some caustic term for the inoffensive cake when he saw her tears. As she turned away the bells on her key ring made a tinkle of protest into the folds of her gown. The sound came to him like a crystal echo from her falling tears. 'My dear,' he called after her. 'All right. Give a party for the helpers. Ask the De Lacey girls. They've done heroic work for me. This will be a treat for them before they emigrate.'

The terrace, the only secluded place since the ravages of the big wind, was chosen for the setting of the cake party. But its seclusion didn't screen the fantasy in flour from George Lucas.

Sir Roderick was in the act of signing the 'bit of paper' that would give Lucas the lease of his wife's holding when the cake was carried to the terrace.

'By the powers of war!—beggin' your Honour's pardon for makin' so bold,' said Lucas, 'is that a real cake?'

It *would* be you, Roderick thought. The last one of his tenants he would wish to have seen the wretched thing. Rumours, ugly whispers about deaths on the Kilsheelin estate had reached him. On the estates of Lord Cullen and Lord Templetown tenants had died of fever; but none of starvation. Through the window both he and Lucas saw young Thomas lurch as he helped the butler and O'Driscoll to carry the cake.

He turned impatiently from the man's thanks for the lease and his good wishes for the afternoon's entertainment. '. . . an' I hope her Ladyship and the children will enjoy the wonderful cake. Sure there's a power of eatin' in it entirely.'

It is probably, thought Roderick, trying to overcome his distaste for the man, that he is not a born tenant. I tend to regard him as an interloper.... His face clouded and he threw the quill from him. Black Pat had been a born, hereditary tenant; sinew and bone of the soil of Kilsheelin.

Surprisingly, Roderick found himself enjoying the afternoon. It seemed eons since he had savoured the grace and charm of social life. The young girls in their crinolines and sashes and flower-laden bonnets looked like a garland of flowers around the cake. They oohed and ahed over it and strained on tiptoe to see the muses. Three of the Delaney girls, despite the short notice, had arrived almost first. From one Bianconi driver to another the invitation had sped from the lodge gates of the castle to the lodge gates of Moormount in Queen's County within an hour and a half.

The bard was enraptured with the cake. He expounded the Gaelic version of the muses to the girls. 'Nine Brightnesses carrying nine lanterns. Only maybe,' he said drolly, 'the great Queen's cook hadn't enough sugar left to make the lanterns.' He looked about him like a naughty child to see if anyone was looking, then broke off a toe from the dancing foot of Terpsichore. He murmured, 'You're a sweet little colleen,' sucking the toe, 'but you won't be so nimble now, gra'gal.' This was the way food should be served; a cake like a snow mountain; a whole side of beef; a pyramid of potatoes. 'Too much talk there is of famine,' he said to the girls. 'Now I remember the Great Scarcity of Seventeen——' Roderick gave him an affectionate shove. 'Go and play for the guests, Bard.'

The old man sat under the cake and winked up at Apollo. 'Yourself and your sugarstick lyre! Listen to this for sweetness.'

Margaret was in billowing white with a great white hat tied beneath her chin. Suddenly Roderick experienced that sentient feeling of having relived this scene before, an afternoon of brilliant sunshine; Margaret in bridal white planning a Belgian honeymoon! He walked towards her. And that tune the bard was playing.... It was the tune the piper had played when they had watched the dance at the crossroads; and, later, tragic little Nonie had flaunted her saucy tune on the violin. Where was she? Where were the boys and girls, the long-haired Naiad? Was it only ten months since he had listened to the piper play that thing the bard was now strumming? And 'twixt the two playings of the lovely melody a million people had died of hunger.

Tiredness flowed back. His head felt strangely light. Mrs. Kennedy-Sherwin looked over her shoulder and drew in the spread of her skirt from that of Mrs. Appleyard with an inviting gesture. He was glad to ease himself down between the billows of their crinolines.

Roderick thought how entrancing was the line of cheek and throat that showed beneath his wife's hat brim. He must tell her ... He must tell her. But he never wanted to stand up again. How blissful to sit for ever in this sun-drenched terrace! A low diapason filled his ears, not sound but vibration, like the buzzing of hundreds of bees. What on earth was Hegarty doing? Standing over him with a sword in his hand? Of course—the damned cake! He must cut it. He struggled to his feet. His body had become an automaton, blindly obeying some inner force that drove relentlessly. As he raised the sword that the butler had handed to him, a movement caught his eye. Only the cuckoo had that curious habit of slipping over a garden wall. Someone used to say something about that habit; someone in his childhood. Funny how many of these childhood associations obtruded of late. Not funny! So many of them were connected with Black Pat. It was Black Pat who used to say that if the garden wall were raised a foot the cuckoo would be trapped and good fortune would come to the garden. The government ought to have raised the nation's sea walls against the cuckoo merchant ships. 'The cuckoo,' he cried to Margaret, pointing his sword towards the wall. But the bird had slithered out of sight. Margaret saw nothing. She merely heard the terrible thing her husband was saying. 'My dear,' he was saying, 'I ought to have raised the wall. Then there might have been no——' No famine was what he meant to say but on a sudden he exclaimed. 'Why then there might have been no need for Fitz's cake!'

He brought the sword down through the cake, unconscious of the sudden silence, unconscious of his wife's white face. She did not possess his lore of wild life. But she did know that the cuckoo was the symbol of unfaithfulness. The guests knew it. It was in their faces. Even Lady Cullen who adored Roderick, thought that he had taken leave of his senses and publicly accused his wife of cuckolding him with the young officer who had presented the cake.

Roderick unconscious of the drama, was prising off sugar muses with his sword tip. Catherine Delaney went all coy and blushing when he handed her Erate and explained that she was the female of Eros, the God of Love. 'What shall I do with it?' she murmured, though everyone knew she would put it under her pillow. 'Keep it for a fast day,' he suggested. 'No, wait!' He took back Eros and gave her another muse.

With Eros poised on the sword tip he crossed to Margaret. 'My dear,' he said making a knightly obeisance, 'the very young do not fully appreciate the significance of Love's symbols.' He was offering her again his own love; but she made no move to accept the figurine. Her face was as white as though the sword tip had pricked her heart.

The little figure toppled from the blade and fell to the ground. Roderick rose wearily. She was keeping up the bitterness! And in front of this crowd! He resumed his seat and closed his eyes.

Sterrin stood forlornly on the empty terrace and watched young Thomas and Hegarty carry away the cake. Where the sword had cut, a brown gash bled a trail of crumbs and fruit. Hungry as she was for sweets, Sterrin had no craving for that monstrous confection. She had a strange feeling of being grown up. It had something to do with the strange look on her papa's face. Sterrin had not known that sorrow could come like that into the midst of fun and brightness. She was sad as she waved goodbye to the Delaney girls. Would there ever again be a truly gay party at Kilsheelin?

CHAPTER 29

Mr. Delaney was dead, struck down by famine fever. Young Thomas was ordered to dress in livery with a mourning swathe about his cockaded hat. Big John and Mike O'Driscoll, with blunderbusses concealed, had to journey for a grain consignment. Young Thomas must supply the ceremonial courtesy for Mr. Delaney's funeral.

It was the strangest funeral Thomas had seen; even of famine funerals. Five of the Delaney girls were ill with fever. Fever was raging madly about the district. The Delaney's nearest neighbours were all down. The three daughters who had been at the tea party at Kilsheelin still wearing their muslin gowns, only sketchily covered by cloaks, looked strange. And strangest of all was the absence of even one clergyman to breathe a prayer at the graveside. The curate had collapsed, plague-stricken, between the hospital beds where he had been administering the viaticum to the dying. The parish priest was struggling single-handed night and day.

Mrs. Delaney looked vaguely about her. She caught the movement of a rose-coloured sash as it fluttered from a cloak. She moved forward and someone said, 'Make way for the widow.' She made way with the others until she realised that they meant herself. *She* was the widow. She, who had deplored all her married life that she was nothing but a widow because Rodney had been so—so gently unobtrusive! She forced back the tears because there was something grievously lacking. Not just the absence of relatives and friends, of tenants and workmen—except those three helping Ned-Rua with the burden that four must carry. It wasn't even the absence of mourning black, Syrilla looked grotesque in a black riding coat over the rose-sprigged white gown she had worn at the tea party. There were but two figures in black; one was her kinsman, Rody O'Carroll. The other looked like an O'Carroll too. But there was no black figure wearing the white linen bandillero of mourning across his shoulders. No priest to breathe a prayer. 'Rody,' she whispered, 'the Latin!'

Roderick swayed out from a trance. 'De profundis clamavi ad te Domine,' he prayed, with a sort of blind obedience that carried him for about two lines. His voice trailed away from the void of his mind into the one that gaped at his feet.

Then out of the silence another voice took up the Latin words, 'Si iniquitates observaveris domine; Domine, quis sustinebit.'

No one seemed to notice that it was a scullery boy who was murmuring that cry from the depths on behalf of the scholarly son of Sir Dowling Delaney. Cathleen Delaney stifled the recollection of some poem the O'Carroll's bard had quoted yesterday—something about a chieftain who had stood like a lance uplifted.

Roderick, after the ceremony wanted to ask the girls to come back to Kilsheelin with him. But already they were rushing back to their plague-stricken sisters.

'It is sweltering there, Rody,' their mother said as she answered his queries. Thomas, holding open the brougham door as erect as 'a lifted lance', heard his own voice saying, 'Put them in the quarry.' Roderick explained about the Scout and the others who, when struck down with the plague, had lain in the quarry in open air and had been cured. The idea didn't shock Mrs. Delaney. It appealed to her sense of the out-of-doors, but Ned-Rua was horrified. 'Miss Katie,' he urged, 'you're not yourself. If you do such a thing I'll—I'll——' Automatically she finished his oft-repeated threat. 'You'll leave me in the morning.'

Ned turned away and wiped his eyes. 'I'll never leave you, Miss Katie.'

On the way home in the brougham Roderick dozed. He awakened with a jolt. Thomas had just made the discovery that he was asleep himself and in a panic had chucked the unoffending horse to a standstill. His master, still fuddled with sleep, had stepped to the ground before he realised that they were halted at a wayside tavern. The clamour of Roderick's weary body and dry throat propelled him inside.

No one answered his knock. When he called, his voice went off through the house on its own. He could hear its echoes. But apparently no one else did. On his way out a man jostled him in the doorway and continued down the length of the shop. Roderick watched him help himself from a big whiskey jar that materialised out of the gloom at the far end of the counter. Copper coins were piled about its base.

The landlord and his household, Roderick learned, were down with fever, as was the entire neighbourhood. People were to help themselves whether they could pay or not. Whiskey was the best antidote for the fever. The man tossed down twopence. 'It's killin' people like flies,' he said. Roderick thought he was alluding to the unrestricted whiskey. 'Particularly,' the man said, 'the gentry. They make no fight. Take another noggin, your Honour.' Roderick did so, then bade the man send in his driver.

Thomas knew he was in for it! The enormity of falling asleep driving was scarcely as terrible as what he had done at the burial when he had suggested putting the Misses Delaney into a quarry. He had no idea how the words came to be said; but when he heard them coming out of his own lips he had the same sensation that he had known in a dream, when he thought he was sitting in his nightshirt in a bianconi, and all the people in the long row opposite him staring out at him over their travelling coats.

The Sir seemed to say drink this! But Thomas knew that the impression was more of the nightshirt-in-a-bianconi feeling and so he kept his lips tight. Then the Sir let out an unmistakable, 'Go on!' and pushed a pewter noggin brimming with whiskey towards him. After that Thomas stopped travelling in his nightshirt in a bianconi. He started floating. He forgot to hold his lips together. Outside they opened involuntarily at the sight of the gossamer web that spread over the bank where the horse had drifted to graze. From grass to twig it spread and from twig to thistle, the shimmering threads woven by innumerable spiders, down the other side of the bank and across the field. 'The winding sheet of Our Lady!' he cried. His inflamed imagination linked the shimmering wraith on the grass from field to field across thousands of miles. 'A land covered by a shroud!' His master recognised the legend of Our Lady's shroud that fell to earth as She was assumed to Heaven but Roderick was just a little drunk and more than a little panicky. He put his boot through the cobweb and turned back towards the stable. He decided to ride home. The house sported a sign proclaiming it as a mail-coach halt. It was bound to have horses. He helped himself to a horse as he had to the whiskey. As he harnessed it he wondered somewhat drunkenly should he pay for it in the same manner by dropping coins in the manger? He strode to the empty kitchen and dropped his card on the table; then, bidding Thomas continue with the brougham, he set the horse for the short cut across the fields and boreens. He must have action; must gallop away from sight or talk of shrouds whether they were woven by spiders or humans.

By the time Thomas drove the brougham down the main-street of Templetown, he was far more lathered than his horse; but then, he reflected, the wise animal had drunk nothing stronger than water. Thomas's stiff hat was making a ridge in his forehead and his tight livery held him in a clammy grip. He stripped off his jacket and took off his hat. There was no one to watch him. The street was deserted except for a few policemen guarding Wright's bakery. Young Thomas wondered if he should speak to them about the sheep that were disappearing from the Sir's pasture. Just the other day they had tried to trap the thief, he and the Sir, lying in wait by the stream. Once they thought they saw a shadow of a man, but before the Sir could raise his gun, a great heron had risen in flight and the man who had disturbed it disappeared from view.

A play bill caught Thomas's eye. He could never resist a play bill; palm trees, minarets, dashing horsemen in colourful uniforms. Pah, a recruiting poster. The picture of the military horsemen recalled something he had been trying to remember. Yes, Lieutenant Fitzharding-Smith. Miss Sterrin had said he was to go see him. He turned the horse's head towards the military barracks.

Lieutenant Fitzharding-Smith was leaving his apartment, followed by a batman laden with books. 'Ah, thought you weren't coming,' the lieutenant said. 'I was just going to dump these.' Thomas was gazing fascinated at a party of Tenth Hussars who were defiling before them. They were resplendent, both horses and men; all that gold in the officers' uniforms was real; so were the leopard skins across their saddles, and the cloth in the uniform jacket cost two whole pounds a yard! 'Not thinking of joining, are you?' said the lieutenant. 'You'd make a fine hussar.'

Thomas tried to shake his head but the effort was too painful.

'I'd never be able to afford the uniform,' he said hoarsely. The lieutenant gave an amused smile and extended his hand. 'You don't have to start there,' he said, nodding towards the glittering Hussar captain. 'You could start at the other end.' Where he pressed the boy's hand there was a gold piece.

Thomas was weaving from side to side in his seat in the brougham. The unshuttered window of a jeweller's shop shed a wanton bizarrerie amid the street's blind and halted commerce. A finger of green light seemed to beckon Thomas. Obediently he dismounted and walked solemnly into the shop. 'How much is that?' he asked, nodding towards the window where the finger of light waved from the green stones of a ring.

'Seven and six.' The jeweller had it out from the window in a flash. Why not? The Blight hadn't extended to rings. Hungry people could purchase all the jewels they wanted. Then an emerald ring in a glass case caught his glance. 'How much is that one?'

The jeweller took in the shirt-sleeved figure and smiled indulgently. Still! One couldn't be sure about people these days! The lad spoke well; a fine appearance too! He might easily be a son of the gentry who were doing their own carting and hauling since they could no longer feed servants.

'Seventy-five guineas,' he said. 'Shall I wrap this?'

Thomas tore his eyes from the lovely emerald. The little ring in the jeweller's hand had gone dim and tawdry. 'N-no,' he answered slowly. His eyes strayed back to the emerald. 'No, I'll wait.'

As the jeweller replaced the ring in the window he recognised the Kilsheelin brougham. A servant boy from the castle! 'You'll wait indeed!' He snorted at the shirt-sleeved figure who was studying the Army recruiting posters outside his shop. He watched Thomas climb into the driver's seat. 'You'll wait a long time, my lad!'

As he shook out the reins, Thomas became aware of his shirt-clad arms and knew for certain that he was dreaming. To drive a carriage in one's shirt-sleeves was more of fantasy than to travel in a public vehicle in one's nightshirt! He fingered the hat on the seat beside him. It felt real and he put it on. He'd better put on the coat too. But he fell asleep instead.

An overhead whirring awakened him. He looked up wildly. The evening sun outlined the wide and placid wings of a heron.

A heron! The sight of the bird spurred him to a sense of urgency about the stolen sheep. He must find that thief. He jumped to the ground. The reins went trailing amongst the horse's feet. He looped them through the whip ring. 'Go home yourself,' Thomas said, and walked off.

He walked in the wake of the heron's flight until a boulder stopped him and he lay where he fell. When he got up he had forgotten about the heron. But he trudged on. There was something that he must do. He heard the sound of running water. It was the Lissnastreenagh, the little stream where he had cooked the picnic trout for Miss Sterrin.

When he stopped to scoop a handful of water, the pain in his head made him stagger, but a firm arm kept him from falling.

'Is it the way that the hunger is on you?' asked the voice of George Lucas.

It hurt Thomas to shake his head. By right he should answer in words but that was strangely difficult. There was genuine concern in the man's face now as he offered to help Thomas back to the castle. Again Thomas shook his head. He must remember not to do that. It let hell loose up there! 'There is something I must do,' he said. Lucas nodded understandingly. 'Them that serve must obey,' he said. 'But the like of you should have no hunger upon you an' you workin' where there is full an' plenty.'

'There is something I must do,' Thomas insisted.

He said it again later to a man with wild hair and clothing; and a face that was not in keeping. For instead of the clay colour of hunger it had the ruddy glow of health, and the blue of his eyes penetrated the clouds of Thomas's brain.

'Who are you?' cried Thomas. 'You are too well fed.' No one had the right to look so vigorous and yet so wild. 'You are the one who is stealing the sheep!'

The man—who could he be?—listened to Thomas's babblings about the Sir who fed the multitude and the thief who had in the haunt of the heron. 'The heron!' he repeated. 'There is sense in your ravings, child! The heron laid twice this season. I guessed that something more than weather had disturbed the clutch it laid in February. No, I'm no sheep thief. I've never tasted meat in my life, nor the potatoes that men are dying for need of. I've bees and goats and a cave that belongs to God. But I'll watch the heron for you—and the thief. Let you rest, for the fever is on you.'

But Thomas wouldn't rest. He bade good day to the hermit and pressed on. He felt as if his body had stepped out from its own skin; out from that tyrannical force that had driven him relentlessly. He wafted on, disembodied, until suddenly weightless, he toppled into masses of fragrance.

His groping hands found blossoms and more blossoms. His eyes strained up through a carnival of lattice branches to the sky. The Scout's face swam towards him, peering as it had done from the quarry outside the fever hospital. But this was no quarry. This was the fairy rath of Lissnastreenagh. This was better than the quarry. A little wind fanned his forehead and gently shook down a frew fragrant petals to dab his moist forehead. His timeless journey was over. No more searching for—a sheep? A heron? Not these. No more searching for—companionship, for human affection.

Where was that hand that had reached to shake his and, instead, had shot about his shoulders and held him against a strangely soft body, in an excess of tenderness. It had waved from a ship and vanished. It waved again through the branches, smaller and smaller, a little hand that could never shoot out about him to enclose him like that other, never bridge the chasm that lay between.

He dozed and a sound awakened him. He dozed again only to awake to the same sound. It was the low musical note of the wind stirring the overhanging branches, bidding them release their blossoms to blanket his shivering fever. It touched with fairy fingers the pine needles in the fir belt so that they vibrated like the tiny strings of a harp and played him a lullaby.

When he awakened it was dawn. The hills were re-echoing with the bleating of lambs that was answered by the deep baaing of their soft-voiced mothers. The sound brought him struggling up. Sheep! They were being stolen. But it was only his thoughts that struggled. His body lay prostrate. His eyes gazed helplessly at the remote and tender sky. It was as blue as—as the eyes of the man who had promised to watch for the thief. Thomas closed his own eyes and let his body slip out from the grasp of the tyrant that drove it. 'I'm staying here—for ever.' The hermit with the blue eyes would not let the Sir be robbed.

When the horse trailed its driverless carriage into the castle yard there was consternation. What accident had befallen young Thomas? Suddenly everyone realised that he had been driven too hard. He had moved among them tirelessly; quiet but all pervading, like the sound of a stream unnoticed until it ceases. Everyone was aware of the cessation, the staff, even the Sir himself. Everyone except Lady O'Carroll, lying on her chaise-longue remote and brooding.

They searched in relays through the night. They retraced the road to Templetown and beyond to the point on the Queen's County road, where Sir Roderick had left Thomas soliloquising about a land covered completely by a shroud. Roderick's conscience reproached him for having left the lad alone with his morbid whimsy.

In the morning there was still no sign. No one dreamed of lonely, haunted Lissnastreenagh. Then the late afternoon brought news that jolted their concern. Constable Humphreys had seen the lad scrutinising the recruiting posters and heard him say that he must go to the barracks; and on the day of his disappearance he had glimpsed him reading the East India recruiting notices beside the jewellers; in his shirtsleeves!

It appeared that the knife boy had run off and 'listed'. The searchers felt foolish. The reference to shirt-sleeves explained the livery coat lying on the driver's seat of the brougham. It also showed a deliberateness of plan that hurt Sterrin and angered her father. The fellow was taking no chances of being referred back to his employer! He had taken the precaution of discarding his livery before presenting himself for enlistment.

Margaret's brooding strengthened to resolve. Somehow she must get to Belgium alone. There was no other way out. Roderick had denounced her before half the county; had insulted and derided her.

Nurse Hogan, coming into the room, showed no surprise at the open valise on her mistress's bed. The Nurse's eyes were blurred with tears. 'Fancy, your Ladyship,' she sobbed. 'Who'd think it of him? To run away at a time like this.'

Roderick came to the door to tell Margaret that he was going to Templetown with the subscriptions from yesterday's post. This was a task that he had gradually come to deputise to young Thomas. And here was the nurse keening about the fellow.

'Stop distressing yourself,' he admonished her. 'Anyone who would run away at a time like this is not worth crying about.'

Margaret sat on her bed beside her valise. The rage that shook her for her husband's flaunting contempt extended to the whole hateful castle, even to the brat of a knife boy whose puling flight had turned the drama of her own departure into farce.

Sterrin, in spite of her hurt, continued to search for him. She wandered down to the stream to the lovely spot where they had had their picnic. No one must know the lonely grief that lay behind the still façade of that small white face. She walked about aimlessly, trying to keep back the tears. And then she found his hat!

Reverently she picked it up from the clump of mosses and speedwells that grew on the spot where Thomas had cooked the tickled trout. 'He's drowned,' she mourned.

Slowly she moved along to where small boulders lashed up the twelve inches of water into a miniature waterfall. There was nothing bigger than a pinkeen in sight. But for Sterrin the translucent streamlet held tragedy. It held the being who was her whole world outside of her parents, of course—and that was a different feeling. Slowly she lifted her gaze to the distant turrets of the castle that would never be the same without young Thomas. Behind her the little pony paced with her, step for step. When she threw her arms about its neck it stood very still and its silky mane guarded the secret of the tears it had dried.

When Roderick saw the hat he wondered for a moment if the boy had sought escape beneath the gossamer shroud of his imaginings. But he turned from his trip to Templetown. He even forgot the sight of the terrible anger that had shocked him on Margaret's face this morning. He rode through every nook and spinney on the estate, seeking to retrieve the trust that he had lost in this boy who had made such unwarranted trespass into his master's affections. Suddenly, he heard a groan. It seemed to come from behind the great circle of blossoming hawthorn trees.

Roderick dismounted stiffly and parted the branches. He saw what looked like a decapitated head, dark and curly, amid the blossoms that covered the slopes and floor of the hollow. It made a faint upward movement that displayed a face with petals clinging to its glistening skin. The effect was comical. Like the violet petals that Margaret used to paste on to her complexion with thick cream.

But there was nothing comical about the spots that interspersed the petals. Roderick had become too familiar with the livid spots that were the sinister blossoms of the plague.

'Young man,' he said, 'you believe in having your fever under idyllic conditions.' He kicked at the blossoms for a footing and landed gently on his back beside his knife boy.

Thomas ejected his swollen tongue a few times. 'The sheep,' he whispered, 'I'll get the thief when I get water. There's water—under the heron.'

Roderick thought he caught the gist of the lad's wanderings. Water. He would get him water; and himself too. But first he must rest. His body beseeched him for rest. And now he was conscious of an unaccountable sense of gladness that seemed to make rest possible.

After an easeful silence his hands groped as though drawing up bedclothes. Blossoms and petals stirred upwards then wafted to rest upon his face and shoulders. 'The babes in the wood,' he murmured, 'bloomin' little robins covering us up with blossoms like the Babes in the Wood.'

Through clouds of sleep he heard a whispered 'Your Honour's Sir!'

'Huh?' Turning his head towards the sound made him wince. The bloated, petal-spattered face was turned towards him.

'They weren't blossoms, your Honour.'

'Huh?'

' 'Twas leaves the robins brought. In their beaks—to cover the babes.'

Roderick digested the information. 'Thank you,' he said solemnly. 'The blossoms must have been carried in the fairies' beaks. Good night!'

But it was still early forenoon. Late that afternoon the riderless Thuckeen was sighted by Sterrin. Another great search began. This time without Big John who chafed aloft on the carriage that waited to bring her Ladyship on some unspecified journey. All afternoon Margaret had wavered, dreading to take the final step towards flight. At last she appeared at the door. Before she reached the carriage she saw the men carrying Roderick on a hurdle. Big John caught her as she swayed. She gripped herself. Roderick had begun to despise these swayings. As they carried him past she saw the plague spots on his face. Behind him they brought young Thomas. She dismissed the carriage.

When Roderick and the knife boy had been put to bed the nurse came to Margaret for the recipe for the cure for cholera that Miss Sarah O'Carroll had sent to Sir Roderick. It was not in her Ladyship's herb book. Margaret hurried to the library to see if he had entered it in his record book. She knew that he had entered some other of Miss Sarah's cures there. As she turned the page she saw his entry of how pretty she had looked at that first Moonlight Ball at the Assembly Rooms. 'Bewitching,' he had written. The tears she had restrained in his presence gushed out. They splashed on the pages as she turned them frantically, looking for last year's records. Her glance was held at a page of entries written in Sir Dominic's hand long before she came here. Something to do with Black Pat Ryan's holding. But in between two lines of her father-in-law's heavy script was an entry in green ink in Roderick's own writing. 'Nonie—Oenone Mansfield —Saint Patrick's Eve, March the Sixteenth Eighteen forty-five.' It was where Roderick had filled in the gap left for Nonie's name by his father, and on an impulse had added the date. It danced out at Margaret, vivid and provocative from the sombre background. Like the owner of the name!

The shock dried the tears that his lovely record of herself had released. The nurse's voice recalled her to the moment's terrible urgency. She flicked the pages. 'Here's the recipe,' she said and frowned. This was not for cholera. This was a recipe for the brewing of the small leaves of the ground ivy. She had drunk this brew herself when she had those swayings. Why was it entered here? She scanned the directions in Roderick's slanting copperplate, and then in brackets she read '... believed to be particularly efficacious in the treatment of madness——'

Madness! A gasp escaped her. Was that why they gave her brew? Why the recipe was kept from her sight?

Nurse Hogan came over and saw the recipe that she had prepared so often.

'Your Ladyship,' she said in a firm voice, 'this is no time to be dwelling on yourself.' She flicked the page. 'Here is what we want—— The Cholera Cure, one-sixth part of camphor dissolved in six parts strong spirits of wine——' She glanced up at her mistress's distended eyes and resolved that she wasn't going to have three patients on her hands. She brought the ingredients to the sick-room and asked Margaret to mix and administer them. Margaret forced back her rising hysteria as she poured two drops of the mixture on to granulated sugar and mixed it with an exact spoonful of cold water. With her watch extended she counted five slow minutes and then repeated the dose. At the end of five minutes more he was still shivering. After the fourth interval of five minutes when a full eight drops had been administered, Margaret had shed all preoccupation with herself. According to the cousins there should be signs of returning warmth before this. They had tried it with Lord Ponsonby and it had been most efficacious.

The nurse urged her to go on with the treatment but Roderick set his teeth against the spoon. 'It is killing the gentry off like flies,' he muttered, 'they make no fight.'

'But it cured Lord Ponsonby,' urged Nurse Hogan with naïve sincerity. 'Miss O'Carroll said so.' What stronger proof of its efficacy? The medicine had cured a peer of the realm!

Roderick dozed. When he awoke the fever was worse. He refused the medicine again. 'It is killing the gentry like flies. They make no fight,' he insisted. Margaret's heart contracted. The treacherous swaying started in her head. She must fight it; because Roderick was refusing to fight. Roderick, who was— deathless—was willing himself to die!

When Mrs. Stacey heard the trend of his wanderings she faced boldly up into the sick-room. 'Master Rody,' she called firmly into his brain, 'you are no gentry to the fever. You had it an' you fosterin' an' you learned how to make a fight. Don't you remember, agra?'

He looked up at her, seeking to remember.

'You had it with Black Pat,' she urged. It was a risk to mention that name but she had to convince him that he was not like the unaccustomed gentry who succumbed. Fever was almost endemic in homes like the one where he had fostered.

He took medicine from her hand. Not the aristocratic kind but the brew she had given him as a child. It seemed to turn his delirium to that time. Repeatedly he spoke Black Pat's name and once Margaret heard him mutter 'Nonie' and then a name like 'Mansfield'.

Gradually Roderick's fever subsided. The time came when he could sit, first at the open window, then in the garden. One afternoon, while he snoozed in the garden, she went to the library. Fearfully she approached the black book. It had acquired an ominous quality; like a locked room that held a grim secret. She gazed fascinated at the entry that Roderick had interposed among his father's records. What had taken place that afternoon that had caused Roderick to come straight here and write her surname beside her *petit non*—Nonie—so gay, so *intime*? For all time! And why in that flaunting green?

Margaret had a sudden recollection of Nonie sitting in her porch, her golden head bent over masses of wool, and about her shoulders a charming green shawl! And then another recollection; Roderick standing in the bedroom in Mountjoy Square telling her about a girl in a green riding habit, a girl with blue flecks in her hazel-green eyes! A girl called Mansfield. Nonie! And Roderick had known all along! Yes, now she understood. Mrs. Black Pat Ryan was the romantic love that had escaped Roderick, only to be recaptured too late.

Margaret turned the pages one by one but there were no further references to the girl; she went back to the entry where the reference to herself as 'bewitching' had caught her eye the evening he had been carried home. '... for the pink creped gown in which my wife looked so bewitching that night when the cowardly Whiteboys terrified her so that the doctor feared for the health of her mind as well as her body——'

The health of her mind! Her mind! She could feel pain pounding at that dull spot in the back of her head. She tore through the pages marked so meticulously with dates of the succeeding years. She came to a page dated simply Repeal Year. Beneath was written the horrible recipe. In that golden year when Ireland had stood on the tiptoes of gaiety and hope, Roderick recorded the treatment for his wife's madness!

The silence in the library was deep. August, Roderick always said was the silent month. The great bird chorus of the year had packed up long ago, and the sap energy had abated in all growth. He knew so much about Nature! Her eyes ranged over the shelves that held his botanical books. She got up and peered at their covers. Here it was! The one that would tell her about the ground ivy. 'A hairy, creeping perennial——' she read and went no further. She dropped the book with a scream as though some horrid thing had crawled on to her skin.

That afternoon Lady Cullen arrived to pay her first call. Roderick was well enough for visitors, and when Lady Cullen was told that Margaret had gone for a walk, the irrepressible old lady decided to speak plain and true.

'How could you, Rody,' she demanded availing herself of the unexpected *tête-à-tête*, 'accuse your wife of unfaithfulness? Before all those people! No,' she said putting up her hand, 'you've used your tongue enough, hinting smart cleveralities with it, like a tradesman hinting for a settlement of accounts. If you suspected your wife of having a lover why the devil's father didn't you stick your sword into his gullet instead of his cake? Dammit, it's not done, Rody.'

Roderick wondered if the old lady were feeling all right. Very gently he suggested that she might be a trifle *'en fièvre'*.

'En fièvre, my foot,' she snorted. 'The others were not *"en fièvre"*. But they were burning, I can tell you; with unholy excitement. I'll wager it was the first time any of them was invited to witness the free spectacle of a gentleman publicly declaring that his wife had cuckolded him. Raise the wall against the cuckoo, indeed!'

Roderick sat astounded. He had gone through that party in a state of fever. 'It is absurd,' he said at last. 'Nobody would dream of putting such an interpretation on my words—not unless they wanted to.'

'Cullen didn't want to. He wanted to call you out. I had to stamp on his toe; the gouty one.'

'But it's fantastic! To make a mountain—a scandal—out of a scrap of pishoguerie! The dammed bird was *there*. For everyone to see.'

'So was the dammed cake—for everyone to see. No one saw the cuckoo.'

When Lady Cullen had departed, another carriage swept in the gate; a resplendent four-horse affair with lackeys erupting from all points; two from the backboard, one from beside the driver, one from the inside; all helped Lord and Lady Strague to alight.

The carriage belonged to Sir Jocelyn Devine, who had set it back with the Stragues. They had been his guests all Summer since Lord Strague's recovery from a gun shot wound received during an armed raid on his grain wagons. Roderick examined the coach with all the curiosity of a boy. He could not resist the sight of anything new in coachwork. This one was the very last word. The slender shafts were attached to a spring to neutralise the motion of the horse; whalebone screwed under the shafts to increase elasticity; every ingenuity to make the carriage glide softly and evenly over rough roads. A fantasy on wheels, Roderick thought.

Minutes later he thought that he must be *listening* to fantasy. Lady Cullen's revelations were followed up by apologies from Lady Strague for Lady Margaret's dreadful experience at the Soupers kitchen conducted by Lord Strague's Vestry committee at Aughnacoll.

'We did not discover until weeks later that the lady who had been trampled down was Lady Margaret, and by that time we were at Jocelyn's place and Strague had developed a fever from the wound.'

The suggestion that Roderick had put to Lady Cullen about being *en fièvre* could not possibly be made to Lady Strague. Her voice was too cool, too assured. It flowed on in a cool recountal of the dreadful scene. After the Stragues had left, Roderick sat in stunned silence. Poor Margaret. She had endured so much for so long. How to make up for it?

Nurse Hogan interrupted his musings. She was worried. 'Her Ladyship ought to have been back from her walk long ago.'

'Worried!' Her master rounded on her as he had never done before. Where was her worry the time her mistress had endured unspeakable horrors? It was the nurse's turn to wonder about fever. Had the Sir suffered a relapse? He was talking of things that might possibly happen in a nightmare. She did recall the evening that her Ladyship had returned like a sleepwalker whose face still held a nightmare's horror! She recalled the filth on her Ladyship's gown!

She told him all she knew. Her Ladyship had never spoken of what had happened. The nurse didn't tell him that her own conclusion had been that some maniac had attacked her Ladyship and she could not bring herself to speak of it. She didn't dare remind him that no one—not even her Ladyship—could speak to him after that night when Black Pat Ryan and his children had died.

The autumn sky deepened to purple and still no sign of Margaret. It was dark when Roderick climbed weakly into the saddle and galloped towards Templetown to search for her. Mrs. Kennedy-Sherwin was finishing up after her turn of duty at the Relief Depot. Roderick felt deep respect for the outrageous little flirt who was proving herself one of the famine's heroines. But Margaret was not there.

Sick with disappointment he turned away; then on an impulse turned back and asked Mrs. Kennedy-Sherwin about that night at the Ryan Duvs.

She told him that she had seen Margaret running along the road towards the Ryans, that Margaret had called out to Mrs. Kennedy-Sherwin as she emerged from her carriage carrying the sick Ryan child. She described how Margaret stood horrified in the doorway of the Ryan house. 'She'd probably been running for help. Poor darling, she must have fallen too. Mud on her face; and her gown!' Mrs. Kennedy-Sherwin's voice shrilled up. 'It was revoltingly ruined! Poor Mrs. Ryan wasn't too cordial to her either.' She sighed. 'The famine changes people; like war. Jeremy says that gentlemen behave queerly under war conditions. Personally, I don't see that it needs either war or famine to justify their queerness——' Sir Roderick was halfway across the road. He turned back to bow and to say that he was in a hurry.

'Who'd have thought it?' she murmured after the thudding hooves. 'What a delicious quarrel that must be! Cuckoos, cakes, gallops by night.' She gave a long sigh. 'Some women have all the luck!'

When the hooves had thudded to a standstill at Kilsheelin there was still no Margaret.

From the oratory window, Sterrin watched with dread as the men started out to search for her mamma. There was something ominous about the slow-moving figures, some carrying lant-horns, others with glowing turf sods impaled on pikestaffs. Out there in the darkness her mamma was lost or ill or—Sterrin shivered, terrified to let the dread word take form in her mind. But it must have formed in Papa's mind. Because he was afraid! She had never thought that such a thing could happen. Now there was no shelter left in all the world.

Young Thomas saw her face at the window as he crossed the yard. They had ordered him to go back to bed. He was but a day or two up and could scarcely crawl. Still he tiptoed into the oratory just as Sterrin had dropped to her knees after the last of the lights had moved into the distance. She turned at the little sound and all at once it was as though shelter was restored. How could she have forgotten the one who was down there in the shadow inside the door? Her heart steadied. There was always young Thomas!

CHAPTER 30

The Ballduff jingle stopped at the crossroads to let down a passenger. Lady O'Carroll stepped up and took the vacant place. At the next crossroads passengers alighted and hurried towards the long bianconi car. She followed them. When they alighted at Thurles railway station she did likewise. As she approached the booking office where they were buying tickets she felt her first nervousness. But she listened while the gentleman in front of her asked for a first-class ticket to Dublin. She moved up into his place and asked for another. Travel was easy!

But when the great monster came chuffing from under the tunnel, clanking and roaring and belching smoke, she panicked.

She stood trembling on the platform while doors opened and banged shut. A porter went on holding the door for her. Everyone else had got in. Timidly she put her foot into the carriage. The engine emitted a fearful shriek. Margaret sprang back. The porter, all sympathy with her shouted to the driver to put a muzzle on his ould chimney. The driver requested him to put a muzzle on his own chimney.

'Come on, ma'am,' urged the porter, 'put yourself in the hands of God an' I'll hold your own hand.' She thought of the dignified stage-coach driver; the ostler handing up his immaculate gloves on the point of departure. As she gave her hand to the porter, the guard blew a whistle and the train gave a preliminary lurch. She withdrew her hand and fled.

Behind her the porter harangued the guard for his bad manners.

'You and your tin whistle! And a lady that's used to the elegance of horse carriages in the middle of makin' up her mind.'

There was no going back to Kilsheelin. That kind of conduct would be just another instance of her madness. She endured a night at the nearby Man o' War and the next morning stepped

283

firmly into the Dublin bound train. The porter almost clapped. 'You've a powerful strong mind,' he commented.

The compliment bore her over the first stage of the journey. This was really nicer than the stage-coach. One was not crushed against undesirable persons. One did not have to watch out for one's flounces. No one spat. A most polite notice requested gentlemen to refrain from doing so. And the sleepers were wooden; not like the granite ones in that train she had travelled in from Dublin to Kingstown, in Repeal Year.

Once she caught her reflection in the carriage window and peered intensely. Strain widened her brown eyes so that they looked wild to her. At last, she thought, she was face to face with her own—Madness. She saw the whiteness of the reflection as a symptom of her malady. The gentleman in the opposite seat was thinking that her pallor glowed with colour as an alabaster lamp glows from the light within.

The children's faces swam in and out of the rushing landscape. Sterrin's so sweet but remote. Dominic, still a baby. Would they miss their mad mother? *Mon Dieu!* Look at the fields! Was her head going to start this treacherous swaying in front of these gentlemen?

'The fields are running.' She spoke without realising. Immediately the gentlemen reassured her.

'One gets that impression when travelling in a train.' The gentleman in the corner said that when he brought his wife for her first train journey, she was terrified at the way the fields seemed to run past the windows.

She thanked them. Her thoughts turned to Roderick. No gentleman would dream of accusing his wife in public. No matter how wickedly she had behaved. Cynthia Appleyard, it was known, indulged in more than just light flirtations; sinful, bed affairs. Yet her husband had fought a duel in her defence! Roderick had used his sword to point fun at his wife in front of their friends.

The gentleman in the corner seat was giving his neighbour advice about travel arrangements. Margaret listened carefully. 'Better drive straight to the packet,' he was saying, 'and stay on board all day instead of waiting to embark in the evening. There will be no getting through the crowds later, on account of the funeral.'

There was no form or purpose to her flight. Like a child she followed these knowledgeable grown-ups. She bade the porter who procured their hackney chaise to procure one for her and drive to the place they had mentioned. She saw the others pay their fares and step aboard. But when she asked her own driver what was his fare. the efficiency of her itinerancy collapsed. The Dublin jarvey's renowned formula, 'I'll lave it to yourself, your Honour,' left her bewildered.

He watched the sovereign emerging from her reticule. 'Will this be enough?' she asked.

He buried it deep under the capes of his surtout, before he answered, 'I'll not ask for a penny more. It is a pleasure to drive such a lovely lady.' Since he wouldn't dare to ask a seasoned traveller for a penny more than one-and-six he threw in a word of advice for good measure. 'I'd put away that reticule of yours, Miss. There'll be a power of purse-snatchers abroad today on account of the funeral.'

His concern touched her. His compliment like the porter's eased the ordeal of going aboard. Travelling on a ship had the quality of travelling over a narrow mountain road. One went where the road went. She paid her money to go where the ship was going.

Her air of distinction, and the shiny contents of her reticule, secured her a nice cabin. When food was brought she realised that she had not eaten since the previous morning. No wonder the famine-hungry were always exhausted. She stretched her tired body on the little bed and the lullaby of the lapping waters sent her into a deep sleep.

She awoke startled and afraid. The little room was moving. Up and down, then sideways. Overhead there was clanking. It was coming down the chimney! It was the turret! Smoke drifted past the window. My God! Where was Mrs. Mansfield? No, Nurse Hogan; 'Roderick, Roderick!' But no one could hear her above the roar of the Big Wind.

With a long-drawn 'Roder-eeck' she stumbled towards the door. It opened and there was Roderick.

She was held firm in the grip of his arms. The noise stopped. The swaying stopped. Everything was suddenly still; only his voice murmuring over and over, 'My darling! My lovely, lost, terrified darling!'

She tried to speak but his kisses stifled over vocal breath. At last he held her from him, her arms gripped. Her lovely graceful

285

arms that had carried a great, full-grown woman! His eyes devoured the elegant form that had lain beneath a corpse, rending her as she dragged herself shrieking from the terrible embrace. His kisses spoke his tribute, reverent, tender, passionate.

She drew away. 'But I don't understand. You ought to be at Kilsheelin, ill.'

'So ought you, but not ill—healthy, sound——'

'I'm not sound.' The interruption rasped out from her, low and tense. 'You know that I am not sound. I am——' She couldn't say the word mad. She looked down at her hands. 'I've read your recipe for—for the leaves of the ground ivy.' She daren't look up to see his face. She ought to have let the thing lie. A sleeping dog! A silent menace between them. He drew her down beside him. His arms still about her. At last his voice spoke very low, 'Is that why you ran away?'

She nodded. Her eyes were still on her hands where a big tear had splashed. He jerked her chin and forced her to look up.

'Margaret,' he said, 'promise me that you will never again let the shadow of such a thought cross your mind.' He looked straight into her eyes, 'The mind that I love.'

His grip on her chin was firm. She had no option but to give back his searching look. Her protests, all the questions she wanted to ask, became void.

Much later she remembered to ask him how he had come to find her. He chuckled. It wasn't hard to trace the lady who held up a whole train and then decided to sleep on the project before attempting another start. He dismissed the memory of his terrible all-night search and the frantic gallop with relays of horses to catch up on that 'special' train. 'That reminds me!' He jumped up. 'We'll miss the arrival. I'd never have reached you in time if I hadn't caught up on the funeral "Special".'

She drew back. Twice today there had been references to a funeral. It had conveyed nothing. There were funerals every day.

'Whose funeral?' she asked.

'The Liberator's, of course.'

She had forgotten that the Liberator's funeral had been winding its slow way across the continent from Italy where he had died. City after city paid homage to his remains. In every port, ships of all nations lowered their flags.

As Roderick and Margaret came on deck, the emigrant ship

286

Birmingham was moving out. When it passed, Margaret saw, to her amazement, a solid mass of humanity, rows and rows, filling the width of the quay and stretching down its length as far as she could see. More people, thought Roderick, than had stood to witness the Liberator pass in triumph to address a million people at Tara.

'I don't understand, Roderick, I thought we were at sea. I felt the boat rocking.'

He explained that what she had felt was when the boat had been hurriedly transferred from its accustomed moorings to accommodate the unusual sea traffic that accompanied the funeral barge.

'Here it comes!'

Slowly the *Duchess of Kent* in a great convoy of vessels, steamers, yachts, fishing craft, came streaming up the bay. The Liberator was making his most impressive entry into the country he had served so nobly.

Nearby a tiny boat floundered wildly. Then another! The fishermen had glimpsed the coffin on the quarter deck, under its vast awning of black crepe. Regardless of safety they knelt in their little crafts to pray.

Suddenly a wild Gaelic keen throbbed over the waters. The *Birmingham* was passing the coffin ship and the emigrants had flung themselves to their knees in a passion of grief for the Great One who had raised them up from the prostration of the Penal Law.

Roderick felt Margaret's tremor. In the strange mood that had accomplished her flight, how could she have endured this scene alone! He gripped her fingers.

Hand in hand they stood on the crowded deck and waited. On the brink of another black harvest, midst pestilence and hunger, midst the keen of the death lamentation, the mighty Tribune was coming to his people in their darkest hour.

Silently the great crowd filed by as the coffin was borne ashore. The quickening throb beneath the deck warned Roderick that the engines were warming for departure. Another minute and they would have been on their way to England.

CHAPTER 31

Thomas often wondered if he had dreamed the strange man he had encountered that day when he had collapsed among the blossoms at Lissnastreenagh. A year had passed since then. The death of Joseph, the footman, of famine fever, left Thomas little time for wandering abroad. He looked at the clock. Now he had an hour and a quarter to himself before the nine o'clock tea-tray went to the drawing-room.

He had crossed two fields before he realised that the footsteps beyond the hedge were padding step for step with his own. He dropped to his knees and peeped. A pair of eyes peeped back at him through the hedge.

'What are you doing there?' he demanded.

'Following you.'

'You are not supposed to do that.'

'Stop preaching and give me a hand through this.'

He pulled her through. She loped beside him panting hard.

'Phew! You set me a devil of a pace.'

'I was not aware that I was pacing anyone; and you should not use the word Devil in your conversation. It is most inelegant.'

'You don't have to correct my speech.'

'No, but I have to take the blame when you speak inelegantly. Then we hear that you are mixing too much with the servants. Meaning, of course, me.' He suddenly remembered to drop her hand.

'You needn't have dropped my hand as if it were something nasty. You *are* rough.'

He stopped and faced her. 'Since I *am* so rough why do you follow me?'

'Because,' she said sweetly, 'you might get lost. If I hadn't followed you last year what would have happened to you?'

His cheeks reddened at his churlishness. In a low voice he answered, 'I should have died.' And now he knew what had

288

really prompted the trail of thought that had led him out here this evening; a wild flower whose name meant 'faithfulness'. He wanted to plant it in the flower-bed he had made for her; a tribute to her faithfulness that kept her searching when the others had given him up as a runaway; a symbol of his own undying faithfulness.

When he told her about the strange man with the intense blue eyes, her own eyes purpled with the dint of mystery.

'Young Thomas,' she breathed, 'and you were keeping this from me. Of course he is the thief.' She grabbed his hand. 'Come on, we'll stalk him.'

But the man needed no stalking. For suddenly there he was; motionless by a rock, like the wild things of nature that merge into the background of the landscape. When he stepped forward their sense of mystery was jolted. There was nothing furtive about him. As he watched them approaching hand in hand, he might have been yielding an audience.

'Is she your sister?'

Thomas dropped Sterrin's hand. 'She is my master's daughter.'

The man scrutinised her. 'God save you, Daughter.' And to Thomas, 'You have been a long time coming back.' With a regal gesture he dismissed Thomas's reply. 'Look down there. Don't speak; keep on looking.' Where he pointed a trickle of men kept moving into the gateway of a farmhouse. George Lucas's farmhouse.

'Is it a wake?' Thomas asked.

'No, and there was no wake a month back when they gathered there. A game of Twenty-five one of them told me. A leg of mutton he said the prize was. But it looked to me that every man carried home a prize beneath his cotha mor.' He put his hand on Sterrin's head. 'Your father's shepherd was missing a sheep that day.' Thomas whistled a breath of enlightenment.

'There was a sheep missing the day before yesterday.'

While Thomas watched the house. Sterrin sped back to Kilsheelin and gasped out the story to her father. Before he could recall her she was gone again. He overtook her, panting over the grass, her red hair flying out behind her like the tail of a hunted fox.

'Go back home. Keep out of this.'

She pleaded with him. '*Please*, Papa! I feel responsible. It was my fault that he came here at all.'

'Come on, then. I suppose you *are* a bit involved.' He hoisted her up.

George Lucas's face turned yellow when his landlord strode into the crowded kitchen. There was no sign of card playing, but a horse skin was displayed prominently.

'It's a raffle we're havin' for the skin, your Honour's Sir.' Lucas's smooth voice was shaking.

The police Night Patrol that Thomas had been sent for were searching the premises.

'Have you found anything?' demanded Sir Roderick.

With unfailing pedantry Constable Humphreys informed him that they had disinterred 'a veritable mutton magazine'.

'Trust old Constable Jawbreaker,' whispered Thomas, but Sterrin's giggle was strained and unnatural. Sir Roderick ordered them outside. As they went they glimpsed the cut-up carcass of a sheep under the stripped floor boards of the adjoining room. They heard words like 'ingrate' and 'thieves' lash out from Sir Roderick as he recognised his own tenants. 'I stripped my lands of flocks to feed you. I stinted my own children——'

An old man with tears running down his face seized Roderick's hand. 'The hand that fed us——' Roderick snatched away the hand. But a story emerged through the old man's babblings. Lucas had led them to believe that Sir Roderick's daughter, because of her mother's delicacy, had lived in fosterage awhile with Lucas and his wife. The men had not questioned the story, 'though I've seen no fosterage since my youth'. No one had questioned it either when it was explained that an occasional gift of a sheep was still sent to Lucas in the old manner. 'Haven't I seen a sheep sent to Black Pat's, Lord rest him?' The meat was sold under cover of a raffle lest his Honour be offended and curtail his benevolence.

Roderick recoiled from the flicker of sheer hate in the eyes of Lucas as he walked past him between two policemen. He thought of how he had been duped into giving him employment the day he came with his tragic story of the Big Wind and of his eviction with nineteen other men because one of Major Darby's sheep had been stolen! Roderick's instincts had been truer than his judgment when he had likened Lucas to the 'darraghadheal', the beetle that had been an accomplice to the betrayal at Gethsemane.

Outside, the hermit brushed aside Roderick's thanks. ''Tis little to do for your father's son, O'Carroll.' Thomas started at the man's familiarity. Roderick assessed the sturdy figure in the green cut-away body coat, knee-breeches, black worsted stockings and old-fashioned square-toed shoes with buckles. The man returned the scrutiny.

'I am the O'Mara of Bannandrum Castle.' He pointed to an ivy gable wall that loomed against the skyline. 'But,' blurted Sterrin, 'you cannot live in a wall?'

'There was a Mansion there once, Daughter, and the silk of the kine grazed on those pastures——' He shook his fist in the direction of Darby's estate. 'Son's son of a black thief!' he shouted.

Sir Roderick was too distracted to cope with the lineage of the curious stranger. There was something about Bannadrum Castle being appropriated under the Penal Code while its owner served in Austria; something too about a son, or was it a grandson, who had grown up half-wild, clinging with imperishable optimism to the crumbling walls?

At his trial Lucas let loose a story of landlordism that shocked the case-hardened court-room. Eyes travelled to where Sir Roderick O'Carroll sat; haughty and aloof; waiting for them to silence the scurrilous wretch. But Lucas's defence was too good to miss—that cake! Lucas increased its circumference from nine feet to fifteen; its height to twelve feet. Three men staggering under its weight—one, a boy, almost falling to the ground. The prisoner had dashed to his assistance. ''Twas torture, your Lordship, the smell of beautiful food so near me.'

Roderick had the impression that the judge sent him a look through his fingers. The prisoner's black eyes missed nothing. Words poured from him in torrent they be suppressed. 'There had been mortal dread on him,' he said, 'since his neighbour, Sir Roderick's own foster-brother, Black Pat Ryan, and three of his children died of hunger; all four of them in one afternoon!'

Roderick braced against the buzz of horror.

Lucas was not deported. He was given one year's sentence in an Irish prison.

'How could anyone believe him?' cried Margaret. 'Believe such things of you!' Roderick sat at the dinner table, tight-lipped and grim; scarcely touching his food. His toil for those terrible years turned into a Famine Folly! A grass-grown road leading nowhere. His home mortgaged! His children futureless!

'People believe facts when they see them—and the Ryan hecatomb was a fact—inescapable.'

Only a few weeks later Sterrin raced across the lawns to where her parents were strolling arm in arm. Just as they had strolled on such a lovely evening as this, unconscious of the Blight that lurked unseen amid the rich growth of that radiant summer.

'Papa, I've just seen the "darraghadheal"—George Lucas.'

Her father frowned impatiently at her. 'Nonsense! The man is in prison.'

'He is not, Papa. I saw him up there.' Where she pointed they could see a small figure moving inside the hedge that separated the front lawn from the adjoining pastures.

'He was peeping in here through the hedge, Papa.'

Sterrin was right. Although the Queen had withheld her clemency from political prisoners, a number of ordinary prisoners had been released under her amnesty. The story of one prisoner in particular had touched her sentimentality. She felt that the long arm of coincidence had guided her clemency towards the wretch who, while starving himself, had assisted a starving servant to carry the great birthday cake that had been presented to herself by the Duke of Devonshire. She had requested that George Lucas be released forthwith.

Tim Lonergan hailed Thomas one morning to tell him that South Tipperary was ready to take the field in rebellion; Thomas Francis Meagher and Smith O'Brien had sent a fierce arousal across Slievenamon to a vast mustering. Tonight Meagher of the Sword would hold a meeting at the crossroads.

Thomas listened at the crossroads enthralled. The knightly grace of the speaker, the glowing words sent pictures flashing across his mind; peasants pouring through the gap of danger; camp fires reddening the darkness. '... shall we snatch victory from death?' cried the rousing voice '... shall the spirit that has survived the penalties, the savageries of centuries, the sword of famine, shall this spirit sink at last? ... then up with the barricades ... should we succeed, the joy, the glory. Should we fail ...'

They failed. Hunger and disease had burrowed too deeply

into the soul of patriotism. The great columns of marching men proved to be a handful of youths. The great revolution was over before Thomas had word of its starting. Meagher and Smith O'Brien and the other leaders were 'on their keeping'; hunted outlaws, stealing through the woods by day, hiding in mountain cabins by night.

Late one night Thomas opened his door at a sound. The Sir, of all people, was moving stealthily down the passage towards the bard's room; behind him moved a slim figure, half military, half civilian, cross-belt, coloured sash, sword hilt over plain dark clothes. The Sir turned sharply at the sound of the opening door and came back. 'What are you doing up so late?' he demanded; without waiting for a reply he went on: 'Forget whatever you may have seen! You understand?' He gave Thomas a penetrating look. Thomas returned it squarely. 'Yes, your Honour.'

Next morning the bard's tray was handed to Thomas by Hegarty instead of by the cook. In addition to the bard's plate of bacon, soft bread and a jug of ale there was a covered silver dish, a pot of coffee and a rack of toast. When Thomas started to lift the cover from the breakfast dish the old man snapped his head off. 'Leave it be and be off about your business,' he said. Then when Thomas stooped over the hearth flags to add more turf the old man became quite agitated. 'Get away from there! Get away!' he kept repeating. When Thomas was half through the doorway he added: 'And don't you be gallivanting near the rath of Lissnastreenagh, Thomas Og. The spells of the Speir-bhean are direful to youths that are comely.' Thomas went off, hoping that his idol would show up for the next meal. But there was no extra food on the next tray. Long before it was due the news of Meagher's arrest had arrived.

Sir Roderick attended the trial in Clonmel and Thomas risked bribing a lad to hold the horse while he ventured into the back of the court. The last time he had stood in a courthouse had been at the trial of the 'darraghadheal'. This time there was no whining protest. The figure that he had seen moving towards the bard's room was standing in the dock, upright, defiant, listening to the death sentence.

Then, miraculously, within hours of the scaffold, came Sir Charles Napier's letter that disclosed how the Prime Minister and some of his colleagues had once, many years ago, plotted treason against the Government. The death sentence was transmuted to transportation for life.

When Thomas told the bard the old man's eyes found their tears. 'Once more,' he quoted, 'shall oft-widowed Erin mourn the loss of her brave young men,' and he made no protest when Thomas busied himself at the hearth slabs. Speir-bhean inagh! thought Thomas. From somewhere under these slabs the exiled patriot had made his way to Lissnastreenagh; not into the direful spells of the Fairy Queen but into those of Her Majesty's police.

CHAPTER 32

Christmas that year was something like the ones that Sterrin vaguely remembered before The Hunger. Dominic had no recollection of such wonderful preparations as were going on in the kitchen. The poultry stock had been built up; turkeys and geese hung over the fires in a molten glow of savoury gold. He was allowed to turn the spits. He took a hand at stirring the vast pudding for the staff dance; joined in threading twine through the holly leaves to make chains for the big barn for the dance. Spicy smells steamed out from the wall ovens where the porter cakes baked.

It was deliciously exciting. And the Sir's Road! Never had he seen such traffic there. Cars spread with mattresses for the women and children were passing that way to town all Christmas Eve.

The church was packed for Confession. Every household had lost someone to be remembered at the Altar next morning. Father Hickey let the people out of the box without delay but the curate in place of the one who had died of the famine fever was a terror. He kept people ages inside. To make matters worse, Sir Roderick O'Carroll took out his timepiece with great deliberateness as each penitent entered the box and took it out again as he or she emerged. His tactics gradually worked the desired effect upon the people in the long row ahead of him. One by one rather than be 'timed before all the world' they surrendered their places and fell back to the very end of Father Hickey's penitents.

There was a dreadful storm on Christmas Day and for the twelve days of festive reunion the rain blew in great sheets. The usual visiting was restricted to the shortest journeys. Sir Roderick, to banish ghosts and memories, fixed Epiphany Night for the staff dance. It had become, too, generally established as the anniversary of the Big Wind. Margaret dreaded the date. The servants dreaded it because the roll of those who had 'seen' Miss

Mansfield's ghost on that night was increasing annually. Sterrin could not forget that her birth and the Big Wind had plunged her mamma in some prolonged and fearful ordeal from which she had never fully recovered.

It was wonderful to sit in the brightly-lit barn and watch the dancing. Big John led Mamma out in the quadrilles. It looked funny to see him dancing and swinging. He was always so stiff and dignified. Papa was in great form. He took Sterrin out for the Cashel Sets and the servants were delighted with the spectacle of the Sir standing in a circle 'clapping home' his partner like the rest of the men.

Thomas, standing in a shadowy corner, wondered if he would dare ask Miss Sterrin to dance. But the sight of her, elegant and unexpectedly tall in her party gown of white voile, filled him with a shyness that he had never felt towards her before. Her papa danced her round and round then swung her off the floor in one final whirl of frills, white lace stockings, ringlets and breathless laughter.

Thomas had splashed the mad extravagance of seven and twopence upon a pair of dancing pumps. Their pointed tips drew glances that ranged upwards to the curled tips of his black hair.

But the knife boy's eyes watched the young daughter of the castle. Suddenly, the floor space between him and that young radiance that was, remotely and strangely, Miss Sterrin, had lengthened out before his eyes until it seemed insuperable. He turned and had reached the entrance when a hand crashed down on his shoulders—and dreams. 'Go and lead out one of them colleens,' ordered the voice of Mike O'Driscoll who was Master of Ceremonies.

He walked Thomas up to a genteel-looking girl. Thomas bowed. 'Permit me the honour of leading you out.'

She glanced him up and down. A servant. But an extremely personable male. She silently extended her finger tips.

You fancy yourself, Miss, he thought. She was the daughter of Lord Templetown's English steward. At the Change Partners they were facing Sir Roderick and Miss Sterrin. 'Young Thomas,' cried Sterrin joyfully. 'Where have you been? I think I am going to fall. My head is dizzy.'

He placed a hand on her waist. 'We'll reverse. That will steady it.' The steward's daughter gazed after them and forgot to dance up to her next partner. He was gazing after them also. Roderick's brain was whirling with wine and dancing. He could not call to mind the youth who was dancing so pleasingly with his daughter. Dancing with that ballet-like quality that is the body's dramatic medium! He must ask Hegarty about him. Hegarty misread his signal and hurried with a flagon on a tray that was slanting at an angle of forty-five degrees. 'Dancing is droothy work, your Honour's Sir.'

'So I see,' said his Honour's Sir, whose vision was on a similar slant. He forgot about his daughter's partner and remembered the steward's daughter. He poured her a negus then whirled her the length of the barn until the next Change Partners restored Margaret to him. 'Get yourself another partner, Big John,' he called gaily.

Next day the shops opened and 'newses' of the past twelve days circulated. The main news item spread horror. On Christmas Day a colony of people had been turned out on to the hillside. Almost a hundred people driven from their cabins in the pitiless rain.

Roderick had withdrawn from public matters since the release of George Lucas. He regarded his release as a public indictment of himself; an official imputation of Landlordism. But the savageries of Christmas Day stirred him to action again. He addressed meetings; wrote to the newspapers; travelled to Dublin with the members of a protest deputation. The Government was assailed on all sides.

And at last it showed mercy. In future, it decided, no eviction was to take place on Christmas Day or on Good Friday. Henceforth, those under notice to quit could shelter quite safely under the shadow of Golgotha; not until the Resurrection eve need they face their own Golgotha; And, Alleluia! Neither would they be shelterless on Christ's Birthday. While angels sang the Birth Hymn they would be free to place the rush lights in the window for the Holy Wanderers. Not until the morrow would they become wanderers themselves.

Father Hickey prayed from the altar for the Christmas outcasts. He referred also to the crop of ghost stories that were holding people in the grip of unholy fear. 'Rest assured,' he told them dryly, 'that those taken to God by the Famine have neither need nor wish to return to this vale of tears.'

Young Thomas gave a cough and sent a sidelong glance

through his fingers at Attracta Scally. She had sworn to him that she had 'seen' the ghost of Felix Downey carrying the 'dead body' of his brother past the front gates of the castle. But the church had hushed to a breathless stillness. Father Hickey had started to call out the Christmas dues. Not a cough nor sound while the congregation strained with godly fervour to catch the amount contributed by every member.

'Lord Cullen of Crannagh Abbey, four pounds; Sir Roderick O'Carroll of Kilsheelin Castle, four pounds; Mrs. Lonergan of Golden Meadows, one pound ten; Mr. Ulick Prendergast, one pound; John Ryan Shake-hands, five shillings; always a decent man and so was his father before him. John Ryan Rua, seven and six and he ploughed my garden—a decent man with ten children to rear.' This list ran on without comment, then an obvious pause. The congregation tensed. There was something good coming. 'Owen Heffernan'—the priest peered out over his spectacles—'five shillings—and if he has one acre by now, he has a hundred and he with neither chick nor child!' Mr. George Lubey was growing impatient to hear his name called from his new mansion. Killincarrig Lodge, former home of the De Laceys had always been called out after Kilsheelin Castle. 'George Lubey——' He sat straight in his pew. 'George Lubey,' repeated the priest, 'of Main Street, two pounds ten.'

The pulpit, Father Hickey indicated, was not for proclaiming the social advancement of parishioners.

Outside in his carriage, Lord Templetown looked again at his watch. He had thought to catch Sir Roderick emerging from Mass long since. He had not reckoned with the Christmas dues and every name in the three parishes called out with 'due' comment.

Sir Roderick yawned and took out his watch; but the list was ending, 'James Keating of Poolgower, four pounds.' The priest descended the steps. Roderick gasped. Four pounds! Before the Big Wind it was a half-crown and an ass load of turf!

The Scout rose for the Gospel. James Keating! The same offering as the Sir of Kilsheelin! The wheel was surely coming round to meet the time when The Keating like The O'Carroll had sent his priest four beeves and a hogshead of wine!

Mass resumed its ritual. 'Dominus Vobiscum' prayed the priest. 'Et cum spiritu tuo' responded the server. Sir Roderick, deep in his missal, turned a page, '... Do Thou we beseech

298

Thee Oh Lord, sanctify this gift offered to Thee——' Four pounds! By the piper of Moses! The Bachach!

Lord Templetown begged permission to enter Sir Roderick's carriage to discuss something important. He wanted to suggest that Sir Roderick stand for the parliamentary vacancy in the north riding. 'No,' he raised a hand against the exploding protests. 'You are an exemplary landlord. You signalised yourself in the famine, while the gentleman who will be your opponent——'

'The gentleman who *will* be my opponent. You seem, my Lord, to take the matter as a *fait accompli*. I hate politics. I am no politician.'

'No politician, true. I should say a potential statesman. Ireland has a plethora of politicians. Our best men do not go into public life. We are represented by mediocrities.'

'What about O'Connell? Davis too. They were scarcely in that category.'

'They were not in any category. They moved in the isolation of their own greatness. Not every century casts up an O'Connell. As for Davis, a genius, a magic personality. He has ploughed the nation's soil. Men like you can guard the seedlings.'

'Metaphors, my Lord, did not avail the seedlings we guarded in '45; and '46; that we cherished in '47?'

Sterrin listened, thrilled. Would Papa go to the British House of Parliament? Would the bard accompany him? The assembly would never give his music the verdict. His knuckles were as big as crab-apples. If only he could be dressed in a suit of rushes!

Roderick was perturbed. Margaret too. He loved his country life. 'We are a quiet family,' he said. 'Worldliness does not become us.'

Lord Templetown looked at the two young faces whose well-bred good looks were the complement of the splendid couple seated opposite him.

'Forgive me if I disagree. You were not designed to browse in dignified rusticity. I envisage you returning from Saint Stephen's to some London Salon of Repeal presided over by Lady O'Carroll.'

There had been a time a few years back when Margaret would have been dazzled by the prospect. But now, out of calamity and misunderstanding, she had found contentment. She asked for nothing but the continued serenity of their present mode of life. Her fingers twined around her husband's. The worldly old gentleman looked at them reflectively. It seemed to him that they followed close to the original plan for living that had been blue-printed for Eden.

'The ground is prepared,' he said. 'Your speeches against the savageries of last Christmas have made a deep impression. I leave the rest to you, Lady O'Carroll.' He took the hand that Lady O'Carroll extended. 'I trust that I have not broken your Sabbath calm.'

During the week when others came for his decision, Roderick's refusal was positive. Politics were dirty, he told Margaret. The estate needed him and he needed it; needed the soil he loved and its workers how, through their recent need of him, he had come to love with a protective tenderness. There was a thousand and one things to be done. Cottages that should be rethatched in autumn against the coming winter had not been thatched in years. Potatoes for next spring's seeding were under his constant surveillance. And this winter he was tasting again the joy of riding out to hounds; riding home at night with a moon like a steel mirror in the sky; coping with his accounts before the blazing turf fire in the library with the red setters stretched at his feet. Abandon all that for the grey winter of London town! Some Salon of Repeal, forsooth!

Then came news of four deaths among the victims of the Christmas Day evictions. A mother and three of her seven children had died in the hospital.

Margaret watched him as he stood gazing out of the window; gazing in the direction of that little boreen; seeing three dead children; two raven-haired; one beautifully fair, as their mother was beautifully fair; a wistful imagery to inspire a man's purpose.

Roderick turned and the purpose was there. In his face; in his voice. 'Margaret, in God's name I'll stand.' He came over to her. 'You don't approve?'

She kept her face over her embroidery. It was the end of something. It was the return of Roderick of the famine period; at the public's beck and call, harassed, irritable. No, the famine had not caused his irritation. *She* had done that, her pettiness! She looked up at last. 'You must do whatever you think is right.'

'This ebbing away of human life is too persistent,' he said. 'A

300

government's first duty is to preserve life.' The phrase had become almost his creed. 'This will give me the opportunity to help to enforce that duty.'

But Margaret knew that this would give him an opportunity to atone before a shrine in his memory.

Repeal buttons flashed again. Margaret listened to floods of oratory. Torchlight processions wound through the darkness to the beat of music. Mrs. Enright started to organise 'Repeal quilting parties'. No easy task, since all available blankets had gone to the famine cause. One day the bard startled Margaret and Roderick by coming to the drawing-room and asking for a new cloak.

'Cloak!' Margaret saw to it that the bard went well shod; well-provided for in linen and woollens, but the great *tour-de-force* of his plaid cloak flowing behind him in warm weather, wrapped about him in cold, was as inextricably part of himself as his white beard. 'Aye,' he mistook their surprise. 'It is not torn yet. 'Twas only got in eighteen five, the last roll of cloth before Hennessey's mills closed. After——'

Roderick stemmed a tide of history. 'You ought to have mentioned this long ago. That stuff must be thinned out after forty-four years.'

'It is thick and warm enough,' said the bard. 'But it is not grand enough for Westminster.'

Roderick cocked an eyebrow at Margaret. The poor old boy was actually envisaging himself preceding his master into the House of Commons in the bygone strut of bardic glory!

'I shouldn't take Westminster for granted, Bard. But you shall have your cloak.'

Margaret decided that she also must have a new cloak, and Sterrin and Dominic. Lord Templetown had placed his London house at their disposal. They couldn't, she said, go to London in their famine rags.

Mrs. Delaney was another who regarded Roderick's election as a *fait accompli*. She had written a letter to the government protesting against her estate being placed on the Encumbered Estates Market. She came hot-foot to Roderick with the government's reply in her hand. 'And it took them an unmannerly long time to answer it, Rody,' she said.

Ned Rua tiptoed in behind her with its envelope. 'I think,' said Roderick, glancing at it, 'that it may have been inadequately addressed.'

The envelope was inscribed—'The Government, England.' It started off 'Dear Government', and pointed out graphically and ungrammatically that the writer had received no rents for two years while she fed and nursed her tenants and a few hundred more of your subjects. She also reminded 'them' of the four hundred beeves her family had sent to London when people there were starving after the fire.

Roderick held his finger over his lips while he read the government's polite regret that it had no knowledge of the fire in question or of the generous gift of beeves alluded to therein. 'They've short memories,' she snorted, as though the Great Fire of London had been a few years ago. 'I came over to tell you what I want you to say to them when you go over, Rody. There is no use in writing letters, I never believed in——'

'Your Honour's Sir,' interrupted Ned Rua. ''Twas the way Miss Kate signed the letter. I warned her. Sure she hasn't written one since she was twelve and she'll be forty-six next——'

'Never mind my age, Ned—God save you, Margaret,' she said. 'I signed it "Yours affectionately", the same as my cousin Lady Judith O'Moore does when she writes to me at Christmas, and she is a Bluestocking who writes for the journals.'

But Ned Rua pointed out that it might have been better to use the phrase that Mr. Wilson, the harness-maker uses when he writes for the money.

'You forget yourself, Ned Rua,' said his mistress with dignity. 'As though I should sign a letter in the fashion of a tradesman demanding money!'

The bard appeared from nowhere and asked her Ladyship if she had got his cloak. From under his old one he produced—all unexpectedly—a small harp. To honour the daughter of The O'Moore, he said, and with his eye to a festive dinner, strummed them unbidden to the dining-room. High time, he muttered very audibly into his beard, that The O'Carroll went to the parliament. Too long this castle had been without feasting and harping!

CHAPTER 33

Roderick rode out on Thuckeen to lead his waiting tenants to the hustings. From the doorway Margaret and the children waved him God-speed. From the turret Ireland's ancient flag, not the green one, the one of Saint Patrick's blue waved proudly.

There was a fine mustering of horsemen at the crossroads. Despite Roderick's repeated insistence that they were free to exercise the franchise without fear or favour of landlordism, they had expressed the wish to ride behind him in array. That was how their fathers, and some of themselves, had ridden behind *his* father!

Roderick's heart lifted as he rode towards them. It was an honour to own the allegiance of such men. Few of them were under six feet in height and their horses were worthy of their riders.

Head and shoulders over the others was Michael Joseph Michael Ryan, on a light chestnut with cream-coloured mane and tail. Beside him was his ancient enemy, Martin Hennessey, the leader of the Hennessey clan that had fought the Ryans in faction fights at every fair day and election. Never before had the Ryans and Hennesseys been known to vote for the same candidate.

The horsemen removed their high hats and greeted Roderick in Gaelic. He answered them in kind and thanked them for their fealty. There was a laugh when he said, 'Is it a thing that I see, a Ryan and a Hennessey riding shoulder to shoulder to vote for the same man?'

'You may thank Father Matthew for that, your Honour,' said Martin. 'Only for him we'd still be splittin' each others skulls; if the Ryans were voting for you, why then, we'd have to vote against you. Indeed, the whole Hennessey clan is mindful of what you did for Mark and his wife and child. 'Twas only yesterday that his brother had word from him from Canada. He

303

said that only for the way you provided for them on the ship they would never have survived the voyage.' His horse side-stepped in the crush of horsemen.

'Canada?' Sir Roderick called after him. But Hennessey's mount was pivoting around on its hind legs, and Ulick Prendergast had reined in beside Sir Roderick.

Ulick owed no vassalage to Kilsheelin, but he had the 'gra' for the O'Carrolls. The old man's face had the haunted look that still lingered on the faces of so many of those who had endured the famine. Ulick might be stingy enough to shave gooseberries for their hair, but he had shown no lack of heart to the hungry.

When he had greeted the old man, Roderick had perforce to greet his son-in-law, John Keating. He expressed his surprise at seeing him here. And Keating answered, 'My vote will always be for you, Sir Roderick.'

Roderick thanked him and rode out in front. The horsemen fell in behind and the road shook with the thunder of hooves.

At the entrance to the town the Repeal band was waiting to play them in.

As they clattered up Main Street, the waiting crowd shouted the old O'Carroll cry, 'The Hawk abu!' The hawk to victory, and then, 'Long live O'Carroll! Long live Repeal!'

'He looks like a Roman centurion at the head of a hundred horsemen,' said Constable Humphreys.

'Whisht!' said the Scout. 'He looks what he is, an Irish chieftain at the head of *two* hundred horsemen.'

Master Hennessey greeted his clansmen. ''Tis the finest cavalcade I have seen riding down this street, and I've seen the pride of Wellington's army ride past.'

A company of dragoons rode by. When their officer had ridden out of sight the soldiers towards the end of the line raised their sabres to the civilian horsemen. 'And here comes the arch-evictor!' cried the Master. Major Darby rode up with a group of horsemen, followed by a brake-load of supporters.

A little dark man with a face smooth, yet shrivelled, like an apple that had been pulled and stored too soon, dismounted from the brake. Wherever he moved, men turned their backs on him. George Lucas was left in the isolation of his treachery.

A sudden blaze of music sounded from the direction of the Mall, and Lord Templetown, preceded by a piper, rode into view at the head of a file of horsemen. Tomorrow would be the coming-of-age of his son. His Lordship had doubled his extravagant arrangements to include the victory celebrations.

Roderick was surounded with well-wishers. They made a path for Lord Cullen, who came tottering up on his Regency cane and brandishing *The Times*. 'Here's your speech for today,' he shouted as he came through. 'Read *that* to the whig supporters!'

He held his snuff box in the hollow of his palm, and unscrewed the top with a practised twist of his little finger. 'There,' he said, indicating the column with the joined finger and thumb that held the pinch of snuff.

Roderick blew the snuff from the paragraph, sneezed and read—'. . . in one year, seventy thousand holdings and their occupiers have been rooted out of the land. This year two hundred and fifty thousand people have emigrated to America. The Irish are going! and going with a vengeance! Now at last after these six hundred years, England has Ireland at her mercy and can deal with her as she pleases.'

Lord Cullen flicked open his fingers and sent a shower of snuff in the direction of Darby's supporters. 'At *their* mercy, egad!'

Roderick did not read out *The Times*'s gloatings but the Scout straightaway procured a copy and read it at the top of his voice to the men who followed Darby. He halted every voter who approached the courthouse and forced him to listen. Between the first and last step of the building he made a number of converts.

The results, as Lord Templetown had hoped, coincided well with the coming-of-age celebrations. When the High Sheriff announced, 'I proclaim Sir Roderick O'Carroll to be duly elected,' the rest of his statement was drowned in cheering. The people went wild with joy.

Tar barrels blazed on the hill behind the castle. The young Scallys were on the road, with ears to the ground for the sound of the carriage. At the first rumble they were up the avenue in a streak. When Roderick, with Margaret and the children, turned in the gates, he saw his people waiting for him.

The flames from the tar barrels cast flickering shadows on the turrets. Lights blazed from every window. Out in front was the bard. And he played this new-fangled air of Mr. Davis's that young Thomas had dinned into all of them. 'It has the sound of marching men,' muttered the old man as he drew forth a rousing chord. The voice of young Thomas soared above the rest when it came to:

> *'For freedom comes from God's right hand,*
> *And needs a godly train;*
> *And righteous men must make our land,*
> *A nation once again.'*

Margaret felt a rush of tears to her eyes. Sterrin glowed with pride to the words young Thomas sang as though he had written them himself for her papa. She was free at last to tell her parents about the secret rehearsals that had taken place in the bard's big room while Papa was electioneering.

Roderick was deeply moved. He would like to have spent this evening here amidst his own people; so generous; so true-hearted; their helplessness that had made them lean on him in the recent, terrible past had endeared them to him a hundred-fold.

For politics he did not give a tinker's curse; but by heaven, he'd use them to see that his people would never again go hungry! He looked at the tall, dark boy who was carrying the great harp indoors and he felt within himself those stirrings of affinity that were not new to him. He must see about that boy. Meantime, politics had made their first demand upon his private life. He must change and return to Templetown House as a public figure.

Sterrin hastened to tell young Thomas of the complimentary things her papa had said about his singing and the way he had arranged the welcome, but she stopped dead at the door of the silver pantry. 'What is the matter with you, young Thomas?'

He was sitting staring at a letter as though he had been stunned by its contents.

He had rushed joyfully to read the letter that Hegarty had just sorted from the post bag. At last! A letter from Kitty and Mark!

His joy was shortlived. No horror that he had witnessed could equal what he had just read in Kitty's letter. Their ship had been fourteen weeks at sea. Because of the fever it had been forbidden to land at New York. When it reached Canada it was one of eighty fever ships put in quarantine at Grosse Island.

Mark had been flung bodily on to the beach with the dead. 'For hours I crawled on all fours through mud and slime and hundreds of prostrate bodies 'til I found him alive, thank God.'

She had found Mrs. Black Pat as well, her children screaming like maniacs around their dead Mammy. The following Sunday, Kitty wrote, the priest who had carried Mrs. Black Pat ashore had led her three children from the sacristy to the altar.

'Here is your sermon for today,' he had said to the amazed congregation. 'Look at them; starved out of their country by bad laws, their father dead in Ireland, their little mother back there in the nameless grave pit of Grosse Island. . . .'

Sterrin went slowly upstairs to tell the news to her papa. He had asked her more than once if young Thomas had heard from his friends.

She found her mamma standing before her mirror dressing for the coming-of-age party at Lord Templetown's. She looked radiant in white with Roderick's diamond necklace, sparkling against her skin. 'Mamma,' breathed Sterrin, 'I've never, never seen you look so beautiful!' Then she told her mother about the letter from America.

Margaret's pleased smile froze. Her ivory skin paled to a frightening white. She reached for the back of a chair to steady herself. Sterrin hadn't thought the news would have such an effect upon her mamma. She looked as though she might faint.

'But, Mamma,' she said, 'the children have got lovely homes. The letter says that the rich people rushed to the altar to take them. The priest had to remind them that they were in the house of God.'

From his dressing-room Roderick called out. Margaret rallied. She put her fingers to her lips. 'Ster-een,' she whispered urgently, 'not a word of this to Papa! We mustn't spoil tonight for him. Tomorrow I shall tell him myself.'

Roderick came in. Like his daughter he halted in admiration of Margaret's beauty. Like Sterrin he declared that never had he seen Margaret look so beautiful.

Lord Templetown, watching the pair enter his drawing-room, felt justified in his statement that Sunday morning that they were designed to perform with *éclat* before the world. At the dinner he placed them on either side of him. He enjoyed the dazzling image of Lady O'Carroll reflected in the empanelled mirrors that duplicated the lights from the candelabra of jasper

307

and filigree and from the great Renaissance candelabrum in the centre of the splendid room.

After the dinner the guests moved out to where the tenants were celebrating. The heir cut the seven-hundred-pound plum pudding with his sword and cut the traditional speech to a fraction.

When the cheering had subsided Lord Templetown led forward the new representative and his beautiful wife. They stood together while the crowd gave them a Three-times-Three.

Roderick said it was too soon to talk of politics while the nation was but rising from her knees after its supplication for bread.

'*The Times*,' he said, 'has told us that at last we are conquered; that at last we are at their mercy. It is true that the famine has succeeded where the oppression of centuries had failed; the Ironsides of Cromwell; the savagery of the Penal Code, availed less than the force of the Great Starvation.

'The lesson of the famine has taught us that Repeal is not a question of political power or party. It is a question of physical existence. The only soup kitchen that will supply adequate nourishment is a Domestic Parliament.'

When he and Margaret at last got through the cheering throng to their carriage they found Lord and Lady Cullen leaning on their canes and on each other. Their grand-nephew Patrick, completely bottled, was standing on a bench reciting to a ring of delighted tenants. On one side he was supported by the heir and on the other by his Trinity classmate, Prince George of Cambridge.

'It sounds extremely bad form,' said Lord Cullen, 'and quite seditious, but pray continue.' Patrick carried on his recitation of a popular squib purporting to be about a conversation between Louis Philippe, hiding in Buckingham Palace after his escape from the Barricades, and Queen Victoria.

Patrick continued—

> '*My dear Vic, sez he,*
> *I'm mighty sick, sez he,*
> *For I've cut me stick, sez he,*
> *Tarnation quick, sez he.*
> *From te divil's breeze, sez he,*
> *At the Tooleyrees, sez he,*

For the Blackguards made, sez he,
A barricade, sez he,
And I was afraid, sez he,
And greatly in dread, sez he,
That I'd lose me head, sez he,
And if I lost that, sez he,
I'd have no place for me hat, sez he.
Stop a while, sez she,
Take off your tile, sez she,
You've come a peg down, sez she,
By the loss of your crown, sez she,
Mille pardon, sez he,
For keepin' it on, sez he,
But my head isn't right, sez he,
Since I took flight, sez he.'

Patrick stopped and rubbed his head. 'My own head is a bit light, sez he....'

'Go on, Patrick,' roared the Prince. 'Finish it!'

'Go on, sir,' roared the tenants. The three young gentlemen supported one another while they racked their brains for the next stanza. Roderick and Margaret entered their carriage laughing. As it moved off they could hear Prince George solemnly intoning—

'Indeed my ould buck, sez she,
You look mighty shook, sez she——'

Roderick sighed comfortably. 'It's been a long day. I own that I'm tired.'

'Oh, Roderick,' she breathed, 'I felt so proud of you!' He raised her fingers to his lips. 'I felt proud of you, too.' They drove in silence for a stretch. Suddenly he turned to her. 'Do you know, I heard today from one of the Hennessey faction that Mark Hennessey and his wife arrived safely in America— Canada he said—but that is probably his mistake. I wonder what can have happened to little—little Mrs. Ryan.'

She half turned to tell him, then stopped. No, tomorrow! She would hold on to this moment. There might never be such another. Her breath caught on her vision of a dainty figure in a chic green shawl, a golden head bent over her knitting, then suddenly looking up out of those long beautiful eyes. Oh, little ghost, why had you come haunting tonight!

He misinterpreted her sharp intake of breath! The tensing of her hand in his.

'Margaret.' He turned to catch her expression in the shadowy light. 'Surely you don't still resent her? She will never trouble either of us again.' She will never cease to trouble us, thought Margaret!

She forced herself to say in a low voice, 'Of course, I don't resent her.' Then in a lighter tone she said, 'What I do resent is this sudden onslaught of public life. It may part us. I couldn't get near you tonight. You will go to London——'

'But you will be in London with me, sooner too than I expected. You must have all your falderals ready by the middle of next week.'

'So soon! And I postponed all preparations, just—just in case.'

'Is that all the faith you had in me?'

'No darling, I had no lack of faith in you. It was just those other times when we made plans. Belgium—then the Blight fell. This time I resolved not to make a single preparation until the election was successfully over.'

'You have had grim reason to be cautious. But all that is behind now. So make no more delay.' He placed his arm about her. 'As for public life parting us! Nothing could do that, my darling.'

A light shot up. They were both startled. But it was only a spurt from a smouldering bonfire. Faintly in the breeze sounded a 'Long Life to O'Carroll!' He replaced his arm across her shoulders and they turned in at the gates in pleasant silence.

Sterrin was leaning from a window watching the last flickering of the bonfire behind the castle. There was still a few revellers round the fire. She felt too excited to go to bed and yield up this wonderful day. Such a proud day. Papa had looked like a prince going to battle at the head of those horsemen. And both he and Mamma had looked *stupendous* tonight.

From the carriage road came the sound of horse-beats. Mamma and Papa returning. She yawned sleepily. Better not let them find her up at this hour. As she crossed the landing she could see the gig lights of the carriage flashing through the gates. Then she heard a shot. She peered through the panes.

310

The carriage had stopped. There was another shot; and a scream! Sterrin rushed down the stairs.

Outside, it was Margaret's shoulders that were braced now to give support. She crouched rigidly by the driveway where Roderick had fallen as he made to leave the carriage. His full weight lay in her arms. His eyes stared up at the face of the woman he had loved so dearly.

As Sterrin dropped to her knees beside them, he was murmuring, 'I was wrong. I thought—nothing—could part us.'

'Oh, Papa!' sobbed Sterrin. A branch cracked and she turned to see a man's figure crashing through to the pasture beyond. ' "The darraghadheal"!' she screamed. She made to rise. Roderick lifted his fingers and let them fall.

'Don't go, my stormling.' In the distance the horses pounded frantically as Big John lashed them to summon priest and doctor.

Margaret cradled Roderick's head in her arms; all her faculties alert. There was a prayer to be said at a time like this. She called it into his ears, then moved her lips to his. They had a coldness that had never been there before. The mad wild shrieks went tearing through her brain but she checked them at her lips. He still had need of her. He strained with his head and she lifted him up while he looked at the castle. A tongue of flame from the bonfire outlined the broken turret. Above it the flag of privilege hoisted for a great occasion lapped gently in the wind. From somewhere beyond, the party cries echoed thinly, 'Long Live Repeal! Long Live O'Carroll!'

He lowered his head on to her breast and as she held him close, her fingers crept to his lips. She could feel the little breaths that beat against them; until they came no more.

Men came, as in a stride, from the polls to the funeral of the one they had voted to victory. Their faces were still stunned from the impact of the tidings. Those whom he had led to the town a few mornings ago now stepped out of line and took it in turns to bear him upon their shoulders. Nearing the brink Big John surrendered the reins of the riderless Thuckeen. He claimed his right to lend a shoulder to the one he had revered.

The pain that the weight aroused in the maimed shoulder was no less agonising than the memory of the night ride that had given him the wound. Sweat drops mingled with the tears as he recalled how he had returned that morning after the Big Wind's storm and found new life and gladness waiting.

'Big John's shoulder must be made sound,' the young Sir had said later to the doctor. 'For we all lean heavily on these shoulders.'

Lord Templetown looked across at the tall, veiled figure who walked with the white-faced girl and the boy. The guilt, he thought, was not entirely with the little dark man with the distorted brain who had fired the shots.

Would there come a time when that stricken woman would point some of the blame towards the man who had entered their carriage that peaceful Sunday morning, who had urged his wishes and gone his way with the urbane hope that he had not disturbed their Sabbath calm? For the hundredth time he asked himself would this have happened if he had *not* intruded upon that Sabbath calm? Would that lovely idyll of their lives be still unfolding?

But Margaret, in the numbness of grief that had followed the initial shock, was no man's accuser. Her eyes followed what they were doing at the opened ground at her feet and through her mind there moved unbidden the lines of some poem.

> *'Dig the grave both wide and deep*
> *For I am sick and fain would sleep ...'*

Across the space something fluttered. Miss Hester dabbing her eyes with a black-bordered handkerchief! Or was it Miss Sarah? The poor old ladies they were so old. And poor old Lady Cullen with Lord Cullen, they were both so old. So were the De Guider gentlemen; and she hadn't realised that Lord Templetown was so old. They were all old—except Roderick—— 'Dig the grave both deep and wide—and let us slumber side by side.'

Someone took the burden from the tortured shoulder of Big John ... 'Dig the grave and make it ready. Lay me on my true love's body.' My true love—Roder-eeck! But no one heard the cry. It had gone echoing down the lonely corridors of her mind.

A hand slipped under her arm and held it firmly. How was it she had never noticed that the features of this white small face beside her were exactly the same as his? The red hair. That was what had clouded the resemblance. But today it was drawn back beneath the black bonnet.

Young Thomas let down the harp at last. Her Ladyship had never liked the harp's sad music. He had hoped that Mr. Maurice O'Carroll, who had arranged everything, would not have sanctioned the bardic lament. But Mr. Maurice insisted. There were few families left who possessed the household bard. Let the Bard of Kilsheelin uphold its tradition.

The old man's fingers forgot their stiffness. The melody they drew from the harp was fraught with such an agony of wild despair that the lament might have been plucked from the strings of his own heart.

Sterrin looked about her in panic. There was no escaping that terrible keen. And now Mamma's arm was trembling. She must stand by her with the support that *he* had given. Oh, for the protection of his strong arms! For the sight of that haughty face when it softened into tenderness and playfulness.

Someone was looking at her. Across the grave she saw young Thomas. He gave her a little smile. Her heart steadied. There was always young Thomas!

PART TWO

CHAPTER 34

The clanging of a bell brought the silent garden to sudden life. Girls of all shapes and sizes in navy gowns and white crochet cuffs and collars came hurrying in response to its sound. In the shadow of a tree by the wall a girl chucked at the pair of legs she was supporting. Their owner ignored the chuck and continued to strain over the wall. Her head pivoted to right and left, watching each end of the road. She was holding on to the top of the wall with her hands while the girl below gripped her legs.

'Sterrin! We'll be murdered. The Confession bell has gone.' But Sterrin had spotted the wagon.

'At last!' she breathed.

A cautious 'Whoa' brought it clattering to a standstill beneath her. 'I was beginning to give up hope,' she said. 'What kept you, Young Thomas?'

'I've been haggling like a dealer to squeeze a few extra shillings so that I could prove to them at home that the price *is* better in this town than in Templetown.' He stood up to hand over the packets of butterscotch. The girl below gave another tug. Sterrin swept the butterscotch down to her. 'Are you sure you can trust her, Miss Sterrin?' She nodded, 'Winifred would die for me. Besides, she loves butterscotch.'

'And you love chocolate.' He pushed a small box towards her.

'Young Thomas!' she cried as surprised as if he had never brought them before. In her excitement she forgot to whisper. 'You know that you mustn't spend your money on me. It's not right.' He knew that it wasn't right to be here at all. If it were discovered in the castle why he was making excuses about higher prices for produce here in this town than in Templetown! It didn't bear thinking of. 'You must have been paid your wages?'

He nodded, 'We were all paid after the harvest.'

317

'Has Thuckeen foaled yet?'

'Thuckeen foaled yesterday,' he told her. 'But be sure you don't let it slip that you know when you are writing. A grand little mahogany bay filly, Miss Sterrin, but not in Thuckeen's class.'

'Oh well,' she said. 'It was only to be expected. The sire wasn't anything *near* Thuckeen's class. It wasn't even a thoroughbred.' She sighed. 'She would never have been allowed to breed outside her class if——' She stopped. Whenever she tried to speak her papa's name the word stuck somewhere in her throat and all the words that should follow got piled up like road traffic behind a balking horse. The bell cut through her confusion and the girl below pulled Sterrin by the legs out of her introspection. 'Jump for it. I'm going,' she hissed. 'Here's Sister Mary Aliquo-five-yards-of-calico.'

Winifred might die for Sterrin but she wasn't going to be caught for her. Sterrin's head and shoulders had gone down for the second time when Thomas realised that her ground support was gone. He flung both arms around her shoulders and held her. She dropped the chocolate box and gripped the back of his collar with her free hand, and that was the moment that Sister Mary Aliquo came through a clearing in the trees with the bell and saw them. She let the bell fall from her hand with one clanging yelp of its metal tongue.

Sister Mary Aliquo closed her eyes and murmured a prayer. When she opened them the vision was still there; the shocking vision of a girl hanging from the wall in the arms of a man! For one terrible moment the nun thought that the immodestly swinging girl was a postulant. She was dressed in black. Then she noticed the auburn hair tied with a black ribbon and she remembered that Sterrin O'Carroll was exempt from wearing school uniform until her two years' mourning was up.

The sound of the fallen bell made Sterrin glance over her shoulder; she saw the nun! The next moment the horse started to move. Sterrin was borne along the inside of the wall for a few yards. Young Thomas called out something about having to let her go. He was being dragged away.

Sterrin landed on all fours and groped about for the chocolate box. The nun regarded this as the crowning insubordination. Any other girl would have jumped straight to her feet, confused and guilty.

318

'What is the meaning of this?' Shock had melted into red-faced anger. Sister Mary Aliquo had frequently to remind herself that Sterrin's seemingly cool, unintimidated manner was due to the subduing effects of her tragic experience; that it wasn't just—superiority that seemed to make such an impression upon her companions—and her teachers.

Sterrin, with one ear tuned to the clatter of wheels and runaway hooves sounding out in the world—every place outside the convent wall was referred to as 'the world'—said simply : 'I lost my footing.'

She rose and waited for the onslaught. But Sister Mary Aliquo was beyond speech. Her soft underlip was wobbling like a motherless foal's. All she wanted was to get away from this unhallowed spot. Her mind groped for the words she would use to make her report to Reverend Mother. That sinful embrace! The spectacle of those—dangling—*extremities*! Sister Aliquo realised that as Mistress of Deportment she must voice some reproof. Conduct came under her particular sphere. But not this conduct! Discipline came to her aid. 'Report to Reverend Mother,' she said in a low, hoarse voice, 'but first go to Confession and see that you examine your conscience on the Sixth Commandment!' She turned and hurried inside.

Sterrin's black brows shot up, 'Is it broken, Sister?' She asked it as though it were something that she had knocked off the wall. 'But, Sister, you told us——' But Sister Aliquo had disappeared.

'So that's what *that* is!' Sterrin paused in the shoe-room to remove her outdoor shoes and reflected that Sister Mary Aliquo-five-yards-of-calico was not very consistent. She had told the girls to skip the Sixth, 'Thou shalt not commit adultery', when they were examining their consciences. It did not concern nice girls.

The Head Prefect came hurrying into the shoe-room. 'What on earth is keeping you?' And then with a sniff, 'Do you think that *you* are above the rules? I happen to be aware of your conduct this afternoon.'

Sterrin put on a black velvet houseshoe and tied the ribbon with a painstaking bow.

'I suppose,' the Head Prefect went on, 'that you are going to tell me he was your brother.'

Sterrin reached for her other slipper. The H.P. was the only girl whom she really disliked. She thought her smug and purse-proud. Her father had cleaned up a fortune on the Great Hunger. He had bought up all the potatoes that had flourished unblighted in the Maharees in Kerry during the famine.

Without looking up Sterrin said evenly, 'I had no intention of telling *you* anything.'

The Head girl flushed. Sterrin's white stillness always struck her as disdain. 'I must say,' she said, 'that your behaviour and your manners do not reflect much credit upon—upon wherever they were acquired,' she ended lamely.

Sterrin thought of the place where she had acquired her manners; and of other places like it, that had drained out their substance while people like this girl fattened. For the first time in two years she felt a vigorous anger sweep through her. 'I will not listen to criticism of my home from any black potato profiteer.'

The remark, crude and earthy as a pelted potato, struck home. The Head girl took a step nearer to Sterrin. Her eyes narrowed, the dark centres filled with rage. 'At least,' she said, 'we didn't gorge ourselves in public on cake while the people starved.' She stepped back. Sterrin dropped the shoe. Her hand shot out and on the cheek where it landed there flamed an angry weal.

Sterrin wheeled and ran through the door, heedless of direction, on down the front avenue; only to get away! Not from fear or guilt of what she had done but from the contagion of those awful words that she associated with the terrible 'Darraghdheal,' who had murdered her father!

She saw the front gates ahead of her without quite realising what they were. Then through the bars she saw a face peeping and behind it the wheels of a wagon. Thank God! There was always young Thomas!

He had driven round to the front and lingered in the hopes of gleaning something about her fate. And here she was racing down the front avenue hoppity-hop in one shoe.

'Get out of my way,' she said to the scandalised gatekeeper who tried to bar her way. She pushed through the wicket. 'Help me up on the wagon, Young Thomas,' she gasped.

'But, Miss Sterrin——'

'Do what you are told!'

He did what he was told; then he wrapped the tarpaulin rug

about her shoulders and listened to the gasped-out story. And he marvelled. Her father's name came out freely; again and again. She even spoke the name that men did not speak to each other; much less to the family; the name of the 'Darraghadheal'. The ringing cadence was back in her voice again and her eyes were purple with anger. Suddenly she began to giggle. 'Oh, Young Thomas,' she spluttered, 'you should have seen the face of Sister Mary Aliquo-five-yards-of-calico when I plopped down at her feet. Oh, I forgot. Did you know that what I—what we—did was adultery?'

'What?'

'Yes, I hadn't realised either. I thought it was something that gentlemen called out other gentlemen for; of course, *you* couldn't be called out. You are not entitled to the "point of honour".'

'No. I'd probably get a horsewhipping.'

'You would not. I wouldn't allow anyone to horsewhip you.' A few big drops spattered down suddenly. She lifted the tarpaulin from across one shoulder and drew it around him, bringing them both together under its fold. She sighed. 'It would be more convenient if you *were* a gentleman.'

'Aye,' Young Thomas agreed, 'a sword is more convenient than a horsewhip. Meantime there's going to be melia[1] murder. What will her Ladyship say when you tell her that you've run away?'

'What will she say but that I did the right thing. Do you think she would have me stay under the same roof as the creature who dared to insult my father's memory?'

Which was exactly her mamma's attitude. 'Except,' said Margaret after the initial consternation and explanations, 'it would have been more appropriate if you had waited for the carriage to come and collect you instead of travelling home in a farm wagon, and if you had worn both your shoes.'

In the general indignation at the dreadful taunt that had been cast at Sterrin her original misbehaviour went unnoticed. But Maurice O'Carroll was not so easily fobbed off. It was he who had insisted upon Sterrin's being sent to school. After her father's assassination, her increasingly distrait eyes, long spells of silence, sheering off from any mention of her father's name, had alarmed him. He insisted that she be removed from the

[1] A homely threat, a 'holy murder'.

scene where she had witnessed so much horror. She needed the company of yougsters of her own age.

Now as he watched her animated expression, heard the vibrancy in her tone as she explained why she had returned, he felt that his decision had been wise; though it had seemed harsh at the time. But he wasn't going to be put off about Sterrin's part in the affair.

Events flowed from causes, he pointed out. 'What, in the first instance,' he demanded of her, 'were you doing up on that wall? And how come that that knife boy fellow happened to be there? Eh, young lady?'

'Well! I knew it was a market day and I heard O'Driscoll say that there were better prices to be had there than in Temple-town—something to do with the iron road. I was looking out in the half hope of seeing him; just to hear word of Mamma, you know—and Dominic.' She paused and added in a small voice wistfully, 'It was lonely there, Cousin Maurice.'

That settled it. He patted her shoulders. 'I suppose it was, gra' gal.'

But at the end of his visit something happened that renewed his suspicions. Margaret had come to the carriage to see him off, but he lingered to bid Sterrin goodbye. She had gone riding on Thuckeen. 'I'd as lief she were back before I go,' he said to Margaret, 'I doubt if she's fit yet to handle that mare.'

Sterrin's red setter, Anna, that had been her father's, came round the terrace end of the castle, barking. It jumped up on Margaret, barking violently. 'Sterrin must be coming,' said Margaret. 'Down, Anna!'

But the setter would not stay down. She continued to jump up barking, then she ran back a few yards and stood waiting, then returned again to Margaret. Suddenly she dashed at Young Thomas who was holding the horse's head. She seized his coat in her teeth and started to pull. He dropped the bridle. 'It's Miss Sterrin,' he cried, 'there's a trouble on the dog, Sir,— it must be Miss Sterrin.' The dog led him across the fields, looking over his shoulder every now and again to make sure Thomas was following.

He found Sterrin lying on the ground; the great black horse standing over her was quivering with the strain of not moving lest it trample her, for her body rested partly against its forelegs.

Young Thomas swooped up the unconscious girl in his arms

322

as though she were no one's concern but his. Maurice, in his preoccupation with the almost swooning Margaret, was vaguely conscious of the action. But when the procession moved towards the house his awareness became acute; the white look on the knife boy's face, he reflected, was something beyond the normal concern of the most loyal servant. When Sterrin was lowered on to her bed she opened her eyes and smiled up at Thomas. Maurice O'Carroll caught the expression on the servant's face as he returned the smile, and made a decision.

'You must not ride Thuckeen again,' Lady O'Carroll said when the doctor had gone and Sterrin was found to be not too much the worse for her fall. 'Cousin Maurice was surprised this afternoon at my permitting you to ride her.' She turned to Maurice. 'You may be sure that she shall not expose herself to *that* danger again.'

But Maurice had come to the conclusion that Sterrin was exposed to a greater danger than that from the great black mare with the gentle eyes.

He beckoned Thomas into the library. 'A word with you, young fellow.'

At four o'clock on a May morning one month later, Young Thomas went away from Kilsheelin Castle and from Miss Sterrin.

He was not due to catch the bianconi for nearly two hours but it was ten to four when he tapped at her bedroom door. She was dressed, waiting. Silently they walked together across the park. Each strove to say something momentous; something that would refer back to all their life together. But every step was shortening their last moments together and still no words would come.

At the wall gap they both turned and looked back. She scraped her throat and said something that sounded 'eejity' to herself. 'Look at the path we have made.' Across the park where they had walked there was a faintly gleaming track surfaced by the dewdrops that their cloaks had brushed from the brown 'traneens'. His eyes followed the track to the shadowy castle that had enfolded his life in its grace; they ranged over the lawns and the fields that held so much memory; they lingered on the haunted field that he had witnessed rising up to the sky on the night that his memory was born; then on the graveyard that held the godchild that he had cherished and the great gentleman whom he had revered. At last they forced themselves back to take the parting look of the one who was the embodiment of all that he was leaving behind.

'Well, it is goodbye, Miss Sterrin.' It was a miserable sort of remark he thought. The tenderness of his smile smashed down the sore, hard pressure behind his eyes. Tears and words burst out together.

'No, no! Not to you—not goodbye to you! Don't go, young Thomas,' she pleaded, then turned away from the futility of her words. She looked towards the castle, her face suddenly fierce, her teeth clenched. 'I shall never forgive Cousin Maurice! Never!'

'Don't blame him, Miss Sterrin. It is true what he said about cutting down staff. He cannot meet the wages. He *is* cutting down staff. He had to make a start somewhere—after all I'm the only outsider on the staff.'

'What about Pakie Scally? There's more to this than meets the eye. What else did Cousin Maurice say to you?'

'I told you before. He asked about my parents——

'And what did you tell him?'

'What could I tell him?—and he asked about my book learning. He said it was wasted here, that there was scope for it outside—that—— Come, they'll be getting up beyond.' He threw his bag over the gap, then climbed up and reached his hands down to draw her up. They balanced on the wall a second, enclosed in the silence of an earth sleeping. A thrush yawned a sleepy trill but a little wind made a husheen-husho in the branches and sent it back to sleep.

The unexpected little bird-note had sharpened the poignancy of the moment for Thomas. It was such a homely, everyday sound belonging to all that had been part of him; the little bird so sure and snug in the nest that it would fly out from in the morning—and all other mornings.

It had stirred Sterrin too. 'I wish that bird had kept its demned beak shut,' she quavered. 'Oh, young Thomas,' she cried huskily. 'No matter who I have waved goodbye to from this gap the loneliness seemed to go from me once I went back to you. I thought I would always have you.' She bent her head. It was so unreal; a most shameful thing to be crying like this. Fancy crying when Mickey-the-turf went to America! She

324

hadn't cried even when Joseph the footman had died of famine fever. But Thomas was so different. That was one of the things she had wanted to say.

He put a hand beneath her chin and lifted up her face. 'You will always have me, Asthore,' he murmured. 'But if I were to stay here for ever and a day I could never have you. There is a whole world between us. It is only by going away from you that I can bridge that world. Do you understand, Sterrin?'

She wasn't sure that she did. Everything was blurred by her sense of loneliness. But she did notice that for the first time in her life he had called her Sterrin without the Miss! He had taken the first step across that bridge which divided their worlds.

He went on looking at her, waiting for her to say she understood. He was still holding the hand she had given him to help her up. At last she nodded.

'Then it is not goodbye. It's *au revoir*. I'm coming back and I mustn't waste another minute till then.' He pushed back the tiny curls from her forehead and in their place he left a kiss. 'God keep you, gra' gal.' He released her hand and straightened up, but she put it on his shoulders and strained on tiptoe to kiss him on the lips. And with that kiss went all the aching pressure of words unspoken.

The same with Thomas. The surging joy of that sudden kiss drove out all sadness. No regrets for Kilsheelin and the memory of his life there, could equal this parting moment. Brightness radiated from his face as he looked at her, dazed with joy. Then he sprang down. He wanted to rush out into the world on the tide of the strength that was flowing from his gladness. She stood there in the wall gap completely still. The castle knife boy had gone; her lifelong companion. But the desolation had gone out from her too. The tall figure striding so purposefully down the Sir's Road was someone else; someone who had brought a new element into her life; an indefinable something—that held wonder.

At the turn he stopped and looked back. The wall on either side of her rose up and held her as in a niche. He let the picture of her sink in. The long school cloak made her look tall. Her hair drawn back out of sight with a black ribbon increased the impression that she might be sixteen or more instead of a four-teen-and-a-half-year-old girsha with hair still slinging.

He doffed his hat and held it high in the air. She raised her hand in return. For one dear moment they stood like that; their thoughts spanning the strip of road that was now the only barrier between them. Then he turned and was gone. Her calm broke up and the heart inside of her gave a wild plunge that bade her jump and follow him through the world. But it was Thomas himself who calmed her as he had always done. The sound of his singing came back to her and she stopped to listen. The sleepy birds listened too and when the last note faded beyond the crossroads seemed to take it up, though not a one of them but Sterrin's own self knew the words—

> '*I love my love in the morning*
> *And I love my love at noon—*
> *For she is bright—*
> *As the Lord of light,*
> *Yet mild as Autumn's moon*
> *And I will love my darling one*
> *Till even the sun shall fade....*'

When she sprang back into the little track they had made, the two of them, had gone. The finger of sun that had reached out across the eastern turret had sopped up the dew drops that had marked its way. What matter! A new path had started.

CHAPTER 35

Thomas had never envisaged himself growing old in the service of Kilsheelin like the other servants. At night in his room, he dreamed of a brilliant career on the stage. He would contrive to get some employment at a theatre. One night, perhaps, some actor declaiming Shakespeare would forget his lines and Thomas, somehow, would be the one to prompt him. His knowledge of Shakespeare and his ability to memorise would create such an impression that he would be offered a part. Or perhaps the actor playing Richard III might hurt his arm and, miraculously, at the last frantic moment it would be discovered that the obscure call-boy was versed in swordsmanship.

He could never quite get the acclaiming audience to its feet. Invariably, at that juncture he would be disenchanted by a voice ordering him to do something like removing the turf ash from the drawing-room fire.

Now that he had left Kilsheelin he was determined to make his fortune. America beckoned grandly. First Liverpool, then America. But once in Liverpool, he was forced to find work in a textile mill to augment his meagre savings. The work was hard and the spectacle of girls working half naked shocked his sensibilities. When one of the girls got caught in a machine and was mangled, Thomas could no longer hold his tongue. He began to exhort the workers to demand decent working conditions. 'I would have the workman be the master of his toil,' he said, 'not its slave.' Those words lost him his job and very nearly cost him his liberty as well. Men had been jailed for twenty years for saying less. A fugitive from justice, Thomas managed to find passage on a convict ship bound for Australia. Thomas quailed at the prospect of journeying down the slopes of the world to the far-off land of Australia. But that was where the ship was going and fugitives from the law could not be choosers. It offered escape.

Often on that deadly voyage he cursed the folly of his outcry.

To have jeopardised his hopes, his dreams, his very liberty, for a pathetic dead girl who had repelled every instinct in him but his pity!

In the Red Sea when pestilence levelled passengers and crew the Captain pressed Thomas into duty. As food supplies went low the winds rose higher. Gales sent the boat rocking off course, until it came within bowing distance of the white bergs of the bleak Antarctic. It bowed so low that at times Thomas didn't see how it could stagger up the sides of another wave. A party of old men and women from County Clare abandoned all hope of meeting the sons and daughters who had gone ahead to purchase the wealth of Australian acres for a few shillings a hundred. Resolutely they struggled into their death habits and lay waiting to go, suitably garbed, to their Creator.

Thomas worked with a will until the day that he refused to add more salt to the salt beef that, with a few scraps of hard biscuits, made up the emigrants' principal meal. Thomas had noticed the salty beef being resalted before each meal and thought it was to maintain its freshness. Soon he discovered that it was an unscrupulous ruse to force the emigrants to pay out money from their pitiful savings for each sip of water for their parched throats.

He reminded the Captain that he was a passenger. He had paid his fare.

The Captain narrowed his eyes and reminded him that he had come aboard in an almighty hurry. The Captain had assessed the anxious haste of the well-spoken young man who boarded the ship at dark of night. Some nob, he had thought, making a getaway from trouble!

Thomas wavered. Just then a child with swollen tongue and staring eyes gasped out something. Its words were drowned in the insane din of men whose starved bodies were reacting to the inferior grog that the Captain doled out at an exorbitant price.

'I won't do it,' he said doggedly.

He was dragged off, fighting like a maniac. They chained him to a fever-stricken convict. 'At least,' said the Captain genially, 'you will have the distinction of being the only one amongst the convicts who has paid his own fare to prison.'

As Thomas lay exhausted, gazing up at the sullen sky, he swore that if liberty was vouchsafed to him ever again he would never risk a moment of it in the lost cause of human pity.

328

The storm blended day and night. Time lost its significance. Days were chaotic periods of space hurled out from eternity. The buffeting winds changed and carried off the sick moanings to which he was fettered. He became disorientated. The creaking timbers turned into the rending of trees. The pinnacle lamp swinging crazily sent flashes that became the sparks from the red burning turf he had held on the pike staff. In their flying glow the Sir guided his horse away from the falling trees to seek help for her Ladyship. The trailing clouds became tendrils of hair In their suffusion, a face formed; nearer it floated until it touched his lips.

Dear God in heaven, what kind of an eejit was I to have flung away my life after receiving such a token! He lashed in impotent fury. The chain bit into his flesh and tugged the sick man into feeble protest. May the devil ride buck-hunting with Mr. Maurice O'Carroll! Why the devil's father did he think a body had acquired learning! White, shadowy, the face floated back in answer. As its lips reached his a rough voice asked him what the effing hell did he mean by lousing down there in comfort and the ship floundering for want of hands.

The speaker was Mr. Jed Ballantyne, the First Mate. He was now in control of the ship. Captain Ebenezer Lancing had the fever.

Thomas raised himself from a clanking chain of dead and half-dead convicts and pointed out the inconsistency of the question.

When they unfettered him he sprang to his feet then landed sprawling on his back. The chains had paralysed his legs into numbness. Once he had massaged them back to life, he forgot everything but the consciousness of freedom. It didn't trouble him that he had to do six men's work.

The sight of land, of the lovely green lowlands of Tasmania's peninsula stirred no glad emotions in Thomas's heart. He had worked hard enough to wipe out his insubordination about the salting of the meat, but he was still not sure whether the Captain really meant what he said about handing him over.

He was ashamed at the relief with which he heard from Mr. Ballantyne that the Captain had died of the fever.

'The old man's snuffed it.' Mr. Ballantyne was beside him.

'Dead!' The Second Mate had died, the Surgeon, emigrants, but somehow Thomas could not imagine the invincible Captain being dropped over the side in a whirling pollution, like that straw!

'What will become of—of the ship?' Thomas almost said, 'What will become of *me*?'

'What'll become of her?' The First Mate spat. 'What became of her these last nine days? There was naught wrong with my skipperin'. And, for that matter, you didn't do too bad yourself. If you'n me was runnin' this ship she wouldn't have gone twelve days off her course.'

'We couldn't have controlled the weather.'

'Weather! 'Twarn't weather; 'twar bad seamanship. That's what 'twar. He claimed in black and white in the newspaper, for all to see, that he was familiar with the coast of Africa, America and Australia; that his ship was sound and seaworthy and provisioned with the finest vittles to last for more'n three months. You saw the kind of vittles them critters got.'

Thomas had seen; to his cost.

Mr. Ballantyne removed his jacket and proceeded to put on the Captain's dress reefer for state occasions. 'Good thing he didn't wear it this voyage. No contagiousness.'

He saluted with an extravagant air. 'Captain Ebenezer Lansing, at your service. You can forget I was ever Jed Ballantyne. He was out off in the bloom of youth, so to speak.'

'What! But that would be a most serious offence. 'Twould be criminal.'

'Gettin' very law-abidin' ain't yeh? You should know all about what's criminal. 'Twarn't for the good of your health you came aboard.' He swept his hand towards the shore. 'Take a look at your hotel waitin'.'

The great black fortress was well in sight. The young man's heart lurched. 'Yes, its nice'n friendly,' jeered the Mate. 'Lackeys will be comin' to take your portmanteau; comin' with their lashes an' muskets. There isn't a convict aboard that has a leg that'd hold a chain.' He looked down at the bronzed well-turned legs beneath the short, ragged trousers. 'Barrin' your own!'

The young man took a long stride as though to assure himself that the chains that had manacled him to a rotting corpse no longer hampered him. He came back to the new Captain. 'What about the other prisoners? Are you going to hand them over?'

'Don't worry about them. We'll fatten them up when we get

provisions here. They'll make good seamen yet. Then we'll set sail for Australia before this wind drops. Australia! There's good cargoes here, and there's men there ready to give lumps of raw gold for a passage to the new gold find in California. Seems once they handle that there gold they'll go to the ends of the earth for more. What about it? Are you goin' to put your scruples over the side or are you goin' to put them purty legs into irons? Take yer choice, and take it quick.'

The fortress was looming nearer and groups stood on the shore watching the approaching vessel. 'All right. It's not a question of choice. It's a question of caution. It would not be manacles if this were discovered. It would be muskets—for all of us. To fail to report the Captain's death could bring us under suspicion of murder—and then there's the question of the Company, the shipowners...'

'The shipowners!' Ballantyne spat. 'Have done with this insubordination if you know what's good for you. Get below and cover them bare shanks. Surgeon Black's clobber will fit you nicely. He was no more a surgeon than yourself, but old Ebenezer warn't askin' no questions as long as the regulations had a wisp of coverin'.'

The young man grinned. The breath of freedom was sweetening the air. 'Aye, aye, sir.' He hurried below but a second later his head came round the bridge rail. 'Excuse me—Captain,' he added with pleasing deference, 'there's just one other point, if I may refer to it.'

The new title made such pleasing hearing that its owner had no objection to listening to any points that followed its sound. 'Be quick about it,' he said.

'What about boarding officials, Captain? Inspectors from the Board of Health, that sort of thing?'

The new Captain guffawed. 'Health inspections, did you say! Look at them. They're holdin' their handkerchiefs to their noses already. With this following wind I'd wager that the whole island has been stunk out this half hour. They won't be too keen to come aboard; 'taint as if 'twas a regular convict ship. Just fill yer nose with that stink, it's the best friend you ever had. Trust that—and me—and we'll get by.'

And they did. They dropped anchor within good smelling distance and formalities were slim and brief. In the dark hour before dawn they set sail for Australia with fresh provisions and a few fresh faces. For the new Captain's consent had been tacit but sure when a few sturdy ticket-of-leave men from the provision boat—prisoners granted a certain amount of freedom for good conduct—had clambered aboard in the darkness.

The new skipper was always in good humour. The remaining handful of Welsh and Irish emigrants came alive under the vigour of fresh water for their bodies and fresh-washed clothes that had danced in the sun-heated breeze.

In the velvet darkness of the First Watch, Mr. Thomas came to know the fate he had escaped. From the four men who had slipped aboard in the darkness, he heard tales that chilled the warmth of the sub-tropical night. 'Eighteen and twenty hangings I seen of a fine morning,' said a Yorkshire man who had not poached for thirteen years. ' 'Twas like as if Ma had forgot to take the bodies out of the washing of a Monday morning,' he chuckled.

An Irish ticket-of-leave man with a scarred face was the only one of the four not anxious to reminisce. The new First Mate watched as he went silently to his tasks, sail-shifting, rope-slicing, hammock-scrubbing. Once when an improvised ball of paper was tossed in his direction he raised his deck-scrub and diverted the ball in mid-air with the skill of a hurler and the splendid teeth showed suddenly in a smile that betokened an earlier gaiety.

As the ball rebounded, Thomas grabbed a brush and caught it aloft with a matching skill that astonished the ticket-of-leave man. 'I shouldn't have thought you were Irish, much less a hurler,' he said. He looked curiously at the First Mate.

Gradually, in the dark of the Night Watch, the scarred man, Bergin, relaxed. He told of a January morning when he was nineteen and very gay and the local lads had clubbed to hire the wagonette for the Carlow races. They were all wagering on the certainty of a one-eyed horse belonging to their landlord—a lady who had reduced all their rents that gale day because she had given birth to a son after ten daughters. Even the brake horse was in a mischievous mood. It couldn't be held from presumptuously galloping abreast with the fine carriage horses of a gentleman who was rumoured to be the wealthiest landlord in Ireland.

' 'Twas he gave me this,' said the ticket-of-leave man, pointing to the scar on his cheek. 'But he wasn't content with that. He

332

got me seventeen years at the next Assizes.'

'It was a savage sentence!'

The scar-faced man turned to him. 'It was a sentence to turn a man into a savage.' There was savagery in his voice. Then it resumed its tonelessness. 'There was a little girl peeping from one of the carriages. Queer, the way a simple thing like that sticks in one's memory! To this day I can see the horror on her face when I got the gash.'

Could the arm of coincidence be so long? For a brief moment the two men, so strangely met, looked out beyond the ocean and the years at the same face. Thomas was learning to restrain his impulses. No need to tell this embittered stranger that that same horrified little girl—for of course it must be Sterrin—had told him all about that incident that had happened on the way to Carlow races in the Repeal year of '43!

'I wonder, will she wait for me?'

Thomas half turned. Had Bergin's mind become unhinged?

An awkward laugh scraped the darkness. 'Someone else I was thinking of. She said she'd wait the length of the sentence for me. Hmph! Romancing; I was the young hero of a drama. Who'd expect a girl to give the whole of her life to waiting for someone who used to please her when she was too young to know her own mind? Who?'

The First Mate didn't feel like doling out bland assurances. His own aspirations had been growing steadily more remote; more improbable. Now, all of a sudden they looked downright silly. He sprang to his feet. 'Look,' he cried with an upward sweep, 'there is the Southern Cross. Over there people are waiting for you also; waiting for men with your fine physique. They say that there are gold nuggets to be picked up there like cabbages.'

Often on the long trek from Melbourne to Ballarat, Thomas regretted his decision not to sail on to America as First Mate to the self-appointed Captain Ballantyne. Compared to this raw, wild territory, America seemed near and homelike; only three thousand miles from Ireland! Kitty and Mark had bought land there with the money they had earned in Canada. John Holohan had become a rich man in Chicago.

It was Christmas Day when Bergin and Thomas reached the gold fields. No one gave thought to the day. No one gave thought to anything but the gold that had decoyed this motley throng from all parts of the world; peers and preachers; bookkeepers and navvies; the scum of Norfolk Island, all bedevilled by the same dream of sudden wealth that so few of them ever realised.

And yet it was here in this outlandish place that Thomas realised—in a dim way—his youthful dream of attaining to the stage of a theatre, through some actor forgetting his lines or becoming ill.

An actor became, not ill, but drunk. The stage was a platform of planks in a canvas entertainment tent. The audience sat on rows of up-turned kegs. Thomas was sitting between Bergin and a young gentleman whom Thomas was assiduously cultivating. The young man, he had discovered, possessed a high and ancient title, temporarily discarded amid the democracy of the gold field. Thomas was wasting no opportunity of equipping himself for the young nobleman's world. It was Sterrin's world. Technically he was word perfect in its speech and its book-learning. He would not, should occasion offer, err by asking for a second helping of soup, by carrying a parcel in the street, by walking abroad without gloves. But all this unapplied knowledge had been gleaned from the wrong side of the green baize door. He longed to apply it in the atmosphere of accepted equality. And, here in this medley of unqueried identities, the young nobleman had accepted Thomas.

In the tent, the audience of diggers chewed and spat and offered rude suggestions to the floundering actor. Suddenly, strangely, from that riffraff group there came a prompt. Thomas looked back. In the dim lamplight, the faces were indistinguishable from one another; all of them caked with the clauber of the day's toil; then, from the clay-matted whiskers and beard of one man, Thomas located the outflow of those lines from Richard III; beautifully enunciated!

The player took up the prompt. When he muffed again Thomas twisted round on his tub watching for the next one; but the anonymous digger had clamped down on his erudition. And suddenly Thomas heard his own voice calling out the lines he had often mouthed silently when he sat at the back of the Assembly Rooms at Templetown and watched them acted forth by the Travelling Players.

Bergin looked at him amazed. 'It's you who should be up

334

there,' he said. The words held a young enthusiasm long lost to the toneless voice.

On the other side, the young nobleman came suddenly to life. He had been lounging, bored and somnolent, his wideawake over his nose, his gauze neck veil clayey and grimy, falling in stiff drapes over his cheeks. He pushed back his hat and sat upright. 'Bergin's right; up you go, chum!'

The occupants of the adjoining tubs supported the motion. Anything for a bit of diversion! They hoisted Thomas from one to another. He was thrust on to the stage just as the actor was being assisted off.

He stood there gaping down at the cheering, jeering, raucous crowd. This was not the dream of his young aspirations. This was a nightmare; like when he used to dream that he was in a crowded bianconi in his nightshirt!

Then his brain cleared. This was no bianconi. This was a crowded play tent; a real audience, real actors, drunk or no; a real stage, even if it wobbled a bit, and by the piper that played before Moses, he was going to stay put on this stage!

With a sweep he tossed his wideawake from him and finished off the interrupted speech. It was King Richard's oration to his army and Thomas as he progressed, started to enjoy himself. Some of the words might have been applied to the mob in front of him. '... A sort of vagabonds, rascals and runaways ... whom their o'er cloyed country vomits forth in desperate adventure....'

Drunkenness was no isolated happening in the canvas theatres that played the gold sites. A few nights later Thomas lent a hand to drag an actor blind drunk from a grog shop within minutes of curtain up. The part was a small one and the theatre manager questioned Thomas about his previous experience. Thomas managed to check himself just as he was about to confess that he had no experience whatever. He assumed the Keep Off The Grass look that he had seen on the titled digger whenever people questioned him about his previous life. That look was enough for the manager. Thomas was a 'quick study'. He got the part, but it only lasted him a night. The players closed in their ranks against 'digger' competition. They decided to postpone all serious drinking until after the performance.

By day, Thomas probed the earth but never did his ears gladden to the music of his pick catching in a nugget. The nobleman's white hands grew hornier with welts and warts. By night, it was he whom Thomas helped from the grog shops.

One morning the claim they worked on filled in with water. Johnny-the-lord pulled Thomas to safety. 'I'm finished with this dump,' he said through chattering teeth. 'I'm off to dig liquid gold from a brandy keg.' Thomas too, was sick of the unrewarding toil; sick of the fanaticism on the faces of men who refused to give in. He decided to go with Johnny-the-lord. He would try to take his chances with the theatre manager. Silently, Bergin fell in with the two.

On the way back they paused to watch a group of men standing around a cavity on a hill. There was something dramatic about the way the men handed the pan of gravel from one to another for inspection. Thomas thought that they must have brought up the colour; but the last man, when he had pawed through the gravel, flung it from him with a gesture of disgust. Without another word the group picked up their belongings and walked off.

A piece of the flying gravel hit Thomas. 'It's all yours,' said the man who had tossed it. Thomas recognised him. He was a London book-keeper who had sold up everything he possessed to seek gold in order to get his employer's consent to marry his daughter.

Bergin looked curiously at the 'cradle'. It was a new type that he hadn't seen before. 'Damn fool,' he said in his grim, toneless way. 'Suit him better to have kept his money and his cushy job in London! Fat chance the likes of him has of marrying the boss's daughter.'

For a weary, sodden moment, Johnny-the-lord reverted to cast and muttered something about the absurdity of a 'clerk-fellow' getting notions because he had learned to push a pen across his employer's ledger.

Thomas, chilled to the bone, felt the sudden heart of rage. He thought feverishly that they had discovered his own foolish aspirations. Who were they, an escaped convict and some discredited squib of nobility, to scoff at the decent aspirations of love?

Some affinity with the hapless clerk who had made such a bid to win his employer's daughter made him reach out his hand to the abandoned crank and set the cradle rocking. The others called him to come on. When he persisted in working it they

336

returned and worked with him. They were loyal mates, as well he realised. What he didn't realise was the rasped state of his mind and body from continuous toil and setbacks; from the continuous bare blueness of the undraped sky above him and the ochre desert of clay all around him. He longed for soft, grey clouds; for little roads that meandered between green hedges; for the sentient winds that breathed into the mind and stirred its thought; but most of all he longed for the softness of lips that had touched his and that held him for ever; ensorcelled to the undeliberate witchery of their magic.

Suddenly he ceased to long; to think. He became a mindless frenzy. In the gravel at the bottom of the 'cradle' his scalded eyes had caught the glitter of yellow streaks. Gold! Gold! They had struck gold!

The strike proved a small one; less than a thousand pounds' worth. Johnny-the-lord went on a spree with his share. Thomas and Bergin put theirs into shares that had started to rise. It might as well be making more money for them while they worked their claim. They reminded each other of the Gaelic saying—'Have a goose and you'll get one'. They had only skimmed the surface. They worked like maniacs. They went on working when water began to pour in. Bergin forgot his past and his bitterness and his half-cherished hopes, just as men there forgot home and wife and child. Thomas forgot at last the face that had haunted his dreams, sleeping and waking.

But it came back to him in fever when he collapsed with dysentery from working waist-deep in the ice-cold water. He reached his burning hand for the bright nugget. It wafted from him, darkening as it went and melting into soft rings and spirals; like the dark gold that sheened around a young girl's face.

When he recovered he had to face calamity. The shares he had purchased had dropped to worthlessness. The pit they were working had caved in. Bergin had escaped with his life. But Johnny-the-lord had not escaped. Johnny with his fine elegant speech; Johnny with the slender hands that had pulled Thomas to safety from the first pit, who had returned against his inclination to the book-keeper's abandoned claim only from loyalty to Thomas! Johnny was entombed in the collapsed mine. He would have been alive but for Thomas's obstinacy over his slighted dream!

337

Thomas felt sick with guilt; sick of the gold fields. He returned to the theatrical manager, but he found him breaking up camp for America ... 'Can you pay your passage to America?' he called as Thomas turned away. Thomas couldn't. The barest necessities of life cost more out here than they had in the blackest pitch of the Famine.

The manager assessed the emaciated features, the dispirited air. Not so cocky this time! He questioned him about previous stage experience and demanded explicit replies. No stand-off-the-grass looks this time! But Thomas had no heart to ape Johnny-the-lord again.

'Are you a convict?' asked the manager. Thomas's quick resentment convinced him; so did his renditions from different dramatists. A born actor, he thought. But he said, 'I don't employ amateurs,' when Thomas confessed to no professional experience. Cannily he watched the hopelessness etch itself around Thomas's lips and nostrils then he made his bargain; good and hard. A signed agreement for Thomas to work for him for an unspecified period in return for having his passage paid to America—and, of course in return for the inestimable value of the experience he would receive.

Thomas would sign anything that would be the means of getting him to America. He grasped the quill to sign with a flourish then suddenly faltered, the quill drooping uncertainly.

The actor-manager noted the hesitation. 'Are you afraid to sign your own name?' he demanded. He was convinced now that the digger was an escaped convict. But Thomas was back floundering in the void of his namelessness; mocked by his own presumptuous aims and apings. He could see the reflection of their folly in the other man's smile. And suddenly with a flash of memory he saw something else! Dublin in Repeal Year, the stage of Crow Street Theatre, Thomas Young, the great actor proclaiming, '... alas, then I was young——' and the gallerite yelling, 'And now you are Winterbottom!'

For the second time in his life he reached for the actor's discarded name.

A few days later Thomas's foot met the ribbed deck of the America-bound ship as though it were a long-lost friend.

CHAPTER 36

Sterrin took the bard's tray from Pakie Scally. It was no great burden to carry these days. Since her father's death the old man had lost his zest for food.

He peered out at her from under his brows. 'The young Sir never brings me my supper tray now.' It's funny, she thought, when Young Thomas used to bring the tray, the bard would call him every name in the family calendar, but it is only since he left that the bard went so far as calling him *that* name.

'He has gone away, Bard. I've told you.'

'He is a long time gone.' She moved and opened the window. The smell of hawthorn blew past on a little wind and there was a lingering scent of apple blossoms. Her eyes followed a little roadeen that went wobbling like a child against the brown shoulder of the hill. 'A year,' she murmured, 'a week, and three days——'

'You are keeping a tight count on the days since that lad left, Miss Sterrin.'

She whirled back. He'd hear the grass growing! 'Bard, there is no knowing you. One minute you talk as if today was a hundred years ago. The next minute you are spotting everything that goes on around you like a pet fox. Young Sir, indeed! And it is Young Thomas you had in mind!'

The old man let out a sigh. 'He was the kind to hang a wreath upon one's harp. Thank you for the snack, Sterrin, Daughter of O'Carroll. Maybe the next time 'twill be a meal.' She chuckled and took the tray. 'I'll get you more. You don't usually eat so much.' She liked to bring his food. He was the one person she could talk to about Young Thomas. In the kitchen they talked of him, but they talked of him as one of themselves. The bard spoke of him as a person. It pleased her, strangely, when he confused Young Thomas with the family.

He watched her as she lifted the tray. 'You're changing,' he muttered, 'and 'tis no harm so. I've always found red-haired

339

women to be treacherous. Your hair is turning into a sweet dark hood for the little face of you. 'Tis a pity about that wart. You inherited that from the princess who married the tinker.'

She looked critically at her reflection in a silver cover dish. 'It is not a wart. It is a mole and I could not inherit things from her once she left the family. She probably passed on her warts to the tinker's line.'

'Oh, she left the tinker and came back with a fine looking male child that had a wart beside his eye.'

'You're making that up, Bard.' She knew every word of the manuscript about the O'Carroll Princess who was so ugly that her father had fobbed her off upon a tinker.

'I don't *have* to make up. I know the O'Carroll breed. Her face might have been ugly but her blood would be proud. It would never let her live out her days, wife to a base-born person without name or home or origin.'

Sterrin picked up the tray. 'I'll send them with some more supper,' she said coldly. Even the bard had no right to go that far!

He watched her leave him without a farewell word, head high, true daughter of all the Sirs and chieftains who had gone before; their chivalric lineage stamped in her features that were cold against him. He called to her pleadingly; she was the sun's warmth coming to him in the winter of his days; she was all of the past glory, coming out of it in gentleness to tend to him.

'You belong in high places, Bright love. Storm and famine, aye and murder too—hell roast them that did it—have kept you too near the ground and the groundlings. You were meant to soar like the golden eaglet that yourself resembles greatly—Eagle to eagle—your father would want it that way. 'Tis soon I'll be meetin' him and it's the short greetin' he'd have for me if I didn't say what has to be said to the little one whom he had to leave unguided. Do you know,' he went on, ' 'twill be a great gathering of us in the parlours of heaven; your father and my father and his grandfather, and my grandfather, that was near a hundred when he died. He was a lad when he came to Kilsheelin from Strague Castle. 'Twas the day that Cromwell rode up to its door and Calvagh O'Carroll handed him up the castle of his fathers without as much as a Go-to-hell. "Whose house is this?" sez Cromwell. " 'Twas mine yesterday, Lord Cromwell, 'tis yours today." My grandfather's father said he would not sully his harp there again.... You were talking about warts gra' gal——'

'I was *not*!'

'What harm: my great-grandfather saw Cromwell that day, a block of a man with coarse nostrils, eyes hard, like a crab that can never ripen into an apple. He was thick in mind and body, and a wart on his chin as big as an onion and another over his right eyebrow. The foolishness of men to rate themselves so high! They are only as important as the little space of life that holds them. Let you go now, gra' gal, for there is an air in my head I must set to music.' He dropped off to sleep.

She tiptoed out, smiling. That air had been in his head for as long as she could remember. But a few nights later it seemed as if he had put it to music at last. The sound of the harp startled Pakie Scally as he carried the tray for her to the bard's door.

''Tis good to hear him play at last, Miss Sterrin, but it is a terrible lonesome tune.' The old man was humming in Gaelic as he plucked at his knee harp. She stood without lowering the tray for the words made her heart lurch with dread.

> 'Long seems to me your coming,
> Old Herald of God
> Oh, friend of friends
> To part me from my pain!
> ... Oh, footstep not heavy!
> Oh, hand in the darkness!
> Your coming seems to me long ...'

When she saw his face she turned, still holding the tray, and made towards the door that had closed on Pakie. She must call someone; but even as the thought rose she knew that she was doing what she had done the night she had turned from her father's prone body—seeking flight from what she had dreaded to face. Mamma, the shrinking one, had stayed at her post like a soldier.

She urged the old man to eat. 'A bird would eat more,' she said.

'Aye,' he said, 'a young bird.' He reached out and touched a curl on her forehead then brought his finger slowly down over the arch of her nose. 'An eagle,' he murmured to himself. 'And

341

it was no grey bird of the eaves that fledged that other; an eagle too, perhaps, or maybe a hawk. A hawk,' he repeated, 'an shouk abu!' And he fell asleep. The next morning, when Pakie Scally went into his room, the bard was dead. The rallying cry of the O'Carrolls, 'an shouk abu', the hawk to victory! were his last words.

Sterrin felt as though she had been cut adrift from all her previous life. Even after her father's death the castle had not become void. Its continuity had persisted; because the bard was there. He was the spirit of the castle; the guardian of all their lives, past and present, linked to him in a chain of history. And now the link was broken. Now they would be an ordinary bardless family like the planters and Anglo-Irish gentry.

To Maurice, when he arrived, Sterrin seemed one with the harps, grouped in bereft silence in the bard's room; the knee harp of Brian Boru, the Tara Harp, the little table lyre that the old man used to carry round with him and the great ceremonial harp of booming applewood. Like them, she seemed to hold within her great throbs of feeling waiting to be evoked.

After the funeral, Sterrin slipped quietly away on Thuckeen. She let the mare break into its beautiful quick canter and bear her away from the sadness. Vitality rushed all about her, in the warm wind, in the little music of birds, in every plant and flower. It was hard to think of the bard lying dead beneath earth that held such life above it. It was hard to think at all with Thuckeen and herself close-knit in this glowing sense of speed and power. She set the mare to a great high bank and soared over; funny how some people were so timid of jumps! No jump ever gave her fear; only people did. They blocked up her thoughts and gave her that feeling that they were good and she was bad, or sinful, or guilty of something.

She saw the hermit of Bawn-na-drum watching her as she cleared the bank and cantered towards him, kin to the wind and the horse and to the great liver-coloured dog, half labrador, half red setter that loped beside her. He noted her light, firm seat on the saddle and as she drew off her glove to dab her moist forehead he sensed the fineness of her hands on the horse's mouth.

'I am sorry for your trouble, Sterrin, Daughter of Roderick O'Carroll,' he said, addressing her in the olden way. ''Tis the end of a great tradition.'

She didn't want to hear any sympathy. She had no wish to be

forced back into the past; she wanted to stay in this glowing moment, and she wanted a drink of water.

When he brought it from his cave in a drinking cup of chased silver she smothered her amazement in a long drink. It would be impolite to show surprise that the old cave dweller should possess a thing so exquisite. Then she saw the bird engraved on the side.

'Is that a hawk?' she exclaimed. She peered close to read the inscription. Underneath was written 'Hapsburgh abu!'

'Aye, but not what you think; not the O'Carroll hawk. It was given to my grandfather by the Sieur O'Carroll who had a set of them given to him by Mari Therèsa.'

He told her that the name of the Austrian royal family, Hapsburg, meant Hawk's Castle. When the Sieur O'Carroll led his Irish soldiers on to the field roaring the O'Carroll war cry, 'The Hawk to Victory!' and his standard with the O'Carroll hawk flying in the wind, the foreign soldiers used to think that he was some Irish branch of the Hapsburgs.

There was a picture somewhere at home she recalled, of the Sieur O'Carroll. He was really the Strague branch of the O'Carrolls—the dispossessed one.

'I have never seen such a beautiful goblet. I am honoured to have been let drink from it.'

'It is I who am honoured,' he replied gravely and he bowed the great head, 'though 'tis few I have proffered it to. Thomas Francis Meagher drank from it and he on his keeping here a few years back, and the one with him of the O'Brien clan and, meaning no disrespect to you, so did the youth who used to serve in your castle. Somehow it did not seem ill-fitting that he should.' He was reaching out for it and on a sudden she drew it back and put it to her lips again, as though to drain the last drop. Young Thomas had drunk from this cup! And then she felt a sense of shame, and that queer feeling of guilt. Young Thomas, and all the others downstairs, had drunk from something or other every day; wooden porringers, thick glasses, cups with Father Matthew's face on them, or maybe the Duke of Wellington's, with painted roses blooming beside his big nose and Waterloo under his chin. What of it! She put the cup into the old man's hand and turned the mare's head. He caught the bridle. 'Don't give too much of your young life grieving over those that are gone. They have lived their lives, your bard and

343

all these.' He raised the cup as though it held the ones he spoke of. 'Be said by my life. If I had to live it again I wouldn't spend it burrowing under a wall that was all that was left to me of old glories; other people's glories. I'd go out and make my own glory. That's what he'll do, I'll be bound.' He tapped the cup and she knew that out of all the people that it contained for him, he meant young Thomas:

She galloped home, ashamed of the singing happiness within her on this sad day! How extraordinary to hear another old man speak so soon again of the symbolic hawk, and in that same breath to speak of Young Thomas! Young Thomas who would make his own glory! Life that had seemed, a while back, to be closing in, suddenly opened out into a lovely beckoning vista.

She found Cousin Maurice waiting for her in the stableyard. 'Didn't I give orders that you were not to ride that mare again?' he demanded. And who might you be to give orders about me, said her mind, but it kept the words to itself.

'I should have sold it long ago,' he went on.

'Sold Thuckeen? What right have you ever to talk of selling Thuckeen.' There was no keeping the words inside now.

He told her of his right. His right, as her father's administrator, to pinch and scrape, dodge and plot to keep the place going until Dominic was of age to take over. 'No enviable right whatever, let me assure you, Miss. That horse is worth too much money to be used as a hack for a thuckeen like you.'

The moisture on her hair made it look black; made her look like her father, he thought, and the words that burst from her made her sound like her father.

'By God, Maurice O'Carroll,' she swore, 'if you sell Thuckeen, you'll sell me with her. Where she goes, I go. My father's horse is no chattel.'

He looked at her silently for a moment. 'In faith,' he said quietly, 'you are no chattel either. You are your father's daughter, but you could have done with a bit longer in that convent. We'll talk about this tomorrow.'

The stragglers that follow funerals—or weddings—still hung around the yard. Sterrin, striding towards the back door, took no notice of an old woman on a crutch who hobbled aside to let her pass.

In her bedroom while she changed from her riding habit she fumed. Sell Thuckeen, would he? This was the last straw.

She'd make a fight for her; this very night after the drawing-room tea she'd rub in hard to Mamma the enormity of letting Papa's horse go to a stranger, and Mamma would back her up on that score, even if it sent her off into a—a what? Not a vapour which was what other girl's mothers had, openly and genteely, with pretty bottles of smelling salts and providing interesting conversation afterwards. But those frightening attacks that had to be coped with behind closed doors and never alluded to afterwards!

Utensils clattered outside and the door opened to admit Mrs. Stacey—of all people—with two copper jugs of hot water. She was up to something. And Sterrin was in no mood to show concern about all this panting from lugging up a load that it was someone's else's duty to carry.

It was because of her cousin, the cook explained. 'My own first cousin, and first cousin to Black Pat Ryan's father, back home this day of all days, after thirty-eight years of service with an English Earl; home on a crutch—only one leg—her other leg amputated a year ago. No more use to the earl's house; no use to anyone, a burden, they said on the Poor Rates, so they gave her three ounces of tea and three ounces of coffee and three two-penny loaves and a shilling and three pence and sent her home to Ireland. Home! All belonging to her dead in the Great Hunger or exiled. Myself is all of home that's left to her and what shelter have I to offer a homeless relative?' She drew her wedding ring up and down her finger and waited.

An hour back Sterrin could have melted to this pathetic tale. Now it exasperated her. Why come to her? Gone was the day when Mrs. Stacey might ask Miss Sterrin to put in a good word for her over some favour she sought. The cook's status had altered since Sir Roderick's death. Her sorrow then had been a personal thing that had brought home to everyone the relationship that had bound her to her master. Lady O'Carroll would be slow to refuse a favour to the foster-mother of her beloved husband. Why this hinting?

For the first time Sterrin noticed how much the cook had aged since that tragedy. And tonight there was a red puffiness of recent tears. Remorse softened her. 'Don't you know well, Banaltra,' she said gently, 'that Mamma will not expect you to turn away your poor cousin?' The term that her father had used towards his foster-mother startled her own ears. It was a while before the cook could answer. When she had wiped the tears with the apron she said, 'I know that, Miss Sterrin,' but she made no move to go.

And then she said what she had come to say. Her cousin had brought 'newses' of Young Thomas.

Sterrin listened in silence. The cook's voice trailed out awkwardly into the silence. What was I thinkin' of, to come barging up here with my story? Times have changed and a servant now is a servant. Young Thomas was a servant and one who had spoken against his betters; preached against them in the public street. An 'agitator', they had called him. This proud silent young lady was not the eager child who had followed at Young Thomas's heels; whom Young Thomas had doted upon, waited on hand and foot. She had grown out of her child's world of the kitchen and the stable the same as she had grown out of her dolls. She is not living in the past like the likes of me. She will side with her caste; that *he* had reneged. Muire Dia, but you've paid for your folly, my splendid boy! Twenty years in Australia, they had told her cousin. A life sentence!

She moved across and left the water, unpoured, on the wash stand. Sterrin knew that the omission was deliberate, because of her own silence. But she dare not part her lips; dare not release their trembling.

Mrs. Stacey turned from the doorway and spoke with unaccustomed quietness. 'I am sorry, Miss Sterrin, for intruding. I had no right in the world to come up here to you with that story.'

Sterrin reached the door in a stride. She clutched the cook towards her by the wide shoulder straps of her apron, and the cook saw the stricken eyes. 'Banaltra!' It was a child's stricken cry; from the child of her loved foster-child. No proud young lady!

'Banaltra, to whom else in the world would you come to with that story?'

Then the door was closed and the cook heard the great key groan protestingly towards its unaccustomed lock.

Reverend Mother held the quill suspended over her correspondence. It was rarely that the traffic on the avenue disturbed her concentration. But there was no ignoring these approaching hooves. Their clamour filled her quiet study with the portent of hasty news; the kind of news that it was the duty of Reverend Mother alone, to break. With a sigh she sanded over the unfinished page. Pray heaven it would not be necessary for her to crush the joy from the life of some unsuspecting child!

Instead of the lay sister's quiet tap there came a quick knock that was an afterthought. The knob was already turned. The figure that stepped up to the table was not a lay sister's. The curtsey it started to drop became shortened to a jerk by saddle stiffness. Words poured out in a rush.

'Reverend Mother, I—I've come back; for good! I shall never run away again. I wish to enter.'

Not for holiness alone is a nun chosen to be Reverend Mother. Mother Berchman looked at her visitor as though it were part of the day's routine for people to come thundering up the drive; forcing their way into her sanctum to make breathless renunciations of the world. Her calm gaze took in the dust-grimed figure. The skirt was coated with dust. Dust masked the eyelids and lashes. A ridge of dust defined the arch of the nose. It gave grotesque emphasis to its arrogance as though the chastening process of the convent had already commenced.

No dust begrimed the lips. The Reverend Mother found herself following the high, full crescent of the upper lip. Had it always looked like that, she wondered. Three years ago when the girl first came here her lips had been too pallid to notice their outline. Now, exertion probably had lent them colour, a curved blob of scarlet that glowed as though it had been freshly painted on to the grey masking of the face. Could a face change so much in—how long was it? Eighteen months? Or had the other, earlier face been masked too; with the filmy mask of young unawakenment that had been held all too rigidly in place by the grip of tragedy?

Suddenly the lips lost their strangeness. They became familiar to the nun, the lips of a young thing; uncertain, trembling.

'I—I have brought my dowry. Oh, not here!' The nun's eyes had dropped to the tight-clutched saddle bag that held a few belongings. 'It is outside. It—she is worth a lot of money.'

Reverend Mother rose and pulled a bell rope.

'Sit down, Sterrin,' she said gently, 'you must first have some refreshment.' She moved to the window and glanced down. A great black horse was quivering and blowing at the hitching ring.

'I think,' she said, 'that your—dowry would do with some refreshment also.'

The first weeks back at the convent were happy ones for Sterrin. It was a relief not to be reminded of Young Thomas at every turn. Of course she missed Dominic and her mother but far better a useful life here than sorrow at Kilsheelin. Even the grim ceremony of the final vow which Sterrin watched a young nun take, failed to dampen her spirits. For a moment when she watched the young nun, newly veiled in black, lie prostrate on the floor, her heart beat wildly in terror. Four nuns held a black pall over the blackrobed figure. The doors were barred for this symbolic entombment. And then as suddenly as they had quickened her heart beats steadied. Sterrin looked across at the nun lying beneath the funeral pall. What was it but a piece of cloth. It would take more than that to frighten her back to her emptied world.

Sterrin was radiant as she made her way towards the common room after the ceremony. She had conquered her doubts. The common room was gay. One of the boarders was playing the piano. But it was a waltz, and four pairs of girls were dancing. Waltzing was strictly forbidden. Sterrin glanced towards the piano. She might have known! No other girl would defy the ban so blatantly. And no other girl could play like that. Sterrin gripped a chair-back to keep her body from following the dreamy rhythm of the music. The pianist, Eileen Morton, was an enchantress at the piano. Away from the piano she was sullen, slangy and uncouth. Her frequent indiscipline was not that of young high spirits. It was a deliberate thing done out of mature resentment. And she knew that she was barely tolerated by the Sisters for the sake of her musical talent.

A great, gangling, Parlour Boarder went up to her and told her to play something else. The pianist told her to go and boil her head and went on playing. When the big P.B. put a restraining hand upon her arm she shrugged it off violently, then lifted her hand over the keys and the entire hall heard her ask what blasted right had *she* to give orders. A current of shock ran through the room. But apart from the 'blasted', Sterrin was in complete agreement with the query. Parlour Boarders had no special authority. They were mostly girls who had returned after their schooling was finished for the sake of companionship; because life at home was too dull and monotonous. A few of them came with the idea of testing their inclination to enter. The one remonstrating the pianist had been here for six years. She had a fortune of twenty thousand pounds, but even the most daring Abduction Club member would have found her difficult to run away with. She was six feet one!

'You are a disgrace to the school,' she said now. 'I feel it my bounden duty to report you.'

The pianist closed the lid of the piano and jumped to her feet 'And I,' she shouted, 'feel it my bounden duty to tell you to go to hell!'

A week later Sterrin watched another ceremony. The whole senior school watched and most of the nuns and governesses. Near the door stood a woman. Sterrin could not place her. Her clothes were shabby and rather townish. Her face would be sharp but for the softening moisture of tears. It was extraordinary, Sterrin thought, the way tears had softened the face of the girl who knelt in the centre of the floor; softened it to pulp. Eileen Morton's eyes were two red blobs. Her lips wobbled pitifully as they strove for the words that she must say.

Rarely it might happen that the parents of a difficult pupil would be asked to withdraw her. But this was the awful ceremony of being Publicly Expelled. It must be like a public court-martial, Sterrin thought; like when an officer is drummed out of his regiment and his commanding officer deprives him of his sword and decorations.

Poor Eileen Morton possessed no decorations, though her father, it seems, had possessed a sword. He *had* been an officer who had married beneath him and had kept the existence of his wife and daughter a secret until his death.

The girl's lips and throat worked convulsively and finally the words came in strangulated gulps.

'I—apologise—for the scandal that I have given to all of you, my classmates, my teachers——' Her red, streaming eyes followed around the watching faces until they rested on her mother's face. She gave a choking sound and covered her face with her hands. Sterrin averted her eyes. They went round the rows of faces that were smugly watching—accepting this act of human abasement. The big Parlour Boarder was the only one seated so as not to obstruct the vision of those behind. She caught Sterrin's glance and gave a self-satisfied nod. Sterrin's disdainful glance travelled down the whole six feet one and a half inches of undesired body length. Sitting there with her feet stuck out and her twenty thousand pounds and a hole as big as a shilling in the sole of her mean blue shoe. As though a blast or a hell would scandalise her.

Something was rising in Sterrin and this time it was not panic. It shook her hopefully, invigoratingly, as water welling up beneath the parched earth shakes the water diviner's testing rod. Mists and uncertainties vanished. Sterrin stepped resolutely from her place and walked down the centre of the hall. All eyes watched her. When she reached the kneeling girl she bowed and smiled her apology for passing in front of her. It was obvious to the amazed assembly where Sterrin O'Carroll's sympathy lay.

Sister Mary Aliquo recovered her composure at last. 'Miss Sterrin O'Carroll!' she called, but Miss Sterrin O'Carroll had taken the forbidden Grand Staircase two steps at a time and was now at Reverend Mother's door.

In the act of knocking she halted to recover her breath. There must be no more headlong entrances.

'Reverend Mother,' she said when she had been summoned inside, 'I wish to renounce my vows.'

Reverend Mother's lips twitched. 'I was not aware that you had taken any vows.'

'I mean—I wish to renounce my decision to take vows.'

Reverend Mother refrained from pointing out that the decision to take vows did not rest entirely with the aspirant.

'What has prompted this sudden change?' she asked.

Sterrin glanced through the window. A group of tiny children were playing on the croquet lawn. One little girl reminded her of Dominic. She had fair hair and brown eyes and the same helpless air. Probably lonely, Sterrin thought. She was one of those boarders whose papas were campaigning in the Crimea and whose mammas had gone to be near them. Sterrin knew that Dominic must be lonely, too.

She turned away. She had meant to express her disapproval to disassociate herself utterly, from the scene she had witnessed downstairs. Instead, to her amazement, to her horror, she heard her own voice saying, 'I wish to get married and have children of my own.'

CHAPTER 37

Nurse Hogan made off with the post bag that lay on the butler's table. Hegarty would be furious but he was up to his eyes in silver polish and her Ladyship could not bear to be kept waiting to know if there was a letter from Miss Sterrin.

She riffled through the fashion catalogues that continued to pour in from London since the Sir's assassination. Themselves and their claims to supply the 'most Lugubrious Appurtenances of mourning. Widows' bonnets weighed to the ground with crepe; mourning rings; lockets to hold the "loved one's hair——"' Suddenly, incredibly, she found herself reading an envelope addressed to Mrs. Hogan, Housekeeper, Kilsheelin Castle. Who in wonder would be writing to *her*? She that hadn't a soul belonging to her since the night of the Big Wind that had robbed her of husband and child!

After ten minutes of speculating that ranged back to her childhood Nurse Hogan decided that the only way to find out who the letter was from was to open it.

Lady O'Carroll, coming through the communication door—the nurse now occupied Sir Roderick's dressing-room—was startled to see the woman who was the bulwark of her life sitting with her face in her hands. But the nurse looked up to the sound of the bells and keys in the chatelaine belt and her eyes were shining. 'It is from Young Thomas, your Ladyship. He is not in Van Diemen's Land; not in prison. He is in America; doing well!'

The news brought no added light to Lady O'Carroll's brown eyes. She murmured some remark that approved his liberty but left no doubt that there her approval ended.

The nurse had finished her reply and was sanding over the envelope when a hackney fly drew up on the gravel. She peeped through the window then with a cry she ran to the next room.

'It is Miss Sterrin, your Ladyship!'

Margaret skimmed across the landing, then suddenly stopped.

351

Nurse Hogan was saying something about having to open her letter and change it—— 'And I had barely finished writing to Young Thomas that Miss Sterrin had left us for ever to take the veil.'

Margaret turned back and faced her purposefully. 'Nurse, do not alter what you have written. Let your letter go as it is.' She moved down a step, then stopped. 'And Nurse,' Margaret was no longer the uncertain personality who leaned upon her companion-nurse-housekeeper, 'I do not wish you to mention to the staff—or'—she glanced towards the hall door—'*anyone* that you have heard from—America. Do you understand?'

The nurse looked beyond her mistress to where a young gentlewoman, with friendly but sure authority, was tossing an order to the butler about paying the hackney driver and seeing to a feed for his animal 'before it drops dead'. Sterrin then ran with arms extended towards her mother.

Nurse Hogan, standing respectfully apart, addressed to the back of her mistress's bombazine gown, 'Yes, your Ladyship. I understand.' She dropped the letter into the leathern post satchel, locked it with her own hands, then handed it to Big John. At Templetown the postmaster, and none but he, would open the bag with his own key. No one at Kilsheelin would ever read the address on that envelope.

Not since the days before the tragedy had Margaret sat up so late. When Sterrin finally reached her bedroom, she found Mrs. Stacey herself drawing the bedwarmer vigorously up and down between the sheets. Hannah wanted to know was there anything else Miss Sterrin required. She half regretted the query when Miss Sterrin actually asked for a bath. Hot water at this hour of the night and the fires ashed down!

But nothing was too much trouble to take for Miss Sterrin. The servants hadn't realised until after she had vanished so inexorably, how much she had meant to them. It was not, they realised, her Ladyship, vague and remote; and certainly not the little 'young sir' timid beyond his years, who was the head of the house. It was the tall, poplar-straight girl with the darkening hair, darkening her looks into a replica of her father's.

With Miss Sterrin the servants sustained the old, homogeneous relationship that had existed between their forebears and hers; an association based upon a tradition of shared disasters in life and hearth, and in creed sustained; unifying master

352

nd man in mood and outlook. That spirit was not in her Lady-ship; no more than in the ordinary gentry. But it was in Miss Sterrin; inculcated into her blood, fostered in her mind by her father and by the bard.

Mrs. Stacey went on drawing the long handle up and down although the bed was as warm as a thrush's nest. She was on thorns to 'draw' Miss Sterrin about what had prompted her to give in at last just when her Ladyship and Mr. Maurice had withdrawn all further opposition and decided that she must have received a True Call. She ducked as a shift came flying over the screen and landed with a slosh at her feet.

'If only I had known you were coming I'd have had hot bricks in the bed all week.' She looked hopefully towards the screen and her eyebrows went up under the frills of her white cap. A long, shapely leg was protruding in mid-air beyond the screen.

The cook had been muting her tones to suit the cloister that still must cling to the body in the hip bath. And here was half that body up in the air—the second leg was there now—stark naked!

Sterrin contemplated her limbs with satisfaction. The clammy rule that had insisted upon her retaining a garment during her bath had irked her at the convent. She waggled her legs. She was free! No cloistering garments. Nothing would ever again induce her to risk her freedom. No matter *what* happened. And nothing ever again could be as terrible as the things that *had* happened.

Sterrin slipped back into youth's heritage. Life stretched out endlessly before her. The desolateness of the bard's passing had cleared from the air. The loneliness for Young Thomas still lingered; but locked in a secret compartment; not weighing her down all the time. Her stay in the convent had given her the strength to shoulder her crosses high. She was glad to be home, and Margaret was delighted to have her back. For she blamed her preoccupation with her own grief for much of Sterrin's unhappiness. Now she fussed over her; took her with her to pay calls. Once again there was a cosy family atmosphere at meals, with Margaret at the head of the table and young Sir Dominic and Sterrin at either side. Margaret even set her music boxes in motion and their tinkling made harmony with the crackling of pear logs on hearths that had lain so long empty. Sterrin felt encompassed with love and protection. Except for that raw, secret place that held her love for Young Thomas.

To forget him was impossible. Once when she fell asleep thinking of their last morning together she was awakened by the stable clock striking four. She jumped from the bed dazedly thinking that it was time for their parting rendezvous. She had started to dress before she realised that she had been dreaming, but she completed her dressing and went out.

As she stood beneath the wall gap with the whole world to herself she deliberately relived that last parting. In the convent she had crushed down its memory. Now she went over everything that he had said and all the things that she ought to have said to him as a quiet brightness crept over the sky. As on that last morning the birds began their faint cheep-cheep until the first ray of sun beamed over the top of the hill above the castle, then the birds leapt from their nests. The grasshoppers awakened and were busy at a stroke. There was a sudden stir in the air that sent her springing up to stand where she and Thomas had stood in the wall gap.

In the field across the road she could see the caps of mushrooms thrusting upwards almost before her very eyes. She was startled to see a blaze of light moving over the slope; but it was only the tin can of a mushroom picker reflecting the sunlight. The sight sent a challenge to her blood that routed melancholy. 'Whoever you are,' she cried, 'I was here first.' She put two fingers beneath the white cap of a mushroom. 'Pretty,' she murmured, 'but you'll be prettier perched on a nice big slice of bacon.'

The thought sent the juices coursing through her gums. She picked a 'trauneen' and strung the mushrooms through its stem like a daisy chain. Her shoes became saturated; but her hair and hands and heart were warming where little floating clouds turned to liquid gold like fairy ships across the deepening blue. Her lips smiled with the smiling morn. She looked no farther ahead than the breakfast of sizzling bacon with the mushrooms that would taste as no other mushroom because she had found them for herself and plucked them out of the dawn's magic.

A whoosh and a bump after the last throb of the breakfast bell proclaimed that Sir Dominic was arriving down the banisters. Then a wafting movement bore the tall slender figure of Lady O'Carroll into the room. Sterrin, rising at her entrance, watched the black swaying that seemed to propel her mother without effort of limbs. Young Thomas had made her aware of the impression; something from a poem by his idol Mr. Davis. 'Her step would scarcely bruise the flowers.' Young Thomas! A cloud soughed by.

'Mamam!' called Sir Dominic. 'May I have breeches?'

'Why, darling, what is the hurry? You are barely past ten.'

'One of the English boys staying at Strague is only nine and a half and *he* has breeches.'

'In another while, darling.'

'Huh! I suppose when the "Morgidge" is paid.' He was promised everything that he asked for 'when the mortage would be paid off'.

Sterrin glanced sideways at him. He had played so long with childish things that he was still regarded as a baby. But he was growing tall. 'Yes, Maman,' she agreed, 'he really ought to be breeched.'

'If I'm not breeched I shall not go to Strague any more,' he announced in a surprisingly firm tone. 'Those English boys keep pulling up my petticoats to see whether I am a boy or a girl.'

Lady O'Carroll choked over her *café-au-lait*. 'Nevair shall you go there again! You shall have a tutor at once.'

'If we can afford one,' said Sterrin grimly. 'Every quarter's day staff is being paid off. I could take over his lessons and he can go to Master Hennessey for Latin.'

Her mother frowned, 'Master Hennessey! He is too—too *du peuple* to impart a classical education to a gentleman's son.'

Sterrin pointed out that he had not been too *du peuple* to give Papa a grounding in the classics before he went to college in England.

A long sigh and a faraway look reminded Sterrin that she had said the wrong thing. Her mother had gone off again down the corridor of memories. It was the same always. Sterrin dare not mention her father's name. She cast about for some safer argument and almost said that Master Hennessey had made a success of teaching the classics to Young Thomas. Young Thomas! Her own sigh mingled with her mother's.

'Look!' cried Dominic, 'it is the fellow with the death message.' He ran to the window. Behind him Sterrin saw that the woman at the lodge was behaving strangely. She had let a vehicle through the gates and instead of returning to the lodge she had dropped on her knees.

Hegarty glanced through the window then hurried to open the hall door. 'The young Sir is right,' he gasped. ' 'Tis the invention that comes when someone is dead.'

Sterrin, framed in the dining-room, was like a stone. The kitchen staff were already crowding the inner hall and someone was whispering. 'It is Mr. Maurice.'

Who else could it be but Cousin Maurice? Whom Sterrin had hated because he had dismissed Young Thomas! Cousin Maurice whose anxious, pleading visits to the convent had but strengthened her resolve to stay there. Who would look after things now? The whole structure of the family would collapse. Already the servants showed signs of going to pieces.

Nurse Hogan hurried forward to take up her place behind her Ladyship. Margaret's fingers crawled towards the sinister, pinkish slip that Hegarty proffered on a shaky salver. The cook had her mouth open for the keen when Sterrin's exclamation cut through the tension. 'May the devil ride buck hunting with Cousin Maurice; arriving by the six o'clock train indeed!'

The telegram boy deemed it no breach of official trust to divulge the contents of the telegram to the Kilsheelin tenants as he drove home. It was friendly and nice to be able to reassure people that there was no bad news. But maybe the news *was* bad! There were queer rumours afloat about Kilsheelin Castle. Maybe this little pink letter from the castle's administrator was the forerunner of the big yellow poster that appeared on the gates of mansions that are forced on to the Encumbered Estates market! And if the owners were forced out the tenants were forced out also, and so the telegram might still be a death message.

Indeed, when Maurice O'Carroll spread out the documents that were the cause of his sudden visit on the table, Sterrin's heart gave a queer thump. 'The Commissioners For the Sale of Encumbered Estates in Ireland,' she read. 'Kilsheelin Castle, situate in the Eli-Fogarty and the Eli-O'Carroll ... the said castle...' There was a list of figures and then stipulations of rentals like offerings of cattle and tuns of wine 'together with one fat beefe and two fat wedders and two pairs of fat capons as ascates ... payable to the prince...' There was a list of tenants' names that were as familiar to Sterrin as her rosary. Lady O'Carroll kept interrupting her as she read them, to make inconsequential remarks like 'Isn't that the mother of the girl who married that good-looking farmer from the Queen's County? Wasn't it a "love match"?'

Sterrin forgot the significance of the document as she noticed a reference to a shooting right granted one hundred and forty years ago to The O'Meara. 'Oh, listen,' she cried. 'It says here that The O'Meara's daughter Tibina was married to the father of Dominic O'Carroll of Strague. Wasn't he the father of the one who was cast out of his castle with nothing but the silver drinking cups that he got from the Empress Mari Therèsa?'

Maurice sighed impatiently. 'You can come out of the past, Sterrin; all of you; of us,' he corrected. 'The mortgage company is foreclosing. The castle is about to be placed on the Encumbered Market.'

Sterrin looked at him; incredulous. This was the kind of thing that happened to others; not to oneself. And then she remembered how she had thought that murder was a faraway unlikely kind of horror, yet it had happened to her—here. But now Papa's murder had become another piece of the historicity of Kilsheelin. The castle was all the more hallowed because it had happened.

She sprang up with a cry, 'Are you mad, Cousin Maurice? Kilsheelin must never be sold.'

'Of course Kilsheelin must never be sold.' Lady O'Carroll's voice was brisk and matter-of-fact. 'You must explain to those persons, Maurice, that Kilsheelin has got to be here for Dominic's coming-of-age.'

Maurice looked at her pityingly. A body could not show exasperation to so much gracious beauty; and such undiminishing beauty at that. She was more damned appealing than ever.

'Margaret, my dear,' he said gently, 'the Commissioners for the Encumbered Estates will not wait for Dominic. There will be no more comings-of-age at Kilsheelin.'

The brown eyes looked wildly round the room. 'Coming-of-age!' The phrase cut sharp through her vagueness; down to the bone of her memory of the tragic return from that last coming-of-age party. Roderick's night of triumph; Roderick's night of death; Roderick's blood on a white ball-gown!

'No,' she said quietly. 'No more coming-of-age.' She put her hand to the back of her head. Sterrin flinched as her father's name sounded out in that long drawn 'Roder-eeck!' And Sterrin knew that she was alone again to face whatever was ahead! And as she bade goodbye to her kinsman he held her hand long in his and studied her face. The spittin' image of her father. A real O'Carroll bred true to the bone. A pity she wasn't the heir. My sorrow, he reminded himself, heir to what?

He leaned out and kissed her again. 'God bless you child! You are having a hard passage. You were born in storm and named for storm. 'Twas the Liberator's idea, that name of yours, I wonder was it wise? I always hold that a name influences a person's life and the dear knows your life seems cast in a stormy mould.'

Without thinking why, she jerked up her chin. 'I'll weather the storm,' she said.

He looked at the determined young face and sighed. 'If you had half as much money as you have spirit you'd weather anything. I must hurry now,' he said, 'or I won't catch this train. A pity they did not bring the iron road along past this way to Templetown. It would have brought some prosperity. Any more word about it?'

'Not that I've heard.'

'Well, goodbye again, girl. I'll do my best with this damned Commission tomorrow.'

That night, as Hannah gave Miss Sterrin's hair its hundred strokes, she kept losing count with the dint of trying to sound out about Mister Maurice's visit. 'Eighty-four, eighty-six, wasn't it a profane sort of thing to send that death telegram into a peaceful house and it only to say he was comin' on a visit? Bad scran' to that telegram boy! A gentleman's life he has. Three shillings and six pence a week and the use of a pony; just to bring bad news! He'd have earned his money in the famine. The Banshee needs no wages. Ninety-ninety-one——'

'You are cheating, Hannah. It is eighty-seven and I've a crick in my neck.' Sterrin was seated at the open window with her hair flowing over her face. Hannah slowed the strokes. 'Miss Sterrin gra'. It's not——' She faltered. 'It's not lookin' for newses that I am, but'—she scraped her throat—'is there any truth in the rumour that Kilsheelin is for the Encumbrancy auction?'

Sterrin remained silent.

'Kilsheelin is hearth and home to all of us,' Hannah said. 'We'd die for it. If this terrible thing is true we'll start prayin'

358

downstairs and we won't stop until our prayers have pierced the clouds.'

'Then start praying.'

Hannah, watching the enmarbled tensity of the features and the long hair flowing over the white wrapper, was minded of a statue in a church; except that Miss Sterrin wasn't looking exactly like a saint.

'Start praying, Hannah,' she repeated. 'But God likes a little help; so while you are piercing the clouds I'll pierce the soil.'

'The soil, Miss Sterrin?'

'Aye, the soil, Hannah. The soil that was taken from us the night that I was born. I'll get it back sod by sod. And once it is back, Kilsheelin will never be taken from me or mine.' She threw her wrapper across the room. 'Get me my riding things.'

'Miss Sterrin, where are you thinkin' of goin' this hour of the night?'

'To Poolgower.'

'But——'

'Don't argue with me.'

A few minutes later she went flying down the backstairs. Big John, from his room over the coach-house, saw her and hurried down. Had she decided to go back to the convent?

When she told him her mission he ventured no remonstrance. Maybe there was madness in the escapade, but there was no denying, he reflected as he watched her go, savouring the flying harmony of horse and rider, that there was some connection between the ups and downs of Poolgower and Kilsheelin. Poolgower was prospering and expanding while Kilsheelin Castle ... He turned away. There were things in the world beyond the wit of man. Mag Miney had been sleek and fed throughout the famine. Her handful of potatoes had never blackened when regiments of potatoes belonging to respectable men had turned to evil-smelling slime.

Yet, he wished Miss Sterrin good luck on her strange errand. One big sod to divide into four to bind the corners of the field the Big Wind had lifted away, that could do it, Big John thought. Perhaps that sod could change the luck of the O'Carrolls, could keep Kilsheelin free for the young Sir and for the gallant girl galloping off into the night.

CHAPTER 38

The watcher in the shadows of the trees relaxed. The marauder was a girl! There was no need to pounce or summon aid. A whinny from the pastures behind him brought forth a strange whinny from the weather-belt of trees where the girl moved stealthily. It was then he discerned the horse. Its docile pacing acknowledged its owner rather than the rein that hung loosely over her elbow.

It was the horse he recognised first. Who didn't know that horse? A bit long in the tooth but still the finest looking animal in the North Riding. So that's who the girl is! But what is she doing at Poolgower at this hour of the night?

She came out into the full moonlight. With a quick sweep of her arm she drew the reins in a double loop round it then dropped to her knees. For a moment he did not heed her strange behaviour because her hood had fallen back and a shaft of moonlight made little sparkles through the waving tendrils and curls of her hair. The horse moved nearer and dropped his muzzle into the silky coil of the nape of her neck.

'Thuckeen! you greedy girl, my hair is not hay.' She wriggled her head and when she turned with a laugh to push away the questing head she saw the young man.

'It is indeed an unexpected honour to have Miss Sterrin O'Carroll trespass upon our lands,' Donal Keating said coldly.

If he expected her to jump confusedly to her feet he was mistaken. She continued to kneel for a few seconds and the gaze that met his was as cold as his own. He could not see the flush that was warming through the magnolia-tinted cheeks because her face was masked with moonlight.

So this was the youngest Keating, she thought as she rose; the one studying law at Trinity! A pity he is not there studying it now instead of trying to impress his knowledge of it on me! With a faint but perceptible movement she avoided the hand that shot out involuntarily to assist her to her feet. 'I am glad that you appreciate the honour,' she said haughtily.

The moon was behind him so his flush also remained unrevealed. 'It would have been still more appreciated,' he replied, 'had you paid your call at a more conventional hour.'

The moonlight did not mask the raised eyebrows and the curled lip as she swept a quick glance towards the house that was steadily expanding into a small mansion. The glance despised his home, and her tone, when she replied, dismissed the suggestion that it could ever aspire for a place on her list of social calls. 'When I pay calls,' she said icily, 'I observe the customary conventions.'

Anger spurred him a step nearer. 'Perhaps Miss O'Carroll can afford to break this convention; but she must not assume that she can afford to break the law with equal impunity. Not only have you trespassed here, you have been guilty also of an act of malicious damage.' He pointed to the square of lea sod she had cut from the ground. For a moment he looked at it with naïve curiosity. What on earth was the girl up to? More of her high-spirited whims! 'Do you realise,' he demanded, 'that it is a serious breach of the law to ... to ...' he floundered, 'to mutilate my father's land like that?'

'*Your* father's?' Her scorn lashed. 'Do you think I recognise his ownership? As for mutilation; that is a subject in which I am not so well versed as you and your family.' She pushed something like a trowel into a saddlebag and gave a fastidious flick with both wrists to shake the soil from her gloved fingers.

Before he could answer she had her foot in the stirrup and the impulse to offer assistance left him at a loss for words. But she had swung on to the saddle and jerked the horse's head away from him so that all that was left for him to do was to stoop for the discarded sod of earth.

'Hadn't you better take your plunder?' he asked.

She looked down at him. 'I've changed my mind. I think, after all, that you had better regard my call as a belated return for the one your family paid ours some years ago. By all accounts it was rather unconventional. Particularly the style of visiting dress. The shirts, strange to say, were worn on the *outside* of the coats. Come on, Thuckeen!'

She set the horse at a gallop for the gate and the breath went out from young Keating in a long, low whistle. No horse had ever jumped that gate before and no rider had ever made the

361

venture. Ye gods! What a jump! What a nerve!

He stood bemused until the hoof-beats had receded, then slowly moved towards the house. As he passed the drawing-room windows he could see his sister-in-law working over her ivory miniature painting. Poor Denise! Life would be deucedly dull for her if it were not for her lovely miniatures. He decided to go in and afford her some sociability. She no longer got any from James since there was no sign of her producing the blue-tinted stock he had hoped for when he sacrificed a rich match to marry a penniless aristocrat.

Donal's father was sitting beyond the fireplace reading the *Tipperary Champion*; and on a low, armless chair in front of the blaze his mother turned now and again to fish out embroidery threads from the well of a mother-of-pearl work table.

Hmph! thought the young man taking in the scene. And this is beneath the recognition of a social call from HER! The arrogant marauder! The tasteful drawing-room of his ladylike mother and his aristocratic sister-in-law! That one wants cooling!

A cloud of smoke puffed out from the big armchair that faced his father and Donal changed his mind about going in to cheer his sister-in-law. Cheer did not thrive in the atmosphere of smug, purse-proud brother James.

A maid was drawing in the French windows in the dining-room. He beckoned to her and made a sign towards the hall door. She nodded and let him in soundlessly. His foot was on the second step of the stairs when the high, thin voice of James called out, 'Is that you, Donal?'

Donal threw a 'yes' over his shoulder and continued up the stairs. The high, thin voice called again, 'Would it be too much trouble to you to come into the room and answer?'

The grace went out of the night as Donal stood in the doorway and faced his brother. The room was filled with the smell of the strong tobacco that belched unchecked from the pipe and clouded the bowed head of the artist.

'Was that someone I heard riding in the "skeugh" field?' The small field that had been surfaced by a windfall on the night of the Big Wind sixteen years before was now distinguished from the many fields that had since been acquired by the deprecatory term 'skeugh', used to describe the hairy grass that grows upon the light soil of boggy land.

Donal did not feel like discussing with his brother the dazzling vision he had just seen disappearing in mid-air over the gate. 'From where I was,' he answered noncommittally, 'I could not hear whatever you heard from here.'

His father pushed his glasses down his nose. 'Can't you answer your brother naturally, Donal?' James spat across his mother's skirt folds into the flowered spittoon.

'The trouble with him is that he can't answer anyone naturally. That's what comes of college and professors at his elbow.'

Their mother's small, shapely hand that had acquired softness too late to uncoil the work-gnarled veins, halted over the work-table in the pointing gesture of enlightenment. 'I'll tell you who it was,' she cried. 'When Bridget was lighting the candles she told me she saw Miss O'Carroll of Kilsheelin pulling in her horse and looking over the hedge at our land. Would it be a thing that she rode in?'

Her husband put down the newspaper. 'Many's the time I saw her father doin' the same thing when he thought no one was looking. Maybe you're right Ma'am. I'll hold a crown 'twas she was in it. They say she has all his ideas. If it were not for her red hair a body would think 'twas himself riding past.'

'Maybe,' said James, ' 'twas trowin' one of *his* begrudging looks at the "skeugh" she was too. A small man he was to begrudge a handful of hairy grass and soil that happened to blow down on a gale of wind....'

'James, don't talk like that,' his mother interrupted. ' 'Twas no stray but God's Own Hand that dropped good soil on a poor field. It is the best one that we have.'

'Well,' he answered with slow portent, 'we'll soon have more where that came from.' His father lowered the newspaper and the ladies stopped working. 'Another windfall from Kilsheelin to Poolgower. The castle is coming on to the Encumbered Estates Market.' James drew loudly on his pipe and let out a great blast of smoke. It fell over his wife like a pall.

She put up her hand to move it aside. Would she ever get used to this horrid smoke? Papa had never smoked in the drawing-room; and never a pipe. His cigars were specially imported even after the Temperance movement had ruined him and caused him to attempt suicide in one of the beer vats in his own brewery. Kilsheelin to come under the Encumbered Estates Act! That proud, ancient citadel! What would become of the lovely Lady O'Carroll and her lovely daughter? She looked through the smoke at her husband. So *he* was planning to buy their estate! For half nothing as he had bought her own father's land; as he had bought herself.

Through the smoke her eyes caught her husband's. She sensed his thoughts. He is wishing that he had waited. The look of pride in the possession of a well-bred wife no longer glowed in those cold, pale eyes.

Denise was right. James was thinking about Sterrin O'Carroll. If only he had waited, he might have bought in the daughter of the castle as a job lot with her family's acres. A mettlesome purchase! But what a possession for a man forbye this colourless sample of gentility who produced bits of painted ivory instead of children.

Donal went from the room, sickened. He, too, had observed the baleful brooding in his brother's eyes. Would the man never be sated? And greater than his passion to possess was his passion to dispossess.

Donal struck the tinder box and carried his candle upstairs, musing on every step over the strange visitor; the strangely lovely visitor and her strange behaviour. The peasants, he reflected, were not the only ones who cut a sod of their native heath to bring with them into exile. If it was true that the estate was really coming on to the Encumbrancy market, it might just be likely that she might wish to take a piece of that famous field as a souvenir. He had known sentimental young ladies who had taken a memento of their dispossessed land to cherish in their trinket boxes. But there was nothing mawkish about that flaming divinity; *nor* about that whacking great dollop of soil she had dug up.

Pakie Scally and Big John watched Sterrin gallop towards the gate. A pity, Pakie thought, as he watched the shadow of horse and rider looming over the moonlit grass, that Miss Sterrin's ringlets had to be put up. It used to stir him strangely to see them flying in the wind as she rode. The long black tail and the mane of the horse and the rider's flaming ringlets used to make a great, stormy outflinging.

He opened the gate for manner's sake. Miss Sterrin would not take time to ride through a gate.

'The young Sir wouldn't do it better,' Big John murmured as

Thuckeen came over the bay hedge without touching a leaf.

'He'll never do it as good,' said Pakie.

Big John looked back at him over his twisted shoulder. 'It wasn't Sir Dominic I was thinkin' of.'

Sterrin tossed him the reign and slid down. 'I had my journey for nothing, Big John.' She felt foolish. Her marvellous scheme to save them all was a child's fantasy. She felt like crying on Big John's shoulder as she had done as a child. But the poor hunched-up shoulder seemed to look to *her* for support. Everyone looked to her. Dominic, sweet and over-childish. Mamma, she looked towards her mother's window. In the moonlight the broken turret seemed to lean towards her too.

'He caught me, Keating's son; down on my knees.'

'James's James?'

'No, the other one.'

'Master Donal?'

'Master!' Her scorn lashed him.

'It is just that he is college-bred, Miss Sterrin, and ... God forgive me, he looks so like a gentleman that ...'

'That you give him a gentleman's title. And to have that parvenu catch me; me! on my knees, on his land! And the worst of it is that I didn't get my big sod, just a little bit of clay with shamrocks.'

'But, Miss Sterrin, 'twas the Sir's own land. 'Twas our land that you were kneeling on. All the same,' he added to himself, 'I'd rather 'twas standing you were.'

'I know what I'll do,' Sterrin was remounting Thuckeen. 'I'll go back. He'll be inside now telling James's James how he spied on me. I'll go back and dig out our sod.'

'Ah, wait until tomorrow,' Big John urged. 'It's tired you are and time for bed.'

Sterrin laughed and patted the hand that lay on her shoulder. 'Go off to your "horsery", Big John. Do you remember when we used to say that?'

The big man looked down at her tenderly. He was seeing the little girl pressed against the window bars of the nursery that was on a level with his own apartment over the coach-house. She used to believe that coachmen slept in 'horseries' just as little girls slept in nurseries. 'Amn't I always remembering that, Miss Sterrin, blait?'[1]

[1] 'Blossom', a term of endearment.

Donal at his window slowly unbuttoned the ruffled shirt and gazed across the field. Maybe she would return! the leaves and branches of a silver birch were wrought into filigree by the moon's silvering. In an oval space framed by the tracery he visioned her face, lovelier than any he had ever seen in his life. But, oh, its scorn! She had looked him as if he were one of the hordes of new beggars that had emerged from the famine with all self-respect gone.

His indignation at her contempt had cooled under James's earth-binding methods. James always spat more fulsomely and spoke more flatly in the presence of his younger brother's gentility. When Donal had reascended the stairs after the drawing-room interview he was no longer the fashionable young legal blade resenting the scorn of a spoilt beauty. He had become the brother of a land-bloated farmer, presuming to his betters.

The sound of hoof-beats came into the silence. They were coming this way. He craned through the window. It was only Doctor Masterson's grey horse cantering past. Donal turned away. 'Visions,' he said to his dog, Bran, 'are not vouchsafed like Hippodrome performances, twice nightly.'

Donal eased out of his tightly stylish pantaloons and pushed his red setter off the night-robe spread out on the quilt. Ten minutes later Bran had decided that he had indulged his master's inconsiderate treatment long enough safely to resume his place on the bed, he heard his name from the pillows. Bran paused guiltily in the crouch of a spring. His master never spoke to him after the candle was this long quenched. 'Bran, you're not fooling me and neither is she, for all her arrogance. She's just a pathetic migrant cutting a nostalgic sod to carry over the ocean.' He turned on his left side and Bran crouched again for the spring. But it was the master who sprang. The covers were thrown back violently. 'Don't follow me,' he said as he put on his dressing-gown, and tiptoed to the door.

The silver surface had been scraped from the landscape by the sharp edge of dawn. It took a few moments before Donal realised that horse and rider were back. Sterrin had returned for her sod. The gap from which it had been cut made a void in the surrounding grey-green but the sod was nowhere in sight. Bran had followed Donal after all, and as Sterrin's slane gripped deep in the earth, the dog bounded out of the shadow.

'Down, dog!' Sterrin said calmly. It's great red plume went

366

waving in delighted apology. She stooped and patted its head.
'You are a beauty,' she said. Before she could straighten up the
animal was on its hind legs and his tongue had stroked her from
chin to brow. A hand reached for the dog's collar and Donal,
his heart pounding violently, said, 'Forgive him, Miss O'Carroll. Tonight he is but human.'

She faltered in the act of mounting. Where on earth had he
appeared from? Why wasn't he inside sleeping? Her foot resumed the stirrup and he came to her side.

'He shall be punished. Shall I shoot him for his profaning?'

She placed her knee over the crutch of the side-saddle and
arranged her skirt and cloak as though he were not there. 'Yup,
Thuckeen,' she crooned. As the horse moved Sterrin looked
down into eyes filled wide with an admiration that the moon
could not hide. 'Do as you please with your own animals. But if
you must continue to make dumb brutes suffer, don't maim the
dog—as you maimed our cattle. Shoot it clean—if you can.'

He stood watching her as she clattered down the road. 'Devil
a fear, my lovely lady, that you won't forget to shoot clean:
clean through the bull's eye.'

Sterrin streaked home once again, defeated for the second
time. The sod lay there ready to be taken, when he appeared.
Sterrin wondered if Donal spent every night in that field. She
took the bay hedge recklessly and Thuckeen's breathing
laboured loud as she cleared the jump.

'You've pushed her hard, Miss Sterrin,' said Big John taking
the horse from her.

'See that Thuckeen gets a good rub down.' She was curt with
him. 'I'm going to bed. I'm very tired.'

At the door Pakie caught up with her. 'Miss Sterrin, beggin'
your pardon, but where will I put this for the time being?' He
was holding a big grassy sod of earth. She looked at it in amazement. It was the one she had cut. 'Where did you find it?'

'Sure, didn't you bring it back with you, Miss Sterrin? When
I took the empty bag from the mare's saddle I thought that you
had your journey for nothing. Then when I unslipped the
saddle girths this fell to the ground.'

And she had never noticed it in her fury. No wonder
Thuckeen had been straining, with *that* banging against her
flank! Tiredness vanished.

'You'll put it no place "for the time being". It is going this minute into the ground where it belongs; for all time. Will you lend a hand, Big John?'

'That I will, Miss Sterrin, with a heart and a half.'

The three of them walked over to the field of the Big Wind. When the last of the four corners had received a piece of the earth that had been stripped from it seventeen years ago, Big John rose stiffly to his feet, removed his hat and said solemnly, 'God send that I may never go out from this place with my soul in my body.'

Pakie uncovered and replied, 'Amen to that.'

Sterrin started to say 'Amen', but a sleepy yawn stifled the sound.

CHAPTER 39

The Commissioners held their melancholy auctions. Lord Templetown's mansion was knocked down to a Liverpool coffin-ship owner. Lord Templetown, beggared by the famine that had enriched his successor, went to live in Dublin.

No one knew who bought Major Darby's estate; no one cared. The famine had not spared him, but unlike Lord Templetown, he had not been softened by it. He saw the tenants he had been compelled to feed as the cause of his downfall. A tenant was simply a rent-paying machine; to have his rent raised or to be evicted. Darby had but to see a new garment on a tenant's child to have an excuse to raise the rent. If it could not be met the tenant and his family were evicted.

Sterrin, riding with Big John who was schooling Sir Dominic on a stocky cob, was amazed to see the change in the Darby estate. Even during the brief months that she had been in the convent there had been wholesale clearance of whole colonies of houses.

'He might as well have left them in their homes,' she said, thinking aloud.

'Aye, Miss Sterrin.' Big John drew abreast, thinking she had addressed him. 'He knows what it is now to be turned from his own home. Thank God that you or yours will never know that fate.'

Maurice O'Carroll had staved off foreclosure with the prices from bits and pieces of land that were not included in the mortgage. But the staff in its relief gave credit for its reprieve to Miss Sterrin. It was her inspiration to take back the castle's plundered soil that had appeased the Fates!

A well-dressed man came through Major Darby's back gates and moved across to where an occasional gable or broken piece of wall marked the site of some twenty homesteads. They watched him as he moved among the ruins then he came towards them. He uncovered to Sterrin but addressed Big John.

'Could you direct me to the whereabouts of Mrs. Landy?'

His tone was grim.

Another upstart owner, Big John thought. A gentleman would not approach a servant and engage him in talk in the presence of his employer.

'Someone of that name went from here to the workhouse eight years ago,' Big John replied guardedly.

'But,' cried Sir Dominic, 'don't you know, Big John, that she has left the poorhouse. She is the woman who is living in the cave.' He pointed up towards the distant slopes where the broken wall of The O'Meara's castle sheltered the entrance to his descendant's cave dwelling.

Sterrin shot a fierce warning glance at her brother.

'I'm afraid we do not know anything of the person you seek. That cave has been occupied by a hermit for as long as anyone remembers. Isn't that right, Big John?'

The stranger saluted her but went purposefully in the direction of the cave.

'Sterrin, why did you tell that man a fib? You brought food to Mrs. Landy at that cave only yesterday.'

'Dominic, could you bid the devil to leave you alone? That new owner seems to be going about enforcing his privileges. He'll smoke Mrs. Landy out of the cave like a badger; maybe get The O'Meara arrested for sheltering her.'

Mrs. Landy's widowed daughter had taken her mother from the poorhouse and had paid the penalty. Derby had evicted her for sheltering an evicted tenant, even though the tenant was her own mother.

They followed at a distance. They saw the hermit come from the cave holding a fowling-piece menacingly.

'My God!' cried Sterrin. 'He'll hang for this. He's never gone that far before.'

Then she saw Mrs. Landy come to the door of the cave; giving herself up to avoid bloodshed.

Sterrin spurred Thuckeen. Over her shoulder she ordered Big John to take Sir Dominic home. 'He mustn't see this kind of thing.'

The O'Meara had sheltered many an outlaw in his cave; peacefully. But this was the first time that he had sheltered a woman. 'I possess the shooting rights over this ground,' she heard him say. The stranger could interpret that any way he liked.

'He is quite right,' Sterrin called out as she reined to. 'This is our land and he has the right to shoot. That woman is under his protection—and mine.'

The stranger uncovered again; more ceremoniously. 'Miss Sterrin, I have no objection to The O'Meara's shooting rights— as long as I am not the target.' He turned to the terrified woman. 'Do you not know me, Mother?'

Mrs. Landy knew her son, Dominic Landy, the Omadhawn of the Wren Boys' procession! Dominic Landy, whom Sterrin had seen marched off among the military when he had raided his own grain cart in the famine!

She rode homewards, bemused; as though she had been part of a dream that had come true. Big John who had not gone too far out of reach to miss the scene was wiping his eyes. He, too, remembered the day he had seen Mrs. Landy following her son as the military marched him towards his exile; for fifteen years. And now! After but eight years!

The horses went off at a gallop, then slowed, then galloped again as the thoughts of the riders set the tempo. One moment they recalled a procession that had wound down the Sir's Road; a hunger-maddened man, an anguished woman straining to keep up, straining to hold the sight of him within her vision. It had always remained as Sterrin's acutest impression of the famine. The weeping woman following the soldiers with their prisoner, his madness exhausted, held for her a suggestion of the procession to Calvary. And now—she spurred the horse—that woman was weeping again, in the arms of the man who owned the estate from which she had been hunted.

'It is a miracle, Miss Sterrin,' Big John said.

And miracles could happen again—to others. In the days that followed the thought kept pushing its way through all her other thoughts. She burned to hear details of this rags to riches romance. Her daily rides began to take her past the Darby estate. Would she ever come to think of it as the Landy estate? But Dominic Landy was not the type of new owner, all leather and whipcord and unaccustomed idleness, to ride a fine horse across his new acres; just for display. He was always in the midst of his workmen, lending a hand or supervising.

Once she saw him outside the church after Sunday Mass helping his mother into a phaeton. 'Mamma, don't you think that we ought to call on the Landy's?'

Her mamma was aghast. One did not call upon the new shopkeeper owners, the gombeen men! The ladies of the old order, shabby, even horseless, were more strongly entrenched in their feudal dignity than when these same shopkeepers came bareheaded to their carriage doors to take their orders. Not that Lady O'Carroll was shabby. Because the castle had escaped the Encumbrancy hammer, she felt encouraged to invest in some of the Sombre Elegance advertised in the catalogues. She had ordered Lubey to send away for some pairs of black silk boots with white satin tops. Today, Sterrin thought her mother looked dashing. She was wearing a daring innovation in mourning wear, white Widow's Cuffs beautifully embroidered in black.

Sterrin pointed out that Dominic Landy had never been a shopkeeper. 'He has been worse,' her mother said. 'He has been a convict.'

Sterrin was quelled. Her conscience pricked her as they drove home in the chill of Margaret's angry silence. It *had* been a bit much to suggest that Lady O'Carroll should call in her carriage upon the Wren Boys' Fool, who had pranced before her in his ridiculous sack disguise for the patronage of her festive food; and upon his mother whom she had fed in the Stirabout Line!

But Sterrin was determined to know how Dominic Landy had acquired the freedom to acquire the wealth. The next time her mother had a migraine that kept her to her room Sterrin purloined the phaeton and drove up to the ex-convict's splendid hall door. She prayed that Mrs. Landy, whom she had furtively fed in a cave a few weeks back, would not receive her at three o'clock in the afternoon in a low décolletée evening gown, all bejewelled, like the potato factors' wives did in some of the old mansions.

Mrs. Landy tiptoed to the door the way she had tiptoed through life for the past incredible weeks. Her starved neck and shoulders were decently covered in a black stuff gown. She clasped Sterrin's hand in both her own. Pathetically she apologised for her presumption in receiving her benefactor in this mansion; like an equal.

At last Sterrin got the story of their new fortune. Dominic had impressed the prison governor as being an honest, industrious man. The governor was one who had retained his humanity. He was capable of realising that the hungry Irish, deported for theft during the famine, were not criminals. It was a case of steal or starve. Dominic had proved to be so conscientious in carrying out his prison duties that he had been entrusted with book-keeping. When two years of his sentence had been served he was let out on parole as a shepherd. Soon he was herding his own sheep; buying his own land, and on that land, alone and unchallenged, he had found gold. By accident, at the London bank where he was depositing the money for the cargo of wool he had brought to England, on his way home he had seen the lists of Irish estates for sale under the Encumbered Estates conditions. English shopkeepers were being offered loans to purchase them. And out from that list stared the name of the man who had called him to his food with the cry 'Suck! ... Suck! ... Suck!' that brings pigs to their swill. More than his banishment, more than his cruel sentence, had the degradation of that summons rankled with Dominic during the lonely years of exile. Sterrin had witnessed the last act of that famine drama. But she had not got what she came for.

'By the way,' she said with great nonchalance as Dominic later assisted her into the phaeton. 'A former servant of ours was sent to penal servitude in Australia—oh, not by us—he was working in England at the time. Do you think he is likely to have his sentence remitted as yours was?'

When he had questioned her about the nature of Young Thomas's offence, Dominic shook his head slowly and with positive certainty. 'The prison authorities regard the like of that as the greatest criminality; worse than thieving, aye or worse sometimes, than murder. Employers out there won't take on "parole men" that have a record for agitation and disturbance among workers. The governor, in my time, wouldn't stand for any leniency to that type of prisoner. He put on my report when he let me out on parole that I was a useful citizen who had been mistreated. He would never consider one who rouses the workers against their employers as a "useful citizen". No, Miss Sterrin, he'll service his sentence—and maybe longer. By the time he is released he won't feel like making any more trouble.'

And that, she said to her face in the mirror that evening, is that! She scrutinised her features. You are going to stop cheapening yourself. You have your life to live. You went on living after your father was murdered. Servants have no right to stir up revolt against their employers. They have no right to—no right to stir up revolt in—she rubbed the glass to wipe a sudden mist but it still blurred her reflection; she wiped her eyes and her reflection swam back;—in the hearts of—of their employer's daughters.

She swirled on a sudden from the face in the mirror; shocked at what she had allowed it to hear. She crossed determinedly to the wash stand, sponged her face with buttermilk, damped down her hair from the rain water ewer until it looked smooth and dark. Then she returned to the mirror, 'Now,' she said to the face that looked out at her, 'that revolt has been successfully put down.' She tapped her heart. 'There shall be no more folly there. Do you hear?' She bent her face into the mirror and drew down her cheek. 'That wart must be seen to, also!'

Thomas peeped through the curtains and shuddered, 'Surely,' he said to the manager, 'you could have omitted that fairground clowning down here?' Beyond the curtain a German-American actor was delivering the inevitable Big Wind recitation in what was meant to be an Irish brogue.

It was the usual showman's trick to attract the Irish; a chair out in front between the acts, and while the scenes were being shifted, no matter how compelling the play, an actor quoting the crude lines '... the night of the "Big Wind" when rich men became poor and poor men became rich...' and for an encore some familiar lines that travestied the famine. The shoddy device never failed to strike an answering chord. It didn't fail tonight. Out through the sophisticated New Orleans audience that had flocked to see and hear the new young actor, rose the familiar reaction. Wherever Irishmen met Irishmen it was 'were you over there for the "gorta mor"' (The Great Hunger)? and then: 'Do you remember the night of the Big Wind?' The tragedies of Shakespeare were fine stirring things to witness; and all the high dramas of the actors' spoken word; but they were not as important as the famine to the men and women who had been both actors and spectators in its grim tragedy, and the dramas of the Big Wind.

They leaned across seats and swapped experiences and after the performance they came backstage and, as usual, the drama of their reminiscences topped the drama of the play. An elegantly dressed man and woman begged to introduce a young gentleman to the manager and to the actor who had spoken the trite entr'acte. The brogue fell softly from their lips as they told of how, two days after the Big Wind, when their emigrant ship was leaving Liverpool, a child of two was sighted crying on the rocks. It had been blown on to the rocks from heaven knows where during the Big Wind and had survived its two day ordeal. A young emigrant couple looked after it on the voyage. 'We are still looking after him,' they laughed. 'It was a Big Wind indeed that gave us a son, for we never had any children of our own.'

The manager escorted them to their carriage. He accepted their invitation to a dinner-party. 'I accepted for you, too,' he said to Thomas. Thomas told him curtly that he had other arrangements.

He had planned to go to his room to write to Kitty and Mark Hennessey, to ask their help in trying to find the woman who had brought him to Kilsheelin Castle in the weeks before the Big Wind. He had always been told that she had gone to America.

'Alter your arrangements,' the manager said.

'I do not take orders about my private arrangements.'

'Don't you indeed? Your—er—trifling successes appear to be sending you beyond yourself. This invitation was accorded to you as a member of my company. As such, I expect you to accept.' The manager threw a dramatic looking cloak about himself. 'It is an order,' he said, stalking off.

'Noises off stage,' said Thomas to his departing figure, 'rude ones.'

He went off to dine with the Liverpool couple. They sent a carriage for him. On the way, the carriage halted to let some wagons pass. Thomas's gaze rested idly on the splendid colonial type house they were passing and as they did, the door opened and a white-clad girl came gliding down the steps. She carried a rose trew on her arm and a piccaninny followed in attendance; just the way the piccaninny 'Young Thomas' used to walk in attendance behind the gliding form of Lady O'Carroll. He craned from the carriage. The girl was beautiful—not as beautiful as Sterrin. No girl could be that beautiful! The house that he would build for Sterrin would be more beautiful than this one. She would float down steps that would be wider, more cascading—but perhaps she might not turn into the floating type. He had to remind himself that when he had last seen her she was still displaying limbs; slender, but unfloatingly vigorous and with a tendency to take two steps at a time.

In the late of that afternoon he took the first step towards building his dream house. His host took him strolling through his grounds and his pastures and showed him great acreage of corn and cotton. 'I was born on a good County Kildare farm and I earned big wages here when I landed, but I told myself that I hadn't come to America to work on other men's land; so bit by bit, I bought my own.' He gave a big sigh. 'I bought too much. I thought I would have children to work and inherit but the one that I made my own has no taste for the land. You saw for yourself just now he is stage-struck. In another while it will be something else.' He pointed to uncultivated acres in the distance. 'I'm going to sell that. Why should I go on troubling myself? I had a mind to build a house there for him. But he is not interested. Someone will get a bargain.'

It was Thomas who got the bargain. A few days later he stood upon his own acres. Tossed on to his lap, he reflected, by the Big Wind that had tossed a poor little mite on to those Liverpool rocks. And to think that he had protested against that trite recitation about the 'Big Wind'. Had the manager agreed, and he had been tempted to suppress the shoddy little entr'acte, the landowner and his wife would never have ventured backstage with their foster-son. Things don't happen by accident. Thomas knew now for certain, and for all time, that his destiny was inextricably bound up with that night of storm that had brought Sterrin into his life.

As he looked up to where his land sloped gently, his enchanted eyes raised up a white house tall enough to meet the enclasping trees. Once he stood enraptured at the sight of a white Colonial-style mansion from which a white-clad girl had floated down the steps, a rose basket on her arm, a piccaninny in attendance. Now in his dreams another white-clad girl floated down the steps—she must float! The roses, somehow, were already in the trew and the little piccaninny carried the secateurs. Other piccaninnies whisked at flies, or made pretence— like Mickey-the-turf used to—of weeding the rose beds. And then, wraithlike, other children glided on to the scene; fair-skinned children with gold-red hair, or maybe black. His children and Sterrin's! He had made real his dream of becoming an actor. Why not this one, too?

Next evening Thomas was astounded to receive a visit from Big John Holohan of Upper Kilsheelin. John and his sweetheart, Molly, the dryad with the wondrous hair had been among a handful of survivors of five hundred passengers who had left Cove in a coffin ship that had justified its name. It had limped over the ocean for two months, all the time jettisoning daily the corpses of its plague-stricken passengers. Weak and horror-wrought, they had gone blindly to the destinations they had been directed to by the unscrupulous employment agents who met the boat. John and Molly were separated by the excited crowds at the pier. John found himself in Chicago, then a swampy village by the lakeside. His prosperity had grown with the village. His business acumen equalled his physical powers. He was a rich man; growing all the time richer and all the time he pursued an unremitting search for his lost sweetheart.

His search led him to New Orleans. This was the last address he had from her one and only letter. John brought Thomas a letter from Nurse Hogan which he had been carrying about for months.

The envelope was covered with crossed-out addresses where it had followed him about for months before being forwarded to John Holohan's address in Chicago. But he could still decipher the thin, reedy writing that had written many a list that he had dispatched with by Nurse Hogan. His fingers tingled at the paper's touch. There would be news of HER. There was bound to be some mention. Wasn't that the real reason that had prompted him to write to Nurse Hogan? Though the dear knows he would have written soon to the woman who had been like a mother to him 'The night of the Big Wind when poor men became rich and rich men became poor——' Nurse Hogan was surely one of those who had become poor that night—in a fearful way; husband, child, home! Thomas opened the envelope with great care.

John moved to the window and looked out to give him privacy. Thomas read quickly once, then again. He folded the letter and stared straight ahead. It was. He had reached the portals of Sterrin's world too late. He was a successful land-owner, a young man of property. He had built the bridge, but Sterrin was no longer waiting.

'Miss Sterrin has left us for ever to take the veil . . .' Nurse Hogan had written.

Sterrin was on her knees tending the sod in one of the four corners of the field of the Big Wind when the bianconi driver waved a letter at her from the gates. It was an invitation to join a house-party at the Delaneys for the Maryborough Horse Show; for the whole family, Lady O'Carroll, Sir Dominic and Sterrin. It was to be an informal, gay affair for young and old, a party like the ones that the De Laceys used to give before the famine. Sir Jocelyn Devine, the principal shareholder of the railway line, was bringing guests in a special train.

Sterrin suddenly recalled what Cousin Maurice had said about the railway line. Where it had cut through private property, the owners had been given big compensations. Not to mention the access it afforded to better markets and prices for their products! She must meet this Sir Jocelyn Devine.

Nurse Hogan joined forces with her to induce Lady O'Carroll to accept. The nurse pointed out that it was the only opportunity of dancing and gaiety that Miss Sterrin was likely to get. There were no more balls at Templetown House. The garrison ladies were off with their husbands at the Crimean war. A gombeen man lived in De Lacey's. A peasant farmer who was also an ex-convict owned Major Darby's estate. It was an opportunity to see the old friends and make new ones. But her Ladyship refused to break her mourning seclusion.

Sterrin rose to her feet. 'Very well, Mamma,' she said with an air of great resolve. 'I'm going back to the convent.'

Her mother assessed the scowl that had knit her daughter's brows into one black sweep across her forehead.

'Aren't you making rather a habit of it?' she countered.

'I mean it. This time I'll stay. At least I'll have companionship.' Lady O'Carroll found the last statement undisputable.

That afternoon they drove to Lubey's to order green velvet for a gown for Sterrin and to enquire why the black silk bootees with the white satin tops had not been delivered to Lady O'Carroll weeks ago.

They had not been delivered, Mr. Lubey explained as he accompanied the ladies to the door without offering to show the velvet, because Lady O'Carroll in her melancholy preoccupation with her lamentable bereavement may have overlooked the fact that her account was so long overdue. Perhaps when Lady O'Carroll's mind had been tranquillised by the settling of the account it would be possible to hasten those dilatory London

378

firms with the silk bootees, the velvet also.

Mr. Lubey's hint cut right down through the years and through the clouds of Lady O'Carroll's remoteness. '*Quelle audacitée!*' she gasped as the carriage rolled down the street. 'Do you realise Sterrin that the person was actually asking me to settle my account? Me!'

'He must be an optimist.'

'Sterrin, I consider your remark to be in very bad taste. Tell Big John to stop at Mr. Hoey's office and I shall instruct him to close Lubey's account.'

'Close it with what, Mamma? A crowbar?'

'Ster-een! Spare me your unladylike terms.'

'Well, perhaps, Mamma, it would have been more genteel had I said hammer—the auction hammer that knocks down the Encumbered Estates.'

'Sterrin, I do not see that the term hammer is any more refined than—crowbar. And I am not familiar with either.'

And I, thought Sterrin, am more familiar with the crowbar than I am with a croquet mallet.

Big John forgot to urge the horses. They paced to the tempo of his thoughts that grieved over his ladies having to return without the finery they had been refused by a gombeen man. They drove so slowly past one turning that involuntarily both ladies turned to glance down a tree-lined road that led to ornamental gates and white railings and beyond, the low roof and white walls of a house that stood embowered in the enclasping woods. The sight of the De Lacey's former home recalled the present owner, Lubey, the 'gombeen' man who had dared to slight Lady O'Carroll with his tradesman's talk. And all of a sudden the two wistful faces became as haughty and remote as though their owners could afford to cover the whole countryside with green velvet.

Hannah had the seamstress installed, waiting to get down to the velvet the moment it arrived. A few months back Sterrin would have blurted out what had happened. Now she said formally. 'Let her go, Hannah. I was unable to get the right shade.'

Upstairs she dropped formality. She went straight to the face in the mirror and gritted her teeth. 'I've got to meet Sir Jocelyn Devine. I must have a gown for that party.'

She rushed up to the attics and rummaged madly through the trunkfuls of bygone grandeur. Velvets, satins, brocades dissolved at her touch like the stuff of dreams. The Big Wind had saturated every trunk and pulped their contents into a gaudy *papier-mâché*.

She rose to her feet and sent the mess flying with a furious kick. It dislodged, of all things, a heap of green velvet. She ran to her mother's boudoir with a pair of breeches. Her mother looked at them sadly. 'Your dear papa's father bowed in them before Marie Antoinette.' Sterrin couldn't resist saying that he must have bowed too low. There was an obvious split down the seat that was not storm damage.

'It will make a breeches for Dominic,' her mother said, ignoring Sterrin's crudity.

There was enough left over from Dominic's breeches to make a short bodice for Sterrin. One of Lady O'Carroll's presentation gowns was transformed into a skirt trimmed round the hem with a row of green velvet leaves. Lady O'Carroll was forced to admire the result of the ingenuity.

She was also, under the sustained threat of Sterrin's return to the convent, forced to permit Sterrin to depart for Delaney's under the chaperonage of Hannah. Two train journeys to Maurice O'Carroll in County Waterford had made Sterrin a veteran of rail travel. But Hannah stood on the platform shivering at the thought of committing herself to the terror of the unknown. When the great iron monster came, clanking and roaring, Dominic slipped his hand into his sister's. Sterrin felt as though he had placed his whole life and world into her protection. The next moment the train had roared past. Hannah was jolted out of her fears, 'There's manners for you,' she gasped, 'think of drivin' past like that and people waitin' to travel!' The porter assured her that it was only the non-stop mail for Dublin. Hannah didn't think this was sufficient justification for bad manners. 'How did they know but 'twas to Dublin we wanted to go? The mail coach wouldn't do the like of that; nor the bianconi.'

The next train stopped, obligingly enough, and brought them at an ambling pace to their destination. Mrs. Delaney, waiting at the station in the maroon carriage had the notion, as they approached, that if she was hoping to marry off some of her surplus daughters she was defeating her own ends in inviting such competition as Sterrin O'Carroll. Not much suggestion here of the white-faced, reddish-haired girl who had moved in the shadow of her mother's beauty; not much suggestion of a nun either. Next day, Mrs. Delaney introduced Sterrin to Sir Jocelyn Devine at the horse show.

'This is Rody O'Carroll's girl,' Mrs. Delaney told Sir Jocelyn.

'Not Sir Roderick O'Carroll's daughter?'

'The same. A calamity!'

Sir Jocelyn reminded himself that Mrs. Delaney had never been given to felicity of speech. He was delighted by this remarkably beautiful young girl. It was immensely flattering the way this sweet young creature was deferring to him and giving him her undivided attention although she was the centre of attraction. Young gentlemen in immaculately cut riding clothes came in recurring procession, making excuses to speak to Mrs. Delaney on the victory of her entry while their eyes wandered to the stunning Miss O'Carroll. But it was on the arm of the middle-aged Sir Jocelyn that she returned to her carriage.

At dinner Sterrin began to fear that she would never get an opportunity to talk to him alone. She had not had a moment even to make a plan since she arrived at Moormount. She shared a bedroom with three other girls. The carriage had been crowded; the Grand Stand had been jammed; at every meal the younger guests sat two on a chair.

She kept her face towards Sir Jocelyn and beamed at every *bon mot* till her face felt stiff. Young girls could not give a conversational lead in the presence of the elderly, but when Sir Jocelyn mentioned that the Dublin gas company was about to give a demonstration of a contraption that would cook food by gas heat, her gasp of amazement caught his flattered attention.

'Isn't science wonderful?' she breathed. 'It makes gas from coal and it makes coal drive railway trains——'

'My dear,' smiled Sir Jocelyn, 'it is refreshing to meet appreciation for the inventions of science in one so young and beautiful.' But Sterrin was disgusted to find that the scientific track she had started him on was not a railroad one. He went on to talk about some impossible invention called a Talking Machine. All the young girls squealed and giggled and someone said that he was a fantastic wag. 'A talking machine, Sir Jocelyn!' cried Mrs. Delaney. 'You must be fooling us now.'

'I vow I am not fooling you, Mrs. Delaney. I saw it at the Vice-Regal Lodge. It can speak and sing and repeat tunes made by musical instruments. This scientifically-minded young lady,' he bowed towards Sterrin, 'would find it more fascinating than the railroad invention.'

Before Sterrin could assure him that nothing in the world just now could fascinate her like a railroad, Mrs. Delaney ordered the young people upstairs to rest before putting on their ball-gowns.

As she climbed the stairs she heard someone calling for Sir Jocelyn's carriage. Her heart sank. After all her scheming! She shook her head impatiently at Fiona Delaney's offer of rags to tie up her ringlets before lying down. Fiona thought that Sterrin O'Carroll needn't be sassy because her ringlets were so natural. But Sterrin just gazed out of the window, regardless of the excited preparations. Belle Delaney was busy pouring urine from a large, flowered chamber-pot into pretty china bowls and adding rosewater and lily-of-the-valley. She handed a bowl to Sterrin. 'If you haven't brought any old kid gloves to wear while this is soaking, I'll lend you a pair,' she said hospitably.

Sterrin spotted Sir Jocelyn's carriage. He's going! She almost wailed it aloud. Belle misinterpreted the consternation on Sterrin's face. 'There is more rosewater in it than the other thing,' she assured her. 'Go on, it will make your hands soft and white.' Sterrin took the bowl but did not use the lotion. Its third ingredient, she reflected, was overdoing hospitality.

But the gay sound of the music drew her heart from its worries. A section of the military band that had played at the show had been kindly lent by the colonel to supplement the fiddlers and pianist. The wallflowers tried not to gaze enviously at Sterrin. They discussed the new paraffin lamps that graced the piano and buffet table. The novelty of the lamps gave them something to focus their eyes upon so that no gentleman would catch their eyes straying in *his* direction.

Sterrin was never off the floor. She had to split her dances to cope with the demand. Then suddenly, blissfully, she found herself dancing with Sir Jocelyn. He had decided to wait for a dance before leaving, he told her, and his look conveyed that it was for a dance with herself that he had waited. Her mind went haring after an opening about the railroad and then she became too aware of the modern-looking lamps on the buffet table.

'May I have some lemonade?' she asked him. 'I've never seen this kind of lamp before,' she went on. 'Are they a new invention of science?'

Mrs. Delaney started to display their mechanism. 'I believe in moving with the times,' she said. 'This does not burn out the way a candle does if you are absent from the room a while. You just turn it down like this——'

'The dear knows what they will invent next,' said an elderly lady. 'First it was the iron road——'

'Yes, indeed!' Sterrin grasped at the cue. 'I think that the iron railroad is the most wonderful of——'

'Then,' continued the lady, 'they invented those horrid little slips for bringing bad news; and now lamps that will burn for hours in one's drawing-room.'

'Yes,' said Mrs. Delaney, delighted at her own progressiveness, 'when you return to the room all you need do is this.' She turned up the wick in a sudden spurt of flame. There was an ominous crack and half the glass chimney crashed on to the uncarpeted floor. 'I think,' said the elderly lady, 'that I shall stick to candles.' And Sir Jocelyn said that it was time for him to go.

Sterrin could almost see the iron tracks disappearing through the door in his wake. Railroad indeed! But it would seem that Sir Jocelyn had arranged for a special train to convey the entire house-party to his mansion on the River Nore for a five o'clock dinner the next afternoon.

Sterrin was the first downstairs next afternoon. The rest were still titivating in an atmosphere of sublimated woman, urinated hand-lotion, singed hair and rice powder.

'Sterrin,' her hostess called, 'will you run back up and hurry them down. We shall be leaving in ten minutes. Yes,' she went on in a lower tone that was not low enough, 'she *is* lovely but a bit flat in the bust. Gentlemen like a well-turned figure. Still she has plenty of time to fill out.' Sterrin decided that she had only ten minutes to fill out.

She slipped behind the screen that concealed the more intimate pieces of toilet ware and pushed a small cushion down her neck. The strain brought a protest from her grandfather's breeches that burst the underarm seam. She tried her heart-shaped pincushion. It produced a curve that was gentle but lopsided. Over the screen she spotted a perfect little velvet apple for holding pins; right in front of Belle Delaney. 'Hurry down, Belle! You are holding up everyone, including me.'

But Belle, holding a big red geranium to her nostrils was

furtively absorbed in her own brand of artifice. As if we didn't know, thought Sterrin, purloining the cushion from under the geranium-covered nose, that she lost her sense of smell after the famine fever and is only trying to dab a bit of colour on her cheeks!

She forced the green velvet apple down inside her gown. It balanced in bulk, not in shape, the heart-shaped pincushion, but the combined effect was more mature and it seemed to be working. During dinner, Sir Jocelyn's gaze kept wandering towards her as she sat in profile from him down the table. The apple-shaped side was turned towards him and he marvelled at its sculptured roundness.

When the gentlemen rejoined the ladies he came straight to her. She had been on thorns listening to the older ladies discussing who was entertaining who, and who behind their fans was rumoured to be THAT WAY! And the younger ones discussing the prices of Jumping Frog Brown walking gowns and North Pole Blue evening gowns. And Sterrin's self refused a few yards of velvet by a tradesman!

'Sir Jocelyn,' she cried eagerly, 'Mamma has told me about your aviary of silver birds. She said it was beautiful beyond words. Would you please permit me to have a peep?'

He bowed. 'My dear, I shall be honoured to have you view my collection. Perhaps some of the others would like to come—you see—er—it is in quite another part of the house.' And delectable as it would be, one might not indulge oneself in her unchaperoned company. But Sterrin was on her feet. 'I should never forgive myself if I did not avail of this opportunity,' she said with complete truth. 'Come, there is no time to delay.' Her eyes and smile diffused the incence of flattery. He forgot his other guests; forgot everything except this sheath of springtime that was awakening responses he had long thought dead.

As they walked down the room he saw their reflected images in a convex wall mirror. No lady, he thought, had befitted his squiring like this tall, graceful, exquisitely-shaped girl.

The spectacle of the aviary startled her from her strategy. On ornamental trees of ebonised mahogany and on branches of palest sycamore perched silver birds of every species, all with shimmering eyes formed from priceless gems. At the base of the trees on a low platform, ranged the glory of the collection, large peacocks of solid silver, their great tails tipped with gold and encrusted with emeralds and rubies.

She moved from tree to tree, touching each bird with reverent fingers, then dropped to her knees to examine the peacocks.

'Oh,' she breathed. 'I have heard Mamma speak of them but I did not dream of anything so glorious.'

He looked down at her gazing up at him, her hands extended to the length of the bird she held from gold-tipped tail to jewelled beak. Neither have I ever dreamed of anything so glorious, he thought. What was it she reminded him of—the young kneeling figure, the rapt expression, the hands extended holding the ornamental bird. Was it of some virgin to the Temple holding out her offering of doves?

Suddenly she remembered that there was no silver metal and costly jewels to weight the wings of the time she was wasting. She replaced the bird and rose swiftly to her knees before he could assist her. 'It will soon be time to catch the train,' she said.

He shrugged the idea. 'The train can wait. It is specially ordered for my guests.'

She beamed. 'How wonderful it must be to have one's own train. We have not even a railway line.'

'I must say I thought it singularly unenterprising of the landlords not to have availed of the opportunity of connecting when the main line was laid.' Her smile shortened a little. Papa had been one of the unenterprising landlords.

'Most of the landlords concerned were preoccupied with postfamine conditions,' she observed.

'Ah yes,' he answered gently, 'and with the forlorn cause of Repeal.'

Her smile vanished. He hastened to recover from his maladroitness. Her father's death, of course, had been one of the final blights in that dwindling movement. For a moment he thought of offering her one of his precious birds.

But she rallied. Disdain would not meet the mortgage; nor Lubey's account. 'A railway line would bring prosperity to the farmers. They have such a limited market for their produce.'

He fingered the replica of a pheasant that he had made rise for three successive seasons without shooting. The young farmer who had subsequently poached it was now happily out of range. There were no preserves in the convict settlements of Botany Bay.

385

'It is touching to see one so young take such an interest in the people. Are there no responsible people to sponsor a railway development without letting a lovely lady like you concern her beautiful head with such mundane matters. Come! Look at this parakeet. Its eyes are fire opals. Don't they give the impression of life and movement?'

'Yes, don't they,' said Sterrin. 'You see, there is no one who could really guarantee the line since Lord Templetown sold out.'

'Ah, it is a question of guaranty! Now, see this bluebird. It is the only specimen where I have used a substance other than jewels. I introduced lapus lazuli for the wings.'

She stroked the blue wing. 'I think this is the prettiest of them all. You know, in the last year the district nearest the railway sent out six thousand firkins of butter over a period that exported only that many hundred before it became linked up with the railway.'

He stopped in the act of reaching for another bird. Butter firkins! Why was this exquisite creature talking like a dairymaid while she was being privileged to view one of the rarest collections in the world?

'Perhaps, my dear, you would prefer if I were to show you over my poultry yard?'

The lapis lazuli dulled somewhat under the blue flash of her eyes. She drew herself taller.

'Yes, it might be interesting to see what laid the eggs that hatched out such birds as these.' She flicked a dismissing finger towards the priceless species.

He drew her hand inside his arm, but made no move to escort her hence. 'Forgive me, my dear. It is not everyone who is privileged to view my aviary.' He placed his finger under her chin and held her face close to his own. 'Why are you concerned about this railway?'

'I . . . it would be wonderful to be connected with the outside world. We are so shut off. It has been so exciting coming here today in your marvellous train. You have no idea. I'm afraid my mind has been full of it.'

But of course! He had travelled too far in life and the world to realise that the novelty of a rail journey meant more to this fresh young mind than the sight of a connoisseur's collection of ornaments.

His silver birds turned to lead as he looked into the intense blue of her eyes set in the white glow of her skin and he marvelled anew at the contrast of jet black brows under the gold-bronze hair. He touched the soft cheek and his trembling was two-fold for the delicious thrill of delight and the fear that his touch might harden her cheek into the Midas texture of his treasure trove. 'And it only needs a guarantor,' he murmured, 'to hack an iron path to the fortress where you have been too long turreted.'

She gazed up with lips parted and eyes more wide and rapt than when they gazed upon the peacock. 'Would you like me to guarantee the railroad?' She sighed with relief. It had been hard work among the silver mummies!

'Would you?' She breathed it like a holy application.

His smile was indulgent. Why not! A few miles of iron rails would not cost as much as a few of these birds and there were always the naïve butter firkins to repay with dividends. 'And if I give you your railroad, my dear, what do I get?'

He hastened to retrench. He noticed the altered look in her eyes, but he did not know it came from the queer crawling in her spine. 'There, my dear. We'll see about this railway.' He brushed her forehead with his lips and his pat on her shoulder was paternal.

Then Dominic opened the door. 'Sterrin,' he said bleakly, 'my breeches!' He was holding both hands over his seat.

'What on earth have you done?' she demanded, though she was never so glad to see him, torn breeches and all.

'I couldn't help it, Sterrin, honestly! I was stooping over the gold fish pond. Now I'll have to go back into petticoats again.' His little fair face was stricken.

'Nonsense,' said Sir Jocelyn. 'Your nurse will put you into fresh breeches.'

'But I have not got another pair of breeches and there's no more velvet to mend these because the rest of grandfather's breeches was put on Sterrin's gown.'

The gaping tear in the seat of Dominic's breeches ventilated light and knowledge straight into Sir Jocelyn's mind. So that explained the sweet little railroad project and all the tender concern for the farmers! The son and daughter of the castle were reduced to sharing their grandfather's trousers! This sweet ingenue was like all the other women whose fingers, in his com-

387

pany, turned into claws that clutched for his gold.

He turned to the child. 'Return to your nurse, Sir Dominic. Your sister will attend to you in a moment.'

Sterrin felt as though she had been plunged suddenly into a torrent. Her body was engulfed. She tried to cry out, but her lips were sealed with some breathing pressure that she gradually realised was a kiss. Like the memory flash of drowning people she recalled other kisses; Papa's, Cousin Maurice's, young Thomas's parting kiss that had been like a benediction; none of them like this strange kiss—so queerly intimately male. She struggled, but her arms were pinioned against her chest. They hurt excruciatingly as though they were being prodded by a hundred pins.

She was released with a quick, angry exclamation. Sir Jocelyn was rubbing his wrists that seemed to be covered with blood. Automatically she rubbed her own stinging forearms without looking at the rash of angry pricks. She was too intent on looking at the face in front of her. It had become quite different; cold and contemptuous; so had the voice that was accusing her of dreadful things. 'You have not omitted one single trick,' it was saying. 'You must be experienced in such overtures to be able to defend yourself so readily with the sordid hatpin trick.'

Rage swept the blood from her face. It choked the words that surged inside her. Damn you, they roared, are you accusing me. Me! of jabbing with a hatpin like a totsie from Love Lane warding off a drunken soldier?

But only her own kind of language escaped from the surge; simple and direct, like the words that she had heard herself say to Reverend Mother on that last morning when she had wanted to hurl forth high-minded phrases about hypocrisy. Curious, he watched her put her hand down her bodice, and as though she were drawing forth a tenderly guarded *billet-doux*, she produced a velvet apple. Heavens, she thought, it is full of pins.

'This is not a weapon,' she said coldly. 'It is my pincushion.' She was too proudly angry to offer an embarrassed excuse about its presence. 'As your guest I did not think it would become necessary for me to defend myself from my host.'

The admiration was back in his face. There was something gallant about her standing there, her depleted figure restored— in part—to its almost boyish lissomness; the velvet apple naïvely outstretched.

'My dear child,' he said, all courtly and benign. 'You have been playing a part that was not worthy of you. And I, in turn, played back to you. I acted towards the wanton you would have me believe that you are as I should not dream of behaving towards the true and gracious lady that I know you to be.' He offered his arm. 'Come, my dear. The whole incident has been a make-believe.'

She did not accept his arm. There had been nothing make-believe about that kiss.

That night she could not sleep for thinking of it. When she did sleep she dreamt that she was struggling in a swirling torrent and when she tried to scream a face came over hers, and lips hard as iron clamped down on her cries. She sat up gasping. Guilt more fearful than she had ever known compressed her. What wicked things had she done? That kiss! Its atmosphere was all about her now. Its queer man maleness! Was this the way girls became Fallen? Driven from home to die in the snow; with a bundle in their arms? She jumped from the bed and ran to the door tearing at the knob. Panic beat in her brain. She tore down the stairs not thinking where. In the grip of sleep and fear all she knew was that she had been overtaken by the fate that caused girls to drown themselves.

At a table in a store room full of boots and leggings and sacks of meal, Ned Rua sat in an agony of accounts. His tongue stuck out across his cheeks. He could add any length of figures in his head without error, but all his accuracy vanished when he had to drag the figures from his brain with a stump of a pencil. 'They don't scoromund[1]—Oh, Holy Mother of God!' He dropped the pencil and made the sign of the cross. A white-draped figure with flowing hair was wafting past the open door. Sterrin slowed at the clatter of an overturned chair. She became conscious of the cold flags under her bare feet. 'I—I wanted some saddle soap for my boots, Ned,' she faltered.

He was as horrified at the idea of her thinking to soil her hands as he had been when he thought she was a ghost. 'Leave them outside your door, Miss Sterrin. I'll collect them myself when I get these to scoromund.[1] I know what oats we bought in and I know what money we paid out, but I can't for the life of me make the two scoromund.'[1]

Poor Ned Rua! He was part of her innocent past! So were

[1] Vernacular for 'correspond'.

the girls she thought, looking at them sleeping so peacefully; so appealingly. Well, maybe not Belle lying on her back with her mouth open; poor Belle! It was that famine fever out in a quarry that had damaged her nose.

She dressed and went from the sleeping house. The urge towards self-destruction was slackening every second. It was that lovely pre-dawning moment when people make hundreds of plans because the young untrammelled air gave strength and hope. Birds were yawning out sleepy trills and here was she planning to—what? She placed a toe in the water. It made a dark patch on the nice green leather. Her shoes would be destroyed. Should she take them off before she—— But then she wouldn't need shoes after . . . A darting movement sent vibrant alertness through her being. She dropped down on her stomach and sidled her hands beneath the water. It was a most unsporting thing to do, but a trout was a trout. Her fingers were just meeting around a scaly belly when a rattle made her look round. 'Hell roast you, Ned Rua! You've made me lose a three pounder at least.'

'Whisht, Miss Sterrin.' Ned put down the feed bucket. 'It's there under that flat stone.'

'I've got it. No I haven't!'

Ned dropped on his stomach beside her. 'There, to the left.' He jogged her elbow and she nearly overbalanced.

'You gomahawk!' she hissed grabbing his arm for support. 'You nearly drowned me.'

Belle Delaney and Sterrin shared a chair at breakfast, and shared the trout, baked in butter on the gridiron. Halfway through the last morsel she suddenly remembered that she had forgotten to drown herself. Anyway, she had made the gesture. Reverend Mother is right, she told herself; I have a vocation for living.

CHAPTER 40

Next afternoon Sterrin, standing at her window over the stable yard in the act of removing her bonnet, saw the Scout come galloping into the yard. He was standing astride the shafts, all pride and purpose. She was minded of the day he came on a white horse to proclaim the news of the Liberator's arrest.

'God save ye!' he cried to the coachman and Mike O'Driscoll and to the inside staff who were crowding to the back door. 'I've beaten Her Majesty's newsbearer. I've whipped the boyo with the telegram.' He mounted the cross board of the cart as though it were a rostrum. 'Once again,' he proclaimed, 'it is my painful duty to be the bearer of ill news to this great house. I have come to inform you that, on the eve of his one hundred and tenth birthday, the great liege lord of Crannagh——' The donkey moved towards a bale of hay and the Scout collapsed with his legs in the air. Sterrin leaned out as his head reappeared. 'Ould Lord Cullen,' he gasped, 'is dead at last.'

Mrs. Stacey halted the start of a keen to ask what had his Lordship died of. The Scout mounted his rostrum. His next lines were not to be thrown away in the floor boards of an ass cart. 'The illness that cut him off before attaining the completion of his eleventh decade was—measles. Youthful to the last, you might say.'

'He mustn't 'a had them an' he a child,' said Mrs. Stacey.

'Perhaps, who knows,' said the Scout stepping down for the funeral ale, 'the illnesses of first childhood may not render one immune in one's second childhood. It's a thirsty day.'

Sterrin saw Mike O'Driscoll removing his straw and his hat to come in for the courtesy drink. 'Begod,' she heard him say as he disappeared underneath her window. 'If he had lived another couple of years he might 'a got the chincough.'

At Lord Cullen's funeral Sterrin met people whom she had not seen for years.

Lord Templetown had come down from Dublin. His former tenants crowded round the elegant, worldly-minded man who had never lacked the saving grace of humanity. Master Hennessey came forward as full of classical quips as ever. 'A noble cortège, My Lord. At least five hundred cars!'

'You are inaccurate, Master,' the Scout interrupted. 'Five hundred and ten, including the hearse. It is heartening to see the fine funerals back again.' He swept off his hat so sweepingly to Lord Templetown that his wig was knocked sideways. 'Man's life,' he misquoted, 'is as the hair of his head, as Tom Moore said.' Master Hennessey looked silently at the bald exposure as though he considered the Scout's prospects were not too bright.

Sterrin shrank back when she saw Sir Jocelyn approaching the carriage. He bowed low to Lady O'Carroll and asked her permission to call at the castle next week. He would have occasion to be in the vicinity next week, with a railway engineer in connection with the proposed new branch line. He was so grave and gentle that Sterrin wondered if she had imagined his previous behaviour. The carriage had moved and he was gone. Sterrin suddenly sat up. Had she imagined what he had said just now? The proposed new branch line!

Sir Jocelyn Devine gave the guarantee and the first line was laid with great *éclat*. The band of the North Tipperary Light Infantry, with unconscious irony, played the Rocky Road to Dublin. The Deputy Lieutenant addressed the big gathering and dwelt hopefully on the prosperity this new link with the outer world would bring to the district. His dreary list of statistics finally came to an end and Lady O'Carroll and Sterrin were free to lead their guests to the first luncheon party that Kilsheelin had known for many a year.

Sir Jocelyn, on the right of his hostess, charmed her with his courtly deference and Sterrin, in new clothes and courage, wondered anew if she could ever have known repulsion from him.

Mrs. Kennedy-Sherwin, watching the animation on Margaret's face as she listened to Sir Jocelyn, scented romance and whispered to young Lady Cullen that it would be the best thing she could do. And Lady Biddy Cullen, remembering that he was supposed to be the richest man in Ireland agreed. 'Look what it would mean to Sterrin,' she whispered behind her fan. 'She could be presented and meet a likely party. There's no one here for her except gombeen men and bankrupts. Wouldn't it be terrible if she were to become an old maid?'

Mrs. Kennedy-Sherwin looked towards the beautiful girl who was in the act of rising in response to her mother's signal for the ladies' withdrawal. What an unintelligent remark for anyone to make about such a glorious creature. Every man in the room was eyeing her. 'Don't be prissy, Biddy!' Sometimes the city-bred urbanity of the former Miss Cuppage-O-Byrne grated. 'The girl will either marry a duke or run off with a ploughman.'

She suddenly remembered something. 'Sterrin,' she said, patting the ottoman invitingly, 'what became of that picturesque-looking groom who used to be here?'

Sterrin drew her dark brows together for a second. 'The only picturesque thing about Mike O'Driscoll is his language. You must mean Big John, the coachman. He is still with us, of course.'

'No, that is not the name, and everyone knows Big John. No this young man was extremely good-looking. The first time I noticed him he was helping to remove that monstrous cake that had been made for the Queen. He had quite an air.'

'Oh!' Sterrin said quietly. 'He has been gone some time. He ...he emigrated.' The slight stammer might have gone unnoticed but there was no mistaking the tell-tale flush. So I was right, thought Mrs. Kennedy-Sherwin, tingling with intrigue. And it is the ploughman instead of the Duke! Oh, this was delicious! But the gentlemen entered the room and Mr. Maurice O'Carroll came up to take his leave of Sterrin.

'Isn't it marvellous, Cousin Maurice?' she said as she accompanied him to the carriage. 'You can travel all the way home by train only changing once and at the same time that horrid mortgage is cleared!'

He looked at her compassionately. 'The *arrears* are cleared, child. That's only...' He changed the subject and complimented her upon her new gown. 'I'll hold a crown you never bought that in Lubeys.' She looked down at the flow of champagne-coloured velvet and then held up her arms to display the blonde valenciennes lace that flowed from elbow to wrist.

'Paris!' she proclaimed. 'Lubey sent boxes of stuff on approbation, and pairs and pairs of the silk evening boots he had refused Mamma, but she sent them all back unopened. The shoneen!'

393

'He is that all right. But don't over antagonise him. He is the biggest shareholder in the iron road and it was a blow to his pride to be the only one you left out of today's party.' He sighed as the carriage rolled down the avenue and wondered how many more times he would visit the old place. Only last week he had parted with his own precious library of priceless books to a Waterford gombeen man. Paris gowns! God help their innocence. And the sum of money from the railroad only a daisy in a bull's mouth!

But Sterrin was jubilant. She was convinced that she had brought prosperity back to Kilsheelin when she had recaptured some of its soil from Poolgower. In the kitchen she was regarded as a saviour. The whole staff had gathered at the back stairhead to watch her as she moved down the stairs in her first formal gown and they gloried in the proud-held head that others mistook for arrogance.

'If the Sir could see her now,' breathed Mrs. Stacey. 'Ye'd think he spat her out of his mouth.'

Big John was the only one who could see over the cook's head. 'If only Young Thomas could see her now,' he said surprisingly. 'She used to come to him with every new stitch she got. He'd criticise it for her as good as any lady of fashion and she had no more pleasure in any garment that he didn't approve.'

Mrs. Stacey brushed the back of her hand over her eyes. 'God be with him,' she murmured as though she spoke of the dead.

They felt strangely embarrassed when Sterrin suddenly appeared among them after the guests had departed. It was seldom she came to the kitchen nowadays and tonight in her long, rich gown she stood apart in the world they lived to serve. But Sterrin wanted to share with them her sense of achievement. Hadn't they shared in the plot that had brought it about? Besides, she wanted Attracta to read her cup.

Pakie Scally helped Mrs. Stacey to lower the rungs of the crane to bring the kettle nearer the flame and as he straightened up he was surprised to see Miss Sterrin's eyes fixed on him intently. To cover his embarrassment he ventured timidly to say that the sods had brought luck, but she scarcely heard him. He was wearing Young Thomas's livery. She was seeing glossy curls instead of Pakie's lank hair and the lithe frame of Young Thomas as he deftly swung the great crane and inserted the kettle hook two holes down when Miss Sterrin came to the kitchen. 'And there's shamrocks spreading all over the place where we put the centre sod, Miss Sterrin.' The curls disappeared and the hands that brushed the crane grime from each other were no longer shapely and well-kept.

'That's unusual,' she said at last. 'I have never found shamrock in that field.'

'Nor anyone else either, Miss Sterrin,' said Hegarty. 'Isn't that right, Big John?'

'It is indeed, Mr. Hegarty,' said the coachman. 'Not even before the night of the Big Wind.'

'Well, in that case,' said Mrs. Stacey, 'we can take it that the luck of Kilsheelin has turned.'

Hannah placed a big napkin across the velvet-covered knees and tucked a corner inside the neck of the lovely gown. ''Twas an answer to prayer, Miss Sterrin. We stormed the heavens.' Sterrin sipped her tea and slowly swirled it round the cup to toss the leaves.

'And I stormed the earth,' she said grimly.

'And there's storms still to come, Miss Sterrin,' said Attracta, peering into the cup. 'Storms and violence. There is an elderly man wishing on you and there's a young man wishing on you too, a fine young man and you'll meet him sooner than you expect, but treachery will part you. I see you standing over a horse, Miss Sterrin.' Attracta was looking out over the rim of the cup into space. 'A horse that is lying down.'

The girl's gaze returned from the dreamy distance. Attracta looked vaguely at her young mistress. 'I can see no more.'

Sterrin got to her feet. 'You are not in your usual form tonight, Attracta. Nothing you have seen links up with anything for me except Thuckeen. It's quite likely that I shall stand over her when she foals.'

Months later Sterrin stood over the prone, prostrate mare and watched the eyes glazing as Thuckeen reached feebly to lick the natal slime from the quivering colt. But the lovely gesture that would reunite the little foal to its dam was never made. The great mare had fought all night and now her questing nuzzle was denied its fulfilment. Before it reached the foal her head fell back. Sterrin in utter and complete abandon, threw herself across the carcass, her arms clasping its neck, her hair mingling with the silky mane she had tended as long as she could remember.

The deep, hoarse sobs unnerved her mother when she came to coax her away. The sight of Thuckeen loosed a flood of memories. Roderick leading the field on the peerless Thuckeen; Roderick smilingly refusing fantastic sums for her; Roderick soaring high over the bay-leaf hedge while she watched with smiling lips and terrified heart.

Nurse Hogan led her Ladyship away and Big John standing beside Mr. Hegarty was crying openly. Tears blinded Mike O'Driscoll as he carried the new-born foal to a foster-mother. He collided with Sir Jocelyn Devine who had sauntered casually towards the stable yard when his knock at the hall door had gone unanswered.

CHAPTER 41

Sterrin paused as she walked up to the gap at Poolgower. She leaned her arms over the ridge. Never, she realised, had she had to climb this gap before. Always, she had sailed over it, clean and straight, never a sod disturbed. Thuckeen had helped her to rise above the crosses that had sprung up so frighteningly in her path; her father's death, the loss of Young Thomas, the death of the bard.

The poignancy of the horse's death had an evocative quality that would not be suppressed. Young Thomas burst through the self-enforced barriers of her memory. She ached for the comfort of his presence. That day, when Sir Jocelyn—Heaven sent—had led her gently, but so firmly away from Thuckeen, there had come a mnemonic flash of a dark, yearning face and a voice that had said, 'You'll always have me, asthore!'

She started to chew a blade of grass but spat it forth. It, too, was evocative; of undigested grass and the green drool on the lips of the famished. And why, she thought inconsequentially did Mrs. Kennedy-Sherwin keep looking at her at the luncheon party when she harped on the scandal of the titled lady in the Queen's County who had run away with the ploughman!

Ploughman indeed! Young Thomas's shapely hands, so fastidiously tended, flicked away the implication. She shifted her head and leaned it sideways on her arms and suddenly the hedge-flowers became a fragrant evocation of the perfumed soap that Young Thomas used to buy out of the crown piece that Papa always gave to him on the anniversary of the Big Wind. The other servants used the dark soap that Mrs. Stacey made from mutton fat, but everything in Young Thomas's room possessed the quality of—not just taste or of apeing his betters—a kind of natural acceptance that his personal belongings should possess quality; but never ostentation. His brushes, bought singly as his wages increased, had been of unadorned ivory. His bookshelves held the library of a cultured mind. Such an accumulation of books since the first one that Lieutenant Fitzharding-Smith had helped her to choose that day in Dublin.

Her cuff button chafed her cheek and she shifted it to the other arm while her eyes dreamed up the crystalline gleam of quartz and mica that Young Thomas's scrubbing had seduced from the granite of his floor. It used to look so exotic around the eastern prayer rug that Lieutenant Fitzharding-Smith had given him when he was dismantling his quarters. What ploughman would show such discernment? Pakie Scally had the room now and no jewels gleamed from its flags.

The sigh that came from her was long and sad. An echoing sigh followed it. Donal Keating had been watching her from the shade of the headland. His sigh turned into a cough.

Sterrin stepped back startled and trod on the tail of one of her two dogs. Its yelping started its companion barking, then the red setter, crouching behind the horse, joined in from sheer boredom.

Donal, holding his handkerchief with one hand, had to drop the reins from his other hand to raise his hat. The horse, already disturbed by the sudden yelping, began to plunge madly.

Habit compelled Sterrin to reach out a hand to restrain the animal. Unwittingly she patted the silk neck whilst instinct brought soothing words from her until the horse quivered into quiescence. Midst all the barking and bolting and coughing she was forced to stand here holding her resentment in check. Now, as he thanked her, it burst forth.

'There would be no need for thanks,' she stormed, 'if you had not been spying on me.'

'I vow and declare, Miss O'Carroll,' he protested, 'that I did not mean to spy upon you.' She did not realise that she was still holding the bridle as she stared straight up into his face.

'Of course you were spying upon me! This is not the first time. Why the devil's father do you do it?'

His sudden laughter set him coughing again; as he dived for the handkerchief in his tail pocket she was forced to take a firmer hold of the bridle.

'Just look what your violent language has done to me!' he spluttered.

The horse's soft nuzzle brushed her. For a nostalgic moment she pressed her cheek against the breathing velvet. Behind the handkerchief he eyed the wistful caress and coughed to prolong

398

its proximity. Finally he gasped, 'Surely if a cat may look at a queen a mere mortal may pause to worship when he is vouchsafed the vision of a goddess....'

'For heaven's sake,' she snapped, 'don't call me a goddess!'

'Yes, it is unoriginal, isn't it?' he grinned. 'But I don't mean a simpering goddess in a niche. I was thinking of a flying goddess of the chase. A Diana!' He bent lower towards her. 'A Diana without her steed.'

She dropped the bridle as though she had been stung. Then with a swish and a froth of petticoats and pantalettes she was over the gap and running down the slope. Oh, to have been able to turn her horse's head and gallop from his odious presence! Instead of standing there holding his damned horse like a lackey! To cast it in my teeth that I am without a horse! The bachach!

At the sound of the train whistle she turned involuntarily; she could still see Donal, watching her. The train! She had a sudden inspiration. I'll let him see that I don't have to travel 'Irish tandem,[1] even if I *am* without a horse! Diana without her steed—dinagh! She ducked behind a tree, pulled up her skirt and fumbled with the strings of her white cambric petticoat and of the white cotton one and the one underneath.

As the train approached the driver saw a young lady waving a large red flag and groaned. He was already half an hour behind and now, willy nilly, he must stop. He had got into trouble a month back for not stopping because the biteen of red had been so small that he had not seen it. But be the power of war, this here flag would stop a bull, much less a train!

An English businessman fumed audibly at the spectacle of a hatless, breathless girl coolly holding up an entire train and jamming herself in among first-class passengers. To make matters worse a donkey strayed on to the tracks and caused further delay. 'This is outrageous,' he said taking forth his repeater. 'I intend to report this.' Sterrin was uncertain whether he meant to report herself or the donkey. The officer in the opposite corner left her in no further doubt. '*I* certainly shall report this matter. Young woman! How dare you inconvenience your betters?'

The 'young woman' was too much for Sterrin's silent composure. 'I inconvenience my "betters",' she answered, 'for my own convenience.' Then, with iciest hauteur she deigned to

[1] On foot.

explain to him that it was her family's privilege, if they wished to travel while the train was passing through their territory, to stop it by waving a red flag.

The officer eyed the now unmistakable young gentlewoman who travelled unescorted in a carriageful of gentlemen, then glanced towards the castle outlined in the near distance. 'I beg your pardon,' he said gruffly.

Sterrin, having disposed of all challengers, both here and outside settled herself comfortably. Then, 'Pardon me, Madam,' the officer beside her, a younger one, was leaning towards her. 'Did you say *flag*?' He adjusted his monocle and directed her gaze downward to where a white string rested upon the gleaming toe of his boot. She froze. Her flag had worked itself from her relaxed grip and hung over her knees, its purpose disclosed. The white tapes from the waistband lay on the officer's shoe. A row of blue and white featherstitching treacherously defined the hemline.

She gazed silently at the revolting garment that had been forced upon her by Nurse Hogan and her mamma to prevent rheumatics after one of her severe wettings on Thuckeen. Then, before anyone had realised what was happening, she was on her feet reaching for the communication cord. The train came to a clanging halt, and Sterrin, her flag slung nonchalantly over one shoulder, stepped from the train, and ran all the way home to Kilsheelin.

She passed the empty rooms to the kitchen where Dominic was listening with delicious terror to one of Attracta's ghost stories. Ghosts! There were too many of them about today. Attracta and her endless lore of Connemara's dead and undead until, as Young Thomas used to quote, 'I thought in my heart and even in my soul that the dead who had died still lived.' She raised the latch that led to the yard and the empty stable she had avoided this week past, but now the foal was giving cause for concern. It was not thriving with its foster-dam.

The slight sound made Attracta turn and as she rose to her feet, Sterrin heard her hiss, 'Ask her now, Master Dominic, sir.' She paused.

'What is it that you want to ask me?' Sterrin's voice and face were so proud and cold that Attracta stood confused. Mrs. Stacey spoke up for her.

''Tis the way Mrs. James Wright—Miss Berry Fogarty that

was—is letting her parlour maid—Attracta's sister—help at the supper next week for the ball in the Assembly Rooms when the gentlemen will bid to redeem the cloaks that the women were forced to pawn in the famine. Attracta was wondering if you would put a word in for her with Nurse Hogan to let her help, too. All the committee ladies are lending their staff.'

Attracta found her voice. ''Tis a great cause, Miss Sterrin,' she murmured timidly. To Attracta, the cause of the cloaks that were handed from mother to daughter was more than great. 'Twas holy. Sterrin wrinkled her brows. She had quite forgotten the dance. 'Weren't all these cloaks redeemed years ago?' she said impatiently. 'Papa gave a big dance in the barn for the ones in this neighbourhood.'

'Will I ever forget that supper!' said Mrs. Stacey branching off into reminiscences. 'There were fifteen hams and . . .'

Sterrin cut her short. 'And there was a ball in the Assembly Rooms as well as lots of quilting parties.'

'But your Honour's miss,' pleaded Attracta, 'these are cloaks belonging to them that were too proud to admit that the clothes off their backs were in pawn and they thought they could redeem them later when times would be better. Oh, 'twould be a terrible thing, Miss Sterrin, for a woman to live her life out with her fine cloak beyond her reach or the right to will it to her daughter!'

Dominic raised a buttery face from his boxtie. 'Don't mind her, Sterrin. It's Lance-Corporal Pluck she wants to meet. He's playing in the band. Isn't he, Attracta?' His mischievous grin vanished when Mrs. Stacey whispered in one ear that she'd never make him another piece of boxtie. In the other Attracta whispered that she'd never tell him another ghost story.

Sterrin strode back into the kitchen and put her arm around her brother. 'Don't attempt to threaten him,' she said with cold anger. She rumpled his curls. 'When you have eaten your boxtie, darling, come up to my room and I'll read you a *cheerful* story. Ghost stories and boxtie are unwholesome diet for a little boy.' The muted servants watched her dignified exit, her red flag still slung over her shoulder, and thought of the times when Miss Sterrin had gorged both ghosts and boxtie until she was too full to stand and too frightened to walk upstairs.

She passed into the yard, hating herself for her unfairness to the two women who doted on the child. Then she stopped dead.

401

It was seldom now that a visiting carriage came driving through the water-filled bawn to cleanse its wheels before the return journey. But it was not the carriage that transfixed her, nor the vague impression of Sir Jocelyn Devine stepping back from the splashes. It was the sight of the horse that looked out at her from Thuckeen's stall! 'Thuckeen! Thuckeen! tais mo croidte! Joy of my heart,' she gasped, 'are you haunting me too?' Her heart steadied and she patted the forehead and ran her hand down the gleaming neck. It was not Thuckeen, but it could be her double—a youthful double. Behind her a quiet voice said,

'You like her, Miss Sterrin?'

She whirled about. 'Oh, Sir Jocelyn, for a moment I thought it was Thuckeen's ghost!'

'Yes, the resemblance is remarkable. Their pedigrees are closely linked.' Sterrin unbolted the door and moved in while the horse reared up.

'She might have out-classed her, even,' she murmured to herself as she soothed the timid creature. When she came out he said,

'Aren't you going to try her out?' She shook her head. 'It would only grig me. It is better for me to become accustomed to being without a horse.'

'On the contrary, my dear, I think it is better that you should accustom yourself to Cloora straight away.'

'Cloora!' It was more a breath than a whisper.

'You can rename her as you please. She is your property.'

'Mine! You mean, Sir Jocelyn, that you are actually *giving* me this beautiful, this valuable horse?'

He shrugged. 'Nothing less would be worthy of you.' Her head spun. Young ladies did not accept gifts from gentlemen unless they were relatives or fiancés. Thuckeen had cost hundreds. This horse outclassed her. One could not appeal to Mamma just now. She drew herself up and made her gesture to the formalities.

'Thank you, Sir Jocelyn. Thank you kindly, but I could not accept so costly a gift.' The amethyst eyes were as wide with renunciation as they had been with concern when she had pleaded for the benefit of a railway for her countryfolk. He played up to the convention of her words and gestured his groom.

The sight of the man moving to unbolt the door was too much for Mike O'Driscoll as he stood beside Big John mingling the sweat of their anxiety. He spat out his straw and hissed, 'Is it gone mad you are, Miss Sterrin?' Big John broke through the decorum of years as he stepped forward, his caroline held above the thick grey waves and said gravely.

'Your Honour's Sir, I ask your pardon for taking a liberty, but if I might make bold to suggest that Miss Sterrin ought to postpone her decision until her Ladyship recovers. It would be only due to you and ...' he looked longingly at the head that poked over Thuckeen's half door, '... to the horse.'

When the carriage had passed under the great arch of the stable gate she turned to the coachman and lifted her hands towards him in a gesture that recalled the days when he used to lift her on to the backs of the horses. She placed them on his shoulders and lightly as she pressed the maimed one, he winced. 'Oh, poor Big John!' she cried remembering. 'Oh, that terrible Big Wind! And,' she added inconsequentially, 'it was all my fault.'

'Miss Sterrin,' he murmured with the gentleness of love, 'if her Ladyship was at herself she would tell you—and so would the young Sir'—she knew he didn't mean Dominic—'that a young lady does not treat the offer of a magnificent blood-horse the same as if it were a box of Limerick gloves.'

She playfully patted the good shoulder. 'And they would also tell me, Big John, my Guardian Angel, that a gentleman does not offer a young lady a horse worth at least a thousand guineas the same as if it were just a box of Limerick gloves.' She turned to where Mike and Pakie were standing in reverence before the animal. 'But, oh, Big John, I'd have died if that glorious creature had gone through that door again and left Thuckeen's stable empty.' Before he could answer she had gone, tearing through the kitchen entrance.

As the wine-coloured carriage rolled behind its four bays towards the lodge, a flying figure came alongside. 'Sir Jocelyn,' she gasped. She couldn't get out another word, for her breath hurt after the mad race. 'It has all been so sudden, like an apparition.' She gulped and swallowed. 'And I don't want to seem disloyal to Thuckeen, but I have never seen anything so lovely in my life as Cloora—Clooreen.'

He watched for a moment the beautiful lips panting out

403

words and breaths that blew warmly against his face. Exertion had reddened them as it did with people of her pallor. Her skin glowed with light instead of colour. Her eyes played no tricks except to cope with the blue shimmering of their own intensity.

'If you have never seen anything lovelier than Cloora, or Clooreen, then go straight to your mirror.' She shot out her underlip and blew a shining curl back from the tip of her nose. A primitively delightful gesture, he thought. 'Goodbye, my dear, I shall be back within the month for your mother's sanction.'

Twenty minutes later she knew again the surging thrill of riding high over the world on the back of a galloping thoroughbred. Straight for Cuilnafunchion she made and tried Clooreen with her first jump at the gap where she had been humbled.

Diana without a steed, Inagh! She gritted, as Clooreen bunched her four dainty hooves beyond coarse contact with the gap. Now let Donal Keating sneer.

The Coats of Arms of such local aristocracy as still lived in the district were picked out on the walls of the Assembly Room with red and white dahlias; but out of appreciation of Lady O'Carroll's great kindness in breaking her long seclusion to lend her patronage, and in recognition of the family's right to fly the ancient flag of blue, there were blue and white flowers on the O'Carroll escutcheon. It was a brilliant occasion. The last of the cloaks was to be redeemed. The ladies looked lovely and pleased. The gentlemen gallant and romantic. For Mrs. Wright, it was a triumph. Yet something was amiss. The second dance was coming to a close but there was no sign of Lady O'Carroll. Mrs. Wright began to feel slighted. She had not enlisted the patronage of the new gentry who occupied the estates purchased in the Encumbered Estates Market. Now, the main feature of the night, the auctioning of the cloaks was due to be announced and Lady O'Carroll not here to set it going. She turned towards a buzzing of excitement near the door. A lovely girl was coming straight towards her. 'My mother became indisposed. She sent me in her place rather than disappoint you.'

Heaven forgive me, Sterrin prayed. Nurse Hogan had almost swooned when she came downstairs with the note of excuse to be despatched by phaeton and saw that Sterrin, resplendent in her Paris gown, intended to deliver the note in person. When the nurse had exhausted her reproaches and remonstrances she concluded with the stock exclamation, 'This could be the death of her Ladyship.'

'If it could then,' Sterrin had replied, 'she must be protected from knowing about it. If this reaches her ears I shall hold you responsible for any consequences.' She was suddenly sick of Nurse Hogan's proprietorial airs and interferences.

Mrs. Wright disposed Sterrin in the seat of honour on the balcony among the non-dancing committee ladies. It was quite obvious to Sterrin that there was no question of her taking part in the dancing. To the committee ladies she was there in the stern purpose of a stern cause. She leaned over the balcony and pretended to take an interest in the crayon drawings on the floor of lovely girls in flowing cloaks of all colours. Her roving eyes could not discern anyone she might entice up here to lead her out.

The Master of Ceremonies announced the first performance in Ireland of King Pippin's Polka, the dance that had taken London by storm. He guaranteed that it would set every toe itching. Sterrin's toes responded to the guarantee immediately but the only offers to relieve their itch came from two semi-invalids. Mr. Enright tapped the region of his enlarged heart and said, in what he thought was a gay doggy manner, that only for THAT he would break through decorum that chained her to do duty for her mother, and seek the honour of leading her out. Lord Patrick Cullen caught sight of the bronze curls among the white caps of the matrons and hastened to pay his respects. He made no effort to conceal his astonishment at finding her at her first public dance unchaperoned.

'A pity,' he said when she explained, 'that they are playing this damned polka. The only dance that I could offer to lead you out in with this damned leg is the waltz.'

They stood behind her at either shoulder, chatting while the gay music wasted its substance and the M.C. announced that the local soprano would sing 'Where Are the Friends of My Youth?': It only needed that, thought Sterrin. Two crippled cavaliers and the committee ladies weeping for the friends of their youth! The ladies put their moist handkerchiefs in their reticules when the song had ended and leaned behind her, debating something that seemed to concern her.

They were perturbed about the correctness of asking her to

405

take her place so prominently on the platform that was being wheeled into the centre of the ballroom. They had planned that Lady O'Carroll would stand there beside the M.C. while he auctioned some new cloaks that had been presented by benefactors. The beautiful stately widow in flowing crepe was scarcely to be substituted in office, however benevolent—by a seventeen-year-old girl who was vividly, challengingly lovely.

'It might be indelicate,' murmured Mrs. Wright. Mrs. Enright found Sterrin's looks disturbing and muttered about 'a snare and a delusion'. Sterrin gave something approaching a wink to Patrick Cullen and said to the mortified Quaker:

'I assure you, Mrs. Enright, that I have not come here on my mother's behalf to either snare or delude.'

Everyone crowded round to reassure her, but the indomitable Quaker held her ground. 'Thee are overready to be loud in self-justification, Sterrin O'Carroll.' But Sterrin wasn't going to be balked of the fun of the auction.

'You want money, don't you? Fussing about etiquette won't keep these unfortunate women warm in the depths of the winter. Why, some of them can't get to church or chapel. It's a great cause,' she added, remembering Attracta. 'Come on, Patrick, start the bidding.'

Her appearance upon the raised daïs a few minutes later had the effect of an apparition. A young lady, not more than a girl, standing up before a crowded ballroom! Such a sight had never been seen there before. She was wearing the *robe de style* that had been sent from Paris for the dinner that had fêted the railroad. Its champagne velvet folds and drapes that fell away to disclose the gold lace valenciennes underskirt were displayed to perfection by the raised daïs that served as a pedestal for gown and wearer.

Mrs. Wright saw to it that the M.C. stressed the fact that Miss O'Carroll, at great personal inconvenience, was taking the last-minute place of her mother, Lady O'Carroll, who was regrettably indisposed, and trusted that the bidders would show their appreciation of her unselfish charity. He then presented a cloak to Sterrin who held it wide for the general inspection while the gold lace fell from her extended arms and revealed them white and shapely. Patrick's bid was drowned at utterance. The sovereigns clattered for the object—it mattered not what—that was displayed between those lovely arms.

From the corners of her eye she saw the crimson cloak tossed to Darcey Lubey, the elegant son of the gombeen man. Dragoons with pinched waists and shoulders ablaze with golden shells pressed round her throne and sought to catch her glance with every bid. She smiled at each and quickly turned with questioning look to demand more and more outrageous bids from the upturned faces and clamouring voices.

The funds mounted beyond the wildest dreams of Mrs. Wright. She was getting uneasy. There was something bizarre to her in the spectacle of the gently-bred girl attracting all those gentlemen about her like moths, dazzled by the flame of her radiance. What if Lady O'Carroll reproached her for this exploitation of her daughter? Mrs. Enright took no joy from the sight of the salver of gold being emptied and replenished. The cause had been gained by means that were ungodly.

But she could not know that Sterrin had swept on to the dais in the surge of feeling from the evening's ride that had yielded rebirth after the long, unyouthful spell of tragedy and calamity and grief and responsibility and depression that seemed to climax with the ending of Thuckeen. Here was an unrehearsed joyousness to which she could respond; acclaim that was balm to a spirit that had been brought too low. Her laughter rang out as bids were disputed and overtopped and daring buyers pushed forward to demand that she cast the cloak about the shoulders of successful bidders.

Suddenly her smile shortened. Donal Keating, coming late to the ballroom, had shouldered his way through the excited crowd. He stood still for a moment staring at the tall, golden girl. A gentleman beside him cried out, 'Ten sovereigns!' Donal called, 'Twelve!' The girl's smile acknowledged the bids then passed to him with a questioning quirk of her black eyebrows that suddenly dropped as she recognised him. 'Fifteen!' called a voice in front of him. Donal's voice drowned the next bid, 'Twenty-five!' he called.

Mrs Enright pulled the M.C.'s sleeve. 'Knock it down to him,' she commanded quite clearly. The auctioneer lifted his mock hammer and reached for the cloak Sterrin held. Not, she thought, if he bid one hundred and twenty-five! With a flick of her wrist she whirled the cloak about her shoulders and, slipping her arms through the inside loops, she held the lovely garment wide, then moved a little to display the graceful flow of its folds. The effect was dramatic. It was the handsomest cloak of the lot. Mrs. Wright had accepted it unwillingly from the wife of the Liverpool coffin-ship owner, who now occupied Lord Templetown's mansion. It was of a lighter shade of blue than the customary type. It had white satin lining and at least fifty yards of velvet ribbon trimmed its hem and hood. Sterrin wished she could own the gorgeous thing. Fancy any farmer's wife lugging eggs to market in this!

There were cries of 'ravishing!' Bids mounted. Mrs. Wright took hold of one of the M.C.'s coat tails. Mrs. Enright grabbed the other. 'Stop it!' they urged. He gave them a mute shrug of helplessness and turned to accept the bids. Donal Keating topped his own bid by another ten pounds. He prayed that James's James might not hear of this night's doings.

Then someone made a gaffe. 'A thousand guineas for the ensemble; cloak and wearer!' a voice cried. In the sudden silence, the M.C. took the cloak from Sterrin's shoulders and announced supper. As he preceded her to the supper room her path was blocked by what looked ominously like a quarrel. A very angry Lord Cullen was speaking to a gentleman with a scarlet cloak dangling from his shoulders. Lady Biddy Cullen was stage-whispering to her husband not to risk being killed in a duel for the sake of defending Sterrin O'Carroll's brazen conduct.

The man with the scarlet cloak turned and recognised Darcey Lubey. He made an elaborate bow. 'Forgive me, Miss O'Carroll, you deputised so admirably for Lady O'Carroll that I was quite carried away.' Sterrin gave him a cool glance, 'Thank you,' she answered. 'I could deputise for my father equally well but when he taught me to fence he explained to me that a tradesman may not lay claim to the point of honour. 'Tis the prerogative of a gentleman.' She sailed into the supper room with head high. A latecomer with the tabs of a captain crowded after her. Could it be possible? The last time he had seen her she was standing on a wall waving him goodbye when he was leaving for India.

The next morning, Sterrin was coming downstairs to join her mother for a carriage promenade when she saw Lady Biddy Cullen's carriage drive up. No inkling of last night's outing had reached her mother. It will reach her now, Sterrin thought, and waited on the landing to be summoned to retribution.

But there was no summons. Through the window she saw the

visitor depart. A moment later she saw her mother enter her own carriage. 'Mamma.' Sterrin was breathless from her rush downstairs. 'Don't you wish me to accompany you?'

Her mother looked at her as though she were seeing her for the first time. 'No, Sterrin,' she said, 'I do not wish you to accompany me.' Her tone dispensed with Sterrin's company for ever more. Her daughter's outrageous behaviour in public was scarcely as shocking to Lady O'Carroll as her deceit and callousness in taking such advantage of her mother's illness.

In Templetown Margaret received a less biased account of the incident. Mrs. Wright was warm in praise of the way Sterrin had taken her mother's place. Margaret relented. Too often in the past had Sterrin had to cover up for her mother!

But her compunction was short-lived. A drove of cattle blocked the carriage as it passed Lubey's. Margaret glanced idly towards the window then sat upright. The big window was bare of its usual merchandise. Instead, down the centre hung a scarlet cloak. In front of it a placard with letters a foot high stated 'As Publicly Displayed by Miss Sterrin O'Carroll of Kilsheelin Castle'.

The auction story blew like chaff at a threshing. The prices Miss O'Carroll seduced for the cloaks mounted higher. The price Darcey Lubey offered for herself grew higher still. When Lady Biddy Cullen gave a carpet dance for her sisters, Sterrin was not bidden. Lady O'Carroll was cut to tears. No function had ever been held at Crannagh without the O'Carrolls.

She called Sterrin to her boudoir. 'I am writing to Sir Jocelyn to ask him to take away his horse.'

'You mean——' Sterrin had to scrape out the words from a choked throat. 'You mean you are not going to let me accept Cloora?'

'So costly a gift to a young lady was *mauvais ton*. After the slight you brought upon yourself from the Lubey person, it is unthinkable.'

Sterrin went towards the stables feeling like a battered fourpenny bit. Mike O'Driscoll was pacing Cloora. Tears pricked at Sterrin as she watched the horse's beautifully held head, its fine action. She felt an affinity with the animal; a creature of the elements; of storm and thunder and rushing winds. There came into her head a text her father used to quote about a fine horse. 'He sniffeth the battle from afar, the thunder of the captains and the shouting.' Clooreen was that sort of horse. 'Unharness her, Mike, I'm not riding her today.' She told him of her mother's decision. Mike lost the straw he was chewing. He had almost lived in Clooreen's stable. He comforted himself with another straw and then he comforted Sterrin.

'Don't be foolish, Miss Sterrin. Get up and ride her while you still have her. There is no use in having a gap between your two front teeth if you can't whistle.' Sterrin's rueful smile brought out her teeth in defence of their perfection.

But the sanction that Sir Jocelyn Devine sought when he called had nothing to do with the horse. He sought the sanction of Lady O'Carroll for permission to propose marriage to her daughter. He would return next week for her answer.

Sterrin was dumbfounded. 'But, Mamma,' she exclaimed, as matter of fact as Mike O'Driscoll, 'why trouble him to make the journey again. Couldn't you have given him his answer?'

'What answer——' Something in her mother's tone made Sterrin's heart give a little quick beat of dread. Surely there was but one answer that her mother could expect her to give to such a proposal!

Her mother *did* think that there was but one answer. She steeled herself for the conflict.

Day after day it waged. An honourable proposal from a distinguished gentleman of great wealth. On the heels of a public bid that was a degradation!

'Do you realise the significance of that terrible bid?' Sterrin had a shrewd idea. She preferred not to think of the way Lubey had looked at her that night.

Sterrin leaned against the mantelpiece in her mother's bedroom and looked down into the turquoise flame of the black turf. Her mother was repeating the arguments that had been arrayed every day. No chance of Sterrin meeting an eligible party, their plight, the mansions occupied by peasants and shopkeepers, no hope of being presented, refused credit by shopkeepers, ostracised by the Cullens, the only people of one's class who maintained even a skeleton of social life. In the flames Sterrin saw a dark face, the one that used to waft in the suffusion of clouds and lace when she used to daydream of her wedding. '. . . and the unmarried officers are all away at the Crimea. I've lost touch with the garrison. Before the famine young officers used to come here . . .'

Sterrin turned from the picture in the flames. There was one young officer who used to come here. Lieutenant Fitzharding-Smith was always hovering around Mamma. And now he was back, a captain. He had been at the dance, Sterrin had met him for a brief moment in all the furore after the auction. How young her mother looked, sitting there on the low *prie-dieu* seat, plaiting her hair! There was a kind of—of unused look about her mother's smooth forehead.

'Mamma, why don't *you* marry?' The words slipped from her. 'You are still very young and very pretty.'

Her mother dropped her plait as though she had been stung. 'Sterrin! What an unseemly suggestion. Me, to marry! After—after—Papa. Why, it would be—sacrilege.'

Sterrin looked across the flickering shadows at the young face and the slim figure. The romance that her mamma had known! The love! 'Sacrilege for *you* to marry,' she said and her voice was angry. She walked to the door then stopped. 'But for me to make this marriage is merely—sacrifice.' Her mother stayed looking at the door that had closed so urgently. She hadn't dreamed that Sterrin was capable of such bitterness. She caught up on Sterrin and threw her arms about her.

'You shall not be sacrificed. *Mon Dieu!* My ewe lamb shall not be sacrificed.'

Reprieved, Sterrin proceeded to read the *Manual For Young Ladies* that Bunzy de Lacey had sent her from America. In the chapter headed 'First Replies to First Proposals', the answer that Bunzy had given to her first beau was heavily underlined. 'I-cannot-love-you-but-I-shall-never-forget-you.' So was 'I-can-not-be-your-wife-but-I-shall-be-a-sister-to-you.' Sterrin tried to see herself going through life being a sister to the elderly and urbane Sir Jocelyn.

She threw the book aside. The writer had no formula for a girl who had a dozen lives depending upon her answer. The workhouse was facing Big John and Mrs. Stacey and the others. What would happen to Mamma? What would become of little, helpless Dominic? She knew now that the compensation for the iron road coming through the property could not begin to clear all Kilsheelin's debts.

Sterrin crossed to the window. In the shadowy light the big yard looked like a city square; fine buildings built in symmetry by ancient craftsmen. In the sentient night air the history of

411

each house breathed out in reproach to her. From the game-keeper's house, O'Driscoll's ancestor had been beaten to death because a Catholic might not carry a walking stick; and in the steward's house there had been a forefather of Hegarty's who had died screening her own forefather. And what has all that to do with me? Am I to become a living mortgage to screen their descendants? And what do I get out of it? Suddenly the full significance of things assailed her. Saving Kilsheelin for the others meant going away from it herself!

Deliberately she unlocked the secret place of her mind that held the hopeless comfort that somewhere, always, there was a heart in which she dwelt; a lover who dare not speak of love; who would go to the end of the earth for her. The end of the earth! 'Oh, Young Thomas, Young Thomas, why had you to be—Young Thomas, the knife boy?'

Sir Jocelyn accepted her rejection courteously. His proposal was, perhaps a little premature?

'You will be taking Clooreen today?'

'Not today,' he told her, noting the relief in her face. The transfer of the horse must await his return from London. 'And when I return, perhaps I may venture to put the same question to you. Meantime, think kindly of me, my dear.'

As she sped towards Clooreen she was already feeling kindly towards him. So generous! And he made her feel like a duchess.

She roamed the country on the magnificent horse, lingering with her in the stable at night, dreading that each goodnight might be the last. Strange men came to inspect the castle and grounds. The gloom their visit cast over Christmas was not dispelled by the scruffy band of Wren Boys who came next day for their share of the feast. Like so many of those who had grown up since the famine they were poorer in physique, less proud in bearing than their predecessors. The famine, people said, had been the end of an era. A race of fine, manly people had died or had gone over the sea before they became accus-tomed to eating the bread of charity. There was none among these Wren Boys, Lady O'Carroll thought, like the handsome giant who had danced with her that Saint Stephen's Day before the famine. Where was he? And where was the girl who had danced with Roderick; the girl with the wonderful hair that had suggested the kneeling Magdalen?

On Epiphany Day, Margaret watched the sky, as always, for

the storm clouds of the big wind. Sterrin did not dare to remind her that today was her birthday. Instead she set out for her last ride on Clooreen. Sir Jocelyn was coming today. As she approached the gap at Cuilnafunchion where she had had the encounter with Donal Keating, she slowed and frowned. Someone had piled up branches over the gap. She dismounted and started removing them, when a man appeared from the other side. 'What do you mean by smashing down that fence?' he said.

Sterrin looked through James Keating as though he were not there. The man, she reflected, must have some post-famine hallucination. She decided to have him warned off the property. But his figure still blocked the gap.

'Please stand aside,' she said coldly.

'You appear to be unaware that it was I who bought this lot of land. I was prepared to buy the whole estate, castle and all, before it was withdrawn from the Encumbrancy auction.' His lips gave a twist that was meant for a smile. 'Withdrawn for a while.'

A lonely silence fell across the landscape. Sterrin felt a chill tremor. It was as though an unspent breath of the storm that had precipitated her birth, that had scooped her father's acres into the sky to fall at this man's feet, had sighed past her. In a drowning flash she saw the castle as the bard had seen it; vanishing fortress with rush-strewn floors and great wolfhounds and the 'yellow-ringleted O'Carroll' holding sway. Near this spot in Queen Elizabeth's day, the O'Carroll had halted his horse and his gallow-glasses[1] to 'bid the English quit his land'. The thought roused her back to life. She raised her whip high over the bachach's head but before it fell he had seized her wrist. He forced it behind her holding her against him. Her left hand held the horse's bridle. As he bent over her he saw her suck in her jaws and her lips formed the kiss he had not hoped to get so readily; they opened and shot into his eyes the spit she had gathered.

Big John heard the thunder of hooves before he saw her. He wondered if she had lost control. The black horse moved as a boat moves before a powerful wind, but instead of spray it cast up sods and stones that fell unheeded on its rider. Men in strange livery looked up and stared as she jumped the bay

[1] Ancient term for 'soldier'.

hedge. In the artificial pond a splendid carriage was discarding the muddy cloggings from its wheels.

Sir Jocelyn Devine thought there was a boyish gallantry about her as she walked down the length of the drawing-room to where he stood. Her riding clothes were mud-spattered. Her hair had escaped from its black snood. It felt like a bewitched barley stack but he saw only the sheening aureole. Had there been no snood but ringlets falling to the shoulder, had there been a moustache instead of the high curved red lip, she might be one of the cavaliers who looked out of their frames, the gentlemen of Kilsheelin who had gone as the Wild Geese to stand by the Old Pretender; who had fought with Prince Charlie. But she was all woman and there was no warm whiteness like the whiteness of her skin.

'Sir Jocelyn! Why have you come today? Is it for your horse?'

He looked into the direct eyes, that would brook no skirmishing by-play. 'I have come to ask again for the honour of your hand in marriage.'

She had no time now for the counsels of the *Manual For Young Ladies* but there was a dignity of ritual about the resolute way she removed her glove and extended her hand to him.

CHAPTER 42

The train clove through the meadows of his native land. How small they looked after the great tracts of America! And had they been as green as this always? He lowered the window and leaned out. The streamlet that ran cheekily with the train was so close that he could see the darting minnow.

An insect with gauzy wings flew past and his heart sank a little. The mayfly would be rising in the castle river. He thought of the excitement when he brought her the word 'the fly is risen'. Up half the night she'd be, tying Green or Grey Drake, and off with her at dawn to follow the river's windings until dark!

More insects swarmed up, dizzy with the ecstasy of their first flight; their first contact with the air and sun that is the wedding ceremony of the mayfly. The ethereal culmination of its two drab years beneath the water. Was it an omen? For he too, after his own drab years of toil and hardship was returning on the gauzy wings of his success to perform at the wedding of an Irish Nabob.

Despondency clouded him. Gone was that bright moment when he had been certain that he could build the bridge to Sterrin's world, when he had bought his land in New Orleans and pictured the elegant white house that he would build for her, and for their children. He had engaged the best architect in the city to design it. That lovely dream was shattered when John Holohan brought him the letter from Nurse Hogan. Thomas still had that letter. He remembered the excitement with which he had torn open the envelope. And the horror with which he had read that Sterrin had returned to the convent. This time to take her vows. What convent had she entered? Surely not the one she had run from that day long ago?

He wished suddenly that he had not accepted the unexpected invitation to break his journey to London and play for Sir Jocelyn Devine's wedding guests at his private theatre. He had

415

sworn never to return; he hated Sir Jocelyn for the cruel wound he had inflicted on Bergin. But the temptation to perform near Kilsheelin had proved too strong; it was a chance to see Bergin again, to find out how he had fared upon his return from Australia. Thomas looked forward, too, to spending a few moments with the kitchen group that had once been family; to the pleasure of bringing lavish gifts to Mrs. Hogan; to all of them; to glimpse the gracious being who was the mother of his lost dream; and to look once again at the setting of a life that was past and a dream that was ended.

Suddenly the train stopped. The guard was arguing with a blue-hooded woman that this was a private train bringing play-actors to the mansion of Sir Jocelyn Devine for the wedding festivities. Out in the middle of the sleepers she stood and pointed to the big growth that hung from her chin and said that if she didn't get to the fair to meet the man with the cure she would be dead before the next day. 'We'll all be dead before the next fair day if we take you up,' said the guard. But she was of the generation that could not understand the unnaturalness of a vehicle—steam or horse—that would pass a foot passenger on any road, whether it were clay or iron.

'And it isn't, she pointed out, 'as though the gentleman that owns it or any of the gentry, except the play-actors, were on the train.'

The engine driver looked at the guard. 'What about the gentleman in the first-class?'

'The one that's over the play-actors?'

'Aye, but isn't he a gentleman, too?'

'He is,' said the guard, 'and for all we know may be a friend or relation of the Big Man.' He turned to the woman. 'Would you mind lettin' the train get past, ma'am. We're off schedule.'

'Indeed, you're not off anything,' she assured him. 'Keep goin' straight ahead.' She waved towards the shining tracks. 'Ye can't miss the road. Let ye not turn right or left an' ye'll be in Kilkenny in a shout. An' sure it isn't leavin' me behind you would?' She coaxed up to the driver. 'Sure, I can see the kind heart of you on your face.'

The guard grew exasperated and waved his flag in front of her. 'Will you get off the line over that, yerself an' yer plamas.[1] There's nothing to be seen on that man's face from one Sunday

[1] Pronounced 'plaumaus'—flattery or soft-talk.

416

to the next but soot.'

The gentleman in the first-class put an end to the discussion. 'Get in here,' he called, standing by the open door. The woman nearly fell out of her standing but she grabbed her basket and rushed.

'Sure, a third-class will do me with the play-actors, Your Honour,' she protested.

'In with you,' commanded his Honour, but at the door she hesitated and looked anxiously in the direction of a stile in the hedge where two, fair, curly heads peeped.

Too late the guard rushed forward to prevent the defilement of their muddy little hooves on the red carpet. The gentleman proved his undoubted gentility by the tone with which he ordered the guard to proceed. 'We've wasted sufficient time, sez he,' repeated the guard to the driver who agreed that it was hard to understand the gentry.

In the first-class, the gentleman swung the large basket on to the rack. 'And if I may say so, madam,' he remarked, 'it is truly a heavy load for a lady who stands in danger of death within the month.'

The lady was all apologies. 'Your Honour shouldn't be dirtying his gloves with the likes of that. There's sixteen an' a half pounds of butter there, eight pounds three ounces in one and eight pounds five ounces in the other.'

His heart gladdened at the sight of the gleaming rolls of golden butter all diamond patted and decorated with rose and shamrock shaped designs. He put back the cabbage leaves and replaced the lid and reminded himself to get wooden, fancy shapes to bring back to Kitty on her Wisconsin farm.

'So, it was your fair day butter and not the growth,' he smiled.

'Sure, your Honour, how could I let me customers down that waits for me in all weathers? An' the growth is no lie either. Look!' She gave him an uninhibited view of the excrescence. 'I have it this ten year,' she said calmly. 'An' listen to the children! Sure, I had to get them to the man with the ass. They're barking like terriers with the chincough.'

Conversation had to yield to the prostrating whoops of the cough but in lulls she discussed the fabulous wedding. He wasn't keenly interested in the wealth displays of Sir Jocelyn Devine.

'He must have money in every pocket,' she was saying. 'She looks a beauty, they say.'

He had not realised that the words that had fallen into the clearing of coughs were addressed to him.

'I beg your pardon,' he said politely.

'The bride, sir. They say she is a beauty out and out.'

He looked back at the scenery. A gentle wind sent the grass rippling to the distant horizon in waves of everlasting green. He felt no interest in the beauty of the nabob's bride. He would prefer if this good woman would permit him to concentrate upon the bronze-haired beauty whose young white face appeared and vanished in each succeeding wave of grass. 'My girl has ringlets rich and rare, by Nature's finger wove.'

'I beg your pardon, madam?'

'I was sayin', your Honour, that it is a great match she's makin' entirely. They say he has money in every pocket but like that again it's a case of "have a goose an' you'll get another". Sure hasn't she a castle herself beyond in Templetown?'

'Did you say Templetown? What castle? What is this Lady's name?' A fit of coughing drowned her reply. She held the child's head out of the window.

'Get it up now, Alannah!' Over her shoulder she excused the indelicacy. 'With respects to your honour, but isn't an empty house better than a bad tenant! She is a titled lady,' she went on, wiping the child's mouth and resuming her seat. 'I disremember her name, Lady Something, but I'd remember the name of the castle if you were just to mention it to me.'

'Would it be Tullow Castle in Templetouhy?'

She shook her head. 'That's not the name, your Honour.'

'The Castle of Ballagh?'

She shook her head.

'Would it be Strague Castle? Or Bawnmadrum Castle?'

She shook her head again. 'It's not Bawnmadrum. That's the old O'Meara place, but 'tis a name like that the lady has. One of the old names.'

He'd been dreading it but now he must cite the name he had withheld. It couldn't be, of course. 'It is scarcely Lady O'Carroll of Kilsheelin Castle?'

She nearly jumped in her seat with the excitement of gratifying the kindly interest of the pleasant gentleman. 'The very one, your Honour!' She went on chatting but suddenly she realised

418

that she had overstepped. The like of her had no right to impose with her talk because the gentleman had shown such friendly condescension. Look at him now, puttin' her in her place with that haughty faraway look!

But he handed out her basket and her children with courtly grace. He swept his high beaver low as though she were a duchess, and he marshalled his flock and his scenery with his wonted efficiency.

A separate carriage bore him to the marble mansion of the man whose wealth was famed even in far off America, and Australia. Every boatload of hunted tenants gave fresh testimony to its hourly increase.

Sir Jocelyn came with courtly condescension to meet the celebrity but his greetings were accepted with such an air of calm equality that, instead of summoning a lackey to show the way to the private theatre, he found himself escorting the distinguished-looking personage there himself. 'I have seen Mr. Macready in "Virginius",' he remarked, 'but the critics hold that you surpass him in the title role.'

The actor inclined his dark head. 'The critics have been most kind.'

'This evening's choice of repertory,' continued the host, 'is that of my fiancée.'

Again the actor inclined his head. 'I trust that her Ladyship will not be disappointed.'

Sir Jocelyn gave him a puzzled look, but as he moved away he paused. 'There will be a ball after the performance,' he said. 'You will not be too fatigued to attend?' The excuse rose and went unspoken. There would be no need to ride through the night to Kilsheelin. Lady O'Carroll too, would be there. Another gem for this marble setting. He tossed from him the picture of a girl in a niche in a wall that was deep grouted with the steadfast mountain grit—a girl waiting!

Waiting, he said to his reflection as he sloshed the coconut butter on his face; waiting for a vagrant; the First Mate of a stolen coffin ship, a strolling player! He pressed in place the short-cropped wig of tight grey curls and clamped about them a bandeau of gold. The chair went backwards to the ground as he pushed it from him to don the Roman toga. A little sugar statue fell on its face as he banged out of the door. He turned and set it up, then touched it slowly in a sort of ceremonial gesture.

Somewhere in the front a woman listened and froze. Out of the past and across the footlights came words that Roderick had quoted—almost with that self-same voice—as she lay on the great carved seat that had been designed by the boy who had ceased his tinkling mid the tea-service to listen also. '... she wished,' she said.

> *'That it had been a man. I answered her,*
> *It was the mother of a race of men,*
> *And paid her for thee with a kiss.'*

The voice from the stage held tones and inflections that beat about her ears with an intimacy that was frightening. She clenched her nails to fight against the credulous fancy. How could this be Roderick's voice!

The actor's voice surged with passion because he was declaiming about a lovely love he had thought could never die; a love that had inspired his whole remembered life and refreshed him in its gentle backwash until it had conditioned his emotions to focus upon the fruit of that love.

'The very flower,' he cried towards Appius on his tribunal, 'our bed connubial grew ...'

First of the enraptured audience to rise in acclaim was the undemonstrative host, Sir Jocelyn. But the cold, averted profile of the lady who remained seated in the shadows of the box was not that of Lady O'Carroll. The white-robed actor, turning again and again before the curtain could pick out no face that recalled her presence.

Suddenly his heart resumed its lilt. Of course! of course! Lady O'Carroll was not the bride at all. She wasn't here. What had he been thinking of to give such credence to the gossip of a woman journeying her children to be cured by a promenade beneath an ass's belly!

In vain the grand audience sought to clap him forth once more, and finally it desisted. To disappear without a curtain speech, was probably, they told each other, some whim of his exclusiveness, the prerogative of fame.

Back in his dressing-room he hurled the flowing robes from him and pulled a fresh white shirt over his head without removing his make-up. 'Oh, sir,' expostulated his dresser, Alphabet, 'you've smeared your nice fresh shirt!'

When the black curls had shaken out through the opening of frilled dawn a streak of yellow ochre showed on every frill. He pulled the shirt from him and threw it on to the floor. 'Get me another,' he ordered. 'And get me into these.' He nodded towards the riding boots.

'A pity to miss the dance, sir,' gasped the dresser as he tugged the boot loops over the limb held horizontally in mid-air.

'No, Alphabet,' said the actor gaily to Anselm Beracium Conceptionez Duignan, 'there is a smell of feet in that ballroom.'

'Oh, Gawney, sir, surely not! Not them ladies and gents!'

Down came the booted leg and up with its shapely companion in embroidered hose. 'No, not them. Little ladies and gents, only they weren't really ladies and gents. That was the trouble. And they weren't sweaty feet, Alphabet. They were sizzling, burning feet performing the dance of death. Remind me to tell you about them someday. *A bientôt*, Alphabet, and go to bed soon. This place is horribly haunted.' A whisk of white satin lining and the tall, cloaked figure was gone.

'Whoever she is,' said Anselm Beracium Conceptionez Duignan to the closed door, 'by the mortal frost, she must be a stunner!'

A few strides brought the actor down a passage and across the marble hall. Silently he slid the great bolt without benefit of butler or footman, and as he pulled the door open a prolonged susurrus of silk and an upward rippling of laughter made him turn. The artist in him lingered on the sudden tableau.

Up the stairs in a swaying procession of colour, hooped white satin, blue brocade, rose moire, climbed a row of lovely girls. Each one held aloft a silver candlestick and its flame glinting in their hair ornaments gave the impression of moving stars. The buckles in their shoes, twinkling out of upheld flounces, looked like starry reflections in the black marble steps that rose wavelike beneath each foaming petticoat. As they wended upward for one final titivation before the ball they chattered and laughed and tossed back words over their shoulders.

'Ye gods, wasn't he divine?'

'Like a Greek god!'

'Not Greek, 'twas a Roman play. He looks like a cast of some Roman emperor.'

'Did you see his eyes?'

'It was his voice that held me. Wasn't it superb, Sterrin?'

The words were tossed over a white shoulder. Then the speaker disappeared in the upper darkness and the girl in the turquoise was alone on the stairway, slowly mounting. Her head was slightly bowed and the diamonds in the suffusion of her hair looked like stars in the bronze clouds of a stormcast sunset. That voice, she thought. Why had it stirred her like this? Why had all these submerged scenes risen upright? Frachans[1] on the hill slopes! Mushrooms in the dewy dawn! Hawthorn blossoms on Lissnastreenagh! A voice, was it across the footlights or across Coolnafunchion that had cried, 'Come on, Rajah! Don't let Thuckeen shame you.' And, linked with all, lifelong, un-uttered, unformed, some vague hope that only now, this grey moment, had finally, despairingly ceased!

A gust of wind guttered her candle. A noise made her turn. How strange to see the door stand open like that at night; and rain and wind coming through the empty hallway!

Then she saw the man who stood at the foot of the stairs gazing up at her. This was a haunted house! Trembling caused grease to drip on the turquoise brocade. This was no ghost! She could see the white of his knuckles from the tensity of his grip on the banister. No convict either! Not this elegant stranger! In all the world there was only one pair of eyes like these that gazed at her with intensity, bluer than ever from the liner that still outlined the unforgettable lashes.

A sudden squall came through the door and up the stairs and moved the pictures on its way and swirled her silken draperies. The candlestick was growing heavy, her arm drooped. With a bound he was beside her and taken the weight from her hand just as he had always done! He held the light to shine on every vestige of the face that was lovelier than he had dreamed. 'Sterrin!'

'Young Thomas!' Their names mingled and then they were silent again. No words would come to either but her throat moved with the congestion of words and questions. Someone was closing the door. The hall came alive. Without speaking he turned to light her up the remaining stairs; just as he had always done. Without thinking she moved upward in the path of light he shed for her.

In the landing he put down the candle and the gesture re-

[1] Bilberries.

leased her voice. 'When did you escape?' But as she spoke she knew the question was out of character. There were years of worldly freedom behind the ease and polish of this elegant man. His smile was as gentle as years ago but it was the quirk of his eyebrow at the question that released just one of all the emotions that strove within her. From the thrill and the wonder and the dazed joy came resentment, fierce and unreasoning. 'Yes, weren't you in prison? You—you *ought* to have been in prison!' He ought to have been because of all the anguish she had endured for him. Lord, the cloud that had shadowed all those years! The slobbering sentimentalising over his broken life. She, running away to share his living entombment. And look at him! The height and breadth of him! The very air about him throbbed with his vitality. She felt cheated. His grandeur mocked her years of mourning pity. She could not know how coldly proud was the mask that covered her humiliation, and seemed to disdain the decked-out finery of the former knife boy. He glanced at his clothes and their grandeur mocked him. He gave a slight bow, 'You are right, I ought to have been in prison. I realise that it was presumptuous of me to be elsewhere. Goodbye, Miss Sterrin.'

'Young Thomas!' He had almost reached the top of the stairs when the name burst from her as it had that morning years ago when she watched him moving down the castle boreen out of her life. He turned. Instead of the black ribbon, there were diamonds holding her hair, instead of the cloak of mourning black there was a gown of blue brocade, but the face above was fine drawn with the same pleading of the girl who had waved from the wall; whose heart was as steadfast as the wall of mountain grit. In one stride he took her in his arms.

'Giola, mo giola!' Brightness of brightness! The old endearment sprang to his lips before they met hers in a long kiss that was her awakening and his fulfilment. When it ended he drew her closer still and buried his face in her hair. 'And if I had taken one more sulky step I might have gone beyond recall for ever and have missed this glorious moment.' He pushed back her hair from her forehead and placed his other hand beneath her chin and gazed deep into the face that had been with him in all his wanderings. How lovely it had become! 'And I see that you still have your wart.' He fingered the speck of brown velvet above her eye.

She drew back. 'Wart, indeed! Let me tell you that my beauty spot is all the rage. All the bridesmaids are wearing ...' her gaiety ebbed.

He drew her back into his arms. 'Are all the bridesmaids wearing warts?' And suddenly he realised with a pang that the warty woman on the train had not been wrong. Lady O'Carroll must be the bride, since Sterrin was here. Here in his arms! The pang gave way to a surging of joy. 'Sterrin, my love,' he murmured, 'if I had thrown away this moment. I think that I must have lived for it since that night when I saw the field taken up to the sky and I thought that the world had ended and was being taken up to Heaven—all the people except the three of us there. Then we reached the castle and I fell asleep and when I awakened you were there. I had a sleepy impression that it was you who had brought calm. Since then you have been my world.' He looked over her head into the shadows. 'You were there when the storm used to crash the waves and clouds together and send the boat into a kind of outer darkness.'

She smiled happily against his shoulder. 'Always the stormy petrel!'

'No, mavourneen.'

She thought that his beautiful voice crooned music into the world.

'You were the white dove of the tempest.'

She gave a sigh of rapture. This was the moment that her life also, had awaited. She twined her arms about him and looked up into his face, 'And I thought that you were in prison—a convict.'

'And I thought that you were in a convent—a nun. Mo cuid de'n naim!' My share of heaven.

She drew back on a sudden. 'But where *have* you been? And what brought you here. You seemed to appear out of the night on the breath of the wind——'

'On the breath of the wind,' he repeated. 'The way you first came. Then you did not recognise me on the stage?'

Realisation smote her. 'So it was you!' she breathed. That was why she had felt so strangely disturbed during his performance. Why Mamma had tensed and agitated her fan so that Sterrin had dreaded the onset of another attack after so long. Young Thomas had always imitated Papa's voice; in a restrained kind of way. But back there in that theatre it had clarioned forth with all Papa's assurance and authority. 'You are the famous Thomas Young!' She was awestruck for a moment, then she gave out a low jet of laughter, 'Oh, Young Thomas, how terribly funny and how terribly like you. You reversed your own name.'

'Not quite. I decided to pick up the name that Mr. Young discarded that time in the Crow Street Theatre in Dublin. Do you remember?'

'I remember. You nearly got Papa arrested, and you had police watching the castle for months. They thought that you were someone dangerous and important—but——' she laid her head against him and she could hear the beating of his heart, 'you were always important to me—your heart is beginning to go thumpity, thump.' She looked up at him. 'It is not really so startling that you should have become an actor. Do you remember the plays we used to get up with Bunzy De Lacey? And do you remember when you acted the Lord Lieutenant at Court Presentations you would not give me the ceremonial kiss?'

'I shall spend the rest of my life atoning for that omission.' His lips met hers and stopped her reminiscences but they failed to stop the little chill of dread at his words. The world around her had returned. They had been play-acting, the two of them, here in this unrehearsed moment of reunion. Now she must face reality.

'Sterrin,' he raised her face from his shoulder. 'what was this about you entering a convent? The news was like a death blow. What happened?'

'Well, you see, Young Thomas—Oh, I must remember to drop the "young". It was always a silly thing. Why you are years older than——' She gazed bleakly into the face that was now so youngly handsome; older only in their own bright sphere. Not in that remote phase of sardonic age that was reaching out from forty years away to grasp her. The same panic that she had experienced in the jewelled aviary began to mount. Then voices came along the corridor and she started back from him. Opened doors threw beams of light and the swish of silken gowns. From the stairs came Sir Jocelyn's voice. She almost dragged Thomas into the room behind her. 'What is wrong?' he asked, 'I have never known you to show this kind of fear. Don't tell me that you are frightened of your future stepfather?'

She seated herself at the dressing-table; her back to him, her face staring whitely from the mirror. Rows of tall candles blazing in mirrored duplicate gave him the impression of an altar ablaze with votive candles. The realisation had a significance unassociated with the time when he used to be in and out of her room every day; to make sure that Mickey-the-turf had replenished the turf holder; to carry in her hip bath and place it just not too near the blazing sods; when he would light her to her room up winding stairs past eerie nooks and crannies. He looked at the sumptuous bed and recalled the time when she had measles and he used to read to her; one hand holding the book the other reaching out to jerk back the red woollen cap that cloustered the red hair over the red-patched face. All that lurid red; the coverlet, the curtains, the red bedjacket, essential colour treatment for measles. This mother-of-pearl bed would have disturbed the treatment. It was—disturbing. He took his eyes from its slender columns embowered in silken drapes and looked back at the face that stared so strangely at him from the mirror.

'Listen, Young Thomas—Thomas. No,' she cried out, 'I mean Young Thomas.' She rose and came back to him. 'Because you *are* young. You will always be "Young Thomas" to me. Always.'

She *had* changed. This was not the Sterrin whom he had known. That Sterrin might blaze with sudden temper but she was never distrait. Even after her father's murder she had conserved her strength to support her mother. 'Sterrin,' he said quietly, 'what is amiss? There is a dread on you.'

Before she could reply there was a tap at the door and Hannah entered. 'Miss Sterrin,' she gasped, 'what are you thinking of? A gentleman blaguardin' in your bedroom!'

'Hannah, you humbug, cried a voice that made her jump out of her standing. 'Don't pretend to be shocked. This is not the first time that you have seen me in Miss Sterrin's bedroom.'

'Glory be to the Hand of God!' she gasped. 'Young Thomas! Didn't I think that you were a gentleman.'

'What a terrible mistake! Why, Hannah, you used to say that you'd know a gentleman if you only saw him walking upside down on the ceiling like a fly.'

'An' I'm looking at one now, Young Thomas asthore; the finest that ever I laid eyes on, barrin' Sir Roderick's own self. Mrs. Stacey will be out of her mind with joy and Big John and indeed Mr. Hegarty, too. He often says that you were his right hand.'

'I'm afraid that you will have to carry them the full of my heart of love and the gifts that I have brought for all of you. I had hoped to risk a flying visit to Kilsheelin tonight. We go to London tomorrow but now that I've discovered Miss Sterrin to be here I shall not risk——'

'But didn't you know she'd be here. Isn't that why we're all here? Sure . . .'

'That's all right, Hannah,' Sterrin interrupted her. 'I shall be down in a moment. And don't breathe a word.' Hannah paused at the doorway; uneasy.

'I don't like it, Miss Sterrin. It's neither wrong nor right and his Honour Sir Jocelyn is asking for you.' Sterrin waved her out impatiently but still the maid hesitated. 'I'm in dread, Miss Sterrin. It's contrary but——' She turned to Thomas. 'You are the full of my eyes. I can't take them off you. Would anyone believe that you ever drew a rusty knife down the centre of a raw potato?'

He opened the door and manoeuvred her through. 'No, Hannah. No one would ever believe such a calumny. My knives were never rusty.'

A man's voice sounded and Sterrin rushed to close the door. 'He'll hear you,' she whispered.

The laughter went from his face. With his hand still gripping the door-knob he said, 'Sterrin, who has put this fear on you! Is it the man whom your mother is going to marry?'

Her eyes were blue-black in the tense white of her face. 'Mamma!' She gave a little laugh that had nothing to do with joy. 'Where have you been, Young Thomas? You cannot have been anywhere in the three kingdoms or you would know the name of the future Lady Devine.'

It was his turn to go white. She noticed the way his knuckles strained white, too, from his grip of the door-knob. A black line of words crawled through his brain. Words like purblind and love-blind and presumptuous fool. But the great actor had no tricks to get his lines across the silence of this unset stage.

'I thought you knew.' So it had been an omen, he was thinking. That mayfly on its wedding flight! 'Do you hear me?' she repeated. 'I thought you knew.' Her voice reached him at last like the prompter's insistent cue penetrating the silence of forgotten lines.

'And thinking I knew,' he said quietly, 'you let me inhale the bouquet.'

'What bouquet?' She said it lifelessly because she knew he was reproaching her in some of his bookish metaphors.

'Sterrin,' he said softly, 'do you remember the Christmas before the famine? Hounds met at Kilsheelin next day and the Wren Boys danced in the hall—oh yes, by the way, Big John Holohan who danced the "double" with that long-haired girl, Molly Heffernan, is on the way to becoming another Croesus. Sir Roderick,' he continued, 'had ordered Hegarty to decant some rare wine for Sir Jocelyn Devine. He was such a connoisseur! Hegarty gave me a lambastin' afterwards because when I filled the decanter I paused for a split second to inhale— to sniff, I should say, I hadn't learn't to "inhale" in those days. Then Sir Jocelyn raised the glass to his lips and savoured it, sip by sip, with slow delight. . . .'

'How dare you!' She had caught his meaning. 'You—you have no right to speak like that to me!'

The white horror on her face recalled him from his reverie. 'No, Achushla, I have no right to speak to you at all.' He twisted the knob and held the door ready. 'But you cannot withdraw from me the breath of fragrance that escaped on its way to the connoisseur. Goodbye, Sterrin.'

Suddenly she was the cool, still girl he remembered. She placed the tip of one white-clad finger on the door and its opening ceased. 'I am sorry to spoil your exit; it deserves applause. You have learned to speak drama magnificently, but this is not a play; it is life; not just mine or Mamma's or Dominic's. It concerns the lives of people like Hegarty whose grandfather gave his life to save Kilsheelin from confiscation; people like Big John and Mrs. Stacey, born in Kilsheelin like their parents before them; and Mike O'Driscoll whose grandfather was flogged to death in the old deer park because he was gamekeeper to a papist when papists were not allowed to have gamekeepers. It concerns the possible eviction of tenants who have occupied our land since—almost since the first Prince of the O'Carrolls lived at Kilsheelin.'

The celebrated actor stood chastened while the descendant of the first Prince of the O'Carrolls rebuked her knife boy; a true princess of her line carrying the burdens of her heritage on the

428

silver and turquoise slopes of her shoulders. Such young shoulders!

'Too young!' It broke from him involuntarily and she misunderstood. Minute by minute she was loving him more, understanding more what had been the meaning of the things he had said when he bade her goodbye over five years ago, and with every minute she was resenting more and more the anguish she had endured on him and the long silence that he had allowed her to suffer. What did he expect to find when he condescended to swoop back in all his glory? A rustic belle wearing the willow for him?

'Too young for what? For whom? Even those who stay at home grow in some direction. They grow old; they even grow rusty ...' His smile angered her while it twisted her heart with its warm sweetness. He was thinking that the qualities that were the antithesis of rust and age, the qualities of youth and brightness stood out from her like another dimension in a full-length aureole.

'I must go down,' she announced in dismissal. 'There is no more time for explanations or reproach.'

He made no move to open the door for her. There was too much to be said. But it opened and Sir Jocelyn Devine said, 'I'm afraid, my dear, we must find time for both, since I find that you are far from reproach.'

Sterrin reflected that she seemed to be observing Young Thomas's knuckles all night. They were shining again through the skin. This time they were clenched. He stepped up to Sir Jocelyn.

'That is an unutterable thing to say to Miss O'Carroll.'

In the turn of Sir Jocelyn's head there was the reptilian savagery of the cobra about to strike. 'I found her,' he replied and his lips scarcely moved, 'in unutterable circumstances and —unutterable company.' Young Thomas almost recoiled from the impact of his contempt. 'I engaged you,' he continued, 'for the entertainment of my betrothed wife.' His eyes moved down the room in the direction of the bed. 'I did not expect you to carry your entertaining powers *this* far.'

Young Thomas felt that for the rest of his life the scaly lustre of mother-of-pearl would always suggest Sir Jocelyn's eyes as they glinted towards the bed. 'Sir,' he said quietly, 'your knowledge of your betrothed wife and your great knowledge of life should reassure you that the circumstances look too black to be real.'

Sir Jocelyn turned from him to Sterrin and said icily, 'How does this man come to be in your bedroom?'

'It would be difficult for me to give an explanation of all the times he has been in my bedroom.'

It was the first time in decades that the baronet's Court-of-Saint James manner boggled.

'He was in my room,' continued Sterrin, 'the morning I was born.' And just as she had once said it when she rose to explain to her father why she had purloined his rarest lilies for the grave of Young Thomas's godchild she said. 'He is of our household.'

'Indeed!' He looked curiously at Young Thomas. 'And what position, pray did this—this person hold in your household?'

Blue flames shot from the diamonds in her hair as her head went up to answer. 'A position of esteem.'

Sir Jocelyn's lips curled. 'Obviously, I do not allow laxities among my servants. Whelps sometimes get swollen from the crumbs that fall from the table of their masters.' His contemptuous look measured Thomas from head to foot. 'Some of them are not even content with crumbs, they sniff their master's wine and become intoxicated.'

'Intoxicated, sir!' cried Thomas. 'If the wine comes from the . . .' he looked significantly round the magnificent room, 'the *vault* of a collector, a whelp might even become exalted.'

Sir Jocelyn threw wide the door. 'Leave this room,' he ordered, but it was Sterrin who stepped across the threshold. With the two gentlemen, one on either side of her in the corridor she made an agreeable spectacle for the two pretty little ladies who rushed after them with a whirring of silk.

'Oh, Sterrin,' they gushed, 'we've been looking out for you. We hoped . . .' they looked coyly at Thomas, 'that you would ask Mr. Young to write a verse in our Confession Books.' Each held a white velvet-bound and gold-clasped book that contained the confessions to the favourite book, flower, colour and poem of their friends and their beaux.

Sir Jocelyn stripped a smile. 'We must not detain Mr. Young. He is leaving at once.' They were all consternation, but Thomas was already scribbling and over his shoulder Fiona Delaney was rapturously reading aloud, 'Can plumes compare thy dark brown hair? Can silks thy neck of snow?'

Her pretty companion presented an open page framed in painted forget-me-nots. Hannah tiptoed fearfully past and Sterrin, on an impulse, turned and called to her. 'Hannah, fetch me my Confession Book.' The maid paused to argue with her mistress that they did not possess such a thing and Sterrin said impatiently, 'The green book in the escritoire.'

The look that passed between them as she handed Young Thomas the green diary he had given her for her fourteenth birthday sent the blood pounding in Sir Jocelyn's temples.

'Sterrin,' he said sharply, 'there is no need to delay Mr. Young further.' He would have bartered his wealth that moment to crane like the two young ladies to glimpse what was being written in the little green book. But it was held too adroitly and in a flash it was returned to its owner. She glanced imperturbably at the lines before she dropped the little diary in her gold reticule.

As she moved down the stairs on the arm of her betrothed, the guests gazed upwards in admiration. They could not guess that her heart was repeating the lines that a trembling hand had scarce made legible, lines written by Thomas Davis of his unsanctioned love.

> *'We told each other to forget,*
> *As if we thought we should,*
> *'Twas said we might not wed, and yet*
> *We kissed as if we could.'*

She danced to its measure no matter the tune. Its message called her mood from joy to sorrow; from exaltation to despair. Sir Jocelyn, leading his fiancée out for the Quadrille, stood transfixed as his actor-guest made an entrance that suggested a fanfare. As Thomas hastened to where his host and Sterrin stood at the top of the line, the pattern of the dance broke up and the dancers gathered around him; the gentlemen clapping, the ladies all dither and delight.

'I crave your pardon, Sir Jocelyn, and yours, Miss O'Carroll, to have been so unpunctual, but I have been detained by the most unforeseen circumstances.'

A lady pushed forward. 'But this is a wonderful surprise,' she gushed. 'We have heard that we were not to have the pleasure.' Thomas bowed gravely.

'I assured Sir Jocelyn on my arrival, when he so kindly in-

431

vited me, that I would be here. Our stay, alas, is all too short and time is precious.' He turned to Sterrin. 'Miss O'Carroll,' he said with a low bow, 'am I too late? Is your programme written out?'

She glanced at her programme. 'The next is a Lancers. It has not been donated.'

'Alas, Miss O'Carroll, I dare not presume to conduct you through the Lancers. I am not competent. The waltz is my one accomplishment.' Under his breath he murmured, 'It is more sociable.'

When he came to claim his waltz, Sir Jocelyn's face was livid. 'You are treading on dangerous ground, sir,' he gritted.

'So I have been warned, Sir Jocelyn, but don't worry. My feet are shod and I shall try to steer my partner past the gridirons.'

A footman passed with a laden tray. 'Are you all right, your Honour's Sir Jocelyn?' he asked timidly.

His employer removed his hand from his eyes as the queer sensation cleared. 'Not that!' He waved away the proffered champagne. 'Get me brandy!'

Eyes were drawn and space unwittingly yielded to the superb couple as they glided down the long ballroom. Dowagers and debutantes watched with the same sub-ache and wondered what he was murmuring down into that upturned face. 'Try not to kick my shins,' he was saying.

And she was murmuring back, 'Those who have had the honour of waltzing with me could vouch that I waltz like a dream.'

He whirled her round a marble pillar. 'And one who had danced the Double Jig with you can vouch here and now that you kick like a mule. Have you read your diary?'

'Yes,' it was only a whisper and he stooped so low to catch it that his lips were caressed by her breath. He danced her back to the centre and up towards the watching eyes of her betrothed, then in and out of the garlanded pillars and banks of flowers and avenue of potted palms, and in a flowered alcove he breathed.

'Sterrin, beloved, you must not marry that gold and marble-inlaid mummy.'

There was impatience in her sigh. 'Young Thomas, such talk does not help. Neither does it help to bait him.'

'Bait! The child-baiting tradition of this house dies hard.'

432

His hand caressed the rounded chin. 'A child still dances to the macabre chimes of its gold.'

She drew back her face. 'What's the use of this, Young Thomas! He has not abducted me. He is a very great gentleman and the highest honour a man can give a woman is his name.'

As though he had received a bullet the arm that still encircled her for the waltz dropped to his side and his face was wounded white and his strangled words were the gasp of pain when he said, 'And mine is but a nickname!'

Her arms were around him and her cheek pressed his and her voice choked with tears as she murmured, 'Young Thomas, Mo bheale Asthore, would you think that I'd own such a thought!' The blood-giving phrase warmed his cheek against hers. Mo bheale Asthore, my life's love. They drew back at the sound from another alcove. It was only a pair of lovers absorbed in the glamour of their own unhappiness. A very young officer of the Blues was urging his plea with a little maiden in gauzy white whose sigh when she murmured, 'Papa would shoot you if you caused another elopement in the family.' She was Winifred Murray, the girl who had supported Sterrin on the convent wall while Sterrin watched out for Thomas.

As the two pairs of clandestine lovers looked at one another from their separate bowers the young officer's mooning look gave way to an officer-and-gentleman frown. He released his arm from its protection duty about the tiny waist and dropped his hand challengingly on his sword hilt. The play-actor was being let see that he was outraging the hospitality—and the honour—of his host.

Thomas stepped towards their bower. 'Sir, your sword arm wrongs Miss O'Carroll. 'Twas better employed before. After all, people who plot elopements cannot even throw pebbles.' The officer went scarlet and Winifred gasped audibly. 'Miss O'Carroll and I are old acquaintances. I have come direct from America. It was a most unexpected pleasure to meet here after years.' Sterrin tapped his arm; the music had stopped. Thomas adopted a persuasive smile, 'Look, sir, and you madam,' he bowed to Winifred, 'could I beg that we exchange partners for a further dance and return here. I should like to speak to Miss O'Carroll again before I leave.'

Sterrin consulted her programme. 'I can give you the next one, Lieutenant O'Hara. It is a schottische. Is yours free, Winifred?' Winifred offered up her programme like an immolation. Sterrin was up to something; just like at the convent, but Winifred felt that she herself would risk her father's shotgun if Mr. Thomas Young suggested elopement. Sir Jocelyn Devine appeared around the pillar looking ominous but his fiancée was on the arm of Lieutenant Joachim O'Hara and the play-actor was signing up Miss Winifred Murray's schottische.

'I say, Miss O'Carroll,' gasped the lieutenant, 'you are expert at this schottische. I haven't quite got the this and the that of it yet.'

'We danced quite a lot at the convent.' Her eyes were following Thomas.

'You surprise me. Isn't it rather wicked? That is, new?'

'It is worse than wicked,' said Sterrin whose eyes were on Winifred; free to hop around openly with Young Thomas.

'You amaze me, Miss O'Carroll. It is scarcely all that wicked.'

She looked at him for the first time. What was he talking about? 'Oh, I mean the waltz. It was forbidden. The nuns thought it was sensuous.'

'Oh!' There was something deucedly disturbing about such a word on the lips of a young lady. This alcove business was disturbing, too. 'I say Miss O'Carroll, oh, I'm so sorry. One, two, three. One—two—three. I mean there's no need to be afraid. Winifred and I won't peach.'

There was a group of girls round Young Thomas. She wanted to go over and pull him away from them. Why hadn't he written? Why has he let this trap close around me? 'You can trust us.' Her eyes returned to her partner. Jove, they were stunning! They had gone purple because their owner wanted to scream; wanted to hit him.

'Are you trying to make a bargain with me?' she asked. 'I'm afraid I don't huckster.' He sweated embarrassment down his side-whiskers, lost his one—two—three and hopped over his sword.

'Oh, perish the thought, Miss O'Carroll.' Damn it she needn't be so glacial. Dancing towards her tryst with one gentleman; on the eve of her wedding to another! And this tryst in the alcove was not meant for a farewell. Sounded more like a beginning. An elopement perhaps. What a tophole infectious thought. Perhaps Winifred might not have to be immune from its contagion.

434

In the alcove Young Thomas had indeed been thinking of elopement; 'But Sterrin,' he resumed where they had left off, ''tis an ungodly sacrifice. The price is too high. Oh, my dove of the storm.' He took her in his arms and murmured into her hair. 'You were never designed for his aviary.' She wanted to stay there, her troubled head on his breast, for ever. She felt like a storm-tossed boat that had come at last to harbour. Then into her peace came a vision of James Keating's face bending over her; of herself placing a hand in solemn pledge into the hand of the man to whom she had fled from Keating. She lifted her face. 'I've made my bargain——' She gave a twisted smile. 'I've told Lieutenant O'Hara that I don't huckster, but I have huckstered for Kilsheelin. I must stand by my word.'

'You have not huckstered, Sterrin. Like great people you have played for great stakes. Kilsheelin and its folks in return for the fairest flower of all its dynasty. But I won't let that happen. There must be a way out.'

She put a hand on either side of his face. 'Young Thomas, if it were just for myself I should not have bartered; but those others; so helpless! They are all like people reprieved. No, there is no way out of this.'

'You must come away with me.' He stepped back and seized her hand. 'I have found you when I thought that I had lost you for ever. I won't let you go. When is the wedding day?'

'Tomorrow fortnight.'

'That gives me time. I must play in London in two days' time. I have arranged for a man to come and meet me here early in the morning before I leave. Bergin. He was with me in the gold fields. He is an escaped convict. He escaped on to the ship that was to have brought me to the settlement—never mind about that now; there is so much that we have to explain to each other. Meantime I believe that I can do something to save Kilsheelin. Don't think that it is no concern of mine, the only home I've known; that gave me bread and life—and love! Do you think that I would let the others, the kitchen family, go on the shaughran? No, we'll hold Kilsheelin.'

Winifred Murray peeped through the palm fronds. 'Oh, Joachim, look at Sterrin's face! She must have decided to elope.'

Joachim looked. 'Now,' he said, 'see what elopement does for a girl. One would never think that she was the same person.'

CHAPTER 43

Thomas repeated the cue but his colleague, Henry Montieth, failed to respond. The audience didn't seem to notice. They were thrilled by Thomas's performance in the revival of *Bertram*. From pit to gallery the applause surged up and down. In the boxes fashionable ladies were rising to acclaim the great American actor. Under the tumult Thomas again threw the cue to the actor who should be struggling to his feet for the curtain line.

Inwardly fuming, Thomas improvised a line and signalled the stagehands. As the curtain came down he called impatiently to the man on the floor. 'Come on, Harry! Get ready to take the curtain.' This was the consequence of treating a cough with whiskey. And this was the actor who was to understudy him on Wednesday while he dashed to Ireland. To Ireland and Sterrin! By Heaven, it would be a pity for the man who would impede those plans.

Thomas swept towards the clamour beyond the curtain but was halted by the sound of a gasp. The principals were lining in from the wings for the first curtain. The leading lady was pointing dramatically, at the same time swooning backwards, on to the shoulder of the handsome juvenile who was staring open-mouthed over her head.

Then Thomas saw what she was pointing at. Henry was lying on the stage, his hands fluttering around his throat. Thomas dropped on his knees and supported the actor's head. Blood flowed from his mouth. The man tried to say something but only a bubble of blood came through lips that were stuck together by yellow ochre and congealed blood. At last the words came and Thomas stooped to catch the pitiful apology. 'I'm s-sorry-Mr. Young. I-I tried to cov——' His head fell back on to Thomas's arm.

Through the curtains the unappeased audience roared for 'Young! Mr. Young! Thomas Young!' Critics who had come prepared to see a passion torn to resplendent tatters had been first puzzled and then fascinated by his technique of restraint and under-emphasis. They stampeded with the rest for the pleasure of his thrilling voice in a curtain speech.

He spoke quietly, just a few words and when he turned to go there was a roar of disappointment. 'Call that a speech, Guvnor?' yelled a galleryite who was settling down to enjoy the cadence for a bit of extra good measure. The bills had prepared them for a famous actor but not for a person and personality who was worth paying to see without any performance.

Reluctantly, Thomas was forced to divulge that one of his cast had taken ill. Only then was he allowed to go. He stepped back. Behind the curtain the actor whose name was billed below his own was making his last exit between two stagehands. Poor Henry Monteith would not be taking his bow. Thomas, following the procession amid silent actors and props suddenly realised the full impact of this catastrophe.

Who would understudy him on Wednesday evening? The programme would have to be changed. All the preparations would have to be scrapped, except his plan to return for Sterrin. Nothing short of his own death would alter that plan!

The players, weary from the strain of their first London audience, shocked by Henry's sudden death, were startled on their way to the stage door by the callboy summoning a complete all-cast muster. They looked at each other. Did this mean that Mr. Young was giving them his usual stage party after all? It wasn't like him, not in these circumstances. They turned without enthusiasm and grouped together as far as possible from the freshly-washed boards.

Thomas addressed them crisply. 'You all know by now that Mr. Monteith is dead. But "the play goes on". Perhaps it was that tradition that contributed to his death. While he lay in the swoon scene a fit of coughing caused a suffusion of blood that he retained until it smothered him.' He broke off on the point of uttering 'needlessly', and turned away sickened, not from the sight of the bloodstains but of himself mouthing platitudes about poor Henry's unnecessary death from false delicacy and misplaced heroics. Out of the shadowy void of the proscenium Sterrin's face shimmered towards him. He turned and paced the deserted end of the stage, then turned in a swirl to face the silent group.

'The play must go on.' His vehemence was startling. 'But not tonight's play,' he continued. 'You did not know that I had arranged with Henry—Mr. Monteith—to understudy me on Wednesday for a few nights, I must return to Ireland on business. . . .' An explosive 'Gawney' from Alcium Beracium Conceptionez Duignan interrupted him. 'And I am putting on the new piece *Romance at the Crossroads*. It went over well the one night we played it before we left America. Audiences don't like their tragedies too distressingly realistic. We must give them something to laugh away tonight's realism. So, everyone on the stage tomorrow morning at nine. Goodnight.' He moved off then stopped. 'I'm sorry that we couldn't have our usual little celebration tonight. Heaven knows, you all deserve one. You must only drink poor Henry's funeral ale. God rest his soul!'

A girl padded after him down the dark passage to the stage door, but Alcium Beracium Conceptionez Duignan with his master's cloak on his arm and obstruction on his mind, kept ahead of her. 'Mr. Young,' she pleaded over the valet's shoulder. Thomas turned impatiently, but when the lamp over the open door shone down upon the girl whose soft brown eyes always recalled Lady O'Carroll, he softened. 'What is it, Miss Du Clos?'

'Mr. Young,' she gasped, breathless with exertion and her own temerity. 'Who are you casting for Sally?' Dear Heaven, was he to cope with casting jealousy at this hour of the night.

'Why you, of course. Who else? Didn't you play it last time . . .' he stopped. She hadn't; another girl, one he had dropped from the company had originally played Sally.

'You see,' exclaimed the girl. 'You *do* see?' She was urging him to see why she had been so presumptuous.

'But,' he said, his brows in a black line across his forehead, 'you were in the cast?'

She nodded. 'As young Peggy; only a few lines.' He nodded as he remembered, but his mind was occupied with the arrangements he must settle tonight; new plans for the performances; lugubrious plans for a funeral; glorious plans for a . . . his heart gave a throb and a surge and his perfect teeth sparkled through a radiant smile at the amazed actress. He held his repeater to the lamp that alternated in the wind with a flash and creak and shadow movement. 'Let me see,' he was almost playful, 'you

438

have almost twenty-four hours to get into the part. You can be word-perfect in that time, can't you, Miss Du Clos?' She could and she was.

She pored over her lines throughout the weary night as she made the role her own. Sparrows were chattering matins as she stubbed out the last of the three candles she had consumed in her all-night concentration.

'Three candles for bad luck,' she rose and stretched her cramped limbs. 'But I didn't have them lighting all together.' She splashed water from a ewer into a basin and bathed her smarting eyes. In the mirror she noticed the network of tiny red veins in the clear blue whites of her eyes. 'Hm! No such luxury as three-candle lighting.' She peered closer at the red veins. 'If I had that I wouldn't have these now. And that horrid Miss Garland won't show me how to bead my eyelashes. She's too angry about not getting the part for herself to help me with make-up. Would I ever dare to ask him to make her? What use is it being word-perfect if my looks let him down. I'm supposed to be a sparkling-eyed sprite, not a bleary-eyed hag.'

Thomas, too, had spent the night in work. Soon after his talk with Dorene du Clos, he had realised that the play was too short. It would under-run timing and it was too long for a curtain-raiser. He had had to write in another scene. To make it worse, Alcium Beracium Conceptionez Duignan came into the Green Room with the news that some of the scenery for *Romance at the Crossroads* was still mislaid at the wharf and added for good measure that he had heard that there was a likelihood of the Holyhead Packet not sailing tomorrow night if this wind continued. 'Nonsense!' snapped Thomas. 'It has sailed in weather a thousand times worse.'

'But it will be very late arriving, sir.' Thomas closed his eyes and tried to think. He had planned everything with Bergin. Horses here, a hackney chaise there, a cross-country dash to make the Great Western route to Dublin while another coach containing Bergin and his faithful sweetheart would decoy pursuit towards the regular Great Southern route from Thurles. It was timed with the precision of a battle campaign. 'I'm not the better of that last crossing yet, sir,' said the valet and his master allowed himself the relief of a smile. Of course! Alphabet had been piling on the forebodings because he thought he was to accompany his master.

'I shall not need you, Alphabet, on this particular—er—business,' he remarked and resumed the correction of his script. But he heard his valet's——

'Oh, *that* kind of business!' through the closing door.

'Duignan!' he roared. His valet returned, quaking. Rarely did his master use his patronymic. It was too long a journey from the first of the christian names. 'Just what kind of business, Alcium Beracium Conceptionez Duignan?' The valet winced under the weight of the names he was so proud of. They didn't sound up to the standard with that thin, slow, enunciation, and with them eyes all narrowed.

'B-business of an important nature, I'm sure, your Honour.'

'Exactly, now go and get me strong tea.'

The valet addressed the ever-boiling kettle. 'Business!' he said. He pelted a fistful of tea into the teapot. Philandering was right and proper, but this business menaced that whole delightful free structure of bachelor existence. 'Business of a most HUMAN nature, and with red hair, I'd swear.' The sound of his own poetry lightened his mood.

Thomas was sipping his tea when the leading lady, Miss Garland, arrived respectfully and conscientiously—she insisted—to query his wisdom in casting one so inexperienced as Miss Du Clos in the exacting role of Sally. Surely someone more mature...? Over his teacup Thomas eyed the mature shelving of Miss Garland's curves and tried to close his mind to the vision of her as the elfin Sally. 'Too bozomatique!' he murmured without thinking.

'Too what, Mr. Young?'

'Too Junoesque, Miss Garland. The piece is but a caprice to lighten a tragedy that has proved too real. A light frivol, not worthy of your,' he eyed her front, he almost said of your chest, 'of your presence.'

When the door closed he drained his cup and rose. 'Fancy that boozalem flopping up and down in a slip jig at the cross-road platform.' He returned at the sound of an obscene guffaw. 'Are you still there, thrice-named? Go out and enquire about that scenery.'

At the rehearsal, Miss Du Clos's achievement of the night, was not noticed. She had trouble with the new scene. She had soared through the original script but her tired brain could not retain the extra lines. Thomas drove her relentlessly. When she had paused a third time to rub her eyes he noticed their strained look. Probably stayed up half the night to learn, he thought, and despatched Alphabet for more tea.

His thoughtfulness restored her more than the tea; she romped through the remainder. The dress rehearsal went without a hitch until she came on, dressed for the new scene. When Thomas had finished his own lines he hurried down front to watch and while he went the actor who was to understudy him next night came to the footlights, and called to her that her brilliant red gown looked magnificent from the stalls. Suddenly a loud groan from Thomas made her eyes flutter in a succession of uncontrollable blinks.

'It won't do. It won't do at all.' It was only now, out front that he received the full impact of the gown. 'Don't you realise that you are supposed to be a country girl? That gown is altogether too smart. Too citified!'

Exhaustion made her sway and see black, but righteous anger revived her. She snatched her script and peered closely, 'It says here, "Enter Sally decked in finery". Surely, Mr. Young,' she urged, looking up, 'if I'm supposed to be appearing at the crossroads dance after a long sojourn in the city it is in character for me to wear city finery?'

'No, it is not,' he roared. 'I won't have city finery. Go and put COW DUNG on your nose!'

A very audible titter from Miss Garland saved Dorene from sobbing outright. 'Take those lines from the beginning again,' he ordered. And so it went on until at last he got the perfection he demanded.

Now the words were right, but Dorene was worried about her make-up. In her dressing-room, she grasped the hard eyeblack and held it to the candle until it ran liquid. She decided to do her eyes before putting on her costume. She dipped a toothpick into the black liquid and held it over her head to fall in beaded drops on every lash. A big black splash fell on her nose and ruined her make-up. By the time it was repaired the hardened eyeblack had to be re-melted, but at last she had the marvellous effect that Miss Garland had denied her. Two black fringes weighted with gleaming beads fanned out her brown eyes making them mysteriously luminous. Dorene stared at her reflection in the mirror and dreamed of the applause she might receive tonight. In her rapt contemplation Thomas's knock went unheard. His voice wishing her good luck brought her hastily to her feet. He gave a startled exclamation. 'Is it possible that you are not dressed yet and you are due on the stage in exactly two minutes!'

There was a snort behind him and Miss Garland pointed over his shoulder. 'Look, Mr. Young,' she said with unctuous emphasis, '*it* has beaded *its* eyelashes!' Thomas ignored her.

'Miss Dorene,' he said more gently, 'when you are pressed for time, which no player should be—today is unusual but lightning does not strike twice—always get into your stage costume first. You can go on without make-up but you cannot go on—like that.' She stooped in an agony to restore the fallen wrapper that had betrayed the curvings of breasts.

It was fortunate that her part called for a breathless, flying entrance. A delighted audience gave her the stimulus to maintain the tempo. She sparkled and tripped through three acts until the new scene where her sweetheart, Thomas, asked her where was his rival. She raised her arm and pointed over his shoulder but no words would come. Twice he smilingly murmured her line. 'He's down there in the green lane behind the orchard!'

In the enthusiasm of the rehearsal she had visualised that green lane as she pointed. Now all she could see was the spectacle of Miss Garland standing in the wings, unseen by the audience, at her old trick of disconcerting the on-stage ingénue.

If only she would stay still, thought Dorene, instead of swelling so ridiculously before disappearing into a black void and then returning to her own size. The prompter raised his voice on the third prompt. The orchestra covered up with a quickening tempo of its rustic dance selection. Thomas allowed his shoulders to follow the music in gentle rhythm. The movement increased the audience's impression, that the speechless pointing girl was indulging in a piece of delightful mime that was completely in character.

At last she found the lines that had eluded her. Down through pounding pain they dropped in black blobs but only Thomas heard her gasp, 'It—it beaded its eyelashes, and it put dow dung on its nose!'

The audience laughed and clapped when she ran swaying from the stage. They were still applauding when Thomas came before the stage and apologised for her non-appearance. She had been called away, he said. He could not tell them, not after last night's apology, that lightning had indeed struck twice. That Miss Du Clos was lying in her dressing-room, her eyes wide open, unable to see.

CHAPTER 44

When the horseman had at last outstripped the leisurely train the passengers withdrew their heads. The landscape held no further interest. The rider, grey-masked with dust, who had paced the train for three unflagging miles, had passed from their view. But the engine-driver's professional pride was challenged. 'Throw on a few more shovelsful!' he ordered the stoker. A few minutes later the entire length of the train passed the rider. He pressed unspurred heels against the horse's flank. It seemed the challenge of a race and carriage by carriage it gained until the engine's ignominious sobs sounded far behind. Suddenly the craning heads sent up a cheer. Horse and rider had risen up in the air, clear over tracks and sleepers and hedgerow into the field beyond.

Thomas drew reign and smiled. It was his first relaxed moment in the headlong dash from Dorene Du Clos's bedside to the train that had seemed to crawl through England; the boat whose engines seemed to be driven by the urgings of his own heart; to the Irish train that had crawled so slowly that he had jumped from it at a junction and hired a succession of livery horses to cut across country.

He patted the blessed animal that had brought him, in that last final bound, to the soil of Kilsheelin. He looked back at the railway line. It had once been a mass path that had led to the hawthorn fort at Lissnastreenagh. Who'd have thought when last he jumped it beside Thuckeen and her rider that it would he turned into an iron railroad. A railroad through the lands of Kilsheelin!

A smell of burning reminded him that the red coals flying from the engine had burned tiny holes in the velvet collar of his coat. 'A burn in your coat is a sign of good luck, according to Mrs. Stacey.' He set the horse at a low gap that brought another flash of memory. He recalled vaulting it on his return from serving the Wedding Mass of Eileen Prendergast to John Keating. With the memory came a pang of hunger like the one he had known that day when, in loyalty to Kilsheelin, he had left before the feasting. He had not eaten since he had gulped down a cup of tea at the station refreshment room early this morning.

Suddenly the broken turret came in view; then the castle itself; and then the murmuring stream and all the gently rich landscape stroked by soft winds. How often had he recalled Kilsheelin's gentle breezes as he set his teeth against the furnace blasts of dusty winds. Where frantic, penniless men babbled about millions as they scrabbled for the swill of the goldfields.

He skirted the demesne wall and cantered towards the niche that had been the scene of his parting from Sterrin. He smiled as he recalled that early dawn after the Ball in Kilkenny, when he had taken a leisurely farewell of his host, Sir Jocelyn and fellow-guests and made a hell-for-leather dash through the fragrance of the May night to his meeting with Bergin. Thomas remembered Bergin's incredulous look when he heard that his old friend was planning to spirit away Sir Jocelyn's bride-to-be. They spent two hours plotting the flight. Then Thomas had returned to Sterrin. She had been waiting between the high topiaried yews that screened them from the house. She listened carefully as he outlined the plans he had made for their elopement. And when they had kissed and clung and kissed again and finally parted only to return for one last kiss, she had left him. A second later she had come flying after him to urge one alteration to their plot. They must meet at the wall gap. It had been the planning ground and starting point of all their escapades, and besides, she had urged, he could see her more easily there as she took her morning canter in the park.

Thomas reached the blessed gap in the wall and stood up in the stirrups. Through the opening he could see most of the park and the fallow field of the Big Wind's caprice and even part of the hill where the cemetery lay. His heart thudded so much at the impact of the familiar scene that he had to grip the wall at either side to keep himself from vaulting over and running across the grass to the great arched gate that led to the stable yard and the big warm kitchen that was home.

Ruefully he thought of the incongruity of his position that barred him from the kitchen since he had now presumed towards the regions beyond the stately hall door that he dared not enter. He thought of the other stately portals that had opened wide to him—in Boston, New York, New Orleans; the gracious ladies who sought the honour of his presence in their drawing-rooms.

A movement on the roof caught his eye. The flag of privilege was flying from the flagstaff. He stared. The last time he had seen it fly high was the day Sir Roderick had been elected. The following day it had flown at half-mast. What possible occasion could this be? of course! It was for tomorrow's wedding. Suddenly all the assurance bred of prosperity and fame deserted him. Once more he was a little bare-legged waif wrapped in a man's brown 'trusty' that was five times too big for him, standing on the gravel sweep there before the hall door, gazing with awe at his own achievement. He alone of all that household had succeeded in raising the flag above the storm-wrecked turret; and beside him the great Sir gazing upwards at the flag that proclaimed his daughter's birth and then turning to bestow a whole crown to the urchin at his feet. 'Don't be too conscientious about taking "advantages",' said the Sir, when the waif had balked at accepting so vast a sum. 'Just grab them!'

The recollection, set in the familiar scenes of his servitude, filled him with the consciousness of his great presumption. What right had he, the castle's scullion, to intrude upon the event the proud flag now proclaimed! The daughter of the castle was going to her rightful heritage. He thought of what awaited her at Kilkenny. Manor, mill and mine, sparkling trout streams, navigable river, woods and pasture lands, all hers! Lawns with pyramids of topiaried yews, pavilions, hothouses that would produce verdant wonders—for HER!

What had he to offer? He dismissed the thought of his great success. Made no inventory of the superb body, the handsome features, the proud head, the massed qualities that brought the hearts of women at his feet. He disregarded that quality of presence that made men everywhere, defer to him. His was just a fine body to display his master's livery and grace the serving of his feast, to lend cachet to the splendour of his coach.

He tightened the drooping reins. For a moment he thought to ride away. Then, a little zephyr of wind set the flag flying into a gentle fluttering that drew his eye again. Why was it today the flag was hoisted? According to castle custom it was flown on the day of the event, not beforehand. Probably Hegarty would have too much to do tomorrow. No battalions of gossoons now,

446

no retainers, no footmen. Still, he wished the old man had waited. It was almost blasphemy that it should be hoisted today to fly high while the daughter of the castle eloped with the boy who used to clean her father's knives. Suddenly he swept his hat off and doffed it towards the flag. From somewhere behind him a burst of music sounded.

He turned. Slowly through the gates came an open carriage. In it sat a bard playing a harp. Thomas stared. But the bard— Bard O'Ryan was dead!

Then in through the gateway swept four magnificent greys drawing an open landau. It held two people, a man and a white-clad girl draped in a bridal veil. Other carriages followed. Great crowds of people were jostling at the lodge gate. Some spectators had climbed the walls. No one saw anything untoward in the spectacle of the solitary horseman who watched through an opening in the wall, his hat held high in homage, doubtless to the bride. As the bridal carriage came level with the wall niche the bride suddenly lifted the veil from her face and looked straight towards the horseman. Across the intervening space each saw the tense whiteness of the other's face.

The procession passed on. Later two men in livery came down from the castle bearing cloth bags. They reached into them for coins that they scattered high into the air and the crowd jostled and scrambled to catch them. Not copper coins for this wedding, but great fistfuls of silver and gold tossed upwards to fall in a gleaming shower.

The motionless horseman took no notice of the scrambling, shouting crowd. His eyes followed the bride. He saw her helped from the carriage, saw her move towards the tall coachman and speak to him, probably to receive his good wishes. The breeze that fluttered the flag tossed the curls over Thomas's forehead. He made no move to replace his hat. He held it aloft as it had been when he had saluted the flag.

He was still that way, arm extended like a posed statue, when Big John, resplendent in new, blue-faced livery, and shining, cockaded hat, came slowly down the side road from the stables.

He paused, startled. Who was this white-faced stranger, as white-faced as his darling had been when she whispered to him just now. Who did he recall? Sir Roderick? Old Sir Dominic? Then the stranger spoke quietly. 'God save you, Big John.'

'Young Thomas! Is it you that's in it, Young Thomas?'

Thomas came to life and dismounted. He placed a hand on each of Big John's shoulders. The older man barely suppressed his wince of pain. Thomas noticed the deformed outline under the stiff precision of the new livery. 'Ah, your poor shoulder. You still bear the token of the Big Wind.'

The coachman took Thomas's hand between his own two and gazed long into his face. 'I thought you were some great gentleman whom she knew. But sure she knew *you*, and you were always a gentleman.' He was recalling the way young gossoons and farmers used to doff their hats to the grown-up Young Thomas.

'So you have prospered and come back to us all. But how did you hit on this day? Did you know that it was her wedding day?'

Thomas drew back his hand and his face was set. 'No,' he said, low and tense. 'That was what I did not know.' The coachman looking at him thought he might be looking at Sir Roderick.

Suddenly it broke upon him. This strange encounter! And the strange words. That is what I did not know! And the stricken look that was etching out of the white features before his eyes, into that pinched look that comes on a dying face. 'Dear God!' he breathed aloud. 'So that is the way it is with you! and with her too. You are the horseman at the gap that I was to take her message to. You!'

The brief word was charged with the enormity of Thomas's presuming. Thomas turned impatiently and pulled at the tired horse that was cropping the side grass. 'Yes, me! And what is her message? Did she say you were to send me away? Or,' he gestured towards the mob. 'Am I bidden to go down there and grub among the canaille for the wedding largesse?'

Big John took the reins from him while he mounted. When he spoke there was infinite pity in his eyes and voice. 'Why didn't I see what was shaping before my eyes and you growing up together. Sure you loved the ground she walked on. But didn't we all? Only you had the learning—and a sort of breeding. I always said it—you were able to come closer to her comprehension. God help you both!' He glanced back over his shoulder. 'Listen, she bid me tell you to ride over to Lissnastreenagh. Go down into the hollow under the hawthorn trees. She'll come to you there, through the underground passage.' He handed up the reins. 'Young Thomas.' His voice was stern. 'Let you not set yourself against God's law nor man's honour. If I thought that you planned aught I swear to you I'll refuse to open the secret door and I'm the only one that knows how.'

Thomas chucked the reins but Big John held on. 'Stand aside,' said Thomas coldly. Big John obeyed.

In the blossom-filled hollow where he had lain with famine fever Thomas waited. Trees bent over him in a circular canopy. Petals fluttered down upon him as they had done when it was his body that was sick. A blossom broke from its branch with a tiny creak and came to rest upon his shoulder. If you break off a branch it is unlucky; but if one falls upon you, it is a sign that you will marry your true love!

He stood there, unconscious of the fragrant beauty that enclasped him. The moments bled away from him. Suddenly the branch drapes parted and she stood there. His exhausted brain could not absorb the realness of her presence. He made no move. She was part of this fairy keep; an apparition in ghostly white.

And then she was in his arms; his love in her espousal robe, his pain, his delight, his every breathing. Her wedding veil enclosed them. The blossoms fell unheeded about their straining bodies. The mingling of their anguish was a consummation.

At last he held her from him. 'What has happened. Why are you in your wedding dress?' She told him. Their farewell embrace that morning after the ball had been witnessed by Sir Jocelyn. 'He went to Mamma,' she whispered. 'He surprised you in my bedroom. He—he described the way he—the way we were when we said goodbye and he let her think that he found us that way in my bedroom. I've never seen Mamma so bad. I truly believed that she would die. But he was able to cope with her; soothed her; said he would shield me. I wrote you to come at once——'

With a groan he took her back into his arms. 'You are not this man's wife. A sacrament is not thrust upon one by force; nor by trickery, for I vow that your letter to me was intercepted. Come, we have wasted enough of life in considering the claims of others.' With one arm he drew her up the slope; with the other he held back the overhanging branches. A shower of blossoms fell all about her, clinging to her veil.

Behind them a door creaked cumbrously. A voice called 'Miss Sterrin,' and immediately corrected itself and said 'Your Ladyship'. Big John stood there. They turned to him. His presence dominated them. Big John's dignity was not a lackey's. It was of the soul. 'Your Ladyship is asked for.' It was the first time that she realised that she was being addressed by her new title. Big John seemed to imbue it with all its obligations. Because you are born noble you have a higher destiny than the peasants! Out of the past came that whimper of memory. Her father's admonition to her when she had complained in the famine that their own table was stinted excessively. You must live honourably so as to give an example——

She withdrew from his embrace. 'Goodbye, Young Thomas!' He took a step after her. 'Mo bheal asthore!' The whispered appeal was frantic. At the sound of the old endearment—My life's love!—she wavered. There were tears in her eyes as she turned to whisper back, 'Mo bheal asthore!'

As she passed through the narrow walls heedless of the crawling green slime that fouled the satin folds of her gown she heard his voice call, 'I'll go on waiting.'

Slowly Big John pushed the heavy door. 'God be with you, Young Thomas,' he said and Thomas was shut out.

He had no idea how long he stood there in the bower that had become a tomb. When he turned at last his footsteps were muffled in the carpet of petals. He kicked savagely through them. They rose in an agitated shower and fell about his shoulders.

From somewhere his bemused senses caught the sound of a bell; the ghostly tolling of the Sanctus bell, that sounded as The O'Carroll slew the priest at the altar? Or was it the fairy bell in the hawthorns? Strange things had happened in this ghostly place.

As he swung into the saddle he saw the top of the great marquee and he knew that the bell was the stable one summoning the tenants and workers to the feast. Without a backward glance he wheeled the horse and spurred it across the fields.

Thomas made no effort to guide his mount. He rode up the hills following a track so old that it was believed to have been beaten out by ancient wolf packs. In the silence a lamb bleated. It was answered by the deep baaing of its mother. A lark planed down to its sitting mate. The horse checked and stopped. A sound of running water bubbling fresh from the hills into the brown pools reached its thirsty senses. It bent over a pool and drank deep and long.

Thomas turned in the saddle. Across the valley he could see the home of his childhood. Behind those walls of mountain grit he had absorbed the creed and tenets of the O'Carrolls. The horse went forward again. Thomas began to recognise his route. Blind instinct had led him up this primitive path. It was leading him towards the mansion that was to receive her to-night.

Much later his eyes, straining frantically, glimpsed a figure that moved whitely in an upper window where light showed.

She was watching the movement of all the little free things in the lake below; conscious of every sound and perfume as never before. Sorrow had acted upon her unawakened senses like a storm upon still waters; had tossed up emotions whose existence she had never dreamed of. She had come a long way from the little river bank where she had thought it her duty to try drowning herself because she felt the shame of a man's kiss.

They had been like Adam and Eve in the ancient garden—the young knife boy and the young girl, happy, carefree, taking each other for granted. Now they were like Adam and Eve after the Fall, knowing good and evil. There had been no apple eaten from the Tree of Knowledge. But the serpent had raised his knowing head. Young Thomas!

The cry screamed through her heart. Dear God, why did I not go with him today? Nothing else mattered; home nor family nor servants, nor marriage vows! My one love, my only love! Where are you?

He stood upwards on the stirrups straining towards the lighted window until the iron cut into his insteps. From the grass came a long sigh. He peered and saw a man and woman lying asleep; tinker man and tinker woman; cleaving to each other and to hell with the world and wealth and rank! The moonlight sparkled on something on the man's collar. A Repeal button! They were not tinkers, then, but the new beggars who had lost the right to their cabin's roof because in the abandonment of their hunger they had sought the workhouse bread. What do you care whether the government sits in Westminster or in Dublin? Governments fall. Dynasties fall. Only men and women matter. The man stirred and flung his arm across the woman. They had each other.

The shrill cry of a moorhen broke the stillness. From the

window the white-robed girl recognised the little mincing gait, the tail flirting with every step. It turned back to the water and made a v-shaped ripple as it swam out to wider freedom. Only the human watchers knew bondage.

A thrush disturbed by the moorhen's cry flew past with a sleepy trill. Its note brought from nowhere the sinister shadow of a kestrel. Panic rose in Sterrin. She tapped the glass and moved her hands as though to wave off this menace to the thrush's freedom.

Suddenly her waving hand was caught in a vice. She was swung around to face her husband. 'Is this another signal? Is your scullion out there?' Her arm hurt where his nails pierced. He had discarded all the crisp trappings that had concealed age; the elaborate stock, the collar, the artificial masticators. She gazed at him horrified. 'I—I didn't know,' she said and stopped; because she almost said that she didn't know that he was so old. 'Answer me! Is he out there?'

Still holding her arm he dragged the heavy curtain across the window. The sight of the great folds shutting out the lovely world of nature and freedom brought back the panic she had felt for the thrush. But now it was for the menace that was closing in about herself.

He mistook the look of dismay that she threw towards the curtain. 'So, he *is* out there. By heavens, if he is trespassing again on my property I'll have him flogged first and then transported!'

'*Your* property.' Her lips disdained his right to query Young Thomas's presence upon Kilsheelin property today.

'Yes, mine. *You* were already *my property when you signalled* your kitchen paramour on the way from the altar today.' His voice thinned upwards. 'Where did you meet him? Where? My charming bride returning to me with her wedding gown smirched from her scullion's abominable trespass.'

She stared at her husband as her thoughts blurred. She saw the green slime from the subterranean walls. It seemed to be coming from the roothless mouthing of those horrible words. Faces floated before her.

Pallid faces strained with the green of rejected grass. But that was Billy Din; whose face had been gentle. The green slime had drooled from his meek hunger. Another face with lips that smiled slowly upwards from perfect teeth. Mo bheal asthore;

452

'You won't signal through this veil.'

A hand was lifting her bronze hair that veiled her shoulders. She steeled herself. No one had ever made *her* faint! 'You are an excellent businesswoman my dear. Now you must keep your bargain.'

Her eyes focused upon the arm that stretched from a brocade sleeve; a sinewy arm, veinous with age, that sought to clutch her. She felt her own arm pinioned. She raised her other, slender, soft, youthful. To do what? To strike the man to whom she had mortgaged her youth, her life? She stared deep into her husband's eyes with a gaze full of hate and fear. Sir Jocelyn grimaced and suddenly fell heavily to the floor.

Sterrin looked down at the figure that lay at her feet. Guilt clamped down on her, not for what she had done, for she had only revealed her true feelings; but for the sense of gladness that had started up inside her. She ran for help. Silently, she watched the servants raise Sir Jocelyn on to the bridal bed; watched them carry in the bleeding bowls; watched them carry them out, dripping red.

CHAPTER 45

Paris was a tonic for Sterrin. She rejoiced in the whim that caused Sir Jocelyn to order this trip as soon as he had recovered. The city was at its gayest in the midst of a joyous celebration in honour of the victory against the Austrians at the bridge of Magenta. Sterrin was delighted by the colour and warmth of the beautiful city. Every day was a holiday and the excitement of it blunted the horror of her marriage to the bitter, cynical man who was her husband. The stroke had paralysed one side of his face. The eye rigid. He blamed her for his illness and was determined to punish her for it. He never left her side, unless in the charge of Margaret's sister, Sterrin's Aunt Yvette, who had been summoned from Belgium to stay with Sterrin. She was a pleasant companion who made Sterrin laugh as she told romantic tales about her childhood. She even made Sir Jocelyn smile.

Parisian society took the young Irish beauty to its heart. Dozens of invitations arrived every day.

Sterrin embarked on an orgy of buying. Milliners with gay bonnet boxes and dressmakers with long boxes beat a path to Sir Jocelyn's château with bolts of silk and satin. They compared colours with the bronze of her hair. Sterrin endured hours of fittings with grace and good humour—a welcome change for the seamstresses who were accustomed to the elegant *ennui* of the court ladies. Madame de Castiglione, deemed the most beautiful woman in the world, sometimes walked in a trance from their measuring tape and roamed the streets burdened with the overpowering consciousness of her own beauty.

There was talk that *la belle* Lady Devine's preoccupation was not with her own looks. Hint of some young *amoureux* whom she had been forced to forsake for the fabulously rich Milord Devine. The empress favoured skirts that displayed the ankle. The dressmakers drew up Sterrin's hem and nodded vigorously. Of a certainty, Milady's ankles could emerge from the shadows.

Out of the bonnet boxes came, not bonnets but hats. Sterrin fitted on a little Eugenie model; a saucy little tricorne affair trimmed with pom-poms. The midinettes threw up ecstatic hands. The new millinery made a perfect foil for milady's hair.

The effect of the hat was too much for Sterrin's vanity. She turned and twisted before the mirror. Suddenly she laughed. Her husband, entering silently, marvelled at what a hat could do for a woman. She had scarcely smiled since her marriage.

He had come to escort her to one of the Empress Eugenie's famous 'Mondays'. It was a purely feminine affair but he was not content with the chaperonage of Sterrin's Aunt Yvette. Impeccably dressed, a taffeta stock wound twice around his neck, a monocle masking the rigidity of his damaged eye and cheek muscles, he escorted her to every function. It was only because gentlemen were not admitted to the Empress's parlours that he left her at the door.

The empress took stock of Sterrin as she swept down for the triple curtsey. When Sterrin's eyes came level with the high Andalusian arches and slim ankles of the Empress, she lingered in the obeisance and missed the timing of the third curtsey. It was the first time that she had seen so much limb displayed below a lady's skirt. '*Miséricorde!*' breathed Eugenie.

She was gazing over Sterrin's head to where a dainty pair of red shoes and stockings rose in the air above a tall screen. '*Quelle frivolité outrée,*' gasped Aunt Yvette.

The feet disappeared and a sleek brown head took their place. The Empress broke into a peal of laughter. 'Ah, it is the *mignon* Countesse Gabrielle. She too, like Italy, has been liberated. Today her annulment came from Rome and, Hop! she go head over heels like *La Liberté.*'

Sterrin listened avidly to what a lady was telling her Aunt behind a fan. 'She has been seeking for years for this divorce . . .' she heard. 'Her marriage was never ... you understand? It was *un mariage du nom seulement. . . .*'

'A marriage in name only,' burst out Sterrin. 'Then she is free to marry again. No wonder she turns head over heels!'

'Stereen!' Aunt Yvette was scandalised. The other lady lowered her fan and stared openly at the young bride who had made such an extraordinary statement.

Sterrin's body felt suddenly, strangely, light enough to do cartwheels. Was it possible that a marriage could be annulled by

455

Rome for being—for being such a marriage as her own? A glimmer of light gleamed down the vista of her hopelessness. She manoeuvred an introduction and congratulated the liberated Countess.

'I take it that you mean to felicitate me upon my culotte, not my matrimonial somersault?'

'I—both!' There was no time to be lost in beating around the bush. She might never again get such an opportunity. 'Look, how is it possible to—to——' Sterrin could not put it into words. 'What was your first step?'

'Ah *that*!' The Countess misunderstood her. 'Simple, *voilà comment!*' She threw out her arms and proceeded to walk on her hands. Sterrin grew desperate.

'It is about your annulment I wish to know. I must know.' But she was addressing a pair of legs that waved on a level with her head. Dear God! I must find out! She glanced over the screen. No one was looking this way. Her husband would be waiting the moment the 'salon' finished; waiting to guard her like a dragon; for ever! She threw her hands down to the floor. The next moment a pair of green shoes walked in the air above the screen beside the red ones. The other girl gave a squeal of delight. 'Hush,' whispered Sterrin, 'I must speak to you, get up.'

'Come, I'll race you first,' the girl insisted. With her head down over the white marble floor, Sterrin whispered things to a stranger that she could not whisper to her own mirror. 'Will you help me?'

It was desperate, but the stakes were high. The head beside her nodded emphatically; unmistakably. Then her hands fell behind. Sterrin was well ahead. No one could beat her at hand walking. Not even Young Thomas. Suddenly she felt gay and reckless. Somewhere in her upended head was the tiny seed of hope that this piece of exhilarating madness might lead hand over hand to—she was gasping—to Young Thomas! Then, hand in hand with Young Thomas! For ever and ever and ever!

'This is carrying frivolity too far!' Sterrin could not hear the stern voice that addressed the Empress. Inside her head there was a storm of silken rustlings from the petticoats that flowered over her ears. She didn't notice the dead silence. There is a lot to be said for these shortened skirts, she was thinking. But the loops that held them draped up from the hem were made of heavy twisted silken cords that banged against her ears. The amethyst drop from one of her earrings hand dropped into her earhole. It tickled. She was tempted to flick it out. Then she saw the boots, small, elegant—but, gentleman's boots!

Up went her hands and down came her feet. Petticoat after petticoat dropped mercifully over her pantalettes; too late. She was standing before Napoleon the Third, Emperor of France. Dear God, let me die now. Let me never walk another step on hand or foot again!

The Emperor watched the glowing face from which the colour was ebbing. Tiny ringlets escaped from her chignon and fell below her earrings. Tendrils, moist from her exertion, clung to her forehead. Her hands pressed straight and hard by her sides as though to hold down the terrible revealing petticoats. She stood like a statue; humiliation made her face more coldly proud. Then she remembered to curtsey. As she rose a voice thin with rage said, 'Sire. I trust I have your permission to present my wife?' She looked beyond the Emperor to the man who stood behind him. She saw the compressed lips, the swelling veins in her husband's temples. It was the first time that Sir Jocelyn Devine had known the satisfaction of seeing fear in her eyes. The Emperor noticed the flickering.

'Ah,' he said, 'I recognise you now. It was difficult when you were upside down. It is perhaps one of your quaint Irish customs to promenade on the hands?'

His anger had not been directed towards the owner of the pair of seductive pantalettes that had walked towards him in mid-air as he had entered the room. It had been for his Empress who had doubtless incited and encouraged her. It looked as if the beautiful acrobat would receive ample punishment from her husband. A twinkle appeared in his eye and an answering one danced in Sterrin's. 'I believe, Sir,' she answered him, 'that my ancestors, a long way back, walked on all fours!'

'So I believe did mine, a long way back.'

His glance fell on Mademoiselle Gabrielle and tightened. He had admonished the Empress more than once about her indulgence towards the unorthodox little Countess. She dropped a curtsey. 'Sire,' she murmured sweetly, 'the regrettable performance was entirely my idea.'

The Emperor inclined his head. 'I do not for a moment doubt

that, Countess.'

'I challenged Lady Devine.' The Emperor looked keenly at Sterrin.

'And I can see,' he answered, 'that Lady Devine is not one to refuse a challenge.'

When Sterrin, close to tears, took her leave, the *ci-devant* countess came flying after her.

'Dear *divine* Lady Devine,' she gasped. 'Don't take it to heart so. The Emperor has ticked off Eugenie, but la! she does not mind. She had won a pair of earrings from Countess Metternich on your win.' She stopped surprised. 'Cherie, you are crying! Whatever can I do to make it up to you?' She had seen the look that had passed between the high-spirited Irish belle and the dandified old satyr to whom she was married.

Sterrin waved off the lackey who was assisting her into her peterine. She clutched Gabrielle's hand. 'You can help me! You must help me! Where can I see you? I shall not be permitted to visit you or have you at the château.'

Gabrielle frowned. 'Let me see! There will be no more "Lundis". They go to Saint Sauvere next Monday. A pity you are not going too.'

'But we *are* going. We have been bidden to join the seaside party, unless,' she said ruefully, 'the invitation is cancelled over this *débâcle*.'

'Pouf!' Gabrielle dismissed the idea with an airy wave. 'You will be the rage. Eugenie will want you to teach her to walk on her hands. Tomorrow,' she continued, 'I go to the theatre to see Mr. Merry, the English actor. I must see his Romeo. I am told it is distractingly romantic. Can you be there?'

Sterrin was dubious. Her husband favoured the opera. Because of his depleted vision, the theatre held little attraction for him. Still, she might be able to arrange it. Sterrin looked to where an elderly dowager was commiserating with Aunt Yvette. 'My Aunt also wishes to see Mr. Merry's Romeo.'

'Good,' said Gabrielle with finality. 'Get her to take you tomorrow. You'll manage it all right. I shall come to your box.'

'But, Mr. Young,' protested Dorene, 'why ever did you agree to Mr. Merry's playing Romeo? Back home in America the critics say you are the best Romeo on the modern stage. Your...' she stopped, embarrassed. She had been going to say

458

your Romeo is the perfection of love-making.

They were driving to the special. Thomas was so deeply pre-occupied with the problem of what to do about her should this Paris doctor offer no help for her sight that at first he did not catch what she was saying. Play Romeo! He shuddered. He would never play that part again.

Romeo had scored Thomas his greatest success. Its setting was so familiar that it was as though he had but to re-live his own memories; Capulet's orchard was the little 'Sir's Road' where the gap had been made in the wall by the Big Wind. When fourteen-year-old Juliet warned Romeo '... the orchard walls are high and hard to climb and the place death considering who thou art', she was really fourteen-year-old Sterrin, standing on her castle's boundary wall taking a fearful farewell of the presuming knife boy. And Dorene wanted to know why he had agreed to let Mr. Merry play tonight's Romeo excerpt!

Thomas thought back to that dreadful day in London after his return from Ireland still numb and bemused, still grief-filled over his loss. When Alphabet had told him that the little actress Dorene Du Clos had not yet recovered her sight. Thomas had gone to her lodgings. As he sat by her bedside his mind, his feelings were muted, his mind numb. When Dorene apologised to him for ruining his scene the night she lost her sight, the significance of her situation struck home.

Those lovely brown eyes had been strained, the doctor said, beyond recall. By him, Thomas thought; by his relentless slave-driving. What was she saying? She was still apologising; weaving her hands aimlessly. She was helpless. Thomas realised that he must find out about her family and get in touch with them.

But Dorene had no family to be notified. The aunt who had reared her had died. She was alone and suddenly she was Thomas's responsibility. He took her to a famous eye doctor. When the specialist, at the end of his examination, shook his head from side to side Thomas began to come back to life. He must help this girl. The doctor had mentioned a specialist in Paris who had done wonders with cases other doctors had given up. Paris! He had been invited to play there for the victory celebrations. The invitation had come while he was in Ireland. He would take this little broken blossom with him. He would leave nothing undone that might restore to her what he had caused her to lose. It might not be too late to accept. Even if it were he would still take her there. They left for Paris the next day.

The carriage was slowing into the kerb. He reached for her hand. 'Come,' he had started to say! 'Cheer up; don't look so sad.' The crassness of it. Must he learn some new phraseology for conversing with the blind? And had not she a right to look sad? Did he suddenly possess the monopoly of all the grief in the world? He stepped out and lifted her bodily from the carriage. 'You are going to be all right,' he murmured and his lips blew the words across her face that was so near to his own.

You are going to be all right. It beat a refrain to the roll of the carriage wheels on the homeward journey. Yes, she was going to be all right. Everyone, the French specialist included, seemed to be in agreement on how All Right poor blind Dorene was going to be. When she had accustomed herself to her incurable blindness! He tried to think of something to say to her. Words were his business; soul stirring, grandiose words, composed by others to be relayed by him; and here, now, in the need of this girl's stricken soul all he could contrive was some stammering half-articulate grunt.

He reached for the hand that lay on the lap rug. It felt like a small, captive bird; a bewildered beat of life. Wordlessly he went on stroking it until at last the slow, hard tears came painfully from between the shuttered lids. Passers-by looked smiling through the windows of the carriage at the charming spectacle of the pretty girl whose bonneted head lay so gracefully upon his shoulder.

That night Thomas forced her to come to the theatre. He was to do a scene from Othello. Mr. Merry had already announced his intention to play Romeo. Mr. Young's acceptance had been so belated that there had been no time for a full collaboration of excerpts from their favourite roles as had been suggested in the invitation. As he leaned with seeming nonchalance against the wall of the box he felt a sudden sense of gladness. The audience, packed tightly, tier upon tier, was gradually bearing in upon his sense of the theatre. The old response to it was not dead. He could feel its mounting stimulation. He turned back and saw the shadowy stillness that was Dorene's face. Was her tragedy greater than his own? His mind evaded the answer. There was no measuring up of each separate tragedy? Or was there? Nothing could compensate this girl for the loss of her sight. And

460

nothing could compensate Thomas for the loss of the love that had been woven into the fabric of his life—its brightest, strongest thread. There rose in the dimness a vision of Sterrin in her bridal loveliness and his breath caught on a quick gasp. Curse John Holohan and his pious prating that day in New Orleans. Holy vows Inagh! Curse John Holohan and his gorilla arms that had pinned him the day he had thought to dash from New Orleans and across the world to snatch her from the convent. Convent! I'll hold a thousand crowns that there was never any convent. It was a plot. They suspected how things were. Mr. Maurice O'Carroll had suspected. Cutting down staff inagh! Why hadn't he cut down on the likes of Pakie Scally, a hanger-on that had no claim on staff status.

'What is it, Mr. Young?' Dorene had heard his gasp. He touched her shoulder. 'Hush! The curtain is going up.' She moved her head from side to side; obediently seeking the direction of the stage that held no interest for her; and then she heard Mr Merry's voice. As she listened she made comparisons; she told herself that Mr. Merry portrayed the form of the drama; but Mr. Young portrayed its soul. She felt another touch on her shoulder. 'I must go behind now.'

He saw the sudden dismay on her face. 'Good gracious,' he said, 'if you could only see your face!' And then he could have bitten off his tongue. How was he ever going to remember not to make these kinds of remarks? 'Immediately I am finished I shall come back here and fetch you. Meantime,' his fingers pressed her shoulder, 'you are to be my sternest critic.' He touched her cheeks.

'Don't grieve Little One,' he said, 'I have not given up hope.'

The door closed gently. Her fingers reached up and pressed the cheek that his fingers had caressed.

CHAPTER 46

Sterrin was glad the *Romeo* extracts were finished. The whole scene and setting had recalled too poignantly Young Thomas and those young days at Kilsheelin. She was on thorns for her meeting with Mademoiselle Hautdoire and it was ridiculous to allow the play to upset her now. In fact she had been so eager to meet Mademoiselle that she hadn't even bothered to enquire about the programme or actors. Actors! There was only one for her! She screwed up the handbill she was given at the entrance and let it fall to the floor. She mustn't display any emotion in front of her husband. It had been difficult enough to get him to come. He had had his fill of Shakespeare in the past and had seen all the great actors. He only came because he was suspicious of letting her out of his sight. Beside her Aunt Yvette was in raptures, completely lost in the actor.

The door of the box opened and before Mademoiselle Hautdoire could move inside Sterrin was on her feet and suggesting that they should go in the promenade in the foyer. Her Aunt Yvette started to accompany her but already they were lost among the promenading audience. The bell for the curtain-up had stopped ringing when they returned. Sir Jocelyn was standing outside the open door of their box, his lips thin drawn with anger. His accustomed courtesy towards ladies strained coldly, when he saw their conspiratorial whispering. He disapproved of this Mademoiselle Hautdoire, but before he could vent his anger some announcement that the stage manager was making brought forth a resounding applause.

'Now perhaps we may have the pleasure of listening to the play,' he said as the door closed. Sterrin laid down her glasses. She wasn't interested in the play or the performers. She was more concerned with what the little ex-Comtesse had whispered to her. It had been worth the flight she had had to make to get there. Suddenly she leaned forward. That voice! Great God, if she went on imagining things like this she would go mad. That quality of tenderness and melody! How it throbbed with passion. She groped for her glasses but could not find them. Heedless of appearance she leaned right over the ledge. In the dim light the black make-up masked the features she scanned. But the commanding figure, the movements, graceful and correct, they belonged to only one man!

He seemed to be speaking direct to her. The very words were meant for her. 'It gives me wonder great as my content, to see you here before me. Oh, my soul's joy! If after every tempest came calms. May the winds blow till they have wakened death. . . .' He stopped suddenly. Now he was looking towards another box, directing his voice there. Near it a white face loomed out, loomed in a mist the way it had been when he was rehearsing the play that had cost Dorene her sight. But this was no misty vision. This was *her* face. She was here! For the first time in his stage life he forgot his lines. His mind was completely blank to everything except that face, like Desdemona's. '. . . that whiter skin of hers than snow and smooth as monumental alabaster.' That was not the line he wanted!

Dorene clenched her hands. What has happened? She had never known him to forget his lines. He had seemed to be speaking towards her. Had the sight of her suggested that awful night when she had broken down and forgotten her own lines? The prompter's whisper was quite audible '. . . and let the labouring bark climb hills of sea Olympus-high. . . .' Dorene mouthed the words and willed them across the footlights. Suddenly Thomas made a quick turn and strode across to the stage centre. He took his line and moved to the stage centre.

'Messieurs and Mesdames,' he cried with a beaming smile and outstretched hands. 'I crave *mille* pardons. Your delightful city has bewitched me. This wonderful audience had beguiled my senses. If you were to drag me forth and hang me from the highest lantern I could not for the life of me recall that—labouring bark.'

The audience went wild with delight. Waves of clapping and 'bravos' rose to the roof. Dorene unclenched her hands and let out her breath.

'Mountebank,' gritted Sir Jocelyn Devine. He was certain that he had been duped into coming. There had been no talk of any actor but Merry and he had not been sufficiently interested in the programme to find out. Sterrin laughed aloud.

Out through the storm of applause her clear voice penetrated to his hearing, 'Bravo, Young Thomas!' she cried. She leaned out of the box completely oblivious of the audience. Her husband reached out a restraining hand. For a moment he had a crazy impression that she might be capable of jumping down on to the stage. Thomas, too, fought a crazy impulse. He wanted to raise himself on to her box and take her in his arms. Instead he raised his fingers to his lips. The perfection of his teeth flashed whitely up at her through the dark-stained features. Opera glasses were levelled towards her. Sir Jocelyn stood up but the house had gone silent. Thomas had plunged into his role. Dorene's hands were clenching again. His acting had taken on another dimension. Its majesty and grandeur were pouring forth in a wild metre that was past her understanding.

'I'll tear her all to pieces!' The cry burst from the heart-wounded Othello in such a power of exquisite agony that Dorene put her hands to her lips to check a cry. Sterrin clenched the plush ledge. Passion undreamed of was surging through her. It poured out from her to meet the torrent of passion that tore across the stage in a mighty flood. A woman screamed. Sir Jocelyn rose and flung his chair backwards. He had been tricked. They were all in it. The ex-Comtesse Thiery, Sterrin's Aunt. She had manoeuvred this pretending that it was Merry whom she wished to see.

'This must be stopped,' he said thickly. 'It is an outrage! The fellow is indecent and so are you! No decent woman would look like—like . . .' He had never been at a loss in his life. The sight of her entranced face, parted lips, eyes moist in a rhapsody of love, was beyond his endurance. 'I'll have him horsewhipped . . . I'll . . .'

Sterrin came out of her trance and turned to her husband. 'You will have him horsewhipped,' she taunted. 'Horsewhipped and then transported! Him!' She swept her arm towards the stage where Thomas, transcendental in his own power had made the Moor his own. The Othello evoked by her presence had borne down all the barriers and was sweeping before him all love and reason and mercy. In a stage box Mr. Merry turned to an American newspaperman. 'Bear witness,' he intoned solemnly, 'I shall never again act Othello. Never shall I hazard a comparison with THAT!'

Outside, Sterrin for the first time in her life had to fight her

464

way through a crowd. She was completely cut off from the carriage. In vain her husband's voice behind her called to lackeys who stood on its backboard to forge a path for them.

'Tell those people to move their carriage from my path,' he stormed.

One of the lackeys forged his way to them. 'They are jammed in, your Honour's Sir. They are gentlemen from the American newspaper waiting to see the great actor.'

'*Gentlemen!* Newspaper fellows. Since when did they become gentlemen?' Sir Jocelyn was beside himself. 'What is the world coming to? A gentleman's carriage held up by a play-actor.'

But all the world was held up for the play-actor. The din of voices, the clip-clop of hooves, the carriages with crests on their panels, the coachmen with cockades in their high silk hats, the footmen in buckskin breeches, the gentlemen in opera cloaks, the ladies with bosoms bare beneath enclustering jewels; they were all here, thought Sterrin as she gained the carriage unaided, because of her father's knife boy! *My* knife boy. And he is waiting for me!

The surge in her body made her light-headed. She leaned back and closed her eyes; and thought of what Mademoiselle Hautdoire had whispered to her in the box. This annulment business involved dreadful disclosures about intimacy. Worse; disclosures about *lack* of intimacy. She squeezed her eyes tight. It would be unbearable; but I'll go through with it. A long, hard fight, Gabrielle had said. I'll fight; hard and long. And at the end there would be Young Thomas! I'll go on waiting, he had said.

A burst of clapping made her open her eyes. Young Thomas was squeezing through the throng; coming this way! She half rose in her seat; then she saw the girl on his arm. Not the conventional linking with an escort, but clinging with the close-held intimacy of a caress. And Thomas was looking down into the girl's face; smiling gently. Sterrin had forgotten; had never started to remember that Thomas could smile like that at anyone else in the whole world. Suddenly he put his arm around the girl and drew her towards the carriage. Sterrin's heart gave a great lurch. She was standing fully upright now. Behind her, her husband's voice was angrily urging her to sit down.

The blood was draining from Sterrin's heart! She watched

Thomas tuck the lap rug round the girl and suddenly into her brain burst the cry that had burst from Othello.

'I'll tear her all to pieces!' Her fingers bent and tensed into claws. She pressed them against her sides to keep them from stretching towards the presumptuous interloper. The dreams she had woven about him, in childhood, in girlhood. A background of lost grandeur. She had dreamed him up when he had left her to fight his way across the bridge that would lead him back to her world; a splendid return with fame and fortune. And when she had believed him in prison, her dreams had opened the gates a hundred times in wild escape. Never for one half moment had it occurred to her that any other woman would dare to penetrate the gossamer that had enmeshed her own Young Thomas, the knife boy, with his—Miss Sterrin!

Primitive rage swept through her. She did not know the words that had flashed into her brain, had reached her lips. Behind her, her horrified husband and aunt heard her clearly say, 'I'll tear her all to pieces.'

Sir Jocelyn snatched the long whip from the coachman and brought it down savagely across the flanks of the nearest pair. The horses plunged and the startled leaders reared up, bringing with them the two grooms who were holding their heads.

The landau scraped Thomas's carriage with a loud scrunch as it passed. He reached out to steady himself and saw her; saw the quick look of her disdain before she turned away. He was close enough to touch her, but not close enough to see the trembling of her underlip, her hands, her knees: all her body trembling with the tenseness of defence. All he saw was a white face, chin high, eyes direct, deigning him no faintest hint of recognition.

'Mo bheal asthore, My life's love,' he whispered.

'What did you say Mr. Young?' It was Dorene asking.

'I said,' he answered and her new sensitivity caught the dullness and the coldness in his voice, 'that I ought to have stuck to cleaning knives.'

As his carriage forced through the dense traffic he did not notice that the Paris *haute monde* was acclaiming the erstwhile knife boy as enthusiastically as it had acclaimed its Emperor a week before.

CHAPTER 47

A pile of invitations arrived for Thomas at his hotel; great names bade him to their salons. He had fought through to her world! Or had he! 'Don't get carried away, my lad! You are just a successful mountebank, a novelty for parading!'

He glanced idly at one with more writing than the rest. It announced that the Comtesse de Souvestre had reverted to her former name of Mademoiselle Hautdoire. She must be one of the wealthy Hautdoire family, a Frenchified version of the O'Dwyers who had come to France with the Wild Geese. A hurried scribble beneath the invitation said that the writer had a very special and urgent reason for asking Mr. Young to come to her soirée.

Mr. Young held the invitation between finger and thumb. This must be from the piece who, rumour had it, had performed a race on her hands—in her underwear—with some other piece of gilded decadence, before the Emperor. 'A very special and urgent reason,' he mimicked. The same special and urgent *ennui* that prompted her tasteless clowning at Court. He threw the card aside.

He pounced upon an envelope with an American stamp addressed in Kitty's handwriting. Dear, steadfast Kitty! No alternating heights and drops in *her* friendship. It had endured through distance and hardships and prosperity from the morning that he had served Mass at her runaway marriage.

She wrote to say that at last she had traced the woman for whom Thomas had searched, the one who had left him with Mrs. Mansfield of Kilsheelin.

'I'll give you her name and whereabouts when you return,' she wrote. 'Mark and I would like to talk to you here first.' Dammit! Why hadn't she written down the address and let him go there at once? The surge of excitement receded. He knew why; as Kitty knew; that the disclosures would prove unpalatable! It was what he had always dreaded; underneath all his

467

fanciful dreaming! He scraped back the chair and jumped to his feet. Whatever it was he must know. There was still time to book a passage in that boat that had just beaten all records and reached France in fifteen days.

He had gone some yards down the boulevard when he bethought himself of Dorene. 'Blast...!' Why must he involve himself in *her* misfortunes? He remembered the brown eyes he had helped to make sightless. He turned back. He couldn't take her back to America without giving her the opportunity of consulting that Swiss specialist who had been suggested by the Paris doctor.

Sir Jocelyn realised at last that he was wasting his breath. Since his wedding night *débâcle* he placed great value on his breath. The dreadful accusations, reproaches, insults that he had vented on his bride all the way from the theatre had brought gasps and sometimes yelps from Aunt Yvette; but they had no effect upon Sterrin. He might as well not have been there. They would leave Paris, he decided. They would go to Switzerland—away from the crowds and from the theatre.

Sterrin was alone; alone as never before. All her remembered life she had been one of two, and the heart of each had been in the bosom of the other. Nothing had altered that; not separation; not prison; not the solemnity of the convent; not even the sacred vow of marriage itself. All the hazards of life and nature, the elements, storm, the ocean, were possible; but not this, another woman, the most elemental of all; blind assured fool that I have been, the most likely!

She was in her bedroom now, the maid fussing at the fastenings of her gown.

'Leave me!'

'But, milady——'

'Leave me, I tell you.' She fumbled and tore at the newfangled hooks and eyes, her unaccustomed fingers dragging out pieces of silk and gauze with the steel contrivances. She flung the gown across the bed and flung herself after it.

From the communicating door her husband watched her anguish liberate itself in shuddering sobs. Display of emotion bored him. He associated them with discarded mistresses; but this was a revelation! This still, cold girl, sensitive and proud, child of an aristocracy, abnegating herself in an agony of be-

468

trayed love. For a bumptious hind, a kitchen boy who had elevated himself into a posturing play-actor! Suddenly he felt that he would barter all his treasures to evoke one breath of love's emotion for this unpossessed treasure. The scenes he had envisioned when he had secured this treasure! His villa on the Adriatic, Sterrin in filmy lace pouring his coffee on its vine-clad loggia; grand salons in London and Paris; impressive entrances with Sterrin by his side, a jewelled flame drawing all eyes, enslaving all hearts but belonging to him. And here was the reality. Sterrin prostrate from degradation, turning his marriage bed like his bridal bed into a bier.

'I'll tear her all to pieces!' Her groping hands clutched the beautiful gown as though it were an effigy of the woman who had dared to encroach upon her heritage of love.

'Tear your rival to pieces by all means, but kindly refrain from tearing the gowns that I have provided for your adornment.'

Her eyes ranged over him as though he were some stranger who had wandered into her apartment. She noted the twisted muscle at his temple; the rigid corner of his lips. *Her* handiwork!

She looked down at the gown that she held gripped between her hands at tearing point: a masterpiece of Worth's, the world-famous designer; twenty yards of gauze over twenty yards of silk and from neckline to hemline flowed shimmering rivers of sequins. Its beauty reproached her.

'You know,' she said in a small voice, 'you don't really deserve this.'

He tried to tilt a cynical eyebrow but it remained rigid and he remembered why. 'I came to tell you,' he said, 'to be prepared to leave for Switzerland at nine o'clock in the morning.'

'But——!' and then she remembered that it didn't matter now. The visit to the royal villa, the fresh wardrobe with its four changes of dress that royal protocol demanded for each day. She had no more desire to face Mademoiselle Hautdoire. Suddenly she realised the enormity of what she had contemplated; to have her marriage annulled; to tear down the sacred edifice of church and law so that she could indulge her deluded passion for a servant, a nameless one at that; someone's byeblow!

'Kindly give heed to what I say. Be ready to leave at nine

469

o'clock.'

She remained looking at the door through which her husband had left, then suddenly rose up with an air of resolve. One by one she discarded the modish-coloured petticoats. White petticoats had become an antiquity in this ancient city that lived youngly. But the nightgown she chose was unrelieved white.

Silently she appeared before him; a white immolation. She felt as she had felt the morning she had appeared before Reverend Mother with her saddle bag in her hand and her dowry tied to the hitching ring outside; a little, too, like the way she used to feel when Nurse Hogan would grip her nostrils and give her a mixture of salts and senna and tell her to offer it up for the souls in Purgatory.

Rarely in his long experience, thought her husband, had he glimpsed the quality that was housed in this graceful form that stood before him. It could arouse passion in men, adoration, madness. Often he had likened her to a flame but never before had he been so conscious of her quivering, luminous warmth. Had the fates reserved for his twilight hour the most exquisite experience of his life?

Almost fearfully he reached out to her, but even as his pulse sent a warning to his heart, he noticed her flicker of revulsion. Pride curdled his desire into venom.

'What apple have you hidden there now?'

'Apple?' She looked down to where his head had gestured, then remembered her trick with the apple-shaped pincushion. She drew aside the lace that covered her bosom.

'There is nothing there,' she said reassuringly then recovered the glimpse of tender white curves. 'You see,' she went on calmly, '*you* see all this differently.' She swept her arm towards the window and the world beyond that held tonight's happenings and all that they signified. Patiently as to a child she explained. 'It was not what ordinary people understand when they speak of love.'

He had to keep very quiet. The blood was chu-chugging through his forehead. He, Jocelyn Devine of the delicious memories, who from his earliest youth had been an epicure in love's art, who understood women better than any man in London or European society, which meant any man alive, was being told by a country-girl not out of her teens that he was incapable of understanding love—that he was ordinary!

470

'*Ordinary* people, like me,' he said at last, 'do not regard the furtive, hole-and-corner precociousness between a servant and his employer's daughters as—love. The fellow should have been dismissed. I am surprised that your father was so hoodwinked.'

Her patience exploded. Young Thomas was no longer worthy of being defended but she would brook no criticism of her father.

'Papa was not the type to be hoodwinked. Papa knew whom he could trust.'

'It would scarcely appear so.'

'I will not allow you to criticise my father.' Then as suddenly as it had blazed, her anger subsided. 'Why,' she went on conversationally, 'when my governess got frightened and lost her head during a bread riot in the famine Papa said that there were to be no more governesses and sent me bird-nesting with—with Young Thomas.'

There was something elemental, he thought about the way she would suddenly lapse back from the dramatic intensity into some simple, direct statement.

'He caught a trout,' she went on, 'and cooked it over a picnic fire on the bank of the stream. It was delicious.' A dreamy smile played over her lips. He could have kissed them but that he wanted to strangle her. The time he had spent conferring with his chef to produce the rarest food and wine for her delectation. And here she was rhapsodising over a crude fish caught and cooked—probably half raw—by her lover.

'And I have no doubt,' he said aloud, 'that he expressed his relish by wiping his mouth with the back of his hand.'

'Oh no,' she answered in that practical way that could be so captivating if he didn't suspect that it was simply contempt for his pettiness.

'He wiped his hands on the grass. You see he had given me his clean linen handkerchief. I suppose,' she went on, 'that it was being so hungry always that made it seem so nice.'

'Hungry. So you have been hungry as well as ragged?'

She ignored the crudity of his reference to the patched-up dress in which she had encompassed his beguilement. She would have worn her hunger as proudly as she had worn her patched-up gown. Not to have been hungry in the famine would have been a shameful thing.

But she had lashed him too severely with the weapon of her

471

crude youth; letting him glimpse that arcadian idyll of a springtime such as she had never known. A picture was shaping out of her reminiscences. The scullion's white handkerchief betokened an early fastidiousness; and that regard for his employer. The haughty young Sir Roderick O'Carroll was not one to indulge familiarity with a presuming servant.

'Why,' continued the voice of her persecutor, 'Papa had been searching for him night and day when they reported that he had run away——'

'Ah, so the prodigy ran away from his benefactors!'

'Indeed, that was just what he did *not* do.' The actor Thomas Young, tonight's stranger, was not worthy of her steel, but the knife boy, Young Thomas, was unassailable. 'He collapsed from famine fever. It was I who found his hat.' She made a gesture that released shafts of blue flame from her diamond rings; as though, he thought, their glory was but to proclaim that this was the hand that had found the scullion's hat. 'Papa found him lying among the hawthorn blossoms of Lissnastreenagh.'

This was fantasy; like something glimpsed in a dream, this girl in bridal white, her bronze hair flowing about her shoulder, here in his bedroom, deigning him glimpses of some young and lovely world. He could almost hear the gay pipes of Pan playing to that feast by the river bank; hear the scamper of his goat-like hooves among the blossoms where her lover had lain. She had been wiser than he when she said that what she had known was not what ordinary people understood when they spoke of love. He put his hand to his forehead. It encountered the knotted vein that was a heritage of his wedding night; the moment of beguilement passed. How dare she come here? Offering him what the scullion had rejected!

He crossed to the bed and pulled the bellrope for his valet. With his back turned to her he said, 'Did I say nine o'clock? Pray be ready to leave at eight o'clock in the morning.'

Back in her room Sterrin released a long breath. She was feeling as she had felt on that last morning in the convent when she had renounced the vows that she had never taken.

At the Swiss station Sterrin had to pick her way through the prostrate bodies of the wounded who had been transported there from Solferino. The sight of their fly-encrusted wounds brought angry protest from Sir Jocelyn. Such repellent sights

472

ought not to be allowed to obtrude upon the sensitivities of travellers; especially travellers come to seek health. Sterrin was roused to a lively anger. 'Have these poor things not the right to seek health,' she flared. The sight of the young, maimed bodies, tunics, hair, faces, blood spattered banished her preoccupation with her own troubles.

But two days later as she drove from the doctor's with her husband, the fragrance of a thousand roses, the sound of little waterfalls chased out of their white snow caps by the sun, the gurglings of nightingales, filled her with a lonely, undefined longing.

The mood was still upon her as she started to ascend the hotel staircase. Then suddenly from overhead there came a voice that set her heart racing. A gentleman came in sight around the staircase bend and Sterrin stopped dead. Here was the one who had involved that undefined longing midst the fragrance and melody of the drive.

Once again the woman was with him; the same woman, his arm tight around her waist, holding her close to him, guiding her down every step in tenderest concern.

He looked up. 'Sterrin!' His startled gasp made the woman stumble within his embrace. Sterrin was here! But why not; was she not everywhere that he went? So many Sterrins, the laughing girl, the lonely lost girl of the assassination days; the runaway schoolgirl; the girl with the soft kissing lips that had come to life beneath his own. But this Sterrin he did not know. The amethyst eyes that had yearned out at him from the wedding veil were the blue of challenging metal. 'Sterrin!' He took a quick step and his companion stumbled again.

The swift, silent drama was splintered by the sound of Sir Jocelyn's voice, 'Don't dare to address my wife with such familiarity! Come, my Lady.'

Sterrin allowed herself to be led away. Dimly she heard her husband cancel their arrangements for a six weeks' stay. 'You will be recompensed,' he said to the expostulating landlord.

From Sterrin there came no expostulation; she had no desire to stay. The perfumes of the roses had gone; the gurglings of the nightingales; the sound of the little waterfalls. Young Thomas had gone from her and all nature had gone with him.

CHAPTER 48

Thomas stared in amazement at the handsome frame house that stood in place of the log house where he had stayed with Mark and Kitty Hennessey on his previous visit to their Wisconsin farm. The first time he had stayed here they were still in the rough log cabin that they had flung together when they had trekked down from Canada. The first winter, while snow covered the ground, he had helped them as they cleared and dug and planted. By the time spring had banished the white mantle from the earth they had cleared several acres of land. In the autumn Thomas had been touring in the region, and he had shared their pride when they gathered in their first fine harvest of potatoes and oats and buckwheat. More and more acres had been cleared and acquired under the Homestead Law. The cabin had been replaced by a comfortable log house. NOW THIS! A finer house than that of the landlord who had starved them out of Ireland in bleak Forty-seven!

'She won't be happy,' Mark chuckled, 'until she has a brick house with pillars and porticoes.'

'And why not?' demanded Kitty. 'John Holohan of Upper Kilsheelin has an army of young men on the road, buying. They can't get enough of our produce.'

Although John Holohan was now a successful businessman in Chicago, to Kitty he was always John Holohan of Upper Kilsheelin. As she led Thomas from room to room through the house, every now and then she stopped and held him at arms length, 'to fill her eyes with the sight of him'. He was a pleasure for any woman's eyes; handsome, tall, and elegant, and beautifully courteous. Where did all those noble qualities come from —in this nameless servant-boy? Well, he'd soon know. Kitty wished now that she had never written to Thomas in Paris.

Thomas had come almost as quickly as his answering letter. He would have come still more swiftly had he not taken Dorene to an eye specialist in Switzerland. She was there now receiving treatment. Thomas had not tarried to hear the doctor's verdict, but he had been less pessimistic than the others.

In the evening the Hennesseys' neighbours came to greet the famous actor who hailed, like all in the settlement, from Tipperary. Thomas marvelled at their ease and independence. Few of them owned less than two hundred acres, yet a decade ago they had been despised tenants, evicted from the few Irish acres that they had held with less right of tenure than the rabbits. On any other occasion he would have enjoyed their quips at each other about having the rent ready for next Gale Day or they'd be evicted; they were all landlords now. But Thomas was afire to talk with Kitty about the reason for his voyage across ocean and continent. He listened with half an ear to the settlers' reminiscences; about the Temperance meetings and the Monster meetings that had awed the world. Maddeningly they capped each others' stories of the night of the Big Wind. And inevitably, though they wished to forget it, they touched on the famine.

'I never put a spade in the ground for the first of the potato crop,' said Mark, 'but there comes a dread on me that brings back the evening of the Blight. Do you remember it Thomas?'

Too well Thomas remembered his master's discovery of acres of evil-smelling slime that had been firm tubers that very morning; remembered his rush through fields of desolation to warn Mark to get his potatoes out of the ground; Mark, silhouetted against the darkening skyline, head bowed over the spade handle, the open drill at his feet releasing its evil-smelling message. Kitty, kneeling in the kitchen beside the cradle, her face pressed for comfort against the face of the baby that was soon to die in the Great Hunger! No wonder that American prosperity had failed to erase the tragedy from her face.

When the guests had gone and the children abed she pleaded with Thomas to drop the quest to learn the truth about his ancestry. She wanted to withhold the precious information that she had unexpectedly stumbled across.

'Aren't you being inconsistent, Kitty? After dragging me across the world?'

'My conscience made me write to you but my heart bids me advise you to leave well enough alone. You might find...' she stopped herself.

'I might find what you always suspected that I'm somebody's by-child; a half-caste with the vices of both parents and the

475

virtues of neither.'

'Don't talk like that, Thomas,' said Mark. His voice held a sharpness never before shown to this man who was dearer to Mark than a brother.

'God has balanced things well for you. If you have missed out in the matter of family it has been made up to you in talents—though to your credit you have multiplied them a hundredfold. You've carved a name for yourself that is famed and honoured. Why hark backwards? None of us want to look back to the past.'

'Don't you?' Thomas smiled. 'It seems to me you did little else all evening, the lot of you.'

There was so much he had wanted to talk about. He would like to have talked with the two Ryan girls whom Kitty and Mark had adopted when their mother had died in Quebec. They had grown into poised young ladies. Of course their mother, Miss Oenone Mansfield, had been born a lady; but she had run off with Black Pat Ryan. Suddenly he remembered to tell them about Dorene.

'Well, isn't it strange now,' said Kitty when he had told her. 'When we were on the ocean before the fever took a real grip I used to go over every last minute with you at the dockside. Your eyes were glued upwards at us—you poor friendless boy, and when a little blind girl bumped against you, you just helped her up the gangway without taking your eyes off us. I cared for her when her mother died of ship fever then I lost sight of her; how could you keep track of one little child? Six thousand they buried under that mound in Quebec—eighty fever ships lined along the river. And the water sparkling and dancing under them!' She gave a little shudder. 'Bring her here, Thomas, if the treatment she's getting in Switzerland doesn't work.'

'Kitty, your heart is bigger than your fine new house. Five children of your own and the two Ryan children—— By the way, you have done more than well by those two. They are polished young ladies.'

She explained to him about the money that Sir Roderick O'Carroll had sent ahead for their mother. 'It was lying in America all the time we were in Canada. John Holohan invested it for them later, and trebled it. The Midas touch, they say he has. We spent it on them, the best schools—everything! Thomas, I'll never understand that mystery; my unfortunate

476

cousin Black Pat to die of hunger and three of his children and yet Sir Roderick—his own foster-brother—thought nothing of sending a big sum of money like that to provide for his widow when she would reach America—God rest her.' she sighed. ''Twas all a mad folly, running off from her fine home with Black Pat, an' maybe it's alive he'd be today if he had married one of his own class. That kind of thing is all right in story books. It doesn't work out in real life.' Weariness descended upon Thomas like a pall. 'Thomas,' she went on, 'is it true that Miss Sterrin O'Carroll ran away from the convent and married the richest man in Ireland?'

He rose abruptly. 'I believe it is true. Kitty, I am exhausted and I must be away at dawn to find your lady.'

She chatted him up the stairs; tested the new-fangled stone jar that proudly replaced the old-fashioned hot bricks between the sheets. Then she put her hands on his shoulders. The last time he had been here he had been two days and nights on the road with little sleep after a season of travelling the whole continent, but he hadn't looked like this—ravaged!

'Thomas, did you go near Kilsheelin? Did you get a glimpse of Miss Sterrin?'

There was no gossip's curiosity in the face so close to his; only the concern that he had cherished when he was a friendless servant boy. He drew out a chair. 'Sit down, Kitty.'

The first cock was crowing when she stood up again. The motive power of Thomas's life had burst its dams. Its torrents still swept over her. The daughter of Sir Roderick O'Carroll and his servant boy! young, nameless, tribeless Thomas! It was like something out of a red-backed novel. No, out of a fairy tale. A pair of children shut off together in a fairy world of castles and grandeur and bygone glory. And no one to warn one of those children, the friendless, bewitched one, that the other would grow up and away into her own proud womanhood. Kitty looked across to Thomas, musing like herself. In troth he had grown into a manhood that seemed just as proud! And will that strange bearing of his grow less assured if it turns out that it has its origin in ignominy.

There was no ignominy. 'But why,' Thomas repeated, 'did you bring me to the back door of the castle?'

The woman-who-had-brought-Young-Thomas had material-

ised from a phrase into Mrs. Willis, a small, neat woman; grey
and severe and—bewildered. Where else but to the back door
would she have brought a ragged, bare-legged boy? One didn't
bring the likes of him to the hall doors of great houses; this
grand gentleman who had knocked at her own hall door must
have travelled too far into prosperity to recall his appearance
and circumstances the day that she brought him to Kilsheelin
Castle. People prospered in America. Hadn't she prospered herself? But America had not given him that—air. She had
always associated it with high birth. The dear knows that there
was nothing grand about *his* birth. He'd have been born in the
ditch if she had not taken in his mother when she collapsed at
her gate.

She had told him all and now she wanted to make tea for him
but Thomas wanted to go on asking questions. Why the back
door, indeed! She was in tumult; the little nurse-boy she had
reared. Parting with him had hurt.

'You must eat,' she twittered and despite his protests she was
gone. Some people found it easier to produce a meal than a
caress.

He thought to follow her. He might lose her again; the face-
less, nameless subject of a lifetime's yearning for identity. He
strode up and down the little room; his feet kept displacing the
rabbit footmats that protected the carpet. He studied the dried
grasses and sea shells on the whatnot in the corner. He turned to
the chiffonier, and there behind the little glass doors on the
upper shelf he saw the silver drinking cup! A thing of artistry
and beauty, startlingly out of place among all the quasi-genteel
trumpery! Once before he had seen such a cup. On the stone
shelf of the hermit's cave.

His face was still pressed to the glass when the woman returned with the tray. Her colour drained away. So that was
what he had come for! She lowered the tray and came over to
the cabinet. 'I never meant to deprive you of what was your
right. A crumb that wasn't mine I've never in my life taken. But
that cup was so long in the little cabinet in the house in Augh-
nacloy then after my husband died and the passage money came
so unexpected from America—a neighbour helped me to pack—
there was only a few days to find a home for you——'

'So my mother had this with her?' All the time she talked
Thomas studied the cup, turning it over and over. It was an

478

exact replica of the one in which The O'Meara had once given him a drink of goat's milk. The hermit had told him that the hawk wrought on its side combined the O'Carroll symbol and the Hapsburgh. A great throb of discovery surged through Thomas as though the cup were a water diviner's rod. It was a while before Mrs. Willis's embarrassed excuses reached him.

He turned to her. 'Please, please don't think that I have come to question what you did with anything that she may have possessed. You shall have a dozen silver cups. It is just that this one has a special significance for me. Meantime, I should love a cup of tea.' Over the tea he probed again for the scant details of his origin. His mother had died the night that he was born. She had asked for water and the woman, thinking she was thirsty, had proffered milk; when it was waved away and water brought, the sick woman had made a desperate effort and struggled up. She poured the water over the baby's head and her voice was steady and clear as she said, 'I baptise you Thomas in the Name of the Father, Son and Holy Ghost.' The words of his Conditional Baptism were the last she spoke.

Thomas was profoundly moved by the infinite pathos of his mother's death. She must have started to die a few nights before when her husband had been killed at his door by the Tithe Proctor's men before they tumbled the house.

'There was a bit of writing pinned inside her mantle——' Thomas jerked out of his reverie.

'Writing? Where is it?'

But it had been handed over with himself to the housekeeper at Kilsheelin Castle and Thomas knew the rest. The Housekeeper had been killed in the Big Wind a few nights later. Her room was one of those that had been destroyed with all their contents. Including the identity of the waif who became Young Thomas here, and Young Thomas there, and you, Young Thomas!

'. . . so I wrapped you in the sheet that she brought. . . .' Mrs. Willis had resumed her story and Thomas uncrossed his legs with a force that slopped his tea. She insisted upon going off for a fresh saucer. He didn't want a fresh saucer. He wanted to know about the sheets. But he had to sit and chafe while the china cupboard was unlocked and a perfectly clean saucer washed. No, it might be dusty. This set is only used once a year.

'There is no use looking for the sheet,' she said when she

returned and her voice had gone edgy. 'It was thin with age even then. I covered you with it for years.'

Thomas brushed aside her self-defence. 'Please, please don't think that I am here to question anything you may have done with her possessions. I can never do enough to repay you for your immense Christianity and kindness to my mother and to myself. But these articles—the cup and the sheet—have a very special significance for me; anything that you can recall about them? What kind of stuff was in the sheet? I mean, was it linen and had it a monogram?'

'A monogram?' Mrs. Willis looked with new interest at the undoubtable gentleman before her. 'There was a bit of embroidery on the corner—an initial maybe or something, I don't know. But it was made of linen all right. Fine linen, the sort that makes good bandages. That's what I did with it afterwards when it was too threadbare to use. I bandaged your leg with it when you cut it on a scythe; a terrible cut.' She paused to savour the recollection of the cut. 'Anything that she possessed I put to your own use. Her clothes were good and I cut them down to clothe you while they lasted. I even gave you her religion. I taught you the Lord's Prayer with a Who instead of a Which and I sent you at night to a neighbour's house to join their rosary. It wasn't an easy thing for me to do at the time,' she concluded.

Thomas fully appreciated how much such an act had meant for his Protestant foster-mother. The Penal Code still lingered at the time. It was a risky thing for a Protestant to shelter a Catholic much less to endeavour to rear one in the Catholic faith. But man's essential humanity had shown itself like a bright, warm thread through all the dull and blood-stained fabric of the terrible Code. Many a Protestant might have enriched himself with the price on the head of a hunted priest had he not chosen instead to grant him the shelter of his home. Just as the Irish Catholics in an earlier persecution had sheltered the fleeing refugees of the Huguenot and Bloody Mary purge. A thought struck him. 'That piece of writing! It was destroyed the night of the Big Wind, but you must remember what was written on it?' She shook her head. She could not read. He was on his feet, the cup neatly parcelled under his arm when another point struck him. 'There were so many gentlemen's places where similar employment was available for me, places like Lord

Strague's or the de Guiders' of Aughnacall or the De Laceys'—any of their places was nearer to you, more convenient when you were so pressed for time. What made you think of Kilsheelin?'

She drew her brows together. What had made her go there? Across the distance of time and ocean one of these places was the same as the other and all of them equally dim in her memory. But the walk to Kilsheelin, she remembered, *had* been longer than to those other places. Oh, she remembered now why she had passed them by. Setting out with the lad that day she had recalled suddenly that his mother, before she collapsed at the gate, had asked how far it was to Kilsheelin Castle. His foster-mother had picked on the place as a sort of omen.

Thomas went still. Things don't happen by chance. After nearly six years his foster-mother had completed his mother's journey: but not her mission! 'And so,' he said quietly, 'you brought me to the back door.'

This time his remark did not strike Mrs. Willis as foolish. There was something like timidity in her voice as she said, 'Would it have made a difference if I had faced up to the front door?' He looked so long and keenly at the viewless window that she thought he was admiring the draped and tasselled curtains in the gleaming brass bands.

'Perhaps,' he said, still gazing through the plush and the lace. 'Perhaps. But,' he said, turning to her with a smile that warmed her, 'it would have made a world of difference if you had not brought me there at all—a lost world of difference.'

There was panic in his heart as he left the neat house and the neat-minded woman whose charity had persisted doggedly up to the blessed urging that had opened to him the back door of a wonder world. Supposing she had dumped him at the De Guiders', the nearest place. He would have got some kindly, hanger-on's employment that would have ensured food and shelter. But his intellect would have remained plunged for ever in darkness. The panic of the fate he had escaped remained with him as he finished the engagement that had justified the trip across the Atlantic to his foster-mother. It kept dogging him in the train between performances. The Big Wind, he thought, might have held for him no meaning but that of a severe storm. He might never have gone out into that rocking amphitheatre of nature: never witnessed from a privileged seat the tumult of the heaven's drama. That night his own sense of drama was born as he watched nature's portrayal of the violently illuminated passions of life, its tragedy, its sombre ferocity, its splendour and again, its mirthless comedy when an antic wind scooped up an entire, unbroken field and tossed it up to the ranting clouds. He would never have encountered that scenic prop of the storm's drama, his own ancestor's uprooted tombstone from which he had learned to read and later to scrawl.

Supposing that the Big Wind had not produced the tragedy of the housekeeper's death! Supposing that she had lived! Would he still have gone with mop and duster to the library where his tallow candle had flickered over the shades of the classic period, Roman and Attic, and on to the pages of the play-actor of Stratford in whose strolling path he now followed? Would he have lingered at the bookshelves absorbing the story of his master's family caracoled in stately fashion down the centuries; awakening to the problematic enigma of heritage?

He took the cup from its wrappings. Reverently he touched the outline of the hawk, the heraldic symbol of the O'Carrolls. 'Which of them are you?' the bard would say. And Thomas had put it down to the vapourings of a bardic mind gone senile. But it was The O'Meara who had started Thomas's odyssey that had led him to this Holy Grail of his heritage. 'May the angels spread a bed for you in Heaven, O'Meara!' He gazed through the window and out of the rolling mists a pair of purple-blue eyes looked up at him in child-wonder. 'Maybe you are a prince in disguise, Young Thomas.' And now, when the prince had succeeded in taking the jewel from the head of the toad, the princess had vanished. And now there was Dorene waiting for him in Switzerland.

Thomas returned to Europe to a jubilant Paris, a once more city *en fête*. This time for Napoleon's vast congress of nations to bring the conditions of Europe under review.

'I believe they are on the brink of Civil War in America,' said a man with whom Thomas shared a compartment on the train to Switzerland. Thomas was startled. He had been living in a wildly swinging world of his own. 'I have heard no war cry,' he said.

Alphabet met him at the Swiss station. The multi-named body-servant had been aggrieved to have to miss an exciting tour in order to escort a blind young lady. The news of Dorene was not encouraging. 'Not that she gave me the specialist's verdict but she intimated it by her manner. I urged her—respectfully—to join the society for improving the conditions of the blind; to make them more *self-supporting*.'

Thomas caught that. He rounded on Alphabet. 'Do you consider yourself *self*-supporting? If I find that you have distressed Miss Du Clos you can support your interfering self at someone else's expense, Duignan!'

Alphabet looked at the stern countenance beside him and trembled for his cushy job. Duignan! Twenty-six Christian names and to be addressed by the far-off surname that was only a weary sigh at the end of his baptismal alphabet! The boss must be proper peeved.

The boss was feeling deflated. In the excitement of his own discoveries he had relegated the problem of the blind girl to the background.

Now she must face it, and the cause of her blindness; a poor innocent caught up in the maelstrom of his frenzy to catch himself a bride from beyond his utmost reach. Besotted, presumptuous fool. What did he know of women? All his life had been a preparation and a dedication. Because he had given his love to a child. Girl-children became women, unpredictable, unfathomable. The memory of his first glimpse of the girl-child turned woman returned. There was no erasing from his memory that tableau of lovely girls moving in procession up the stairway, their candles flickering over the black marble; and, last and loveliest, the girl in turquoise blue.

He took out a gold cigarette case and tapped it savagely. Fool! Damned, quixotic, romantic fool! I've lived too long in the world of make believe. He struck the long sulphur match. It quenched immediately under the cold cloud of his breath.

'A superior servant,' he said aloud to the second match, 'is neither fish, flesh nor good red herring.'

Alphabet turned to him. 'I do my best, sir, but I do appreciate that you appreciate that I *am* superior.'

Thomas blew out a cloud of smoke. 'And an actor is no better. Romance and tragedy are his stock in trade. I returned to her at a propitious moment; the prelude to a splendid marriage that lacked but one thing—romance; and the strolling player supplied it from his repertoire.'

483

He sought out Dorene immediately, dreading the interview; but at the door of the sitting-room he stopped dead. She was seated at the piano playing, of all things, a gay gallop. It was amazing the dexterity with which her fingers raced up and down the keyboard, never fumbling a note. Ornaments on the piano, lustres on the mantelpiece tinkled and danced to the force of her playing. Thomas was at a loss to define his reaction. It was like hearing rollicking music hopping out of a church organ. What had he expected? A blind Cecilia strumming mystic melodies!

Somehow it was all out of character. A person stricken down with blindness would not play with that reckless gaiety; and suddenly the explanation dawned on him. Of course! She was hardly going to tell Alphabet. The news was good and she was keeping it to surprise him.

She sent a ripple of graceful notes running down the board and lifted her hands with a flourish.

'Bravo!'

She gave a startled shriek and whirled around on the stool. Her eyelids lifted over a flash of brown, then drooped weakly as she groped to her feet. His arm went round her as she swayed uncertainly.

'I'm sorry I startled you, but it was such a rousing performance. I don't have to ask what had induced such *élan*; the news is good. It is, isn't it?' It had to be. It couldn't be otherwise. She had expressed it in every note; and yet, she was silent.

The news was not good. The doctor could do nothing for her. Thomas took her chin in his hand and forced her face up. 'Look at me!' He cursed himself. But wasn't there a bloom on her cheek like a sunkissed peach? Wasn't there rejoicing in her spirit?

She twisted her face from his grasp. 'I'm sorry that you have to be disappointed——'

'To the devil with *my* disappointment—forgive me my dear. It is your disappointment that matters. Dammit, I must see the doctor at once.'

'No! No!' The vehemence in her voice startled him. Or was it that her voice was becoming more mobile; acquiring the power of expression denied her eyes? She could become a better actress than before. 'He can tell you nothing that he has not told to myself. It is not nice hearing, and it doesn't improve by

484

repetition.' For the first time since her blindness, he discerned bitterness in her voice. Who could blame her. 'He—the doctor—did everything that he could for me and when there was no improvement I asked for the truth. I asked him not to spare me. I see no mercy in giving false hope—I see no mercy anywhere but——' her voice cracked, 'that's only because I can't see anything.'

His arm that had assisted her from the piano tightened around her waist. 'It is all right, Mr. Young. I'm not going to be hysterical. I'm going to be sensible; very sensible. That was why I was practising that dance tune just now. The new railway round the Simplon is bringing a great many people here for winter holidays. Madame Kohlat, the proprietress, told me that there would be plenty of employment for me playing for carpet dances after dinner. I thought I would earn enough to go to America.'

The poor child! Trying to earn what would release her from this prison of snow and silence.

'I was longer than I expected to be. There were some tempting engagements offered. Did you think that I was going to leave you here to turn into an icicle?'

'It was nice in the summer. The summer catered for the other senses. There was life in all those lovely smells from shrubs and roses; in the sound of the waterfalls from the little streams of melted snow always rushing and gurgling down the mountain, and in and out through their sound I could hear the nightingales. It was like a constant orchestra. Then everything went away, the orchestra, the roses, the waterfalls, the nightingales....'

Poor child, he thought again. To be blind within sight of Mont Blanc! To be blind at Lake Leman! Not to glimpse it through branches of tulip trees and clumps of crimson rhododendrons!

He understood what she felt about that cessation of life. It had been the same with him when the separate stream of Sterrin's life had ceased to flow within him. The little waterfalls bereft of sun had frozen into silence. His fingers caressed the soft cheek.

'No more worries, little one,' he murmured into her hair. 'I'll guide those little footsteps all the rest of the way.'

CHAPTER 49

If she kept busy enough, life at Kilkenny was just supportable. There were plenty of young officers around, but Sterrin could not forget that the military were there to supervise the evictions of Sir Jocelyn's tenants, who were being driven off their land to make room for a new breed of cattle he wished to develop. Tonight there was to be a party, the first evening of a house-party for the officers and some of Sir Jocelyn's friends. Lady O'Carroll had been invited and Sterrin was pathetically eager to see her mother again. In truth, Sterrin was looking forward to the party. But there was something that clouded her expectation. To Sterrin's dismay, she discovered that Donal Keating of Poolgower was one of those invited. She protested angrily to her husband and told him she did not wish to entertain the Keatings. She explained about the night of the Big Wind and how her father's field had landed on the Keating's land. She even told him about the Whiteboy raid that almost killed her mother. But Sir Jocelyn was not the least bit interested in Sterrin's feelings about the Keatings or, indeed, about anything else. He simply remarked that he hoped she would wear one of her new dresses from Paris.

Hannah draped the novel Grecian-cum-Renaissance gown over her mistress's head and after a certain amount of fumbling managed to fasten the hooks and eyes. With a sigh of relief, she stood back to review her handiwork.

The gown was a revolution from the swinging crinolines. It was moulded so tightly that Hannah was embarrassed at its revelation of the lines and curves of a woman's body. Moulded breasts, flat stomach; it was indecent after the outbulging years of horsehair petticoats and the steel cage that had supported the crinolines. And these thighs! Hannah had never before associated thighs with a lady. The prophecies of Saint Columcille were beginning to come true. Women, said that holy prophet, will wear trousers.

Her eyes fell to the shortened hemline that revealed two inches of ankle. The sight drove her to speech. 'God never meant *them* to be seen.'

Sterrin raised the skirt and revealed a pair of shapely legs. 'How do you know that God meant them to be hidden, Hannah? I doubt if HE bothers about such things.' She swung her leg forward. 'There is nothing to be ashamed of about them.'

'Ah, Miss Sterrin, you are changing. You were often a wild colleen but you never used to make light of holy things.'

'There is nothing holy about these,' said Sterrin, dropping her skirt. She put a hand on the maid's shoulder. 'I shan't keep you waiting long. There will be no music tonight on account of Lady Murray's bereavement.'

Svelte and regal, Sterrin seemed to cleave a path through the crowding crinolines. She gave a cool nod towards Donal Keating and pretended not to notice that officers were raising their monocles.

One of them took her down to dinner. 'You have great courage, my Lady,' he said, 'to blaze this new trail; or should I say train?' He indicated the train that flowed out from her as they descended.

'Thank you, Captain,' she said. 'Do you find that it takes courage to face all these people whom you have been evicting this week?' He busied himself with the train over the dining-room threshold. His hostess's tact, he thought, did not march with her beauty. Evicting her husband's tenantry was not quite his cup of tea.

'I should have thought,' she resumed when they were seated, 'that it would be a soldier's duty to protect women and children—and their homes.' Her clear voice fell into the shallows that precede the flowing of dinner talk. So did his answer, though it was almost a whisper. 'It was not I who ordered the evictions, Lady Devine.'

With ponderous tact the wife of the Deputy Lieutenant for the county roared in with some questions about the gay doings at the French Court. 'Your charming wife,' she said to her host, 'seems to be a devotee of the French Empress. I believe that it was she who started this new vogue.'

'Yes, indeed,' said Sir Jocelyn. 'Eugenie's edict banning the crinoline overshadowed the Emperor's New Year speech.'

'Humph,' said the lady. 'She is not *my* Empress. She won't

ban *my* crinoline.'

Sterrin contemplated the lady's bulging proportions then leaned forward with great deference and said, 'That would be most unkind of the Empress, Madam, to ban your crinoline, I mean. It is much more becoming to your—style.'

Sir Jocelyn looked down in surprise at his wife. Her remark to a lady so much older was not in character with herself. In all fairness he admitted to himself that while she was mettlesome and hot tempered, he had never heard her make unpleasant remarks to other ladies. Her laughter was brittle and frequent; but tonight too frequent; her dinner partner seemed fascinated. And of course this old haybag had asked for the dig she had been administered. But it was unfortunate that it had been administered by the hostess.

The Deputy Lieutenant's lady was waving her fan as though to drive off apoplexy. 'I'll wager,' she said to her other neighbour, 'that she is a rebel.' The fan blew the wager down to Sterrin.

Another lady said that she had happened to be in Austria during Eugenie's visit. 'She was wearing a gown that fully disclosed her ankles. In broad daylight. Ankles, did I say? A lot more could be seen. I'm told the Emperor Franz Joseph averted his eyes while she was stepping into the carriage and when his own Empress Elizabeth was about to step in after her, he stepped forward and completely screened her and everyone heard him say, "Careful, my dear. Someone might see your feet." Of course it was obvious that he did not allude to the sweet Empress Sissi, as they call her. *Her* gown was long and flowing—and, completely decorous.'

Sterrin was outraged and bored. Without waiting until the footmen came in to remove the cloth she gave a quick signal to the ladies and rose to her feet.

'What execrably bad form!' she said as she rose. 'The Emperor Franz Joseph's, I mean.' Sterrin smiled reassuringly at the astounded ladies. It was bad enough being summoned from the table before the cloth was removed; but to be accused of bad form.

'One might forgive bad taste in dress,' Sterrin said, 'but in speech! Never!' Tall, sheath-like, her train establishing a regal distance between her and the others, she swept out.

Her husband, standing at the head of the table, watched her, gratified in spite of herself, at her curtain speech. The others, he thought, swaying from side to side in the crinolines that he had once thought so graceful looked suddenly, like waddling ducks. She was such a hostess, as he had always envisaged; such a wife?

That night, when Hannah was still struggling with the hooks and eyes of the dress, he came to Sterrin's bedroom. 'Get out!' he ordered the maid. He groped at the complicated fastenings that strained against her taut muscles.

Sterrin tensed.

It had to happen some time. Marriage is a bargain, and she had collected plenty of the profits; and so had Mamma, Dominic, the servants, the tenants. Marriage holds no romantic moments with romantic bridegrooms. That sort of thing is thought up by writers of yellow-backed trash and by—by deluded fools brought up in convents and castles. This is life; this is—— There was no sense seeking words. The surge within her was not a thing of words or defined thought; just a jabber-jabber of sentience to dull the pounding of her heart. A hook tore over her flesh.

'God'll mighty!' she exploded. 'Do you have to tear the flesh off my bones?' She looked over her shoulder. 'Ugh!' The exclamation was not for her scratched flesh; but for the spectacle of his artificial masticators. His gasping breaths had dislocated their guttapercha gums. They were projecting all purple and slobbery.

Her disgust was the last straw. The wave of passion roused by the sight of her beautiful body making its sweeping exit had beaten itself out in the conflict with the hooks and eyes. He turned and looked at himself in the long, pier glass.

'One would think that I was a monster,' he muttered to his image. The grotesque gums were in position again.

'You *are* a monster, no,' she raised her hand as he turned, 'not because of this.' She rubbed her smarting back. 'I mean that private army out there in the park; your bloodless victory. Six hundred people turned from their homes. To them you are a monster.'

'I am not concerned with how I seem to the *canaille*.'

'They are not *canaille*.' Her low-pitched voice spiralled. She blazed at him. 'They are human beings with the right to humanity. My father never evicted. He held that to deprive

489

people of their homes was to deprive them slowly of their right to live.'

He tapped his snuff box. 'And I don't have to remind you of how your tenants repaid your father's humanity. Since you are so concerned with human rights let me remind you that I, too, have my rights.'

'You are free to take your rights,' she said quietly.

He looked at her reflection in the mirror; standing so passively, arms at her sides, the palms out; a sort of self-abnegating surrender. To him! There rose before him a vision of two countesses who once almost gouged each other's eyes out for the favours of his couch.

In a flash of revelation he saw her as she had been the day she had accepted his proposal of marriage; swinging towards him down the drawing-room of the castle with a sort of desperate courage that had delighted him; the high gallantry of her caste. Sir Jocelyn, why have you come today? It is for the horse? That heroic gesture; the glove withdrawn, the hand proffered in surrender. By heaven he had sold herself to him for the horse!

'Take off your glove!' The words ripped out from him.

She lifted her hands slightly then glanced towards the dressing-table where her long gloves lay. Was this another rush of blood to the head? He had babbled this way after they had bled him on his wedding night.

'Gloves?' she asked.

He turned from the mirror and seized her dress at the neck. 'This,' he cried, 'this gauntlet.' With one savage wrench he tore the stately *robe à l'Imperatrice* apart from neck to hem. For a moment he stared at her splendid, youthful body. He felt a sense of renewed potency and vigour as he pulled her towards the bed.

A wick spurted in the silent blackness. In its sudden light Sterrin saw her reflection in the pier glass; lying in the rags that he had made of the *robe à l'Imperatrice*. And then she became aware of her husband standing by the bed. Looking down at her abasement! The thought gave direction to the spirit that was floundering somewhere in a pit of shame and degradation.

She raised herself on to her elbow. By twisting her lips tightly into a smile she managed to control their wobbling. They must look like Sister Mary Aliquo's did that day in the convent garden. And was *this* what Sister Mary Aliquo-five-yards-of-calico was alluding to when she used to teach us that nice girls had no need to examine their conscience on the Sixth Commandment? Bitterness etched her smile into steadiness; but in the flickering light all that her husband noticed was the elusive, enchanting smile that he remembered from betrothal days. Her composure astounded him. He watched her swing a pair of long legs over the side of the bed, kick back the train that adhered to one half of the robe, slough off the upper portion from her shoulders, stretch luxuriously then rise slowly like a hibernating snake emerging from its winter sleep.

She crossed the room. Now I'll never challenge Mademoiselle Hautdoire to walk on her hands; such a silly thought to go forging its way through her shocked senses. But now, of course, there could be no more talk of annulment.

He watched her cross the room. Not a snake, he thought; a thoroughbred Persian cat daintily picking its way across a crowded street; disdainful of its surroundings; more concerned about wetting her feet than in avoiding the traffic.

She picked up a peignoir, tied it about her, and order seemed restored. He felt cheated. His act drained of manliness.

'You have evaded your obligation long enough,' he said.

Her answer was so low that he had to crane to catch it. 'One does not rivet on one's own chains.' She glanced up and for a fleeting moment, beneath the proudly-held poise he glimpsed her sick misery and horror. But her expression changed so quickly that he thought that he must have been thinking wishfully. 'It was a debt of honour,' she went on in a clearer tone. 'One always gets round to meeting that kind of debt.' It might have been a wager on a horse.

When Hannah heard him back in his own room she tapped at her mistress's door, but got no answer. It was dawn before a sound made her tap again. 'Help me with these boots, Hannah.' Miss Sterrin's ladyship was in riding dress! The maid almost tripped over the mound of silken gown that lay inside the door. So obviously flung there. 'Leave that thing and do as I tell you.'

When her mistress had gone Hannah picked up the gown again. A great jagged opening parted the front from neck to hem. The back was still held by the new, scientific hooks and eyes; except for the top one. Science inagh! She appraised the disorder of the unslept-in bed. By the looks of these endra-martins[1] the prophecies might not come true in this generation. 'A Miller will come without Thumbs—no. A Spaniard will rule and ruin Ireland——' Musha sure these are the prophecies of Saint Columcille. Its want of sleep is on me. As if a saint would concern himself with the sinful andramartins of the Quality. Not, of course, that it is sinful when they are married. No, it's not a prophecy that I am tryin' to remember. It is a curse. The one that was put on this house when the little children died here; dancing for the Quality on hot gridirons. The curse that no child would be born in this house to inherit it. It would always be passed on sideways, to nephews and cousins and the like. Hannah rearranged the counterpane and freshened the pillows. Well, by the look of things it might be that Miss Sterrin's Ladyship might be the one to break that same curse.

Sterrin had forgotten about the soldiers in the park. She wheeled from the sight of each encampment and finally rode towards the distant farmyard. The soldiers watched her set her horse at its high gate. She'd never do it! 'Twas a reckless jump. 'Ye Gods!' gasped a young subaltern. 'She rides like an Arab!'

The road held no retreat. It was filled with the grim cause of the soldiers' presence in the park. Even though she had to pull into the grass margin to avoid the endless procession of dispirited men and weary women and children, she was only vaguely aware of them as a roadblock. They trudged past aimlessly; some glanced up at her, then turned away from her cold, proud face. 'Mammy, I want a drink of water—Daddy, carry me. I can't keep up with you ... I'm tired.'

The plaint recurred like a chorus until its metre beat into her brain. She looked down. Mothers carrying babies; fathers carrying older ones; boys and girls carrying toddlers; others lagging behind, tugging at the grown-ups.

Sterrin shook her head sadly. She saw clearly that her pre-occupation with herself was immature emotionalism; that she was running away from reality. She moved back in the saddle with some idea of making room for an exhausted child. The space she made would scarcely hold one small child. And at her feet a whole tide of humanity crawled past.

Six hundred families. It was what Papa meant when he used to talk about the Diaspora of the Gaels. The wailing hundreds

[1] Carryings-on.

he had seen when he was despatching some of the tenants to America had suggested to him the Jewish Diaspora, when the Jews went out from Israel. This scene reminded Sterrin of the famine years when the roads used to be thronged with the starving. But then, there had been men like Papa and like Lord Templetown and other charitable landlords, racking their brains and their fortunes to cope; and there were the quaintly-clad Quakers, tirelessly moving through the countryside, and the parish priest and the Protestant vicar, out by day and night; united in the cause of mercy. But here there was no tempering mercy. The great overlord had the right to rid his land of humans as though they were crop-destroying vermin. And the Government showed its approval by manpower, military and police, to assist in the extermination. The people looked at her, not with hostility, but without friendship. It was a relief to realise, gradually, that at least they did not recognise her. She had arrived too recently. And she had hoped in time, to get acquainted with them, to establish the same friendly relationship with them as with the tenants at home!

As she walked her horse in tempo with the march of the outcasts she heard an outcry behind and wheeled. A group of men with crowbars were prodding awake some old people and children who had rested beneath a hedge and had fallen asleep. She spurred her horse towards a man in riding-breeches and leggings, who was holding a horsewhip menacingly.

'Stop those men!' she cried, reining her mount to its haunches. 'How dare they touch these people!'

The man looked at her for a moment before raising his hat. He didn't recognise her, but she was a very grand lady on a very grand horse, and she spoke with quelling authority.

'It is against the law, ma'am,' he said, 'for evicted people to shelter beneath the hedges.'

'What law?' she demanded.

He shrugged. 'Oh, I don't know.' His tone was not over respectful. 'Anyway, it is against my orders.' He turned impatiently and raised his whip. 'Hi, get you up!' he shouted to an old man deep in sleep.

Sterrin raised her own whip. 'Don't you dare to touch him!' she cried. 'I am Lady Devine. You will take your orders from me.'

A murmur rippled through the crowd. The overseer with the

whip went flabby with obsequiousness. Apathy went from the hunted; some showed hostility. Some drew away respectfully. A few came near her, sensing hope. A middle-aged man got stiffly to his feet and rubbed his knees. He moved over to Sterrin. 'I'm thankful to your Ladyship for the concession of resting beneath my own hedge.' The overseer made to intervene, but Sterrin raised her whip.

'Yes,' continued the man. 'I made that dyke. I ditched-in that land, as far as that bend.' He waved down the road. 'And I ditched in the fields back there as far as the hill. I was too good a farmer, I made my land too valuable. For every bit of fertilising and every bit of ditching and every bit of building I carried out, my rent went up and up until it was beyond all hope of paying. But if I had done nothing the result would have been the same. I'd still have been thrown out—for being shiftless and lazy. That's what he was told.' He indicated the man beside him. 'And these others. Sir Jocelyn Devine, with respects to you, my Lady, had brought a new breed of cattle from the Continent and the human stock on his land was in the way. Up there,' he pointed to the hills, 'the people were turned out because the pheasant hatcheries were trebled this year to make a bigger shoot.'

Sterrin felt a sick heat rising from her stomach to her head. She had known nothing of this. She shifted her whip to the hands that held the reins and put her free hand to her forehead. The man mistook the gesture. 'I'm sorry, my Lady, to distress you with the tale of our miseries.'

'No!' she said dully. 'It is not your telling me. It is your misery itself, the misery of all of you, that distresses me.' She drew on the rein and the man put out a restraining hand. For a second she thought he might be seeking to impede. She was uncertain about his attitude. He was well spoken but his voice held cynicism, as well as respect. She noticed another man who had been moving towards the speaker, a well-dressed man with a scarred face, who carried a sports gun. He had been watching her while the other was speaking and at the back of her mind there was a sense of familiarity.

'John,' he said to the man who had spoken to Sterrin, 'I am sorry to see you this way. I have come to offer the shelter of my home to you and yours.'

The overseer moved forward. 'Are you aware, my man,' he

asked, 'of the penalty for harbouring an evicted tenant? Every man jack of your family and clan can be fined for it. Aye, and turned out too.'

The scarfaced man's grip on his gun became less casual. 'Listen, whipmaster,' he said slowly. 'Don't "my man" me. I'm no chattel of your misbegotten master.' Sterrin flinched. Did he face towards her at the word 'chattel'? She remembered him now. It was Bergin, Thomas's friend who had watched for her here in these grounds over a year ago to help Thomas with his plan for elopement. How much did this man know? Did he know of his friend's volatile loves? Of her own humiliation? He uncovered sketchily towards her then turned back to the overseer.

'Nobody questions my right to receive friends under my roof. John,' he said to the man who still held Sterrin's bridle, 'that is my boat down there. When you get across the river you are on my land.' He looked meaningly at the overseer. 'Let anyone try molesting you there!'

Sterrin rode back across the path like one possessed. Soldiers scurried from her path, once she rode through a smouldering fire and sent sparks flying in all directions. An army cook stared open-mouthed after her, the contents of his skillet pouring down his apron. A footman appeared before she dismounted. She tossed him the reins and had reached the stairs-foot before she paused to toss a brief apology to the young gentleman whom she had almost up-ended in the hallway.

'Pray don't apologise,' said Donal Keating coldly. 'No person has the right to obstruct the path of Lady Devine!'

Sterrin hurried upstairs and didn't wait for an answer to her tap at her husband's door. 'Sir Jocelyn!' she exploded:

The presence of the valet bending over his master at the dressing-table checked her outburst. She paused, expecting the man to be dismissed. Her husband sent his eyebrows up in what was intended as sardonic surprise. Only one eyebrow responded. The contortion produced in the mirror disgusted his fastidious vanity. He reminded himself that his disfigurement had been caused by the beautiful tyro who was standing there pouring out breathless expostulations about suffering humanity.

'You must do something, at once!' She paused for breath. He leaned closer to the mirror.

'Bring it a little more forward,' he said to the valet. The man was drawing forth a lock of hair to shape into a curl over the twisted muscle that bulged over his master's eyebrow. 'One might of course, wear a wig,' he murmured, 'but then wigs are so *démodé*—aren't they, my dear?'

She had the feeling as she looked back at him that the Chinese dragons on his yellow silk robe were crawling over him. 'Out there,' she said, low and tense, 'there is a blemish that is a reproach to humanity. How do you propose to conceal it?'

He drew the curl a little more forward. 'You mean those demolished houses, don't you, my dear? They *are* an eyesore, I must admit, but I hope soon to have all traces of them cleared away.'

She turned away in disgust, but the thought of the homeless spurred her back. 'Won't you make arrangements to feed the people, even soup kitchens? They are starving and they are being forced along in a—death march. Even the cattle are free to move over the pastures.'

He stood up. 'They will have much more freedom now,' he said, 'and it will be possible to have many more cattle.' He threw his gown from him. 'This conversation has gone far enough. I am paying sufficient rates to maintain the Poorhouse. Let these people go there. Let them go to America, if it is fool enough to take them in. But don't bother me about them again. It is time you changed out of those clothes. Your duty at the moment is to your guests.'

496

CHAPTER 50

The chef looked up in amazement at the spectacle of her Ladyship entering the kitchen. When he heard the cause of her presence his eyes and mouth gaped. 'Milady! *C'est impossible*. Cook for six hundred people!' His assistant, a Professed Cook from London, folded her hands and prepared for battle. Her skill was the complement of his artistry. As a team they had worked together for years, dedicated to the holy cause of their Master's palate and securely entrenched in his appreciation.

Sterrin's eyes roved over the strange territory of this modern kitchen; the great range burning anthracite coal that cooked and heated without the gaiety of flames; the brownstone trough where a maid was washing vegetables in water that poured effortlessly from a tap in a wall; no Johnny-the-bucket. No human hand to fetch or carry it away. No hand human enough to stretch from such a kitchen to help the hungry. She recalled the Kilsheelin kitchen straining at its seams to cope with the famine; wall ovens steaming all day; never a spare hook in the great crane that swung its full complement of bastibles, bakepots and kettles over the eight fires in the hearth.

She turned away. Kilsheelin kitchen and its occupants were far away in some other civilisation. In the passage outside, hurrying servants flattened themselves against the wall; wide-eyed at the spectacle of her Ladyship coming out from the kitchen.

She found her dinner partner of last night gazing tenderly down the muzzle of a sports rifle. He transferred the look to his hostess. When he heard her request his breath went out in a whistle. 'Lady Devine, for me to order my men to fix up a field kitchen for your husband's tenantry would be—mutiny!'

'Why should it be? As an officer you can surely give orders to your men. You have ordered them to distribute food in the famine regions of India. You told me so yourself.'

Why should a man be compelled to turn from the appeal in

these lovely eyes? He laid down the gun and smoothed his moustache as though to clear the path for the words that were about to emerge. 'Lady Devine, in India I should not dare to countermand the orders of a Maharajah. Your husband's sway here is just as powerful as a Maharajah's and he is just as——' He stopped and went scarlet. He had almost said HE is just as cruel. 'I mean, er, as a magistrate he has the most amazing powers; far more so than magistrates in England. Over here they are being granted more and more power all the time; even over the ordinary public, much less over their own tenants.'

A servant entered. 'Sir Jocelyn's compliments, your Ladyship, and the shooting brake is ready to start.'

As she passed through the door that the captain held for her she said, 'I might have known that you wouldn't understand.' She swept out. He hurried after her, protesting. She silenced him with a gesture. 'I must make certain that adequate hampers have been prepared. The shoot is a long way off. Our guests must not go hungry.'

He caught up with her and barred her way. 'I'll broach the matter to Sir Jocelyn,' and then almost into her ear he murmured. 'I would put an army into the field for you.'

Sterrin moved on to where the luncheon hampers awaited her inspection before being fastened. 'Loaves and fishes.' She thought wistfully of miracles. The butler and housekeeper exchanged looks. 'No, your Ladyship,' the butler corrected her respectfully but firmly. 'These leaves are packed around ice for the champagne; not for fish. These here contain truffled partridges and——'

'What's over there?' Without waiting for an answer she crossed a passage to where a servant was emerging with a great scoop of flour. The captain, followed by Donal Keating, came seeking her down the passage. She went on assessing the bins of flour and meal that lined the long room. 'There is sufficient here to feed six hundred people. Isn't there?'

Mrs. Ledwidge explained that supplies had been increased to supplement the soldiers' rations. 'Soldiers?' Sterrin turned angrily, then saw the officer. He sketched a rueful gesture. His mission had failed. His host had told him courteously to mind his own business. She turned back to the housekeeper. 'How many cakes of soda bread can you produce from that bin?' The housekeeper looked as delicately pained as though she had been asked how many yards of buttermilk would make breeches for a bull. Impossible woman. 'Have you not coped with the famine?' Sterrin's voice was sharp with contempt.

The housekeeper looked worse than pained. She looked positively wounded. What could one expect, she thought, from a ladyship who would walk down to her own kitchen? What could one expect from a ladyship who saw fit to walk in her underwear before the Emperor of France? She folded her hands together over her black sateen apron. Sterrin assessed the gesture and waited. Here was another pair teamed against her. These two had been running this household before she was born.

'Your Ladyship,' the housekeeper took an impressively deep breath. 'I have been accustomed to cope only with the needs of the nobility and I have always given satisfaction. If I may say so, your Ladyship, I have always been where there was full and plenty.'

'You have been most fortunate,' was all that she said; and she said it gently. 'And now,' she turned to a bin, 'since you appear to have no idea of how many cakes of soda bread this can produce let me enlighten you. It can produce fifty; bastible size, each one adequate for six persons.'

'Indeed, your Ladyship?'

'Yes!' Now the butler as well as the housekeeper recoiled. Her Ladyship's voice had become a crack of a whip. 'Fifty cakes of soda bread,' she repeated, 'and that is what I want from every one of these bins. See to it immediately.'

'B-but, your Ladyship——' The woman's smugness had crumpled before the force of authority in Sterrin's voice. 'The ovens of a coal range could never cope with such numbers—the chef——'

'Waste no further time in questioning my orders.' Sterrin's features could have been fashioned from ice. 'Set your maids to scouring these disused bastibles. Have them slung over the fires in the boiling houses. I shall return in something over an hour. Have the bread ready for me. Yes,' she turned to where the footman had reappeared at the door, 'tell your master that I am coming.'

Sterrin paused at the door to tell the butler that he might close down the hampers. 'They are most satisfactory,' she smiled.

The smell of baking bread reached down the avenue to greet

her when she returned—on pretext of a headache—exactly an hour and a half later. The staff, subdued and perspiring, awaited her instructions about the mounds of soda cakes that steamed from shelves and tables. When she had seen them despatched to where the homeless were camping on a common beyond the estate boundary she wandered, deflated down the little path that led to the river.

Her brief sense of victory was over. Victory inagh! A bit of bread for those who had been deprived of their right to grow and make their own bread; and she would not have gained that victory, she would have been humiliated before her menials had she given them time to contact their master. Their veiled hostility had never troubled her before. She had been aware of it, but in some nebulous way—connected with the little French comtesse who had won the victory of her freedom from her unconsummated marriage—she had regarded her presence here as a transient thing. Somehow, some way, down some vista of time she would be Sterrin O'Carroll again. But after last night, that hope was erased. She felt chilled and solitary. As she approached the river, she saw Donal Keating pacing its bank. 'Why are you not with the shoot?' The sharpness in her voice startled her own hearing as well as his. It had erupted from her self-loathing; and from the loathing in which she held every male human being.

'I told your husband that I did not feel like slaughter today,' and his voice went a shade colder.

She came through the little wicket gate and walked beside him. She said slowly, 'Don't antagonise my husband.' He stopped and demanded impatiently. 'What can he do to *me*?' She found herself envying him his independence of her husband. He can turn you away from here, too, she thought. And suddenly she knew that she did not want that to happen. He was her own particular enemy; part of all those feudal enmities of Kilsheelin that time or distance had neutralised. 'And anyway,' continued Donal, 'why does he have me here? I have no claim to the distinction of his kind of guest.'

She could not tell him now that it gave her husband a twisted satisfaction to foist what he considered 'the young upstart's obnoxious presence' upon his wife. Instead she said, 'By all accounts you have attained distinction in your profession and, for myself, well I am glad that you are here.' She was surprised by what she had said. Yet it was true.

He flushed with pleasure. 'I never thought to hear that from you; the business of the field went deep with you; with your father.'

'It was that "Whiteboy" raid on my first birthday that implanted the bitterness about the field. A moment earlier and I would have been in the spot where the bullet hit. My mother never fully recovered, she——'

His startled exclamation halted her. She noted the way the colour ebbed from his face as he groped for speech. 'Lady Devine, you horrify me. I had never heard of any raid until that night when you came for a sod of the field to bring, as I thought, to America. You spoke contemptuously of a "call" that my family had made upon yours, of shirts worn over their clothes. Next day my mother explained. She didn't approve of the raid. But I swear to you, Lady Devine, that neither she nor my father dreamed that there was anything but a warning shot fired into the air outside. Your mother wounded! My God! I would never have—never have——' He recalled his bumptious badinage that night when he first laid eyes upon her, kneeling on the 'skeough' field in the moonlight; and again, as she walked with her dogs up Collnafunchion. 'I would never have faced you, much less flaunt myself here as your guest.'

A pulse beat in his cheek. His boyish distress clouded up the recollections of all that he stood for in her life. She found herself reassuring him.

'My mother was not wounded. Her—illness—had started on the night of the Big Wind when I was born.'

'You were born the night that the field fell upon us? You see,' he went on rapidly, 'I was cut off early from close touch with my family. I was sent away to school at a much earlier age than other boys; again something to do with your family. My eldest brother resented the patronage of having my brother John's Wedding Mass served by some young servant lad in your household who knew Latin; a picturesque-looking chap. I thought he was some college boy home for the holidays.'

But my Lady was not listening. Another flush tinted his pale cheeks. Servants as a topic of conversation, as in all things else, was beneath the interest of such as she. He apologised for his bad form. 'I merely mentioned him, my Lady, because his presence there sparked off something that cut me off too soon from early association with home and its happenings. In a way, he had an influence upon my life.'

Influence upon *your* life, she was thinking. If he only knew the influence that that picturesque-looking servant has had upon my life.

'You see,' he went on, aghast at her disclosures about the raid on her home, 'the rest of my family do not see eye to eye with my eldest brother. He goes his own way, broods over ancient wrongs, keeps reading the old family manuscripts.'

She raised her eyebrows. 'Have you one of those?'

He raised his. 'We did not sprout out of your sky-borne field —as your family seems to think. We have been in abeyance for a couple of generations, but those records have helped us to hang on—oh,' he exploded. 'I wish that I could give you back your field. I wish that I could carry it back to you, all wrapped up in an apron. There is a legend about a lake in Kilsheelin that was supposed to have been brought there wrapped up in a fairy woman's apron. You wouldn't know about that kind of rustic lore.'

'Wouldn't I?' She proceeded to give him chapter and verse of the tale of the disappearing lake; how Nora, a fairy woman from Killarney, had carried one of the lakes of Killarney in her apron to oblige another fairy woman in Upper Kilsheelin when there was a drought there. 'It was on the strict understanding that it was to be returned, but when years passed Nora had to come and fetch it away in her apron. Scientists give all kinds of highfalutin explanations for its strange behaviour, but,' she paused to blow a curl up from her forehead, 'that is the true explanation.'

She really believes it, he thought, as he watched her eyes turned dark purple and wistful. He felt that he was being privileged to glimpse that remote and lovely world she had known in childhood.

'I forgot,' he said, 'that you had a family bard to keep you posted in lore and legend.'

'It was not the bard,' she said dreamily, 'it was Young Thomas who told me about Nora and the lake.'

'Is Young Thomas your brother?'

Had he said something wrong again? The look of dreaming reminiscence that had made her face look like some soft flower was shuttered inside its everyday mask of cool stillness. She did not reply. Voices sounded on the river behind them. Two men were getting into a boat. A woman with a maid wheeling a bassinette waved to them then turned back up the hill.

Sterrin recognised the scar-faced man. The other was the man who had rested under the hedge earlier in the day. The woman must be the girl who had promised to wait for Bergin the whole seventeen years of his sentence. What must it have felt like, that glorious moment of reunion? And it was the girl who had made that possible; she it was who had gone on waiting. The man had but to return. Dear God, why didn't I?

The other man was speaking to her. 'I should like to apologise to your Ladyship for the way that I spoke to you yesterday.' Before she could answer he went on: 'That house up there,' he said, pointing to the remains of the fine stone house that had been his home, 'is more than a mass of stones and rafters. My father, my grandfather, aye and his grandfather were born there and died there. My seven children were born there; two of them died there. Something of all our lives went into those stones and rafters. It had a double door.' He was reminiscing to himself now. 'The inner one blew away the night of the Big Wind. When we were replacing it my father added an outer one that would stand up to any storm. Mavrone! What chance had it against the crowbar?' He came back to his surroundings. 'I beg your Ladyship's pardon for forcing my troubles on you. I only intended asking if you had any objection to my going on up there to steal a piece of soil to bring with me to America. Maybe it will bring luck to whatever land I may be able to come by over there.'

A joyless laugh grated out from Bergin in the stern. '*Steal* a sod of his own soil. The soil that belonged to the Graces—both sides of this river—since the Graces were sovereigns of Kilkenny and Kilkenny was the sovereign city of Ireland.' A stroke of his oar carried the boat past her without waiting for her permission.

Donal watched her seat herself on the river bank. He couldn't know that her knees had started to give way. The bard had told her about a man called Grace who had mustered four hundred men from these parts to fight with King James at the Battle of the Boyne. King William's great general had been so impressed with him that when the battle was over and Grace heading home with his forty survivors, he sent a message after

503

him offering him high honours if he would join the victorious Orangemen. Grace read the tempting offer then on the back of the Six of Diamonds he scribbled his reply. 'I despise your offer.'

And here was his descendant ousted from his land by the man to whom she was wife; begging *her* permission to steal a sod. She put her hands to her face and wept as she had not wept since her discovery of Mickey-the-turf stealing the jelly that she had been sacrificing before the shrine of the Child Jesus that the famine might end. The sacrifice of her marriage, though it had saved Kilsheelin and its tenants, seemed almost as futile as that of the jelly. It had not been able to save those six hundred families. The horror of that spectacle of the morning, the horror that she had suppressed last night, came forth now in a bursting dam of tears.

Suddenly her hands were drawn away from her face; a big fragrant handkerchief dried her eyes and face. She was helped to her feet. 'There is no sense of sitting around on damp grass.' Donal was coughing as he spoke. 'That's what gave me this,' he tapped his chest with his free hand, 'the night that you came to our place for that sod. By the way, did you find the one that I tied to your leathers the next night?' She nodded.

They walked in silence for a moment, his hand still holding hers. She glanced sideways at him through the pom-poms that dangled from her sports hat. The fine skin of his face flushes too readily, she thought. It wasn't just a cough he caught that night when she had gone twice to Poolgower.

'I thought you, too, wanted to take a sod to America,' he said. She could never let him know why she had been there. And then with a sudden, angry clarity she realised that it was for the same reason that she was here in this place; to save Kilsheelin from the Keatings; from the threat of that loathsome elder brother. Donal felt his hand vacated as though it were a contamination. She hurried ahead. The triangles of silk peeping through the slits of her sports skirt made a sound like an angry sail flapping against the mast. 'Bring back the field in an apron inagh!' She stopped and confronted him. 'What about those other fields?'

Donal was lighthearted. He couldn't keep up with her moods; besides he had not had breakfast.

'My Lady,' he stammered, 'they were bought in open market.

They were offered for sale——'

'The castle was not offered for sale. Your brother gloated to me that he was going to get it, that——'

'My brother did that? Lady Devine, I swear to you——'

'Oh, don't tell me that you knew nothing. You are all chickens of the blue hen. Your brother did worse than that, let me tell you.' Instantly she was sorry; she was taking a mean advantage of a guest; a vulnerable one. He looked white enough to faint. 'What did James's James do? What in God's name could the lout have done? I must know what it was that he did, Lady Devine.'

She shook her head. 'It is finished. I ought not to have mentioned it. Anyway, I've halted his march.' He watched her eyes narrow and the soft mouth crumple into something like bitterness. 'At least, in our direction.'

He took a step towards her. 'You are speaking of things that I swear to you I know nothing of. It is hard for you to believe that; but by heavens I shall get to the root of it. Whatever wrong has been done you shall be righted.'

She looked at him for a long moment and when she finally spoke he was shocked at the dull despair in the clear young voice. 'There is nothing that you can do. What is done can never be undone; never!'

And then Donal knew with a certainty that lashed him, that she was speaking of her marriage. He saw her as he had seen her this morning, confronting those hostile servants; a spray of starry clematis plucked from its protecting wall; a white moth torn by rough hands. Suddenly he saw his brother's hands, big, unkempt. He saw them impatiently brushing aside flowers because they were a waste of useful ground; saw them knocking to the floor his wife's exquisite miniatures because they were time-absorbers for the children who ought to have absorbed her leisure. He saw those hands plucking at the clematis; tearing the moth's white wings; depriving it for ever of freedom. He turned from the sight. 'Where are you going?' He had not realised that he had turned from her too. 'I am going away. It is the only thing that I can do.' She knew what he meant; then a movement caught her eye. The lodge-keeper was opening the gates for the shooting brake. Panic seized her. They were coming back, her husband and the rest, to enclose her. She was alone as she had been when she sent Thomas from the wall gap. Only then she was confident that some unchartered vista of freedom lay ahead. Today she was trapped.

She knew she must not let this Donal Keating go out of her life. There was an affinity between them that was not with these others. They had mutual acquaintances: like Fairy Nora and her apronful of lake; and wouldn't the tale of the flying field sound as improbable a piece of magic to these others as that of the disappearing lake? She seized the hand that she had dropped the moment before. 'Listen, let us end the land dispute; for ever.' He tried to think of something to say; something high-sounding that would abjure and repudiate all that his family had meant to her; he wanted to drop to his knee and proffer her the sword that he had never possessed. 'If the damned field,' she was saying, 'had to fall upon anyone I'm glad that it fell on you.'

He was moved by her inelegant phrase. He raised her hand to his lips and said, 'My Lady, you'd coax a haggert full of sparrows.'

They watched the cart with the 'bag' move away from the wagonette towards the back premises. They could see the great pyramid of slaughtered birds. 'And now,' murmured Donal, 'the Lord sent a flight of quails over the sea and down to where the camp was.'

'What is that about quails?'

'I was referring to a "shoot" in the desert; a flight of quails that came miraculously to feed the Jews in their wandering after the Diaspora.'

'Diaspora! Fancy your using that word!'

He had to remind himself of the enormity of his brother's presuming to prevent himself making a cynical reply. He thought she was being patronising about his learning.

'Yes,' she went on, 'this morning as I watched those homeless people I bethought of how Papa described the famine emigrations as the Diaspora of the Gaels——' She stopped dead. 'Quails, did you say? What price pheasants? Come on, Donal.'

The amazement of the kitchen staff at the spectacle of her Ladyship coming to the kitchen was duplicated in the yard men at the spectacle of her sprinting into the yard and breathlessly ordering them to stop unloading the bag. One of them ventured something abour Mr. Wilson's instructions, but Sterrin merely called to Donal to climb up.

'Cl-climb up! On that? You are not going to——'

'I am.' She had the horse started towards the gate as the gamekeeper's phaeton drove in. There were contented puffs rising from Mr. Wilson's pipe. It had been a brave day. And a powerful brave bag. Allowing for a couple of dozen for the table and gifts, the rest would be his perquisite. Suddenly his eyes gaped. His mouth opened and out fell his fine pipe and crashed in pieces on the floorboards.

The gamekeeper was far too prosaic a man to imagine things. Much less to imagine that it was her Ladyship who was sitting up there driving a farm cart. Then he saw a young gentleman clambering all over the precious birds. This was carrying a prank too far. A prank? The young gentleman, as he passed, was protesting to her Ladyship that her gesture would be none the less charitable for having been carried out by a workman.

'A workman,' said Sterrin, forcing the gamekeeper's phaeton out of her path, 'would have been challenged by him, and by then my hus—by then the others would have been on the scene. Anyway don't be prissy. My mother carried a six-foot woman for over a mile to a soup kitchen; and didn't you say that the Lord drove a flight of quails down to where the camp was?'

Donal wondered if the Israelites had looked like these homeless ones; gazing at the beautiful apparition that had come to succour them in their dereliction. 'Cead mile blessings,' murmured an old woman. 'Manna from Heaven!' Children eating slices of hot bread gathered round the cart.

'Not manna,' Sterrin smiled at the woman. 'Just quails and I'm afraid not from Heaven.'

A man lifted out a brace of birds. 'Beggin' your Lady's pardon, them's not quails; them's a sight better; them's pheasants.'

Sterrin tightened herself against the flutter of fear at the sight of her husband standing grim and ominous in the middle of the stable yard. But her first word scattered the protest that was intended to annihilate her. 'Jocelyn,' she called out, dropping—for the first time—his title, 'it has been marvellous! I haven't driven in a farm wagon since I was a little girl.' He resisted a thrill of exultation. She had succumbed like all those who had gone before her; that mnemonic array of beautiful women. The great lover was restored to his prowess. He turned to her and his joy withered to anger. In the amethyst depths of her eyes he saw mockery. 'The bag,' he gritted. 'The birds; what have you done

507

with them?' He hated the sound imposed upon his voice by his unpolished agitation.

'The bag?' She withdrew her hand and waved it towards the gentlemen who were discussing the day's sport at the hall door, 'Captain Saint John, my husband and I are discussing the bag. Really I haven't seen anything like it since—since my father's time, but,' she beamed around the circle, 'I have a confession to make. Already I have taken a liberty with your trophy for some of my less fortunate friends.' Captain Saint John knew what she meant. He glanced at his host. Could the loss of a few birds cause a man to show such naked venom? And how much longer could this pinioned beauty continue to oppose her husband? The other men gathered around their charming young hostess. To have given her pleasure, they insisted conferred the accolade upon their day's achievement. It was an interesting moment. Sir Jocelyn was prevented from replying by the arrival of an enormous and eccentric-looking carriage drawn by two spanking greys. 'The Delaneys,' cried Sterrin delightedly.

Sir Jocelyn raised the mobile eyebrow. 'I understood that they had written to be excused.'

'Oh, I suspected that that was just shortage of ball-gowns. I sent a note this morning by the bia driver not to miss the Assizes' Ball for the sake of a ball-gown.'

'Hm, lack of a ball-gown would not deter *you* from your purpose. Did the demoiselles Delaney not have at least one grandfather?'

Smilingly, she tossed him back his thrust. 'The Delaney grandfather, Sir Dowling, was only five feet high. My grandfather was six feet four. One can do a lot with breeches of that size.'

Sterrin and Sir Jocelyn were moving towards the carriage, to all appearances chatting cosily while the ritual of Mrs. Delaney's arrival was enacted; her babet[1] removed, her bonnet that dangled from a hook in the roof, donned and tied, the little red-carpeted staircase unfolded from somewhere inside the unfashionable high carriage and placed carefully in position by the faithful Ned Rua.

Mrs. Delaney was very much the Grande Dame as she greeted her host. Sterrin was surprised at such unwonted formality from the friendly and uninhibited lady. She learned the reason

[1] An indoor headgear worn by ladies of fashion.

for it as she led her up the stairs. 'I had no intention of entering this house ever again,' said Mrs. Delaney, 'but I took it kindly your writing today about the ball-gowns. I had not the heart to deprive them of the Ball, but,' she halted on a step, 'Sterrin O'Carroll, is it a thing that your father's daughter could not raise a hand to prevent six hundred people from being turned from their homes?'

'She could not.'

Mrs. Delaney looked up startled at the abrupt tone. The face in front of her had the same unreadable look that it had on its owner's wedding day; and the dear knows happiness is easy enough to read.

Mrs. Delaney's gaze followed the great pillars of black marble that rose up all the way to the roof whose ceiling was of the brothers Adam, then on to the walls whose panels Angelica Hoffman had painted. 'The waste of it,' she murmured. And then, surprisingly, for her, she quoted, 'Unless God build the house they labour in vain that dwell there.'

Sterrin interrupted the meditations to ask why Rory had not come.

'Rory has gone to America.'

'You don't mean that he has—emigrated?'

Mrs. Delaney gave a sad little nod. 'The sons of the gentry are emigrating, too; but the prosperity is slow catching up on them until they forget their gentility.'

Sterrin, conditioned from childhood to the awareness of suffering, saw that it had taken the parting from Rory, the heir born miraculously after ten daughters, to bring out at last on his mother's face all the strain of the poverty and debt that dogged the surviving landlords of the famine era. 'I've made my son an exile. I carried my tenants on my back; your father too; six hundred!'

Sterrin, after a brief vision of Mrs. Delaney carrying her Papa on her back the way Mamma had carried Mrs. Holohan, deciphered the ambiguity. Even her closest friends, kin to her father who had carried her own tenants upon his back, were charging her with a share in the guilt of this fiendish eviction. She would never escape from it. Panic gripped her; she must get out from here; to where? Not another gallop-by-night to the convent.

The girls were giving little ecstatic shrieks. Sterrin had preceded them to their room where gowns, exquisite beyond their wildest dreams, were arrayed for their choosing. Mrs. Delaney, softened by Sterrin's thoughtfulness, sought to make amends. She asked about the day's shoot; when she heard its amount her sporting enthusiasm was stirred. 'That should be worth seeing. I must go down.'

'No, no.' The girls stopped their fitting and preening to look towards their hostess. Sterrin O'Carroll had been held up to them always as an example of poise and ladylike control. There was nothing poised about her expression now; nor about the sound of her voice. It was almost hysterical; over nothing.

Sterrin explained about the bag. And then, childishly needing to be understood, she told about the bread.

Mrs. Delaney looked at her with something like awe. 'You got bread baked here for six hundred people? That took more than kindness. It took courage; and high courage.' But Sterrin felt only guilt for their praise.

'Courage,' she repeated dully. 'It feels more like cheek; like offering a poor woman one of her own halfpennies when you have stolen her savings.'

All the county was at the Assizes' Ball that night. Sterrin, entering on her husband's arm caused quite a stir. This was the first public appearance of the bride of the wealthy Sir Jocelyn. Her beauty, they had heard, matched his wealth; and her *diablerie*, by all accounts, matched that of the Castiglions and Metternichs of the French courts. Her gown, people said, must be the *dernier cri* that had silenced the creak of the crinoline. A deaf dowager raised her lorgnettes. 'What's all the fuss about? It is a striking gown, but not revealing.'

The judge's wife murmured into the dowager's ear trumpet that while the gown did not reveal it definitely suggested. The dowager had an absent-minded way of putting her ear trumpet to her mouth to reply. 'Suggestion is the secret of allure.' The statement came in a trumpet blast and everyone stopped to listen. 'When I was a girl the ball-gowns held open display and the gentlemen wouldn't trouble to give a second look. What is concealed yet discreetly suggested is much more provocative.' Everyone looked towards the target of the trumpet blasts. Sterrin felt naked.

The colonel of whatever regiment supplied the band had the privilege of leading out the lady of his choice in the first folk dance of the programme. The Deputy Lieutenant's wife, anticipating the honour, started to compress her hoops. The judge's wife likewise snapped her fan shut. The bandmaster waited with raised baton. The colonel bowed before young Lady Devine. The chosen lady had the privilege of calling the tune, 'I think,' she murmured after demure reflection, 'that I should like *Paddies Evermore*.' She ignored her husband's startled protest and went on, 'You see, it was written by his Lordship, Mr. Justice O'Hagan.'

The colonel beckoned a subaltern. 'That should please our legal guests,' he beamed. The subaltern was stammering; making no move to go. 'Hurry!' snapped the colonel. The subaltern hurried; the bandsman passed on his instruction, then turned in consternation. Next minute the subaltern was back whispering to the colonel, 'Egad! Do you tell me so? A rebel song?' Down the length of the room, the dancers ranged in formation, every right foot poised, heard the exclamation. The Deputy Lieutenant's wife had been led out by the judge. She gave him a look of perplexity. But the judge was wishing for someone to lead himself out: out from this embarrassing dilemma. The song had been written by his learned colleague back in the days when a coterie of young barristers had helped Davis to sound in verse the Reveille of a whole people. The judge had written a few incendiary verses himself at that time. But legal honours had dimmed the vision of young patriotism, and the judge's ermine had muffled the last sound of its clamour. Now here he was, expected to dance to a tune for which he would have indicted these people had they been ranged before his Bench instead of on the floor of a ballroom.

But the lady of the dance had stopped for her green brocade train. Donal and two juniors draped it over her arm. The dance began, topped and tailed by the Assize judge, and the Colonel of Her Majesty's 49th Foot, footing it to as seditious a sound as ever jailed a rebel. '... our fathers bled of yore,' carolled a group of juniors as they stood during the Ladies' Chain. 'And we stand here today like them, True Paddies Evermore.'

The colonel's bow was short at the finish. 'A bit rebellious, my Lady,' he said mopping his brow. 'I shouldn't have thought such sentiments were quite your dish of tea.' Sterrin gave him a knowing look over her fan.

'I did hear the sentiments from the ear trumpet; about what

511

is concealed being more discreetly provocative.'

This time his bow was more clanking. 'You have a nimble wit, my Lady,' he said and he forgot sedition in the reflection that the eyes that were twinkling at him were as bright as the diamonds in the lovely hair above them.

Sterrin forgot things too. Her saucy victory, as she led her mainly mutinous corps down the ballroom, had gone to her head to mix with the praise and the clamouring for dances. She was exalted. She remembered only that she was young. Overhead a thousand candles bent with heat and sent their weary substance dripping down to bespatter the shoulders of her partners. She stopped troubling to peal off the particles of hot wax that landed on her face and neck; even dared to dim out the brilliance of her diamonds.

The depression returned as she left the ball in the stark light of dawn. All around the carriage stood the homeless; in groups or moving a few paces and stopping, afraid to fall asleep less they be arrested for vagrancy. Sir Jocelyn could scarcely wait for her to enter the carriage to start the attack about her choice of tune; about her public degradation of her husband, of herself. 'Sheer clowning; nothing else; in the worst possible taste.'

Sterrin lay back on the upholstery with eyes closed, wishing that Mrs. Delaney would hurry on so that they could get away from these despairing looks that reproached her to the bone. Her husband might as well have been whistling jigs to milestones. 'You should display *some* concern for the feelings of others.'

Sterrin sat up abruptly and faced him. 'The feelings of others?' she repeated very softly. She swept a gesture towards the window. 'Do you mean the feelings of these out there?'

'I mean,' he snapped, 'the feelings of Colonel de la Sarthe. He paid me a great tribute when he honoured you.'

Sterrin went deflated. Everything that she did seemed to turn back on her. The business of the bread yesterday. A daisy in a bull's mouth! The purloining of the 'bag'; a childish escapade. The choice of a dance tune; boorishness. Mrs. Delaney got herself inside at last.

'You led that poor colonel the divil's own dance, Sterrin. Yourself and your *Paddies Evermore!*'

She eased herself back against the upholstery. 'And as for the judge, he looked as though he were dancing on a hot gridiron.'

The icy silence recalled to Mrs. Delaney the legend of the children who had danced on the hot gridirons. She decided that she was not making a fist of her conversational gambits. Before she could think of something to amend her lapse a stone was flung at the carriage.

Suddenly, strangely, a long-forgotten scene came to Sterrin's mind. A hunger-maddened mob was raiding Wright's bread van. It overflowed around the pony trap. The terrified governess had dropped the reins and allowed the pony to bolt while she sat there screaming her terror. An adult, Papa had said that night when Sterrin awoke from a nightmare, should control her fears; at least in the presence of a child. And here was her husband, his aplomb shattered, screaming like a woman for the footmen; for the police.

When the police arrived the crowd had vanished in the direction of the workhouse. Sir Jocelyn turned in fury to Sterrin. 'There go your "Paddies evermore". They stone you for your pains, then run to the workhouse to shelter at my expense——'

'At two and twopence halfpenny per pauper per week,' said Mrs. Delaney and the dignified modulation, so different from her usual offhand speech, compelled his attention. 'They will not burden you for long; the expectation of life maintained at that price level is very short indeed.'

'Anyway,' said Sterrin, 'they ought not to be hunted by police for simply throwing a stone. If anyone had made *me* homeless I should not be satisfied with a stone. I should fire a bullet.'

The English footman, fussing with Sir Jocelyn's lap rug, was caught off guard. He gave a startled gasp. Sir Jocelyn dismissed him with an angry flip. He would like to have dismissed Mrs. Delaney, too, but at least she had the good taste to go to sleep; deeply asleep, since no lady in possession of her senses would snore like that in the presence of a gentleman.

He leaned towards Sterrin. 'Now I know,' he started. Sterrin's head was leaning towards Mrs. Delaney's shoulder. He shook her knee but her head landed comfortably. 'Listen to me,' he whispered. She replied with a gentle snore; then for good measure she added a little nasal click like Mrs. Delaney's.

After breakfast the younger members of the house-party were assembled on the lawn as eager for their morning's ride as if they had slept all night. Some of the mounted grooms wore

513

massive belts for the support of the more fragile young ladies who took their horse exercise pillion style. Sterrin was scandalised to see Belle Delaney mounting a block and taking her place behind a groom. Belle, like herself, had always scorned the mounting block. Much less to ride pillion! And then Mrs. Delaney, of all people, hurried out and linked the hooks in her daughter's buckle to the one at the back of the groom's belt.

'Mrs. Delaney,' Sterrin called, 'what on earth is Belle doing riding pillion?'

'Doctor's orders.' Then grasping Sterrin's bridle she reached up and whispered, 'Internal.'

'What!' A thrill of delicious horror ran through Sterrin.

'I'm surprised at you to think such a thing,' said Mrs. Delaney. 'The girl may be a bit of a tomboy in the way of riding but she has never been permitted to forget that she is a lady. Knows nothing about that kind of thing; doesn't know how she came into the world, thank heavens. It is just that these doctors are finding out more about our insides. I told Doctor Drennan that he was insulting us. Cut him dead at the Meet.'

Sterrin's mount was growing restive. 'Be careful of yourself, too, Sterrin. You've had one miscarriage already.'

'What!'

'Oh, now,' said Mrs. Delaney, soothingly. 'Sure it is no secret that you had a terrible miscarriage as a result of your little walk the wrong way up in front of the Emperor.'

'Who said that?' Sterrin's voice was very quiet.

'Oh,' she was informed, 'Sir Jocelyn himself said it, well, not in so many words but he inferred it.'

Sterrin turned her horse's head towards the avenue. But her mind was seething. Now she knew that Sir Jocelyn, suspecting that she had swapped confidences with the little ex-comtesse in Paris, had found a way to hit back.

She brought her whip down and the horse rose in the air before galloping wildly down the park. Grooms with pillion-riders were hard set to restrain their mounts that stampeded in pursuit. She cleared the park and a field before steadying to a canter.

Voices hallooed and Eva Delaney reined alongside. 'Phew!' she gasped. 'You've led us a nice dance. Like you did last night. Shall I ever forget the bandmaster's face when you asked for *Paddies Evermore*. Hadn't you the nerve?' When there was no

514

answer she said, 'Do you know, I don't believe, Sterrin, that you have heard one word that I've been saying.'

Sterrin recollected herself. 'By the way,' she said, 'it must be an affliction on Belle to have to ride pillion.' Eva shrugged.

'This was my turn for the riding habit. Belle wore it to the Maryborough Show last week.'

Sterrin turned and regarded Eva's costume. If anything it was more perfectly cut than her own. 'Nothing but the best material; the most flawless cut, would satisfy Mrs. Delaney for her own or her family's riding clothes. They were never very strong on gowns but at least they always had one riding costume apiece. Fancy Mrs. Delaney covering up with such an outrageous whopper.

'Then there's nothing wrong with her health?'

'Oh, she has some trouble with the interior mystery; but nothing that a riding habit wouldn't cure as far as keeping her from riding is concerned. Didn't Mamma hunt all day until a half an hour before Belle was born? That's why Belle is still expected to believe that she was found in a covert. Come on, I'll race you to the gap.'

The two tore across the field, a splendid pair of horsewomen, superbly matched and mounted. The others slowed to watch and cheer. Beyond the gap lay the road gate. Eva made for it and soared over. Sterrin, in the act of following, recalled the scene she had jumped into yesterday morning. She turned aside; Donal followed her. The others jumped the gate after Eva.

Donal strove to keep pace with Sterrin. The railroad tracks intruded. She took them with a jump and landed safely on the far side. Donal, leading his horse along the embankment, saw her slow to speak to a group of children. They were running and screaming after a blue-cloaked woman. Sterrin spurred after her. 'Why don't you wait for the children?' she demanded.

'Don't stop me,' the woman panted. When she raised her head the folds of her hood fell away from a fleshy growth beneath her chin. 'I'm going to America,' she said.

'And deserting your children?' Sterrin was horrified. The woman never slowed. 'God forbid! It is to have them with me that I'm going to work for another home over there.' A train whistle sounded. The woman doubled her speed; behind her the children called frantically. 'He turned us out.' The words came in breathless sobs. 'Out of our lovely home an' their father'—she choked—'their father not three weeks dead.'

Round the bend came a puff of smoke. She raised her arm high over her head and waved towards the train. 'Mammy! Mammy!' The smallest toddler had stumbled and fallen. Its mother returned and lifted the child in a fierce caress and covered its face with kisses. 'My baby; my baby. Here, Storeen!' She shoved a penny into its hand. 'Buy sweets. Mammy will be back tonight.' She put the child down and fled.

The train halted. The guard reached out, took the bundle, and the little peeping sod of the ground from which she had been uprooted and drew her gently inside. 'Keep clear of the line, children. Your mammy will be back shortly.'

Donal came to his senses as the train moved off. He grasped the carriage window and galloped alongside. 'Do you know where you are going to? Have you friends over there?' She leaned out. 'I'll be all right that way, sir. I'm goin' to a place a few miles beyond America, Quebec, it's called. There's a neighbour's son works there, or in the next ploughland from it. He'll get me a situation.' The train pulled ahead of Donal.

Sterrin was squatting among the children, the reins looped over her arm; just as he had seen her on that first occasion. A girl crouching in the moonlight, curls tumbling over her forehead, her arm linked through the reins of a horse that muzzled at her hair. She rose to her feet and squeezed the handkerchief that had mopped their little wet faces. 'Does she know where she is going?' The children could not hear what the beautiful lady was whispering to the gentleman. He continued to look after the train while he replied. 'She is going across the world to a place called Quebec where anyone will tell her the way to her neighbour's son in the next ploughland.' He raised his hat towards the vanishing train. 'God carry you safely,' he said grimly, 'to that next ploughland. It is probably a thousand miles from Quebec.'

Sir Jocelyn was replacing one of his precious birds when his wife burst into his silent aviary. Words came tumbling from her; nameless babies; a mother torn from her children; travelling alone to some unknown destination at the other side of the world. 'Get her back! The express train would overtake her. Bring her back to her poor little children.'

He held the bird up to the light. 'I do believe that there is a chip in the eye of this bird and, yes, the setting is loose. How on earth can that have happened.'

'God'll mighty!' she stormed, 'you are not a dummy like—like these lumps of metal. You have a soul. You have to face your God. You are answerable for these children. For the fate of their mother——'

'I shall have to send to Dublin for a silversmith,' he murmured gently. He replaced the bird on its polished branch. 'No, I shall go there myself though I suppose that means that I must wait until the house-party has finished. I must not take you away from your guests.'

Words halted themselves within her in a shocked surge. Nobody could be this callous. Nobody in all God's world! 'I shall take myself away.' At last she said, 'It would be a crime for me to continue to live here and sanction such—such abominations.'

He came close to her. 'Where will you go to, my dear? To Bankrupt Castle? Or perhaps to Quebec and send back later for your own homeless ones?'

A feeling of futility assailed her and suddenly she knew it again for the feeling she had experienced in those bleak, almost foodless days of the famine when the great sacrifice of her precious jelly had turned into something ridiculous.

'They *shall* be homeless you know; if you withdraw your collateral.'

'Collateral? Isn't that something in a bank? And isn't that an unnecessary taunt? I don't possess such a thing.'

'Oh, but you do, my dear. Collateral has many forms. Clever women use their bodies as collateral; as you did.'

He watched her deep-set eyes rise level to their brink. They became like painted eyes done in primitive colour upon bleached-white linen; then he saw her crop go up and he sidestepped like a dancing master. It landed on the bird that he had replaced and sent it clattering to the floor.

The silence stretched out like doom. Gradually she became aware of the way he was looking at her. His lips were drawn back over the maroon guttapercha gums of his false teeth. She felt a shiver. 'I have told you,' he was saying, thin and low, 'that some day you might go too far. This, I think is the day.'

There was no time to assess the meaning of his remark; no time to carry out her threat of a dramatic departure. The guests were waiting for her and tonight those little motherless children would be waiting also. She had arranged with them. But the devil himself, she felt, was inside the younger guests that evening. There was no getting away. They clamoured for carpet-dancing, charades, treasure hunts; anything rather than dissipate their festive spirits in sleep.

When she finally escaped she had to weave in and out through the concealed paths of the maze and hug the margin of the artificial lake where the soldiery dare not intrude. The Brennan children gazed at her in awe. Her shimmering cloak suggested to them a church; something on a pedestal or on a stained glass window. Worth had called it his 'esperatum' cloak but he had never designed it for concealing a big kitchen basket of food.

The four of them gathered round the basket and timidly savoured the wonderful dainties that she had brought to them. Soon food and friendliness released their tongues.

The eldest boy, the little girls were saying, had a terrible distance to go. He was staying with relatives miles off. The other three were divided among two households. They had to be disposed of that way, unobtrusively, since the law forbade any householder to take in evicted tenants or their families.

The hug she gave them at parting had more than pity in its warmth. It had something of affinity. And though it had saddened her to find that they were not to have at least the solace of each other's company there was a new excitement in her wistfulness.

She hurried away, making plans for them in a surge of compassion. She had moved from the grass back to the ornamental paths when she heard footsteps behind her. Her heart lurched. Inside or outside, there was no place here that was free from the hauntings of those little children and their ghostly footsteps! The darkness of the night with its great immensity of stars turned all the world into a ghostliness. She quickened to a run. The footsteps became less ghostlike. She turned. 'So it's you!'

She was in no mood for Donal Keating. Her cloak caught in one of the walls of topariæd yew. Donal released it.

'You remind me,' he said, 'of Queen Elizabeth of Hungary with her basket of food that turned into roses when her tyrannical husband overtook her on her errand of mercy. Allow me.' He reached for the basket then dropped his arm abruptly. She had pulled the basket in close to herself. He misinterpreted the gesture. 'Forgive me my familiarity,' he said, 'the remark about

Queen Elizabeth's husband was not intended to be personal.'

The basket started to cut through the folds of her cloak and dress with the dint of her clutching; for suddenly, it was holding again the food that she was sneaking off to the young Ryanduvs, the children of her father's foster-brother and someone had made a grab at it; someone with black curls and curvy lips that were demanding: 'Who do you think you are? Queen Elizabeth of Hungary? I've a good mind to tell your papa.' A dire threat. Papa would have seen fit to spank her if he were to discover that she had exposed herself to the risk of famine fever by stinting her own nourishment.

'I must leave tomorrow.'

She came back to her surroundings. Oh dear, he's getting huffy again. And small blame to him. How could he be expected to keep up with her moods when she could not keep track with them herself. She had come out tonight resolved to stop playing at life. The plight of that woman parting from her children had finally jolted Sterrin into reality.

'Oh, please don't go on taking offence. Don't go. You've got to help me with those children.' She told him about the way they had been severed from each other. 'How could their uncle do such a thing to them? Their mother left money with him for their keep.'

'He daren't risk eviction for himself and his own children. The terror of eviction chills natural humanity.'

At the corner of the house they parted; for all the world like sweethearts, thought Hannah as she waited for Sterrin at the conservatory door.

Captain Saint John, returning from the camp felt much as Hannah did. He felt disappointed too. Somehow, it dimmed his image of her that she should be conducting an illicit intrigue. She had looked so gallant this morning fighting her lone battle for those unfortunate wretches. Who could have drawn her heart? The hall light flashed on the face of the young barrister chap who had been with her among the flour bins.

In the drawing-room Sterrin came straight to the captain. 'I have been looking for you, Captain Saint John. I hear that you sing beautifully.' And you, he thought, lie as beautifully as you do everything else.

'You can't have looked too far,' he murmured. 'I too, was outside.' His glance flickered towards Donal. Before she could answer, Sir Jocelyn came up and led her towards the harp. The title of the piece that he had chosen for her to play was Moore's *Love Thee Dearest*.

The jewels on her fingers flashed as she plucked a defiant ripple from the strings. 'I'll play one of the songs that our old bard taught me.' The opening line was a mother's reproach to her daughter. 'Is there ne'er a man in Ireland to please your discontent?' Sterrin looked straight at the captain as she sang the reply. 'There are men enough in Ireland but none at all for me. For I never loved but one young man and he's beyond the sea.'

Was she trying to convey to him, the captain wondered, that he had misjudged what he had just seen outside? That the young man who parted with her so stealthily and who was looking at her now with such adoration meant nothing to her? He glanced at his host to see how he was taking the song; but there was nothing to be gleaned there. Sir Jocelyn was gazing down at his young wife, his courtesy a walled city about him. The captain felt a thrust of distaste, and then, a sense of relief at the realisation that his duty here would end tomorrow. Evicting women and children; battering down their homes, was not his idea of martial glory. But his gaze returned to the gold-clad figure at the harp, this lovely enigma was perilously near his idea of feminine glory.

On the morrow others were finding excuses for abrupt departures. The atmosphere of the evictions was beginning to pall; the presence of the military; the reproachful eyes of the homeless. Landlords, themselves not over-lenient, sent their servants with messages of polite regret. Unforeseen circumstances, they were all pleading, forced them to cancel their acceptances for the functions, the concerts and plays in the private theatre, the banquets, the balls that had been planned for this elaborate house-party. One message of regret enclosed a clipping from the London *Times* setting the final seal on the general disapproval. 'Sir Jocelyn Devine,' it said, 'has always done things on a massive scale. He maintained his standards in these recent evictions ... the affair at Kilkenny,' it concluded, 'was not fragrant.'

Sterrin's heart sank into utter misery when a letter came from Kilsheelin cancelling Lady O'Carroll's visit. She had been counting the hours until she would meet her mother again.

When the last guest had departed Sterrin was summoned to the silver aviary. Her husband was holding the bird she had damaged. 'Isn't it time,' he said, without looking up from his scrutiny of the bird, 'that Clooreen was brought here from Kilsheelin?'

'Naturally, she will come here when she has foaled,' she replied. 'That was understood.'

'In that case there is no further need for her to remain there. I desire you to go to Kilsheelin and see to her transfer yourself.' He went on stroking the bird as though he were soothing the wound of a living creature. She restrained an urge to knock it out of his hand. It looked so lumpish compared to a live bird captured in one's grasp. No substance; but warm; and soft with the frantic beat of life. So Clooreen had foaled. She suppressed another impulse. She must not ask him what it was, a filly? a colt? She must show no enthusiasm for anything; for anyone. And what the devil's father was he up to? He had but to despatch grooms for the mare. Was it thinking of selling Clooreen that he was? At last he looked up at her. 'I leave for Dublin next week.'

She made no sign. Her face was masked over with the stillness that had once captured him. No eager questions about the horse. Where was the girl who had chased his carriage down Kilsheelin avenue to thank him for the gift of Clooreen; the beautiful lips panting out words and breaths that blew warmly against his face? 'On urgent business,' he added. No question of her accompanying him, though she was free now of her hostess duties. But still she made no comment. He was up to something; something of more significance than the repairing of that shapeless lump of silver in his hand. What matter! She was going to Kilsheelin; and on her own! An unhoped-for joy. She would bring her grandest gowns to divert Mamma. Poor Mamma, who had had to experience the ignominy of having rude comments about Evictions shouted after her carriage.

A week later, on the eve of his departure, Sir Jocelyn suffered another rush of blood to his head. Sterrin, counting the hours till her first meeting with her mamma since her wedding, had to cancel her visit to Kilsheelin. She was compelled to spend long hours in the sick-room reading wearisome newspaper reports that he could have got his secretary to read. He kept making her go back over big words that she had mispronounced. One day, when he had been ill a month, she skipped the word 'unpredic tability'.

'Kindly spell out the word that you have omitted,' he demanded.

With a tearing rattle she threw the newspaper to the ground. 'Damn the soul of it!' she shouted. 'A body would need to have been sleeping with a schoolteacher!' Her head felt strangely light. It seemed to have lost contact with her tongue. 'Unpre whatever-the-devil you call it. No lady has any call to use such words. I . . .'

'Exactly. I beg you to refrain from such uncouth utterances.

'I never read a newspaper,' she went on, 'much less a thing called a—a Leading Article.'

'Surely you read—and hoard—the *Theatrical News*?'

She rose abruptly. Once and for all she was going to put an end to the gibing on that subject. Just then the doctor's voice sounded outside. As he came towards her she dropped a slight curtsey that included the bed and the doctor. 'If you will excuse me, I am feeling tired.'

The doctor peered at her professionally. 'You have been over taxing yourself, my Lady, cooped up here in the sick-room for a month.' He darted a closer look. 'Or would it be anything else, Hey, my Lady?'

'Yes, it would.' In the expectant silence a displaced pillow made a slithering sound as it fell. Sir Jocelyn was working himself upwards. 'You mean. . . ?' he began.

'I mean that I am sickening for smallpox.' She closed the door on a panic-stricken outcry from the bed. Sir Jocelyn had been above the recent vaccination law. No official or doctor would presume to enforce the filthy, protective virus of small pox into his sacred, scented body.

As she left the house it still clamoured with his bedside bell demanding the doctor, protection, immunisation. 'That will learn them,' she fumed as she sped through the maze. This twelve months past one dare not show a hint of tiredness, not even after two successive nights' dancing, without becoming the bridal target for coy innuendo.

The children were not waiting at the usual rendezvous. She continued to walk in the direction that they usually came from until she spied them sitting listlessly outside a cottage. When they saw her, instead of running towards her, as usual, they

ctually made a move inwards. Sterrin, who had not bargained
or walking two Irish miles of rough road in her velvet and satin
bootees, was in no mood for wilfulness. She rapped out a summons that brought them wheeling back on the double. The
younger one looked at the foot from which her Ladyship had
removed the shoe. 'It's a foot,' she gasped, 'like anyone else's.'
Sterrin picked two pebbles from the lacy stocking. 'What did
you expect?' she snapped, rubbing her sore instep.

'She means, your Nobility,' said the other, 'that she thought
something grander would come out of boots like them.' Sterrin
had the stocking off now and the speck of blood from thorns
and pebbles was not blue, but red like the blood that so frequently coloured their own clayey feet.

'It would have felt grander, anyway,' grumbled Sterrin, 'if
you had been where you ought to have been. Why weren't you?'

They looked at each other then hung their heads. At last she
dragged it from them. Their uncle had warned them against
her. She was the landlord's wife. They were not to trust her and
her for-God's-sake-la-de-da charity. There was nothing la-de-
da, Sterrin thought angrily, about this long walk that had exhausted her so strangely; and all those baskets of food! The
idea!

Their little sister, the sad little voice was saying, had been
despatched to other relatives. They didn't know where their
brother was. Sterrin's eyes closed wearily as the recital went on.
He had been put away from the relatives to whom their uncle
had transferred him. '. . . and next week the two of us are going
to the workhouse.' Sterrin sat upright and pulled on her bootee.
'By the livin' God you won't!' She didn't know how she was
going to stop it, but stop it she would.

She rushed from them after a hug and the contents of her
reticule; a few chocolates and little tea biscuits. La-de-da
charity was right. Preening herself over an odd basket of food!
A sop from the woman whose husband had torn their mother
and home from them.

As she emerged from the maze through the little wicket gate,
she glimpsed her husband reclining on a long cane chair, all
cushioned and rugged, basking in the late autumn sunshine in
the fountain court. The smallpox scare apparently had not induced another rush of blood to the head. Still—she wasn't
ready for battle.

She limped wearily around by the the kitchen premises. She ignored the curious glances of servants as she walked along the back passage. The store-room door was open. Without thinking she entered. She leaned an arm on a bin either side of her and surveyed the rows that lined the walls. The sight of them gave her a sense of her own futility. Never, before, in her rather exalted existence had life revealed herself as superfluous. 'What good am I? I can strum the harp, sing in Italian—badly, in French, a bit better.' She looked up at a dangling spider. 'I can embroider as finely as you, and mind you,' she addressed the spider seriously, 'I embroider better than most, except perhaps Mamma but she . . .' a sound at the door stopped her.

Mrs. Ledwidge, the housekeeper was gaping—there was no other word, her mask of superior servility had slipped—at the spectacle of her haughty Ladyship leaning nonchalantly against a bin of oaten meal; chewing the stuff and talking—right out loud to a big black spider. 'His Honour, Sir Jocelyn, would like to see you in the fountain court.' Her gaze fixed itself on Sterrin's mouth.

To Sterrin's amazement Sir Jocelyn informed her that he had decided to travel to Dublin that very day, without waiting for lunch. 'I find,' he said, 'that the business that takes me there has been too long postponed.' There was a measured significance about his words that Sterrin was to recall later. A footman came and gathered the rugs and instead of taking them to the house went on through a grille doorway that gave on to the front of the house where a carriage awaited. She realised then that her husband was dressed for travelling. He must have been merely awaiting in the fountain court the preparations for his departure. It was a very sudden decision. She said so aloud.

'Are you sure that you feel up to the journey?'

'It is too late now for you to show concern for my health.' He paused as though to let the statement sink in. 'Your conduct this morning showed poor consideration for it. I prefer not to discuss it. I have sent for you to impress on you to go immediately to Kilsheelin, not later than tomorrow, and bring Clooreen here. I have arranged for grooms to go and travel back with her.' A little cloud shadowed the court. Sterrin longed to see Clooreen but somehow the lovely mare belonged to Kilsheelin as Thuckeen had belonged there. Why this urgency? There were hundreds of horses here.

'Our own grooms can accompany her from Kilsheelin,' she replied. 'She is more accustomed to them.'

'She must accustom herself to *my* grooms. Good day, my Lady.'

Somehow, it suddenly seemed utterly unnatural to part from someone going on a journey, someone part of one's family, without a gesture of farewell. She would have flung her arms around Papa; she always embraced Cousin Maurice; she even kissed Big John whenever she went away from Kilsheelin. In fact, she recalled she used to kiss Sir Jocelyn when he would drive off from Kilsheelin in their betrothal days. She was clearing her throat to get out 'God-carry-you-safely' when he turned again.

'You don't seem to be aware that your face needs washing. There is meal on your mouth.'

She reached down to her little handkerchief pocket, then stopped. She'd be damned if she was going to obey orders to wipe her mouth as though she were a grubby child. She shot out her underlip and blew upwards in the old careless way. He remembered how she had done that when she came panting and blowing after his carriage to thank him for Clooreen, blowing the moist curls from the lovely white forehead. The sight of the meal irritated him. It outlined the lovely pouting curve of her upper lip. He was ashamed of the urge, raw as the meal itself, to kiss away the clinging particles. She turned from him with her kissing mouth that still quivered in debate over a last-minute farewell salute and then his final words hardened its indecision.

'You will refrain from tampering with the domestic stores for your misplaced acts of charity. My staff has its orders.' He went through to the waiting carriage.

Sterrin strode determinedly down through the green baize door to the bin-room. It was locked.

'Does your Ladyship desire anything?' It was Mrs. Ledwidge.

Sterrin repressed a desire to smack this smug face that seemed to materialise out of a void so often of late; then her mind recoiled from the unseemliness of such intensity towards a servant. What is coming over me? Quietly she requested the housekeeper to unlock the door.

The housekeeper reared like a viper then as suddenly wilted. Without altering its expression the face in front of her seemed suddenly to have unsheathed the authority of centuries. She

525

took the key from her belt and opened the door for her mistres:

I'm behaving like a child, Sterrin thought, when she wa
alone among the bins; coming here for defiance! I want noth
ing. Or did she? She put a handful of meal in her mouth an
felt better. It seemed to satisfy some moist, gnawing within he:
How pimply those children had become! She took anothe
handful and chewed and ruminated like a young heifer; and ou
of her rumination she reached a decision about the childre:
Tomorrow she was going to Kilsheelin. She would take ther
with her. It was as simple as that. Why hadn't she thought of
before? Kilsheelin solved all her problems. Had she not taken
father and his five children into the castle when their potatoe
had blackened at the start of the famine? And there was mor
room there now; no teeming servants. Johnny-the-buckets was
field worker, Mickey-the-turf had gone to America. The knif
boy was gone. She sped up the stairs on the heels of her resolu
tion. For the first time in her remembered life she had liste
Young Thomas with the other *garçonnerie* of the kitcher
without a distinguishing thought; without his name that ha
been engraved on every ridge of her mind.

She went from room to room, taking a child's delight i
having all their wonders to herself; thrilled for the first time a
the realisation that she was mistress of all this. The cavernou
wardrobes in her husband's dressing-room were like Aladdin
cave. Blue shafts of light blazed from the jewels that formed th
buttons on his waistcoats. In his bedroom she spied a pair o
gold heels peeping out from the satin fold of the bed where the
touched the floor.

As she picked them up a musical sound throbbed through he
body like a smitten harp. Hannah came running at the strang
sound.

'They are musical shoes,' Sterrin told her. 'We saw a dance
in Paris performing in a pair.' As she tied them on, it occurre
to her that the valet must have received very sudden orders fo
packing to have left them lying about so carelessly.

Hannah watched entranced as her young mistress, her skir
held high over her long slim legs, beat out a jig to the music o
the shoes. It was like the grand days long ago when Miss Sterri
and Young Thomas used to dance jigs in the kitchen to th
music of Paddy-the-rat's fiddle. Poor Paddy-the-rat. God re:
his soul. He'd drop dead in his grave if he were to see musi

oming out of a pair of feet!

Sterrin threw herself on the bed, panting and coughing.

'You are overdoin' it, your Ladyship's gra' gal. I'm thinking 's a chill you've caught with them little wet, satin slippers an' ou overtired with the dint of such walkin'.' She insisted upon terrin's staying in her own room instead of going down to unch.

'What would you like me to bring your Ladyship?'

All her Ladyship wanted was some oaten meal.

When Hannah returned a few minutes later with a silver dish f oaten meal mixed with perfumed toilet water. Sterrin let out n unladylike expletive.

'How the devil's father do you expect me to eat that mess?' he exploded.

'Eat it? I thought that 'twas to put on your face that you anted it.'

She went off for another foray to the bin room only to return few minutes later with empty hands. The room was locked nd the housekeeper had gone out on business. The keys were ith her.

'Blast her!'

'Miss Sterrin!' Hannah forgot the title in her shock.

'It is not to be borne. Could you imagine Mamma locked out rom her own stores?'

Sterrin was weaving her stockinged feet back and forth agiatedly and suddenly they hit something that gave a metallic ound that was not of musical shoes. She swooped. Sir Jocelyn's ig bunch of keys lying where they must have fallen unnoticed n his so uncharacteristic rush of departure. But Sterrin was not asting conjectures.

'It is an answer to prayer,' she breathed.

Hannah rolled up her eyes. 'Prayer!' she ejaculated. Her misress handed her the keys and gave her a playful push towards he door then pulled her back by the streamers of her apron.

'Wait!' she hurried to her room, dragged down a Parisian and-box, emptied it of its millinery and handed it to Hannah. Get a supply while we have the key.'

Fifteen minutes later Hannah shook her head over the specacle of her mistress eating meal from an elegant pink and white triped hat box, like—like? A shaft of light lit up threads of red n the dark bronze hair—like—a Rhode Island Red hen!

Next morning Sterrin awakened in a high fever. 'And r
wonder,' grumbled Hannah, as she wielded the long bed
warmer up and down beneath the blankets. Hannah was bitter
disappointed. Here she was with everything packed; all th
lovely gowns to show Lady O'Carroll, and she herself countin
the minutes to be back in the big, happy kitchen of Kilsheel
where the staff was the same as the closest blood to her, and no
Miss Sterrin's Ladyship was laid up with a shivering chil
burning one minute, cold the next. 'Traipsing after them chi
dren all that distance and nothing between your little feet an
the ground but a pair of satin bootees.'

Hannah put the warmer down on the floor. She laid a har
on the hot forehead. 'Mo bla ban na Sterrin.' Concern ha
routed anger; formality too. Lady Devine was once aga
Hannah's bla ban na Sterrin. Her white blossom of the storm
She pulled violently on the bell rope.

'What the devil's father are you doing that for?' The blosso
was white indeed, but uncrushed.

'Ringin' I am to rush someone for a doctor. You are in
roarin' fever.'

'I never want to see oaten meal again,' Sterrin gasped.

'Thank Heaven for that, anyway,' said Hannah.

'B-but,' chattered Sterrin, 'I must get to Kilsheelin. I mu
get that key copied.' Hannah put a hand on the hot forehead.

'Are you sure that you are at yourself, Acquanie? What f
would you have need of the key when you have taken the tur
against the meal?'

'I resent the indignity of having to ask my own servant for i
Mamma has a key to every room in the castle. Could yc
imagine her having to plead with Nurse Hogan or Mrs. Stace
or Hegarty to unlock a handful of meal for her?'

'Hmph! I couldn't imagine your mamma's Ladyship stoop
ing to anything so vulgar as to eat dry meal. Say this I mus
whether you like it or not. You are lettin' down the family
home; them that were there away back in Time when the lik
of these'—she waved a deprecatory hand at the surroundin
splendour—'were only in the cow's horn. When your Lady
ship's mamma craved for anything it was for a peach steeped i
champagne.'

Sterrin drew herself up in anger, but fell back in weakness.

'Who,' she demanded in a croak that was meant to be a shou

'said anything about "cravings"? I chew meal to keep myself from eating chocolates because they are spoiling my waistline. That's why Eugenie's ladies-in-waiting smoke cigarettes.'

'Aye,' muttered Hannah, going to the fire to replenish the bed-warmer, 'by the look of the carry-ons 'twasn't chocolate that bulged some of *their* waistlines.'

For a week Sterrin throbbed in pain and fever but fiercely resisted every suggestion of a doctor. The day before Sir Jocelyn was due back she was up at dawn, with the carriage ordered for Mrs. Delaney's place. The forge at Moormount was the same old time, all-purpose type as the one at Kilsheelin Castle. Its blacksmith could forge a thimble or a scissors or a key as readily as he could a set of horse shoes.

'Why this one only?' asked Mrs. Delaney when Sterrin, her mission explained, had detached the store room key from the rest. 'Why not have them all copied. It is up to you to know what lies behind locked doors and drawers.' Then with a sapient nod of her head she added, 'Knowledge is power.'

It was the small hours when Sterrin reached home. Her husband's key-ring had held a lot of locksmith and Sterrin now had a perfect copy of every key, safe in her reticule.

Sir Jocelyn's agitation at not finding Clooreen in the stables seemed to Sterrin out of all proportion.

'But she ought to be here! Here in these stables.' He kept repeating the words as though it were of some very special significance that the mare should be back; and at that particular time.

When he heard what had prevented Sterrin from carrying out his instructions, he became still more agitated. 'You've been ill? What was wrong? What did the doctor say? Why wasn't I informed?'

'For heaven's sake!' Sterrin exploded. 'I was much too busy sneezing to send a medical bulletin to Dublin.' She had the feeling that his anxiety was linked with this Clooreen business. It had no concern for herself.

Next day she slipped away and went to see the relatives to whom the boy's uncle had handed him on. They disclaimed all knowledge of his whereabouts. She rode on, brooding over the cruel fate of the little chap; his sisters and brother too. As she skirted a shrub the horse swerved and reared up. Next moment the figure of a boy emerged and started running wildly. She called after him, but he redoubled his efforts. When she caught up on him he was trembling with exhaustion and terror.

'Surely you are not afraid of me?' she called.

But he was. He knew her identity now. She was the wife of the terrible man who had torn his mother away from him to the ends of the earth and made him an outcast.

He was scarcely recognisable from the plum-cheeked boy who had dipped into her basket of goodies that August night. He was gaunt and unkempt from hunger and exposure. When she pressed money upon him he backed away again. 'They will say that I stole it.' But she insisted upon him taking it back to his relatives. It would sustain him while she made arrangements to get him to America. The boy took it fearfully. A widow, he told her, who had lived for fifty years in the house next to his uncle had been evicted for taking in her widowed daughter who had been turned out in the mass evictions last August.

It was early December when a letter arrived from Donal Keating telling her that the sorrows of the boy and his sisters were at an end. He had written to the Emigration Society in America. One of its most prominent members was John Holohan of Upper Kilsheelin. He had arranged for passages for the children. They would be met at Castle Gardens and looked after until they could be reunited with their mother.

The news so heartened her that she decided to ride out that morning to her first Meet of Hounds. Her husband and his doctor were standing in the hall as she came down. She included them both in a gay good morning as she passed without slowing. Sir Jocelyn halted her. 'Doctor Denning thinks that you ought not to hunt today.'

She turned to the doctor. 'Is there contagion abroad?' Her husband came close and peered through the thick veil that was drawn tight against her face and secured behind over the curled brim of her tall silk hat.

'Your look suggests to him that you might possibly be exposing yourself to risk by hunting. Are you concealing what it is my right to know? It is imperative that I know—immediately.'

For all his sophistication, she thought, with a string of mistresses behind him, he sounded like an old maid. Concealing what is his right to know indeed!

'Fiddlesticks,' she said, 'I'm as healthy as a salmon.' She

strode across to the waiting groom, ignored his proffered knee and swung herself into the saddle.

What was so imperative for him to know! She flicked her horse to outstrip her thoughts; because she knew the answer. The only consequence to the revolting experience that night last August that Sterrin had ever considered was that it had ended her hopes of annulment. It had rendered her marriage consummated. But it was too unnatural a deed, too gross, for any other consequence. She lashed the horse into a full gallop. If she rode hard enough she would outdistance this shackling menace. Nothing would happen!

Pink-coated men on fine horses looked appreciatively at the splendid horsewoman who rode so recklessly, but so sure. They shouldered and jostled their mounts nearer. All that they could glimpse under the thick veil was the deep pit of her eyes, the moulding of her cheek bones, the poreless pallor of white skin. But the body showed its perfection in the tight hunting coat of darkest green.

Cattle scampered out of her way. A little donkey ran alongside her till the first fence, then brayed pitiably when she left it behind. Laughter rippled across Sterrin's mind and broke upon her lips. She forgot everything but the joy of the hunt. She thought only of her mount's easy grace; of the tall fences that its feet despised; the great wall that had loomed and vanished; the sparkle of water in streamlets, so lightly crossed, like that problem back there.

The Master was straight in front of her heading for the next ditch. Beside it stood a riderless horse. As the Master approached the ditch the tousled head and muddied shoulders of its rider rose up. The Master had barely time to shout, 'Duck, Peregrine!' and over with him. A cloud of divots came hurtling into Sterrin's vision. The head of the unfortunate Peregrine was within four inches of the feet of her mount before she saw him. If she chucked sideways, herself and her mount would be in the green-bronze water of the ditch. There was nothing for it. Here goes! 'Duck Peregrine!' she yelled, and Peregrine ducked for dear life. Sterrin soared over, high and sure and never a touch of iron on the ditch. Her spirits soared. She might as well have been riding a cloud as a horse. Laughter bubbled out on the steam of her breath, as over her shoulder she glanced the benighted Peregrine, whoever he was, going down for the third time.

From a hilly lie there came a whimper. A patch of geese cackled as hounds waded in. There was no covert for the small brown thing that lurked in the gorse. It broke and slipped through a hedge, down a boreen that led to a house. Hounds followed in full cry, jaws mouthing towards its hunt. Suddenly their cries changed to whines.

A voice said, 'Have they made a kill?'

Sterrin flung herself from her horse, barely conscious of a pain that rent her back. The circle of hounds, no longer baying, were backing away from the body that lay in their midst. She lifted it and held it in her arms.

'They've made a kill. Oh, God, they've killed the little hunted boy.'

A voice said, 'These were not made by hounds.' It was Bergin who had dismounted beside her. He pointed to the hands manacled behind the boy's back, to the fingers crusted with blood.

There was a house near by in the clearing. A face appeared at the window, then the curtain was drawn. Sterrin looked down at the body of the boy, then her eyes focused on the blood on the lintel and on the ground in front of the door of the house. She looked up at Bergin.

'Who could have done this? Who could have chained him this way?' Her eyes were hard and unforgiving.

Bergin dashed for the house. He forced the frightful story from the man and woman who lived there. Twice last night they had hunted the boy away. When he returned the second time they had chained his hands and brought him to his uncle's door. All night the boy had banged his manacled hands against his uncle's door. When Bergin returned to where Sterrin still cradled the child's body on her knee, a neighbour came forward and said that he had heard the wailing but thought it was the Banshee. Another spoke up and said he had heard a voice crying, 'Put me on my feet.'

Sterrin listened to Bergin tell of how the boy had been left to die, pleading for shelter, for humanity, for the right to live.

Bergin stooped and took the body. As Sterrin attempted to swing herself into the saddle the pain reasserted itself. She jerked on the reins for support. The horse responded and moved forward, dragging her along with one foot in the stirrup. Two men rushed to help her. As they jerked her upwards a wild pain went rending through her then everything went black.

Sir Jocelyn watched as the men carried Sterrin upstairs. At brief intervals he rapped on her door and demanded reports from the harassed doctor. Finally he broke in without knocking.

'Is there no hope of saving the child?'

Faint but clear his wife's voice answered. 'The child was already dead when we found him. He had been——'

'Pshaw! That brat!' He dismissed the dead boy as so much vermin. 'My child! My child that you have deprived of——' He looked wildly about to assess what his child had been deprived of. He had been about to say 'existence', but it was too meagre a term for the plenitude of life that awaited the being of his creating. Beneath all his sophistry and cynicism he had maintained a superstitious acceptance of the tradition that no child would inherit the property direct. It had zig-zagged over the years from one distant relative to another; an oblique heritage. Somehow to him had been vouchsafed the privilege of stabilising the heritage; the founding of a dynasty. His voice spiralled to a scream.

From her bed, Sterrin had the sensation of having died and was witnessing the judgment of a soul. This man who had held the power of life and death, the dereliction of six hundred lives, stood confronted by the spectacle of his own futility. He was powerless to recall the embryo life that would have crowned his own. She wanted to tell him that he had had a long crack of the whip, that God is not mocked, but her voice sounded calm and assuring as it announced that she would have other children. Her husband was startled into silence, then he turned and let them lead him away. He sensed that it was her own young body that she was reassuring.

CHAPTER 51

The child's lonely death sent a throb of horror around the world. In Westminster, Mr. Bright raised his beautiful voice and this time a shocked House listened in moved silence. All over England right-minded men and women clamoured against a government policy that could expose a helpless child to such a fate. Not since the famine had so concerted a feeling pulsed through the nations.

The American press was outraged. Newspapers edited by men of Irish blood expressed rage and sympathy in terms that an Irish tenant would have been afraid to whisper in his secret heart. Articles were written by young men who had been homeless, evicted boys a decade before. In black captions they dared to cite the names of Irish landlords. They dared to suggest assassination. They urged homeless men who still dared to shelter beneath Irish hedges to rise up against their oppressors.

It was a misty, muffling afternoon in December when Sterrin drove up the avenue after a round of calls. She was back sooner than was expected. The calls were but a card-leaving and the lamps were not lighted. With a word to the waiting footman she turned and walked across the lawn where a little gate gave on to the river path.

It amazed her to see masses of blue beneath the beech trees. She drew near and hundreds of pigeons that were gorging themselves on the masts they had drawn from the beech sheaths rose up in flight. She looked up at the blue cloud they made. Their long-drawn cooing with the great overtones of their winging made a symphony of muted thunder. She was saddened when a potshot sounded; but no bird fell.

A few yards further on she came upon her husband's body.

For a numbed second she stood looking down. Was this the threatened stroke? A blue-grey feather wafted down and settled on his face. The gentle encroachment defined its white stillness. Jocelyn was dead!

She dropped to her knees. There was something she must do; something her mother had done when she had held Papa's dying body in her arms. As she bent to breathe into his ear the prayer for mercy she noticed, as one notices the trivial in the moment of solemnity, the judicially placed curl. The valet had placed it where it would conceal a distorted muscle. She pushed the hair from over his ear and displaced the pomaded curl. It disclosed a bullet hole!

She raised her head and saw Bergin standing on the path. Her eyes travelled slowly and rested on the gun held so nonchalantly beneath his arm.

'It was you!' she breathed. Her eyes widened with horror.

He shrugged. 'What I killed is back there.' He gestured over his shoulder. His assurance ridiculed her suspicion. 'Shall I summon aid—for you?' he asked.

'I——' she was about to give a cold refusal; but no words came. The shock was beginning to tell. He raised his hat and replaced it quickly. The respect was for her and not for Death's presence.

'I shall inform them at the house,' he said. As he opened the little gate he looked up at the sky. 'The outriders should have reached there by now,' he said grimly. 'No doubt the gates will have been flung wide!' He passed unhurriedly through the gate to the great mansion. Before his mind flashed a vision of the lashings he had received in that penal fortress where he had spent his youth and early manhood. His hand unwittingly went to his gashed cheek. 'I wonder,' he said. He pulled the bell with great strength. It clanged long after he had given his news.

Sterrin continued to kneel there, Sir Jocelyn's head on her arm. She had prayed automatically. But she couldn't continue to pray; nor even to think. Since the boy's death she had scarcely spoken to her husband. But now she knew no sense of relief; nor any grief. She recalled her mother's passionate grief as she fondled her husband's dead body in her arms.

The river flowed on, indifferent to the passing of the overlord. It swept as usual to the bend that hid it from her sight. Her husband's head grew heavy on her arm. Already the twisted muscle was relaxing into the sculpted modelling of death. And death presented him with an impressive nobility; a reminder of what might have been! He must have been a remarkably handsome man. She studied his features without dread. She had

535

never before held him in her arms; never been so close except that night when he had taken her. Had he been less cruel would she have come to care for him? She would have at least respected him. But, like her mother, she was capable of but one great love. There are women like that!

When the rain fell that night there were people who still cowered beneath the hedges; still evading the workhouse; without hope of the passage money to the Promised Land of America. They looked at each other as the news spread, but they still dared not speak their thoughts!

Not so their neighbours who had reached America. When the news came over the waters they had freedom to tell each other that justice had been done. A San Francisco paper offered a reward to the assassin. The city's working girls read the news without regret. Bankers estimated that within the year these girls had sent a million dollars to maintain the homes the crowbars had levelled.

The reward went uncollected. The assassin was never revealed. Bergin was questioned; his gun examined. The shell of the solitary cartridge discharged was found near the carcase of the bird it had killed. Routine, said his questioners apologetically. Bergin was no vengeful evictee. He was an estate owner; a rich one.

Sterrin was nearly all packed. She stood over the open trunks watching the maids fill them with her gowns and cloaks. She had not reached upon wearing a quarter of them. And now it would be at least two years before she could wear them again.

'There was no room for any more, your Ladyship.' The sewing maid put the lid on the last trunk.

'Make room!' Her Ladyship rapped out the command. The maid looked up startled at the set, cold face.

'Get more trunks; get valises, get anything.'

The maids hurried out and Sterrin turned to Hannah. 'See that nothing is left behind. You understand?'

Hannah nodded ruefully.

'Too well I understand, gra' gal. You can trust me to see that there is not a stitch left behind.'

A footman tapped and announced that Major Devine would appreciate it if Lady Devine could spare him a moment in the library before she left.

The new owner, Sir Jocelyn's cousin, came straight to the point 'As you are leaving this afternoon I thought I should like to discuss with you the matter of having the horse, Clooreen, returned to the stables here.'

'Clooreen is my personal property. She belongs where she is.'

'But, my cousin Jocelyn, was most precise on this. He was most anxious that the horse be brought here without further delay and, er...' The major gave an embarrassed cough, 'according to the terms of the Will——'

'The Will,' she broke in, 'bequeathed you all the horses in the stables at Noremount Manor. Clooreen is not one of these.' But she was meant to be. The reason for her husband's agitation at not finding the horse here on his return became clear to her; so much about that odious Will was clear; that morning when she had struck the silver bird in the aviary and her husband had said, 'I have told you that some day you might go too far. This, I think is the day,' and the other morning when she had made the unfortunate quip about smallpox and he decided so unexpectedly to go to Dublin. 'I find that the business that takes me there,' he had said, 'has been too long postponed.' And the business, as she might well have suspected was this vindictive Will that had disowned her. The only thing he had omitted to cut off from her was the elaborate wardrobe of garments that she was making certain to have packed.

'As you will,' Major Devine said. 'Now,' he consulted a list in front of him. 'There is a casket of jewels mentioned here. It is not in the safe.'

'It is in my room.' She spoke with quiet assurance.

'Oh!' There was a challenging note in the exclamation. Did she think she could claim the jewels also?

'I will bring it to you.' She turned away. He stepped after her.

'I will go up with you.'

She stopped and looked him full in the eyes without speaking. He wilted under the gaze.

'You must not trouble yourself, I shall send a servant.'

'Major Devine,' she said firmly. 'I will hand you over the casket myself. It has been kept always in my room, but Sir Jocelyn retained the key. That is it.' She pointed to a small but complicated-looking key on the bunch that lay on the desk. He looked down at it, relieved. 'As you will,' he said again.

He accompanied her to the door and watched her slowly mount the stairs. Once inside her door she made a dash for the little watch pocket in the bed drapes. Thank heavens they were still there! She had forgotten about the keys since that night when she had returned from Mrs. Delaney. And thank heaven for Mrs. Delaney, who had insisted upon her having all the other keys duplicated as well as the store key. 'You are at least entitled to know what is behind locked doors and drawers,' that sound woman had said. 'Knowledge is power.'

The casket held the less opulent jewellery, including many of the gifts purchased for her during her engagement. The grand parures and diadems and necklaces for great occasions were kept elsewhere. She rummaged feverishly, then drew forth a locket, a simple affair on a slim gold chain, its pendant of mosaic of flowers done in enamel and surrounded by pearls. She pressed the spring at the back. It was there, a shiny black curl. She pushed the locked inside the neck of her gown. 'You are not going round the fat neck of Mrs. Theopholus Devine.'

In the act of replacing a pair of amethyst earrings, she paused. Her husband had bought them because he thought that they matched her eyes. 'They may as well go on matching them.' She pushed them down after the locket. Rage at his base suspicion had her fingers still trembling as she locked the casket. 'He'll accompany me, indeed!' On a sudden she unlocked it and drew out a handful of rings. She removed her indoor mittens and thrust a ring on every available finger. 'That will steady them,' she gritted.

There was no sign of her agitation as she entered the library holding the casket.

'Would you care to check the contents?' she asked placing it in front of him on the writing table. 'I presume you have a list.' She didn't presume anything of the kind except, perhaps, for such of the jewels as were heirlooms. 'And hadn't you better take these too—my betrothal ring and its keeper?' She made a gesture of withdrawing her left mitten. He backed away expostulating and embarrassed. For a moment he thought to offer her back the casket, then he recalled the rumours that she might have done the murder herself. The overseer who had supervised the evictions had seen her enter the little wicket gate to that lonely path a moment before the shot sounded. The footman who had tucked Sir Jocelyn into the carriage after the Assizes Ball, when a stone had been flung at the carriage, had heard her say, 'If anyone turned me out of my house I wouldn't be content to throw a stone at him, I'd shoot him.' Everyone knew that she was a whizzer with a gun.

He swept an arm around to indicate all the priceless *objets d'art* that crowded the room. 'If there are any of these, or anything elsewhere that you would like to take, any souvenirs?'

She looked around her and felt her first tug of deprivation. If she had taken more care; if she had acknowledged the existence within her of the child that she had lost, she would not be surrendering her possessions in this ignominious fashion. The inheritance would not have gone on tilting sideways to still another indirect heir. But she had not acknowledged the existence of the child even to herself. It had just been a nebulous surge; a suppressed conjecture; instinctive as the urge that had driven her down in the night hours for the oatmeal; as the one that had impelled her just now to retrieve the locket with Young Thomas's hair.

Her gaze came back to his. 'I do not covet any souvenirs of my stay here.'

More to avoid the look in those fearless eyes he turned to place the casket in the great bookcase, where a drop-leaf door in the centre was down revealing a recessed compartment. He lifted some parchment documents out of his way and left them on the writing table while he disposed of the casket. She glanced indifferently at them, then the inscription on one of them forced itself into her consciousness. Her heart gave a lurch. There was a momentary cessation of existence, then her knees buckled and she sat down abruptly. He turned at the slight sound.

'You are ill, my Lady?'

The blood had gone from her face. Its whiteness was no longer of a white rose, but of thin lime. He darted to the bell rope and her wits returned sufficiently for her to curse herself. Why hadn't she grabbed the document while his back was turned, instead of wasting time collapsing. She fought back the waves of weakness and got to her feet. She braced her shoulders against the mad pounding of her heart. She assured him that there was nothing amiss with her and left the room with head high.

Inside her bedroom she leaned against the door. Hannah

looked up startled from sewing the cloak.

'Oh, Hannah, Hannah, this is the worst of all!'

The maid half-carried her to the chaise longue. 'Twasn't in nature to go on enduring the likes of what this poor white blossom had faced; to come upon her husband murdered as she had come upon her father; and after losin' the hopes of her little child!

'Hannah!' It was only a whisper. 'Hannah, how will I face them? I've sacrificed everything. It has all been for nothing. Poor Mamma! Poor Dominic! The poor servants.' She had looked up at the anxious face, 'And yourself, Hannah.' The maid stiffened. Cead mile curses upon the head of that footman. The rumour must have drifted to her Ladyship that 'twas her own true aim had fired the shot.

'He has it, Hannah. The castle. I saw it. Down there in the big bookcase.' The maid put her hand on the forehead that was pressed to her bosom. Would she be going a bit like her mamma? Next minute her hand was pushed away and Sterrin was on her feet.

'By the livin' God, what am I wasting time ullagoaning for? God never made a gap but he grew a bush to stop it with.'

Major Devine looked up impatiently from the great roll of parchment, then jumped politely to his feet. It was Lady Devine who had tapped.

'I'm afraid,' she began gently, 'that I must encroach upon your hospitality for another night. I really don't feel up to the journey this afternoon.' He was all concern and reassurances.

'By all means——' He barely stopped himself in time from saying, 'stay as long as you wish'. That might be a bit too long.

She made no move to go. 'There is something else.' She gave him a shy, pleading look. 'You were kind enough to ask me if there was anything that I should like to have as a souvenir. I'm afraid that I was not very courteous.'

What could she be coveting? Whatever it was, it would be impossible to resist these eyes. She opened the big tapestry embroidery bag that swung from her arm. He watched curiously.

'You'll probably think me very silly, but I should like to keep these.'

To his amazement she produced a highly ornate pair of shoes with jewelled heels. 'They would scarcely fit you. You are much

540

bigger than Sir Jocelyn.'

'But, my dear lady,' he gasped, 'if you wished for something so personal belonging to Jocelyn, why not——'

'But you see,' she interrupted, 'these are musical shoes. Look!' She whisked off her shoes and put on the others then stood up and with her skirt drawn up a few inches tapped out a tune. 'Aren't they delightful?' she asked.

'They are truly delightful,' he agreed, his eyes glued to the slender ankle and shapely display of limb that rounded slimly up into the hint of white lace threaded with black ribbon. She dropped her skirt and resumed her seat.

'Then I may have them?' Her eyes wistful and pleading held him while her toe pushed one musical shoe gently towards the massive fold of window curtain beside the table leg.

What a child she was! She was on her feet again, drawing the string of her bag and securing it on to her arm with a little pat of satisfaction. A strange mixture of childlikeness and dignity, he thought. Circus shoes and all. Dammit, she managed to go out like an abdicating queen.

There was a smoky darkness in the library that night when Sterrin slipped into it. Those anthracite fumes, so different from the turf, always caught at her throat. Tonight they seemed worse than usual. But since her miscarrage her sense of smell—in fact all her sense had quickened. She tiptoed to the bookcase and foosthered with her keys. One after the other failed in the lock. Her heart was thudding and her fingers, as each key failed her, began to tremble. Hurrying footsteps went racing past the door. From somewhere there came a sound of agitated voices. Strange at this hour. This night of all nights. Dear God, let this key work. She had to stop to force a handkerchief into her mouth to muffle the cough. The fumes were unbearable. At last a key engaged. She groped frantically and found, not one but three rolls of parchment. Which one was it? She raced to the fireplace. There was only the faintest red in the dying creesach. One roll after another she tried, the evil sulphuric fumes choking her until tears streamed from her eyes, and she was within a dog's bark of pitching the lot into the fire, when the mean red eye of the creesach showed up a familiar word. At that moment Hannah's voice called out her name; again and again, at the top of her voice.

'Miss Sterrin! Miss Sterrin! Your Ladyship!' The woman

must have taken leave of her senses to betray me like this. Oh, Mother of God! And then came Major Devine's voice, startled, angry; 'Do you mean to say that your mistress is in there?'

The door was pushed open. 'Lady Devine, what in God's name are you doing there?' He lifted the candelabrum high over his head.

There was no one down there where the great gothic bookcase stood, undisturbed, as he had left it. The wind bellied a curtain. There was a flash of fire on the ground: there was a banner of flame in the room. It showed Lady Devine on her knees groping in the folds of the curtain near the writing table. He saw her fish out something and hold it aloft.

'I came down to look for this. I found that I had only one in the bag.' It was one of the musical shoes.

He bore down on her. 'Are you mad, girl? Do you realise that the house is on fire?' He pulled her roughly to her feet and dragged her towards the door. A buffet of fiery air struck them and drove them back. The Major pushed Sterrin towards the window. There was a tinkle of glass and she was out in the cool air. From behind came a wail like a banshee. Sterrin stepped back into the burning room. The Major tried to pull her back but she fought him like a tiger.

'You've caused enough trouble looking for your damned silly shoes.'

'Let me go!' she yelled. 'It is not shoes now but a human being.'

She dived for something white from which the wails were proceeding, but could get no grip; only something bumpy and fleshy and eerie, then realised that it was Hannah's face, which the maid had had the presence of mind to cover with an apron; but there was no more presence of mind left. She stood there blinded, terrified, yelling. Sterrin pawed, found hair and pulled.

'Shut up!' she hissed. 'If I've to drop what's in my other hand to pull you out you'll be sorry later that I saved your life.'

And that's just what happened. As she dragged the maid through the window Sterrin dropped the precious object that was pressed tight to her side beneath the Vesperatum cloak. Major Devine looking up from directing the human chain of buckets from the fountain court, saw the windows of the ground floor fill with great orange whorls and curling waves of

542

fire. As he looked, a figure in something shimmering went in through the window, as a diver goes towards the water, head-first.

'Come back, for God's sake,' he shouted, but his voice was lost against the steady roar of the flame that was like a great wind.

Inside, Sterrin pawed and clawed along the burning floor. Flames licked the back of her hand and ran up her arm. Her quickened senses could distinguish the intimate singeing smell of her forehead curls. And then she found the bag and was through the window again, the bag held over her face.

'I've got it. I've got it. I've got it.' She couldn't stop saying it.

'You deserve to burn, to expose the lives of others for the sake of a toy.'

His voice was savage and so was his grip on her arm. His cousin, Sir Jocelyn, knew what he was doing when he disinherited this nitwit. God in heaven, what sane woman would venture into that inferno for a musical toy! She broke from him and ran. There was lurid light on the lawn. It guided her to the shelter of the trees, black, immense, shivering in the red darkness. He must not find her. He would take her bag from her. She must never go down there again. All around her the birds were aroused and fluttered in the air with shrill cries of alarm and wonder. A swarm of wasps routed from their nest against the eaves of the house hummed in the night air with savage anger. Rats came from the cellars and galloped like grotesque diminutive horses, in the long grass near the trees. She screamed and the sound guided Hannah to her.

A man's voice spoke to her; not the Major's, a grating leaden voice. The wind blew the words away. It keened and moaned above her in the black indignant trees.

Bergin touched her arm and she whimpered with pain. The face she turned to him was stunned and horror-stricken; as it had been when he last saw it above the dead boy's: as it had been when he first saw it, a little girl's face peeping from a carriage window at the whiplash that had laid open his cheek.

'I've come to take you to my house, Lady Devine.'

He was making no move to help put out the fire. He had brought no workmen as other neighbours were doing. She caught the words and shook her head.

'I must go home.'

'There is no home there to go to.' He nodded towards the blazing, roaring house.

'Not there. That's not my home.' She knew no regret for the great, grand house that opened its doors wide in hospitality to great, grand people and never a welcome; never a crust for the hungry.

'The little children won't dance there any more. The gridirons have set fire to the house. The little children should have worn musical shoes. They would have protected their flesh. Burned flesh is so painful.' A low moan shuddered through her.

Bergin ignored her protests and carried her to the river and his boat. But Sterrin was not deranged. The fire that drove her was not the one that raged back there. She must get to Kilsheelin. It was in danger, and she held its safety.

On the opposite bank of the river away from the obscene smoke she planted her feet on the cool ground and would not budge. A dark hedge outlined an avenue. Its darkness was the darkness of night, she knew its colour would be green and sane but she would not linger in the house it led to.

'Thank you kindly,' she said to his urgings, 'but it is imperative that I get home tonight; if you could afford me transport? As far as Moormount, the Delaneys' place, would do.'

'I'll drive you there,' he said. If he didn't, he knew that she would try walking it on her scorched feet.

Mrs. Delaney, the voluble, made no comment at the sight of Sterrin's face. While Ned-Rua, roused from sleep, prepared the carriage, she put cool linen on Sterrin's arms and painted egg white on her cheeks and on the scorchmarks where the glossy brows used to wing across the white forehead, that was white no longer.

'You've lived up to the name the Liberator chose for you, Blah na Sterrin. Blossom of the storm. Inagh! You've known more storm than blossoming; but you'll know your blossoming yet. I feel it in my bones, gra' gal.'

She kept hushing Sterrin's thanks.

'But,' gasped Sterrin, 'it is for the keys I'm thanking—only for them—one of them unlocked the deeds of Kilsheelin Castle——' she spoke in jerks and gasps her lips swollen from blisters and sealing with egg white. 'I didn't know that he had them. I must get home——'

'Is he after you?' Mrs. Delaney, startled, cracked an egg on to the carpet.

Sterrin shook her head. 'He doesn't know, I think. I'm not sure, but if I get them to Kilsheelin he can do his damnedest.'

'More power to you, girl! Here,' she splashed a big jorum of whiskey into a tumbler, 'try and take a sip of this.' Sterrin tossed the lot down in a gulp. Mrs. Delaney took the empty glass and looked reverently from it to Sterrin.

'Oh, you'll blossom again all right,' she said, 'if your spirit was only half the strength of your swallow, you'll blossom.'

CHAPTER 52

The old peacock gave its proud, high scream as Sterrin drove up the avenue to the home of her childhood. The castle was scarcely visible; just a deeper greyness looming out of the greyness of the dawn, but its buttressing arms reached out and enfolded her. And then out of the clanging awakement it was her mother's arms and Dominic's and Nurse Hogan's.

Down in the kitchen the fan wheel was set-to furiously and one by one the eight fires came to life under their cranes. Sleepy servants came towards their glow, buttoning livery and tying aprons and talking in shocked tones about the face that had gone from here in such loveliness less than two years ago. Hannah was put in the butler's big chair in the inglenook while her shins and hands were tended to. They gave her the soothing herb brew that had sent Miss Sterrin's Ladyship to sleep, and before it took effect she retold them what she had told Lady O'Carroll about the night's horror that was like that of the night of the Big Wind; and with the mention of that night of nights they digressed as people always did. Poor Miss Sterrin was lucky to be born that night and they had been disappointed that she had not been the heir, but had not it proved lucky for all of them that she was not? If she hadn't gone back through the flames a second time to save the deeds after going back to save Hannah they would all be facing the road now. And not one of them, from her Ladyship down, with a solitary notion that the castle was in danger!

'She's a hero,' said Mrs. Stacey.

Mr. Hegarty removed his pipe and requested her not to betray her ignorance. 'She's a hero-ess,' he said.

' 'Tis a great credit to God the way he made her,' Mrs. Stacey continued. 'There is not her equal in the human world and when she dies the angels will make room before the fire of Heaven for her to warm her purty shins.' Hannah drew back her own aching shins a little from the heavenly vision.

'Yes,' she agreed, 'but you shouldn't have let her see you make the sign of the Cross when you caught sight of her face and I know she heard you saying that eyebrows never grow again. There was no good in askin' her to bid the divil good morrow until she has to meet him.'

Mr. Hegarty rose to his feet and set the staff about their business and threatened, as he had threatened after every exciting disruption of routine for the past twenty-five years, that 'there would be law and order in this kitchen from this day forth'.

No pursuer came on the heels of Sterrin's gallop-by-night. But she was taking no chances. She had them send for Cousin Maurice, and until his arrival lay the embroider bag with its incongruously assorted contents beside her on the counterpane. No one dared touch it. It had cost her too dear. The doctor kept her under sleep as much as possible but in its intervals she lay in her bandages and relived the moments that, for her, represented the different sums that had made up the purchase price. The wedding night, the terrible night last August, the morning when she lifted the dead boy in her arms; the afternoon when she raised her husband's murdered body in her arms, arms, arms. She lifted her bandaged arms and the movement brought a groan of pain.

It was on the sound of her groan that Maurice O'Carroll entered the room. At the sight of her face he barely succeeded in suppressing an exclamation. He forced himself to be hearty and plunged into the matter of the deeds.

'You are sure,' he asked as he unrolled the parchment, 'that there was no specific mention of them in the Will?'

She shook her head; then in slow, pain-filled phrases she told him about the codicil that had been added recently in Dublin. 'All horses in the stables at Noremount. That let Clooreen out.' He could see that the grin she essayed was an effort. Ah, the lovely mouth of her; like a flower divided! And the brows that had been as soft and as delicate as moss. What had they done to the sweet, brave colleen?

'The same,' she went on, 'with the documents in the library, deeds of certain properties and the titles thereto.'

'Has the heir seen this?' Maurice tapped the parchment.

'I doubt it. He only arrived the night before the fire, late.'

'I fail to understand,' Maurice said slowly, his eyes poring over the deeds, 'why this was not handed over to you after your

547

marriage. It was to have been part of your husband's settlement upon you. He undertook to clear the mortgage and restore to you the unencumbered property. I simply cannot understand it.'

A throb of guilt broke the rhythm of Sterrin's pulse. She could not tell Maurice of all people, that it was Young Thomas, the servant whom he had dismissed, who lay behind all the bitterness that had terminated in merciless reprisal against them all.

'Anyway,' said Maurice, rolling up the parchment, 'you've got it back, gra' gal, and let anyone try taking it from you again. No gentleman would lay claim to this in the circumstances. But let him try and by God, I'll call him out; law or no law.'

Sterrin dragged herself upward. 'If you don't, she said grimly, 'I will.'

He put her back gently.

'You've done more than your share, child. What you have to do now is to get well.' He ran his fingers through where the silky curls used to cluster over her forehead but they recoiled from the scorched stubble that they encountered.

When he had gone Sterrin asked for a hand mirror. Her cousin's repressed start when he entered the room had not gone unnoticed. This was what Hannah had been dreading.

'Miss Sterrin,' she pleaded, 'haven't you had enough excitement for one day?'

'Is the first glimpse of my face after so long to prove another excitement?'

Hannah busied herself picking up things as though she had not heard.

'Hannah,' called Sterrin as sweetly as her puffed lips would allow. 'Do you remember when I had measles and you covered the mirror when I asked to see my spots. You said that it was Halloween and that if I looked in the mirror on that day I might see the devil. What are you afraid that I might see now?'

'Miss Sterrin's Ladyship, it is the way that the doctor said you are to sleep as much as possible that you have had a great shock and that——'

'And that if I see my face I'll get another shock. Hand me over that mirror.'

A long-drawn wail of horror brought Maurice and Lady O'Carroll hurrying up from the drawing-room. Sterrin was lying face downwards, her whole body heaving with deep, hoarse sobs, her bandaged hand still clutching the mirror.

Days became weeks. She studied the mirror by the hour hoping for the improvement that the doctor promised her, though he doubted it himself. At last Hannah suggested to her what she had suggested in desperation to Sir Roderick the night of the Big Wind when no doctor could travel and Miss Sterrin near losin' her fight to be born; that they call in Mag Miney.

The old woman had reached the landing from the back stairs when Lady O'Carroll spied her. The sight of her brought back to Margaret the sight and the smell of the rancid butter with its growth of greenish black fur that Mag, after delivering Sterrin was about to apply when the doctor arrived and bundled her out. And now, before she could reach Sterrin's door, she was bundled out again.

Her mother's display of authority prompted Sterrin's first urge towards the renewing of her life. 'Get me into my clothes, Hannah. We'll go to old Mag. I didn't haul this castle back under my arm after being near roasted alive just to return to being treated like a child again.'

But at the cottage she shuddered away from the evil-smelling concoction made mostly of stale, thick goat's milk on which a hairy fur had grown.

'The cure is in that hairy fur, your Honour's Ladyship.'

But Sterrin would not tolerate it near her face. At last she yielded to an application on her arms. On the way home she forgot its smelly presence in the first sight of the great boglands rising up behind the castle. She had missed the bogs in Kilkenny. The spring bustle of farming was in progress. Ploughmen were shearing through the black soil, the great, patient horses pulling; crows solemnly following the fresh-turned furrows and the sowers moving in harmony, dipping into the great slings about their shoulders and making the wide, splendid, ritual gesture of sowing the grain. She looked at the home that had seen her birth and the birth of her ancestors; great-hearted heroic men. The other home that she had seen die in its flames had been but a lodging. Here was peace. Here was hospitality. Here, old servants lived happily. And by the heels of Christ they'll go on living happily here! Did that upstart back in Kilkenny dare to think that he would ever warm his backside here? He nor his that had never fought an inch for it; never spilled blood as Normans and Elizabethans, and Cromwellians had, to win themselves a lien on the earth of Kilsheelin! The cure had started, not in her arms but in her spirit.

After a few visits to Mag the dreadful scarifying marks on her arms seemed to grow less, but nothing would induce her to endure the filthy mess upon her face. She took to wearing a veil when she rode abroad on Clooreen and at sight of anyone she knew drew it down over her face. Once as she rode, unveiled, up to Coolnafunchion, savouring the cool fresh breath of the air upon her cheeks a horseman slowed towards her and raised his caroline. A thrill of pleasure shot through her as she recognised Donal Keating but it was stifled at birth by the recollection of her lost beauty. She tugged the veil down over her disfigured face and rode past him without a sign of recognition.

He gazed after her, stunned. Oh, but this was too much. Was she starting her capricious tricks again? Only a few short months ago and they were corresponding amicably over the disposal of the Brennan children. And now not even a thank-you for his trouble in getting those little girls off to America while she was ill.

Kitty took the newspaper from the post-cart driver. 'Here Dorene,' she said to the quiet figure waiting in the doorway 'give this to Thomas. The driver tells me there has been some big landlord assassinated in Ireland.'

Some time later Kitty came into the sitting-room saying 'Who was the landlord, Thomas?'

'Oh, Madame Hennessey,' exclaimed Dorene, 'I have been too busy pleading with Thomas to take me with him to see the house that he is building on his land in the South.'

'What is the use when you won't be able to see it,' said Norisheen brutally. Kitty frowned at her warningly.

'The weather is cold for you to travel so far,' she said to Dorene. In emphasis, she threw a quite unnecessary log on the fire. 'And indeed for you too, Thomas, after your long tour would you not wait till the spring?'

Dorene lifted her head from Thomas's shoulder. 'But Madame Hennessey, we must get our house started. We cannot stay with you indefinitely.'

Thomas answered Kitty as though Dorene had not spoken. '

am booked up for the rest of the winter, right into the middle of spring, besides,' his tone became less explanatory, 'my—kinsman expects me.'

Kitty stepped back from the scorching flames that suddenly held a shiver of bleakness like the east wind's breath filtering through the May sunshine. She had hoped that with Miss Sterrin's marriage he would have given up this dream of building one of those old colonial mansions on the land that he had purchased when he first toured the South. The South had seemed so far away, so improbable to Kitty when she had been all of home and kin to Thomas. But now that he had traced this O'Carroll kin somewhere in the region of his own property, it was 'my kinsman' expects me!

The irrepressible Norisheen mimicked his words. 'My kinsman expects me. Hoity-toity, let no dog bark!'

Thomas burst out laughing then turned to Dorene. 'I've told you Dorene, it is a long journey and it has got to be a quick one. I cannot be——' he stopped as he was about to say 'hampered' and now he wanted to be alone, untrammelled when for the first time in his life he would meet someone in whose veins ran the same blood as in his own. 'I shall be very busy in New York, signing and attesting and what-not for my citizenship.' He had postponed seeking out American citizenship until he had finally established his identity. Not under a nickname reversed would he register himself as a citizen of America.

'Pleece, Tòmas, pleece!' Dorene linked his arm and entwined her fingers in his. He gently extricated himself and left the room. After a moment Dorene followed him, sure-footed in the space that had been left clear of obstacles for her progress from the sofa beyond the fireplace to the door.

'I believe,' said Norisheen, 'that she waves those hands of hers helplessly in front of him, just to impress on him how pretty they are. She's always creaming them and buffing her nails.'

'Hush, Norisheen,' Kitty answered. 'She has as much right to cultivate as you have. It is good that she has the heart to. When a woman loses her vanity she loses her flavour.' She picked up the newspaper from behind the cushion where Dorene had sat.

'Well,' said Norisheen, 'I think that she piles on that foreign accent.'

Kitty didn't answer. She was deep in the newspaper's account of the assassination of Sir Jocelyn Devine. That night, she wrote to New York to Fintan, her brother, who had left Ireland in Repeal Year and studied by night after his day's labour, to make himself a solicitor.

Marcus O'Carroll read aloud the document that Thomas handed him—the accomplishment of the odyssey that had brought him on his long journey.

'...and we, Richard and Dermot Rourke of Molesworth Street, Dublin and The Parade, Kilkenny, Notaries by Royal authority, do hereby testify that according to references made in the record office of the Exchequer concerning ... hm ... hm ... and attesting the accuracy of extracts made from the cantelury of the monastery of Holy Cross and papers in the public archives in Paris ... Thomas O'Carroll to be a gentleman recognised reputed and qualified by patronage ... issue of the illustrious house and family of O'Carroll....' The American looked over the top of the document, 'And you claim to be this Thomas O'Carroll?'

Thomas felt sorry that he had come here. He crossed his legs and took out his cigarettes. 'May I smoke?' He leaned back and gestured towards the document. '*That* Thomas O'Carroll was my father and I did not come here to make claims——'

But his host was on his feet, proffering cigars, pulling the bell-rope for refreshment; making up for his initial reserve. Even without the credentials he had been favourably impressed; but one had to move guardedly. His family had had no truck with the acting profession. And the Irish were great ones for claiming greatness.

'I've come at this particular time,' Thomas started, but his new kinsman held up his hand in sudden enlightenment.

'You don't have to tell me. I might have known. They are all coming to me; young relatives I haven't seen since they were in smocks and pinafores; ones I've never seen. You've come to join in my regiment.'

Thomas had forgotten all about the war.

Long into the night the two men sat traversing the centuries that had diffused the bloodstream stemming from their joint ancestor; the one who had been informed against and disinherited by his youngest son.

'And now,' smiled Marcus O'Carroll, 'it is my turn to be disinherited. I mean from my place on the tree. You see, we had taken it for granted that it was the eldest son, the disinherited heir, who had come over here and started this branch.'

Thomas's documents had revealed that there were four sons. The two middle ones had gone to the American colonies.

'Where did the eldest go?' asked Marcus.

'Nowhere. He became a raparee.'

'A what?'

Thomas explained that the raparees were bands of young men belonging to dispossessed families. They clung doggedly to the vicinity of their old homes; hid in bogs and mountains and made plundering raids on the usurpers. They were the fore-runners of the Tories and the Whiteboys.

'Later,' resumed Thomas, 'he settled in to the humble home where his father had ended his days. He married the beautiful daughter of his father's foster-brother but could not adapt him-self to the crude life of a farmer. He would drink from nothing but the silver cups given to his father by the Empress Maria Terèsa, but was incapable of earning anything to maintain their standards. Eventually he was given a position as Collector of Hearths and Window Tax and lived the life of Reilly, dining at all the big mansions where there were plenty of windows and hearths and often scorning to collect the tax because the hosts were so hospitable. But his grandson, Thomas O'Carroll—that Thomas O'Carroll,' Thomas nodded towards the document, 'wasn't content to live on the filmy claims of past grandeur. He worked his farm industriously until two days before I was born. But it was the time of the Tithe War, when the Catholics started to resist paying Tithes and Cess for the support of the Protestant clergy and the maintenance of their churches. My father was shot at his door for his refusal to pay. My mother died while journeying to Kilsheelin Castle with the papers of my identity and ancestry.' He went on to explain how the papers came to be destroyed the night of the Big Wind.

Suddenly Young Thomas was Cousin Thomas. Marcus O'Carroll introduced him to friends and neighbours all over the county as our 'cousin'. When gracious ladies floated across their drawing-rooms to greet him as Cousin Thomas, he experienced a feeling of unreality. Any moment he would wake up and someone would order Thomas to replenish the turf chests by the drawing-room fireside. 'Cousin Thomas I want you to meet——' 'young Thomas, I want you to empty the ashes.

Hurry up with them knives, young Thomas, or I'll leather your backside!'

But Thomas didn't wake up. The wonderful reality of his visit stretched from days to weeks and from weeks to months. It was more than three months after he had started out on the visit when he called on his way back to the firm of solicitors where Kitty's brother, Fintan, was a junior partner. Fintan, he was told, was at the harbour meeting an immigrant boat. He was representing one of the committees that looked after the welfare of disembarking emigrants. Thomas himself, under the direction of John Holohan, had often helped at Castle Garden when his engagements permitted. But today he had no time for benevolence. He was impatient at having to trail like this after his solicitor. He watched the white-faced passengers disembarking. And the efforts of zealous social workers to obstruct the actions of unscrupulous employment agents and white slave emissaries. But there was no one to obstruct the Recruiting Officer. He was there, resplendent in his best uniform, to dazzle the hunted outcasts of Irish evictions. A fine life awaited them in the American army! Grand uniform, good food. As soon as this war was over, the American army would be coming over to fight for Ireland's freedom! Then no more evictions. How old are you? Most of them didn't know. Some had been born in the famine. No one had thought to register their births. How old were you the night of the Big Wind. Oh, hazily, I was breeched that year! I was born in Black Forty-seven! I believe I was born the day-twelve-months after the Big Wind. The Big Wind was a date on history's calendar. The satisfactory thing, thought Thomas, was that they had been born, born to flee across the ocean from the landlord's bailiff, straight into the arms of the Recruiting Officer!

He finally sighted Fintan, resplendent in a blue officer's uniform. Now Thomas knew why there had been such a delay with his citizenship papers. Fintan had been too busy getting an officer's commission to attend to Thomas's naturalisation. To add insult to injury, he seemed to think it unreasonable of Thomas to be so annoyed about it.

'Can't you get it rushed through for me now?'

But Fintan would be with the 69th. One of the older men at the office would see to the matter. 'All the younger ones have joined up.'

Thomas thought he detected in the statement a hint of reproach to himself. Over his shoulder Fintan called, 'I may see you at the wedding if I can wangle leave.'

'Whose wedding?'

'Norisheen's. She made a sudden decision when her beau joined up.'

Thomas was amazed to find Hennessey's big parlour filled with military men. All the young men he had met here when he had come in response to Kitty's news about his foster-mother, were in blue uniform. There had been a Station planned for the next day and Norisheen had decided to avail of the presence of a priest in the house to rush forward a marriage that she had previously tended to postpone. Other young couples in the room had, likewise, decided to avail of the Station function.

Towering above the wedding guests was Private John Holohan. The millionaire who could procure commissions for others would not hear of one for himself. Thomas made his way towards Kitty, Dorene clinging to his arm. Kitty seemed preoccupied and not inclined to indulge him in his annoyance with her brother, Fintan, over the papers. John Holohan, glass in hand, broke into *The Wedding at Ballyporeen*—the song he had sung at the platform dance the afternoon of the blight. Then in a voice as booming as his singing he asked Thomas why had he not joined up under the command of Thomas Francis Meagher, the idol of his youth. Meagher of the Sword.

Thomas explained that he was to play in New York in two nights. 'Anyway, I haven't got my citizenship, thanks to Fintan.'

'You don't need citizenship,' said Mark Hennessey.

'I know,' said Thomas crisply. 'I've seen Ireland's evicted citizens, her surplus stock, being picked off the ships like so much fodder.'

'What's come over you, Thomas?' said Mark. Kitty hurried over and handed Thomas a letter.

'It came this morning,' she said.

It was from his new-found Kinsman, Marcus O'Carroll. '...I am here at the head of my regiment,' he wrote. 'We are all in fine fettle and spirit with no doubt whatever about the outcome of this conflict. The spirit of our ancestor—yours and mine—who fought with Washington will not be found lacking——'

'I met Tim Lonergan at the barracks,' said John. 'You remember Tim Lonergan of Golden Meadows?'

Thomas nodded and tried to resume the letter.

'I thought he'd be an officer an' he college bred,' John went on. 'But, of course, Thomas, if you decide to fight you'd get a commission in the 69th.'

Thomas looked up from the letter and around at the watching and listening faces. He felt strangely rasped. What right had they to take him for granted? As one of themselves. He wasn't one of them. His oneness was with the writer of this letter. 'If I decide to fight,' he said, 'I shall not fight with the 69th.'

'You'd renege on the Meagher of the Sword?' exclaimed Mark.

'And what regiment have you got in mind?' asked John.

Thomas looked down at the letter. 'I am here at the head of my regiment. . . .' The words stared up at him. He looked back at John Holohan.

'If I decide to fight,' he repeated slowly, 'I shall fight with the South.'

The room went silent. Small sounds took over; Dorene's little intake of breathe, the crackling of the fire logs. Then the crash of a giant fist on the table and a bellow from the millionaire private. He accused Thomas of treachery to the country of his adoption.

'It hasn't adopted me yet.'

'It gave you success—wealth.'

'My talent gave me success. My fortune was struck in Australia.'

'I multiplied it. You ingrate!'

Thomas was tossing back frivolous arguments because John wanted arguments, explanations. Mark, too. All of them. And he couldn't give them the true reason, that was based on the simplest most elemental emotion. That he was following the trail of his kind. He could not explain to them that as a child, aye and as a growing gossoon, he could not pass a cabin where children sat with parents around a hearth or table without wanting to crawl in among them on his belly like a little stray terrier and plead to be let stay with them. He could not explain to these angry, smug men, who were assured in the consciousness of an identity set in ancestry, what bleak outsideness of his

556

nameless existence had been. What it meant to him now to find people who had the same blood as his in their veins. Who had taken him to themselves and called him kin. Their cause was his cause.

Soon after dawn, Thomas, from his window, saw the priest arrive; and then the blue-bonneted brides, for all the world like the Shrovetide brides whose Masses he used to serve long ago. On a sudden, he strode across the corridor to Mark and Kitty's bedroom door.

'Mark!' he called.

There was silence. 'Mark,' he repeated.

Kitty opened the door slightly. 'I'm not quite dressed, Thomas. I've been up half the night.'

'It is Mark I want.'

'He's asleep Thomas.'

'He is not. I heard him moving. Mark!' he called over her head. 'I want you to do me a slight favour, act as my Best Man, then Dorene and I will go away——'

Mark came and stood behind Kitty. 'There can be nothing between us.' He made to close the door. Thomas pushed it back. 'There need be nothing more after this.'

A girl came up the stairs towards the door, calling Kitty. Thomas murmured something quickly. Mark shook his head and closed the door in his face. Thomas heard the key turn.

He stood there for a stunned moment, then turned and went slowly down the stairs. Young men were queuing on one knee outside a room for Confession. They looked up then resumed their preparations.

Kitty caught up on him outside the hall door. 'Where are you going, Thomas?'

He looked at her without replying, his face livid, nostrils flaring. 'I don't know,' he said. And then collecting himself, 'I'm going to make arrangements to take Dorene away—I can't leave her here.'

'You can, Thomas. You can! Where would you take her to now?'

'Kitty, my plans are all upset. I can't come back here again. I'll send you an address in a couple of days. Could you let one of the girls take Dorene to me?'

'I'll take her to you myself, Thomas.' She threw her arms about him, tears streaming down her cheeks. 'Oh, Thomas, I've

557

read that there is no war so bitter as the war of brothers. I never thought such a state should come to pass between us!' She watched him go and remembered watching him another time as he walked away from their cottage after bringing them food and cheer in the famine desolation. He had looked back and called something to them in Latin from the Mass. And he had called it to them again when he had watched the emigrant ship taking them to America; taking them away from her. She said the words after him now. 'Sursum Corda.' Thomas stopped. She saw the tenseness of his face soften into the old smile. He raised his soft hat and the heart inside him responded to the words she had given him back.

'Sursum Corda!' Lift up your hearts!

CHAPTER 53

People in the street were pointing in the direction of the Templetown Assembly Rooms. A flag was being slowly hoisted over its roof. Soon a furious pair of elbows was flaying through the gathering crowd and the Scout was demanding newses right and left.

'Who won?' he clamoured as the Stars and Stripes ballooned out to their fullest to proclaim the first great battle of the American Civil War.

It was with proud feelings that he heard that the Federals had won at Bull Run, was not his son with the 69th, under Captain Thomas Francis Meagher? 'Why wasn't I told?' he demanded fiercely. But soon he was told without seeking. A Canadian ship arrived at an Irish port three days later with details of the battle of Fredericksburg where more than 10,000 of Meagher's Irish Brigade had perished. The Scout's son was among them. He groped in his tails for his handkerchief to mop his streaming eyes. 'He has paid his debt to America,' he said.

Lady O'Carroll and Sterrin came to call on him. There was an air of comfort in the little house due to the money that had been sent so regularly by the lad whose body lay buried so far away. Sterrin was startled to glimpse in the room beyond the kitchen the symbols of a wake. A bed was covered with the finest white linen and draped with black crepe. A candle burned at its four corners and women keened and prayed about it though it held only a soldier's badge and rosary beads.

'These are his earthly remains,' said the Scout, indicating the beads and badge. 'It was a kind thought on the part of young Mike Hennessey, to send them to me. Your Ladyship will remember young Mike, the Master's nephew?' Sterrin nodded. Big John, another relative, had told her that Mike had won his officer's sword and shoulder badges on the battlefield.

'It is a most compressive day, your Ladyships,' said the Scout, and Sterrin was glad that the presence of a body was not

559

added to the 'compressiveness' of the wake.

'It was such a day as this that the Reverend Mr. Sealy Debenham, the Protestant minister, God rest him, carried me all the way from here to the hospital in his arms, as though I were a baby; and he a lad of sixteen years. The poor Vicar was dead in a week with the famine fever he caught from me and I walked out of the quarry where I had been left to die, cured.'

He bowed them to the door of their carriage like a grandee. 'It was gracious of you, Lady Sterrin, to step out of your own sorrow to visit me in mine. Have they apprehended the pulpit yet?'

'Pulpit?' Sterrin had almost forgotten the Scout's misplaced pedantry. Before she solved his question he looked up at the sky.

'Oh, the pulpit.' She shook her head.

'Why, I wonder, was my boy spared that untimely death under his native sky only to meet one as untimely beneath a foreign sky? Why? But there's no use in askin' life a question beforehand. A body has to live it first and find the answer later; too late, maybe.'

The Scout's profundities found an echo in Sterrin's mind as she drove out of the lane. Too frequently did she ask herself why, when she reflected upon the useless sacrifice of her marriage. She had benefited no one. She felt like telling the Scout that you don't find the answer even after you have lived your inexplicable experiences.

Two dashing-looking officers walked past while the carriage was halted outside a shop. She heard one of them say, 'Which of them is the young widow?' She was dressed in the same black drapes as her mother. She was the identical height. Even the distinction of being a trifle slimmer was denied her by all the clustering drapes and weeds.

'I might as well be forty instead of twenty-two,' she thought and, forgetting her scars, flung the veils right back over her crepe bonnet. They slowed almost to a standstill. It had been intriguing to speculate upon what lay behind the dark screen of dual widowhood; their first impression was of vivid beauty and then they stared—crudely. Gradually, through her remoteness and her weeds, Lady O'Carroll became aware of the scrutiny of two strange military gentlemen on the sidewalk. Behind her crepe barriers she frowned with the effort of trying to recall if they were old acquaintances. But instinct rushed over the bogging fences of memory and reassured her that no gentleman of her acquaintance would think of staring at her that way. A sound beside her drew her eyes to the spectacle of her daughter's unveiled face. 'Sterrin!' she gasped. 'Cover your face immediately!'

Sterrin drew down the veil and turned her head towards the window beside her. They drove out of the town in silence. About two miles outside, Lady O'Carroll turned suddenly at the sound of a sob.

'Why, Sterrin, darling!'

Sterrin was quivering from head to foot. She pulled angrily away from her mother.

'How could you be so cruel,' she sobbed, 'to order me like that to cover my face. I—I had forgotten when I raised my veil that I look like a monster.'

Her mother was astonished. 'Sterrin, I never dreamed of your poor face. I was thinking of the impropriety of a widow unveiling in public before she is at *least* two years bereaved——'

'I've never been even two *minutes* bereaved,' Sterrin said.

Cousin Maurice was waiting for them at the castle. Sterrin had come to associate the visits of her cousin with the mortgage or the probable sale of Kilsheelin. With funerals too, Papa's, and Jocelyn's and, as far as she was concerned, her own wedding had been a funeral to justify a visit. She was sure that this time it must be the mortgage.

Dominic thought the same when he returned home after dinner with Lord Cullen and Captain Fitzharding-Smith. Dominic shouldered off the suggestion that he should join Cousin Maurice in the library to discuss business.

'I mustn't neglect my guests. Forget business, Cousin Maurice, and join us in a rubber.'

'Well, read that first,' said his cousin, handing him an official-looking document.

Dominic whistled. 'As bad as that! It's all Sterrin's fault,' he said childishly.

'Your sentiments do you no credit, Dominic. Your sister has done her part. God! When I think of that child's face when she returned here.'

'Nevertheless,' said her brother angrily, 'it is damnably hard to hear the things that are being said about her.'

'Who said anything about Sterrin?' Maurice's voice was roaring the words as the pair entered the drawing-room.

'So you've heard?' said Patrick Cullen, seating himself at the card table and stretching his lame leg out on a chair. Maurice stood still. Patrick looked so obviously like someone who had let the cat out of the bag; and Captain Fitzharding-Smith was raising his eyebrows and coughing in a warning kind of way. Dominic took up the cards and shuffled them.

'Come, Maurice!' said Dominic dealing them out.

Captain Fitzharding-Smith almost grabbed a hand. 'What shall we play for? Your usual, Dominic? Though I vow I've no livestock in my purse.'

'Faith, then,' replied Dominic, 'I've no ready cash in *my* purse; it has got to be the usual; a sheep a point and a bullock on the rubber.'

Maurice threw down the cards. 'I won't play for stock. There is little enough of it on the land as it is.'

Sterrin came in and stood behind him. She had often seen Maurice play away a whole herd. This must have something to do with whatever Dominic had been saying to him about herself.

'Look here,' he said, 'what is all the mystery? You are not afraid to lose a sheep or a few bullocks. Who said what about me? Out with it! I'm going to know.' She turned to Dominic. 'Come on, Dominic, you'll tell me if I have to shoot it out of you!'

Her choice of threat caught the unsubtle Patrick off guard. 'There's been enough of shooting for one day,' he said and immediately drenched his treacherous tongue with a long drink of port that emptied a full goblet.

Out came the story. Dominic had fought a duel over Sterrin, that very afternoon. He had spied the carriage and as it emerged from Love Lane and had reined-in in time only to overhear the officers' remark about his sister's face.

Dominic wasn't sure whether Sterrin was going to faint or explode. He put an arm around her. 'I—I'm sorry I didn't kill the bounder,' he said in his gentle voice. Maurice regained his lost composure.

'Don't talk nonsense, boy! Duelling is no longer a pastime. It is murder. Why didn't you stop it, Basil? As for you, Patrick, you ought to have had more sense.'

Patrick was getting a bit muddled and muttered something

562

about chivalry and loyalty to one's friends. And Captain Fitz-harding-Smith, it seemed, had galloped, hell for leather, after the two officers immediately he got wind of the affair. By the time he had arrived at the rendezvous the offending party was nursing a wounded elbow. 'Went through clean as a whistle,' said Patrick and began tittering in a way that was irritatingly reminiscent of old Lord Cullen.

'Stop laughing, Patrick,' snapped Sterrin, 'I don't relish being the subject of your amusement.'

Patrick choked, halfway down another goblet. 'Hoity-Toity!' he spluttered. 'You are a nice one to talk. I'll wager you amused His Imperial Majesty with your hand-springs and what not.' His fuddled brain was trying to sieve some salacious titbit about Sterrin's sojourn in Paris.

Sterrin took a quick turn into the centre of the room, pulled off her belt and tied her skirts around her knees with it.

'Look!' she said briefly. Before they realised what she was about she had swept up her arms and the next moment a pair of shapely legs in plaid stockings were weaving high in the air. She walked on her hands till the tips of her toes set the dangling glasses of the chandelier chiming. 'Now,' she panted, straightening up, 'there is the sum total of my behaviour in front of the Emperor. And it was at the Empress's *soirée*. The Emperor only surprised us at the finish. Does that justify duels and gossip and the loss of a lady's reputation? Does it?' she blazed, untying her skirts and pushing back her hair into its snood.

Captain Fitzharding-Smith and Maurice O'Carroll, looking into the fearless eyes, wide and dark with anger, could readily imagine the harmless romp that had caused such pother.

Dominic, at any other time would have relished the performance. But the remark that had really made him fight the duel was not one about a frolicsome somersault. There had been an oblique reference to an actor; something about his being surprised in a bedroom—with his sister! It was, of course, unthinkable. All his life he had looked up to Sterrin; followed her lead in every prank. He fought with her, most of the time; but he revered her. She would never be capable of anything so furtive, or messy. Still, he had argued all evening to himself, her husband had been a bit long in the tooth, and Sterrin was so hellishly good looking. It wasn't for turning somersaults that she had been cut out of that heritage of delicious wealth. There must have been something. He, too, looked into her indignant eyes and knew that he would never challenge her.

Did she know, he wondered, how much slanderous gossip she courted? It had been less malicious when it had been assumed that she was an extremely wealthy young widow. Now that it had been established that she had been completely disinherited the gossips were saying 'I told you so' and telling more so. How could an old man wreak vengeance upon anyone so young and sweet! His eye ran over the morsel of lace edging on the snood that restrained her chignon. It was the merest concession towards the widow's cap.

'Sterrin,' said Cousin Maurice, 'you promised to show me that talking contraption that Tom Steele invented.'

A crate from Kilkenny, that someone had thought contained some of Lady Devine's packed clothing, had been found on arrival at Kilsheelin to contain a Talking Machine that Sir Jocelyn had ordered before his death. Captain Fitzharding-Smith was diverted.

'I didn't know that Mr. Steele was an inventor,' he said.

'Indeed he was,' said Maurice, 'he has contributed most valuable improvements to this new incandescent lighting. There was a great inventor lost in him only he insisted upon traipsing after lost causes. Back in 1820 he was on the track of something in artificial lighting that has only been discovered recently by the modern scientists. But nothing would do for him but go off and help the Spanish patriots against Frederick VII.'

The gentlemen gathered round as she assembled the different parts. 'Mr. Steele didn't invent this,' she explained, 'he was carrying out experiments upon it before he died.'

Dominic's carefully assumed *sang-froid* was tilted to an open-mouthed amazement, when suddenly a human voice—a man's—came singing from the speaking trumpet. A woman's voice joined in, but the mingled words grew shrill and out of tune. Sterrin turned the winch frantically and the voices sang in tune to the end.

'By Jove,' exclaimed the captain, 'that's incredible! I've never heard anything like it. I've heard attempts in Paris, but they were scarcely recognisable. They haven't got that far in America yet.'

Cousin Maurice was so dumbfounded that Sterrin offered to wind him into speech. 'It is not right,' he said at last. 'It is taking an ungodly liberty. Our bodies are the temples of the Holy Ghost. I don't believe that it was ever envisaged in the Divine scheme of creation that man should extract that portion of the body that is the human voice and put it, for amusement, into a—a joke like that!' He sat back and mopped his forehead. 'Is there any more to it?' Curiosity oozed through his disapproval.

Sterrin removed the disc and put in another. Out of the machine, with startling suddenness, came a weird voice that just missed being sepulchral, owing to the tinny *timbre* of the mechanism.

'You are engaged in blood,' said the voice, 'and are strengthening the enemies of your long suffering country——'

'My God,' breathed Maurice, 'it is Steele himself——'

'Now I address these words to you in the hope that, through the power of science, my voice may come to you and direct you from your folly. The prophetic utterance of the Liberator has come true. Before his lamented death, he said, "I shall not be six months in my grave before the flag of rebellion will be unfurled in Ireland"——'

'Stop it, Sterrin! Stop it, for God's sake,' cried Maurice.

She lifted the rotary spike from the groove. Dominic's face was white. 'Is it—is it one of those spiritualist things, a mechanical séance medium?' he asked shakily.

'Not at all, Dominic,' she assured him, 'Mr. Steele was just experimenting with his own voice to test the machine. That is the way he used to address the Whiteboys during the Repeal Movement.'

A knock at the drawing-room door brought Nurse Hogan to say that her Ladyship had got the impression that she had heard singing and in view of Lady Sterrin's recent bereavement—— She looked at the closed piano. Over in its corner the great harp stood as silent as ever. Some of her Ladyship's hallucinations, she thought, as she withdrew. She returned to say that her Ladyship had some embroidery silk and other materials ready for her cousins in Virginia for Mr. Maurice to send off. Nurse Hogan would bring them down straight away as her Ladyship might not be up when he would be leaving in the morning.

'I doubt,' said Maurice, when she had gone, 'if there is much use in sending any more gifts. I've had absolutely no acknowledgements and I've sent two separate consignments of stuff to

Virginia. They used to acknowledge by the first possible boat.'

'It is like the famine days,' said Fitzharding-Smith, 'only the situation is reversed. Now Ireland is sending food and things to America.'

'With the difference that then every ship on the sea was co-operating to get the stuff here. Now they are trying to prevent a little humane help getting to the South—— Look, Patrick is falling asleep. Call the carriage.' Maurice turned back at the door. 'Sterrin, for God's sake get rid of that contraption. Destroy it. It may be scientific, but it is also diabolical. There is something irreverent about letting the voice of a dead man be heard after the grave has closed over him.'

When the gentlemen had gone, she stood looking down at the machine. She put her finger abstractedly on the rotary arm. Nurse Hogan shifted the bulky packet to open the drawing-room door. Her Ladyship had made up a lot of little luxuries and elegancies for her cousins, the O'Regans of Virginia. The poor ladies must miss their comforts. And they used to be so kind; sending all that food during the famine. 'Twas to be hoped that Mr. Maurice would be able to get it out from the Strand of the Little Music to some America-bound ship.

She peered into the shadowy drawing-room. There was no one there. She could have sworn that she had heard a voice. Sterrin, on a mischievous impulse, stepped back behind the window embrasure. Nurse Hogan took another step and froze. In the empty space a terrible voice was saying over and over—'I shall not be six months in my grave—I shall not be six months in my grave.' She dropped the parcel and ran screaming from the room.

Hegarty came rushing in. 'Twasn't like Nurse Hogan to be-have queer except in a very bad storm. Mother of God! She was telling the truth! He turned with a wailing gasp and collided with Pakie Scally. They grappled with each other to get away from the ghostly voice that repeated over and over 'I-shall-not-be-six-months-in-my-grave——' until the instrument jammed and ran out.

The following day was perfect for the regatta on Lough Dergh; the air was clear, the water sparkling. Sterrin's black bombazine was conspicuous among the gay coloured gowns of the other ladies. It proclaimed more than her widowhood and its identity. It suggested heartlessness and lack of respect for the convention, her venturing to a festivity after so recent a bereavement, but what could be expected! It also gave excuses for coy glances towards the fair good looks of Dominic.

'It doesn't look quite *de rigueur*,' said Dominic withdrawing his eyes from the brown ones that ogled invitingly from beneath a red parasol.

'I quite agree,' said his sister, 'a *red* parasol over that complexion is disastrous!'

'Don't be catty. I mean your being here.'

Sterrin trailed her fingers through the waters. Like the sparkling waters, she refused to be ruffled. A military band was playing the *Cricket's Ramble Through the Hearth*. There was a sort of kinship between her and this lake. Once upon a time the O'Carroll chief had been known as the Lord of Lough Dergh and its lakes and waters where they would have their hamper lunch was full of their family lore.

'I say, Sterrin, you really do have no regard for conventions. I suppose that's from being so much in the kitchen. I remember the way you used to trail about after that chap who cleaned the knives.' It was a shot in the dark but he noticed that her hand came out of the water with a sudden jerk. 'I just barely remember him,' said Dominic. 'Didn't some of the servants say he became an actor?'

Something stirred in his mind. An actor! The officer he had challenged had made an unsavoury reference to an actor and— Lady Devine. Sterrin! The way she removed her hand from the water! Her face had gone still. She had been so vivid. All the way along she had been gay and full of laughing reminiscence and despite the black veil she looked like a schoolgirl in her ridiculous little straw bonnet.

A shot went off for the start of a race. Sterrin turned her head glad of the excuse not to answer. If Dominic were to guess! But Dominic was guessing already. He was adding two and two and almost making five. Ye gods! A servant! He had often thought his sister was an enigma. Especially when her face went remotely still like it was now. So that was why she had never seemed to bother about the men who hovered about her! That's why she didn't trouble to make more of a success of her marriage!

They picnicked on an island. Sterrin showed Dominic the

spot that was haunted by Teresa De Burgha and the last O'Carroll to hold the title of Lord of Lough Dergh. Young Lord O'Carroll had come to keep a tryst with Teresa, daughter of the De Burgha, the Norman Chief, who had seized his property. De Burgha bored holes in O'Carroll's boat, not knowing that his daughter planned to elope in it. The lovers were drowned as they eloped and their shadows were supposed to haunt the waters.

'The O'Carrolls were not fortunate in their loves,' she concluded dreamily.

'What about Mamma and Papa?' he asked. 'Their romance had a lake for its setting, the Lake of Nightingales. They were very happy.'

'But not for long,' said Sterrin. 'Mamma can never forget her lost happiness,' and to herself she murmured, 'but at least she had it, however short it lasted.'

Dominic had no more doubts. Ye gods! She was still hankering after a servant-cum-actor! As Mamma loved Papa! But Papa was a great gentleman. He almost said it to her.

'I wish,' he said instead, 'that I had known the people you used to know, the bard and all his stories, but most of all Papa. I remember so little of him.'

'He was a lovely Papa,' said Sterrin and then she spoke his own thoughts aloud, 'and he was a very great gentleman.'

Dominic lay back on the sward and closed his eyes. Sterrin's remarks about Papa set him thinking. She was the replica of her father. Her standards were as high; her assessments as keen. If she loved an inferior, he could be no inferior person. He tried to recall something of the chap. Tall, well set up; well spoken too, as good with horses as Big John, more deft in the house than Hegarty. Now that he bothered to recollect him, Dominic recalled that he had become a sort of young major domo before he went away. Egad! Was that why Mamma had urged Sterrin to marry Devine?

As they started the homeward drive they found the roads thronged with people moving against them. Not the regatta onlookers but farmers, peasants and shopkeepers. There was a good flow of smart phaetons. Among the horsemen she recognised Donal Keating. He passed the carriage looking straight ahead. Dominic hailed a barrister friend to ask him what it was all about. He tried to halt but was borne on by the crush. Suddenly

568

the landau came to a standstill and Big John clambered stiffly down and examined the horses' feet. One of them had cast a shoe. 'There's a forge not fifty yards down the road,' a gentleman passing in a phaeton pointed back. As he pointed a tall, broad-shouldered man pushed towards them. He raised his hat to the occupants of the carriage and then turned to Big John. 'I don't doubt but it is to my forge you are pointing. It's sorry I am to disappoint you, but it is closed till the meeting is over.'

The crowds were heading for a meeting on the slopes of Slievenamon. 'But surely,' said Dominic, 'that is not sufficient cause to leave us stranded. We have fifteen miles to travel. I am Sir Dominic O'Carroll.'

The man raised his hat again. 'I would be proud any other time to oblige an O'Carroll of Ely O'Carroll, but this is no ordinary meeting, sir. High officers from the American War will speak and Mr. Kickham will preside at the meeting——'

'The writer—the man who writes for the *Irish People*, in Dublin?' asked Dominic.

'Yes, sir, there are other writers to speak also. Mr. O'Leary and Mr. Thomas Clark-Lubey——' Dominic turned to Sterrin.

'Mr. Lubey is a scholar of Trinity. I've heard about him.' He turned to the blacksmith. 'You will only miss a few moments of your meeting by shoeing our horse. Your attitude is scarcely obliging.'

The man took out a heavy watch. 'I cannot afford to miss these few moments, Sir Dominic.' There was an independence in the friendly tone. 'I happen to be on the committee of the meeting.'

He did not miss Dominic's raised brows, 'But,' he continued, 'if you would like to attend it, there is a short cut down a boreen at the back of my field. You could wait there away from the crowd. I think of the young lady waiting——'

'You won't keep me waiting,' said Sterrin, standing up, 'I'm going to the meeting.' She reached him her hand but the blacksmith cupped her waist with his great hands and swung her to the ground delightedly. Dominic sat on for a moment in dignity then found himself following his sister's lead as he had done all his life. As they passed through the empty forge he nudged Sterrin towards a stack of newly-forged pikes leaning against a corner.

'Nice peaceful implements for a forge! So that's why they

have a blacksmith on their committee!'

'For that matter,' said Sterrin, 'they have a blacksmith's son on their committee in America. Look at Mr. Lincoln!'

'Where is he?' For a panting moment as they climbed the slopes of Slievenamon, Dominic thought she had seen the President of America among the many bronze-faced men whose complexions and accents were so unmistakably American.

The blacksmith clove a path through and they followed him to the summit. Dominic marvelled that there was no condescension in the leaders' greeting to the blacksmith. All of them bore the stamp of breeding and culture. The American officers were big, stern-looking men with countenances aged too soon as the price of bloody victories in the battlefields of their adopted country.

On the faces of the spectators there was a grim purposefulness that had not been on those who had attended O'Connell's Monster meetings. These people had lived through an experience that O'Connell's followers had not known. They had suffered the Great Hunger and they had witnessed the Great Death. Now they were living through the Great Exodus of the evictions that was draining away the life of the nation.

Sterrin recognised the faded Repeal Button in the lapels of many of the older men. But these men were no longer interested in Repeal, only in the ownership of the soil that was their birth's heritage and their life's labour, that they now held with less right of tenure than rabbits. They had come to this meeting on Slievenamon Mountain, 15th August 1863, as members of the new Tenant League, hoping to hear of some plan or purpose to help them resist being made beggars, landless and houseless under the government system of eviction.

The speakers were outspoken in their criticism of O'Connell. To Sterrin, born in the reign of the Liberator and nurtured in his Repeal doctrine, they sounded profane. She studied the elegant form and features of Thomas Clark-Lubey, the patriotic son of a Protestant minister; reared in the airs of an ascendency household, prejudiced against Ireland but passionately espousing its cause; noted the arched brows, the bright eyes, gloomy and glorious as a poet's dream. Dominic listened avidly to the polished sentences shaped by a refined, subtle intellect. Clark-Lubey told the great assembly that Ireland should no longer sit weeping over the tombs of her hopes and her wrongs. He urged them without florid oratory to bestir themselves and waste no further time recounting the centuries of their country's misgovernment. The remedy lay within themselves. And Dominic, gazing about him saw to his amazement that the people knew what he meant and were filled with grim assent.

'Better for men to die as men than as paupers! Can the outcome of any struggle be any worse than to be driven from the families they love? The homes they adore...?'

In some countries, such a speech might be the prelude to fame and honour, here it was likely to be a prelude to the gallows.

Dominic was drinking in every word. Sterrin too. These words recalled the terrible evictions from those Kilkenny farmsteads. To her dying day she would never forget the spectacle of the dead boy; of the blood on face and hands, on the cobblestones and door lintel, where it proclaimed his pitiful struggle for the simple right to shelter in a home.

The writer Kickham spoke about the two-fold purpose of the assembly; land rights and leases and fee-simples and other legal terms that Sterrin scarcely understood. He said that the second purpose of their meeting upon this mountain was to declare their resolution of labouring to the death for the liberty of their enslaved country. Kickham had the weapon of the famine. He pointed it down the rich slopes of Slievenamon to the verdant valleys and yellow cornlands of the Golden Vale. He bade his audience look.

Down beneath them the silver waters of the Suir defined the broad golden acres. In that silent moment both men and crops were listening. The warm August wind sent a whispering ripple that only the crops could hear. It was a scene of peace and plenty. Men gazed and remembered the hunger they had known amid its richness. Down there men had died of starvation—in a year when forty-five million pounds worth of food had been produced. The absent landlords had taken possession of that harvest when the tenants had neither substance nor seed. Now the new landlords were taking possession of their homes!

An American officer with one armless sleeve stepped forward. He spoke of the work of the Fenian movement in America, of the great outdoor gatherings, that pledged support to Ireland, to hasten here at the first stir of revolt; to take up arms against England if she went to war against the United States.

He held up a green flag, and when the cheering ceased he told them that when the horse of Captain Thomas Francis Meagher had been shot from beneath him he had jumped to the nearest parapet and pointed with his sword.

' "Boys," he cried, through the storm of bullets, "look at that flag and remember Fontenoy——" '

The officer couldn't go on for cheering. 'Listen,' he cried, 'there was only one insubordinate man that day. A young lad emigrated by eviction from that valley below you. When the colonel ordered him to lower the flag because it was too conspicuous, he said: "No, sir, I'll never lower it". A bullet killed him immediately but before the flag could fall from his hand another man sprang to retrieve it. It went from hand to hand as they fell; but not a man in the regiment would lower it.'

Sterrin knew a moment of panic as the great storm of cheers surged across the mountain and went echoing down in the valley round her. Her brother put an arm about her and their two hearts quickened to the same exaltation as they looked at the tall captain holding the green flag in his left hand. Behind him another officer upheld the Stars and Stripes.

Later, as the blacksmith shoed their horse, he told them that the American captain had lost his right arm as he swooped to retrieve the flag when the last of his company fell.

The landau rolled homeward behind the horses' leisurely clop-clop. Its steady rhythm beat into the day's fatigue, the heads of brother and sister lolled backwards and forwards till they rested in sleep against the cushions.

It was the sudden silence as wheels and hooves passed over the grass at the crossroads that awakened them.

'Jove!' exclaimed Dominic. 'Are we here already? I must have been asleep. The excitement of the meeting and the long climb tired me.'

'It wasn't meant to make people sleep,' said Sterrin. 'It impressed me as a—a kind of awakening.'

'For heaven's sake, Sterrin,' said Dominic. 'Why should people like us become involved? We've never evicted. We've never rackrented——'

'I have,' said Sterrin in a low voice. 'I'll never forget the reproachful way they looked; all those women and those exhausted children; and that poor little boy. I can't shut out the sight of him running from me the last time I saw him alive.' A sob shuddered up and she put her hands over her face.

Dominic was dismayed. Sterrin never gave way to tears. She had always been his strength; the one who had dried his own young tears. He moved over beside her, gently drew down her hands and proffered a handkerchief. He had been feeling just a tiny bit of a fool over that damned duel yesterday. But now by God, he'd like to fight it over again.

The gate lodge-keeper rose stiffly as the landau rounded the bend. He didn't want to be caught with his ear to the ground like a gossoon. But he was getting a bit hard of hearing and every carriage had its own sound. There was a time when he'd known all the family vehicles by their rumble in the ground before they'd reach the cross. Sterrin returned the handkerchief as they drove in the gates. For want of something more comforting to say, Dominic told her to keep it for another while in case she'd want it again.

That night Dominic fell asleep over his claret. Sterrin stood a moment looking down at the chiselled features, the fair hair that waved softly back, the fragile look stirred a chord of tenderness. The duel had established its strain before the meeting and played on his emotion—both their emotions.

'Come on, old chap,' she said, 'I'll give you a hand upstairs when I have quenched these damned candles. I wish Mamma would consent to have lamps.'

Upstairs, when they had said good night, Dominic said suddenly, 'Do you know, Sterrin, that must have been a horrible experience for you, that monster eviction and that poor boy. Sir Jocelyn can't have been such a nice person as I thought. He was always so jolly decent to me: slipped me a tenner every time. And you seemed to be having such high jinks. And then to be left high and dry without a bean! It's like bequeathing an insult to a lady; a public accusation from the grave.' He stopped struggling with a knotted bootlace.

'Accusation of what?' Sterrin stooped down. 'Here let me help you with that lace.'

'Do you know,' he went on, 'all those chaps today, and those American officers; they all seem to have a sort of dedicated spirit. There's a terrible antithesis in this business of tens of thousands of Irishmen slaughtering each other in America, the ones in the North against the ones in the South. I suppose it's a sort of reverberation of all the evils they have suffered here, the famine and the evictions.' He chucked the other bootlace and made another knot. 'I keep on thinking of them. The way they placed the flag above their own lives. Being killed didn't matter as much as keeping the flag afloat. It made me think how little we value our flag, the genuine pre-conquest flag, and what it must have cost our ancestors in blood and valour to earn the right to hoist it over the house. Yet we seem to be detached from all this struggle; sitting smug because we are safe.'

'Safe!' hooted Sterrin, 'we're nearly out of the door.'

'Oh, surely not?'

'Didn't you see the billet Maurice brought last night?' She yawned and stretched. 'We're never but a step away from the auctioneer's hammer. Go to bed, dear Dominic. At least tonight we know we have a roof over our heads.' And tomorrow, she thought, I will find out more about the Fenians.

CHAPTER 54

Through the blue cloud of smoke that had settled across the frozen plains, Captain Thomas O'Carroll saw a sea of brave, green nosegays. Wave after wave of green sprigs like offshoots of the boughs of peace that had made a moving forest of human beings marching peacefully to Tara. But the wearers of these nosegays were not marching to Tara; nor to Peace. It was the Irish Brigade swinging up towards the Confederate position on the high ridge west of Fredericksburg.

Behind him, Thomas heard his men muttering, 'By God, we're for it. They are Meagher's men!' And then from beyond the stone wall where Thomas's men were waiting a voice rang out. Thomas had heard that voice for the first time as he sat on the carriage outside Conciliation Hall just before the blight. 'Abhor the sword?' Meagher had said. 'Stigmatise the sword? No, my Lord, for at its blow and in the crimson of its quivering glance a giant nation sprang up from the waters of the Atlantic——' And now, before him at Mayre's Heights in Fredericksburg, sword in hand, at the head of the Irish Brigade of the Union Army was Meagher of the Sword.

'It's Greek to Greek today, boys!' cried that orator of revolution. Thomas, recalling his Euripides groaned, 'In Greece, alas, how ill things ordered are!' And he led his men to give battle against the hero of his youth; to lower the flag of the land that had given succour and asylum to millions of his countrymen.

Waves of Irish charged forward, many to meet their fellow countrymen, man to man, eye to eye, bayonet to bayonet. One of Thomas's officers, Lieutenant Hubert De Lacey, suddenly found himself face to face with Tim Lonergan, who was carrying the green flag of Meagher's gallant Irish troops.

In spite of the tumult, the noise, the men falling all around, Hubert recognised the flag-bearer instantly and shouted, 'Tim Lonergan.' The wounded Federal did not recognise his boyhood's companion, matured and unfamiliar in the Confederate uniform. But there was no doubt as to the identity of the Captain who rushed with revolver levelled to give Tim the *coup de grâce*. Uniform did not confuse *this* identity. It sharpened the sense of familiarity. For Tim had seen this young man in another uniform, the blue-grey with royal blue facings and gilt buttons, the servant's livery of the O'Carrolls. The Captain lowered his gun as the wounded Tim gasped out the nameless name of his servitude.

Hubert De Lacey, half kneeling, watched the trail of blood as Tim Lonergan staggered back to his men, colours dipping and swaying, but never falling from his grasp. There came to him in that unlikely place the memory of young Tim Lonergan beckoning him mysteriously up a steep path that led to that rare find, a sparrow-hawk's nest. High above two fierce eyes had singled out a prey and swooped. Backwards and forwards a curlew twisted in the sparrow-hawk's grip; but its tender breast was ripped off neatly as though done with a knife, a bayonet. The rest of its body was left untouched and a faint trail of beads of blood led towards the nest. Hubert had felt the same squeamish feeling that he felt as he watched the trail of blood that marked Tim Lonergan's staggered dash back to his regiment.

'But he held on to the flag. Every time it dipped to the ground it came up again with a fresh splodge of blood,' he said to Captain O'Carroll in the field hospital where they both lay wounded, prisoners of the Federal Army. Irishmen from both sides, the wounded, the captured, lay about them in the crowded tent. From every state, from every city, town and village, from the forests they had cleared; from the hills and plains and prairies that their toil and industry had created; from the mine, from the desk, wherever the Irish were, they obeyed the summons of their adopted country. North or South, they had not paused to argue the righteousness of the cause. They had acted as they felt; with the community with which they lived. The Irish of the South standing with the state to which they felt they owed their first allegiance; each side of the line loving America; each fighting with two-fold purpose, the claim of the country of their adoption and the honour of the country of their birth.

'It was when he discarded the bough of peace that he learned how to cling to the bloodstained flag of war,' said Captain

O'Carroll. Lieutenant De Lacey turned quickly.

'Did you know him?' For Hubert had never associated that tall, broad-shouldered officer in the grey uniform with the blue liveried youth who used to hold little Sterrin O'Carroll's pony on a leading rein when she came to visit his sister Bunzy.

Thomas lay on the straw with his hands behind his head and thought back through the years to the night when he had been posted in the darkness to turn back the men who came marching to Clontarf; every one armed with the bough of peace. He could see, despite its dust mask, the hurt, angry look on Tim Lonergan's face as he cast the futile peace bough from him and turned for home. O'Carroll's peaceful caution had spared Tim for the death storm at Marye's Heights at Fredericksburg!

'I knew the parent bough of the green sprig that he wore.' Hubert was surprised at the unusual grimness in the voice of the debonair captain. 'A thousand green sprigs,' it went on, 'on a thousand bodies on the glory of another country's battlefield.'

Just then, a huge soldier in Federal uniform walked into the tent bearing a Southern soldier in his arms. Thomas thought of Milo of Crotona bearing the bronze statue of himself through the stadium to the Altis. It was John Holohan, the Chicago millionaire, from Upper Kilsheelin. His burden protested noisily that he needed no help from any damned Yankee. He proved it by sinking to the floor when he was put on his feet.

John Holohan picked him up and placed him on the straw next to Thomas, without a sign of recognition, and walked away without acknowledging the 'God Save You John', that Thomas gave him in Gaelic.

Later, Private Holohan came and squatted beside Thomas. 'I want to speak to you,' he said in gruff Gaelic. He spoke for a quarter of an hour about a task he had in mind for Thomas, a complicated mission which, if Thomas undertook it, could gain him freedom. 'Yes,' Big John concluded. 'For that purpose you will be set free.'

The Confederate Captain looked up lazily at the millionaire soldier in the Federal uniform. 'For that purpose,' he repeated, 'merely to convert the British Army to Fenianism; get British soldiers to support the Irish? Are you quite sure you have no other little commission that you would like me to take on, en route? You would not like me to break my journey and slip up to Russia to endeavour to make a Fenian out of the Czar? The

British Army in Ireland! You are not asking much! A rebel in Ireland is a felon of the lowest degree; fit only for hanging, flogging or deportation—or all three. A rebel in America is a gallant Southern gentleman.'

'You ought to know.' John's face had gone grim again. 'You chose to become one of them. Why, it beats me to think.'

Thomas replied that it beat him, also, to think of being asked to go to Ireland to help free it from British thraldom, 'while over here you try your damndest to trample the liberties of a people fighting for their independence; fighting, like the Irish at home, against complete extermination.'

'Will you go?'

'If I do not, since I may not continue to slaughter my fellow countrymen, I suppose the alternative is to be held prisoner? And you, I suppose, will continue in the holy cause of the slaves who are better fed and housed than Irish peasants.'

'Will you go?' asked John grimly. 'Will it make a difference if I tell you Sir Jocelyn has been murdered and Sterrin is ill. I had it from my mother last week.'

Thomas did not answer. Sterrin's husband dead?

'Will you go?' John asked for the third time.

YES, the answer roared through his brain. I'll go now; to my little white love! He even made a movement of his wounded foot. Pain brought reasoning. He moistened his lips. They were suddenly parched; for water; for the touch of vivid soft lips that glowed from a bridal veil?

'Give me time,' he said.

'Time!' John Holohan almost spat the word. 'They are too fond of time in the old country. That's not the way to get things done over here.'

'No?' Thomas smiled mockingly to cover the thudding of his heart. 'Has this great Union discovered some other element?'

'Ach! You haven't to look over your shoulder for a word. And you know how to use it; and to direct it. And, your profession has trained you for disguise. You are not likely to get caught straight off the boat like the other chaps we sent over.'

'Speaking of disguise, perhaps you could procure something to disguise my feet. They look so obvious without boots. Mine were removed for my leg to be dressed. They have vanished.'

The millionaire soldier who refused to become an officer while pouring his wealth into the Federal funds—and now into the

578

Fenian funds—could procure most things. Once Thomas's foot had healed, John Holohan procured all the essentials to assure Thomas's safe transit to New York where he played in a Command Performance for Colonel Michael Corcoran of the 69th Regiment, back from his long imprisonment in Richmond.

New York staged the greatest public display that the city had ever seen for Corcoran, a brave Irishman whose regiment had fought a glorious battle. Under the shower of bouquets, in the midst of the handshaking and speeches Corcoran turned to speak to Thomas about his mission to Ireland. Briefly he outlined a plan of campaign. He talked rapidly in between frequent interruptions by dignitaries with testimonials. At last the din of bands and fire bells and church bells proved too much. Corcoran gave an exasperated shrug and turned towards the crowd. Thomas edged closer. He had absorbed his instructions. He wanted to say goodbye. The boat left for Ireland this very evening.

There came a lull in the clangour. Corcoran called over his shoulder.

'This,' he said, as he waved his hand at the cheering crowd, 'This is not for me. This is America on her knees to Ireland!'

There was something different about the Fenians and their plans for rebellion. They were a brave, grim-faced band. Their firmness of will and organisation were even more impressive than their oath of secrecy and the guns they smuggled in from America. They were not like the men who had followed O'Connell or Davis. Even Cousin Maurice O'Carroll noticed it in the men who waited in his cave for the long oilcloth-covered weapons that were carried from off-shore vessels.

'Do you know, Sterrin,' he had said on his last visit to Kilsheelin, 'I don't think this next affair will fail. There is a frightening efficiency about these Fenians. The men were not young hellrakes of rebels. They are old–young fired by a relentless purpose. The famine did that; cheated them out of boyhood and fun. Even the military are leaning towards Fenianism. I drank a few noggins of claret at the club the other day with a Hussar officer and by God he made no secret of his sympathy.'

Sterrin felt it too. When she visited Denis, the blacksmith who had taken Dominic and her to the meeting, she heard similar accounts of the military sympathy. Denis had administered the oath to nearly every soldier in Clonmel Barracks.

'They are ready to admit the Fenian insurgents when the time comes and fight side by side with them.'

'And when will that time come?' A man moved out of the shadows. Sterrin recognised Bergin. He always seemed to materialise from shadows. Later, Denis explained that Bergin was afraid. But it was a different fear from most. Something inside him had broken in the terrible settlement in New Zealand. He was chaffing for the first shot of revolt; prepared to die therein; but to be caught beforehand for a lesser treason and Sent Over again was a prospect that he could not face.

'Clonmel is not the only barracks to be taken over,' said Bergin. 'I've travelled all over the country organising, and everywhere I have found disaffected regiments and pregnable forts. We are at the peak hour to strike, yet James Stevens counsels us to wait, and meanwhile he writes columns of highfalutin patriotism in the *Irish People*. He is not a soldier. He is a dilettante. The time that he, and others, is hoarding will not mount up like ammunition stored. It will melt in this fever of waiting like gold in a crucible.'

'We must wait for the Americans,' the blacksmith said. 'It won't be much longer. As soon as we've helped them to dispose of their own war, they will come and help us to win ours. They've promised.'

Bergin gave something like a snort. 'I can't see it happening. The Americans are not idealists. The moment their war is over they will rush back to their factories and their shops and their offices. Their first concern will be to restore their own prosperity.'

Sterrin's exasperation with the man broke its bounds. 'Why must you be so bitter always?'

Berlin looked down at her where she sat on a rough seat near the furnace and he spoke, a stumble of words and then a cascade. Here was another depleted life, thought Sterrin as she listened, like those Cousin Maurice had spoken of, who had been rushed through the forcing house of the famine from childhood to a grim manhood. He had been in the glory of youth, an athlete, hurler, footballer, the best dancer on any crossroads platform. He described how he had got the gash on that rollicking journey to the Carlow Races. Sterrin was stunned as she realised that she had witnessed that scene from the carriage window; that here was another of her husband's victims. No wonder he hated her. Was it to punish her he was telling her this?

The wound had festered. Erysipelas had developed. Women shrank openly from the sight of his face. This was far worse, Bergin said, than the horror of the convict settlement, worse than the slavery, the starvation, the floggings, the spectacle of hangings.

Sterrin felt abused. Why must he lash this into me? Lash, lash, lash of toneless words!

'Dammit!' she rose angrily to her feet. 'The day you got that lash I was four years old—— Why should you——'

He stepped closer. 'You thought fit to ask about me being bitter. I'm sorry that I am slow at words. My own bitterness with life was cured by—by someone who loved you.' He could hear her quick intake of breath. 'A girl had promised to wait for me. I didn't think to hold her to young promises, to bring her my battered face and spirit. But *he* told me that she would be waiting for me—that . . .'

'Did he know her?'

'He knew you.'

She was startled. The quiet statement lingered in the quiet darkness.

'He based his faith in all womankind on you.'

And now it was her turn to pour forth a cascade of words. A young girl's gush of eager questions about her sweetheart. What did he say about me? Did he say I was—— How did he—— Tell me more. He didn't hear the words. They were unuttered; silent jets spraying through her hurt spirit.

'I shall never forget his anguish that day when he came and told me that the plans for the elopement were off. You were married to someone else.' The toneless words fell like stones. Where the spraying jets had bedewed was now aridity.

'He consoled himself very quickly.'

Bergin felt his own bitterness could scarcely equal hers. 'Did he get married?' He was startled out of his tonelessness.

'I assume,' she answered, 'that the woman who was with him in Paris became his wife. They were together in Switzerland, too.'

He shook his head, too surprised to speak. He knew now that he would not tell her, as he had thought, that his bitterness towards her sprang from the memory of her walking hand in hand with Donal Keating along the river; gallivanting, as he had thought, behind her husband's back.

He scraped his throat and started to frame some embarrassed apology for his misjudgment, but she had jumped to her feet. She hadn't come here to listen to his condemnation of her conduct—not his self-pitying whining. Did he expect her to stand at the coach stop every night like—like the girl who had waited for himself?

'You didn't do too bad, did you? How many men have known similar misfortunes without being crowned with such success. You were able to buy a big estate. My husband wanted to buy it.'

'That's why I bought it.'

'So that you could be within shooting distance of him?' It was one of those utterances that seemed to escape from her unaware to startle her own ears. She waited for his outburst. But as though she had never uttered the terrible charge; as though he hadn't heard, he said,

'I owe my wealth also to the man who loved you—and *because* of his love for you.' He told her the story of the mine shaft abandoned by the London clerk who had hoped to marry his employer's daughter. 'It was sympathy with the young man's hopes, because of his own aspirations, that made him go back and work it. We tried to argue him out of it.'

She sat down again. Her knees felt weak. Nothing else. And out of that shaft that Thomas had tried—for her sake, was it?—Bergin had found wealth enough to enable him to come home and shoot her husband with the maximum of security. It *must* have been he—— The hundreds of her husband's victims had diffused suspicion; it was eerie, some thread of fate linking this man with her and her husband and with young Thomas. So young Thomas had made a fortune! It wasn't just his salary as an actor! The old ache of yearning came upon her like a vapour. He had kept his promise. He had made a fortune for her. And then to go and throw it at the feet of another woman! God, how could he have comforted himself so quickly? And suddenly she thought she saw the explanation. He had probably been engaged to this girl that time when he had come to play in Kilkenny. Hadn't he said something about having been told that she herself had entered a convent!

She little knew how decorative she seemed to the two men as

she stood there, tall and graceful. Denis spoke his thoughts.

'My Lady. You do us too much honour to come here. You belong in high places. To see you there in your lovely cloak, one would think 'twas for a palace or a ball you were dressed instead of for my dirty old forge.'

He would not take the hand she offered. 'I'd dirty it with my black paws.' He displayed the big, grimy palm, all calloused and blistered. She didn't offer her hand to Bergin. Suddenly she felt that she couldn't touch the hand of her husband's murderer.

CHAPTER 55

In the month that followed, Sterrin's activities crowded out the thoughts of Thomas. There were too many victims of eviction to be succoured. Seldom a week passed that Sterrin did not journey to the scene of an eviction, her saddle-bags bulging with food. The police and military were finding her an embarrassment. It was an offence to render assistance at these operations, but Lady Devine was a haughty piece, without fear. The rank and file level regarded the heavily-veiled face with something of superstitious dread. The officers with thoughts of intrigue. Was it true that the face had been hideously disfigured? Their eyes took liberties probing the veil, admiring the lissom grace of the proud head poised on the neck like some dark blossom on its stem.

By accident, Sterrin chanced upon the eviction of Ryan Ha-Lad. The familiar thud of the crowbar reached her as she mounted the summit of a low hill.

'My God!' she spurred the horse and the next moment flung herself to the ground in time to drag an infant from beneath a lurching wall. The wall fell in on its back. It had a gay wallpaper; a tasty house, roofed with braided thatch. The falling rain bedewed the flowers on the wallpaper. Children screamed at the sight of the four walls that had held them in the happy safety of a home now lying prone and battered like murdered things. Their mother, too, lay prone. She was in the last stage of her labour; and then the heavens sided with the demolition squad. Their clouds opened and let down sheets of icy rain.

A word of command sounded above the din. Police and military assembled to march away in proud formation. Sterrin barred the way of the first line. 'You cannot leave these people like this. The woman needs immediate attention.'

'Madam,' the police officer replied, 'we are representatives of the law. We had a duty to perform and we have performed it. We are not midwives.'

She stopped herself from wasting her breath on outraged reproach. He was doltish and smug. He thought he had said something cleverly quelling. Instead she reached to the kitchen table that lay upended.

'Help me get this to that hedge,' she said. 'It will shelter her till the doctor arrives.'

His neck swelled inside his tunic. He put a shiny gloved hand to his sword hilt. He, said the gesture, was a sub-inspector of police, with sword and epaulettes and the power of life and death over men.

'Madam', he barked, 'I warn you that you are violating the law that forbids intervention or interference at evictions. Stand aside!'

He called out a word of command to his men. For answer Sterrin jerked the massive table upwards and pulled it across the front line of men. The men with right legs raised in precision for the first step were thrown backwards on the line behind. Sterrin, assisted by some of the children, continued to pull the table until it was past the men and in the shelter of the hedge. When she tried to drag the woman beneath its shelter, she shrieked with agony. Cruelly, inexorably the bony gates of life were being forced open. With the imperishable optimism of the human race, another member was thrusting and forcing, demanding, pain by pain, its right to know hunger and cold and homelessness.

'Take the baby! Miss, take the baby!' The woman must be delirious. There was no sign of a baby except the one that was trying to play with the wallpaper. 'Take it, Miss! Oh take it. It's there.'

Sterrin's heart turned over. Deliver the baby, that's what the woman meant. Nausea rose in her gorge. She had never been near a birth. Never heard the details. There was before; there was after; but there was a gross part and this was it. She dragged off her gloves. She groped down there but she couldn't look. Her eyes fixed themselves on the flowers on the wallpaper but they denied her a focus. Rain was smudging them to a running blob of colour. Her fingers touched natal slime. They cringed with repulsion. Nausea rose again. And then, miraculously her fingers found their sensitivity. They thrilled to the contact of Life, frail, quivering but substantial. A wave of exultation surged through her. Fingertips that were separate entities grew over-bold as they drew the life away from its background o mystery. The woman cried out in panic.

'The cord! Miss! Your Ladyship! The cord, you'll choke the child.'

Disgust returned. How could a woman with such a tastefu home use twine so sluttishly? Dear Lord, what was keeping Ryan Ha-Lad, her husband, with the doctor? A pleasant voic said, 'How are you managing?'

She straightened up. 'I was beginning to—to manage, but she —she seems to have got herself—got the child entangled with cord or twine or something.' It was one thing for a woman to secrete a packet of tea down the neck of her gown, but to have twine—in such a context—endangering a child's birth! 'It's most careless,' she said aloud.

'Yes, isn't it?' The doctor spared her a whimsical glance ove his shoulders. A moment later he handed her the new-born child.

'Have you never heard of the umbilical cord, Lady Devine? She hadn't, but with instant knowledge grasped his meaning. She felt a thousand prissy fools. Why had it to be like this always, she thought, while she rummaged among the scattered furniture for baby clothes? This inane reticence about the mos vital of all matters, life itself. The wonder of this mystery had never been described to her. But then who could have done it. Not her mother surely. Not the nuns at the convent.

Someone was saying something to her. She couldn't quite catch because the new baby was proclaiming its presence as loudly as if it had suddenly realised its folly in letting itself in for such an existence. Sterrin's brain felt as sodden as her cloth-ing. The only positive act she could recall having ever per-formed for a tiny baby was when she bit off Dominic's nails when no one was looking because Mrs. Stacey had said that tha would keep the fairies from getting him. She stooped in a sudden and then it occurred to her to put the baby in its mother's arms.

In the poor little happy silence of their meeting Sterrin at las managed to catch what the man was saying. Fear flooded through all the crevices of her being. Another man's voice said, 'Are you mad? Do you realise what you are saying?' Donal Keating sprang from the dogcart in which he had driven his brother-in-law to the patient. 'Do you?'

The sub-inspector did realise. He repeated his words. He said to Sterrin. 'I arrest you, in the name of the law——' He went on to talk about her obstruction of himself and of his men in the performance of their duty. He omitted to say that she had made him a fool before his men; that there had been a suppressed snigger when she had turned their parade into a burlesque. All the time that he talked she observed how the macassar on his hair resisted the raindrops; and all the time the fear hardened within her until her mind was made up. That was what she was afraid of. Not of what he might do to her, but of what she knew that she was going to do to him. 'I'll kill him,' she thought. 'I'll kill this bloodless popinjay, just as soon as it takes me to get home and get a gun. I'll shoot him through clean as a whistle.'

But there was no returning home.

Sterrin could never recall the exact moment when the handcuffs were placed on her wrists. One minute there was a void in the girdle of her arms where the little soft body had nestled. The next, they were closed together, manacled at the wrists with an iron chain. There was a vacuum silence; like the aftermath of a great blast that has swept away the air. Sterrin found her voice. 'Remove these!' She said it as though it had but to be said to be obeyed.

The officer gave a signal. Two policemen closed in on either side. Fear of a different kind swept through Sterrin. Panic! This was real. They were actually daring to lay hands on her— Sterrin O'Carroll. She didn't think of herself as Lady Devine. They were going to shut her up some place. She brought the manacled hands down over the horse's neck and tried to swing herself up. For the first time since she had learned to ride the pony with the fairy blood she bungled and staggered. For a moment she ran alongside the animal; her hands achieved the mane. With super-human strength she held on until she was in the saddle with a 'Yup Clooreen' and the mare breaking into a beautiful canter. Police and military jumped from her path. Sterrin was away.

But not for long. Scarlet uniforms and uniforms of bottle-green ran alongside. The bridle was seized. The great, black horse reared up fearsomely; uselessly.

Donal Keating, following in the phaeton, called out something about bail and rode out ahead. Later in the blockage of a drove of cattle, the strange procession caught up on him; scarlet

587

soldiers with sabres; bottle-green police with carbines; in the midst the veiled horsewoman, proud, straight-backed. The profile beneath the veil made him think of a young eagle in a close-meshed cage. He could have touched her, they were so close in the little rough road but he called out again about getting bail. She nodded silently. He could see a swallowing in her throat that made him lash the horse and blink the sudden moisture from his eyes.

Ryan Ha-Lad rode a naked donkey, no saddle or reins across field and dyke to Kilsheelin Castle. When he gave the news it was like the night of the Sir's assassination. The household was stunned with horror. Then the sound of wailing Hannah's and Mrs. Stacey's, reached Lady O'Carroll before the news itself; and like on that terrible night it was Margaret who took control. She calmed the others and went with Dominic to the gun room.

'Go instead to Mr. Hoey,' she urged. 'It is a solicitor she needs, not a gun.'

But Dominic, white-faced and grim as never before, went undeterred.

It was Mike O'Driscoll who rode like the heels of hell for Patrick Hoey, the family solicitor. Big John had gone quietly to his room, lifted a loose floorboard and taken out a brass-bound box, then ridden off in the wake of Ryan Ha-Lad's little donkey.

People said that it was like a horse fair or—God between us and all harm—a sudden illness and the friends and relatives dashing to the bedside. There seemed to be a continuous thunder of hooves up the avenue of the house of the magistrate who was holding the Summary Court. News of the arrest had flown like chaff in high wind. Ryan Ha-Lad, short-cutting through Major Darby's former estate, gasped it out to a workman. On the fastest horse in his stable Dominic Landy, the ex-convict owner, came galloping to the rescue of the woman who had succoured his mother. He tossed gold in front of the magistrate. 'Is that enough?' Dominic Landy demanded and without waiting for an answer tossed down more. On his heels came dapper little James de Guider, looking, at close quarters, not so dapper, and holding a little red money bag, not quarter full, in front of him like a child holding a bag of sweets. Pathetically aware of its inadequacy he did not say, 'Is this enough?' he merely said, 'Will this help?' Sterrin was touched to the heart

And then Big John. The towering coachman looked with stern disapproval at the sacrilegious policeman, ignored the magistrate and laid his offering before his mistress.

'Your Ladyship, I have brought the bail money. There is thirty-eight pounds and eighteen shillings here.' Poor Big John. His savings since the famine!

Sir Dominic strode into the makeshift court-room like an avenging, mudspattered god. Hand over holster. He demanded his sister's liberty; he demanded satisfaction. He threatened the law on them; the crown. He was Sir Dominic of the O'Carrolls. Release my Lady, his sister! The sub-inspector stepped forward ominously. It was looking as if there was going to be another arrest when Doctor Quigley-Greyson arrived in the midst of the outburst. He described and ridiculed the police officer's obstruction charge. Far from Lady Devine obstructing the law, she herself was obstructed in an act of humanity.

The magistrate had been feeling mildly piqued at not being able to get a squint behind that thick veil she was wearing and his gout was giving him severe pain, a fact which Sterrin had not failed to observe. When, during the doctor's recital his glances in the prisoner's direction altered, Sterrin availed of the chance to raise her veil sufficiently to allow of a delicate dab at her nostril and to cause the magistrate to reflect that if the rest of her face matched up to that mouth it must be a very beautiful one indeed.

He rounded on the officer who had brought him on gouty foot from his bed of pain and icily informed him that it was the primary duty of the police to protect life, and that instead of assisting this charitable lady in her great act of mercy he had actually obstructed; therefore, and in view of all the facts he would now, with deep apologies for the distress and humiliation inflicted upon Lady Devine, dismiss the case and rule that the bail money of one hundred pounds be returned. He lifted a cheque in the direction of a young gentleman, who stepped from the shadow of a tall policeman and, for the first time, the runners in the ransom race became aware of Donal Keating.

Outside, afterwards, Sir Dominic's tone was cool and distant as he offered his thanks to Donal.

'Of course, we couldn't have accepted...'

'We could and we did,' said Sterrin crisply. 'What did you expect me to do? Go to prison comforted by the fact that you had got yourself arrested, too? Charging in with a gun. You might at least have brought along a batch of bullocks and some sheep. Do you not think me worth as much as a few rubbers of whist?'

She could afford to rag him now that she was safe but her heart had contracted with dread at the sight of him coming in all doughty and feudal. She kissed him.

'Thank you, you darling, gallant thing.' Her voice felt a bit gravelly with tears. 'What would I have done if they had arrested you? What would Mamma have? I'm not worth risking your safety.' Before he could say anything she turned to Donal. 'And thank *you*, Donal,' she said offering her hand. 'I can never thank you enough.'

Lady O'Carroll stood at the oratory window like one of its statues. Dread had turned her heart to stone. Every few minutes she would go and kneel at the altar but she could not keep up any sustained prayer. What were they doing to Sterrin—a delicately-nurtured lady in the hands of rough police and military? And what would they do to Dominic? Dominic, her darling. Would they execute him if he used that gun?

The rain had stopped and the fragrance of the flowers blew towards her with kindness and a bird murmured sympathetically in the trees. Was that a hoof-beat? No, 'twas her imagination. Her children would never come back here again; back to the castle for which Sterrin had risked her beauty and her life. What would Roderick say? His daughter—proud, lovely— arrested like a thief. Was that a hoof-beat? There was no doubt about it this time; a great, urgent clattering of many hooves. Ah, *Sacrée Vièrge*, give me strength for what I must hear.

In through the gate rode Sterrin; beside her rode a strange young gentleman and behind—— Oh God be praised! Dominic. A whole cavalcade followed and then something like a dray with someone lying on it and children's heads bobbing and alongside the man riding the donkey again, the man who had brought the news of Sterrin's arrest.

Margaret, skimming down the stairs, absorbing things in that sentient way of hers, without concrete thought sensed that the callers in the dray cart and its outrider, had come to stay. Another family to take up residence in the fever hut like the one that Sterrin had installed there in the famine.

In the blessed relief of reunion, Lady O'Carroll did not realise

ll later that the farmerish looking man she had received in her
drawing-room and fed in her dining-room was one of her
daughter's would-be saviours, was the convict she had seen
arrested for raiding the grain carts and whose mother she had
fed in the stirabout line in the stable yard. The world was upside down indeed! The genteel daughters of the former owner
of this man's mansion were doing discreet home laundry in
England. Genteel washerwomen! But did Sterrin really need to
have him here as a guest? After all, he was only repaying a debt.
Roderick had gone to great extremes to save him from prison
and deportation. But Sterrin was a law unto herself. And then
Margaret stiffened to cold anger when she realised the identity
of the handsome young gentleman she had been chatting to so
graciously and thanking so warmly for having put up the bail
money, was none other than one of those crude, criminal Keatings, who had once fired into the castle and just missed killing
her.

Under cover she scrutinised him. Frank, open. Nothing murderous there; nothing crude; gentle eyes; but they were devouring Sterrin. The presumption! But it was blood treachery to
have brought him here. What was she thinking now, in face of
that ardent gaze? There was no knowing behind that dreadful
veil. And then Lady O'Carroll realised that it was not a dreadful veil. It was beautiful. Sterrin might protest that she was no
longer interested in her appearance, but there was interest indicated in the choosing of that veil and, hein, it *was* intriguing. It
was drawing all the men's eyes to the mystery that lay behind.

When her excited guests had departed, Margaret went out to
where the fever hut lay in the lea of a low hill out of sight of the
castle. Windows had been added to the once miniature fortress
designed to lock contagion away from the healthy. Mrs. Ryan
Ha-Lad lay in the bed near a bright fire and the children played
happily in and out between the two apartments, thrilled to be
within the safety of not just four sturdy walls, but eight—for
the hut, as big as their own house, was octagonal.

Mrs. Ryan Ha-Lad's outpourings of gratitude and praise for
Lady Devine were so fervent that Margaret reflected that any-
one might think that Sterrin had delivered the child. Mrs. Ryan
Ha-Lad, like most women basking in the aftermath of a satis-
factorily concluded labour went on to dwell on the details. Lady
O'Carroll felt one of her swayings coming on. She reeled. Ster-

rin *had* delivered the child.

She hurried to Sterrin's room. As Sterrin listened to her mother she felt a growing ... growing sensation of the one she had felt on the morning that she had witnessed Eileen Morton' odisasement. 'I thought,' concluded her mamma, 'you had merely helped them to shelter and secure a doctor, but—to take part—to witness. You! A young lady of your background! You poor child, it must have been hideous for you.'

'It was a privilege.' Sterrin was sitting in a low chair near the fire; her back to the dressing-table mirror. A small ornamental mirror that used to stand on the mantelpiece had been removed Anything that could reflect her face had been removed. Her hair was down and she was holding a strip of linen to either side of her face. It irritated Margaret mildly the way Sterrin shook the hair down over her face whenever she entered her bedroom She, her mamma, who had tended to all her childhood's ailments, all the tenants' too, for that matter. *Including* skin ailments!

'The only "hideous" thing about the experience was that made a silly fool of myself. I expressed something like disgust to the doctor because Mrs. Ha-Lad mentioned something about cord. I thought it was some crudeness of dress.'

'What else could you be expected to think? Girls like you——'

'Girls like me, I suppose, don't come into the world attached to cord; or are they attached to something silken? Like this? She flicked the braid on the satin cushion. 'Girls like me,' she went on, 'are only fit to be pushed blindfolded into marriage and find out all the natural things, or should I say the "hideous" things—in a hideous way——' Her mother's quick intake of breath halted her for a moment.

What awful experiences must this child have gone through to make her speak with such bitterness. It was not today's terrible ordeal; nor her maiming, nor her being disinherited.

'I'm sorry, Mamma,' Sterrin went on. 'But my values have changed. I've been through more in the past two years than any nice girl would have to endure in ten long lifetimes. I've no more time for sham dressed up as gentility. The real things in life, the raw things, have been covered in stupid mystery. Mrs Ha-Lad has known more happiness than ever I have. You should have seen Ryan Ha-Lad crying when she moaned in her.

592

labour. He was more concerned about his wife than about the loss of his house. He cried again when he took the new baby in his arms, cried for joy.'

'But darling, Hannah told me that Sir Jocelyn was frantic with concern when—when you had the mishap.'

'He was frantic for the fate of the inheritance—savagely so.'

Lady O'Carroll wondered was she going to hear the true facts at last. She could readily credit the savagery part. She would never forget the cold thin anger he had displayed the time that actor, who had been in service here, had presumed into Sterrin's bedroom. *Vraiment!* The anger, partly justified, had been terrifying to regard.

But Sterrin sat silent, her elbows on her knees, her hands holding the pieces of linen to her cheeks. Margaret tiptoed to her and kissed the top of her head. 'Would you let me see your poor face?' Sterrin twisted her head further away.

'When you saw it that first time I saw *your* face, and I saw Cousin Maurice's and I saw Mrs. Stacey making the sign of the Cross.' There was no reaching this Sterrin. Her mother left another kiss on the bent head.

'You have had a dreadful experience today. *Dieu*, when I think of it!'

'Did you—did you collapse, Mamma?'

It was Margaret's turn for hurt. 'There are times, Sterrin, when I, too, manage to face up to things.'

Sterrin dropped the ointment-smeared linen. 'Oh, Mamma, I did not mean it like that. Too well I know how you can stand up to things. It was the memory of the way you held Papa in your arms when he was shot and—and did whatever had to be done; no hysteria; no panic; and all those other times. The horrible sights out there in the stirabout line and the way you carried that giant's mother all the way to the soup kitchen. It was your example, I say, that kept me from running away or doing something dreadful when—when.' She broke off, fearful of having said too much. She had never touched so close to the actual moment of her mother's tragedy. But this moment that was between them was sane and close as never before. 'It was a grim coincidence,' she spoke into the flames, her face in her hands again, her hair hanging forward, 'both of us, mother and daughter, both to know our husbands assassinated; but you, of course, lost more.' Margaret was touched to a yearning pity. But

593

you, of course lost more. The naïve little sentence dismissed wealth, power and glamour compared to the loss of love. She stooped low and kissed a little white patch of forehead that showed between the drapes of hair. 'Drink your *tilleul*, my darling. It will make you sleep.'

She paused in the opening of the door. 'Darling, you spoke of being "pushed blindfolded into marriage". Have you forgotten that I had completely withdrawn from the notion of your marriage. There was no one more surprised that I when you told me that you had given Sir Jocelyn your consent.'

'The Keatings were on the point of buying the castle. That justified anything; marriage or murder.'

'And yet you could bring one of them here today? Under *this* roof? Sterrin, my dear, you never cease to amaze me.'

Lady O'Carroll would have been further amazed late next night had she seen Sterrin waiting in the Sir's Road for the horse that Big John was leading with cloth-muffled hooves across the cobbled yard.

'You know what you are doing, your Ladyship?' His voice was an anxious whisper. Her voice whispered back.

'This is something that has been laid upon me by my conscience.'

More than an hour and a half later she stood in the blacksmith's forge and gave the same answer to the same question. The blacksmith then turned to a man standing in the shadow. 'It's only for a minute that we'll be turning you out, Mr. Keating. Sure you know that yourself.' Donal, in the knowledge that no third person must be present, moved out without a word.

Sterrin, standing in the dark red gloam of the forge, her right hand upraised, felt a momentary dread. It was like being part of some cabalistic rite held in some sinister, underground cave. Fortunately for her purpose, the dimness cloaked her wavering and Denis marvelled to himself at the resolute quality in her low-pitched voice as she repeated after him—'In the presence of God, I, Sterrin Mary O'Carroll. . . .' To the last unrelenting word of the Fenian oath, she never faltered, as some that he would have thought more intrepid might have done. 'You are the fifty-first this night that I have given the oath to. The other fifty were of the Highland regiment widin' in the town. There's more than half the regiment with us. Aye,' he said at her exclamation, 'ten minutes ago I couldn't have told you that.'

Donal had come back. 'Was there any great need to bind Lady Devine to an oath? O'Donovan Rossa, our greatest leader in the movement has no oath.'

Denis bent over the furnace to put a kettle on for tea. He put Sterrin in mind of Big John; so utterly dependable and, that same unpretentious dignity that commanded one's respect. He looked up with a smile, 'I suppose they think the ladies are so tender that their hearts would need to be spancelled to their heads by an oath or they might let it run away with them.'

A teapot stood on a stone shelf and beside it a white mug; ostensibly his own, for Sterrin noticed when he moved a slab in the wall that there were other white mugs there. In readiness for grim tea parties! For grim men coming by night across Ireland; across the Atlantic? Denis started to pour then suddenly stopped and with a 'where's my manners' hurried out.

Donal moved over to Sterrin. 'Do you have to do this?' he whispered. 'Isn't it sufficient for someone like you to—well, exist?' It was something he realised, to be said looking into a woman's eyes. In this red darkness that was like the blood-tinted darkness behind closed eyelids, it sounded banal. Even that damned veil couldn't conceal her impatience. It came seeping through the mesh.

She turned towards his whisper. 'Is that a gibe or a compliment? No, forgive me. I shouldn't say such a thing to you after what you did for me when they arrested me. But no one knows better than you why I must do this.'

He knew that she was alluding to the six hundred evicted from her husband's land and to the fate of the little hunted boy. As she gazed into the glowing furnace she spoke of the famine horrors and he saw through her eyes the macabre scenes that had shadowed her childhood.

'All these things have happened because people like me—our class—have been content to, just exist. Most of them have been living on their tenants like warm well-fed fleas in a skinny dog's coat. Papa used to say that in other countries it was the aristocrats who used to lead their people against oppression. Here the aristocrats hold aloof. That's why all our rebellions have failed and——'

'This one won't!' His voice cut through like a blade. Her revelations made him feel that he had scarcely skimmed the

595

surface of life. 'Look,' he pleaded, 'when I spoke of you—just existing—I meant that it was enough that you should add grace to the lives of others, that—oh hang it, I was alluding to your beauty. If——' 'Beauty!' He recoiled from the savagery in her voice. He watched her hands tear at the fastenings of her veil, then just as suddenly they fell limply to her knees. Vanity was stronger than bitterness. Anyway, she reflected, it is too dark here to let him have the full blast of what had caused Mrs. Stacey to make a sign of the Cross. He watched the deliberate way she unbuttoned her glove. 'Look,' she reached him her bare hand. 'My face is like that mark there.' Since the morning when she had snubbed him he had caught a wisp of rumour that she avoided people because of some disfigurement incurred through saving her maid from the fire; but all he could see now was a shapely whiteness.

He held the soft hand in his and felt the quiver of her misery. Suddenly he stooped and she felt his lips on her palm and then on every finger. Nothing Frenchified, a throbbing caress that sent an answering throb through all her being. She wanted to throw herself forward and feel his young arms about her body and his warm questing lips upon her own. Then there was a clink of china.

The blacksmith moved forward. 'This is more becoming to you, my Lady,' he said as though he had never seen her draw her hand from the clasp of Mr. Keating. She gripped the little cup. Its gold rim glinted in the glow. To regain control she focused on its hand-painted flowers. 'Pansies for remembrance,' she murmured.

The words, a stop-gap, drifted into silence then suddenly they rebounded; impelling her to remember. She knew now who Denis, busy at the furnace with kettle and teapot, reminded her of. Not Big John at all! Those wide shoulders, lissom and straight! Poor Big John's were bunched from that terrible accident on the night of the Big Wind. The blacksmith looked up and took the cup from her to fill it and the sudden blue flash of his eyes recalled eyes that were bluer still. The fantasy persisted in the play of flames upon his crisp dark hair; lending a suggestion of moving curls, shining and jet black! The emotions aroused by Donal's kiss went surging through her veins, clamouring for someone who was not Donal. She was no longer a sworn soldier of the Irish Republican Sisterhood. She was all woman; craving for the one man in all the world whom she could ever love!

When the tea was finished Denis put the cup away in the secret place; giving it dark purpose; making her one with it. But all the way home the longing for lost beauty that was ensorcelled to lost love stayed with her; unconscious of the love that rode and flowed beside her.

The first beam of sun was starting to stretch with a lazy warmth out of the east when Sterrin rapped at Mag Miney's door. 'A Mairead!' she called out in Gaelic. 'I have decided to try that messy cure of yours.'

The old woman opened the door and peered up. 'I knew you wouldn't stay sittin' up behind that black screen much longer; frightenin' crows and little childer. Come in, my pulse!'

Half an hour later, Sterrin, half fainting from the smell, clamoured for the abomination to be removed. 'Another quarter of an hour, my pulse,' pleaded Mag.

'Not another minute.'

She washed her face in a tin basin of rain water into which she flung a half dozen of the scented washballs she had filched from her mother's bedroom. But she came again the next morning and the next.

One morning, returning from her treatment and on her way to discharge her first task for the Fenians at the Campions' farmhouse, she met Donal. They dismounted and strolled along a bridle path that skirted Owen Heffernan's house. Sterrin thanked heaven for the scented washballs. Mrs. Heffernan came to the back door to drain the three-legged pot of breakfast potatoes. 'The potatoes are the merest aperitif,' Donal told Sterrin. 'When Owen goes to the fields his dainty little wife will cook a breakfast for herself that would choke a horse, and more power to her, he is a dreadful old skinflint.'

Sterrin laughed at her own recollections of Owen. 'When I was a child one of the brides picked for him ran away from the altar when she got her first glimpse of him. Another one, a beautiful, but very poor girl, called Kitty Dowling had run away from him before that. While the matchmaker and her parents were disposing of her to old Owen, her own sweetheart, Mark Hennessey, arrived in the orchard and whistled her out to tell her that he was in a position to marry her. He had found some bank-notes that day in a hedge while he was ditching.

They had been lying there for years since the night that the Big Wind blew thatched roofs with people's life savings all over the country.'

'And did they live happily ever after?' He watched the heavily-veiled head shake slowly.

'They are now, I hear, and rich. Their first child died of hunger. They nearly died themselves. My father despatched them to America with the widow and the children of his own foster-brother.'

'Black Pat Ryan?' He cursed the interjection that betrayed raw curiosity. The mystery of the hunger deaths of Sir Roderick O'Carroll's foster-brother and three of his six children, all in one evening, was still debated locally. It *had* been hunger—not the famine fever that had killed the fat as well as the starving—and yet they had lived in a good holding and Ryan was said to ride a horse that was as splendid as that of his foster-brother.

He sensed her angry silence as she walked ahead, leading her mount. He stumbled and gave an angry exclamation. She looked back over her shoulder.

'I walked on an egg-shell,' he explained. 'It is a habit I seem to have when I'm with you.' Her laughter rippled back at him. He was so dear and companionable! And that fierce and secret oath that bound them was so much bigger than their separate entities.

'It was his wife's pride.' She vouchsafed him an explanation. 'She had been a lady of well-to-do family, who ran away with Ryan. Her family cut her off. Calamities suddenly hit them; loss of livestock as well as crops. None of us knew that they were hungry. They never let on.' A wave of guilt smote her. They had let on. The younger ones had howled with disappointment the day her father had discovered her little drama of putting her own dinner in the trunk of a tree for them.

'If you were to run away with someone—beneath you.'

This time it was she who stumbled. Dammit, did he know that too?

'And you were hungry, would you let on? Would you ask for food?'

'I couldn't see myself begging for food; not if I knew where it was to be had.'

'You mean that you would steal it?'

She shrugged and halted to mount where the track gave on to

a boreen.

'I say,' cried Donal, 'let's ride to Lissnastreenagh. The blossoms are out.'

Lissnastreenagh with its fields like some wonderful carpet of pink and white on a green ground from fallen blossoms and its circle of hawthorns in full bloom; a great tent of blossoms over the intertwining branches. Don't break off a blossom, Young Thomas! It is not lucky! But if the blossoms fall on you themselves, you will marry your true love. And the blossoms fell on his curly black hair; and they fell on his bloated, fever-stricken face when he collapsed there after the famine; and they fell on his hair and shoulders and on hers and on her bridal veil when he crushed her to him and swore he would go on waiting for her. Your true love, inagh!

Donal's voice brought her out of her reverie. He was starting to apologise stiffly. The Fort-of-the-blossoms was on Kilsheelin territory. The whole world might go to view the wonder of it, but not one of the Keatings of Poolgower. She interrupted him.

'I haven't been there since——' and then without thinking she said, 'I'll face it.'

Before he could ask her what was there to face, she cried out, 'I'll race you!' and galloped off.

She was there before him; sitting erect, silent, rigid; every line of her body betraying tenseness. The blossoms were too newly out to have started to drop down their magic carpet but the great circle of hawthorns that bent over the deep hollow was completely roofed and walled with pink and white flowers. Their fragrance filled the air. Waves of memory wafted through her with every wave of perfume. A sadness more desolate than that she had known on her wedding day swept through her. Then, there had been ecstasy too.

'One should never go back,' she murmured. He finished the sentence for her '—to where one has known happiness that has fled.'

What could this nice young man know of happiness that has fled? Of the happiness of racing against young Thomas, he on Rajah, she on her Connemara pony; happiness, after that two days' search, when she had found the half-conscious young Thomas lying hidden among these blossoms; when she had come to him here straight from plighting her vows at the altar, there had been happiness in her anguish. How else could it have

599

been and she to have his arms about her. Ah God, to feel them about her now!

When she had ridden a while she glanced back and then wheeled and returned to where Donal still stayed his horse.

'Little Fido didn't follow,' he said.

'I'm sorry for going off like that. This place gives me shivers. It's haunted.'

'By what?'

'By—by the ghost of a priest who was slain by an ancestor of mine; slain at the altar for daring to start Mass before his Chieftain had arrived. There were vestments found down there in that hollow; chalices too.'

'I wish you would take off that veil so that I might see how you look when you are lying.'

'Are you accusing me of telling lies?'

'Yes. Your castle, they say, swarms with ghosts. I expect that they come haunting every night, with Hippodrome performances on Mondays, Wednesdays and Saturdays. I don't think that ghosts trouble you sufficiently, my Lady, to make you ride away from them. Who did the blossoms fall upon—or fail to fall upon?'

He could almost see her jawline harden behind the veil. 'I don't believe in pishoguerie.' She made to shake up the reins but he reached out and grabbed the bridle.

'We all believe in pishoguerie, my Lady fair, when it is the pishoguerie of romance. This morning I had the presumption to invoke the fairies to let their blossoms fall upon me.'

'Why should that be presumptuous?'

Immediately she regretted the query. The last thing that she wanted was a declaration from him, from anyone. She was free as never before. She wanted to stay that way.

'There is no presuming about my loving you. To do that is as natural as to breathe. It was in testing the blossoms to see if my love was returned that I presumed.'

His grip on her bridle tightened. Presumed indeed, but there had been no presuming when it was a servant boy who had spoken his love here and the blossoms had showered their benison upon him. An arm of sun reached down upon the branches and unstoppered a new fragrance; provocative, inveigling their senses. The bird song resumed with a saucy piping of finches, and then, what must traitorous Clooreen do but reach out and start nuzzling Donal's mount with velvety kisses!

Sterrin felt the antennae of her womanhood reach out like Clooreen's velvet nuzzle, to absorb this moment that was bathing all her senses in a sweet suffusion. In another moment the human heads must meet in harmony above their mounts. Then a startled exclamation broke from her and brought the horses apart.

'Ye gods! I had forgotten about Campion's "station". You and your blossoms!'

He watched her ride away. He, too, had completely forgotten that she was on a secret mission of her Fenian oath. Her voice came back to him.

'It is too soon to expect the blossoms to fall upon you.'

His heart surged. Too soon! Dolt that he was; of course, it had been too soon in her widowhood. He spurred after her. 'Does that mean——?'

'It means,' she called back with blithe unconcern, 'that the blossoms are too new. You must wait till they are full blown if you want them to fall on you. Yup, Clooreen!' She was over the hedge and away.

CHAPTER 56

Men in groups outside the Campion farmhouse ceased their chattering as Sterrin rode in. Which one of these is my 'contact' she wondered. The clatter of preparation for the Station break-fast muted as women's faces peered through the windows of the front kitchen.

'It is Lady Devine.' Mrs. Campion straightened up from the chickens she was basting and came forward. 'What broke a rib-bon of Lady Devine, Miss Sterrin O'Carroll, that was, to come to this Station? None of them had ever come to one before, or to any other Station, and why should they with a chapel in their own house?'

She greeted Sterrin with a quiet dignity. She was no longer the plump, jolly woman who had enlivened the wedding that had roused such a stir in the castle long ago because young Thomas had served its Mass. She had the 'ha'anted' look of the famine's visitation. Its fever had taken her husband and two of her daughters. She turned to a young girl in the doorway and bade her have someone see to Lady Devine's horse.

The girl glanced towards the horse and back to its owner.

'Will Lady Devine be staying for the Station?'

There was a polite surprise in her tone and in the eyebrows that seemed to ride towards Sterrin's riding hat and down to her riding boots. Sterrin realised that the girl was wearing a school uniform with the little white veil that boarders wore in convent chapels; that people were alighting from phaetons and jauntings cars and farm carts, all in their Sunday garb. The porch was ablaze with blooms. Every plant had been forced into bloom. The roof had a new thatch; the walls a fresh coat of lime. Suddenly Sterrin understood that quick up-and-down glance. This thuckeen of a girl was no goat's toe. She had made Lady Devine realise that she had come spanking in to a religious function as if she were entering for a Point-to-point.

She managed a gracious apology for her attire and then to her

602

dismay, she found herself placed at the head of the penitents who knelt in a line from outside the parlour door across the long kitchen and up every step of the stairs. Confession! Sterrin hadn't bargained for that.

Her examination of conscience got a sudden jolt from the penitent whose place in the queue she had supplanted. Old Mrs. Hannigan's knees were killing her. Her fasting gurglings after her five-mile walk on an empty stomach were killing the meditations of the other penitents. But at last she had reached the head of the line. And then, shutting out the light of heaven from her, Mrs. Campion comes and planks down fornint her a young lady that looked as if it 'twas to hunt foxes she was goin' instead of to confession. The susurrus of Mrs. Hannigan's 'Hail Marys' grew louder and angrier. Recognition dawned. She pinned down the seventh 'Hail Mary' with her thumb and called to her hostess. 'Whisper! Is she,' she nodded towards Sterrin's head, 'the one who danced before the King of France in her drawers?'

'. . . and forgive us our trespasses as we forgive—the blasted old bachach!' Sterrin swayed on her knees; grappling with her fury and her soul. The spirit triumphed. Those within earshot, not certain if they had heard aright, decided that they had not when they saw Lady Devine rise to her feet and gesture the old woman to resume the place that she had been deprived of. Mrs. Hannigan shuffled gratefully forward on her knees. 'And anyway,' she remarked with kindly ambiguity, 'your Ladyship would have needed more time to count your sins.'

Sterrin knelt on, in conflict with herself and her surroundings. Was it a thing that the luxury of her married life had left her no longer *en rapport* with this life and its people? That's ridiculous. It is because of the people that I am here. But that was the cause of her unease. Using a religious gathering for a political purpose! No, it's these damned flags. Oh, heavens, such language and I preparing for confession. She buried her face in her hands. Mrs. Hannigan's gurglings got through their defence. So did the unmistakable consumptive cough of new arrivals; overheated from tramping the long dogged miles on empty stomachs. The smell of roasting chickens and boiling hams sent out their tantalising beguilement.

Something came to her from her spiritual readings when she had aspired to take the veil. Saint Teresa of Avila had such trouble in concentrating on her prayers that she started counting the nails of the boots of the nun kneeling in front of her and offered each nail as a prayer. Sterrin dropped her hands from her face. The hobnails in Mrs. Hannigan's boots were arranged in little clusters of three, like shamrocks. Sterrin counted them separately and offered them up in sets of three 'Hail Marys'. She had reached halfway down the sole of the right boot where a piece of dung covered the cluster of nails and shattered her concentration.

The parlour door opened to discharge a penitent and boots and nails disappeared as Mrs. Hannigan rose to her feet, but the opening was blocked by the figure of Father Hickey.

'I just thought I'd see what has happened to the men.' He assessed the few males among the kneeling women; young boys and old men. Mrs. Campion was torn in all directions; basting chickens, cutting bread, supervising the tables spread out in the barn. Father Hickey saw Lorcan Campion talking with a well-dressed stranger—a man with a cruel scar on his cheek—listening with head bent as though he were deeply interested in the pattern that his toes made in the gravel. It seemed it was always strangers, from some distant part, who came to give orders and to impart the Fenian oath. No 'Circle' knew from whom its orders came and so no person could betray. All around the yard men were talking, low and stern, instead of goshering[1] about cattle and the prospects of the harvests as at previous Stations.

'What brings them here since they will take no part in the ceremonies?' the priest asked; and he shook his head with infinite sadness as though he knew the answer. They had probably been excommunicated in their own diocese; like in Kerry where a Fenian had shot a member of the Crown forces and the bishop had made that terrible pronouncement that 'Hell is not hot enough nor eternity long enough for whoever did the deed'.

Sterrin was put beside Father Hickey at breakfast and found that her partner on the other side was Mrs. Lonergan. She turned to greet her but to her surprise, the old lady took advantage of the cup of tea that was put in front of her just then to take a very long, appreciative draught and then leaned across to say, 'It is too fond of the tea an old woman like myself is, Father. When the Gorta Mor was on us I didn't know the taste of it. I was glad of porridge made with yellow meal from India. But now, the only thing I'll miss when I go to Heaven is the sup

[1] Chattering.

of tay.' She pronounced it 'tay' not so much from brogue but that she had received her schooling from a band of French nuns who had found refuge from the French Revolution in her father's house. The priest looked pityingly at the patient face. She had been through so much. But hadn't they all? Every face at the table bore the strong lines of suffering endured. He recalled when five rooms in this house held typhus patients and the two eldest girls and the father had died. His hand went abstractedly to the piece of turnip in his pocket. He had never lost the habit of carrying a piece since the time when it used to be the only thing that broke his fast on the long journeys by dark and day, bearing the Viaticum to the stricken.

'And who,' he asked, 'told you that you would have to go without your tay in Heaven? Won't you have Te Deum and Laudamus Te and Glorificatum Te. Sure isn't it Te, Te, Te, all the time in Heaven?'

Mrs. Campion stopped pouring over the shoulders of her guests. 'Is it jokin' you are, Father? Bad manners to me to doubt your word. Didn't I always hear that there wasn't the beating of you in Rome for Teeology?'

Mrs. Lonergan sighed. 'The dear knows I'll be glad to go even without all that nice Latin tay. This world can do no more to me.' She sighed again. 'A queer, modern world, wars and trains and telegrams. Indeed we get the bad news as quick without the telegrams. I heard the banshee the night before Tim was killed. I heard it as——'

'Tim!' Sterrin put down her knife and fork and turned. 'Mrs. Lonergan, I didn't know. How did it happen?'

Talk and clatter quietened. For a moment Sterrin thought that she was going to be publicly slighted, then Mrs. Lonergan for the first time raised her head from the down-drag of spirit that held it in its grip. Her eyes looked straight into Sterrin's.

'Naturally, you didn't know. The fate of one ordinary Irish soldier would be of no consequence to *your* kinsman.'

'My kinsman?' Sterrin was mystified.

'Aye, your kinsman . . . the officer who killed my son . . . from here. His name is O'Carroll.'

The whole table had gone silent.

'But Mrs. Lonergan I have no relative fighting in the Civil War. Ancestors of mine went to the American colonies more than a hundred years ago. We cannot be held responsible for

605

what their descendants do. We have no knowledge of them; no contact.'

'No contact?' Mrs. Lonergan repeated. 'Yet you send them food.'

'But not to any O'Carrolls. We send food to relatives of my mother called O'Regan. And,' Sterrin bridled, 'why shouldn't we? They sent big consignments of food here in the famine. Shiploads! My father used to go armed with guns to protect the wagons all the way from Waterford. It would be very strange if we would not send help to them now when they are in want themselves.'

There was a murmur of agreement. Mrs. Lonergan looked appealingly towards the priest. 'Would there be a mistake, Father?'

She turned to Sterrin and her voice held its old caressing quality. 'It was a chaplain in America who sent the story of what happened. I don't know what to think.'

Sterrin was glad to have calmed the sweet old lady, and glad of the chicken and ham and griskins and all the delicious dishes that followed. She realised that it was nearly one o'clock and that she had been riding since six this morning with nothing to eat since the nine o'clock tea in the drawing-room the night before.

The priest followed her to the yard as she was mounting to leave. He noticed that the man with the scar seemed about to speak to her. 'Are you sure, Lady Devine, that there is none of your family here fighting with the South in the Civil War?'

Sterrin shook her head. 'Who could there be from here but Sir Dominic? My cousin Maurice of Waterford is the only other relative. He has no children.'

'It is strange,' said the priest. 'My informant seemed certain. Tim didn't die immediately on the battlefield. He told the chaplain who attended him in hospital that he had recognised the officer who followed on the heels of the two rebels who had given him the final lunge. He was seen to speak something to the officer and the recognition appeared to be mutual.'

Sterrin shook her head again. 'I don't understand it. There could be a great many of our name out there for all I know. It is a big war.'

'A big war, indeed,' the priest agreed. 'No war is as hate-inspiring as a Civil War. Ah, the wanton waste of those young

606

ives that went out from here in friendship with each other; neighbours' children killing each other.'

Out of the corner of her eye Sterrin saw Bergin watching her. He must be her contact. But the priest was not finished. He drew his piece of turnip to the tip of his pocket and then dropped it back, but made no move to go.

'What's this I hear about a talking head at the castle?'

'Talking head?' Sterrin was puzzled. 'Oh, you must mean the talking machine. Would you like to hear it? I'm afraid the discs that contain the sound have gone silent. They need to be kept in a certain temperature and the castle is so damp. But if you care to hear Mr. Steele's voice, his disc is a bit better than the others. He adjusted it himself.'

The priest shook his grey locks. 'No, I knew that Mr. Steele had the inventive faculty, but, the human voice!' He shook his head again. 'To seek to perpetuate it in a separate mechanical existence is—is a presuming on the divine power of creation—it savours too much of Deism and Spiritualism.'

Sterrin glanced towards Bergin. He was waiting for her. She reached her hand down. 'Goodbye. Father. It will do no more harm. It has been silenced.'

'That's good. That is what Saint Thomas Aquinas did as far back as the thirteenth century. A philosopher called Magnus invented a thing called a Talking Head. He introduced the mechanism into a skull. The saint had it smashed.' Sterrin pulled one rein a little, but the priest had taken out his piece of turnip and was taking a nibble as he always did in preoccupation. 'Sterrin, I may call you that since I had the pleasure of knowing you since your infancy. There are people here today who did not come to participate in the sacred functions of the gathering. It is heartening to see you here, though.' He nibbled at his piece of turnip. 'I have never before encountered you at any but the one in your own oratory. I have witnessed your charitable activities among the unfortunate people but don't allow your pity to lead you into dangerous paths. Young people are being led into taking rash oaths that are a profanation of the sacred name of God. They have grievances, the dear knows, but oppression is better than putting their necks in the halter by disturbing the peace of society. No rulers on earth will permit any order of men to overturn established law, by private author-ity. My Lady, Sterrin child, your mother has had her share of sorrow.'

And with that cryptic remark he moved towards his phaeton. There was no sign of the scar-faced man as Sterrin rode out. Her mind was so torn with the unease of the priest's very pointed homily and concern that it might have caused her to lose her 'contact'. But before she emerged from the boreen on to the high road he emerged from a field.

'I waited to give you the password.'

She reined in. 'You gave it to me last week,' she said coldly. 'I passed it on that same night.'

'It must be changed immediately. There is an informer in the circle. The whole group was surprised last night. One of them was captured a few hours back and shot!'

'Without a trial?'

He nodded. 'They have orders to shoot at sight, if necessary, and apparently they deem it "necessary" to shoot men drilling with shillelaghs and a few pikes. But they *did* hold an inquest upon this one. He was of sufficient consequence. The verdict this morning was—justifiable manslaughter.'

Her heart turned over. Would they have caught Donal after she left him? Not Donal! 'Was it Donal—Mr. Keating?'

A suspicious look narrowed his eyes. Would Keating be the cause of her zeal for Fenianism?

'Our mutual friend of the anvil must be warned. They are looking for him,' and then he answered her query. 'No, not Keating,' he said shortly. 'Listen,' he went on. He spoke the password and made her repeat it. 'Pei Marier.' It is good to be quiet. He had chosen the watchword of the Maories of Pei Marier. She took up the reins. Over her shoulder she tossed a taunt.

'Are you quite sure that you can trust me to pass it on?'

His constant air of cold watchfulness was beginning to get on her nerves. He swung up to the saddle.

'This time,' he said as he wheeled his horse towards the bridle path, 'I take it there is no inducement to make you break faith.'

The crack of her whip made a duet with the larrup he gave his own horse as they made off in different directions. The insufferable churl! It was the very devil, thought Sterrin, to have to take instructions from him. But she couldn't allow Denis O'Flanagan, the blacksmith, to incur the risk of the wrong password.

She thought to rush straight off to warn him, but Mamma must be very worried about her not returning to breakfast, much less lunch, and also she would need to change horses. Clooreen would be overworked before nightfall. As she turned in the stable yard she saw the Delaney equipage, being wheeled back and forth through the carriage-cleaning pond.

'It must have been hard driven,' she said to Mike O'Driscoll. 'Too hard,' he said. 'But it had hard reason.'

'What reason?' Sterrin asked and looked curiously at the faces round the pond, Big John's, Ned-Rua's and Mike's. There was a definite something in the air. Mike took out his straw to explain, but Ned-Rua intervened.

'Let your Ladyship go inside. Miss Katie will tell you herself. Some people,' he looked angrily at Mike, 'are inclined to forget their place.'

Mike put back his straw. 'Someone has forgot their place *now* with a vengeance!' said Mike.

In the drawing-room Sterrin found Mrs. Delaney as near to a vapour as it would be possible for her to achieve. The 'someone' who had forgotten his place was the young groom with whom Belle was in the habit of pillion riding. The pair had eloped.

'What!' Sterrin was scandalised.

They had been seen by a bianconi driver heading towards Templetown. 'We caught up on them but we lost them in Templetown; another bianconi driver said he saw them heading for the Thurles road, but at your cross the lynch pin came loose. It finished me altogether to find you away. I was counting on you.'

'Where were you, Sterrin?' her mother demanded. 'I have been distracted with anxiety.'

'She's here now.' Mrs. Delaney was impatient of petty grievances in the face of such calamity. 'You'll go after her, Sterrin dear?' She mistook the look of consternation on Sterrin's face. 'I suppose it is too much to expect from you.'

Sterrin dropped on her knees in front of Mrs. Delaney and gripped her hands. 'Nothing is too much for you to expect from me.'

She was thinking of the night of the fire when Mrs. Delaney could not do enough for her; but she was thinking, too, of her commitments to the secret cause she was sworn to. Why did she have to swear that terrible oath? And Father Hickey said that it

609

was a profanation. But if she didn't start out soon Denis, the blacksmith, would have set out for the night's rendezvous; his freedom was at stake; his life. She trusted the big man with his quiet strength; his quality of utter reliability. And the blacksmith had rewarded her confidence with his implicit trust.

Every foot of the wood and mountains was familiar to her and the haunts of the wild bird and its cry. Sometimes men scattered over The Devil's Bit 'on their keeping' would hear the sweet musical cry of the Grey Lag Geese long before it was time to look upwards for the V-line gaggle. They would know then that someone was telling them that men had come over the Atlantic; Americans to drill and equip them. And if some hidden outlaw spied Lady Devine roaming on horseback over the hilltop he did not suspect that it was her lips that had uttered the wild goose cry.

Denis was surprised to see the carriage draw in at the forge. Always she came by horseback and by night. She passed on the warning. There was an informer among them. The blacksmith was able to put her on the trail of the elopers. A body wouldn't need to look twice to know what they were up to. Ill assorted and guilt-marked, they had been spotted easily.

'Ah, youth is a drover,' was his comment. 'There is a clamouring inside it like the sounds from a red-hot anvil. High or low, it makes no difference. But he should have respected her—and, she should have respected herself.'

Sterrin was surprised at the calm way he had taken her warning. No anxiety, no drama. The little saucepan spat out its own warning. He opened the cupboard that contained the little china cup. The sight of it, flowered and fragile among the big, stark mugs reminded her of herself among those stark revolutionaries except Donal. The hovering cloud melted into the recollection of him.

'You will pass my message to Donal ... Mr. Keating if he comes tonight.'

Denis paused. 'Now *there's* a young gentleman who knows how to respect a lady, even though he might adore the ground she'd walk on. The big men tell me that he is a brilliant barrister with a great career ahead. They tell me that when he is in Clonmel Assizes the ladies actually condescend to go into a court-room; just to listen to him.'

He escorted her to the carriage and gave directions to Big

John where to find the inn that the lovers had enquired about.

'Don't kill yourself rushing after them. There won't be a bianconi passing that way for more than an hour and, I'm thinkin', by the looks of her she will be glad to see you. She has had her fling.'

He was right.

Belle threw herself straight into Sterrin's arms. The groom stood sheepishly by the table, fearful to seat himself in the unaccustomed setting of carpets and mahogany and brass; disorientated. Sterrin curtly ordered him on to the box seat and bustled Belle into the carriage. How could she! she thought, but she uttered no reproach. Belle unfolded the story of her love and of her disenchantment. Mamma had forbidden her to go horse-riding, only pillion riding, doctor's orders. Sterrin recalled the spectacle of Belle fastened to the groom by a hook attached to her big pillion belt and holding on to him around the waist. For nearly two years now they had roamed the countryside up hill and dale in an embrace that had lost its exigency in affection.

'But, oh Sterrin, he hadn't enough money for the dinner and he called the waiter "Sir".'

Mike O'Driscoll intervened for the unfortunate groom against the onslaught of Mrs. Delaney. 'It was askin' for trouble, Miss Katie. Up there behind him on the same horse; her arms around him day after day. Him sittin' there ridin' within her hoult.'

'There was no need to ride within her hold,' stormed Mrs. Delaney. 'She was attached to him by a strong iron hook.'

'Iron hook, how are you, Miss Katie! Hadn't she a pair of arms too? and where was she to put them only around his waist? Women's flesh is very temptin'.'

Back in the drawing-room, Mrs. Delaney admitted that Dr. Drennan had said something that must have meant the same thing. 'He called it "pro-Pink" something.'

'Propinquity,' said Lady O'Carroll and looked, unwittingly towards Sterrin. That was the word that Cousin Maurice had used the day Sterrin had fallen from the horse and the knife boy had carried her home. Sterrin fumed. It had never occurred to her that there was any resemblance between this squalid affair and her association with the knife boy. Comparing young Thomas to an oaf who said 'Sir' to the waiter and couldn't order a meal. Young Thomas, who from childhood had ordered the *garçonniere* like a commander-in-chief; spoken with authority to shop assistants; respectable farmers had uncovered to him. She recalled that night after the ball in Kilkenny when she had conspired with him to elope—God, why hadn't she gone with him that night—the easeful authority with which he had spoken to the bodyservant with the alphabet of names. Propinquity! That was an unjust dig.

'I have never been able to accustom myself,' Lady O'Carroll went on, 'to the fraternising with servants that prevails in Irish households. Servants are bound to take advantage. At home in my country the relationship is more *de-haut-en-bas*.'

When Mrs. Delaney had gone, Sterrin strolled to the little table beside her Mamma's chair. 'May I have a cigarette, Mamma?' Without waiting for a reply she reached into the embroidery bag and drew out a little satin-covered box inscribed in gold, 'Ma Chérie'. She proceeded to light one of the tiny cigarettes that were the vice her mother thought no one knew about.

'Sterrin!' Force of habit brought the shocked remonstrance to Margaret's lips. Guilt brought colour all through her creamy pallor. 'When did you start to smoke?' she brought out lamely, just to prevent herself saying 'How did you know that I smoked!'

'I started,' Sterrin told her, 'with a clay pipe in the kitchen when I was about six. I progressed from that to cigar butts in the turf ricks. Unlike the fortunate little girls in Belgium there wasn't always the concern available for me about "fraternising" and "*de-haut-en-bas*" and the consequences of "propinquity"!' She went out in a puff of smoke, feeling mean for giving her mother one in the eye for all those long spells of near neglect when the household revolved around her mother's malaise. In the corridor she collided into Hegarty.

'Miss Sterrin!' The butler was scandalised. She removed her cigarette.

'Yes, Hegarty?' She was very much *de-haut-en-bas*.

'Your Ladyship, I—er—I must see to the lights in the drawing-room.' He hurried on. He'd have a word about this with her other Ladyship.

Margaret had got the full impact of Sterrin's words. They held a whole lifetime of reproach; she put her hand to her head.

There was no swaying there. It was only when she felt that queer, violent pain in the back of her head that the swaying started up. *Had* she neglected Sterrin? Had she been left too much with that knife boy, though indeed he was genteel, not like that uncouth groom. Too genteel. To think of his going straight to Sterrin's bedroom when he came to play at Sir Jocelyn's house in Kilkenny! It must have been a frightful shock to Sir Jocelyn to have found him there. He could easily have broken off the engagement, instead of pushing the marriage forward before the scandal could leak out, perhaps into the papers even, Sir Jocelyn had said, because the actor was so prominent. Margaret wished she had a shoulder to lean on; she reached for the little satin box.

Hegarty came softly into the room and coughed. 'Your Ladyship——' Then he stopped dead. Her Ladyship was blowing a cloud of perfumed smoke from her lips.

'Yes, Hegarty?'

'Er—shall I light the candles, your Ladyship?'

'Of course, why ask?' She made no effort to conceal the cigarette. The cat could stay out of the bag. Hegarty had neither taper nor tinder. He made his escape to the kitchen and blurted his tale into the still seething excitement about the elopement.

Mrs. Stacey took the clay pipe from her mouth. 'Cigarettes,' she gasped, 'the two of them at it!' Then with supreme disregard for consistency she went on. 'Do you know what I am goin' to tell you?' They had a shrewd idea. 'I'm goin' to tell you that the prophecies are coming true.'

'Saint Columcille never prophesied that women, ladies—would smoke cigarettes,' said Ellen scornfully.

'No,' said Mrs. Stacey, 'but he prophesied something not far from it. He prophesied that women would wear trousers—it's the same kind of ungenteel thing. There's not a gra'dle of differ between a cigarette in a woman's mouth an' a trousers on a woman's legs.'

O'Driscoll got to his feet. He had been the centre of interest over the way he had stood up to Mrs. Delaney. 'I go against you, ma'am. I'm thinkin' that a pair of trousers would cover more than a cigarette would; more's the pity.' He ducked from the aim of a turf sod and Hegarty said that there would be law and order in this kitchen from this day forth!

CHAPTER 57

Sterrin tossed the little cigarette into her bedroom fire. It was as puny as her own exposure of Mamma's secret addiction. The odd time that Sterrin took a pull, she liked it to be male and pungent. Sterrin was exhausted. It had been a day of varied excitements. She made Hannah set up the hip bath and have the water made hot. Depression was not to be tolerated. She would throw it and her stiffness out together. In the distance beyond the window a light spurted up, then another. She wondered idly as she threw scent balls into the tub what it might be. Probably travelling tinsmiths. Then Pakie Scally poured in the big jugfuls of hot water. He gossiped as he poured.

'There was a young lad in the kitchen asking for milk for the evicted people.' He nodded in the direction of the distant flames.

So that was what the flame was, she thought.

'There were Peelers all over the place!'

Any ordinary evening she would have been bringing food to the encampment. 'Peelers!' she repeated. Police! The word alerted all her senses. Blast Belle and her ploughboy! They had driven all thought of the password out of her head. She had not even given it to Denis the blacksmith, but at least she had warned him to keep away. Dear God, to have fallen down upon such a trust! The lives of men at stake! She turned from the enticement of the warm, fragrant bath, every bone in her body aching. The bath would have to wait.

Surely, she brooded, as she rode up the hill towards the fort, there must be some other way of helping people besides all this cloak and dagger stuff? Lawlessness, grim oaths and men like the unhappy Bergin. How he would gloat over her failure to do her duty. Why did he ever take the trouble to help her during the fire? Oh, this is no life for a lady! I should be lying in my bath. I should be dancing. I'm not the dedicated type. And then that inexorable phantom procession approached, the six hundred trudging wearily past, raising reproachful eyes to her; the

614

little gaunt boy running from her, from all that she represented. No one could not fight that kind of thing alone. One had to belong to an organisation that had discipline—and ruthlessness. That was the only way to tackle and overthrow the system that perpetrated such inhumanity. No good in doing Lady Bountiful with a basket of food to some homeless encampment.

Revolution was the only solution, and revolutions, as the French leader, Monsieur Landu Rollins, had said of O'Connell's peaceful methods, cannot be fought with rose-water. How often had she heard Papa quote that! Well, here is your daughter, Papa, wearing the Red cap of Revolution!

'Halt!' Her heart missed a beat. A file of policemen had emerged from a thicket. She thought to urge the horse into a gallop, but caution prevailed. High-horsing would not avail this time. She recalled her scornful taunt to Bergin this morning. 'Are you sure you can trust me with the password?'

The officer in charge bade someone uncover the lantern. It was held up to her face. 'Your name, Madam,' She gave it coldly. 'What is your business abroad?'

'I am not in the habit of accounting for my presence on my own *property*. What is your business on our land?'

The interrogator was not Sub-Inspector Bible, but his authority was more compelling. 'Madam,' he said with quiet insistence, 'somewhere on *your property* there is unlawful assembly and drilling. This is an unorthodox hour for a lady to go horse-promenading.'

She twisted around and pointed her whip to two bulging saddle-bags. 'This is my business abroad—food for those people down there.' She nodded towards the red glow. She gave silent thanks for the expediency that had prompted her charity.

'Indeed,' she went on with a smiling change of front. 'I ought to have been there long ago, but I was busy over another type of lawlessness. I had to travel quite a distance in pursuit of an eloping couple and bring the young lady back to her mother.'

'Ah,' the officer allowed himself to smile too. 'We had been apprised of that abduction. I'm glad that you were able to restore the young lady to her mother. And now, we must not detain you any longer.'

He caught the bridle and with calm deliberateness turned the horse the opposite way round until it faced directly the distant smoke from the evictees encampment.

'Did you know,' he said blandly, 'that you were heading in the wrong direction?' With a quick word of command he turned back in the direction in which Sterrin had been riding. She had not hoodwinked him. She had led them straight back to the spot they had just missed. The password! The police officer would give the other password and the door would be opened to them and twenty—maybe thirty men would be—'shot at sight'? Given life sentences in the colonies? Hanged? The one in charge would certainly be shot, perhaps 'at sight'—Donal. She raised a hand as though to stop the raiders. The folded whip dropped to the ground from her limp grip. Suddenly there came an excited shout from the raiders. They had found the entrance to the Danish fort. The shout summoned her to her senses. She dropped the reins, placed a finger on either side of her pursed lips and uttered a wild, whistling, lonely cry. Would Donal, if he were inside, recognise the sound drawn from the lonely heart of a betrayed bird. Was she too far away for her voice to penetrate the thick walls of the fort?

Donal, tensed at an earhole in the fort, heard the strange cry of the domestic goose when the gander that has been its love since Spring, hears the distant cry of the wild geese and suddenly, in response to some primal instinct, deserts her for his wild brethren. He warned the sentinel not to open the door. The password was in the wrong hands.

Sterrin tethered the horse a distance away and when the raiding party, thwarted, had long departed, she tiptoed to the entrance.

'Donal,' she called softly. It was a complete violation of the rules. Names were never used; only initials, and not one's own. And of course it would be a sentinel who would be posted inside the entrance—demanding the password. Oh, dear! Tonight she was a completely demoralised soldier of the Irish Republican Sisterhood; completely untrustworthy. That silly frivolous Belle and her absurd elopement.

But it was Donal who answered. And he too forgot the conspiratorial initial. Instinct prompted him to respond to that unmistakable voice.

'Sterrin,' he answered, and drew back the massive bolts. On straw in a corner lay a youth of about seventeen. A half-suppressed moan escaped and Donal dropped her hand and went to the lad. In the dim light of a lantern she saw his white, pinched

616

eatures.

The boy, Donal told her, was his nephew, James Prendergast Keating, son of that pair whose wedding long ago had caused such a furore in the castle; and the near dismissal of a certain knife boy. James was supposed to be visiting with his grandparents at Poolgower before starting his Law studies. He had escaped with a bullet in the leg from the raid that Bergin had told her of, where the leader had been shot dead on sight.

'He must get to a doctor,' Donal whispered. 'The leg might mortify. Even if it does not he is not robust enough to bear prolonged pain.'

Sterrin looked at Donal's strained white face. It didn't seem to her as if he either was robust enough to continue the prolonged hardship of his mountain outlawry. 'If I could get him to Poolgower, my brother-in-law is there.'

'What about your brother?' She knew that he had made open pronouncements against the Fenians.

'James's James?' he said bitterly. 'He wouldn't think twice of informing upon me. Fortunately, he is away on business.'

'Come then,' she said. 'I'll help you with this James.' They half-carried, half-dragged him along the tunnel to the secret exit and on down to the dyke where the mare was tethered. Just as they were hoisting him on the pommel they heard sounds. The figures of men loomed out of the wet mist. Sterrin jumped bodily into the wet dyke and took the lower part of the boy's body in her arms. Donal crouched beside her holding the upper part. She prayed that there were no mounted troops. Their horses might seduce a coquettish whinny from the concealed Clooreen. But it was the police patrol returning. Over the bank the two could see them hammering at the fort. The sentinel would have plenty of time to escape through the passage and burrow out to the hilltop.

When the raiding party was out of sight, Sterrin bade Donal take the mare and go alone for the doctor. 'We'll never get him out of this now. I've got him in a fairly comfortable position.'

Donal tried to remonstrate. It was raining heavily. Sterrin was soaked. 'I cannot leave him like this. Hurry, you're wasting time.'

He eased the boy's body against the bank and clambered out. A swirl of rain sent him sideways. He saw her stoop her head to thumb her hood forward without disturbing the boy. 'Your

617

cloak is ruined. You'll be drowned.'

'Ssh,' she hushed him. ''Tis no time to think of finery. Take De Lacey's fields—Lubey's, I mean. He won't be about at this hour. You'll get to Poolgower that way in no time. I'd ride it in twenty minutes.'

'*You* would!' he smiled and disappeared.

He made the ride in twenty minutes, but not the return ride with his brother-in-law, Dr. Greyson-Quigley. It was an hour and twenty minutes before sound of their horses gladdened Sterrin's ears. She held the boy's limbs out of the water and her own were cramped and chilled. Sometimes he moaned. Once he moved his head and spoke.

'I say, I feel an awful rotter forcing a lady into such a predicament. You must be suffering frightfully.'

'Don't worry about my suffering. It's the kind that will dry out.'

After Donal and the doctor lifted the boy over the dyke, they had to lift Sterrin in the same way. She longed to rub her limbs I'll probably have to walk on my hands in earnest tonight, she thought with a grin. She had to squeeze back the tears. It was agony to try putting her legs to the ground. But she wouldn't hear of Dr. Greyson-Quigley's suggestion to come back for her when the patient was fixed up.

'No, they are waiting for me down there. I promised. I feel better already.'

As she neared the glow of the fires she heard footsteps padding hard behind her. Heavens, she thought, it must be one of the police raiders. But it was Donal.

'I forgot to give you this. Your cramp put your wetness out of my head. Put it on!' He helped her down and drew the horse out of sight of the squatters beyond the hedgerows. She was glad to undo her sodden cloak and put on the cloak he had brought her. The combs fell from her wet hair and a sudden red glow from the campfires showed her standing there with her hair cascading over her shoulders. He reached out and touched it gently.

'"A sacred forest covering the mysteries of thought..."' he quoted. She laughed and wrung the water from it.

'There is no mystery in my thoughts just now; only to dispose of this food then get home.'

He watched as she twisted it and pushed it up under the

oak's hood and he went on quoting...

' "Its wanton ringlets waved as the vine curls the tendrils." '
She untied the food bag. 'How on earth can you be romantic
n a night like this!' He took the bag from her and walked the
orse beside her.

'I can always be romantic where you are. It would take more
aan rain to damp the ardour I feel for you. Sterrin, will you
ot change your mind?'

She stopped.

'Donal, I will not face another loveless marriage.'

'Loveless! How could our marriage be loveless and the love
aat I have for you.'

'It isn't fair to ask you to do all the loving.'

'Oh, Sterrin, I'd do it with a heart and a half and for ever.
emember the happiest marriages are those where one loves
nd one permits herself to be loved.'

His tender logic sent a faltering through her where his love
ad failed. Why not let herself be loved? She could never hope
o know those transports of love she had known for another.
Vhy should she condemn herself to go through life—probably
s a sort of spinster widowed aunt eventually to Dominic's
hildren? She put out a hand.

'Perhaps when all this is over I—I shall permit myself to be
oved.'

The words sounded condescending to her but they were the
esponse to his reasoning and her hand pressed his with a
entleness that held no condescension. He held it as gently, then
aised it to his lips.

'When all this is over!' His pleasant voice was almost bitter.
When will that be?'

She had never heard him express doubt. Always he held out
igh glad hope that Ireland at last was on the verge of absolute
reedom.

'But, surely, it will be any day now. America will send aid.
Ve must be patient. Her officers have done splendid work
lready. The men are all ready; drilled and eager.'

'Drilled to carry pikes and walking sticks against millions of
reech-loaders and the cannons of the British fleet? Yes, the
nen are drilled and eager. They are on the topmost of their
agerness. They can go no further in that direction; only back-
vards. We might wait too long for America. She has her own

war to finish. Meanwhile, we have sixty per cent of the Britis
military in Ireland on our side. We have a fair stock from th
police barracks that have surrendered to us. We could make
start before the disaffected regiments are shipped out of Irelan
But, no, our leader keeps preaching patience. Stephens ha
done his work. His secret society is functioning. He is a brilliar
organiser, but not a soldier. He will wait too long.'

Sterrin was startled at such criticism of the great patriot wh
was the supreme Head of the Fenians! And from Donal!

'Yes, authority and power have gone to his head. Why doesn
he lead the men he has organised into battle? Why protract th
business of secret assembly, this cloak and dagger play? Th
secret administration of oaths. The men over there behind th
hedge need no oath administered to them. If they were n
Fenians already they became ones the moment the picka
brought the first wall down on their hearthstones.'

Before she could break the silence he coughed violently. Im
pulsively she put out her hand to him again.

'Donal, you are doing too much. Promise me that you will g
home tonight and rest. Get out of these clothes. I'll bring bac
your cloak tomorrow.'

They were on the outskirts now of the firelight and he dre
back from it in fear of recognition. From the shadow his voic
called softly.

'Keep it. It is my dearest treasure. I never hoped to see yo
wear it.'

What a funny thing for him to say, she thought, as she move
on to meet the evicted.

She thought of it later as she sat up in bed sipping hot mil
laced with poteen. Hannah picked up her sodden clothes—
'Now *that*, your Ladyship, is what I would call a beautifu
cloak.'

Sterrin, her face coated in layers of ointment, looked at th
cloak that the maid was holding out fully extended—a blu
barathea affair, lined with white satin and heavily trimmed wit
bands of velvet. Now she recognised it. It was the cloak tha
Donal bid so heavily for at the Auction—and with recognitio
she realised what he had meant about its being his deares
treasure. She had been too weary and wet to take in the implica
tion.

'That isn't the cloak you wore going out, your Ladyship.'

vas as near as Hannah dared approach to asking where it had
materialised from.

'I was loaned it when my own got saturated. I shall return it
omorrow.'

'Where will I tell Pakie Scally to return it to, your Lady-
hip?' Hannah was consumed with curiosity.

'No place, Hannah, and thank you kindly,' said Sterrin
weetly. 'I shall return it myself tomorrow.'

Sterrin did not return the cloak the next day. When she
woke in the morning her body ached from head to toe. She was
acked with pain and spent the day in bed. In the evening a
arty of military rode up the avenue. All in the castle held their
reath.

The lieutenant in charge explained his mission to Dominic.
The captain was on his way. He was here with his men to give
rotection or arms against the Fenians.

Captain Fitzharding-Smith was ushered in in time to hear
Dominic give the reply that the father he scarce remembered
ad given to Captain Fitzharding-Smith twenty-three years be-
ore, when the then lieutenant had suggested that he seek pro-
ection against the Whiteboys. His family, Dominic said, had
ever sought military aid against their tenants or any of their
ountrymen.

The young lieutenant interpreted Dominic's refusal as a per-
onal thing that slighted his own powers of protection—and
erhaps his swordsmanship. He smoothed his long moustache
nd gave a curt word of command and he marched his men off
he premises. Captain Fitzharding-Smith lingered on. He had
oped for a private word with Sterrin. He was worried about
er. He had heard mention of her name in connection with a
ideout where Fenians met and trained. He had listened to the
nexorable order—Fenians to be shot at sight, and he had seen
n lonely places, in the wake of patrols, the unarmed, unidenti-
ied bodies of young men from God-knows where. Lady O'Car-
oll came down and told him of Sterrin's illness. He expressed
is concern but the news brought him a strange sense of satis-
action. No warning of his, he felt, would have caused my Lady
Sterrin to lie low.

When Dominic sauntered into Sterrin's room with the news
f the military visit he was hardset to hold her down from
ushing to warn the men in the fort. Eventually he got the

password from her '—though I doubt if it will avail,' he grumbled, 'if the military get there first. They'll use explosives not passwords.'

'Take the short cut,' she urged and then she recalled him to give a warning signal in case the military were ahead of him.

She lay restless, refusing draughts that might betray her into sleep. Lady O'Carroll delayed the late drawing-room tea because Dominic had told her he would be back for it. When Hegarty came to quench the drawing-room lights, she bade him wait. At midnight she decided that Dominic had been thrown from his horse. The men servants organised a search. In the kitchen the women kept vigil. Mrs. Stacey turned the fanwheel round and round with her thoughts until the roar of eight blazing fires stayed her hand. At two o'clock Sterrin tossed the bedclothes from her.

'Are you crazy, Miss Sterrin's Ladyship?'

Sterrin pushed the maid from her path. In the stable yard Big John pleaded with her. She rode out, fever, pain completely overborne by the force of her dread for her brother.

The forty was empty. By the light of the lantern that she had carried inside her cloak she saw the door lying on the ground. There was a strange acrid smell in the air. It was as Dominic had said. The military had used explosives instead of passwords. But where, dear God, was Dominic?

The mare walked her home unguided almost a dead weight across her shoulders. In the stable yard Big John was just in time to lift her as she slid to the ground.

Captain Fitzharding-Smith came early in the morning to break the news to Lady O'Carroll that her son had been arrested.

Dominic had been turning away from the fort, his message delivered, when the military came charging up towards him with bayonets drawn. As they seized him, he implicated himself completely by sounding the bird cry that Sterrin had given him. The men inside heard and burrowed through the labyrinth to safety.

In the days that followed the staff at Kilsheelin were helpless and bewildered. It seemed to them as though the citadel of their lives was falling down through the centuries upon their unprotected heads. Their Ladyships, both prostrated upstairs. Their young master about to go on trial. For his life maybe. The end of a dynasty! When they heard the name of the Assize Judge they were filled with despair. His grandfather used to try the rebels of Ninety-eight. Twenty a day he would sentence to hanging, they recalled to each other, and he would crack jokes with the black cap on his head. This grandson cracked no jokes, but he found the black cap no burden. To Fenian rebels, high or low, he was merciless.

Upstairs Sterrin lay half delirious in fever. Dominic! The sensitive boy who had taken so long to grow into his years. It seemed like yesterday that he was an unbreeched lad rejoicing in his first pair of trousers, made from his great-grandfather's velvet breeches. And now, the grey frieze of the convict. For all the lovely hours of his youth. And she had sent him! The last of the O'Carrolls. A wailing shriek went out from her. It echoed down the corridors and stairs and into the great kitchen that had known the echoes of her laughter.

Mrs. Stacey hesitated no longer. She looked at the faces round her, Big John's, Hegarty's, Mike O'Driscoll's, Ellen's and in an outer sphere, not of their close-knit kin, Pakie Scally; gratitude for the home that had reared him yielding to the loyalty that was theirs by generations of association. Milesian servant and Milesian lord fighting the same odds, sharing the same destiny. Mrs. Stacey's milk had nourished Sir Roderick, the father of Master Dominic, her darling. At the breast of Hegarty's mother, old Sir Dominic had been nursed in foster-age. Big John too, his blood was linked with the O'Carrolls by the milk of his womenfolk.

'I'll do it!' The big cook rose slowly to her full height, grim with purpose, she dwarfed them all; even the coachman no longer towered. His good shoulder drooped in sorrow to meet its maimed comrade. They knew what she meant. In the night hours it had been whispered on a stillborn breath—a thought too terrible to voice. Hegarty broke the silence. 'In God's name then!'

Big John turned towards Pakie Scally, 'Yoke the back-to-back.' He turned back to the cook. 'I'll drive you—Mary!' A frightened gasp went from Ellen. 'Mary!'

It had started.

They drove first to the house of the widow of George Lucas —the murderer of Sir Roderick who had died in jail. She listened and went pale. 'I've never had anything to do with the like——'

'Mary Lucas,' interrupted Mrs. Stacey sternly. 'Lady Sterrin is your foster-child. Sir Dominic is the last of his line. If his father's young life had not been taken from him by your husband——'

'You have no need to tell me,' the woman whispered. 'I know.' She looked about her fearfully, then whispered. 'I'll be there.'

Josie Scally, neat and lissom in her parlourmaid's dress, opened the back door of Mrs. Wright's private residence beside the shop. 'But, Mrs. Stacey, ma'am,' she said when she heard, 'my name isn't right. I'm Josie——'

'And Mary too,' the big cook interrupted. 'You were christened Mary Josephine.' And then solemnly, 'We have need of you, Mary Josephine Scally.'

Dread lent a greenish hue to the olive pallor of the Connemara girl.

'All right, Mrs. Stacey,' she whispered, 'I'll be there.'

Among the tenants five more women named Mary were enlisted. 'We will get the others at the Crossroads dance on the Holy Day,' Mrs. Stacey said. 'The crowds of the world will be there.'

But on the Holy Day the American flag waved forlornly over the empty dance sward. Where fiddlers and melodeon players were to have played for the dancers it was a time of mourning. Boats still brought lists of dead from the battlefield at Fredericksburg. There were bereavements in every townsland; still worse, neighbour glanced askance at neighbour, for neighbour's son had killed neighbour's son. It was said that of the fourteen hundred Meagher took into battle, only two hundred and fifty survived. Some told of bodies lying on the frozen plains still unburied. At Mass on that Assumption Day it was like Palm Sunday. Every second prayerbook held a green sprig; not of blessed palm but of the evergreen that had been plucked, at General Meagher's suggestion, by the great Irish Sixty-Ninth and worn in their tunics as they rushed to meet the death storm of Mayre's Heights.

After Mass, Mrs. Stacey waited at the Crossroads but the mourning women drove past her and past the flag their sons had died for; no lingering or gosthering. Mrs. Stacey drove on, her dread purpose unfulfilled. The Assize Judge drew nearer on his circuit, and in the barracks day after day, Dominic, frail but inflexible, faced his questioners. Mrs. Stacey went to the railroad station where the mothers and widows of the fallen men were to collect their pay. She spoke to the black-cloaked women. Some turned from her. But Mrs. Ryan Fortynine, a cousin of Black Pat Ryan's, listened and nodded her head. One or two others did the same.

Sterrin's fever abated. As her strength came back, she felt an overpowering surge to be up making some effort for her brother; anything, throw herself on the mercy of the court, give herself up; go plead with the Deputy Lieutenant of the County. He had been entertained here at the lunch for the opening of the railroad. Her legs felt strangely stiff and weak as she made her first effort across the room while it was empty. She rested awhile on the chaise longue then moved restlessly to the window and rested her warm forehead on the cool glass. Gradually as one plan after another chased around her frantic brain she became conscious of something unusual going on in the yard beneath. Every few moments, a woman, cloak-muffled, would flit almost furtively across the yard towards the kitchen entrance. As a fourth woman entered the yard towards the kitchen Sterrin raised the window. In the shaft of light as the kitchen door opened to her knock, Sterrin thought she recognised Mrs. Ryan Fortynine. She leaned out and caught a low murmur of greeting—'God be with you, Mary,' and the visitor's response, 'And with you, too, Mary.'

What on earth would Mrs. Ryan Fortynine be doing here at this hour? So far from her little shop in Templetown. Sterrin was not likely to mistake Mrs. Ryan Fortynine. Every year at Christmas, when she was a little girl, she used to give her a quart can of sweets. Another figure appeared. This time, even before the light flashed, Sterrin recognised Mrs. Ryan Ha-Lad. But she was a regular visitor to the kitchen nowadays. Why this furtive approach, almost tiptoeing and lookings to right and left? The greeting was repeated. Each addressed the other as Mary and now Sterrin was certain that the one who greeted the visitors was Mrs. Stacey. She had never heard Mrs. Stacey addressed by her Christian name. There was something eerie about all this. These women were not dropping in for a friendly coordheec[1] in the kitchen. They were coming stealthily as

[1] Visit.

though their purpose was sinister. A shiver of memory ran through Sterrin. Still another figure was flitting through the dusk and in the flash from the doorway Sterrin recognised Josie Scally, the sister of Pakie and Attracta. She was conscious of something like relief that there was a break in the dark chain of Marys—But no! 'God be with you, Mary,' said the voice of Mrs. Stacey. 'And you, too, Mary.' Mary! From the homeless mite who had materialised long ago in the kitchen from under her dead mother's cloak that had draped two other sisters as well, and when they had given their names the High Priestess of the kitchen had said to her, 'Mary Josephine is too long. I'll call you Josie.'

There was no one about. Hannah was helping Nurse Hogan with Lady O'Carroll, who was crushed with worry about Dominic. Sterrin tiptoed slowly down the back stairs, clinging to the banisters, amazed that she could not take two steps at a time.

No voices sounded from the kitchen. It was strangely quiet as though some distant torrent had suddenly ceased. She peeped in. Ellen sat crouched over the fireplace, hands limp, no knitting, no crochet. Attracta sat at a table, her face in her hands. The men, Hegarty, O'Driscoll and Pakie Scally, stood around, their eyes straying towards a passage beyond the yard door. From where they watched there came a low diapason of sound.

Sterrin grasped the door and tried to quieten her breathing. It was labouring as never before. But she must see what was happening. Suspicion was hardening into certainty. The only way that she could get to that passage without going through the kitchen would be to retrace her steps up the servants' stairs and across the gallery and down the main staircase across the hall to where a little passage branched off the kitchen to the bard's quarters.

To contemplate that way, it seemed endless. She who should accomplish it with a hop, step and a jump! She set her teeth, gripped the banisters and started to climb. When she finally dragged herself across the gallery she leaned over the polished banisters and slide down the front staircase on her stomach, the way she had done as a child. At last she reached the passage outside the bard's bedroom where the strange noise was coming from. Soundlessly she turned the knob. The door was locked. She moved on and let herself into the big music room, where he had spent his years since the Big Wind had damaged the outer wall of his bedroom. Soundlessly again she turned the knob of the inner door. It yielded and a gasp of horror escaped her. The bard's bed was dressed for a deathbed. Around the bed the black-cloaked women bowed and writhed and brought their hands together in silent claps and from their lips came the subdued wails of the death lament. The focus of their keening was a small black object that lay in the centre of the corpseless bed.

And Sterrin knew that she was witnessing the terrible Wake of the Thirteen Marys.

She turned to flee the horrible scene but her limbs were powerless. Then she heard Dominic's name, but the black article on the bed did not belong to Dominic; not as the rosary beads and the military medals of the Scout's son and of others like him had been waked instead of their young bodies that lay under American skies. Dominic was alive and no one would wake the living youth, unless those who wished him dead. And this wake was to wish him life. Another name was mentioned. The women clapped and moaned in a grief that was almost satiric. Sterrin knew the name. In the Fenian 'circle' it was uttered with dread. The Judge who bore it left a trail of hangings and transportations and floggings in the path of his circuit. Tomorrow he would pass sentence on Dominic.

Sterrin moved to stop the frightful orgy, but Dominic's face swam before her, the gentle brown eyes, the fair hair. Calvagh O'Carroll had had fair hair too, and he was hanged. Nonchalant as a French aristo in a tumbril he had helped the hangman to tie the knot. And the citadel of the O'Carrolls had dwindled further. And the little boys of old Sir Dominic had died of the cholera. All but Papa. And Papa had been murdered. Murdered by the husband of that woman over there, writhing and moaning with the others to save the life of his victim's son. The last of the splendid line.

Something stirred in the pre-Celtic roots of her being. She dropped the hand raised to protest. She closed the door and left them to it.

It is only a silly superstition, she told her labouring heart as she climbed back. Like putting one's clothes on the floor in the shape of a 'T' on Hallowe'en night. Like pouring melted lead through——! 'Hannah!' The maid was rushing along opening doors as she went. 'Miss Sterrin, where were you?'

627

Sterrin threw herself in the maid's arms.

'Hannah, don't leave me. Hannah, stay with me all night.'

The maid carried her to her bed.

'You were down there, Miss Sterrin,' she spoke in a fearful whisper. 'I see it in your face.' She didn't realise that the face was naked of masks or bandages or veil. She saw only the terror-filled eyes, the mouth trembling as never before.

'You saw them!' She made the sign of the cross. 'Don't think of it, Miss Sterrin.'

'I shall always think of it. I shall never be able to forget it, Hannah. Never!'

The day of the trial extra police were drafted in from neighbouring towns. They stood with fixed bayonets round the courthouse. Every tenant turned out. Young Sir Dominic was beloved of them all. While they crowded the front entrance a cab brought him to the back entrance. Inside the panoply of justice was arrayed. The world must know that Sir Dominic O'Carroll would not be the victim of an indiscriminate order. No shooting at sight. A jury waited in the wings. Many of them, landlords, were incensed, not because of treason against Her Majesty, but because of this business of Lady Devine. The idea of feeding and pampering tenants whom *they* had chosen to evict.

The minutes dragged by. Court officials whispered. In the gallery Maurice O'Carroll and Lord Cullen looked at watches and conferred. Lady Biddy Cullen was there and Mrs. Delaney. Mr. and Mrs. James Wright and Miss Berry Comerford. Ulick Prendergast waited as he had waited in sympathy for the father of the boy that last day of his life. So did Michael Joseph, Michael Ryan and Marty Hennessey and as many of their faction as could squeeze in. James de Guider assisted his brother Stephen into the court—the first time the lame old gentleman had been in Templetown since the famine. Their relative Patrick de Guider was there, the sole survivor of the fourteen brothers who had died of famine fever contracted from the stirabout line of Connemara migrants.

The Clerk of the Crown Peace came into the Court and announced that the trial must be postponed. The judge was ill!

Pakie Scally erupted from the court. He went to the Kilsheelin carriage and whispered to Big John. The coachman looked down to where his cousin, Mary Hennessey, stood looking up. He nodded—a prearranged signal—and she turned to Mary Ryan and to Mary Lucas and behind them was Josie Scally, christened Mary, who had crept out in her mistress's absence. They were there; all of them. The women who had keened the terrible Wake of the Thirteen Marys.

Mrs. Stacey tensed at a window in the castle as she saw Pakie Scally coming at full gallop. He gave her the news. The judge was ill at his lodgings; gravely ill. He had felt poorly starting out from the last Assizes town. The doctors had advised him to desist, but he had pursued his circuit. And now he lay at his Templetown lodgings in an agony of colic from which he could scarce recover.

She moved into the room she had made ready with her own hands. She quenched the candles that still burned round the empty, black-draped bed where she and the women she had summoned had keened the living judge. She lifted the three-cornered black object from the centre of the bed and handed it to Pakie.

'Get it back to where it came from,' she said.

That night the judge died.

Another came in his place. His name brought a glint of hope to Sterrin. She went to the kitchen.

'This time,' she said, 'let justice take its course.' It was the only indication she allowed them of her knowledge of the wake. At the door she paused. 'The last judge died as a result of something that the doctors are calling appendicitis.' She looked meaningly around the circle of faces; 'Something inside him that burst.'

When the door had closed on her Mrs. Stacey broke the silence. Low and grim she muttered: 'It waited till the right time to burst.' She swung the crane from the fire to remove a pot. 'What's this young Thomas used to say when no butter but turf would come in the milk an' we churnin', an' across the bog at the same time Mag Miney would churn pounds of butter from a taschain of cream? There's more things in heaven and earth, he used to say, than anyone in this world dreams of.'

Sterrin went to her room and put on the black water-silk gown she had long since laid aside. She ran her hands down over her body. Illness had whittled down her waistline. She

629

could almost span it with her two hands. That was something anyway! She felt a sudden resurgence of her old pride in her looks and took a step towards the mirror then stopped. No, not now. If I look at it I won't be able to go on. Her marred face would not fit in with her plan to help 'the course of justice'. She dragged her hair from its chignon and pinned it in bunched-up ringlets that fell on either cheek. The new style was a help to her scars, though she hated the podgy look of those barrel curls dangling on women's faces. She preferred to drape her hair across her ears and secure it back in a knot on her neck. Grecian they called it, though the bard used it to say it was the old Irish fashion. Ah, Bard, what would you say if you knew that the last of the family was on trial for his life? And what would you say Bard, if you were to know the paltry part myself is trying to play in this cause? Pride and shame halted her, but suddenly she recalled the bard in his bawdy moments.

I know what he'd say, her thoughts took tongue with the din of her desperation. He'd say, More power to you, Sterrin. Daughter of Roderick O'Carroll. Go in there to Templetown and beguile the daylights out of that man. She pinned an exquisite veil of finest Carrickmacross lace over her face. She rummaged for lip salve and longed after the French lip rouge in jewelled boxes that had gone with the flames. Ah well! Her eyes fell on the red-backed novel beside her bed. She seized it. Any port in a storm! She moistened the cover and rubbed its red dye through the lip salve, then with the aid of a tiny pocket mirror that barely showed her mouth, she raised the veil and reddened the pouting outline. She threw Donal's cloak about her shoulders and from the doorway darted one frantic look towards the mirror.

In his Templetown lodgings the judge frowned at the sound of a tap on his sitting-room door. Hadn't he given orders that he was not to be disturbed? Without waiting for his response the door opened. Despite the veil his first impression was that the intruder was a beautiful woman. The slender frame, the poise of the head, the suffusion of hair, the set of the shoulder. The face was framed in the white satin lining of the hood that rested upon her shoulder in classic folds. His eyes, narrow from assessing men right through their faces to their hearts to see if they held guilt, tried to penetrate the very attractive veil, but all that he could see was a glow of red defining a mouth that would ve allured in the days of his susceptibility!

'Madam, this is——'

'I am Lady Devine. I——' She was about to recall their meet-
g at the Assizes Ball at Kilkenny when she remembered her
adacious choice of a rebel song when it was her prerogative to
ll the tune; *and* his embarrassment. Till now, all she had
membered was his appreciative glances and the fan-fluttered
nts of his amorous past. 'You visited us at Nore Hall,' she
mended.

If this was a belated return visit, it was as disconcerting as her
noice of dance tune! But he was on his feet to his former
ostess. 'I heard, with deep regret, of its demolition by fire. I
eard, too, that you suffered injuries saving the life of your
naid.'

A glove ready unbuttoned was removed from beneath her
oak. He saw her draw her hand from beneath her cloak as
hough it were a nervous gesture of unconscious reaction; noted
quick glance at a red scar on a pretty hand then it was back
eneath the folds.

'I have come about my brother——'

His hand shot up. 'My Lady! This is something that cannot
e discussed between us. You may not tamper with justice. The
risoner who will stand before me tomorrow cannot be tried as
nyone's brother or son. He will be tried as a rebel and given a
air trial.'

'He is no rebel,' she flashed. 'It is I who am the rebel.'

I can well believe it, he thought. And a dangerous one. The
ind of rebel the young men would follow madly and think
was Caitlin Ni Houlihan herself. Ireland the Queen, with that
egal head of hers and that clear voice. He'd follow her himself,
egod, if he were twenty years younger, ay fifteen years younger.

'I can well believe it, my Lady,' he repeated aloud, 'I seem to
ecall a certain rebel song called for at a certain hall.'

'Ah, that was naughty of me!'

'There is nothing I can do, Milady,' the judge was firm.

'Sir, he is so young, sensitive, immature——' The clear voice
vas cutting through the surge of memory. 'He is the last of
s—my mother—— You see, sir, I asked him to take a message.
Ie had no idea of its implication. I rushed him because I was ill
nyself.'

'Otherwise you would have brought it yourself. What was the

631

message pray?' Dammit. What am I saying? This was parleyin
with her.

'Just to warn brave men that *they* were to be denied th
benefit of appearing before you in "fair trial". They were to b
shot at sight!'

A nimble wit, by gad. It could be titillating to draw it furthe

'A daring admission! My Lady, I regret that I must end thi
interview; this discussion. It is extremely unethical.' Suddenl
he frowned. 'There have been other unethical methods tried o
your brother's behalf. Some absurd superstitious rites. Stupid
of course, but ruthless, murderous even, in their concept.'

In the Bar mess that evening the barristers had talked o
nothing else. Grand Jurors, they said, were laughing at the ide
of it, while looking over their shoulders apprehensively.

'Surely, my Lady, you don't believe in that kind of thing?'

'My father did.'

'He was superstitious?'

'Far from it. He was intolerant of all superstition except tha
one. But, that, of course, was merely an association with him. I
his childhood some women held the Wake of the Thirtee
Marys on a priest.'

'You surprise me. I didn't think that they would wreak suc
hatred upon their priest.'

'It was not that they hated the priest whom they waked. I
was that they loved so much his predecessor who had bee
transferred. They wanted him back.'

'What happened?'

'The new priest died. But of course,' she commented reassur
ingly, 'it was of a broken heart that he died.'

'It is monstrous,' said the judge. 'Ghoulish—such practice
should be investigated by the law and punished. Tell me, m
Lady, this orgy, this er—wake, is it still in progress?'

She gave a slow shrug. 'Who knows? People—*our* peopl
would do anything if they thought it would save my brothe
but——' she paused and her eyes seemed to compel him. H
could not see their colour. Colour never mattered to him. It wa
the setting that he had ever bothered to observe. He could detec
the almond sweep in the deep pit of those eyes behind the veil

'Yes?'

'They would do anything for me too *if*'—she paused on th
slight emphasis—'if I were to ask them.'

The little niggling cloud that had shadowed the judge since he had heard of the wake seemed suddenly to melt. His rest tonight would be all the more peaceful for the assurance that a circle of harpies was not trying to keen him out of existence. Her ungloved hand was extended to him, high-arched, inviting. He took it and turned the scar upwards.

'A brave scar, my Lady.' He raised it to his lips. 'You are a very gallant person, Lady Devine.'

Next day on the bench, through interlaced fingers, he watched Donal Keating conduct Sir Dominic's defence. Donal's name was not yet on the Hue and Cry list. No one suspected that he was a Fenian leader.

The testing time had not found Dominic lacking. He had divulged no name to his questioners. The judge listened to the impassioned plea, the prisoner's youth, his family's great prestige, and of course, his complete innocence. He didn't miss the equally impassioned looks that escaped from the Defence Lawyer towards the veiled figure in the public gallery. Whatever was behind that veil now, there were women who could exude the quality of beauty even though they were as plain as bedamned. I'd take me oath he's pleading for the sister's love as well as for the brother's release! The learned Counsel looked a lot thinner than on the night of the Kilkenny Assizes Ball, when he danced after her, holding up her train and singing, *Paddies Evermore*. The solemn-faced judge sighed nostalgically. Didn't I do it all myself? Rebellions, love, poetising, until the serious things, fame, money, rank, caused him to put them away like a gay costume after a Bal Masqué.

After his release, Sir Dominic was carried from the Court on the shoulders of his cheering tenants. In the outsurging crowd Sterrin got separated from Maurice who had come from Waterford for the trial. Jammed in the doorway crush she saw the redoubtable Scout; sadly out of character; no longer the thrusting, elbowing newsmonger clamouring to know 'Why wasn't I told?', the supreme newsbearer who had bribed with gold a wagoner so that he, Scout Doyle, would be the first to proclaim to Templetown the astounding news of O'Connell's arrest. Sterrin had a flash of memory of the doughty Scout arriving at a lumbering gallop up the front avenue, no less, to proclaim the great news to her Papa. As she passed him Sterrin said, 'It is great news Mr. Doyle.' The sad face quickened at her recognition. The chimney-pot hat swept high.

'An *aus*pital occasion, my Lady. Most momentatious! My heart mourned with the mother's heart of Lady O'Carroll in her hour of decrepitude.'

Sterrin had a feeling that the verdict had deprived him of sharing an equality of grief with her mother. On a sudden impulse she said:

'I wish we could get the news more quickly to her.' She nodded to where the eager supporters were endeavouring to unharness the horses and draw the carriage themselves. 'Would you be so kind, Mr. Doyle, as to hire a horse, or fly chaise, in my name at Mullally's and hurry ahead of us to Kilsheelin?'

Like the old war horse that scented the battle from afar, the Scout was back in his role. The horny elbows were flailing right and left beating a path for the bearer of 'momentatious' news.

Another voice murmured into her ear as she forced through the cheering mob. The blacksmith, under cover of assisting her to the carriage where Cousin Maurice O'Carroll was waiting, had something else to convey to her with his congratulations. She gave him a quick look of apprehension.

'My cousin insists on taking me to Waterford tomorrow—but—only to recuperate. No more of the other—I have involved my family too far.'

'Your Ladyship, nothing could be more opportune for us now than your trip.'

She had never heard such urgency in the quiet voice.

'It was yourself who spoke of your uncle's Castle, his Sacred Cove. Let him allow our ships to land guns in that cove. Your Ladyship, please! This is the last demand I shall make of you. We are within a heartbeat of success. No more trials and transportations.'

Maurice O'Carroll drew her to the carriage. Sterrin struggled to hold back the tears. She had reached breaking point, and was shaking from exhaustion and fear. The opening of the carriage door seemed a reprieve from the sinister commitments of secret oaths. But as she placed her foot on the step she gave a quick glance over her shoulder and nodded her head to the blacksmith.

CHAPTER 58

Thomas came from his hotel room drawing on his gloves. Immediately, two big obvious-looking men rose from an ottoman and approached him. One of them spoke to him, 'Are you Captain O'Carroll of the American Army?'

Thomas was outraged. '*I* am Thomas Young, the actor.' He spoke with an elegant mince. The plain clothes men looked at each other. 'But sir,' said the man, 'we have reason to believe that you have documents that declare your commission in the American Army.'

A long, slow dawning played elaborately across Thomas's face. 'Those! But they are belonging to poor O'Carroll who went down in that awful charge led by General Hooker——' He covered his face. 'God, I hate to recollect it. I was to play there, and would you believe it, the theatre had been converted into a hospital! Blood! I simply loathe the sight of it!' His voice fluted into femininity.

'Poor O'Carroll,' he resumed, 'he asked me to bring some belongings to relatives in Londonderry—he was positively saturated with this—*Seltic*—sentimentality—I thought Londonderry was some suburb of London, but Major de Waters of the 10th Hussars—I'm supping with him tonight after the performance—tells me that the place is away in the north of this country, a whole day's journey off. It is most inconvenient.'

The two policemen looked at each other. The 10th Hussars! The crack regiment of the British Army!

They started an apologetic withdrawal when the door next to Thomas's room opened.

'Excuse me, sir,' said Alphabet Dignam. 'His Excellency's lady kong brought this. It is for tomorrow's reception at the Vice Regal——' Thomas flicked it a negligent glance and closed his eyes. Blast Alphabet! He gestured the card towards the police. 'Do you wish to see this?' Pray God you don't! 'If you have any further doubts.' The police 'not-at-alled' and turned.

Thomas was releasing his breath when they turned back from whispered conference.

'Might we just ask you this man's name?'

'That is a difficult question. You see,' said Thomas, 'th answer requires more time than I can spare.' He started enumerating on his fingers, 'Alcium, Beracium, Conceptione Dionysius, Ephraim—look here, I have to be on the stage in twenty minutes and he has a Christian name for every letter in the alphabet—show the gentlemen your baptismal certificate Alphabet! The surname is Duignam. It was his father's idea the plethora of Christian names.' The police had reached the stairshead. Thomas drew out his card and scribbled.

'Perhaps you would like to see the performance? This wil admit you to two seats, with my compliments.'

They thanked him and withdrew. Thomas rounded on his body-servant. 'You damned idiot! What did you mean by but ting in? And could you find nothing more convincing than card for the Fenian picnic at Cincinnati?'

'I thought it would add vermilion to your statement, sir.'

'It almost did,' said Thomas grimly. 'Go peep over the ban sters and see what they are about.'

Alphabet returned with the information that the policeme had just passed out through the front door. 'They seemed satis fied, sir, that you were not a Fenian. One of them just tappe his forehead and shrugged. The gesture alluded to you, sir.'

It was the first shadow on Thomas's luck. It was also the firs time in years that he had put on the play in which poor Henr Monteith, his leading man, had died. As Thomas lay on th Gaiety stage in Henry's part he almost yawned. He had spen the previous night on the Dublin mountains drilling volunteer and he was sleepy.

Up in the gods an impatient wag prodded him awake. 'Ye're long time dyin', Misther Young.' The interrupter was chide from the opposite side of the gallery.

'Shut up, you bosthoon! Some people have no appreciashu of dhrama.' Thomas, in the process of getting up, nearly fe back when his sympathiser called down, 'Taker your time Misther Young! Die away there!'

Drill, thought Thomas, as he released his yawn in his dressing room, does not blend with drama. But he kept his suppe appointment at the officers' mess in Island Bridge barracks. An he kept his appointment for the slopes of the Dublin hills at two in the morning, and of the two hundred British soldiers to whom he administered the Fenian oath there, at least eighty belonged to the dashing Tenth Hussars.

Sterrin, lying on the chaise longue in her mother's boudoir, read the account of Thomas's run at the Gaiety. She was still convalescing from the rheumatic fever she had contracted and wasn't supposed to strain her heart by horse promenading or strenuous walking, yet here she was lying completely still and her heart was beating as violently as if she had climbed the Devil's Bit on foot! She resented the horrid thudding; not only because her heart had been growing strong but because it had started to know peace. Since Dominic's trial she had made up her mind about Donal. His passionate plea in her brother's defence had stirred more response in her heart than the pleas he had made to herself. Donal appealed to her heart though he could not compel it. And never could he cause it to beat as it was going now.

'Mamma, will you be needing Big John this afternoon?' she asked.

'No, darling. Unless you wish me to accompany you on a carriage promenade.'

Sterrin did not want to be accompanied. She wanted to go alone to the forge. The blacksmith would contact Donal for her.

As she started out for the forge Big John told her that it had been raided. It was a year since she had seen the blacksmith. She dreaded to find that he might have had to go forth 'on his keepin''. Still, all seemed well when they got there. She could hear the smith's voice, a rich rumble of melody, as she entered the forge. He broke off with a startled exclamation as she followed in the wake of the horse Big John led in. 'Which shoe is it?' he asked. Then from somewhere under the horse's belly he said, 'None of these shoes is loose.' He must be under some strain, she thought. Normally, he accepted that the horse was merely led in to cover her visit.

Just then the police arrived. They seemed strangely surprised to see the smith here but they ransacked the place just the same. Constable Younghusband went up the chimney and when his feet had dangled down like a pair of churns for ten minutes he plumped to the ground. He held out something with an air of triumph to the officer. 'I found the implements for making cartridges, sir.'

Sub-Inspector Bible examined them and threw them aside. 'These are muddlers for making punch.' The constable hadn't looked too bright not even without all the soot on his face and his shako not askew.

Another constable brought forth an ominous-looking iron pole. 'Ah!' the sub-inspector was pleased. 'A pike!' The smith lifted a shoe from the furnace. Without looking up he said, 'Mrs. O'Hanlon doesn't call it that. It is the stake she has tethered the goat to for the last forty years.'

The officer brought the pole nearer the fire. 'Of course,' said the blacksmith. 'I may be wrong about the goat, sir, it may not always have been the same one, but it is the same stake.' The officer flung the stake from him and told the smith peremptorily that he was sending his horse, the grey, down immediately for shoeing.

'Certainly, sir,' he said cheerfully. 'Isn't it extraordinary,' he continued chattily, 'how fashions change! When my father had the livery stable he used to charge five pounds extra to hire out a grey. Now, greys are quite out of fashion. A body couldn't hire one out at all if there was any other colour available.' He tightened his leather apron. 'It is the same with women's hair. There was a time when a body would cross the street out of the path of a red-haired woman. Now, red hair is all the fashion.'

A shower of sparks showed Sterrin palely proud, the red lights in her hair intensified by the reddened darkness. The officer had seen the elegant carriage outside. To offset the smith's over-familiar remarks he saluted in her direction then withdrew.

Sterrin was puzzled Denis never made facetious remarks. But she was not surprised that the inspector's manner had rattled him. It had rattled herself. 'I want you to get a message to Donal—to Mr. Keating,' she said.

He looked up quickly. 'No,' she reassured him, 'it is not anything to do with the "circle". It—it is something—personal. Well, you know the way it is.'

'Er—yes,' he said respectfully. 'I know the way it is.'

'I have decided'—she hesitated—'to take your advice.'

She was surprised that he had no eager comment. Something was amiss. But what? In the silence her eyes lighted on the little

638

iron kettle. 'Constable Younghusband hasn't spilled all the water,' she said, 'with those feet of his. Don't you think there would be sufficient left for tea?' He looked vaguely round. 'Here it is!' She picked up the little rusty caddy that the police had pushed from its usual place.

The great fire had subsided. Only the rattle of bridle and bits and the occasional stamping of hooves showed that a horse stood in the dark shadows behind the glow.

He filled the big mug and extended it towards her.

She looked down at it startled. No apology for its uncouthness. 'What has happened to my cup?' A flame spurted up and played on the mug, on the black fingers, black as soot, down to the last graceful, tapering point! Not the work-hardened, calloused blunt, blistered fingers that Denis had spread out to show their unworthiness of her handshake.

'Who are you?' she whispered. She made no effort to take the mug. A flame spurted upwards towards his face and answered her question.

'You!' she breathed.

'Sterrin!'

Often she had wondered what would she do, what would she say, if she were to meet him again; this man who had filled her heart so full that there was no comfortable space left for any other man. She would pass him by! Look through him haughtily. She scraped her throat. 'Where is—"L"?' That wasn't what she meant to say and, Oh, God, she had let slip the initial by which Denis was known in the 'Circle'.

He gave a startled exclamation. 'You know that?'

Wheels sounded on the cobbles outside.

'He is on his keeping.' It was a whisper. 'I am covering for him to get away while the search is hot.'

There were other things she wanted to know. 'Are you in love with that woman? Who is she? How did you come to marry her so quickly.' But all she said was 'Are you a Fenian?'

He nodded. 'I am—"V". Sterrin, listen.' He put down the mug. They were alone in the warm sensuous darkness. Her heart was racing. It was not supposed to incur excitement. Behind her the horse champed, shook its head and set all its bits rattling. Thomas strained through the veil and glimpsed the deep pit of her eye, the poreless pallor of skin. 'Sterrin!' Big John blocked the horseshoe opening. 'Have you finished the

639

shoeing,' he said meaningly and withdrew.

Thomas stretched forth to take her hand. Involuntarily she took a step back. He mistook her gesture. How could he know that if he threw those blackened arms around her and crushed her against Denis's grubby leather apron she would have rested there; never to leave. 'I had forgotten the black,' he said.

Words came to her. The wrong ones. 'You forget quickly.' Her voice was tense and strained with the dint of keeping it low. 'Your hands reach out too readily to women! The woman you flaunted before me, pawing her, caressing her in public, so soon after—in Paris in——'

'Sub-Inspector Bible wants his horse shod immediately.' A policeman entered, followed by a groom leading a horse.

'Right you are,' the blacksmith called back. 'Thank you, your Ladyship,' he said, 'I'll just lead out your horse and give the coachman a hand.'

The policeman saluted Lady Devine as she passed. Outside two policemen guarding the forge saluted. The blacksmith backed the horse into the shafts and as he stooped to fasten the leathers, he murmured just loud enough for Sterrin to hear. 'The "pawing" was necessary. She is blind!'

The doctor had told Sterrin she needed rest and care. There was nothing that rest and care could not cure. Nothing. Sterrin agreed, as she stared out of the window of the coach. She was cured of the excitements that had disturbed her heart. Heart strain! No sickness of the body would have made her heart plunge as the sight of *him* had done that day. No sickness could drag it down with such a lurch as had those words 'she is blind'. All the suppressed, unformulated hopes had died in that moment: the inventive love, half guilty, half yearning, prompting her that he would tire of the other. She's some fast actress who caught him on the rebound; embracing him in public. She might have known that Young Thomas of the gentle smile would never indulge such behaviour. Oh that smile that had flashed its comfort at her across her father's grave! But wasn't he the one who had come well out of the *débâcle* of that star-crossed love? Hadn't he got himself a wife who was young and comely, who would hold him for ever with the mystique of her blindness and its pleading pathos that would ensure for ever that pity which is so closely akin to love?

No, no more excitement.

The pace at Kilsheelin slowed perceptibly. Sterrin took solitary walks. She brooded in Sir Roderick's study. She received calls but returned them with cards left by Pakie Scally, pressed into service as a footman, in the livery that had been bought out of her lavish trousseau account. Were it not for Mrs. Kennedy-Sherwin, now living with the Crimea-wrecked Jeremy, nobody at the castle would have known that Pakie guarding the immaculacy of his white gloves until almost the very opening of each door had held the cards grasped in his moist hands.

'One never has to read the inscription on the cards he leaves,' thrilled the still irrepressible little lady. 'One only had to glance down at the salver on the ones that have black smudges.' Big John had nearly died of shame.

There were few visitors at Kilsheelin. The Delaneys called occasionally. James de Guider dropped in quite frequently. sometimes to talk, sometimes to ask for help in tracing his family genealogy. Soon after Sterrin's return from the convent James had married his housekeeper. At the time Sterrin had attached little significance to James's marriage. To be sure, it was a come-down for a dandified and aristocratic gentleman, but James was impoverished, as well as very lonely. Lady O'Carroll had refused to call on Mrs. de Guider. She felt that James had let Roderick down by this misalliance.

Now James was seeking the trail of his kind. The spectacle of his two little sons being brought up without the graces and refinements that he had known in his own childhood had spurred him to start another manuscript of his family genealogy. The old one had been destroyed by the Big Wind. The Famine had finished the downward tread of their fortunes. Its pestilence had taken fourteen of his married brother's fifteen sons. The surviving one was an invalid. James felt that since he could not give his sons fortune of a gentleman's education, it was incumbent upon himself to leave them at least a record of a lineage of which they could be proud.

During his visits to the castle, James pored over the bard's records and prowled around the old roofless church in the O'Carroll burying ground, where so many of the de Guiders had been buried. Once Sterrin went with him to the graveyard and scraped lichen from monuments that proclaimed that The

Comerford of The Devil's Bit had brought two hundred foot soldiers to help The O'Carroll drive from his lands the 'Four Men of Cheshire' to whom Queen Elizabeth had given over Tipperary. The daughter of The Comerford, ancestors of James's mother, had married The O'Carroll and was buried beneath the stone. But what James had hoped to find was some record of one of the Strague O'Carrolls who had been dispossessed by his youngest son. A Timothy de Guider, who had been High Constable for the North Riding of Tipperary at the time had appointed the elder son O'Carroll to a position as Collector of Hearths and Window taxes, and one of his descendants, Thomas O'Carroll, had married James's very young Aunt Johanna de Guider—youngest of eighteen children. Her husband, James discovered, had been killed protecting his holding against the Tithe Proctor's in 1833. That same week his wife had given birth to a son in a neighbouring house, but there was no trace of the house, mother or child. 'And this child,' Sterrin interrupted excitedly, 'would actually be the lawful heir to Strague Castle?'

James nodded. 'And my children's cousin. Yes.'

She wondered did the Stragues know about this Thomas O'Carroll.

Sterrin had an inspiration. She told him about the silver drinking cup that the old hermit of Bawn na Drum Castle had shown her. His grandfather had got it from the dispossessed O'Carroll. 'He might be able to trace the boy you are looking for.'

As they wandered back through the tombstones, she came upon the tiny grave of little Theobald Hennessey, Young Thomas's god-child. She recalled how Mark, the father, and young Thomas had taken turns carrying the little wooden box and how the tears had flowed down young Thomas's face and he couldn't take his hands from the box to wipe them away. For the first time she realised what it must have meant to him to lose the first, the only, human being to whom he could claim some form of relationship. Was there ever anyone so bereft of family?

A horseman was reined-in on the little road that separated the cemetery from the bog. When James de Guider had driven off in a little new-fangled trap, he dismounted and came toward her. It was Bergin. She hadn't seen him since that day at the Campion 'Station'. He told her that Thomas had been arrested. The veil could not hide her quick short breaths. She managed

642

ome adequate words; then, with a murmured apology about
eing in a hurry, left him. He watched her move along the road,
lower and slower. Obviously she was in no hurry. And who was
.e, he asked himself, to be wounding her always? There was a
errible love between those two.

Around the corner she sat on a low wall. She had begun to be
appy. She was enjoying the little social whirl that poor Mam-
na was trying to whip up. The visits of the Delaney girls, the
it-bits of scandal from Mrs. Kennedy-Sherwin. Tracing family
vith James de Guider had been like the old times with the bard.
And now!

She sprang to her feet. Why should it worry me? Let his
lind love do the worrying! She thought of her mad gallop to
he convent when she was told of his arrest, away from the
vorld that contained him no longer. But then she had been a
hild. Now she was a woman. She quickened her step and then
he had to stop and grope for a handkerchief. God'll mighty, is
t crying I am! If she hadn't gone up there to the little church
vith James, she wouldn't have recalled that gruesome little box
nd the one who carried it crying. But someone must shed tears
or a lonely soul taken to prison and only an unfortunate blind
voman to weep for him. How did he come to marry her? Was
t because he had to marry someone and better one who couldn't
ee that he loved someone else. Because he *does*; still. It was in
iis face in the forge that day, and in his voice.

A few days later Mrs. Kennedy-Sherwin's bulletin made farce
of Sterrin's drama. 'My dears!' the outburst started, as usual, at
he drawing-room door, 'have you heard about that devastating
Fenian from America—the one they've been looking for for
nonths! He used so many disguises there was no catching him,
nd do you know why? He is actually the famous actor,
Thomas Young. They brought him to the barracks and, my
lears, I would have been out much sooner, but I've been angling
or an opportunity to see him. They say he is positively *deevy*!
And then the very next evening didn't he go and escape?
Wasn't it infuriating, Sterrin? My dear, I don't believe you are
istening. But wait till you hear—he is really Captain O'Carroll,
. Confederate officer—drove out the barrack gate in a bread
van!'

'Captain O'Carroll,' exclaimed Lady O'Carroll. She had been
ingularly quiet during the recital. No fan fluttering to conceal

laughter.

When the visitor had gone she came and sat on the ottoman beside Sterrin. 'I have never referred to your meeting in Kilkenny in Sir Jocelyn's house with that actor—that mountebank who used to clean our knives.'

'Then don't refer to it now.'

'Sterrin! How dare you speak to me like that.'

'I dare because I won't be taken to task as though I were a child. I am going on twenty-seven, a woman *and* a widow.'

'I don't care what age you are.' Margaret jumped to her feet, her great brown eyes blazing, the keys and bells on her chatelaine belt jangling. Sterrin remembered that once, in childhood, she had seen her mother like this with Papa.

'This—this *canaille*, this servant—to dare to take our family name. *Sacré Dieu!*' She was beside herself. 'He never knew his place and you—you spoilt him instead of keeping him down.'

'He could not be kept down,' Sterrin's voice lifted itself, 'because he had it in him to rise. You saw his ability. His refinement. You praised his artistry about the big tree—you—' Hegarty, coming to remove the tea things, backed out in horror. Their Ladyships were nearly shouting at each other.

'I'm not concerned with the talents and refinements of underlings. I believe in keeping them in their place.'

'Like you did Mrs. Black Pat Ryan.' The words dropped out of Sterrin's sudden recollection of the incident where her mother had looked, and behaved, as she did now. There was no getting them back.

Margaret stood very still. She looked down silently at Sterrin and then she whispered, 'You are right. You are not a child. You are a woman; a *wicked* woman!' She put her hand up to the back of her head. Sterrin's hand shot out too. 'Control yourself, Mamma!' Her voice was only a gasp, but strangely authoritative. It brought her mother up short. 'Because——'

'Because what?' asked Sterrin's brain. Her voice answered, 'because I'm the one who is going to faint.' And she did, straight away.

Once Margaret saw that Sterrin was all right, she went to her room. She did not emerge for weeks.

Sterrin knew bitter remorse. It was a terrible gibe to hurl at her mother. She started sending little notes to her mamma's room. There were no replies.

Sterrin took strolls in the demesne always ending in the direction of Coolnafunchion; but never a sight of Donal. If he came to her now and asked her to marry him she would give him the answer she yearned for. He was lying low. She had heard he had come under suspicion. She wished him dear luck, for she knew the fear and loneliness of the hunted.

Sometimes men 'on their keeping' would contact her and she would shelter them until it was safe for them to press on on their secret purpose. She put them in the bard's room for a few days. Even Americans came, Northerners as well as Confederates. Men seasoned in the smoke of battle. Men convinced of the Fenian cause. They showed her a gentle deference as she arranged for their comfort. Only the hereditary servants might bring food to the guests' in the bard's room. 'You can trust them?' the strangers would ask and watch the tantalising white gleam that was her smile behind the veil. Her cause, she assured them, was her servants'. As her ancestors' cause had been the cause of *their* ancestors.

It was strange, Sterrin thought, to see these men who had fought against each other so fiercely in America, now joining together in the common cause of Ireland. She remembered how kindly Mrs. Lonergan had turned against her under the delusion that Tim had been killed by one of her name and kin. One of her name! A shock of enlightenment shot through Sterrin. Mrs. Lonergan's son had been killed at the hands—or the orders of young Thomas, the servant boy she had indulged with the hospitality of her fine home and the friendship of her son. And I, we, to bear the blame of that killing because he had the audacity to take our name. But was it audacity? Couldn't it have been—sentiment? She turned from the treacherous tenderness.

The landscape seemed bleak wherever she looked, the Movement was faltering; its march stumbling to a slower tempo. Dublin Castle had hunted James Stephens out of Ireland. But even if he had remained, the Brotherhood had lost its faith in him. He had beguiled them over long with high hopes and glowing promises. When he slipped away to Paris no regretful glances turned that way. He was in the right setting for dilettante revolutionaries.

News from Canada brought some short-lived joy. The Fenians had crossed over the borders of Canada. The detachments of Canadian volunteer forces, mustered to meet the in vaders, had been overwhelmed. The regiment of the Queen' Own, rushed from Toronto had been routed. King James di not run from the Battle of the Boyne as quickly as did Colone Booker, the Commander of the Queen's Own, on his charger But the American government pursued the pursuers and seize the Fenian arms. The Fenians crossed back into America wit only the trophies and flags that they had captured.

At last Sterrin received a note from Donal. He wished t speak with her about a matter of some importance. They met i the Hermit's cave at Bawn na Drum. 'I cannot understand it she said to him, 'when I was a little girl and the Liberator wa conducting the Repeal campaign the American Presiden warned England that he would invade Canada if it fired on Repeal gathering...' she faltered.

Donal did not want to talk about politics. He wanted to tal about Sterrin. He wanted her to marry him. It was a strang setting for a proposal, she thought. She looked round the cave it reminded her of the forge. But the heart inside of her was no turning over as it had in the forge. It was calm. It had burne itself out on the flame of its own passion. In such a setting a this her dream love had received its final blow. Donal was urg ing his own love; enough for two. The flame from the sod burning in a makeshift hearth in the corner flickered across hi face and showed it handsome, attractive, but white: too white too thin. In the flicker a silver cup glinted on a stone shelf. A cup, china, gold-edged, had glinted on the stone shelf of th forge, too. Why should Donal have to love for two? He de served the full measure of love. And why should I go withou love; if he has so much to give? 'What a place to propos marriage to me; and what a way to rush me here by night!'

It was half-flippant, half-angry, wholly temporising. Sh shrank from the final commitment of acceptance. There was s much to be considered. Her mother would never consent. Ster rin to marry a Keating of Poolgower? Her father would di again in his grave. She herself would probably have died in he mother's arms on the night of her first birthday if the horribl James's James Keating had fired into the drawing-room fiv minutes earlier. She might never have lived to receive hi brother's proposal! Never have lived to receive the insult of hi own—assault—— And almost as the acceptance trembled upo

…r lips she remembered that it was to punish James's James …eating she had married Sir Jocelyn Devine—and made havoc …her life—and looks—and by-passed her life's love. She stepped …ck, irresolute. Donal shook his head sadly.

'What is it you want?' he asked low and tense. 'If it is a …mantic setting you need, remember that I asked you under the …ossoms of Lissnastreenagh. You said then that they had not …ossomed enough, I should wait for them to fall. I waited and …ey fell and they bloomed again, and fell; season after season …d still I've waited.'

'You've waited a long time,' she murmured gently.

'I can wait no longer.' His tone startled her.

An ultimatum? Was he intimating that he was not going to …ear the willow for her. 'You've made up your mind to marry, …not me then someone else? Thank you for the honour of first …oice!'

'There is no one else. There never could be. Caitlin Ni Houli…n is the only other woman in my heart and—she is calling …ry urgently.'

'The insurrection?' she breathed. 'But—it has—dissolved?'

'No, the Canadian thing has put new heart into the move…ent. The men turned back from Canada are pouring in here. …h Sterrin! We have been through so much together, must I go …to the crucible without something more from you than half-…omises and withdrawals? I must go to take my stand against …r enemies. I seek no mercy and I shall make no compromise. …nd somehow, Sterrin, I see this attitude to my enemies as the …titude to the woman I love with all my soul and being. I want … mercy, no compromise, from her.'

The gentle face was resolute as never before. Suddenly the …ll portent of his words came upon her. It was one thing to …lk of rebellions, to plan and hope, but here was the reality! …his splendid life; the brilliant intellect, the heart so tender to …man sufferings; the heart that was her one sure resource. 'No, …onal,' the cry burst from her heart, 'don't go—the sacrifice is … great.'

'No lesser sacrifice will serve; but if I return——' He put his …nds on either side of her face. She stiffened and his hands …opped, despairingly.

'No,' she cried again, 'it is *because* of my face. You haven't …en it.

'It is not by the skin of your face that I measure your soul. still glimpse your eyes behind that veil. Their spirit is the sam as when it challenged your hostile servants and made them fe the multitude. I remember the beauty of your face when danced with you at the Assizes ball, but more vividly do I r member the tenderness of your face next day, when you he those bereft children in your arms on that railway bank. Ay and your head is poised as proud and graceful as when you ro between the lines of your captors—to jail, maybe.'

'And you ransomed me. Oh Donal!' Her head rested on h shoulders. His arms went about her.

There was a sound at the cave's entrance. The old herm came in, upright, not a hair of the great curled head missin 'The patrol has reached the top of the hill. It will be starting return, but it will be half an hour before it winds this way the road. You'll have crossed the bog long before then.' handed Donal a vaulting pole. 'I have left a burning sod of tu on every foothold. It will light your way. Jump from one to th other.' He went out.

Donal laid aside the pole and took Sterrin in his arms. I pushed up the veil and kissed her lips. He stroked the har where she had once shown him the scars and on the finger th he kissed she glimpsed, through her tears, a shimmering whit ness. Then he took up the pole and it was like a lance as he wei forth to his rendezvous with Caitlin Ni Houlihan.

CHAPTER 59

From end to end of Ireland there was something in the air. It seethed in the earth. It rode on the night wind. Men straightened their shoulders and told each other that Fenianism was no longer an idle theory. The Fenians could have swept through Canada! The men took heart again and drilled in the forts and raths. There were many arrests, many more than before. But now the men from America came, men who had fought against each other at Fredericksburg and Gettysburg, survived the war to unite under the Fenian banner and march side by side to Buffalo, sleeping on its sidewalks waiting to carry the green flag over the frontier into Canada. They carried it instead to Ireland and with it the Stars and Stripes that they had fought for. Twin banners equally loved; equally sacred. 'Soon or Never,' was the Fenian cry. Now it was to be soon.

Thomas travelled through the heart of the country alerting men to the coming rebellion. He noticed birds that he had not seen so far inland since the afternoon of that Twelfth Day in 1839 when he had scurried over the bogs and fields with Lady O'Carroll's gift to Lady Cullen. That day the prescience of some terrible storm drove the birds far inland. Now this March day of 1867 he noticed birds that should be starting on their journey to the islands of the Hebrides and Iceland sitting in rows discussing the wisdom of undertaking the journey. Never had spring wind blown so cold. The wind whittled through the flesh of the men as they struggled across the mountains and through the hidden ways to their long-delayed tryst with rebellion. Many fell in their tracks, and lay there. Only time dare move, and halt their purpose.

When the storm quietened the men rose again. Then the snow fell pensively, and without wind. It betrayed the footsteps of the tiring rebels, then relented and covered them again. The snow continued to fall with the silence of a multitude. And now it covered their fallen bodies. Men remembered no storm so cruel.

The older men recalled the Big Wind but that had been a manly storm—a storm that lashed a man's blood to warmth. This snow was mean and biting. It slowed the march. It betrayed the cause, and simplified the task of the police and the military.

It was easy to track down those whose feet were fettered by frostbite; whose hands were manacled with its numbness. The government acted in other ways, too. Thomas tried to contact Major de Waters but he had been transferred overnight, with his Fenian-tainted regiment, to India. Every disaffected regiment had been transferred from Ireland. The Channel Fleet had been drafted to Bantry Bay.

Thomas rode to the Waterford coast to watch for a vessel that had left New York with arms and ammunition and with officers who had been trained at West Point, tried at Gettysburg. It was a lonely, frigid watch. The cliffs that curved around the fairy cove where Maurice O'Carroll's house stood, had become an ice cathedral, and Thomas wondered if the half moon alone in the great grey sky was feeling as bleak as himself. It answered his thoughts with a spectral beam that revealed the outlines of the ship.

It flew the green flag bearing the proud motto: 'Erin Resurgante', waving like a taunt in the face of Ireland's despair. Thomas signalled his presence and slowly rowed out to the ship. He brought the men aboard the same tale of defeat they had heard from messengers at other coves along the coast. The storm, he told them, that had delayed the ship had scattered and disorganised the battalions of seasoned troops who had endured and waited its coming. Most of them had been arrested, some already on the high seas to deportation and were imprisoned in Arbour Hill Barracks over the graves of the executed rebels of '98. Some were already aboard ships *en route* to penal deportation. His own work among the military gone for naught. And those who were left had pitifully few arms. It would be futile to land. The officers and men bade Thomas a grim farewell, helped him into his boat and watched him to shore. Then the ship that one week ago might have precipitated the capture of Munster, the prelude to ultimate freedom, turned round and faced west into the gale.

Thomas galloped through the snow to where Donal Keating and Bergin waited near the coast with other survivors of the storm. A sod of turf blazing on a pike's head guided him down he rugged track to a camp fire in a hidden glen. Donal, on a knoll away from the fire, had watched through the night alone; guiding the stragglers by signals; shivering and dreaming warm dreams of Ireland's liberation. The night of her slavery would soon be brightened by the gleam of patriot steel; her centuries of slumber broken by the music of patriot cannons!

He listened to Thomas in silence as he watched the distant light of their ship of hope going from them back across the Atlantic to freedom: to transatlantic Ireland with its thousands of disbanded Irish soldiers ready and waiting to come and free their land of the thraldom that had made them exiles. It was not to be soon. It was to be never. 'I told them in Dublin that we were delaying too long,' Donal said bitterly. 'Why did Stephens wait so long? I told him in Dublin nearly two years ago that we should not place our hopes entirely upon American aid and upon the arms in British barracks. I suggested that we purchase supplies from England. There was absolutely no restriction upon their sale at that time. A few hundred armed rebels to meet that ship would have altered the course of Irish history.'

Thomas, too, fixed his eyes on the receding speck of light, trying to hold it back. 'That is what they said out there. But to have landed without some armed co-operation would have been madness. Now we must send these men back to their homes! I'll go and divert the rest.'

All night Thomas met the stragglers as they arrived, the unpaid soldiers of Ireland, exhausted, but exultant at having won through the gale. It reminded him of Tom Steele waving his peace bough at the weary hopeful marchers who had converged on Clontarf for the last, glorious rally of the Monster meeting that was to have brought Repeal to Ireland. 'Go back! Go back!' the Head Pacificator had cried, 'there is no meeting.' 'Go back! Go back!' cried Thomas to their sons. 'There is no rebellion.' They listened dumbfounded.

'Fate is on the side of England,' said Bergin. 'Nothing could have defeated us in 1796 if the Expedition that Wolfe Tone sent from France had not been scattered by a hurricane, with thousands of troops and ammunition for the rebels waiting as we are; the hand of God is against Ireland.'

'Don't blame God,' said Donal, 'it is bad leadership.'

'Bah!' fumed Bergin, 'there was nothing wrong with Davis's leadership in '45. He had the entire country marshalled to a

651

victory march! It was the hand of God who withdrew hir
from us. And on top of that the Famine. My grief to see brav
men deserted!'

'Enough of this defeatist talk,' said Thomas. 'Every rebellio
is a step nearer freedom. The next rising will gain us our free
dom.'

It was the afternoon of the next day before the three reache
the Tipperary hide-out rest. As Donal slept, Thomas studied th
exhausted face of the young lawyer who had been prepared t
toss away the prospect of a brilliant career. But lots of patriot
had prospects of brilliant careers. What man had such a pros
pect as Sterrin? What were they to each other? Husband an
wife? Betrothed? He had not passed on her message at th
forge. He must do it now when Donal awakened.

Bergin's scar gaped hideously against the weary whiteness o
his face. Sleep was gradually relaxing the bitter lines of hi
mouth. Thomas leaned up on his elbow. A mouth capable c
tenderness; a handsome face before it had been disfigured by he
husband.

Donal stirred and muttered a word. Thomas heard it. Sh
was everywhere. Her husband's brand on Bergin's face, he
name on Donal's lips.

Clouds of sleep draped his brain. He would anchor a loyalt
to his poor, blind Dorene. Of heart he had none to give her, bu
he would give her—give her—his lids drooped—kindliness an
—and—courtesy—his possessions. He would look no longe
across the sea to that fairy turret whose occupant had become—
a mortal.

Three hours later he was shaken forcibly awake. A battle wa
in progress. General Burke had taken the field a few miles be
yond Tipperary town. Thomas's spirits rose. He had serve
under Burke. All was not lost. Thomas, Bergin and Dona
jumped on their horses and galloped off to the battle.

It was a sorry rising. Near the fort that was to be the gather
ing point Thomas met some of the men whom he had trainec
Like the rebels whom he had been forced to send home las
night, these too had been dispersed without firing a shot. 'W
hadn't a gun to fire one,' a Yankee private said bitterly. He hel
up his arm. 'That's the only arm I've left. I'd have gladly give
it if I had the opportunity to make one stand for my ow
country.'

Thomas spurred in the direction the men told him Burke had taken. A few moments later he had to pull his horse hastily into the shade of the trees. Ahead of him was a party of military and even as he sighted them he saw Burke fall from his horse; saw him manacled by the British and marched to captivity. Thomas beat his hand against the saddle in helpless fury. The ignominy of it. A gallant officer like Burke. Captured in this pitiful, sterile expedition.

A burst of firing behind him brought him weaving back to where he had left Bergin and Donal. The firing was nothing; just a few bravado shots fired at random after the dispersing rebels. Thomas found Bergin almost at once. They spied Donal's horse a few paces away; riderless. Donal had been thrown; but he made no move to remount. When Thomas reached Donal's side he saw at once the crimson stain spreading across his shirt. One of those random bullets had found a rebel's heart. Donal smiled faintly, at Thomas, whispered something, sighed and closed his eyes. 'Give her——' He paused. Thomas bent closer. 'Give her my eternal love.'

CHAPTER 60

Sterrin glanced through the library window. The snowdrop
had melted. She could see the violets studding the tree boles o
the avenue. In every bush and tree the blackbirds, thrushes an
chaffinches were discussing their marriage and housing plan
But Sterrin could plan no more.

Why, she asked herself, for the thousandth time, had sh
deprived Donal of the happiness of those past few years : herse
too? She could not have failed to be happy with him. He wa
incapable of making anyone unhappy. His goodness had bee
transparent. It had a distinct presence. That was what ha
made her so impervious to the bitter background between thei
two families. That was what had been the well-spring of h
joyousness.

Hegarty opened the door without knocking. 'Is it there yo
are, Miss Sterrin?' Age was dulling his formality as well as h
vigour. 'It's Mr. de Guider. He's in the hall.'

She shook her head. 'Make my excuses.' Then custor
asserted itself. 'In the hall? What are you thinking of, Hegarty
Show him into the drawing-room. Mamma is there.'

'It's yourself he wants to see first. It's private and important

James de Guider made a tiptoed entrance. He waited f
Hegarty to leave. 'I was entrusted to give you this.' He drew
letter from inside his coat and handed it to her.

'Who gave you this?'

'Read it,' was all he would say. He was portentous wit
mystery.

She read :

Dear Lady Devine—Before Mr. Keating died he regaine
consciousness briefly. He whispered a message that I feel wa
intended for you. It was—'Give her my eternal love.' Earlie
that afternoon I had conveyed to him the message that yo
passed on to me in Deegan's forge. It was the first oppo
tunity that I had of doing so.

He died bravely. May his gentle soul rest in peace.

I beg to remain
Your obedient servant,
Thomas O'Carroll.

James de Guider hurried towards her. 'Sterrin, Lady Devine! Are you faint? Shall I summon someone?'

She didn't answer him. Her head was bowed down over the letter. 'Oh God,' he heard her moan, 'this is beyond bearing. Oh Donal!' The poignancy of his message was rending her; then helplessly, she began to cry. Till now her grief, as always, had dried her eyes the way the east wind dries the soil.

She felt a touch on her bowed head. 'I shall not intrude further. I had no idea—the——' She looked up; aware of James, then down at the letter: aware too for the first time of its signature. Donal's message had dimmed out the rest of the letter.

'Thomas O'Carroll?' She looked up. A slow wonderment knifing through the numbness of anguish. 'Who gave you this? How do you come to know about—about Mr. Keating?'

James took a step towards her, the eagerness he had been compelled to restrain bursting forth. 'Sterrin, forgive me, I mean Lady Devine—I know nothing about Mr. Keating in relation to your letter—except the lamentable knowledge of his untimely death. But, but—the one who wrote the letter, who gave me—it is incredible, he is the one I have been looking for, the son of my father's sister—and it was you who led me to him: through the old hermit.'

This fantasy, set in the grim reality of Donal's death was too much to absorb.

'Mr. James,' she said, addressing him as she had been taught in her childhood, 'this is an assumed name. This person performs on the stage under another assumed name—Thomas Young. Before that he worked here on the staff. He was one of our house servants——'

'I know, Sterrin—Lady Devine. He was young Thomas, your knife boy. I remember him well. He used to come and milk our cows twice a day when our staff was down with famine fever.' Excitement drove his voice to a thin penetrating pitch. On the other side of the door Hegarty was able to catch the rest of the words without further strain. 'Young Thomas,' he heard, 'your

former knife boy is the lineal descendant of Sieur Dominiqu
O'Carroll, dispossessed by his youngest son on an act of Dis
closure. Young Thomas should be the heir to Strague Castle

Not for over half a century, not since his own knife-boy day
had Hegarty scurried kitchenward like now. He burst into th
kitchen. 'Wait till ye hear——'

Eight minutes later he came through the hall with a tea-tra
not due for another quarter of an hour. Mr. de Guider was i
the hall and Miss Sterrin's Ladyship was on for making hi
stop. 'No, don't leave it till another day. Tell her now. I'
prefer that she would hear it from you.'

Hegarty, completely outside of himself, and agape for mor
oared in with: 'It isn't goin' you are, Mr. James? Sure I've pu
you in the teapot.'

Tea was served in the drawing-room. Foosthering among th
china, dragging out the ritual of service, Hegarty didn't miss
syllable.

'But what started him—I mean,' Lady O'Carroll was askin
'what first gave him the idea that he might be other than wh
he was——?'

'Other than one of the *canaille*?' Sterrin put in.

Hegarty, recalling his French, wondered at such contemp
from Miss Sterrin, of all people, that should be leppin' out
her skin.

'It was Bard O'Ryan,' James de Guider explained, 'things h
used to say. Thomas told me that he sometimes would call hi
Calvagh and sometimes he would say, "Are you Roderic
Achilles, or some other name?" But only to Thomas, never t
any other servant.'

'Oh that's the truth, many's the time I heard him an——'

'Hegarty!'

'I beg your Ladyship's pardon. I'm not at myself with th
dint of excitement. I've heard talk so often of The O'Carro
who was cast out by his son——'

'And, of course, Mamma,' Sterrin interrupted, 'Hegarty'
grandfather was killed while protecting *my* great-grandfathe
That is why it is so difficult sometimes to be *de-haut-en-ba*
with one's servants.'

Lady O'Carroll noticed Sterrin twisting the pearl ring on he
engagement finger. She became aware of Sterrin's hands an
fingers. They had been covered with rings when she returne

656

from Kilkenny. Unconsciously she said, 'I've never noticed that ring before, Sterrin. It is a strange ring. So pale—pale for tears they say.'

'Yes, Mamma. All the others were so dazzling. They outshone it. But not any more. They are all gone. Sold. It is my happy function in life to part with what I have—my jewels, myself, so that Kilsheelin stands and we can all be frightfully *de-haut-en-bas*. Isn't it, Mamma?'

'Stereen! But you are bitter!'

'No, Mamma. I am not bitter; not anything. I am past feeling.'

The two might have been alone, regardless of the men—guest and servant.

James de Guider tactfully intervened with a request to be allowed to see the portrait of the Sieur Dominique O'Carroll, which hung in the gallery.

'Yes,' he said, when they brought him there, 'it is there. The likeness persists.'

The castle staff seethed. Hannah was waiting for Sterrin. 'Can you get over it, Miss Sterrin!' She was 'Miss Sterrin' now as in the days of young Thomas. Mrs. Stacey laboured up the backstairs. 'It's like a fairy tale, Miss Sterrin.'

Maybe you are a fairy prince, young Thomas! It was a dull thud of memory.

'Sure it happened to others—Lord Templetown, meaning no disrespect to him, has no real claim to that title. His father was lorded for votin' for the Union. The last real Lord Templetown was working in a livery stable. There is many like him, if only they could come into their own. Big John says it doesn't surprise him at all. He always expected to hear something like that about young Thomas.'

Nurse Hogan had the same to say. 'He was the only one of the lads who could speak English to me when I came. An' teaching himself to write from the tombstones 'twas as if something deep inside him was striving upwards. I never heard from him since the day you came from the convent and he wrote to say how well he was doing on the stage and he never in a jail at all only——' she stopped herself: too late.

'You knew that he was not imprisoned?'

The nurse looked apprehensively towards Lady O'Carroll's room.

Sterrin took her first quick step since the news of Donal. As she entered the room her mamma turned from the open wardrobe. In full view, not out of sight, as always, hung the white satin gown: the dark brown splotches clearly visible on the skirt; and on the bodice where his head had rested, Papa's blood! Sterrin turned and went out, the reproach unuttered. Margaret wondered what she had been going to say when her glance rested on the blood-stained gown.

Sterrin went back to the library to the book of poems she had been looking up when James de Guider had been announced; some lines she wanted that had run wordlessly through her brain since the news of Donal. Here it was! 'And once again shall oft-widowed Erin mourn the loss of her brave young men' ... the print blurred out. She banged it shut and pulled another towards her. It was Papa's black Book of Records.

She glanced through it indifferently. Incidents of his life since he took over from his own father stood out in his graceful continual slant. They read like a novel. His meeting with Margaret; the clothes for her wedding; the homecoming to the castle; the parties for her.

'On the night of January the sixth in the year of Our Lord one thousand eight hundred and thirty-nine, a great wind blew across Ireland. It caused havoc and disaster and the loss of many lives, how many it is not yet known. In the course of this storm, nigh five acres of the land that my forefathers have held through centuries against all unwarranted approaches, was raised skywards in my presence and borne out of my sight. The seventh of January of this same year I rode forth to the lands of James Keating of Poolgower and there did witness my own land lying unbroken as it went from me. I pray God that this act of Nature will not affect the lives of those whose heritage has been so strangely visited.'

Sterrin snatched up a quill: 'On the night of March the fifth, 1865—a snow storm blew across Ireland——' She paused. She thought to write something about Donal—weren't the fortunes linked? He was part of their heritage. Their field had 'visited' his family and stayed. And Donal's life was affected. She threw down the quill. This was superstition. And suddenly she remembered the one whose life had really been affected by the storm's visitation—the little boy whose identity had been blown away. She turned from the thought of him and read the entry about her own birth. The writing was less meticulous—a hurried entry: 'An afterthought,' she said aloud, and then she gave an exclamation. 'I wasn't born the night of the Big Wind. I was born the morning after! I'm a day younger than I thought.' No one had ever bothered to refer to the fact. She had never known a birthday treat; never received a gift! Except once! On her fourteenth birthday the knife boy had given her a little leather-bound diary—the one on which he had later written—'They told us we should never wed—and yet we kissed as though we should . . .' It was gone in the flames.

On a sudden impulse she drew his letter from her reticule. The irony of it! That the only writing he had ever again penned to her was to convey to her another man's undying love! Beyond the sunlit windows the chaffinches and blackbirds and thrushes were at it again! Moidering her senses. She rang for Clooreen to be saddled. It was a long time since she had gone riding.

The mare was led round by Mike O'Driscoll, eager to discuss the knife boy to knight-errant saga. But he was deflated at Lady Sterrin's indifference. Did they expect her to hoist the flag over the castle? she thought as she rode out. Let his blind wife do the jubilating.

The air rushed towards her. It brushed past her face soft, soothing. She avoided Coolnafunchion, her favourite ride. That was where Donal used to watch out for her. She took the little bog road—a famine folly—for its champagne air, but she jumped a low hedge into a field before it reached the spot where it ended in stark bog. Across that strip, narrow but deadly to the unwary, was the hermit's cave, and between it, half hidden under purple pools of brown skeough grass, lay the stepping-stones that Donal had trod so surefootedly going forth to the rebellion.

As she jumped back into the little road on her return she glimpsed a vehicle landed in an impasse. Nothing but bog in front and no room in the little road to turn the vehicle round. They must be complete strangers. This was just one of those roads leading to nowhere that had been built in the famine to make the hungry work for their fivepence-halfpenny a day Relief money. A young lady stepped from the chaise and came hurrying towards her.

'Excuse me,' she said, 'but could you direct me to a road called the Wolf Track? It is a narrow road like this.' She spoke with an accent that might be American. An extremely pretty lady, very dark and vivid. Sterrin took in the saucy hat, the elegant fur-trimmed travelling coat.

The Wolf Track! It was years since she had heard the road called by that name.

'You would need to circle all that bog to reach it, but actually it is only a short distance down there.' She pointed down the fields. 'It lies behind the railroad. There!'

'Why, of course!' the girl cried, 'we have been down that way already, but the tracks confused me. There was no railroad when I used to live down there.'

If she lived down that road, Sterrin reflected, then she must belong to one of the tenants, but she wasn't the usual 'returned Yank'. Her assurance was that of breeding.

'I guess,' the girl went on, 'that it would not take me long to walk down there, to run down; that is if the owners do not set their dogs on me for trespassing.'

'That is unlikely,' Sterrin smiled. 'What is the name of the people you are visiting?'

The girl gave a faint shrug. 'I am not visiting people. I am visiting a house; taking a peep rather—and a quick one at that. There is no one of my name there now.

'And what, may I ask, is your name?'

'Oh, my name has no significance. Butler is my name. It was my late husband's name. I never got used to it as mine. He went off to war the morning we were married. My father's name was Ryan. He died in the famine.' She looked over her shoulder. Someone was calling her from the chaise.

'Will you excuse me, please?' she said and with a little bow and a smile she turned in the direction of the chaise, called out something to another lady then went skimming across the field.

Sterrin sat her horse, astounded. The girl was surely one of Black Pat Ryan's daughters; one of the children with whom she used to share her own dinner. She had the dark good looks and independence of her Papa's foster-brother; the breeding of her mother—Nonie Mansfield. The strange encounter had thawed a little of the frozen casings around Sterrin's heart. If ever anyone had met with sorrow, with tragedy, it was that blithe being hurrying over the fields as to a bridal. Her mother dead of ship's fever—and now this reference to her 'late' husband. More tragedy! Yet there was no bitterness on the girl's face; no blank numbness, no sign of emotional paralysis. She just took her fences like a thoroughbred hunter. Sterrin straightened in the saddle. Her head lifted. In the distance she could just see the top of the broken turret. It was a God's disgrace not to have had it mended long ago. There were a few pounds left from the sale of her jewellery. Every penny that came her way seemed to go into that maw of a castle. But wasn't it good to have held on to it, not to have let it go to some Scottish game-keeper, English shop-keeper or Irish Gombeen man—or James's James Keating?

A light footstep sounded behind her. She turned and saw another girl approaching. Beyond her the chaise driver was forcing the unfortunate horse back into contortions in an endeavour to turn the vehicle round.

'What are you trying to do, you stupid man?' Sterrin rode down to him and dismounted. 'Don't you know that you'll never turn there unless you take the horse out of the shafts.' It infuriated her to see animals ill-treated. She let Clooreen crop and took hold of the hackney horse's bridle to soothe him. She was on the brink of the bog, the very spot she wanted to avoid. Another hand, in a kid glove, reached beside her own to pat the animal's forehead.

'You seem to have wonderful control over horses. I'm terrified of them.' The voice had a foreign intonation that was attractive, something like Mamma's. Sterrin turned to the speaker. This must be another Ryan girl.

'Are you not going to visit your old home, too?' Sterrin asked. She tried to study the girl's face but it was partly concealed by the peak of a very pretty bonnet; one of the new small type that perched on the top of the head, but it was not fashionable to have the peak down shading the face like this one.

'I came to see—a person. I have come specially all the way from America. He is here, in this district, but there is so much secrecy. He is one of those Fenians.'

'If he is a Fenian, you are risking his safety to make enquiries about him from strangers.'

The girl was stroking the animal inside a diamond-shaped patch of white on its forehead. She went on stroking without replying; her finger tracing the diamond outline. Then very quietly she said, 'You are not a stranger.'

Sterrin was startled. Most people round here knew her by sight. But this was an American—and the girl hadn't even looked at her. The driver led the horse out of the shafts. Sterrin stepped back. Across the bog she saw the old hermit coming to the entrance of his cave and peering across at her. Suddenly she remembered the American officers she had harboured. Ah! That must be the link. She waited a moment for the girl to establish herself, then she said:

'I do hope you trace who you are looking for. I'm afraid I cannot help you. Good day.'

The girl took a step after her. 'You *can* help me. You know Mr. Young. I believe it is because of you that—Thomas is focusing his—*patriotism* in this area.'

It seemed a long space of time that the two faced each other in that wilderness; so desolate that even the grouse and mountain hare avoided it.

Sterrin started to say something but her treacherous heart was at its thudding again. It always made her voice shaky and now as never before she needed it steady, controlled. She tried to see the girl's eyes, but that damned ospried peak was too concealing.

'Are you another daughter of Black Pat Ryan's?'

The girl shook her head. 'Thomas brought me to Madame Hennessey—Norisheen's relation. He was to have come back there for me after the War, but instead he came here. I've waited for him all that time but——' the mouth, a pretty one, made a bitter moue, 'you had become a widow meantime and he became a Fenian.'

Behind the veil Sterrin's eyes probed frantically. This couldn't be the woman who had been with him—she had an irritating way of holding her head at an angle. All Sterrin could assess was the flawless skin, and out of the chaos inside herself there emerged a clear-cut envy. Something else emerged.

'How do you come to know who I am?' Norisheen, quite unmistakably had had no idea.

'You—you rode out of that castle when we were on the other road and, oh, anyway, Thomas described you.'

'And how did he describe me?' No shake in the voice now.

'Oh,' there was hesitancy. 'Tall, horsy——' The eyes seemed to flicker upwards, 'dark hair—I forget.' Her back was to the bog. Behind her Sterrin saw a movement at the cave entrance. Another man had joined the hermit.

'He described you to me also.' The other man had started to move forward. It was Thomas. 'He told me you were blind. I will lead you to him.'

Sterrin put her two hands on the girl's shoulders, with one swirl she propelled her to the brink of the bog. 'Walk straight in front of you and you will find him. He is only a few yards across from where we are standing.'

She gave her a gentle push. A hump of solid ground rose immediately beside her out of the bog, beyond was a sheer down-suck of quagmire. The girl stepped on to the hump.

'Go on,' Sterrin said, her heart had shifted to her throat. I won't raise a hand to help her. One foot was raised towards the hump. From the other side came a warning shout.

The girl stepped off the hump; not forward into the ooze; sideways to where a half-concealed piece of turf gave a solid footing then forward to another foothold, then sideways again, then forward. There had been lighted sods on them to guide Donal, but even by day one might miss the footholds if one hadn't good sight.

'Dorene!' It burst from Thomas in astonishment. And then, 'You have recovered your sight. You can see!'

She can see, all right! Sterrin couldn't say it aloud. She was trembling from head to foot and he was calling something to her, something like, 'My God, what were you thinking to do?' and the 'blind' one clinging to him like a limpet. Blind inagh! She moved towards the horse and tried to swing up.

'Will I give you a hoist, Miss?' It was the hackney driver. For once in her life she was glad of a leg up.

Horsy am I? I'd take my oath he never said it. Yup, Clooreen. Dark hair! It wasn't even dark red that time when he returned before the wedding. You put your foot in it there, my lassie! Divil a fear of you putting your foot in the bog!

Dowling's dog barked as Thomas came down their boreen that night. Dowling's dog had barked the first night he went there, in Repeal year, with dripping from Mrs. Stacey as an excuse to get her the 'newses' of a match-making between Kitty and Owen Heffernan. A different dog. The roof of the two-storey farmhouse was different from the thatched one of 1843. It was

663

slated; with American money. Prosperous looking, but less picturesque.

Kitty opened the door. She drew him hurriedly inside. 'You took a risk to come. They tell me that even the rabbits are looking out for you.'

'I'd take a bigger risk to see you.' He swung her off the ground and kissed her. 'You could have knocked me down when I met Norisheen and heard you were on a visit.' He put her down and looked at the black dress the bunch of crepe tied at the neck with the widow's brooch. 'Poor Mark! I felt as if I had lost my right hand when she told me that he had been killed. I had no inkling. I knew from John Holohan that he had come through the slaughter of Fredericksburg.'

She nodded sadly. 'He came through everything and then, when all was over—nothing would do him but to join the Fenian attack on Canada. The irony of it! If he had been killed in the war they'd have said he died gloriously. "Never were men so brave" and all that, but because he died in the Canadian affair he died—needlessly.'

'Aye,' murmured Thomas, 'and irony too in the bitterness that came between us. No brother could have been dearer to me than Mark. We are all united now in the cause for which he died. I couldn't believe that any cause would make him turn from me in hostility as he did that morning—because our loyalties differed!'

'It was not at all like what it looked. It had to do with Dorene, Thomas.' Kitty took his hand and led him to the sitting-room and set him by the fire. He glanced around. 'Dorene is not here? And Norisheen?'

'She is staying with Mark's people. But Dorene has gone to a hotel in the town.'

'You heard what happened today?'

She nodded.

'It should have happened long ago. No,' she put up her hand, 'I don't mean about being pushed in—and I doubt that——'

'I saw it happen.'

'Well, maybe Lady Devine had her doubts too, like the rest of us.'

'But Kitty, she—Dorene—explained to me that sight came to her in desperation; some "blind" instinct that forced her to see. She said she has had such temporary flashes before—when she

664

sensed danger. You know it is quite feasible, Kitty. The instinct of self-preservation is very powerful.'

Kitty was silent for a moment. She took Thomas's hand again. 'Thomas. I don't know where to begin. Many a time I tried to put things into letters, but gave up; and since you came to Ireland you were harder to find even than the others. They had their assigned areas. You were everywhere, on account of being able to disguise yourself. Dorene was on for coming here more than a year ago. Once she did leave and we thought that she had come here, but it turned out that she had gone back to the stage for a while—a blind girl's part she was playing. So she said, anyway.'

Thomas leaned forward. 'Kitty, are you trying to tell me that Dorene has been deceiving me about her blindness? It is absurd. I brought her to eminent specialists. She could not deceive them. The one in Switzerland was recommended to me as the world's greatest.'

'Did *he* say that she was incurable?'

Thomas paused to recollect. The Swiss doctor had held out some hope at the first examination. He undertook to treat her. Then when Thomas returned from America, Dorene said it was hopeless. He gave an exclamation. It was not the doctor who had told him. It was Dorene. He suddenly recalled the rollicking music he had interrupted when he returned to her Swiss lodgings. He had taken it to mean that she had recovered. A girl who had received the final pronouncement of her doom would not—could not have played like that. He recalled too, how vehemently, fiercely she had opposed his going to the doctor. 'And,' he exploded into speech, 'I didn't even pay him. I went away without seeing him.'

Kitty watched the dawning recollection on the tired face. It was going to be a bitter disillusionment. 'Thomas,' she said on a sudden, 'wouldn't you give up the Fenian work? There is little prospect of success now. You look worn out. You have been too long "on your keeping" sleeping in caves and the like.'

'I'm sleeping at de Guider's house tonight but I use the cave by day. There's a big price on my head. I could not risk staying openly with the de Guiders—even though they are my cousins. Did you know that, Kitty? My full first cousins.'

'No! They couldn't be. They are too old.'

'My mother was the youngest of eighteen children. Those two

665

are her eldest brother's, Stephen Achilles de Guider's children; born before my mother.'

'It is a wonder that you talk to us at all with all the grand relatives you are acquiring.'

'Hmph! I wonder would they have found me so acceptable if I had turned up to them as the bedraggled servant boy with no one but you and Mark to befriend me. However,' he turned from the reflection, 'I should have been gone after the *débâcle* of our ill-fated rebellion but I waited for General Burke's trial and now I am waiting to see if the death penalty will be repealed. I doubt if the Government will go that far. There is too much indignation in America. He is an American citizen which, by the way, is more than I am. Thanks to Fintan. But Kitty, we are talking in circles. Let us get back to this matter of Dorene. This is—unspeakable; if it is true.'

'It is true, Thomas. It is a long story. It goes back very far— and that matter of your naturalisation papers is part of it. 'Twas I who got them held up.' She put her hand up as he started to exclaim. 'One day, when Dorene was with us about a week and you were off some place tying up the last loose threads about your people, Mark began to get suspicious. He thought he saw her reading a book one day. He began probing; setting little traps for her; drawing her out about her past. One afternoon the post car driver, when he handed me the newspaper, mentioned—casual like—that some very big landlord had been assassinated in Ireland. I repeated the story to Dorene—not thinking who it might be—and told her to give you the paper. That evening, after you had gone to visit your people in the South, I found the paper behind the cushion where Dorene had been sitting. It was opened and folded back at the page that had the account of the assassination—a big headline that you couldn't miss. His name staring out at you, so——'

'I never saw it. My God!'

'I guessed as much. So that night I wrote to Fintan and gave him an inkling of our suspicions and I asked him to hold up the naturalisation papers. I suppose it was wrong of me but I knew you were bent on not taking out those papers till you had had your own name established. You always said you wouldn't become an American citizen under a nickname—even if it was a stage name—and famous—and the same went for getting married. So we thought we'd postpone the marriage till we made

666

enquiries. And we knew you were marrying out of pity and a sense of obligation.'

Kitty paused. She felt a longing to take Thomas in her arms and comfort him. For all the little silver lights that dappled the black curls on his temples he had a look of young hurt upon his face. Oh Muire Dia, but the world and life and the elements had made a plaything out of him. You'd wonder why his mother was allowed to deposit him in this world before her arms were taken from about him. Tossed by the wind, cheated of his name, tricked by women!

He lifted his head. 'What had Dorene to do with Mark's behaviour that last morning?'

'When you told him, through the bedroom door, that you had decided to Marry Dorene straight away that morning with the other couples, and wanted Mark for Best Man, we knew it was the only way you could take her away with you from a house that had rejected you. And remembering about that first night when you took my message from this house to tell him I had decided to elope with him, and how he promised to be your friend for ever—and of how you served our Wedding Mass—it near broke his heart. But hell roast it, Thomas! He couldn't let you walk into it. You were more to him than any brother. You'd never have taken his word against Dorene's if he told you that he just suspected you were not the cause of her blindness, when he couldn't give the proof; not just then, anyway. His anger over your—betrayal of Meagher made it easy for him to refuse you.'

'Betrayal! That's hard hitting.'

'Be fair, Thomas, Mark never heard of Thomas Francis Meagher until you quoted his speeches to him. Meagher himself could not rouse men's blood more than you did when you re-cited his big speech. Mark couldn't understand why you wouldn't want to fight for the North with Meagher.' She noticed how his nostrils quivered in the still whiteness of his face. She had gone too far. She reached across and put her hand on his knees.

'Thomas avourneen, put the past behind you. You still have a prospect of happiness——'

'Happiness?' His mouth twisted in bitterness. '*That* may be added to the past that I too put behind me.'

She stood up. 'Let's stop mincing and pretending. Miss

667

Sterrin—Lady Devine is free——'

He was gazing into the turf flames, the same bitter twist on his lips. Without altering his gaze he said. 'Miss Sterrin's romantic attachment for her servant-companion finished years ago. The deep and mature love of Lady Devine was for someone else. He died in my arms. It was my dubious privilege to convey a last message to her. The nature of it was too sacred to allow of my obtruding my earth-bound sentiments.' He shook his head at the pictures in the flames. It would be unthinkable.'

Kitty gave a sigh of impatience. 'She's alive, isn't she? The pair of you are on this earth. Believe me, it's the only damn thing that matters after you've come up against the blank wall of eternity....'

'She despises me.'

'If she does, why did she take the trouble to push Dorene into the bog?'

His gaze came up at last from the flame tableau. 'That now, Kitty, is something I should like to find out.'

'Then ask herself.'

'I'll do that.'

Thomas did ask Sterrin about her strange behaviour at the bog, but not until after he had sent his profound apologies to the Swiss doctor about his account and had received the doctor's assurance that the debt had been discharged by the patient, and the doctor's sincere hope that she continued to maintain the splendid recovery that she had made during her stay in Switzerland.

Sterrin, when next he saw her, was walking up the hilly field that skirted the bog road. From behind the ditch he watched her pause and lean against an upstanding rock.

She had walked further than she intended and what, she asked herself, brought her this way again? Evening was coming and the call of the pee-wits sounded sad and weird across the distant bog. To drown the sadness she whistled out the long, low warble of a thrush, flutelike, melodious.

From behind her came an answering trill. So vibrant, that a male thrush went hurrying to see if its affianced bride was philandering. Sterrin glanced back. The sound came from where two rocks leaning together formed a shelter known as the Witches Rock. It wasn't a thrush who had answered her warble.

It was a man. And once upon a time he had taught her how to imitate a thrush. She should move away.

There was a weariness, Thomas thought about the way she was leaning against the rock. She must be grieving for Keating. He could not charge in straight away now to challenge her about Dorene. He approached her quietly, almost casually. He spoke about Donal. She listened, looking straight ahead.

After a pause he said, 'Were you married to him?'

Still looking ahead, she answered, 'We were about to be married.'

In the distance he could see the Devil's Bit withdrawing beneath the shadows. The whole world was withdrawing itself quietly so as to leave them alone. Musingly, almost to himself he murmured, 'It is hardly credible.'

'What do you mean?' she said at last.

'I mean—a Keating of Poolgower. Over there,' he said indicating the distant turret, 'there was a time when a servant would be dismissed for having anything to do with a Keating marriage.'

She also had a faint recollection of the time she had implored her papa not to dismiss the knife boy for serving a Keating's Wedding Mass.

'Any woman,' she said coldly, 'would have been proud to marry Mr. Keating. I don't consider myself as having been worthy of him.'

'I quite agree.'

She rounded on him. 'How dare you?'

'There is nothing worthy about making murderous attempts upon the lives of others. Pushing people down bog holes!'

'I didn't push her down a bog. She asked me to direct her to you and I did. Your wife is not blind.'

'I know that.'

'Then why did you tell me that she was blind?'

'Because I thought so. All along, until you gave me your convincing demonstration to the contrary.'

'You mean——' Amazement had routed all her dignified reserve. 'You mean that she deceived you? That she pretended to be blind?'

He nodded.

'Is that——' her voice scraped, 'is that why you married her?'

'I did not marry her.'

In the silence a drop of rain fell upon her face. She had a sudden sense of refreshment. And then the real significance of the words struck her. 'You mean she is your—tu-tu? How revolting! Allow me to pass.'

He grasped her arm firmly. 'The time has come Sterrin Daughter of Roderick O'Carroll, as the bard used to say, for you and I to get things straight between us. There have been too many misunderstandings, too many missions and obligations. Now you listen....'

He talked and he talked and at first she would interrupt with questions. And he would put his hand over her mouth. And finally she gave up, content to listen. For his voice had become like a violin bow across her heart-strings.

The rain fell. They shifted to the shelter of the Witches Rock; her head shifted to his shoulder. Where else could she put it? There wasn't room for two heads where the rocks met in a point. And it was easier that way when it came to recount her version of the years and events that had parted them. She told him everything. As he listened, he felt as if his bones had turned to water. The strength she had shown! 'Twas her blood. The blood of her people! His heart exulted far inside him, strong and sure, flowed a tributary of that same blood.

'Tell me,' he said on a changing note, 'what was it made you suspect Dorene?'

Her brows pondered the reason. 'She didn't act blind; I know so many blind people in Templetown; those who were blinded when the orphanage went on fire, the night of the Big Wind and those blinded in the famine.' Then she remembered the fingers accurately outlining the white diamond on the horse's forehead and other things. 'Now you tell me something. Did you tell her that I went striding about slapping my hips with a riding crop and talking about drenches, fetlocks and brood mares?'

'Good heavens! Did she say I did?'

'She said you said I was "horsy". It's the same.'

'That is one thing you are not. Superb horsewoman though you are.'

She gave a little sigh. 'I knew you didn't say it. What will happen about her now?' She could feel pity for the girl now. The conniving years, the waste of living.

'She has told Kitty that in a strange way she is relieved we know the truth, that she will be glad to get back to the stage. I can help her there.' His voice went grim. 'But she will scarcely need my help. She has played an exacting role with superlative skill.'

Her head got a little jolt where he had shrugged away the memory. He put up his hand and gently fixed her head more comfortably into his shoulder.

'Listen,' he said, and the old deludering raillery was back in his voice, 'did you hear who young Thomas, the knife boy, turned out to be?'

Her head shot up, charged with all the excitement and wonder that had failed her previously. 'It is now that I am realising it. Now that you are not turning out to be someone else's fairy prince. Young Thomas! To think that you might have been the owner of Strague.'

He pressed her head back again. 'I *will* be the owner of Strague Castle, Sterrin, my weary little blossom of the storm.'

'But hasn't it gone? It was on the Emcumbrance Market— Lubey had his eye on it.'

'It has not gone and Lubey will never warm his backside in Strague Castle—pardon the language, my lady fair. It is the knife boy breaking out in me.'

'Oh, that's all right—I heard Papa saying the same when Lubey had his eye on Kilsheelin. Only Papa used a briefer term.'

'He was more privileged. Tomorrow morning I shall see Patrick John-the-Baptist Hoey, the solicitor. Tomorrow evening I shall present you with the Deeds, or the equivalent thereto, of Strague Castle, I regret, though, that I shall not be able to have them suitably accompanied by a pair of musical shoes.'

They were walking now towards the castle, for the soft April evening was tending towards a chill night. She turned to face him.

'And what,' she asked softly, 'would I be doing with the deeds of Strague Castle?'

The birds had ceased their singing for the day and the daisies had closed their faces to the night and the love between Sterrin and Thomas was as natural as all this; but never a word of it had they spoken. They had come too far along a trail of disappointment and heartbreak and frustration for sudden flights of rapture. It was like long ago when they spoke by silence, each aware of the other, in harmony, thinking their dreaming thoughts.

'You would be guarding them for me again the day when you would cross its threshold, chatelaine of the castle. Woman of my house. Your own home; that we will share in peace. Och! What happens to one's words when one wants the use of them at a time like this.'

She just stood there looking at him until he saw a tear escape the veil.

He touched the veil. 'This must be what Nurse Hogan had meant when she wrote me long ago to say that you had taken the veil. Why cover your lovely face?' He felt her start from him sensing something wrong.

Ah God, it had to come! 'I told you about the fire,' she cried. 'Did you not understand that I am disfigured?' She turned from him.

He gripped her arms so that they hurt. 'Wear your veil! Always and for ever if you wish it that way. But don't turn from me ever. What do I care about disfigurements? You are part of my life. I've loved you since the morning that I hoisted the flag to proclaim that you were born. What use to me would be the perfection of any other woman's face?' He drew her into his arms and held her to him and she could feel his body trembling. 'You frightened me just now. You have turned away so often.'

He was at the end of his tether. She could feel the panic in his body. 'Don't leave me, Sterrin. Don't leave me!'

She put up her arms about him. 'Never! Young Thomas, Never! Mo bhead asthore!'

Thomas was emerging from the solicitor Hoey's office in Templetown, when Mr. Lubey arrived with his son. Ten minutes later the Lubeys picked a crumb of comfort from telling the dour James's James Keating that he also was too late. Strague Castle had been bought privately.

The three men watched Thomas as he went into the Livery Stables.

'A play-actor!' young Lubey sneered, 'and by all accounts, a former servant at the castle!'

672

Thomas came towards them from the Livery Stables. Desperately, young Lubey pressed in against the wall of the sidewalk. 'I never,' he sneered again, 'yield the inside of the path to
upstart!'

Thomas slowed. 'Indeed!' he exclaimed. Then he stepped on
the muddy road and gestured the side path with a sweep of
his arm. 'I always do!' He uncovered courteously and moved on.

James's James Keating never forgot a face. A former servant
of the castle! He remembered a castle servant who had served
his brother's Wedding Mass. He studied Thomas during the
little passage of arms. James's James was always watching when
people didn't suspect; watching in hidden places for the brother
who had been 'on his keeping'; watching Kilsheelin Castle that
he had coveted; watching its daughter that he had coveted
more. He had watched her yesterday in the arms of her former
servant. He remembered how Sterrin had spat in his face.

That evening James watched as Sterrin waited inside the
niche in the castle wall. He watched her lover arriving and
smiled when he heard the cry: 'Halt! In the Queen's name!'

Thomas did not halt. He set the horse to its haunches and as
it sprang over the wall, he tossed an envelope to Sterrin. She
called a word to him. The police inspector, in the act of following, was nearly thrown from his horse. Sterrin had jumped into
the niche as his horse's forefeet approached. 'This is private
property,' she said quietly.

The inspector turned and made for the road where the British military had arrived. Thomas galloped across the park, over
the haunted field, up the Slopes of the Embroidering Women,
past Lissnastreenagh's bowery shelter and on to the old mountain road. The military, outdistanced on the road, came within
firing distance of him on the narrow track. Thomas fired back
till his horse was shot from under him. He gave his last bullet to
the screaming animal, then ran.

The shouting and thudding had long faded away when
Thomas crept out from a dyke made by a stream between the
mountain and the moor. It was almost dark. Thomas crawled
across the moor top until increasingly large tufts of heather
forced him to his feet. Their crackling brought a hare bounding
out with ears alert for its cause. From another tuft came an
officer also alerted by the sudden crackling. His revolver rang
out but missed its aim in the uncertain light—then the sound of

futile clicking told Thomas that the officer's gun was as emp
as his own. He started to run. The officer sprang and caug
him. They grappled and struggled, wrestling each other to t
ground. They rolled over, displacing great sections of bog to
ped with heather and leaving bare patches of black, mould, sli
pery as butter. They skidded down the hill till they met gra
and ended up in a great clump of nettles. Thomas made o
final effort to rise but a grab at his legs brought him down wi
a yelp of pain. He lay gasping for a moment then sat up a
rolled up his trousers to disclose a great zig-zag gash, bare
healed. 'Sorry—about—that,' gasped the officer looking at t
wound.

''S all right.' Thomas took a long, painful breath. 'I do
mind bullet wounds at all—but'—gasp—'I simply loathe net
stings.'

'So do I!' said the officer rolling up his cuffs.

Thomas looked about him and made a sudden move. T
officer grabbed.

'It's all right,' said Thomas. 'I just wanted to get these do
leaves. That's what I like about nature. She holds no spite. S
always produces a cure for the stings she inflicts. Here ye
are!'

They sat side by side doctoring each other's stings with th
soothing dock leaves.

The officer looked at Thomas's ugly wound. 'Which side we
you on?' he asked.

'Confederate. I was with Cleburne when I got this.'

'Tragic about him. From around here, wasn't he?'

'No, Cork. But his father, like myself, came from aroun
here.'

The captain economised on breath and let his face show h
surprise.

Thomas nodded in the direction of the distant castle. 'Gre
up over there.' Laboured breathing made conversation staccat
'Remember?'

Captain Fitzharding-Smith, dock leaf suspended in han
turned round and looked hard at Thomas. He knew that he ha
made the prize capture of the Movement; the mystery man wh
had baffled the authorities and demoralised the army fo
eighteen months and who had proved, incredibly, to be the cele
brated actor, Thomas Young. Back in the mess they wer

674

king wagers about his capture.

'I still have a book that you chose for me,' Thomas went on, 'aint John's Eve, it is still my favourite.'

A speck of white showed on the heather. An instant's hesita—n—and then away—a white hare with black fringes to its rs. Together the two men watched it run like a thing with nged heels; barely touching the ground till it disappeared ound the shoulder of the hill. 'People,' said Captain Fitzhard-g-Smith, 'call that kind of hare a witch in disguise.'

The officer turned back to him. 'You have thought of a great any disguises. How is the leg?'

Thomas's eyes still followed the hare's course. To its right he uld glimpse the tip of the canopy where the circle of haw-orn trees sheltered the dell that held the underground passage. nis evening as he jumped the wall niche she had whispered, issnastreenagh,' and he knew that the secret door would be t unbarred.

'Up there,' he answered, 'there are dock leaves with special operties.'

They eyed each other. 'Could you find them?' asked the ficer.

Thomas nodded. 'Do you wish me to bring back some?'

The officer helped Thomas to his feet.

'No thanks,' he said. 'I've got to find my horse. I got unseated a damned ravine full of boulders.' He moved off then stopped. y the way,' he called, 'if you should find it——'

From the hedge behind sounded a crackling. A voice called, re you all right, sir?' and a redcoat struggled through. 'What ppened to your horse, sir?' he asked. 'Shall I——?' He spied e tall figure limping up the hill and bounded in pursuit.

His commanding officer raised up his voice. 'I left my horse the ravine behind that scrub up there to the left.'

Thomas swerved to the left. More smashing in the hedge lmitted a gaggle of police who streaked after the soldier. homas disappeared into the ravine. The soldier jumped. A oment later Captain Fitzharding-Smith saw his horse clearing e ravine with Thomas on its back.

'Why the devil did you let him get away with my horse?' he emanded when he caught up with the crestfallen soldier. The sping man could only look away to the distance where homas was disappearing into a dense circle of trees.

CHAPTER 61

All of Kilsheelin seemed to be assembled in the bard's roo
Sterrin, white-faced, sat slumped in a chair. Hegarty was
one knee, his head down, listening at an opening in the hear
A large slab of carved stone stood upended in the fireplace. M
Stacey stood by the window, while Sir Dominic paced up a
down. Only Lady O'Carroll was missing. She was to be to
later about her new kinsman and the danger he faced.

Suddenly, Hegarty cried out, 'They're here!' All watch
silently as Big John pulled himself through the hearth-openin
Once through, he turned back to grasp another pair of hand
But with a spring Thomas was in the room. He is in the castl
Sterrin thought, but still not through the front door. M
Stacey had taken the initiative. With a 'Cead mile failte, Your
Thomas, a boucaleen,' she had thrown her arms around hir
Then, as if suddenly conscious of something about the voi
that answered her, she realised that this was no 'boucaleen'
the kitchen that she was greeting with such familiarity, s
stepped back. 'It's forgetting my manners I am—making
free.' Hegarty, with a hand outstretched, edged her away ar
told her that indeed she was forgetting her manners, then reali
ing that he was forgetting his own, made way for his master.

Sir Dominic, expecting the former servant to be overwhelme
to be greeted as a kinsman, was formulating a reception th
would be reassuring, yet tinged with a judicious touch of cor
descension. He found himself according a youthful deference
a dignity that out-matched his own.

It was in the dining-room later that Thomas felt ove
whelmed. For after a whispered order from his master Hegart
like an ancient Ganymede offering the wine cup to a god, can
solemnly to the table bearing a four-sided cup of yew wood ar
silver, and placed it before his master.

'The Mether cup!' The words burst from Thomas with
kind of awe. Sir Dominic had indeed made a gesture of hig

ute. Sterrin, moved almost to tears, realised that the ceremonial cup had not figured at her wedding. No one had
ought of it and Dominic had been too immature. She felt a
sh of gladness for the omission. Here was its true occasion.

When was it last filled, Hegarty?' she asked.

'It was filled, my Lady, when the Liberator—God rest him—
ank your health from it a few nights after you were born. It
s a great occasion but'—he turned to Thomas—'this, too, is a
eat occasion, if I may make so bold as to say so and proud I
Young Tho—Mr. Thomas, sir, to carry the Mether cup to
e table in your honour.'

Dominic took hold of one of the cup's silver handles. 'I drink
Thomas O'Carroll of Strague Castle.' Still holding the
ndle he moved the cup to Sterrin. She gripped a handle. 'I
ink to——' She looked out over the cup to Thomas, 'to
ung Thomas.' She pushed it gently towards him. He reached
a handle and their three hands held the cup while he sipped
response.

Thomas felt incapable of speech. His mind was a suffusion of
nder; of fraternity, of shelter after storm; of a fine-drawn
otion too exquisite to bear. At last he said in a low, tired
ice,

'You do me too much honour.' Then to cover his emotion he
d them of the silver cup he had got from his foster-mother
at was a replica of the one owned by the hermit of Bawn na
rum. Sterrin told him how she had drunk from the hermit's
p and been told its history. 'Little dreaming——' she broke
. 'Young Thomas—your eyes are closing with sleep.'

He gave his head a shake. 'Not sleep, they are just dazzled
—everything.'

Sir Dominic observed the look that passed between them. He
d been so taken up with the romance of this splendid clansman
ho had materialised out of the mists of the dawn, that he had
rgotten that it had other aspects. His sister had turned the
stle upside down last night. She had insisted on opening the
bterranean passage for the first time in God knows how long
d she herself had kept vigil at the exit! Dominic rose from
e table with a remark about seeing that a guest-room was
epared. Sterrin smiled at the subterfuge. As if a pull of the
llrope would not suffice!

When he had gone Thomas reached across the table and took

her hands. And as he did he realised that in all his years in t[he]
house, in this room, this was the first time that he had sat at [the]
same table with her. For a moment they sat silent, their ar[ms]
forming a bridge between them.

'Do you know what this recalls to me?' he said gently. [He]
inclined his head towards their outstretched arms and clasp[ed]
hands. 'It reminds me of that early morning, how many ye[ars]
ago—when I went from you because I had to cross the brid[ge]
between your world and mine.' He drew her closer and reach[ed]
to kiss her forehead as he had done that morning. 'It has bee[n a]
long journey, asthore, but I seem to have crossed the bridge [at]
last.' His humility swept through her with a tearing pain. S[he]
placed her head on her arms in an excess of humbleness. Th[at]
such a man should have had to journey so far and so lon[g,]
should have had to suffer, to demonstrate his worthiness [to]
her!

'Oh, Young Thomas, avourneen! What must God think [of]
us—of people brought up like me? We seem to expect him [to]
create special beings to be worthy of our class. That the[re]
should ever have been a bridge 'twixt you and me! And sure[ly]
God never built a bridge to divide people like Denis, the blac[k-]
smith, from us. Donal too, I used to look at him from acros[s a]
bridge.' She lifted her head. 'People shouldn't trouble to jour[ney]
across such bridges. They should smash them!'

'And why, my stormling,' he answered, 'do you think th[at]
there are so many wars and revolutions? People everywhere a[re]
beginning to do what you suggest; to smash the bridges betwe[en]
one class and another. Oh, Sterrin a gra, but I'm weary.' H[e]
dropped his head on his arms, but raised it instantly. 'Forgi[ve]
me,' he murmured sleepily.

He rose to his feet, dizzy with fatigue and the ache of h[is]
wound. He refused to go to a guest-room, just somewhere with [a]
quick exit. For the first time she noticed that he limped.

'Did Basil Fitzharding-Smith do that?' she asked, as sh[e]
helped him to the couch in the bard's room.

He shook his head. 'America's *very* Civil War—a fellow-Iris[h-]
man. He had a miniature bough of peace in his hat—and a lon[g-]
range rifle in his hand.' He closed his eyes. 'Like Cromwe[ll]
exterminating the Irish with a Bible in one hand and a sword [in]
the other.'

He opened them again to the touch of her lips on his forehea[d.]

678

the sight of her face bending over him as she tucked rugs
ut him. 'It is only a dream,' he murmured, 'I shall wake and
d that you have vanished. You always do.'

She tiptoed from the room. When she reached her own room,
flung herself down on the chaise longue, too tired even to
dress.

That afternoon, when she awoke from an exhausted sleep,
e tiptoed again. A few steps, then stopped, then tiptoed again;
rfully she raised her hands to the fastenings of her veil then
opped them again.

'Go on, Miss Sterrin,' Hannah had come up behind her in the
ror.

'Oh, Hannah, I daren't face up to what I might see.'

'You've faced up to worse, Miss Sterrin. Go on.' She tensed
her mistress pulled the veil with a desperate tug, without
pinning it from the band of velvet that held it.

The two women gazed into the mirror, wordless. At last
errin turned to the maid. 'I don't understand it, Hannah,' she
eathed. Hannah continued to stare. Close as she had been to
r mistress this was the first time in years that she had seen her
e without being covered either by thick layers of ointment or
a veil.

'You should have taken if off long ago. I often told you.' She
uched Sterrin's face. 'It's as soft as a baby's bottom. You can
arcely see the scars. I should have used the ointment all the
ne the way you did! My legs are still purple!'

Sterrin had her face pressed to the glass in rapture. 'No,
annah,' she answered. 'You should have gone to Mag Miney
ery morning at the crack of dawn like my Ladyship did.'

'No! Miss Sterrin, you never!'

Sterrin nodded. 'Filthy, smelly stuff with hair two inches
ng. You'd think it was the inside of a dead rat that she was
plying to your face.'

Hannah made a grimace of disgust. 'But you ran from her at
st. When did you go back to her?'

With a sudden pang, Sterrin realised that it was after Donal
d told her that he loved her, that night when she took the
nian oath, that interest in her looks had been reborn.

Poor darling Donal! She looked at his ring gleaming on her
gagement finger; then deliberately she changed it over to the
ght hand. You wouldn't begrudge me my happiness, Donal,

679

and the dear knows it is not too soon. She unpinned the ring
that dangled over her cheeks and drew her hair back int
figure eight on the nape of her neck.

Lady O'Carroll, descending the staircase, glancing back o
her shoulder at the spectacle of her daughter tripping down
a schoolgirl.

'When am I going to meet our distinguished guest?'
began and then she stopped and stared. 'Sterrin! Your fac
She reached up her hands as Sterrin came abreast of her. 'St
rin, what has happened? You are transformed!'

Before Sterrin could reply a great clanging sounded at
hall door. Dominic came hurrying from the drawing-room a
opened it. A police officer stepped over the threshold with
being invited.

'I have reason to believe,' he said, 'that a dangerous a
wanted criminal has gained access to this castle.'

Margaret reached for Sterrin. Her eyes, detached from sen
tion, noticed in this moment of crisis, the scars that
emerged from the quenched radiance of her daughter's face.

Dominic was demanding the officer's warrant and the offi
was saying something about special powers of entry and sear

The hall filled with policemen gripping carbines. Ster
darted away from her mother straight down the passage to
bard's room. Lady O'Carroll took a frightened step backwar
She lost her footing and fell heavily, striking the back of
head. Dominic lunged up the stairs, shoving policemen asi
and lifted his mother from the staircase and carried her to
room.

Sterrin, unaware of her mother's fall, burst into the bar
room.

Big John was looking down at the sleeping Thomas. 'He loo
a bit like he did the morning you were born, a little white-fac
gossoon stretched out across two chairs, dead to the world, a
the wet black curls plastered on his forehead.' She had to
him go on talking while she stood panting against the do
struggling to get her breath. 'The Sir gave him a long look a
said—"Put covering on that boy".'

'Big John,' she gasped at last, 'he needs covering now. Th
are out there—the police—like hounds that have drawn a cov
and found hot scent.'

The coachman moved back the stone on the hearth wh

rrin awakened Thomas.

I'll send Pakie with a horse to Lissnastreenagh,' she told him.
.ere will be a train passing the Lissnafunchion fields. He'll
p it for you with a flag and explain that you are one of us.
u will be able to connect with the Waterford train and get to
usin Maurice's.'

Ie took her in his arms. 'Will you join me there? I won't
ve Ireland without you. I meant to plan all this out with
—we would get away to America by way of your Cousin's
ve of the Fairy Music, then later come back to Strague when
ngs have quietened.'

She clung to him. 'Do you think I'd let you dare to leave
land without me? I'll travel down to Waterford tomorrow.
d be with you.'

She sped along the passages to Pakie Scally. But Pakie, the
tler informed her, had been despatched for the doctor.
Driscoll then, she thought. 'The doctor!' Sterrin's dismay
s tinged with impatience. 'Don't tell me that Mamma has
d one of her attacks?'

The butler took out his handkerchief and wiped his eyes. Too
ich was happening too quickly for the bewildered old man.
wasn't I let them peelers into the castle. Her poor Lady-
ip!'

There was no mystery or swaying in her mother's room. Lady
Carroll lay unconscious. Heavy footsteps sounded on the cor-
lor. Sterrin suppressed a cry and dropped on her knees beside
e bed. The door opened without a knock and two policemen
tered. Sir Dominic sprang up from his seat. 'Get out!' he
dered. They looked at the unconscious figure in the bed, then
oked enquiringly at the sub-inspector who had followed them
. Dominic strode to him, his face livid, his eyes blazing. 'Get
ese men out of this house! Get them out! Look at what you
ve done! We are awaiting the priest and doctor!'

A gasp sounded from behind him as the door closed. 'The
iest, Dominic? She's not—she's not dying?'

Nurse Hogan assisted her to her feet.

'Your mamma's colour is improving. She cut the back of her
ead. I just took advantage of there being a Station down the
ad to send O'Driscoll there for the priest.'

O'Driscoll not available either! What would become of Young
homas? Sterrin could not stir from her mamma. 'What, in

681

God's name, will I do?' It burst from her.

The nurse misunderstood her. 'There is nothing anyone c
do, your Ladyship. We must only wait until the doc
arrives.'

And mercifully, the doctor arrived just then. Scally had be
able to intercept him at a patient's nearby.

The doctor, with an arm around Sterrin's shoulder, let h
out of the room. 'Leave your mamma to me. She seems to
coming round.' He was closing the door on her when he open
it again. 'What's wrong with your face?'

Dully she put her hand to it. 'Nothing,' she said.

'So I see,' said the doctor.

She reached the bard's room as Big John was emerging fr
the concealed passage. 'Did he get away?' she whispered. Befc
he could answer Young Thomas climbed out. 'There are pol
in the hollow. They haven't found the door, but it is only
matter of time.' Heavy footsteps sounded in the kitchen passa;
He jumped back down and Sterrin, as she helped to batt
down the flag over the dark curls, felt as if she were helping
entomb him.

The footsteps moved on to the kitchen. Mrs. Stacey, wi
magnificent unconcern for the presence of the police, was ma
ing pastry. Her high-cauled cap towered over the highe
shako. They plied her with questions but she only shook h
head.

'Is she deaf?' one of them asked.

Sterrin entered the room. 'She does not understand Englis
The cook looked as if she were about to treat them to son
choice English. Sterrin spoke to her in Gaelic. The listeni;
police assumed that she was interpreting for them. Mrs. Stac
gave her an understanding look, then, placing the pastry in t
bastible, she stalked off with it to the bard's room. Th
watched her draw burning sods from the fire she had light
there that day for Thomas, flatten them on the massive hear
slab, place the bastible on them, put more red embers on the li
then seat herself, take off her shoes and proceed to pick h
corns.

They tapped the walls. They dragged the massive bed fro
its place, the great armchair, the couch. 'Whose room is this
demanded the sub-inspector.

Sterrin told him it was Mrs. Stacey's.

Hm, a very impressive room for a servant!'

Mrs. Stacey was my father's foster-mother.' Sterrin said it as
he reason was supreme.

The sub-inspector moved upstairs again. He had overlooked
 oratory. There would surely be some old penal day escape-
e for priests.

Sterrin went out and up the back stairs. She reached the
lery just as Dominic, a lighted, blessed candle in his hand
s preceding the priest upstairs. Sterrin dropped on her knees
reverence for the Viaticum he bore with him. Dread clamped
wn on all her being. Mamma was about to receive the last
es of the Church! She rose and groped towards the oratory.
When the sub-inspector and his minions, following her
sely, entered the oratory Sterrin was kneeling before the altar,
 face buried in her hands, her shoulders shaking. She reined that way, oblivious of them—while they searched.
ddenly she lifted her head. The officer stared. Downstairs her
e had been hidden in the shadows of the doorway. It had
en veiled when he had arrested her for obstructing an eviction.
ways it had been veiled. Now for the first time he saw it un-
vered—lovely—no arrogance; soft with grief. The flame of the
ar candles made a sapphire shimmering of the tear-filled eyes.
ars overflowed unchecked down her cheeks in a heartburst of
ef. He murmured something and withdrew.

Later Dominic came. He knelt beside her and put an arm
out her. Mamma was going to be all right, he assured her. She
s fully conscious and the doctor had some queer idea that the
ury to her head was going to do her good.

It wasn't a faint this time, Sterrin; not one of her queer
uts. She just slipped and hurt her head. He says he often
ndered if some of those flying debris had struck her the night
u were born. She was never able to remember except that she
d that queer pain in the back of her head. It is not there now;
d no tension; just soreness.'

She bowed her head again. 'Thank God,' she sobbed.

Someone else came into the oratory. She looked up. It was
omas. He gestured them to silence. Mrs. Stacey, he told
m, had released him, 'from under the apple pie' when the
lice had gone——

'But they've only withdrawn because of my mother,' inter-
ted Dominic. 'They'll be back.'

'I know and I shall give myself up—no——' He put his ha[nd]
up again. 'She told me about your mother. I've done this [to]
her.'

Sterrin watched the way he strove for words; so unlike h[im.]
He always said things the way one would have liked to say th[em]
oneself. His face was ghastly; and there were traces of sli[me]
where his sleeves had brushed against those subterranean wa[lls.]
Like the smear on her wedding dress.

While they argued and pleaded with him the priest ca[me]
quietly into the oratory. He placed a hand on Sterrin's head.

'Your mother is in no danger.' He stopped at the sight [of]
Thomas stepping forward from the shadows. Sterrin introduc[ed]
him and hurriedly explained what was afoot.

The old priest gazed at him in quiet wonderment. 'You[ng]
Thomas,' he murmured. 'The young Latin pupil who used [to]
serve Mass for me. So you are the famous outlaw.' He show[ed]
signs of reminiscing.

Sterrin said quickly. 'He wants to give himself up. It wo[uld]
mean the death sentence.'

The priest nodded sadly. 'It would, I fear. I wonder——' [He]
looked at Thomas speculatively. 'I wonder is there any disgu[ise]
you could think of, and maybe you could drive away with m[e in]
the old phaeton.'

Thomas shook his head. Before he could answer there cam[e a]
violent knocking at the door. Sterrin tensed. Then her m[ind]
raced in all directions. Somewhere behind the altar there wa[s a]
panel but the steps that led from it had caved in with the stor[m.]
'Twas too late. Everything was too late. The priest was look[ing]
at Thomas with infinite pity. They could hear voices. Domi[nic]
stepped out to the gallery. 'It's the military,' they heard him s[ay.]
A minute later he was accompanying a military officer into [the]
room.

Without preamble the officer addressed Thomas. 'Get i[nto]
this quickly.' He handed him a bulky parcel. 'There isn'[t a]
moment to lose. If you are caught on the premises Sir Domi[nic]
is to be arrested for harbouring a felon.'

In the waiting lull Sterrin whispered a while to the prie[st,]
then hastened to see her mother. The doctor was coming fr[om]
her room.

'Let her sleep, Sterrin. There is no fear of her.' He talked [to]
her as she returned to the oratory. Vaguely she was aware of [the]

vants crowding in the rear of the hall; upturned faces, a
ispering tension. Hadn't there been a queer stern urgency,
y commented, in the arrival of the friendly captain?

When Thomas reappeared in the oratory, Captain Fitzhard-
-Smith barely suppressed a whistle of amazement. 'It be-
nes you better than it did poor Orlando de Trafford. I once
d you that you'd make a fine hussar.'

But you told me that I should begin at the other end.'

The captain turned to the door. 'Come, there is not a moment
spare.'

Sterrin reached out a hand to him. 'There is one moment you
ust spare.'

The waiting servants watched her appear at the gallery head.
annah,' she called, and then she added. 'All of you! Come!'
They crowded into the oratory, looking in wonder at each
er. What was happening? Dr. Mitchell was standing there,
d the priest wore his stole, and two splendid officers standing
front of him. There was a sort of ceremonial quality about
e way the young Sir took his sister's arm and led her a step
ward to stand beside one of the officers, then with a click of
s finger beckoned Hannah to stand behind her.

'Twas then it struck into their minds. The splendid officer
side Captain Fitzharding-Smith wasn't a splendid officer at
. He was their own young Thomas, the knife boy and the
iest was marrying him to their own Miss Sterrin.

The moment was over. Captain Fitzharding-Smith drew
errin from her husband's embrace.

'I will wave to you from the wall gap,' she whispered tremu-
usly.

'You will do no such thing.' It was a command from an
nfamiliar Captain Fitzharding-Smith. He was in his own
alm; indisputable.

'Then,' she turned pleadingly to Thomas, 'look back when
u reach the gate—just, only look back.'

A few minutes later, the lodge-keeper hurried to open the gates
the two officers came cantering down the avenue. No sound
tween them but the clink of scabbard against stirrup.

As they passed through the gates one of the officers slowed,
en halted. The castle was closed and silent. No lights showed
om the windows. Then as they watched, a tiny flickering light
owed in the broken turret. A figure loomed there, then van-

ished. There was another movement above the tiny light. 'Tw
it and the waving moon the flag of Kilsheelin was lapp
gently; full-masted; proudly.

A great event had taken place in the castle.

THE END

The MS READ-a-thon needs young readers!

Boys and girls between 6 and 14 can join the MS READ-a-thon and help find a cure for Multiple Sclerosis by reading books. And they get two rewards — the enjoyment of reading, and the great feeling that comes from helping others.

For complete information call your local MS chapter, or call toll-free (800) 243-6000. Or mail the coupon below.

Kids can help, too!

A Gift of Romance

Six novels of passion ... fire ... and triumph!